Praise for Walter McCloskey's suspenseful debut novel

Risking Elizabeth

"Sensitive portrayals of the city and psychological characterization compound this novel's excellence."
—*Library Journal*

"McCloskey adds a few new twists along with a pinch of John Grisham . . . the perfect read."
—*New Orleans Times-Picayune*

"Walter McCloskey's first novel carefully evokes a New Orleans that is six parts the author's youth and four parts gritty, end-of-an-era reality from a city whose legendary grace is steadily edging toward urban nightmare . . . The end product is a very good read."
—*Greensboro News & Record* (North Carolina)

"The author's affection for New Orleans permeates his descriptions of the city and its inhabitants, easily conveying the sights, sounds, and smells that are unique to New Orleans. He writes with elegance and style."
—*Richmond Times-Dispatch*

RISKING
ELIZABETH

Walter McCloskey

𝔅
BERKLEY BOOKS, NEW YORK

If you purchased this book without a cover, you should be aware that this book is stolen property. It was reported as "unsold and destroyed" to the publisher, and neither the author nor the publisher has received any payment for this "stripped book."

This book is a work of fiction. Names, characters, places, and incidents either are products of the author's imagination or are used fictitiously. Any resemblance to actual events or locales or persons, living or dead, is entirely coincidental.

"Way Down Yonder in New Orleans," words and music by Henry Creamer and J. Turner Layton, copyright © 1922 Shapiro, Bernstein & Co., Inc. New York. Copyright renewed. International copyright secured. All rights reserved. Used by permission.

RISKING ELIZABETH

A Berkley Book / published by arrangement with Simon & Schuster, Inc.

PRINTING HISTORY
Simon & Schuster, Inc. edition published 1997
Berkley edition / August 1998

All rights reserved.
Copyright © 1997 by Walter McCloskey.
Author photo by Josephine Sacabo.
This book may not be reproduced in whole or in part, by mimeograph or any other means, without permission.
For information address: Simon & Schuster, Rockefeller Center, 1230 Avenue of the Americas, New York, New York 10020.

The Penguin Putnam Inc. World Wide Web site address is
http://www.penguinputnam.com

ISBN: 0-425-16413-6

BERKLEY®
Berkley Books are published by The Berkley Publishing Group,
a member of Penguin Putnam Inc.,
200 Madison Avenue, New York, New York 10016.
BERKLEY and the "B" design
are trademarks belonging to Berkley Publishing Corporation.

PRINTED IN THE UNITED STATES OF AMERICA

10 9 8 7 6 5 4 3 2 1

Acknowledgments

I WANT TO express deep thanks, for reasons each will know, and roughly in order of their appearance, to Max Nathan, Anne Parker, Ann Porter, Philip Andrews, Elise O'Shaughnessy, Alfred Hero, Doug Fricke, Kathy Robbins and her associates at the Robbins office, and Bob Mecoy at Simon & Schuster. Kathy is a rarity: someone who measured up to her advance billing. She and Bob are the best teachers I've ever had.

Anne Parker's assistance has been invaluable from the start. Her beauty is matched by her intelligence and judgment.

For my family

and

Bessie Zaban Jones

Author's Note

THIS IS A work of fiction. That means that I have felt free to create Carnival organizations, route a parade, alter Latin American history, and modify the geography and geology of the area outside New Orleans. I have even opened Galatoire's on a Monday.

The discussion of divorce in Chapter 10 is based on laws current in 1981.

In Chapter 25, the spelling of the term ''olographic'' (usually ''holographic'') is, like so much else, peculiar to Louisiana.

Full fathom five thy father lies;
  Of his bones are coral made;
Those are pearls that were his eyes:
  Nothing of him that doth fade
But doth suffer a sea-change
Into something rich and strange.
Sea-nymphs hourly ring his knell.

—SHAKESPEARE, *The Tempest*, I, ii

RISKING
ELIZABETH

Walter McCloskey

PART ONE

Downtown, Uptown:
New Orleans, 1981

ONE

I WAS URGING Ike into the clothes Grandmother had set out for him when, at exactly six, jazz rose from the courtyard below. I couldn't have named what time-worn song the hired musicians played, but it was so jubilant that something inside me, dormant until then, abruptly sat up and took notice.

"Dad? Am I staying back in the kitchen tonight?"

"Well, Leona's fixing you dinner."

"But I want to see the people."

"You've seen them before."

"They're better than the zoo."

Ike's eyes held me. Enormous, round, with ice-blue irises circled and pinpointed by black, they reminded me what a shrewd observer he was.

"Okay," I said. "For a little while anyway."

Grandmother's property stretched from Esplanade to Barracks Street and was fronted by a brick wall surmounted by baroque iron grillwork. The grillwork was the first reason tourists stopped to stare: when they stayed to peer through the wrought-iron gate they saw an expanse of lawn, in the center of which was a raised marble fountain, and the brick façade of the house itself, with its balconies, its row of tall French windows, and its general air of slightly faded grandeur. In the rear was the flagstoned courtyard where the mu-

sicians were playing, another fountain—this one submerged
and banked by recently pruned jungle—and the carriage
house in which, for the past six months, Ike and I had been
camping out. Fifty years before, it had housed Grandmother's chauffeur, but those days were long gone.

Outside, it was New Orleans in February, ten days before
Mardi Gras. That meant the weather was temperamental: in
this case, lukewarm and sticky, with a descending ceiling of
swollen, gunmetal-gray clouds. Any colder and the musicians
would have had to be stationed inside, as they often had
been, at the far end of the front hall, where their echoing
trumpet blasts not only cut through the cocktail babble but
also threatened to bring the house down. The courtyard was
illuminated by hurricane lamps in which candles fitfully
burned. When Ike and I crossed to the main house, the trumpeter was exercising his blistered lips so furiously that his
eyes looked about to explode. "Can't we turn that down?"
Ike asked.

Grandmother stepped through one of the windows that
opened from the dining room onto the terrace. Motioning us
to a marble bench in the corner of the courtyard, she whispered, "Wait, don't go in. I have something to tell you."

At seventy-nine, Grandmother was a tall, slender woman
who carried herself—shoulders erect, jaw jutting forward—
with the air of one who knows that she is, or has been, a
great beauty. On this occasion she wore, as usual, something
black. At the base of the deep V in front was a gardenia that
matched exactly the ivory pallor of her skin. She leaned forward to kiss Ike, then turned to me and said almost defiantly,
"I may be selling the house, Harry. I just thought you should
know."

"What happened to being carried out feetfirst?"

"I'd still prefer that. But Cousin Charles says with the
way things are going I ought to start living off capital. This
house, as it turns out, is my chief asset."

"True enough. Did he tell you what it's worth?"

"We didn't get down to that."

"Seven hundred thousand. Maybe eight. If you find the
right buyer and the market holds steady."

Her great dark eyes expanded. She took my arm. "I'd

better sit down.'' She remained standing. ''How do you know?''

''Lawyers have to know something about property values.''

''Why didn't you tell me?''

''You never asked.''

''But I had no idea. Charles talked mostly about what a liability the house is. How it needs structural repairs that I can't possibly afford and's getting to be an albatross, a white elephant strung around my neck.''

Ike laughed. Grandmother did, too.

''What should I do, Harry?'' she said.

Behind her, through the windows, I could see figures moving in the dining room. White shirtfronts, some headless in shadow, a gold-skinned back in a backless dress.

''Right now, go in to your guests. We'll talk about this tomorrow.''

''Oh, the guests,'' Grandmother said. ''That's the other thing I need to tell you. I've been giving the same party for fifty years, but this time I decided to make the guest list more, well, democratic.''

''In what sense?''

''Friends have been saying for years that I'm not in touch with the real New Orleans anymore. They say that with this oil boom there're all sorts and kinds of people out there''— she gestured broadly to include whatever and whoever lay beyond the brick wall—''who're taking over the city. So tonight I branched out: I invited Monopoly money. That's money so big it doesn't seem real, darling,'' she said to Ike, then turned back to me. ''Of course, you'll see the usual faces as well, but the point is to let these other people get a look at the house in case I decide to sell it. A glimpse of old New Orleans as a lure. Is that too shameful?''

''On the contrary. But I've handled cases for some of these people, Grandmother. The way you talk, they might be gangsters, white slavers, or dope peddlers. They're just business-people like any others, only more successful than most.'' I might have added, ''So far, at least,'' but I didn't. The oil boom was still so frenzied that each day saw some new high roller emerge from the woodwork. I wasn't alone in figuring that it couldn't last.

"I don't think I was brought up to trust that kind of success."

"Great-great-grandfather Haynesworth wouldn't like your admitting that."

She laughed delightedly. "That robber baron," she said, caressing the phrase. "But that was so long ago, Harry."

"The world hasn't changed that much."

"Mine has." She turned toward the house. "I've got to face the crowd. I just wanted to alert you."

Two

GRANDMOTHER WAS WRONG if she thought her new guests would stand out from the rest like scum on the surface of a pond. If they stood out at all it was because some spoke with a twang rather than a drawl or because the men were leaner and more fit and the women, even those with plain pioneer faces, wore jewels that glittered rather than gray diamonds stuck in antiquated settings. Otherwise there were the usual number of couples in early middle age and a handful of debutantes and their escorts—grace notes of youth and beauty—but half the guests appeared to be about seventy-five, and of these many were women who had long been widows and whose smiles were as fixed as their helmets of white or steel-gray hair. In spite of the new additions it was still the same old Saturday-night crowd. These were the people Andrew Jackson meant when he said he had come to fight a war while the natives went off to dance. Thirty minutes into the party, the level of raucous animation was already reaching a crescendo.

Which was just as Grandmother would have wished. She had firm views on what makes a good party. First, "Strong drink and plenty of it. The party takes off right away and maybe, if you're lucky, the guests will leave early." She always had bars set up in the front hall and dining room, and another in the courtyard during warm weather. Elsewhere, in order not to block the flow of traffic, waiters passed trays of deep amber-colored drinks. But Grandmother's guests rarely left early, because she gave them as much to eat as to drink. As Ike and I passed through the dining room, I saw that along with the usual ham and burnished turkey the table held chafing dishes of creamed crabmeat and mushrooms, silver platters of daube glacé and whole fish in capered mayonnaise, sitting beside crystal bowls filled with iced shrimp. Behind a table near the pantry a man was shucking oysters to order.

"Do you want any of this?" I said to Ike as I took an oyster, squeezed lemon on it, and swallowed its briny fatness whole.

"Ugh." He grabbed my hand and pulled me toward the living room.

We stood in the doorway before going in. When I looked down at Ike, he was vibrating like a tuning fork, scrutinizing the crowd as if they were performers on a stage. The room itself had taken on a theatrical aspect. It was sixteen feet high with two walls of French windows that rose toward a ceiling bordered by tiers of elaborate plaster scrollwork. The walls needed paint, but this evening Grandmother had lighted the room only with candles—great numbers of candles in silver candelabra—and the diffused golden glow treated the room tenderly, as it did the faces of the women in it who were past their prime. I had to hand it to Grandmother. She knew a lot of ploys, all of them artful.

Jazz, muted by distance, drifted with the damp air through the windows and filled the room with a cynical and melancholy gaiety, like a voice wearied by excess but still determined to charm.

Over near the front gallery, on the far side of the room, an amorphous cluster of familiar and not-so-familiar faces had gathered. From this perspective, they seemed to be struggling to preserve their identity as a group against the invasion of barbarian tribes.

"Catch the lineup over there."

Ike nodded. "Family."

"How many of those characters can you name?"

"Let's see. Two Haynesworths. Four Careres. One Hobson. One Pickwick. Two Eastmans. I've seen three others before but I don't remember their names."

"Impressive even so. We should go over and pay our respects."

"Not yet."

I couldn't tell what had caught Ike's attention, but mine stayed with the group across the room. Some were distant cousins, by blood or marriage, whom I scarcely ever saw except at this yearly event. Others, like Grandmother's second-cousin Charles Haynesworth, senior partner in the law firm where I worked, figured more crucially in my life. On Charles's left and making some effort, if only polite and political, to merge with Grandmother's newer guests were Charles's daughter Diana, a matronly figure in red satin, and her blandly affable husband, Rudolph Carere, instantly identifiable by the single black eyebrow that traversed his forehead perhaps only an inch and a half below his hairline. I spotted Diana and Rudolph's daughter Emily, a debutante that year, off to her grandfather's left, talking to a young couple her own age. As I watched, she burst out laughing, then clapped a hand over her mouth and turned to whisper something to her grandfather. Charles's expression didn't change, but he bent his elegant, parchment-covered skull close to the always avid ear of his ninety-five-year-old aunt Bessie Eastman Pickwick, down from the family house near Donaldsonville for Carnival Week and seated, at that moment, in one of Grandmother's straight-backed gilt chairs. My first glimpse of Aunt Bessie had been at a New Year's Eve party fifteen years before, where, at age eighty, she had astonished the crowd by swiveling a wicked twist with one of the younger male guests.

"Look over there at Charles," I said. "What do you think he's telling Aunt Bessie?"

Ike frowned and shifted his head to indicate two middle-aged women on his left, one dressed in green and the other in black, both strangers to me, who stood talking to each other, eyebrows raised, in that insinuating local drawl that always meant gossip.

In the crowd swirling around them, Grandmother's formula was working its wizardry. Appraising stares had yielded to smiles, open-mouthed hoots of merriment; caught up in a rhythm, the variegated partygoers moved to it in unison. For the moment, Ike had forgotten the crowd. His face was rapt but unrevealing. What, I wondered, could he possibly make of what the two women were saying?

". . . got so rowdy the party flew out of control. One of the wives danced topless on top of the table—"

"Not Diana!"

"Diana wasn't always so heavy. And there was plenty of fooling around *un*der the table. The upshot was Miss Ella wrote Rudolph a letter saying don't ever come back to Commander's. Look at him standing over there, our next King of Neptune, smug as you please."

"That was so long ago, Tatine. We all did naughty things back then. Now it's our children's turn to do those same things. What fun those cherubs must be having."

"Well, now that you mention it."

"I don't get you."

"The Carere boy."

"Jamie?"

"That talk last summer about nude—"

"Let's go." I took Ike's shoulder to propel him in another direction. "Enough's enough," I said.

"But Dad, I want to hear about Jamie."

"Sorry, son. Time to move on."

I had grabbed a glass from one of the floating trays. The room's glow had deepened. Its heat was intense but consoling. All the women in it were now beautiful, and their beauty was essential: how they might see themselves in their dreams or had always wanted others to see them. Holding Ike's hand, I searched the crowd for that gold-skinned back that had flashed across the dining room window not ten minutes before.

"All hail the hostess!" a male voice boomed out. "The only woman who's lived in the Quarter forever without—"

"Turning into Blanche DuBois," someone else yelled. "And she's still holding on to Belle Rêve!"

This toast was greeted with whoops of laughter and hoisted glasses that glinted in the light of the candle flames.

From the other side of the room Emily Carere waved, then

headed toward us. Although her progress was direct, she seemed to sashay, turning her head from right to left, smiling brightly, working the crowd like a professional. Born to be a Carnival queen, on Wednesday she would be one: she was slated to be Queen of Atlantis, two days after her father was King of Neptune. Emily was a small-boned brunette whose red dress, almost the same shade as her mother Diana's, dwarfed her with its abundance.

"Forget Jamie Carere," I said to Ike. "You'll have to settle for his sister."

"Harry and Ike, you two adorable men." Emily kissed me moistly on the mouth and then kissed Ike on both cheeks.

"Ike, I'm not supposed to talk about next Wednesday night, but I want you to know I always planned to have you be a page in my court. Mama said it just wasn't the best time for you, so I had to get someone else. But I did think of you first."

"What's a page?"

"You've seen pictures. They dress in little costumes and wear blond wigs and get to carry the queen's train."

Ike said nothing. He just gazed at his fourth cousin with a politely neutral expression.

"Harry, let me borrow this sweet boy for a minute. I want him to meet Beau. He's as big a fan of Dr. J as Ike is. Beau's my date, over there in the corner talking sports as usual. He and Ike'll get on like a house afire."

Ike shifted his bland gaze to me. I winked.

"Bring him right back, Emily. His dinner's waiting."

"Don't go off, Dad."

"I'll stay just where I am."

Left alone, I renewed my search of the crowd. The two women on my left were still talking.

"... upstairs room in some kind of annex. Private, of course, but waiters came and went. So did the whores. Jamie Carere was at one end of the table and the groom-to-be was at the other end, and each one was being serviced, if you know what I mean, in different ways by a whore."

"What I can't figure is how those bad boys keep a hard-on with so many people watching."

"Lou!"

"But I'll bet you something, sweetheart. Antoine's isn't about to send a letter of reprimand to Jamie Carere the way Miss Ella did to Rudolph. At Antoine's it's just business as usual."

The two women were approached by a round-faced man in a dark suit and black-and-white-checked tie. I recognized him as the owner of a well-known antique store on Royal. "Break it up, you two. I have an announcement to make and I'm telling you first because I want the whole world to know. But wait a minute." A hand tapped my shoulder. "Harry Preston, is that you with your back to us?"

"That it is, Spencer."

"Come join us. I was just springing some news on these ladies, and you might as well hear too."

"Shoot."

"Call me a rat if you want, but after what's happened I'm jumping off this sinking ship. That means selling the house on Camp Street and moving to Covington. How the mighty are falling."

"Spencer, you of all people," the woman named Tatine said. Her face made small movements of concern.

"Let's face it. The balance has been tipped. This city's divided into two warring halves, each getting ready for Armageddon. Thieves are robbing us blind. Saturday morning I was drinking my coffee on the sunporch out back when Tommy, my yardman, came to tell me most of my plants on the front porch were missing."

I half listened as Spencer talked, but my glance wandered the room, resting first on Ike over by the bookcase with Emily and her boyfriend, then prowling among the groups that formed, shifted, and dissolved. Anyhow, Spencer's story was familiar, with a couple of twists. Coming home late from a party, his next-door neighbor had seen the plant thief—a tall black woman with a large shopping bag—and followed her home in his car to a double on Magazine, only six blocks away. Spencer drove there, spotted his plants in the yard, and loaded them into his station wagon. As he was leaving, an old man came out of the shotgun cottage next door.

"He was a chinless Asian with big staring eyes. I said, 'You tell the thieving bitch who lives here to stay away from my house on Camp Street.' He said, 'She no she. She he. She work as drag queen downtown.' I said, 'He, she—it's all the same to me. Just tell her if she bugs me again I'll haul her in front of the judge and have her ass shipped to Angola. They'll grind it to mincemeat.' ''

"But Spencer," Lou said, "what'll happen to your shop if you move out of town?"

"I'll keep the shop and a pied-à-terre upstairs. After all, business is business. Speaking of which, Harry, this party was one of Julia's brilliant strokes. A mix-and-match party. I've already acquired two new clients, oil barons who probably can't sign their own names but whose wallets are bursting with new money. I love new money, but the people who have it want it to look old. When I sell them high-priced junk and other people's ancestral portraits, they start feeling better about themselves. After tonight, I owe Julia a commission."

"I'll tell her to take you up on it."

I felt a tug at my sleeve. "Dad, I'm back. Enough's enough."

"Why, here's your son," Spencer said, as the two women murmured appreciation. "Ike, right? It's hard to believe you're Julia's great-grandson. How old are you now, Ike?"

"Nine."

"What big blue eyes you have."

"The better to see you with."

This was the closest Ike had ever come to making a flip remark in public, but Spencer threw his head back and laughed.

"This young man has your number, Spencer," Lou said.

"He's not the only one. But I meant it, Harry, when I said I owe Julia. Clients like these are lambs in search of the slaughterhouse. In my business you've got to plan for the rainy days ahead."

"So would the city and the state if they learned a lesson from their own histories." The speaker was a tall, heavyset man in his sixties whose wispy gray hair stuck up from his head. He had been standing on the edge of the conversation. "But politicians hereabouts never plan for the future. They take the money and run. What do you think the city's going to fall back on when the bubble bursts?''

Tatine glared at the stranger. "What makes you so sure the bubble will burst?''

"It always has.''

"Some people think the glory days are here to stay," Tatine said grimly. "I'm talking about prominent local businesspeople. Where did you say you're from?''

"I live in Atlanta, but I was born and bred in this briar patch.''

"You ought to move back before you claim the right to bad-mouth your birthplace.''

"I might just do that. I spend my nights, if not my days, missing New Orleans." His eyes gleamed. "But love doesn't have to be blind.''

"You'd better watch what you say to Tatine," Lou said. "For such a well-bred lady she's got a mighty short fuse.''

"Lou, I do not.''

"I've been specially careful ever since she started packing that pistol.''

All of us, Ike included, laughed. We stopped when we saw Tatine's face.

"Lou, you weren't supposed to tell.''

"It's nothing to be ashamed of, darling. Show these men what you have in your purse.''

Tatine raised her eyebrows. Her glances darted to right and left. She smiled slyly.

"Buzzy made me start carrying it after I got mugged. A black man smashed my car window when I was stopped at a light and grabbed my purse at knifepoint.''

"Buzzy's such a thoughtful husband," Lou said. "Now go ahead, show us your new toy.''

Tatine opened her handbag a few inches and lowered it. Inside, partially obscured by a lace handkerchief, we could see what looked like a chrome cap pistol with a mother-of-pearl handle.

"Buzzy bought it at some antique shop in the Quarter. Right down the street from you, Spencer." Tatine looked at Ike. Still smiling, she extended the bag. "I bet you're just dying to hold it.''

Ike peered up at me questioningly.

"Maybe some other time. Right now Ike and I have to excuse ourselves. This talk has been fascinating and more instructive than you might guess. Spencer, I'll urge Grandmother to collect that commission."

As we moved into the crowd, I whispered to Ike, "A zoo is right. Tell me, how much of that talk did you really understand?"

"Maybe more than I think I did. Would that lady really have let me hold her gun?"

Just then, lightning flashed outside. A slow rumble was followed by a resounding crash. Wind whipped a curtain into the room. When someone yelled "Batten down the hatches!" the level of hilarity abruptly escalated. An old man near the fireplace leaned back as if to steady himself and knocked a half-empty champagne glass off the mantelpiece. The woman talking to him caught the glass in midair and drained it dry, all in one sweeping gesture of her jeweled wrist.

The trumpeter stepped through one of the French windows. "Aw-right, le's take it from the top!" He raised his instrument. Eyes popping, he hit the pickup notes of "When the Saints Go Marching In." Aunt Bessie rose from her chair like a wound-up toy and headed the line that began to form. Elbows pumping, hands clapping, fingers snapping, the guests burst uproariously into song. Then they pranced into the dining room behind the cakewalking trumpeter as he blasted his clarion call through ceilings and roof into the low-lying dome of heaven beyond.

"At this rate," I said, "they'll have to cart some of the guests home on stretchers. We'd better find Aunt Bessie while we can."

But we never made it to Aunt Bessie. As we headed across the room, Ike said, "Dad, over there. That woman in the white dress."

"Don't point," I said, turning to look where he pointed.

To the left of the fireplace, a young man and woman stood talking. Or rather, he was talking and she was listening, if she was listening at all, with a face ready to explode.

It shouldn't have surprised me, but it did, that Ike had singled out the guest I had been looking for.

The man was about my age, in his thirties, and seemed familiar. He was handsome, trim, and conspicuously well dressed. His eyes were glazed and his mouth worked incessantly, like the mouth of a fish.

The woman was something else. With her deep-set eyes, wide mouth, and noble shoulders, she looked like a young Clytemnestra. Her thick black hair and eyebrows had lives of their own. She might have chosen her white dress to show off her skin but she wore it indifferently as if she had pulled it from someone else's closet. If you had pointed out to her the wine stain or mud stain on the skirt, just above her right knee, she would probably have received the news with stony unconcern.

"A fine room, a handsome architectural memento," the young man was saying. "But it needs to be revitalized by a more contemporary concept, one that plays off the old against the new. We could give it dead-white walls—"

"Oh, screw those dead-white walls. Please, please, Jack, don't talk about what *we* could do. We're finished. You know we're finished."

He looked down at her. "Don't get hysterical. Control yourself, Elizabeth." His voice slid from smug to nasty so quickly I thought he must be drunk, or worse. "Take a pill, take a drink, go back for some more shock treatment. Better still, a frontal lobotomy."

She threw the rest of her drink in his face. This included two ice cubes that landed on the floor with the clatter of large dice.

Her gesture was so abrupt, like the gestures in dreams, that she was out of the room before I could fully register what had happened. Ike had of course taken it all in.

"Did you see that, Dad? Right in the old kisser."

The young man stood motionless, staring dazedly at himself in the gilt mirror above the fireplace. Our eyes met in the mirror. Then he took his handkerchief from his breast pocket and dabbed at his face. It was possible that no one else had even noticed what had happened. At least, anyone who had was pretending not to.

It had been an ugly exchange on both sides. But the woman was like no one else I had ever seen, and her stricken look the moment before she threw her drink stayed with me. Without her, the crowded room seemed empty.

Leona appeared in the doorway behind Ike and signaled me that it was time for his dinner. When I led him to her, she took his hand from mine and said, "How's my man? Wait'll you see what Leona's got for you—something real special."

"Wait a minute, Leona. I want to say something to Dad." He fixed his eyes on mine. One was slightly larger than the other, with a higher eyebrow. "Are you going to find that woman?"

As usual, he was one step ahead of me. "I might just do that," I said.

*T*HREE

SHE WASN'T HARD to find. Smoking a cigarette, she was standing by one of the raised brick flower beds that bordered the alley leading from the front to the rear courtyard. Her white dress shone in the dim glow that spilled from the dining-room windows. The flagstones were filmed with light rainfall from the aborted storm.

She spoke first. "You saw that, didn't you?" She did not turn to face me directly.

I made no reply.

"Not a pretty spectacle. But ends of marriages rarely are."

"Is it the end?"

"It is. It lasted all of three years. He married me for money, I guess, and I married him—I don't know why I married him. Yes I do. I had run my course in this town and I thought he would give me something new to work with. That sounds awful—no, it *is* awful—but it's true. And he seemed straight enough at the time, or maybe it was his family that did."

"Aren't you straight?"

She laughed. As laughs go, it was genuine, if a little too rat-a-tat-tat. "I am beautiful and I am smart and I am rich," she recited in a self-mocking singsong, "but straight I am not." She turned then and gave me an appraising stare. "And who are you?"

"Harry Preston. Mrs. Hobson's grandson. My son and I live in the place out back."

This interested her. "What else?"

"I'm a lawyer."

"And a father." She paused. "And a husband?"

"My wife died last year."

I was glad that she did not make the usual response to this statement. She said simply, "I want a drink, Harry, and I don't want to go back inside. Can we go to your place?"

"Sure."

Rain had driven the musicians to the shelter of the front gallery. From that welcome distance I could hear them playing "Marie Laveau, the Voodoo Queen" when I opened the door to the stairwell that led to my apartment above the garage. We climbed the steep stairs, I switched on the light in the living room, and she said, "This is a good room. It's like the rooms in the main house but on a smaller scale."

"I thought your husband was the one interested in houses."

"You *were* attending, weren't you?" She threw her purse on the sofa. "No, I'm interested in houses, too—some houses. Actually, it's a fairly recent interest, and one of the few Jack and I have in common. Maybe it's because I grew up in an awful house by the park. Big and grand and in bad taste—all the bad taste that money could buy."

"Why not tell me your name?"

"My married name is Bennett." She said this so carefully that I wondered what other name she was hiding. "Elizabeth Bennett. Like Jane Austen's heroine, but with two *t*'s."

"Elizabeth. Of the fine eyes and superior moral intelligence?"

"A lawyer who reads."

"Some do."

"Not my husband, and he calls himself a lawyer. Nothing more demanding than *GQ* and *Architectural Digest*."

"We all went to school once."

"With some it doesn't take." She abruptly moved across the room as if executing a dance step and came to rest by my desk, where she incuriously fingered some papers on the surface. "Why don't I know you?" she asked.

"You're younger than I am. And obviously we don't travel in the same circles."

"What circles do you travel in?"

"None in particular."

"I've traveled in so many I don't know whether I'm coming or going." She lit a cigarette. "But tell me. You didn't grow up here, did you?"

It seemed to worry her that she couldn't pigeonhole me. "Not really. I came here during the summers with Mother, but I grew up in Connecticut. After college I decided to come here to law school at Tulane. Then I went to work, got married, Ike was born, Ann died. After she died I didn't want to go on living in the same house, so Ike and I moved down here. Temporarily, but here we are."

"You make life sound simple."

"It's a life like any other."

"No lives are like each other. Where's that drink?"

"Whiskey or vodka?"

"Whiskey. No water and not much ice."

I fixed drinks, she took hers, downed it like medicine, shuddered and gagged a little. We fell silent and studied each other. She looked to be in her late twenties. If her beauty was what you saw first, next was her agitation. Her slight trembling—she had been trembling since we had entered the room—didn't stop but seemed to become more controllable as she drank.

"I'll be all right," she said. "But I need another drink. Don't bother getting it, I'll get it myself," and she did.

She came back to the sofa and sat down facing me with one leg folded under her. Then she riveted me with her gaze. It was direct and glittering.

"All right," she said, "let's get down to cases. What did you come after me for?"

The trumpeter held a distant, wailing note, then the band stopped playing. The silence in the room hummed.

"You're not very talkative, are you?" she said. "Is that your way of hedging bets?"

"I talk when I have something to say."

"Right now you don't?"

"You asked a question I don't exactly know the answer to."

"Then put it this way, Harry Preston. What is it that you want from me?"

"Not one thing."

"Yes you do," she said, nodding slowly. "What made you think I was a pushover?"

"I didn't and don't."

"You just may be telling the truth." She set her glass on the table, leaned forward, and looking into my eyes, rested her right hand on my left knee, so lightly that her thumb's pressure on my inner thigh was almost weightless. It connected, though, and she saw that it had. I placed my hand over hers.

"Not now."

"No?"

"Bad timing."

"Not from the look of things."

"I meant for you. For me too."

"Is it possible you're just a nice guy?" she said. "A nice guy who's read a book or two?"

"Sure, that's me. But not quite a pushover."

"You're right. It was bad timing." She reached for her glass and, seeing that it was empty, started to stand up.

I took the glass from her hand. "My turn."

When I sat down again, I said, "You know, you needn't feel that you have to take charge."

"Take charge?"

"Run the show."

"But Harry. If you don't try to run the show, at least try, then it runs you."

"Is that so bad?"

"In my experience."

"Pretend this evening's different, then. Just take it as it comes."

"That's easy to say." But in a quick single movement she reversed her position on the sofa so that she lay back facing the room, with her head resting lightly on my shoulder. "Just like a first date," she said.

"Well, maybe it is."

"My God, you're right." She kicked off her shoes—scuffed white shoes with cruel and absurd high heels—and put her feet on the low table in front of the sofa. "So what's next?"

"I don't have a schedule."

"What about your son?"

"He's waiting for me back at Grandmother's."

She laughed softly. "In that case you won't be asking me to stay over. Children do make the best guardians."

"You need a place to stay?"

"I couldn't face Jack again tonight."

"What about calling a friend? Or a hotel?"

"Right now, I don't want to explain anything to anyone. As for hotels, you forget this is Carnival time. But there is one place—"

"Use this phone or the one in the kitchen."

When she returned from the kitchen she said, "I can't move there until tomorrow," but that was all the explanation she offered.

As it happened, the matter was settled when the phone rang a short time later. It was Ike. "Dad, if it's all right with you, I'm sleeping at Granny's tonight."

"How come?"

"Leona says I can watch the party from the top of the stairs. Just like I used to when you and Mom had people over."

Nothing in Ike's voice suggested that he didn't mean exactly what he said.

"You're sure that's what you want?"

"Sure I'm sure. Night, Dad."

"Good night, son."

When I rang off I turned back to Elizabeth, who was now sitting up, staring at me. I hesitated more than a moment before saying, "It looks as if my guardian has plans of his own."

She reached over, took my hand, and pressed the palm against her cheek. "I don't always act tough," she said quietly. "Just when I think I have to."

"I understand."

"Joking aside, would you mind if I slept here?"

"Of course not."

"And can you understand this, too? What I want now, what I need has nothing to do with sex. What I need is a safe harbor."

"I do understand. You'll stay in Ike's room."

"He wouldn't mind?"

"Not at all."

And that was the way things started.

We had another drink, then I went into the kitchen to get us something to eat. I peered into the nearly empty refrigerator. Luckily, Leona had given Ike and me a container of red beans and another of rice. I heated the beans in the microwave. Then I removed the chunks of sausage and coarsely pureed the beans in the food processor, thinning them only enough to achieve a barely liquid consistency. The thick soup went into two large bowls; in the center of each I floated an ice-cream scoopful of heated rice and surrounded the rice with sliced sausage. I brought the bowls in on a tray, along with a bottle of pepper vinegar, an already open bottle of red wine, and what was left of a French loaf I had bought that morning from a pastry shop near Jackson Square.

Elizabeth was lying on the sofa. At first I thought she was asleep, but she sat up abruptly. "God, does that smell good. Even when I think I can't eat anything, I'm always, always wrong."

We ate silently like companions of long standing. She took the same pleasure in this simple food that I did, using pepper sauce liberally and wiping her bowl clean with the heel of the loaf. She seemed completely at home in a stranger's living room, maybe because, at the moment, she had no real home of her own. As she ate she kept her thoughts to herself.

Around ten I showed her to Ike's room. She took in the posters, books, toys, and the narrow bed. "Someone lives here," she said. She brushed my arm with her hand, then closed the door without turning to face me.

In the middle of the night, I woke with the sense of there being someone else in my room. She was standing just inside the doorway, outlined by the light I had left on in the hall.

"Is something wrong?" I said.

"I woke up scared. Then I started thinking of you in the next room. Do you mind company?"

"I should tell you that it's been a while."

"No matter." She drew back the sheet and slid in next to me. The sudden touch of her bare skin on mine was electric. I had never known skin like hers, so smooth it might have been poreless: except for its warmth it felt like rare silk. Our mouths met. At once my body came to life.

"There, you see." She drew back. "Now lie still for a minute. Don't move."

"I want to move."

"Don't. First," she said softly, her mass of hair sweeping down my chest, "let me do this." Then, more softly still, "And now this."

"I've got to move."

"Not quite yet," but she didn't resist, only stiffened slightly, when I placed my left palm on the small of her back and reversed our positions in bed.

"This isn't a solo performance," I said.

"So you want to be old-fashioned?"

"It's not a bad place to start."

She clung to me and lifted herself as I pulled a pillow down under her. When I knelt between her legs, she reached forward and guided me into her very slowly as into a sheath, then held me fast. I sensed the pleasure she took in trying to make my body the prisoner of hers, but what the hell, at that moment I was a more-than-willing prisoner. Then I said, "Don't move."

She laughed. "I want to move."

"First let me do this."

"Oh, God."

"Now this."

"That drives me crazy."

"You can move now. If you really want to."

Throughout our lovemaking she was generous but impersonal until the moment that she said, "Harry," only once, but as if she really knew who I was. My own burning release was like a closed door being thrown open. It left me shaken.

Later, lying against me with her head on my chest and her right hand resting lightly on my stomach, she began talking again in that cool analytical tone that she had used at first.

"Don't talk," I whispered. I pulled her face toward me and kissed her eyelids: her bristly lashes tickled my lips. For the first time in months my body was happy and my head empty. Nothing mattered now except balls, cock, heart—tender lust for this complicated, smooth-skinned stranger. What I felt was simple enough. Couldn't complication wait?

"I wanted to say I was sorry—"

"Don't be sorry." I lifted her forward so that I could kiss her vertebrae, shoulder blades, and slim, strong neck. When I kissed her neck she shivered like a cat and laughed.

"Sorry for what I said earlier—"

"Did you say anything?" I bit her earlobe gently.

"Don't do that. I meant the bit about being rich and smart and beautiful. Of course, it's not entirely untrue, but to say it is a childish—"

The laugh that erupted when I put my tongue in her ear shot up through her stomach from the soles of her feet.

"Forget it. Anyway, you said it with irony. Now lean forward. Let me move here. Move forward again. Now come back slowly. Give me some help—"

"Don't count on my irony," she said. "It comes and—Harry. My God."

When she laughed explosively again, I felt every spasm. For me, this time was like being pulled inside out.

I woke lying on my stomach. One sheet was tangled on the floor. Winter sunlight slanted through yellow curtains, giving rise to wishful thinking. Where the curtains parted I saw a strip of two blues—the indigo façade of the house opposite, beneath a colder blue strip of sky. I felt unseasonably expectant, like a boy looking forward to his long summer's day.

When I turned over I saw Elizabeth standing before the mirror in her white dress, back to me, brushing her hair with quick violent strokes.

"What's going on?" I stretched. My groin ached with pleasure. "Come back to bed."

Filtered light bathed Elizabeth in a new golden glow. If I could keep her from talking, maybe things would stay simple. But no such luck.

"I've got to get out of here," she said.

"Why rush? Unless your husband's having you tailed."

"Don't joke. It's Ike I was thinking about. I don't want to be one of those shady ladies motherless little boys meet in the dawn's early light."

"Ike's still asleep over at Grandmother's." I stretched again. "It's Sunday morning. Let's hang around here. We'll make a plan."

"You've got a plan," she said, eyeing me in the mirror. "It's painfully obvious."

"Come ease the pain. As for Ike, there's nothing he'd like better than to meet you."

"Why do you say that?"

"At the party last night—Ike noticed you first," I said, lying just a little.

"Did he? That's flattering. But if and when I meet him I want to stage it somewhere terrific like Galatoire's, where I can ply him with luscious food and play the great lady."

"He might prefer a shady lady at Burger King. Better yet, come back to bed and we'll all three go to lunch later on. We'll keep it simple."

She turned toward me. "You are a nice guy, Harry. I haven't met many, but I recognize one when I see him. Even so, you aren't simple, and you know things aren't simple for me."

"I could make things simple," I said without thinking. "If only for—"

"Do you mean that?" She set the hairbrush on the chest of drawers. She studied me. I was suddenly aware of her being fully dressed while I lay naked in bed. Somehow this gave her an advantage. I got up and went over to embrace her, but she stepped back, shaking her head.

"Tomorrow," she said. "I'll buy you lunch tomorrow, Burger King _or_ Galatoire's, if—"

"If what?"

"I want a formal appointment. Well, fairly formal. I'll call your secretary and set it up."

"I still don't get—"

"You did say you were a lawyer, Harry, didn't you? Well,

I'm in bad need of a lawyer. One I can trust. As of last night," she said, "that's you."

Things definitely weren't simple now. "You can trust me, Elizabeth, and I'll give you some free advice if you want. But I'll never be your lawyer. Because of last night, if for no other reason."

She kissed me lightly. "So rigid and upright. Let's not argue. Free advice will be a good place to start."

ℐOUR

WHEN I ENTERED Grandmother's kitchen later that morning, Leona and Ike, familiar as an old married couple, were polishing crystal and silver goblets with soft cloths and setting them neatly in rows on the counter. Leona had been with Grandmother longer than either of them could remember. Massively handsome, with pale eyes and high cheekbones, she had a presence that even the vaulted space of Grandmother's kitchen couldn't minimize.

"Look at you two," I said.

"Leona let me stay up till after ten, Dad."

"And we're trying to settle on what I'm giving him for breakfast."

"Sausages, Leona, please."

"Sausages, then. But remember I got work to do."

"And biscuits?"

"No biscuits. French bread buttered and toasted, eggs, grits, sausages, but no biscuits."

"Biscuits?"

"They'll take a while."

"Biscuits."

"Okay, biscuits." A smile flashed across her face. "Nothing I wouldn't do for my boy."

I said, "You can throw an egg in for me while you're at

it," then left them to their flirtatious kitchen rituals. In the living room I found Grandmother sitting in front of the small inlaid table where she played her endless games of solitaire. Several windows were open to the day, and the room itself had been restored as if magically to its usual order and serenity, with no trace, except for a staleness in the air, of the whiskey-swilling horde that twelve hours before had been shaking the house to its foundations. In her black-and-white housecoat, with her pale skin and tightly coiled silver hair, Grandmother looked as serene and unshaken as this room in which, seated erect in her straight-backed chair, she habitually presided like some queen or minor deity. In an enormous crystal ashtray that was almost unbreakable, and big enough to smash a man's skull, burned one of her inevitable cigarettes: a local brand called Picayune that were strong as small cigars. She dealt her deck with such staccato precision that each card struck the table with a pistol-like report.

"Well, hello." Her glance was amused. "Now don't worry, I'm worldly enough not to—"

"I'm not worried. I was only following your lead."

"My lead?"

"Branching out."

"So that's what it's called."

"Besides, Ike was in good hands. The best. Now tell me what you know about Elizabeth Bennett."

"Berenson that was." She kept her voice neutral and her eyes on the cards. "She'll always be Berenson no matter how many other names she attaches along the way."

Berenson. The name had the special resonance of names you see on libraries and hospital wings, but for a moment I couldn't place it. Then I remembered.

"International Fruit. Is that Berenson her father?"

"Grandfather. Old man Berenson. He's the one who counts around here."

"You mean money?"

"Big money. What I was talking about last night. For years it was enough that he was International Fruit, but he's more than that now. Land—a lot of land. Oil and gas and who knows what else. Now he's so rich he makes most of the locals look like paupers."

"Berenson's not local? The name's been around forever."

"About as long as I have—not quite forever." Squinting, with her right thumb she lifted the corners of the cards in her left hand, extracted a black seven, and placed it on the red eight that was faceup on the table. "He's from Russia or the Ukraine or someplace. Came over here with an un-pronounceable name that he finally whittled down to Berenson. If you want to know more about him, ask Cousin Charles. He was Berenson's lawyer back in the thirties but he pulled out early because he was afraid he might dirty his hands."

"How?"

"Something political. Remember: Berenson's the sort who didn't just buy up things, he bought people. He even bought countries, then turned them into banana republics. I don't know what else he did. Ask Charles."

"And the girl?"

"I've only heard rumors. That's all I know about anybody. Maybe that's all there is to know."

"Skip the philosophy. Let's have the rumors."

She dealt the final card, observed the results, sighed fatal-istically, and lit another cigarette. She smoked in a masculine style that had always struck me as incongruous. She held the cigarette between thumb and forefinger, inhaled deeply, then emitted twin jets of smoke, dragonlike, from her nostrils. Watching her smoke, I somehow found it easier to believe that she had remained an excellent horsewoman into her six-ties, that she had been Grandfather's companion on hunting and fishing trips, and that she was in fact the crack shot she was reputed to be.

"I'm tired of talking. All I've heard is she's a handful. Always into trouble, in and out of schools and mental hos-pitals, now this marriage. Of course, one problem is that she had all that money but no one knew just where to place her."

"Place her?"

"It's the way of the world. Her mother was from Boston, one of those names you read about in history books. Then something happened to the father, I can't remember what, and old Berenson and his wife got custody of the girl. Every-one was surprised when young Bennett married her, but they shouldn't've been. The Bennetts have been broke for so long they grabbed the first life raft that floated by. And there's no denying, the girl is pretty.''

"Pretty!"

"Striking, then," she said mock-grudgingly. "I just wish you wouldn't get mixed up with her, Harry."

"Not because—"

"Of course not. It's the other thing. All that talk about insanity and mental hospitals."

"You mean the girl has 'tainted blood'?"

"Don't joke. No Haynesworth has ever been institutionalized."

"Quite a few should have been."

"Possibly. The fact is they weren't."

"No. They preferred drink, pills, and suicide."

She looked at me silently for some time. Finally she said, in an altered, shaken voice, "I refuse to believe that my daughter committed suicide."

"Maybe Mother didn't. Not exactly. But you know the way she and Father lived. And you know the way they died."

As if to steady herself, she placed her hands on the table in front of her.

I felt driven to go on without wanting to. "One of us," I said, "even had the bad taste to marry someone who got herself murdered."

"Don't. Please don't. Some things shouldn't be spoken of, at least not that way."

She turned and stared out the window. I had often thought that, given the chance, Grandmother would have built a moat outside the wall in order to keep the world, or the vast part of the world that offended her, at an even greater remove. I understood the way she felt even though I had, without knowing why, tried hard not to let her see it.

"Your poor Ann," she said, with her face still averted. "That poor, poor child. If she had stuck to her own way of life it wouldn't have happened. But no. She had to take that job at the hospital. She wanted to *help* people. She wanted to reha*bil*itate whores and lunatics and addicts, lost souls who should probably be allowed to stay lost. No wonder one of them turned against her, in that terrible way . . ."

The flood of memory, always imperfectly dammed, poured through. "It was a fluke, Grandmother. The man had been released. No one knows why he turned up at our house. No one knows why he did what he did. He was crazy. That's the point: there isn't any point." I could feel myself losing control.

"No, Harry. There is a point. When Ann took that job at Charity she opened the door to another world. And when she opened the door of your house the day she died—because we know she did open the door—that other world destroyed her. That's all I'm trying to tell you now. When you open a door, be careful what you let in."

I pulled up a chair next to hers. "Grandmother, you make Ann sound like a do-gooding innocent. She wasn't. She told me more than once she wasn't even very trusting."

"It's your turn to explain," she said, putting her hand over mine.

"Ann knew what her patients were capable of. She knew some of them were psychopaths, sociopaths. When she opened the door to that man, she just wasn't thinking. That's why I wake up at night grinding my teeth, furious with her and missing her too."

"It's strange you should say that." Grandmother leaned against my shoulder. The lemony scent of her cologne floated above the deeper aroma of Picayune tobacco. Elizabeth's hair had smelled of tobacco, but a different tobacco. My body held the smell and recent memory of hers. How long would I remember Ann's body, which had always smelled exactly of itself?

"I felt that way toward my Harry," Grandmother said. "With his heart, he wasn't supposed to go hunting and fishing, but he kept right on doing it. Then one day I got a call, and he just wasn't there anymore. The cases aren't the same, but this business of what to do with the rest of our lives is."

𝒻IVE

IKE AND I often spent Sundays shuttling between Grandmother's house and our apartment, and this Sunday was no exception. We were in Ike's room most of the morning. He did homework at his desk, while I lay on his bed reading the Sunday paper. Absorbed in his assignment, which at this point involved studying two printouts his teacher had given him, Ike radiated his usual intensity in repose.

Occasionally I would raise my eyes from a column of newsprint to watch him working. Then I remembered how Ann, always leery of making Ike self-conscious, had prevented herself from gazing at him for long periods of time, as she well could have, in what she had once called a trance beyond loving. Still, when we three had been in a room together I had liked the way she responded when he asked a question. The mutual clarity of their blue eyes had reflected light piercingly. Those times belonged to the past, but on this Sunday, as on others, I was often startled anew by the generosity of curved lashes, Ann's lashes, on Ike's cheek, as he bent over his desk, or his heavy eyelid that echoed hers. Elizabeth's eyes were an almost black green, her lashes thick but straight.

Ike turned to me. "Dad, what do you remember about fairy tales?"

"Not much. Why?"

"Mr. Cassidy read a book that talked about good and bad fairy tales. I mean ones that end the right way or the wrong way. He's given us two that end the wrong way. We're supposed to choose one and rewrite the ending."

"Sounds like a good assignment."

"But what if the wrong endings seem to be the right ones?"

"Do they?"

"I'm not sure yet. Does Othermama know about fairy tales?"

This was a private name Ike had given Grandmother after Ann's death. He did not call her by it to her face, although I think she would have been pleased if he had.

"Well, she probably remembers more than I do. Why not ask when we see her later on?"

"I will."

I felt guilty when I couldn't readily enter Ike's world. For too many months he had been my lifeline, and I knew that he sensed this, as children will, at that deeper level where meaning is. But it was an unfair responsibility I wanted to free him of.

Meeting Elizabeth had disturbed something that had been stagnant inside me. Now I was pulled as if by a strong current that could lead me out of myself and into a different place. I felt myself giving in to it. But I wanted to choose to give in.

Ike interrupted my thoughts, as he often did, with a remark that connected with them. "You know, Dad, this room smells different. Like a woman's been here."

"Perfume?"

"No, a little like Mama, but different." He rarely spoke of Ann.

"Well, a woman did sleep here last night." I didn't add: for part of the night.

"That woman at the party?"

"Yes. Her name's Elizabeth. She needed a place to stay, and I told her you wouldn't mind if she slept in your bed. Do you?"

His gaze held mine. "No, I don't mind. I like her smell."

I got up, went over to him, and placed my palm lightly on top of his head. His hair was thick and so blond it felt different from other hair, like fine-textured hay.

When he drew back and looked up at me, he blinked once. "I mean it, Dad," he said, then turned to the work on his desk.

$\mathcal{S}$IX

THAT AFTERNOON WE were slated to go with Grandmother to a parade party at Cousin Charles Haynesworth's house on St. Charles Avenue. The parade was Dionysus and marked the official beginning of Carnival Week. I still had enough New England in me never to have gotten quite used to this week—a dreamlike, time-out period punctuated by parades at odd hours, drunken clients calling to cancel appointments, a buoyant air of truancy intensified by twinges of guilt that swept through the town. Like other parents of young children, Ann and I had taken Ike to every parade we could, but that Sunday I was feeling lazy and private, in no mood to mingle. When Grandmother called at two to tell me she was ready, I said, "Why don't Ike and I drop you off? We'll take in a movie, then collect you afterwards."

With me, Grandmother's policy was usually hands-off, but today she said, "Harry, I won't let you become a recluse."

"Skipping a parade party won't make me a recluse!"

She laughed. "Some might take it as the first symptom. Besides, Ike loves parades and you know how much Charles cares about these social things."

She was right about that. Even before I had joined the firm, Charles had swamped Ann and me with invitations to Carnival Balls, cocktail parties for everything from Thanks-

giving and Christmas to Mardi Gras and Easter, parade parties, picnics across the Lake, New Year's at the Jackson
Club, lunches at the races, random family celebrations.
Whenever a new invitation had arrived, Ann would give me
one of her candid stares. "Only if you say we have to. Otherwise, the lady regrets." After Ike's birth we had used him
shamelessly as an excuse to decline. Because Ann's background had been out-of-town and academic, she had little
patience with the city's relentless party-going rituals. Apart
from this, Ann had never really cottoned to Cousin Charles.
"He has an empty space where his heart should be," she
had said to me once. "No, not empty: I see an engraved
invitation prominently displayed."

"He's stuffy, I admit, but aren't you being rough on
him?"

She shook her head. "Another thing: if he could, he would
pull you into that empty space."

"What do you mean?"

"Didn't you say he had a son who died?"

"Yes, Jeremy. He was only seventeen when he fell off a
Carnival float and a truck ran over his head."

"Another local horror story. Well, I sympathize with
Charles wanting you for a son, but he's not the right father
figure for you. Sometimes when I see you together I think
he's trying to brainwash you."

"I don't brainwash easily."

"But you can seem easygoing and pliable, Harry, and that
may have given Charles the wrong impression. Only *I*
know," she said, "that you're really stubborn as a mule."

When I said, "Anyhow, I'm not in the market for a father
figure," she had given me another look.

"Just don't forget that when the next invitation rolls in."

But Ann was dead, and although I had started to beg off
I had my own reasons for going to this party, not just for
Ike's sake; if I still owed Charles anything after all these
years, now was the time to pay it back any way that I could.
Grandmother was waiting in the courtyard when we went
down, wearing a gray and black dress that seemed to go with
her silver hair. "Two charming escorts," she said, taking us

each by a hand, "when I'd feel lucky to have only one."
Her hand felt powdery and soft.

The early promise of sun had waned and the day was now
overcast, cool but humid enough to bring sweat to my forehead. Above Jackson Avenue crowds had already gathered
under the live oaks on both sides of St. Charles and on the
neutral ground where, on ordinary days, streetcars rattled to
and from the Quarter. Fathers were erecting ladders for their
children to stand on, and the children were munching mouth-
fuls of pink cotton candy. No sign yet of mounted policemen;
we opened the car windows and listened in vain for drums.

Cousin Charles lived in a white Victorian Gothic edifice
that occupied nearly half a block facing the Avenue in the
Garden District and conveyed a sense of permanence and
solidity. "How long has Charles lived here?" I asked Grandmother as we parked at the side entrance. "Was this house
in the Haynesworth family?"

"Lord, no. I must have told you before, Charles grew up
with a name and the memory of money. His father was one
of those Haynesworths who blew everything, and I don't
think Charles ever forgave him for it. He had to put himself
through law school, then afterwards—" She paused. "Actually, I think Charles made his first real money by marrying
Eleanor. This house belonged to her family. They've spent
a lot on it through the years even though Eleanor insists on
keeping it the way her parents, the old Huberwalls, had it at
the turn of the century. Dark mahogany paneling. Red damask walls and velvet curtains. Orientals even in dead summer." She sighed. "Not even a trace of Adam or
Hepplewhite."

"What's Hepplewhite?" Ike asked.

"Lightness and elegance, dear heart. Two antidotes to op-
pressive gloom."

$\mathcal{S}$EVEN

A FAMILIAR CROWD milled in the blood-red main hall and dining room to the right. On this occasion its ranks were extended by large numbers of small children and teenagers. Waiters passed silver trays of milk punches and Bloody Marys and fluted glasses of champagne. Grandmother left me to lead Ike toward the library, where some of his young cousins were playing. As I headed toward the dining room I saw Cousin Charles coming toward me with an extended hand. Although he was pushing seventy-five, his step was still nimble.

"Harry, my boy. It's a treat to see you at one of these affairs. How is your grandmother, the amazing Julia? And Ike? Are they here, too?"

Cousin Charles Haynesworth was a worldly man. That is: his victory in the world, especially in the isolated inner world of this city, was total. He had been the King of the Carnival without ever showing that he cared about it, and his daughter Diana had been Queen of Comus. These weren't social and civic honors that he had campaigned for directly—unless you regarded his entire life as a kind of campaign. His acquired fortune was rumored to be either "considerable" or "vast." His household was managed by an unobtrusive black butler of reputable antiquity. He had a vacation compound across

Lake Pontchartrain. The impeccable manners of his still-beautiful wife Eleanor allowed her to show flashes of humor, if not of insight. At his dinner parties the food and wine were locally famous, but he himself only picked at his plate. Abstention and mild disdain were so intrinsic to his manner that his success seemed to have courted him, not he it. I had once observed Charles playing cards, after lunch, with the dining-room crowd at the Jackson Club. His dapper figure, ascetic features, and saturnine eyebrows isolated him from his food-loving, moonfaced cohorts. Unlike them, he never drank while he was playing cards, and he won more often than not.

Through Mother's family I was *of* the city even if I often chose not to be *in* it. Through her marriage to Bennett, Elizabeth might be in the city but she would never be of it. Charles was both of the city and, by choice, in it up to his neck.

"Grandmother's in the library with Ike," I said. "She seems to have survived last night's fracas, and so has her house."

"I don't think I saw you at her party."

"Oh, I was there, but not for long. Something came up."

"I see." He smiled slightly. "But don't forget, Harry, we all have social obligations, no matter how onerous they become."

Charles's tone was such that I started to lie to him. I almost said: "But I have a young son, sir, who requires attention." Remembering the night before, I kept my mouth shut.

"You know," he said, "you're privileged to have Julia for a grandmother. She's a woman of rare qualities. I can still remember as a young man, and I was just that much younger than she, walking into Antoine's one day and being told by the waiter, 'Your cousin Mrs. Hobson's in the Rex Room. Everyone's trying to get a glimpse of her.' That man's voice was positively reverent." Familial satisfaction flooded Charles's face. "Yes, Julia's amazing. And that house suits her well. Frankly, I'm sorry she's thinking about selling it."

"That's funny. I thought you had urged her to sell."

"If Julia said that, she overstated. I was only pointing out pros and cons. In any case, it would be a shame for that house to go out of the family. If Julia decides to sell, Diana and Rudolph might be interested in buying it. That way Julia wouldn't have to traffic with brokers. I know how such dealings offend her."

What Charles said and what he meant weren't always the same. I decided to test him.

"What gets me, Charles, is how out of touch Grandmother is. She had no idea what that property is really worth."

"But you knew? And you told her?" He seemed surprised. "Of course. Good. We can't let Julia make any rash decisions, my boy."

An overweight, overdressed couple pressed forward then to claim Charles's attention. I knew the husband only by his nickname, "Melonbelly"—one that I hesitated to use. He shoved his moist red face close to my cousin's and shouted: "Charles, your parade party means Mardi Gras has officially arrived."

Charles recoiled perceptibly but held his expression free of distaste.

A phalanx of children, Ike among them, charged toward us from the rear hall. Ike grabbed my hand. "Let's go outside, Dad. The parade's coming. I just heard the first oompah-pah."

Approaching drumbeats can quicken the most jaded heart, and Ike's wasn't jaded. My heart quickened in response to his. This would be his first Carnival without Ann: it was up to me to make it as special as I could. Outside, the parade crowd that had gathered on the divided Avenue was thicker than before. We made our way as far as we could toward the front, then, though Ike was really too old for it, I hoisted him onto my shoulders as so many other fathers had their children. To steady himself he placed one hand on either side of my head. Drums pounded and the crowd roared as maskers riding the floats pelted them with glass beads and other trash.

Freeing his right hand to catch what he could, Ike gripped my hair with his left. The parade lurched across our line of vision. Each crayon-colored papier-mâché float portrayed an episode from the myth of Theseus. Procrustes's bed was followed by dreadlocked Medea and her poisoned cup; the Minotaur in the labyrinth and Ariadne's thread, by the patricidal black sail on the voyage home from Crete; Amazonian love and Hippolytus's fatal chariot ride, by Phaedra's suicide, the encounter with Oedipus in the Grove of the Furies reserved till the end. By then Ike had fistfuls of treasure and I had a cramp in my neck, but it was a small price to pay.

The last float disappeared, but more was to come. Teeny-bopper cheerleaders in skimpy satin and sequined outfits strutted by in formation, twirling their batons and twitching their bottoms to a prerecorded voice that chanted: "I want it, and I want it *now!*" Some of the girls looked scarcely older than Ike.

When we got into the car to go home, I said to Grandmother, "Did Charles tell you Diana was interested in buying your house?"

"He certainly did not." She gave an abrupt little laugh. "Harry, do you think that's why Charles didn't tell me what my house is really worth?"

"Maybe he doesn't know what the market is in the Quarter."

"Charles? Why, Charles knows what everything's worth in this city. And everybody. Much as I respect him, all he's ever been interested in is making money—the only Haynesworth in our generation of whom *that* could be said. Diana's greedy, too: she's not his daughter for nothing. Once I saw her, a grown woman, pass up dessert at a family party, then steal a piece of cake from a child's plate when the poor little thing's back was turned. He howled bloody murder when he saw it was gone."

"Grandmother, is there anything damaging about anybody that you *don't* know?"

"Plenty. But I know more than I need to." She laughed softly to herself. "About Diana's husband, Rudolph, for instance. No, it's too wicked to speak of poor Rudolph. This time I really shouldn't. Not in front of Ike."

"Granny, please tell about Rudolph," Ike said. "I promise I won't listen."

Grandmother laughed again. Old age and temperament had largely liberated her from the discretion she had been taught in her youth. Like many good storytellers, she couldn't resist an eager ear.

"Well, there's his family. The Careres. Old Creoles who think their Mallard beds justify aristocratic pretensions but who're rigidly petit bourgeois at heart, inbred and so stingy they keep the butter locked in an armoire so the cook won't waste it."

"How could you possibly know that?" I asked.

"Because I *knew* Rudolph's aunt when we were girls! We were in school together that one year I went to the Sacred Heart Convent, before Mama decided education and religion didn't mix. And of course all the older Careres turned into serious drinkers of the worst type—"

"You got types?"

"Just listen. When Rudolph's parents sold their house down the block from mine on Esplanade, the buyers had to haul out truckloads of bottles from the crawl space underneath. There was even a chute in a second-floor bedroom that the Careres pitched bottles down so neighbors couldn't count them in the trash. These weren't whiskey bottles, either, these were liqueur bottles and absinthe bottles, sticky-sweet stuff only Creoles could stomach. You do know why absinthe was outlawed in this country, don't you? Because wormwood pickles the brain. Maybe that explains poor Rudolph—"

"Why do you keep saying poor Rudolph?"

"Have you ever talked to him?"

"At a hundred family gatherings."

"Do you remember anything he said?"

"Not really, but—"

"Oh, I know, I know," she said impatiently. "At first Rudolph doesn't sound any different from the other men in his group. They all talk that private language made up of fatuous banalities. My point is, that's worked to Rudolph's advantage. He gets by just sitting there like a swarthy wax dummy, a fixed smile on his face. But the truth about Rudolph is that he's always been the tiniest bit backward. His parents brought him up to believe decent manners could get him through life—even through school. And in a way, they have."

"He's done pretty well for himself, hasn't he?"

"Well, Charles set Rudolph up in the oil business back in the early sixties. But everyone supposes Charles pulls the strings. That's Charles's way, you know. Take the matter of my house. I'll bet Charles has been pushing Diana and Rudolph to buy it. He's always had a thing about my house."

"If you want to keep the house, Grandmother, why won't you let me help with expenses or at least pay rent?"

"I've never had a tenant. Why should my grandson pay rent? I offered you that apartment as a gift. A gift that's not freely given, one that's taken back or has strings attached, is worse than no gift at all."

"Then let me gently insist. First, that you rent the apartment to help pay the upkeep on your house and second, that you allow Ike and me to be your first tenants—paying tenants—until we get settled elsewhere. Everyone gains."

She hesitated. "Well, since you are my lawyer—"

"One who's giving sound counsel."

"Then I could still leave the house to you and Ike."

"That's not what I had in mind."

"I know. But it's something I want to do." She sat up. "Right, then. All settled." She giggled. "And this way we have the added pleasure of depriving grabby Diana. Now let's celebrate. I'm famished. I was so family-trapped at Charles's that I didn't even make it to the dining room. Drive around the corner to the Pontchartrain Coffee Shop. Ike can order a hamburger and mile-high pie. Harry, you and I'll have crabmeat au gratin and those delicious muffins they serve. And one ice-cold martini first. Only one. Straight up. Clear as crystal. With just a sliver of pinched lemon zest floating at the bottom."

Ike said, "Granny, you know how to make people have fun."

"Why not? Having fun's next best to being happy."

When we reached St. Charles and Jackson Avenue, Grandmother said in a different voice, "Living here as long as I have, you can't even drive a block without staring your past in the face. Pull over here, Harry. Just for a minute. I want to tell Ike a story.

"Ike, do you see that gas station on the corner? That's

where your great-granny grew up, centuries ago. Can you believe Papa's house stood there once? Whitewashed brick, three stories high, with narrow Corinthian columns, and a formal rose garden in back. Papa lost it during the Depression, and so help me, the city let the next buyers tear it down to put up that monstrosity." She paused as if to let the past come into focus. "Anyhow, here's where we lived. Sister and I, that's Adele who died before you were born, Ike, we were so overprotected we scarcely crossed the street without a maid behind us. Know who that maid was? Inez, Leona's mother—that's how far back she and I go. Adele and I were spoiled rotten, too. Wasn't anything Papa wouldn't give us, me especially. Everyone knew I was his favorite, and even Adele didn't seem to mind. It was just the way things were. He didn't think I could do any wrong, wrong by his standards, I mean, and that was why he was so furious when I eloped with his friend Harry Hobson."

I said, "You eloped with Grandfather? I never knew that."

She smiled. "Hard as it is to believe, I slipped out the front door, rode the streetcar downtown, met Harry at the St. Louis Cathedral, and we were married that noon. The problem was that Papa had grandiose plans for me to marry a French count he and Mama had met on one of their trips to Europe: a perfectly charming man, except that I wasn't in love with him. Not that Papa had anything against Harry; he just didn't see him as a husband for me. As I said, he was one of Papa's friends, and I first met him when Papa brought him home for a drink. They were in the living room when I came in. Harry was standing with his elbow on the mantel, framed by that same gilt mirror that's over my fireplace now. I saw his profile first, then he turned when I said hello. I nearly fell over: he was the handsomest man I ever saw. But let me add quickly that he was also one of the least vain and self-centered: my Harry was no peacock. After we eloped, Papa and Mama didn't speak to him for a year, but I brought them round in the end. One Sunday we went over for dinner as if nothing had happened. That was the way people could be in those days."

"Why didn't they see Grandfather as a husband for you?"

"Age, to begin with: he was more their generation than

mine. Then religion: the usual—I was Catholic and he wasn't. Not that I cared, especially since we were married by a priest. Papa talked about money, too, and what an irony that he lost his seven years later. After all, your grandfather ran a perfectly decent import-export business that allowed us to do pretty much what we wanted. He just wasn't the sort to devote himself to the money thing. But the truth is, I think Papa was jealous that I loved him so.''

"Any regrets?''

"Only that he died long before me, but that was the risk I took, and I knew it when I married him. So remember, Ike, when you grow up and start to think about marrying, remember your great-granny married for love in a day when not everyone did.''

As I drew up to park across from the Pontchartrain Hotel, Ike said from the backseat: "Look over there, Dad. That woman again: Elizabeth. The one who slept in my bed.''

"Where is she?''

"She just went into the hotel.''

"Suddenly I'm tired," Grandmother said with a sigh. "Why go to the Pontchartrain when we have so many leftovers at home? Like that heavenly crabmeat ravigote, so much better the next day. Ike, we'll get you a hamburger from Ruby Red's on Esplanade. Then your father and I'll be able to put our feet up, so to speak. Is that all right?''

"Okay with me.''

"With me too," I said. I wondered whether Grandmother saw me smiling. She had rarely been this transparent. But I didn't want to encounter Elizabeth so soon again anyway, least of all with Grandmother in tow.

After supper, I lighted the fire Leona had laid in Grandmother's oversized living-room fireplace. Then I stretched out on the sofa and stared at it while she and Ike tackled his writing assignment at the oval rosewood table behind me.

"Child, why change the ending of 'The Little Mermaid'? It's meant to be a cautionary tale.''

"What's that, Granny?''

"One that points out stupid risks you shouldn't take. Surely you can't have her end up with the prince. He's meant to marry one of his own kind.''

It had never occurred to Grandmother not to speak to a child with such certitude. But Ike had always known how to deal with her.

"Then let's let her have a life in this world, at least. Let's let her walk without those sword pains in her feet."

"That was the witch's condition she accepted when she risked everything on the off chance of winning the prince's love. The point is, she lost. She was meant to have a tail and live under the sea."

Her emphasis made me wonder whether it was aimed at me.

"But Granny," Ike said, "you took a risk once. And you weren't sorry."

Silence. Then: "You have a point there, child. But it was a calculated risk, and I did end up with the prince. If only for a time."

&IGHT

DURING MY EARLY years at Eastman and Haynesworth I had often had occasion to ponder the distinction, if any, between being an innocent and being a fool. Ann had told me once: people trust you because you're trusting. But how many years ago had that been? If my first impulse was still to take people and situations at face value, I preferred to think it wasn't because I was innocent but rather because most forms of deception required so much wasted effort. I had long since accepted that I lived and worked in a world of appearances that often proved at least partly false. I didn't have any illusions left about the nature of the firm for which I worked. I didn't even have illusions, though I could have used some, about why I had gone on working there as long as I had. No matter how much I tried to distance myself from what I regarded as the system, I continued to accept the special rewards that it alone could confer.

In my second year with the firm, Mike Shushan, an associate who had been there a year longer than I, came into my office one day with the look of news on his face.

"Congratulate me, Harry. You're staring at the newest associate of Macauley and Stein."

"Sure, I congratulate you if it's what you want. But you

surprise me, Mike. I didn't even know you were job hunting.''

''I can guess what you're thinking. Macauley, Stein doesn't carry the same local clout as an old-line outfit like this one. But they're giving me a salary hike—modest, I'll admit—and a promise of partnership.''

''What about here?''

He looked at me quizzically.

''I mean what about your chance of partnership here? Judge Eastman sings your praises, and not just inside these walls. He calls you a tax wizard. This firm will be sorry to lose you.''

''Harry, you'll always be the man I have in mind when I say some of my best friends could have been Christians.''

I laughed, but he must have seen that I didn't fully catch his meaning.

''Eastman, Haynesworth doesn't take Jewish partners. They never have and probably never will. I knew that when I came here. I only wanted to smooth a few of my rough edges and raise my market value.''

''What if Eastman endorses you?''

''Eastman's on the way out. He's already had one stroke. He hasn't brought in any significant new business in years. If he has another stroke and survives, he'll be shoved upstairs and acknowledged as the figurehead he's already become. That will leave Haynesworth in charge, and about him I have no doubts.''

''Again, how can you be sure?''

''I'll answer you this way. How many Jewish members does Rex have?''

''How would I know that?''

''Not many, and most of them ride together on the same floats. Yet these characters are only too eager to be members. You know what other Jews call them? White Jews. Even if your cousin Haynesworth made me a partner, which he wouldn't, I'd have to become one of those white Jews. That's not for me.''

''I've never paid attention to these things.''

''Why would you? You're connected. That's what counts around here. Believe me, this firm will take a black partner before it takes a Jew. When it does, it'll simply be bowing to the inevitable. But that black will have to be the whitest black you've ever seen in these parts. Not an Oreo—the filling *in* the Oreo. For now, the next associate in this firm to make partner will be you. Not that you won't deserve it. You work as hard as the rest of us and you're smarter than most. But those won't be the only reasons you're tapped.''

In the eight years I had been with the firm since, nothing had happened that contradicted Mike's assessment of the way things were. Tacitly I had bought into the firm's unstated system of values. I had been made a junior partner at twenty-nine, and now I could count on a hundred and fifty thousand a year, sometimes more if my performance merited a few of the percentage points held in reserve. My education in the East had been liberal. My upbringing had been liberal but unsettled, even chaotic. In exchange for the semblance of stability, I had learned to bite my tongue. This was easy enough in my line of business, especially since conversations such as the one I had with Mike had never occurred since, or not within the walls of Eastman, Haynesworth. Even Ann and I rarely discussed the silent pact I had made.

In my fourth year with the firm, I brought off a deal that convinced Charles not only that I was a capable negotiator, but also that I had learned my way around to a degree that he could take seriously where profit was concerned. That June my name moved above the line on the firm's door that separated partners from associates. But this wasn't why the case remained so clearly in mind. Nor had it connected with anything else in my life the way other cases sometimes had. Instead, it had come to stand for this place and time, New Orleans during its latest and maybe last boom period. The elements of the case were familiar—family and land, past and present brought together as progress was superimposed on decay in the kind of steaming, layered compost that dissolved the distinction between them. The case also bore out the truth of what Grandmother had once told me: ''You don't need brains to get rich around here. All you need is a patch of swamp somebody ceded to your grandfather in payment of a bad debt.''

The client in question was a shrewd Cajun and would-be

developer from La Place named Clet Dupepe. A former client
for whom I had handled a tricky piece of intrafamilial diplo-
macy had recommended me to Dupepe. Beyond that, Dupepe
came to me because he wanted a young lawyer in an established firm. He had made enough money in offshore navigation to pursue what he called the path of progress, and he
felt that only a young lawyer should walk that path with him;
but he also wanted the image of respectability that an old-
line firm like Eastman, Haynesworth could provide. For Clet
Dupepe the path led across the river from New Orleans to
the area known as West Bank, even though on a map it
looked like east. Driving around in his Jeep (he reserved his
Jaguar for evening use) on a land-scouting expedition, he had
come across a swampy, barren tract, not too far from the
Mississippi River Bridge, on which he envisioned a shopping
center. Dupepe proposed that I handle everything: acquisition, financing, plans, and specs. He figured the cost of the
shopping center at close to three million. When I offered to
take a reduced fee in exchange for a ten percent interest in
the center as a kicker, or bonus, if the project reached frui-
tion, he readily agreed.

The trickiest stage in this transaction proved to be the initial one: acquisition of the land. It was owned by two brothers and a sister, heirs of a notorious political boss and white
supremacist from Belle Chasse named Adonis Coco. The Cocos' power dated back several generations. Grandmother said
the family had been a nest of vipers in their glory days, but
the present-day Cocos proved to be harmless as grass snakes.
With the elder Coco's death, the family's fortunes had
waned. As with so many sons of tyrannical fathers, the brothers were alike in their shiftless bonhomie. Since the family
had already drilled for oil on the land, without success, the
brothers were eager to sell it. But the sister, who had married
an old New Orleans name and lived in the Garden District,
opposed the sale. It was in convincing her to sell that my
real achievement lay.

Alta was the third wife of an older man whose coffee
business was inherited and whose temperament was held to
be as domineering as her father's. Her air was that of the
convent schoolgirl she had once been. She wanted to hold

onto the land because marriage had given her apparent financial security, and the land played into her fantasy of her family's plantation past. That was when I decided to do some research. After consulting the rumor mill and a private detective, I learned the complexities of Alta's situation.

Her husband had already established a pattern of discarding wives in favor of younger trophies. Presently he was meeting a blond divorcée twice a week at a downtown motel that rented rooms by the hour. Alta was pushing forty and her marriage had been childless. My belief that she could benefit from my counsel made me more than usually persuasive. When we met apart from her brothers, her conflicting characteristics began to emerge. She had defied family tradition when she married a divorced man. I sensed a steely element under her deferential manner. She was one of those women, not unusual in the South, in whom childish romanticism coexisted uneasily with a street-smart practicality that I tapped into and that she may well have owed to her father. I showed her how much she stood to lose in the case of a forced partition and public sale of the land. Without discussing her marriage, I showed her what she stood to gain. Since she had inherited her share of the land before her marriage, whatever money she made from its sale would be hers alone; instead of relying on the men in her life as she had been trained to do, she would achieve a measure of true independence. This was the argument that convinced her.

Two years later I represented Alta when her husband sued for divorce. Alta had long suspected his infidelity but couldn't prove it. She herself was free from fault. She never questioned my using evidence of her husband's adultery that I had gathered earlier to win alimony from him now, alimony which would continue until her remarriage. "But I'll probably never marry again," she said to me when we drank to her victory in my office. "I have you to thank, Harry. You showed me the stupidity of dependence. I owe something to my father, too. When I stopped fighting the sale of that land I remembered something he once told me. He said you should always know what fights to run away from. How did he put it? 'When you fight and run away, you live to fight another day.' " She raised her glass. "This alimony fight was the one worth winning."

As it turned out, the path of progress had led directly to the West Bank shopping center. After six years its resounding success still provided Eastman, Haynesworth with a substantial annual return. But progress was capricious: in another year those crowded malls might be empty.

I had gained more from this transaction than a partnership and a clearer sense of how this city worked. I learned how crucial and how easy it was to collect information within its closed-in limits. Growing up, I had avoided gossip. This reflex wasn't principled. I had simply heard too much of it at home. Mother had carried North with her the nonworking Southern woman's habit of spending much of her morning on the phone with women friends, "catching up," as she called it. Although on occasion, like Grandmother, she could raise gossip to the level of an oral art form, more often the conversations I caught snatches of were aimless nattering. Or so they had struck me then.

Now I saw the professional value of catching up. I began calling people, some friends, some no more than childhood summer acquaintances, to get the scoop on local characters and situations. It continued to amaze me how few of my sources could resist the impulse to talk. If anything, they appeared to be flattered that I might regard them as authorities. No one swore me to secrecy, but since I didn't repeat what I learned I gained a reputation for discretion, a rarity in these parts. The truth was, I regarded gossip impersonally, as research. "Give me a reading," I would say. "Just tell me what I need to know."

That Monday, as usual, I dropped Ike off at his school uptown on Jefferson Avenue, then drove back downtown to work.

As I negotiated the morning traffic at Lee Circle I wondered whom I should call first to get a full or at least fair account of Elizabeth's background and family. About Elizabeth herself I decided to make do with what Grandmother had told me: Elizabeth needed a chance to be known in her own way and time. As for her grandfather, Grandmother had said: ask Charles; but whatever his association with Berenson had been, I knew better than to rely on Charles for an unbiased view. Mike Shushan came to mind, as he often had recently, and not merely because he knew the Jewish community. If Elizabeth really did need a lawyer, she couldn't do much better than Mike—but that, too, would work itself out. Mulling over these options, I couldn't know that the information I needed was on its way to me, not exactly unbidden but like a long-silent witness who demanded to be heard at last.

The offices of Eastman, Haynesworth occupied the twenty-second floor of one of the newer steel, concrete, and glass structures downtown near the river. In shifting its location from the old Hibernia Bank Building to this one on Poydras, the firm, notably Charles Haynesworth, had meant to show a willingness to move with the times. But the way the offices had been decorated intentionally conveyed a different message. The atmosphere was that of a traditional men's club, conservative almost, but not quite to the point of shabbiness: old wood gleamed with wax, brass shone, the oil portrait of Eastman (wearing the official robes of his four years as a federal judge) in the reception room had recently been cleaned, as had the slightly worn but extremely valuable Persian rug.

In outfitting the corner office Charles had assigned me when I made junior partner I had tried to sustain the prevailing image of unshakable security, permanence, and excellence. But neither my grandfather's desk nor a mahogany breakfront filled with books and photographs could subdue the main feature of the room: two floor-to-ceiling, wall-to-wall windows, apparently designed less to create an illusion of space than to inspire vertigo. From this vantage point I could look out over the tar-papered, heat-blistered roofs of lesser buildings and see, in the distance, the muddy curve of the Mississippi and one of the bridges that spanned it. It was through these windows that my clients, weaving their gaudy fantasies, pointed in conflicting directions toward the path of progress.

My secretary's desk was positioned in the eternal fluorescent noon of the hall outside my office. When I stopped to collect my mail, she looked up from her typing and said, "You've already got a visitor, Mr. Preston. Name's Bennett. Said she knows you. Said she wanted to wait in your office, wouldn't take no for an answer. Seemed mighty worked up to me, so I let her in. Did I do right?" A middle-aged woman with dyed auburn hair and an ample bosom, she peered at me over the tortoiseshell rims of her bifocals. Her name was Esther Rabbitt.

"You did right, Esther."

"I told her you had an early appointment and have to go to court at ten, but I don't think she heard me. Seemed mighty set on her own business. Kind of intense, know what I mean? Somebody'd be doing her a favor if they told her she was missing two buttons from that nice Ultrasuede suit, but I didn't think it was my place."

"Thanks, Esther."

Elizabeth was staring out the window when I opened the door. She wheeled around to face me.

"I thought you were going to call first," I said.

"I know. I'm sorry, Harry, but I couldn't wait. I went home yesterday morning, threw some things in a bag while Jack was mercifully still asleep, and checked into the Pontchartrain. It's Carnival Week, but Grandad keeps a suite there for business, and they let me use that. All day yesterday I walked and walked. I wanted to call you, but I knew I should give you a chance to breathe. Then last night I couldn't sleep—my nerves felt on fire—so I got up early, dressed, and came down here." Her self-mocking laugh was like a dry cough. "It sounds ridiculous, but I've been waiting outside since six-thirty, first on the sidewalk, then in the lobby."

"I'm afraid you'll have to wait a little longer, Elizabeth."

"Longer?"

"My first appointment is due any minute."

"But I can't wait longer."

"You'll just have to." I spoke very calmly. "I'll put you in one of the conference rooms. Esther will bring you coffee—on a silver tray in a thin china cup—and something to eat, if you like. Fresh orange juice? Croissant? Brioche?"

"Are you serious?"

"This firm can provide those services. But it's hard for me to take seriously that it can."

"I was going to say just coffee." She lit a cigarette. I noticed then that she smoked the way Grandmother did, though her hands were trembling. "But maybe I will have—"

"Take it up with Esther. I'll send her in to you."

I led Elizabeth down the hall past the main conference room. Through the glass wall I saw Charles's head profiled and reflected in the window wall beyond, as he sat facing five or six men I recognized as the group he met with once a month that always included his son-in-law, Rudolph. Charles looked up as we passed. I acknowledged his blank stare with a nod.

When I returned to Esther's desk after getting Elizabeth settled, I said, "If young Bradford's here, send him in. And please, dear Esther, take good care of Mrs. Bennett. Don't let her run around loose."

Jason Bradford was a twenty-one-year-old senior at Washington and Lee with whom Ann and I had sometimes played tennis at an uptown club. On Friday he had appeared at my office unannounced and as anxious as Elizabeth. In the fifteen minutes I could spare him he had blurted a sorry but not unfamiliar story.

When the IRS claimed Jason had failed to report some $20,000 of income, he had gone to his father for an explanation. He went to him only because he couldn't think of an alternative. Jason knew enough about his father to make him wish he knew less. He knew that his father had, at best, an uneasy relationship with truth. This prepared him for the elder Bradford's shifty-eyed evasions and subsequent charges of ingratitude. When the explanation did come, it was fragmentary and accompanied by maudlin excuses and promises of restitution. That had been three months ago. Jason had tried to raise the issue again twice since, but his father had left the room and the house both times.

In a sense, the explanation, or what Jason had extracted of it, was simple enough. When he was four years old his maternal grandmother had established a sizable trust in his name, with his father as trustee until Jason reached his majority. This grandmother had been dead for twelve years; his mother had died of cancer two years later, when Jason was eleven. Jason's father had never told him that the trust existed. What he now admitted was only that he had lent some of the income from the trust to the ailing wholesale hardware firm that had, he reminded Jason, been in the Bradford family for generations and that Jason stood to inherit.

When Jason had telephoned his mother's brother, Uncle Patrick, in Opelousas, Patrick had said, "I was afraid this might happen. I warned Momma years ago not to make Curtis trustee but all Momma said was, 'Curtis is such good family, Marylee's lucky to have got him.' 'But Momma,' I said, 'good family doesn't mean diddly-shit when it comes to money.' And Momma said, 'Patrick, don't be crude.'" Patrick had given Jason the name of the law firm in Opelousas that had set up the trust. Then Jason had come to see me.

When Esther announced him today, I went out to greet him. His dark curly hair was matted, his eyes bloodshot, and his face pale. I wondered whether he looked this way from worry or because he ran with Jamie Carere's crowd, which I knew he did. His gratitude when Esther brought him a tall glass of orange juice was more than good manners. He might have been twenty-one, but he still needed someone to look out for him.

When we were alone, "Jason," I said, "the first thing you have to decide is how far you're willing to take this."

"How far is far?"

"We don't know how much your father owes your trust fund. If he's been stealing from you for years—and ugly as it sounds, he may have been doing just that—then he might owe more than he can pay back. But he can't discharge that debt by declaring bankruptcy. Not if he's committed fraud. If he's broken his fiduciary duty, for example, or taken unfair advantage. In other words, this could end up in a lawsuit. Would you take your father to court?"

"I'm not sure."

"Situations like this can blow families apart. Would you risk alienating your father, maybe permanently?"

"I honestly don't know. There's just the two of us, but it's not as if we had the greatest father-son relationship before this came up. Dad's not exactly into the role model or male bonding sort of thing. He never has been. The truth is, he's been out of control for years.''

''In what sense?''

''Drinking. Partying. Screwing around. God knows what else. He stays out later than I do sometimes. Over Christmas vacation I've come down in the morning and found him asleep behind the steering wheel of his car in front of the house. I guess he's lucky to have gotten home at all, but the car must have been on automatic pilot. I don't know how he keeps it up at his age.''

''He's not the only one.''

''Don't I know it! Dad's forty-six but the guys he hangs out with act like they're still in college. Buzzy Maclean, Potter Landrieu, Duncan Strong—those guys are wild men! And Charlie Parkerson! Know what he did? At his last birthday party he dressed in an Elvis suit and drove his Harley-Davidson into the house up some special ramp right onto the dining table and into the birthday cake! Rudy Carere used to be in that group too, but he's cleaned up his act in the past few years, or so Jamie tells me. I wish Dad would follow his lead, but no such luck. I really worry about some of the things Dad's getting into, Harry. There's this character they've all taken up with, some sleazeball lawyer named Renny something. I think that guy's pushing drugs. He pulls into our driveway late at night, and Dad goes outside and gets in the car and they just sit there, you know? Then when Dad comes back in the house he acts sort of shifty and paranoid. He peers into empty rooms and looks behind curtains. Jesus!'' He shook his head. ''The poor guy really needs a caretaker.''

''Then you're not unsympathetic.''

''No way. I've acted pretty dumb myself sometimes. If I could make Dad take care of himself, I would. No wonder his business is slipping—half the time he doesn't make it to work. But I can't sit back and let him steal from me, can I? Especially if he's just blowing the money.''

''Some children would.''

''Should I?''

''I don't think so. There's something you should know if

you don't already, Jason. Your father's gotten pretty heavily
into gambling.''

''I know he plays poker sometimes.''

''I've heard talk around this office. I've seen your father
myself, in that back room down at the Jackson Club. Charles
Haynesworth, he's senior partner here, is one of your father's
poker buddies. The stakes can get high. Charles has won a
lot off your father. In fact, your father owes him money now.
And Charles isn't the only one he owes.''

''You're getting at something, Harry.''

''I am. If your father's into gambling along with whatever
else, you can't afford to assume responsibility for him or his
debts. His own parents aren't alive, are they?''

''No.''

''Does he have brothers or sisters?''

''He's an only child, like me.''

''And me. I'm not unfamiliar with situations like this.
Truly, you can't be your father's keeper. If he won't listen
to reason, the most you can do is take care of yourself. In
doing that, you may be doing the best thing for him, too, in
the long run.''

''Then you'll help me?''

''That's something else I was getting at. I'm giving you
the name of a lawyer with a different firm. Mike Shushan,
an old friend of mine. He's with Macauley and Stein, just
around the corner. Smart as a whip and cuts right through
bullshit. He also has the advantage of having grown up in
Baton Rouge.''

''Why not you?''

''I would be glad to act in your behalf, Jason. But this
isn't the right firm for you.'' I saw just how true this was.
''A relatively small firm like this one, whose senior partner
plays poker with your father, and trounces him, a man your
father owes money to, who's in the same clubs and Carnival
organizations he's in—let's say this firm might put pressure
on me to handle your father more gently than would be in
your best interests.''

''You wouldn't give in to them, would you?''

''Not if I represented you. Believe me, though, it's better
to avoid the situation entirely. The Bradfords have been en-

trenched here for a long time. You want a lawyer outside of the old-boy network whose firm will back him up. Your father's got to see from the start that you mean business. If you agree, I'll tell Mike to expect to hear from you. And Jason, I'll give him and you any help I can.''

When Jason left, I rang Mike at his office. "I'm sending you a client. A college kid who needs a hard-nosed lawyer.''

He laughed. ''So you thought of me. What's his problem?''

''Papa's been dipping into his trust fund. But talk to him first. Then we'll talk. I think you'll understand why I referred him to you.''

''I haven't seen you in a while, Harry. How've you been doing?''

''I never thanked you for your note. I should have.''

''Forget that. I want to know how you are.''

''I'm doing okay now. You could say my life's been on hold.''

''Naturally.''

''As a matter of fact, something happened a while back I meant to tell you about. Then everything shut down. Do you have a minute now?''

''More than a minute.''

''About eight months ago a whiz kid named Harris applied for a job here. Grew up in Shreveport. Yale undergraduate, Tulane Law School, Law Review, third in his class. After he interviewed Harris, Charles Haynesworth came to my office. Clearly he'd been impressed. But that's not what he wanted to talk about. What he wanted was for me to make a call to you. 'You remember that acquaintance of yours, Mike Shushan, who was here in the early seventies?' he said. 'You've kept up with him, haven't you?' I said I had. 'Then why don't you give him a ring and ask him about young Harris.' Ask him what? I said. 'Well, Harris is an attractive prospect but we don't really know that much about him, do we?' I said his record and interview spoke for themselves. 'To a point,' Charles said. 'But only to a point. The question is, would he be suitable here? Would he feel comfortable?' I said since we would be lucky to get Harris, Harris would have to decide whether he would be happy with us. That was when Charles got impatient. 'Are you deliberately being obtuse, Harry? I want you to call Shushan and find out whether Harris is a Jew. If he is, this firm may not be the right place for him.'

"I stared at Charles for about thirty seconds, Mike. Then I told him I wouldn't feel right about making that call. I said it would be offensive, to both you and me. He decided to throw down the gauntlet. 'Do you mean you won't ask Shushan about Harris?' I said yes, that's what I meant.

"But I know what you'll say, Mike, about what I did in the end. You'll say I was trying to have it both ways at once, as usual. I finally said, 'I don't have to make that call, Charles. I know the answer to your question.' I did, Mike. I had been in law school with Harris's older brother, who went back to practice in Shreveport. I knew Harris was Jewish. Here's the way I reasoned. You remember our conversation years ago, when you talked about having to become a white Jew if you worked for a firm like this?''

"I remember.''

"You knew what you were doing when you applied here. Maybe Harris did, too. But maybe he didn't. I figured he shouldn't work for a firm whose senior partner didn't want to hire Jews. I figured Harris *wouldn't* be comfortable here. I know what I'm saying about myself, of course. Anyhow I told Charles that Harris was Jewish. 'You might have told me sooner,' he said. 'You're not slow on the uptake, Harry. You forced me to spell things out.' It ended there. But he didn't ask Harris back for another interview.''

Mike was silent for a time. Then, ''Did you know we hired Harris?''

''No, I didn't.''

''As you say, he's a whiz kid. You did us a favor. So, for that matter, did your worthy Cousin Charles. Now I have a proposal to make. Why don't you come to work for us too? The amenities may not be up to your standard, but we'll make the move worth your while. You see, we're short on a certain kind of lawyer. We could use someone with old-guard connections who's a little sick of playing the game.''

''Only one? That's rank tokenism.''

''Even so, I think you'd feel right at home.''

I laughed. "I probably would. Thanks, Mike. I've been thinking about making a switch. Oh, and Mike. There's someone else—something else I want to discuss with you. Not a client or a case exactly . . ." I thought of Elizabeth in the room down the hall. "This just isn't the right moment."

"Call back anytime, Harry. I'll be in and out all day."

ℰNINE

WHEN ELIZABETH AND I were again alone in my office, I said, "All right. Sit down and let's have it."

"I'm too nervous to sit."

"Stand, sit, whatever. Just tell me what's on your mind."

"It's hard to know where to begin."

"Start somewhere."

She crossed the room, stopping to smash her cigarette out in the official-looking brass ashtray on my desk. In the course of the conversation, she filled the ashtray with smashed cigarette butt piled on smashed butt. Behind her the cityscape reeled—empty-eyed vertical grids, a sky that seemed a single dull cloud.

"Rico Famiglietti," she said. "I'll start with him."

"Isn't he one of Marcello's boys?"

"In a small-time way."

"What's Famiglietti got to do with you?"

"I met him years ago. I was around seventeen at the time."

I shifted my gaze into neutral.

"It's not what you think. He owned a bar over on Decatur, a dive called the Gin Mill, and I used to spend a lot of time there. He still owns the place but now he calls it the Trade

Winds.'' She let out one of her barking laughs. ''You can guess the sort of trade it traffics in.''

''Stick to the point,'' I said, and then, as she talked, tried to angle my way into a place somewhere between my personal and professional perspectives. Elizabeth's candor was unsettling: I didn't question it, but she chose her words with finicky precision, and her obvious omissions, when they occurred, urged my imagination up paths it didn't want to pursue.

This character Famiglietti was someone she had known in an earlier life, a time when she had done what she called stupid, careless things, and she was taken by surprise when, the week before, he had called her up and started rambling on about how he wanted to expand his nightclub. At first she had assumed he was looking for backers, but it had turned out to be more complicated than that. Next to Famiglietti's bar was a building that he wanted to buy. Unoccupied but not on the market, it was owned by one of Elizabeth's grandfather's corporations. As it happened, according to Famiglietti, Elizabeth was listed on the board of that corporation. This hadn't come as a complete surprise. Elizabeth knew that she was nominally on the board of a number of corporations. Her grandfather had set up a trust for her when she was very young—maybe more than one trust.

''It's complicated and I've never really tried to understand it,'' she said. ''All I know is it's irrevocable, if that's the right word. And staggered. That means—''

''I know what it means.''

What it had come down to was that Famiglietti had wanted Elizabeth to persuade the corporation to sell him the building. Elizabeth explained that she didn't have the influence: her grandfather was old and ill, she hadn't seen him in two months, and all his affairs were handled by lawyers over whom she had no influence whatsoever. Quite the contrary. She received a monthly check and that, she had told him, was that. But Famiglietti hadn't let the issue go.

''That was when he reminded me that he had some mementos, as he called them, from my youth.''

''What kind of mementos?''

"The worst kind. A photograph. Actually, two photographs."

I would not have asked what was in them. Elizabeth's dark gaze was fearless because she wanted to keep it fearless. Lip biting and chain-smoking told a different story.

"What are you saying, Elizabeth? Is he trying to blackmail you?"

"I don't think that's his game, not exactly. Apparently he keeps a file of this sort of thing in case it might come in handy."

"Did he say what he might do with the pictures?"

She shook her head.

"Who he might show them to, I mean."

"I know what you mean. You mean: in the end, who would care that I had ever put myself in that position?" She grimaced at her own choice of words. "It boils down to three people: Jack, Mother, and Grandad. My grandmother doesn't count. She was always out of it; now that she's eighty she gets the credit for being senile. Mother and Jack don't really count either, unless Jack could find a way to use this to his advantage."

"Why doesn't your mother count?"

She stiffened. She went to the window and stared out. "I remember the day Mother left for Boston." Her voice was diminished, as if she had fallen through a trapdoor. "She came to Grandad's house on Walnut Street. I was ten. When I came downstairs she was standing in the hall. The door was open behind her. The sun was so bright I couldn't see her face. 'Don't try to understand,' she said. 'You're just too young.' Then she was gone. I don't know how long I stood there. Someone put a hand on my shoulder. It was Grandad. He had missed her on purpose—I could tell that. All he said was, 'No promises, Elizabeth, but I'll do what I can to teach you to fly.' He did, too. But growing up, the problem was—" She turned back to me. Her eyes clouded, and her voice assumed a cutting edge. "Grandad had to be away so often that I was usually left to Miss Taylor's tender mercies."

"Miss Taylor?"

"A Scottish governess Grandad picked up in some slave

market. At least she started out as a governess; now she's a self-styled majordomo."

"And your mother?"

"She made a new life for herself."

"What kind of life?"

"She's headmistress of a girls' school outside Boston. Ames Academy—founded by one of Mother's high-minded ancestors nearly two hundred years ago. She lives and breathes that school. She's even resumed her maiden name. Mother's recycled herself," she said acidly, "into a sort of virgin queen. Nowadays she treats everyone the same—like servants or irresponsible children."

"Including you?"

"Oh, Mother's condescension is democratic: in that sense, she's a true New England liberal. But I've managed to make my presence felt. In person when I visited during the holidays, then again when I was at Radcliffe—briefly at Radcliffe. Even, sometimes, long distance."

She lit another cigarette and expelled smoke in actressy fashion. She looked like a child playing the sophisticate. Just as often, she seemed the reverse.

"You're saying it's your grandfather who would count."

She nodded. "He put up with grief from me and always bailed me out. The last time I saw him was right after his stroke. His left arm was paralyzed and his mouth drooped, but his eyes were sharp as ever. I wouldn't want him hurt by something as cheap as this."

While she talked, I had seated myself in the chair behind my desk. Now I saw that in doing so I had tacitly agreed to put our relationship on a professional basis. I wasn't sure what I wanted our relationship to be, but this wasn't it.

Nevertheless I said, "How can I help?"

"I'm going to see Famiglietti tonight. Come with me, Harry. I don't want to do or say the wrong thing. If I bring a lawyer with me, Famiglietti'll know I'm not going to be intimidated easily."

I saw her point. Before I could make any sort of reply Esther's voice came over the intercom. "Don't want to interrupt, Mr. Preston, but it's nine forty-five and if you don't get going you're going to be late for court."

I stood up and started sifting through papers on my desk. "Sorry, Elizabeth. If you had called earlier . . ."

"But I'm not finished, Harry. This is only part of it. I'm not finished!" In her voice was a shrill insistency that evoked the kind of child she had once been and maybe still was. Apparently sensing this, she got control of her voice. "Let's have that lunch, then." She smiled. True or false, it was an amazing smile, stretching wide chiseled lips over glittering teeth. "Talking to you, even this much, has made all the difference. Who knows why? Maybe," she said playfully, "I've shifted the responsibility for my life, from myself onto you."

"I don't want that responsibility, Elizabeth."

"Of course you don't, Harry. No one in his right mind would."

Then for the first time she sat down in the chair facing me, hands folded in her lap like the hands of a good little girl. I still stood at the desk, trying to collect my papers and my wits. "I was overstating as usual," she said. "It means a lot to talk to somebody I can trust. Of course I have Dr. Jasper, but he's a psychiatrist and there's a limit to how much he can help me with the more practical aspects of life. Real life, so called."

She got up and came around the desk. She put her hands gently on mine. "Trust is what counts, Harry. You know that."

My pulse jumped.

As if she had slipped into a trance, she said dreamily, "I'll go to Galatoire's before twelve and get us a table. I'll be waiting when you get there. Since you're running my life, tell me: what will I do until then?"

I withdrew my hands from hers. I snapped my briefcase shut. Then I said the first thing that came to me.

"Esther says you're missing two buttons. Go buy some."

She fingered the lapels of her jacket, then chuckled self-indulgently.

"Well, Esther's right. But where do I go to buy this sort of button? Who'll sew them on?"

She touched my left cheek lightly with the fingers of her right hand.

"It's much easier to do this." She slipped her jacket off and tossed it into the wastepaper basket by the side of my desk. "Easy come, easy go. This way you won't be embarrassed and I won't have to worry about buttons."

I retrieved the coat and placed it around her shoulders. "Don't be such a grandstand player." I grabbed my briefcase and ushered her out of the office. "I'll see you at Galatoire's around twelve."

$\mathscr{T}$EN

THE CASE THAT took me to court that morning was tedious and, in its quiet way, tawdry. The two grown daughters of what the newspapers called "a prominent civic leader," a businessman who had died virtually bankrupt, were suing his woman friend for the return of some property—a house, their dead mother's jewelry—that their father had given her before his death. Under the archaic intricacies of Louisiana law, they did in fact have a claim, though I had warned them that it depended on a careful weighing of the assets against the liabilities of their father's estate. On this occasion, the woman friend was presenting in court her edited version of her relationship with the dead man.

In response to my questions she staunchly asserted that she had never received any gifts from him other than candy, flowers, and books: gifts any lady could accept without reproach. She somehow managed to weave into her testimony the irrelevant fact that, in spite of her own straitened circumstances, her daughter had made her debut the year before; she offered this as if it were proof of respectability, which in this city it was sometimes taken to be. Indeed, with her subdued clothes and her air of debilitated gentility, doubtless she was the lady she claimed to be. Legally, of course, she had good reason to lie. And as she droned on in her hushed drawl, the cynical Mediterranean face of Judge Mancusco grew wearier and wearier, registering her statements for the hypocrisies they were even though he might finally have to decide in her favor.

Through it all I could not get rid of the image of Elizabeth's blatant smile that bared her strong white teeth.

When I arrived at the restaurant it was a quarter past noon. Already a long line of customers stretched around the corner from Bourbon onto Iberville. I wondered why Elizabeth had decided on Galatoire's if she wanted a place to talk. This was a restaurant with the appearance and privacy of a barbershop. It comprised a single large room with white tiled floors and mirrored walls in which one could see, from various and shifting perspectives, not only oneself but the backsides, profiles, and full faces of those who were eating or about to be fed.

I pushed past the line, entered the restaurant, and spotted Elizabeth immediately. She had secured a small table on the right-hand side of the room, and without even looking up she caught my attention. She didn't have to try.

The restaurant was occupied chiefly by people who looked like tourists and by New Orleans matrons of a certain sort, not unlike the woman I had just left in court. Then there was Elizabeth. With her clean sharp bones and vigorous eyebrows, her dashing clothes worn with slapdash disregard, she stood out like a barbaric princess displaced among hoi polloi.

When I sat down opposite her, she said, "I was so hungry that I couldn't wait." This was not an apology, simply a statement of fact. In front of her were an empty cocktail glass, a half-emptied plate of shrimp rémoulade, and a napkin-wrapped pile of small French loaves, one of which had been largely consumed.

"I'll call the waiter," she said.

She addressed the waiter by name. His name was Alphonse. He addressed her by name, too. He was old and bent. She treated him with polite authority, and he treated her with deference.

It soon became clear that Elizabeth had chosen this restaurant for the simplest reason, that she could not get enough of its food. Although she talked throughout lunch, she contrived almost never to stop eating. She ate with a child's rapacity only partly governed by an adult's sense of purpose. She had already established herself as something of a sloven, but her manner of eating, though unconventional, was not slovenly. To the extent that it was possible she ate with her fingers and the help of small pieces of bread. Slowly but voraciously she would break off a piece of bread, make an open-faced sandwich of the bread and some of whatever was on the plate in front of her at the time—first the shrimp, then trout swimming in butter and almonds, then salad shot through with garlic—and place this carefully in her mouth. She managed to eat without ever distending her face and also to go on talking but never with her mouth sufficiently open so that the food in it was visible. She wasn't self-conscious about the way she ate, yet the practiced skill that went into it was obvious.

"I was hungry as a wolf," she said, smiling.

I replied that I could believe it.

"And you will go with me to see Famiglietti?"

"Yes, but I won't be free till after ten. I've got to make an appearance at that ball tonight." I was hoping she would put the whole thing off. I should have known better.

"Then I'll meet you at Famiglietti's at ten-thirty. It's two blocks below Canal on Decatur."

Her attention seemed to drift then. She glanced indifferently around the restaurant and drained her wineglass.

"There's something else, Harry. I want you to get me my divorce. As soon as possible."

I set my fork on my plate.

"Under the circumstances, Elizabeth, that's not possible."

She laughed blithely. "You mean the other night. Who knows about that except us?"

"That's the point. I do."

"Don't be such a prig, Harry. Divorce is a routine matter. So is a one-night stand." She paused to gauge my reaction.

"For some." I looked her in the eye. "Not for others."

"I meant: unless it turns out to be special," she said in a different voice.

"And could happen again."

"And most likely will."

"Elizabeth, you call divorce a routine matter. More often it isn't. From the glimpse I got of your husband, he doesn't want a divorce."

"True. Jack plans ahead and I'm necessary to those plans."

"If he contests it, divorce can be a sticky business."

"But there must be some way."

"Sure." I recited without blinking: "If you can prove he's committed adultery, you can get a divorce immediately. Or if he's been imprisoned for a felony. Otherwise, you can live apart for a year and then file suit."

"A year! That's ridiculous." She lavishly buttered another piece of bread, broke it in two, and placed one piece in her mouth.

"I won't argue that point. You must have a lawyer. Take it up with him."

"Listen, Harry. The only lawyers I know are Grandad's lawyers, and I'm not about to ask them to handle something like this. They've always made me feel like a ward of the state. Oh, they're terribly polite, even unctuous, especially Mr. McIntyre. Uncle Mac, I'm supposed to call him. All he knows is how to kiss ass. Uriah Heep with a brain the size of a chicken's."

"Then I'll give you a list of some reputable lawyers. With a friend named Mike Shushan at the top."

For the first time she stopped eating. "I don't want the names of reputable lawyers." She italicized "reputable" as if it were a questionable term in some foreign tongue. "I just want you to—"

"Goddammit, Elizabeth, why can't you get it through your head? I'm not the man for this job. Not yesterday, today, or tomorrow. Accept that, because it's true."

"I'll accept it." Her look was sullen. "Now let's get on with the advice."

We both laughed at once.

"You can always pay," I said.

"Pay?"

"Make a settlement."

"How much?"

"Don't be a child, Elizabeth. It's not a fixed sum. It has to be worked out."

"I bought him once," she murmured, "and it galls me to have to buy him off now."

The amount of contempt and self-contempt that went into this statement hung above the table like a noxious cloud.

"For the record," she went on, "I receive a sizable income but I haven't the faintest idea how much capital I can lay my hands on. I've never bothered to check."

"That's easy enough to do. What other assets do you have? A house?"

She nodded. "A cottage in the Garden District. On Philip Street. I bought it years ago, before I even met Jack. I don't know what it's worth now."

"A lot, probably. But wait. If you bought it before you were married, then it's not even community property. Your husband doesn't have any claim to it. It's yours free and clear."

"Does that matter?"

"It gives you something to work with."

"Well, Jack may have no claim to the place, but he's put a lot of himself into it." She shuddered. "He's turned it into his idea of where chic young marrieds should live. It has what you might call a tiptoe quality. Everything perfect and in its proper place. Or it would be," she laughed, "if I hadn't been living there too."

"Would you be willing to let him have it?"

"I don't care about the house as such. But if, as you say, he has no legal right to it, then I'll be damned if I'll sign it over to him for nothing."

A clarity of purpose began to assert itself in her voice. It was easy to imagine that, growing up, she had always taken money for granted without ever becoming interested in the details of where it came from, how it was made. Like so many children of the very rich, she may even have been afraid to know, or not really allowed to learn. If her emotional history had been as chaotic as Grandmother's rumors claimed and as she herself implied, then there may never have been a time when she could have educated herself in her own affairs. But now she looked and sounded like a woman who, having made a bad bargain, sees it for what it is and wants to set it straight, without coming out on the short end.

"I don't owe Jack anything." Her voice was decisive. "We don't live together, Harry. We never did. We just occupy the same cage."

By now the diners were well into their second oversized drink, women were table-hopping to greet old friends, and volleys of laughter and gossip richocheted off the mirrored walls. I had to lean forward to hear Elizabeth describe her first meeting with Jack Bennett. She had been at a friend's cocktail party and feeling blue, when Jack appeared out of the crowd. He had seemed just another beer-guzzling Deke from Tulane, but a very good-looking one. "I've always been a fool for looks," she told me. Sauntering up, he had said: "So you're the Elizabeth Berenson I've heard so much about. Is all they say true?" She had almost groaned at that one, but his teasing tone caught her. When she gave him some version of the rich-beautiful-smart routine, he replied without skipping a beat: "It *is* true, then. I was just wondering."

"Maybe it was that little joke that got to me. But I swear, Harry, he really has done a Jekyll and Hyde. His sadistic streak didn't show up until after we were married, after he got used to spending my money and resenting me for it at the same time. Then he switched from beer to cocaine: it did wonders for his waistline but Lord, what it's done to his head." She hesitated before saying: "I want to go back to something you mentioned earlier. This matter of adultery. Of course I can't prove Jack's committed adultery any more than he can prove it of me. But since we've been married his tastes have certainly changed in any number of ways. 'Broadened' is the way he'd probably put it."

"That's vague."

"I mean it to be. After all, I'm not a complete bitch and I'm hardly in a position to throw stones. But I need to know if this sort of thing could be relevant."

"What sort of thing?"

"I spoke of Jack's grandiose fantasies. Well, some of his fantasies are both grandiose and bizarre. This Second World

War business—this thing he's got about Nazis.''

"*Nazis*?"

"Hold on. Last year a German Army tank turned up in the side yard. Complete with artillery. It's still there, decaying in the damp like the carcass of some prehistoric animal. When I asked Jack where he got it, he smiled spookily and said, 'People traffic in stranger things than this, Elizabeth.' ''

"What did he mean?"

"The tank's an obvious absurdity. But now he's collecting costumes, implements, artifacts. He has a closet full of storm troopers' uniforms, God knows how many Lugers, an ashtray that belonged to Goebbels, and most recently a lamp shade he says was made by Ilse Koch.'' Her eyes widened. "From human skin.''

I felt as if someone had placed a lump of dry ice at the base of my spine. I said, "Well, maybe you could use some of this to claim he's pathological, but—"

"There's more to it than the collecting, Harry. He's started going to fancy-dress parties, and I don't mean as a masker in a Carnival Ball. He asked me to go along once. He showed me the costume he wanted me to wear. A mask and feathered cloak made from the skin and wings of a vulture. If I wanted proof of what part I played in his fantasies, I didn't need it after that. I said, 'Jack, I'll give you the name of a good psychiatrist, but count me out of your social life.' He looked as if he might hit me, but then he said, 'Jew bitch. You're the crazy one around here. That's common knowledge.' He must have known I was serious, though, because since then he's left me alone.''

She paused to light a cigarette but when she looked up she dropped the cigarette onto the table. Her face froze. "Guess who just walked in.''

I didn't have to guess. My back was to the door, but glancing in the mirror to my right I saw Jack and another young man, as sleek as he, standing inside the restaurant's entrance. They were obviously waiting to be shown to a table; and then Bennett spotted us. For the second time his eyes locked with mine in a mirror.

"Damn him,'' Elizabeth said. "I haven't even had dessert. And he's heading this way.''

He was indeed. Under its midwinter tan his face burned red with rage. Then he was standing beside our table, fists clenched.

"Elizabeth, what the hell are you doing here?"

"What does it look like, Jack?"

"I mean where the hell have you been for the last day and a half?"

"I checked out. Permanently."

"You can't do that."

"Can do and have done. My only regret is that I didn't do it sooner." She indicated me. "Jack, this is—"

"I know Preston," he cut her short.

"Well, not really," I said.

Ignoring me, he addressed her again. "What's Preston's business with you?"

"He's my lawyer." She said this with such flat finality that I would not, at that moment, have undercut her by denying it.

"Since when?"

"Since today."

"Preston's not your lawyer. I'm your lawyer. If Preston's anything, he's your latest playmate."

The partial accuracy of his guess touched a nerve. "Whoa, boy," I said. Since I was taller than he was, I stood up. Heads turned in our direction.

"Don't 'boy' me. Elizabeth, I'll expect you tonight. At home."

"I wouldn't wait up."

"What does that mean?"

"It means I'm not coming home. It means this marriage of convenience is no longer convenient."

"Is this Preston's doing?"

"It's no one's doing but my own."

He tried to make his voice reasonable. "You can't get a divorce, Elizabeth. I've been working on something. I could prove to you now, if you would listen, that you're not capable of running your own affairs. You're certainly not capable of running your life."

"And you are? Look around you, Jack. People are staring at you. Well, I'm fed up with this conversation. If you and your friend over there don't clear out of here now, this minute, I'll create a public spectacle that'll make Saturday night look like child's play. You once accused me of liking to make scenes, Jack. You were wrong, but I certainly know how if I have to. And I have the advantage. I don't give a hoot what anyone thinks and it's all you care about. That and your freaky games.''

Jack tried to stand his ground. A pale angry eye glared in his profile like the eye of a fish. Elizabeth glared back. He turned and rapidly made his way to the door, where his friend stood waiting with a bewildered look on his face. Bennett said something to him, and they were gone.

People had stared, but if the festive roar had subsided momentarily it now surged over us once again.

Elizabeth said, "I may not have any appetite left, but that bastard's not going to cheat me out of dessert." She beckoned to Alphonse. "I'll have crêpes maison. What'll you have, Harry?" She was staring down at the table. Her chin was trembling.

I reached over and lifted her chin so that she had to look at me. "Thanks, but I've had enough."

She didn't draw away. "Just as long as it's not more than enough," she said.

$\mathcal{E}$LEVEN

THE JACKSON CLUB was located in what had once been a private mansion on Carondelet Street. Wedged now between a men's shop and a bar, its blank white façade and front door with a frosted-glass panel did not solicit or receive attention from passersby. When I entered, I felt even more removed from the world outside than I did in Grandmother's living room. Since this was primarily a men's luncheon club, most of the activity, including the card playing, took place in the dining room at the rear. The muffled silence of the entrance hall and unused library was profound, like the silence at the bottom of a well.

I asked the white-jacketed black waiter named Welman to tell Charles Haynesworth I had arrived. Then I went into the library and sat down in a wing chair by the front window. I stared out through the slanted slats of an interior shutter at what I could see of the sidewalk outside. Only forty-eight inches separated me from the feet passing on the pavement and yet, if I believed in the unwritten codes of this city, I could not have been more distant from them.

I rarely used this club except for an occasional business lunch, but when I had gotten back to the office after leaving Galatoire's, Esther had handed me a note from Charles, asking me to meet him here at four.

When my cousin appeared, I rose to greet him. "Harry," he said, "thank you for finding time to see me."

I could remember when Charles's avuncular authority had put me at ease, but no longer. "Is this something urgent? I don't mean to rush things but I'm supposed to pick Ike up at school in an hour."

"Of course. I wanted to see you about—but let's sit down first." When we were seated he said: "I'll call it a conflict of interests."

"I don't understand."

"I'm speaking of the Berenson woman."

"Grandmother's been talking to you?"

"She's only thinking of your welfare. Yours and Ike's."

"I still don't see the problem."

"You've taken her on as a client?"

I hadn't. I wouldn't. But since I didn't like being pressured, I said, "Would you object?"

"It might not be wise."

"Why not?" Adopting his usual view that profit was all, I said, "Elizabeth is her grandfather's only living descendant. A lot of her inheritance will be tied up in trust, but a lot more probably won't be. If she wants her own lawyer, the yearly retainer alone would be considerable. Besides, she needs a lawyer to handle her divorce from Bennett."

"It wouldn't be wise for you to get involved."

"You still haven't said why."

"Trust me, you don't know all there is to know."

"Grandmother told me quite a bit."

"No doubt, and I'm sure you took it in. But remember, New Orleans is a hothouse compared to that Connecticut town you were raised in. I mean it's a society operating by homegrown laws that must seem exotic to outsiders. You and I happen to be lucky, Harry. We occupy a privileged place in the hothouse."

The "you and I" was obligatory and meant to be complimentary. If there was humor in his tone, and there rarely was, I couldn't detect it. "I'm not sure what this has to do with the Berensons, Charles. Why don't you just tell me what I need to know."

"It's better not to talk of these things. Let me put it to

you this way: the doors of the city are open to you now. You may choose not to take full advantage of that, but they are open. On the other hand, this is a wicked city for closing doors, too.''

"Grandmother said you worked for Berenson once."

"Did she now? I'm surprised Julia even remembers that, it was so long ago."

"But it's true?"

"Yes, it's true. In fact," Charles said, sitting forward in his chair as if rising to a challenge, "I'll use it as my case in point. I was young, fresh out of law school, and Berenson needed New Orleans connections. Ours was never a match made in heaven, though, and it didn't take me long to figure out the kind of pirate he was. Coming up from nothing, the hard way, he had to rely on his birthright: the unscrupulous know-how of the East European Jew. I think it amused him to put my own values to the test. Once he called me into his office. 'Charles,' he said, 'tell me something. Would you say you try to live by the Good Book?' I could only reply rather lamely, 'If you mean the Bible, I suppose the answer is yes.' 'That would be the New Testament, of course,' he said. 'The Sermon on the Mount. Lilies of the field, turn the other cheek, the lame shall enter first.' This time I made no reply. I couldn't see what he was getting at until he said, 'Well, my code is more primitive. Justice without mercy. An eye for an eye. Right now our codes are in an uneasy equipoise, as you can see. I trust you'll let me know when the balance is tipped and your disapproval of me becomes insupportable.' ''

In what Charles said, Berenson's voice came through to me clearly. It was hard, though, to imagine Charles as an innocent someone else had toyed with. While he talked, Welman had silently padded into the high, shadowed room with its dark oil paintings and gilded mirrors, turned on standing lamps in dim corners, even though we were still the only occupants, and now hovered nearby holding a tray with two glasses on it. Charles motioned to him.

"Mister Preston wants that bourbon and water. I'll take the Perrier."

"Thanks, Welman, but I'll pass."

Charles studied me, took his glass and a measured sip from it. "Where was I?" he said.

I thought: he knows perfectly well where he was. What obscure game was he playing in asking me to give him his cue? It occurred to me that he was testing me in some way, as he claimed Berenson had once tested him.

"Disapproval. Berenson said he hoped you would let him know when your disapproval of him became—I think your word was 'insupportable.' " I kept my tone as flat as possible.

"Actually, that was his word." He took another sip from his glass. "Well, not long after that it did. You may have heard of—no, I don't suppose you would, but it was a rather notorious affair at the time. Berenson staged a behind-the-scenes stockholders' coup at International and fired the managing officers."

"What was notorious about that?"

"Listen to me, son. I don't make the rules, I just play by them. What you need to understand is that in spite of his great personal fortune, Berenson was never accepted in this city. Of course he wanted to get in the clubs and Carnival organizations, and he was galled when he couldn't. His origins were against him, to be sure, and his accent was thick enough to cut. But more than that, on his way up he had been involved in all sorts of activities that made him unacceptable on another level—gunrunning, staging revolutions, setting up puppet governments. When New Orleans snubbed him, he decided to get back the only way he could."

"You're saying this so-called coup was nothing more than revenge?"

"Decide for yourself. Berenson was a major stockholder in International. Then he started accumulating proxies to give him the deciding vote. I even helped him gain those proxies: that was one of my first assignments. You can guess how I felt later, when—"

"How could it concern you?"

"Berenson was testing me again." Charles narrowed his eyes. "The board of directors were men my parents knew—Bringier, Lee, Claiborne. One of them was even my godfather, Jonathan Freret. These men belonged to those organizations that had shut Berenson out. Berenson always played his cards close to his chest, and I was so green I couldn't see what he had in mind until it happened.''

"What did happen?"

"At the next meeting he dismissed the board."

"But he had to give reasons."

"It's easy to find reasons. He cited incompetence. He cited the drop in the value of his stock, but after all, it was the Depression and International wasn't the only company that was hurting. No, his real reason was revenge. I've never forgotten how he used my inexperience to help him get it."

Abruptly Charles stopped talking. His ivory-colored face slowly turned a deep red. I had never seen him lose his composure before. He didn't really lose it even then. He remained silent, breathed deeply, then his face regained its usual pallor.

"I didn't want to speak of these things," he said. "Since I have, I should add this. Like any other young man starting out, especially one whose father has died—yourself for instance—I needed a mentor. Berenson couldn't be that for me. Jonathan Freret never got over being fired. He was a ruined man in every sense. I left Berenson and went to work for Eastman. I should have done that to begin with—Eastman's kin, after all—but I was fool enough to take Berenson's offer of more money. When I told Berenson I was leaving, he said, 'So the balance has been tipped? It's later than I thought it might be. Still, I always knew you were a man of principle.' Luckily, I cleared out before Berenson started making land deals with Huey Long. We don't have to speak of politics, ethics, or morality. The point is that anyone who trafficked with Long became a pariah. I could never have risked letting that rub off on me.''

"What about this man McIntyre?"

"So you know about him, too?"

"From Elizabeth."

"Well, I met Mac in law school. He came from a small Mississippi town, and working for Berenson, he didn't have as much to lose as I had. In one sense he had everything to gain. He knew he could never do better than Berenson, and I did too. That's why I got Mac the job in the first place. You could say I named my own successor. I guess it's all

panned out for Mac. He lives across the Lake, where he
handles Berenson's oil land, so I don't see him much—not
that I would in any case. When I do see him, he seems
contented with his lot.''

"So he didn't pay a price."

"He didn't have a price to pay."

"Then what about Bennett? I don't come here much, but
isn't he a member of this club?"

My cousin's right eyebrow shot up as if triggered by an
internal mechanism. He took a sip of his Perrier and set it
on the table. "Bennett's father put him up for this club the
day he was born, and he was still in college when he was
elected a member. Unless he stops paying his dues he'll be
a member until the day he-dies. That doesn't mean doors
haven't been closed to him, and not just because of his marriage to the Berenson girl. We've all heard the stories about
Bennett. My point is that if you represent the girl and air
those stories in court, some of the mud will land on you."

I didn't like the idea of mud. On the other hand, I didn't
care much about it one way or another. But we seemed to
have arrived at a similar conclusion from a different set of
assumptions or premises, though I did not want him to know
it. "What do you think I should do?"

"Get her to turn the case over to Mac."

"She doesn't trust him."

"Good Lord, why not? Mac is eminently trustworthy."

"Well, maybe not trust. She says he's a fool. She says he
has a brain the size of a chicken's."

My cousin never laughed but he came close to it then. The
sound erupted from deep within him, as abrupt and inelegant
as a belch.

"Well, Mac's never had much upstairs, as the saying goes,
but he knows how to take orders. With Berenson, that's all
he's had to do. However, you want a solution to your problem." His eyes searched the ceiling for inspiration. "Here's
what you do. Refer the Berenson woman to a lawyer in another firm, preferably someone from out of town, and keep
an eye on things from the sideline. That way you can honor
this feeling you have for her without having to compromise
yourself.''

"Do you have a lawyer in mind?"

"I'll leave that to you. Oh, wait," he said, fixing me with an icily opaque regard. "What about your friend Shushan over at Macauley and Stein? He might be suitable in any number of ways."

I wondered how many levels of irony and awareness were contained in this suggestion, or whether he intended any irony at all.

"He might at that," I said.

Charles stood up. "I have to go, and I know you do too. Just remember, Harry, Julia and I have your interests at heart. In the end, that's what counts."

TWELVE

CONVENTIONAL WISDOM TOLD me that the French Quarter wasn't the best place for a child. Common sense told me that Ike and I should get settled on our own, somewhere uptown nearer his school and other children his age. Still, I knew that so far, at least, Ike had not only derived special comfort from Grandmother and Leona but also enjoyed the human spectacle the Quarter afforded. Often in the afternoon Ike would play at a friend's house until I picked him up before dinner. Less often, Grandmother or Leona might pick him up, using taxicabs or my car since Grandmother no longer kept one. This routine had worked surprisingly well for six months, so I had let decision-making slide.

Grandmother had lived in the Quarter so long—sticking with it through the unfashionable years, when her neighbors threw garbage into her courtyard—that it had become her natural habitat. Now it was fashionable all over again, but no matter how tarted up the Quarter had become in recent years, with developers buying cottages that had been built for small change at the turn of the century, renovating them, and unloading them for two or three hundred grand, its essential nature remained unchanged. That was its appeal: the cheek-by-jowl mixture of elegance and sleaze. In the Quarter, as out-of-town Baptists well knew, anything went. The attitude that pervaded the city—let the good times roll—was at its most intense here, where it was possible to find those good times without the irksome pretense of respectability. Two blocks away, Bourbon Street now announced in gaudiest neon the specialized entertainments that had always been available, but in the past only to the cognoscenti.

Grandmother had a network of neighbors and friends to rely on but the neighborhood itself was scarcely immune to the crime that had swept the city. Her next-door neighbor, a widow like herself, had waked one night to see a strange man at the foot of her bed, and it was only chance that her caterwauling had caused him to bolt rather than to slit her throat. Her story sounded wild, but she had a smashed window and two elephantine footprints to prove it. Now the wall of her courtyard was topped by a row of jagged glass teeth embedded in concrete gums. Often, when I was blue, these images would present themselves forcefully. On the other hand, I knew that an uptown address did not guarantee safety. I would remind myself that the mother of a colleague had recently been found in her Garden District house with her head split open like an eggshell. The only things missing from the house were two silver candlesticks, a color TV, and a case of Tanqueray gin.

And always there was Ann. We had lived in an upper middle-class cocoon near Tulane, and that had been no protection at all.

Early that evening a wave of Carnival Week traffic carried families like flotsam and jetsam from the edges of the city into the center, where they would watch the Neptune parade. Driving Ike home, I was caught in several crosscurrents. It was after six when we reached Barracks Street. Clouds that on Saturday had begun to descend now weighed on rooftops. Houses were pressed like paper cutouts against an equally depthless sky. It was not a night to go to a club called the Trade Winds. It was a night to stay home with Ike and play Stratego.

I pulled up in front of the faded green wooden gates of the service courtyard where I kept the car. Ike started to get out to open the gates, then paused.

"Wait, Dad. Look in the rearview mirror. See that car parked in front of the Wilsons'?"

In the diminished light all I could make out was the outline of a dark sedan. It looked empty.

"What about it?"

"That car came and went at least five times yesterday. Four times when I was working at my desk by the window. Once last night after we came back from Othermama's. I saw it pull up under the streetlight."

"Maybe the Wilsons have a guest."

He shook his head. "Not this guy. He's creepy. He looks like he was put together from pieces of other people."

"So?"

"He parks the car and gets out and walks up and down the block. Sometimes he goes around the corner."

"Well, if I know the Wilsons, they'll have his car towed if he leaves it there too long."

"No, he's never gone for more than five, ten minutes at most."

"What conclusions do you draw?"

"None. Unless he's casing the joint."

"Which joint?"

He considered this. "That's not easy to tell."

Some reflex almost made me say, "You've been watching too many movies," but I didn't. Separately and together, in the months following Ann's death, Ike and I had seen a psychologist, as Ann herself would have urged; but even without those visits I would have known enough not to undercut Ike's watchfulness or his suspicions. To do that would have been to deny both his experience and my own. It was Ike who, coming home from school in the afternoon, had found Ann dead. Haphazardly slashed with a bread knife from our kitchen and lying in so much of her blood that the rug had become a mushy sponge.

When we had moved down to Grandmother's, I urged her to have an alarm system installed. She adamantly refused. Dealing out the cards, she would say: "Absolutely not. I'll move out before I live that way. This house is too old. It's always settling, sinking. I'd have to live with the alarm going off and the place crawling with policemen. Put one in your place if you want, but I'm old enough to live without the illusion of safety. Or *de*lusion."

When we entered the apartment that evening, Ike went straight to one of the windows that looked down on Barracks and pulled back the curtain.

"Look, Dad. There he is."

I had gone into the kitchen and by the time I reached the window the man was inside his car. I could see nothing more than a dark mass behind the steering wheel. Then the car pulled away from the curb and disappeared around the corner.

"You missed him." Ike's voice was more disappointed than accusatory.

When I put my hand on his shoulder, he turned from the window to face me.

"Son, I don't know who this character might be. I don't say you're wrong to wonder what he's up to. You're more observant than I am, and especially since your mother died you're more suspicious too. That seems right to me."

"Why aren't you suspicious?"

"Probably I just don't want to be."

There was a lot I still needed to say to Ike about Ann's death. That night, instinct sent me in another direction.

"We can't ever know what's going to happen, Ike, but we can make a plan. How's this? If you spot that car again, memorize the plate number and write it down. I'll call a guy I know in the registry office and find out the owner. That way, even if we can't tell what this character's up to, we will know his name. Okay?"

"Okay." He nodded twice, thoughtfully. My wisp of a plan had meant more than talk could. Maybe he saw plans as safeguards against chance, but probably not. He already understood that they were simply the best we could do.

THIRTEEN

GRANDMOTHER RARELY ASKED for favors except during Carnival season. Tonight Rudolph Carere would be King of Neptune, and Grandmother, who had been queen of this ball nearly sixty years before, would sit with other former queens in a front-row box. Visibly hesitant, she had asked me to take her to the Municipal Auditorium at nine, adding quickly that she didn't care how long I stayed.

Putting on formal clothes, especially white tie, had always pissed me. I owned the paraphernalia, most of it Father's or Grandfather's, but too often I had to search for some stud or cuff link, and impatience made my fingers clumsy. That evening, though, instead of being impatient I observed the ritual with detached curiosity. How broad this getup made my shoulders look, how narrow my waist. Although I had trouble tying the tie without Ann's help, I felt in the end that I had stepped into a different world from the one I usually inhabited. Charles might have said this proved I would always be a newcomer in the city. For the people Charles had grown up with, these transformations were common practice.

I went into Ike's room where he was working at his desk. "How do I look?"

"Funny but good. Good and funny."

If I went out at night, Ike slept at Grandmother's. This

evening, since Grandmother and I would be leaving together, Leona was staying the night. When I walked Ike to the main house a little after eight lights were ablaze in the living and dining rooms. "What's going on?" I said to Leona as we entered the kitchen.

"She's at it again."

"People?"

"Mm—hmmm."

"How does she keep it up?"

"Lord knows."

"I told Ike he could watch TV."

"Fine with me."

"Or maybe we can play gin," Ike said.

"Now you're talking."

In front of one of the living-room bookcases an elaborate drinks table had been set up. A silver tray held decanters of various heights and shapes, some heavy crystal, others deep red and gold Bohemian glass, each with a silver label depending from its neck on a silver chain. But most of the guests—ten or fifteen old regulars in formal dress—were filling their tumblers from ordinary bourbon and vodka bottles left over from Saturday's party.

Grandmother came over when she saw me in the doorway. "You look a perfect swell," she said with a laugh. "As you can see, there's been a slight change in plans. So many friends are going to Neptune I thought we'd meet here first. And Charles called to say he'd have his limousine stop for you and me on his way to the auditorium."

"If you don't need me to take you, I think I'll walk instead."

"You're not mad, are you?"

"Of course not. But it's a good chance to clear my head."

Spencer, standing with glass in hand, as usual, was talking to old Aunt Bessie, who sat on one of the sofas by the fireplace. She was wearing blue lace and a tiara that made me wonder whether she, too, had been queen of the ball some fifteen years before Grandmother.

"Miss Bessie," Spencer said, "the other night I threatened to move to the country and now my decision's firm."

"What swayed you?"

"A lot of things, but here's the most recent. When the roofer came today to examine some new leaks he discovered bullets lodged in the slates. Bullets? I said. Why would anyone shoot a roof? For one wild moment I thought a fleeced client had staged an antic revenge. But no. The roofer told me it was now a common problem in the Garden District. Turns out the St. Thomas Project, the one below Jackson Avenue, has become an armed camp. Especially on New Year's Eve the natives stoke themselves with joy-juice and smack and go crazy. The night air zings with bullets fired at random. Some end up in our roofs but that's not the worst of it. Last New Year's—you must have read about it—a girl walking on Magazine was lobotomized when a bullet dropped into her brain right out of the blue. For God's sake, Miss Bessie, I refuse to wear a helmet when I walk out my front door. You've done right to stay up there in Donaldsonville all these years."

"I only come to the city for parties. Then I beat a hasty retreat."

"What's the longest you were ever away from home?"

"When I was married to Frank Pickwick."

"How long was that?"

"I married Frank seventy-five years ago. It lasted four months."

"Only four months?"

Aunt Bessie looked up at him with liquid, wicked eyes. "Marriage proved to be a revelation," she drawled softly. "But it was a revelation that failed to please."

"Spencer, don't get Bessie started on marriage," Grandmother said. "Age hasn't withered her scorn." She took my arm. "Harry, come meet one of your grandfather's transplanted cousins. Douglas Hobson from Atlanta, this is my grandson Harry Preston."

"We met the other night but not formally," I said as I shook hands with the tall, professorial stranger who this evening wore tails and had his hair slicked down. "One of our local ladies objected to your bleak economic forecast."

"Ah, yes. She made me feel like Tiresias—a prophet without honor. But nothing I said was original. I was only restating the obvious."

"There's a mind-set that regards truth telling as treason."

"The same mind-set still fights the Civil War."

"Douglas has been forecasting again," Grandmother said. "He says when the boom ends and the city falls back on tourism, the local dealmakers will start pumping up the volume in the Quarter."

"How?"

"Added attractions."

"What's left to add?"

Douglas shrugged. "How about gambling on a big-time scale?"

"Would the city council permit that?"

"It'll be the old argument: job opportunities. That's like citing biblical authority. You're either a believer or a heretic. Remember the Louisiana Lottery? Conceived during Reconstruction and born in iniquity?"

"Douglas, when you get going on local history you're as bad as Bessie on marriage. Oh, Lord," Grandmother said, "there's the front bell. It must be Charles's driver. I'll have to send everyone on his way."

"And I'll be on my way. Tell Charles I needed some exercise. Douglas, I'll see you shortly. When there's time, I'll gladly listen to any story you want to tell."

Grandmother said, "Harry, you will dance with me once before you sneak off early from the ball."

"Of course I will."

"Don't worry about Julia," Douglas said. "I'll watch out for her. I've had a crush on her since I was a kid and she first married Cousin Harry."

"And now you're an old man," Grandmother said. "How old do you think that makes *me* feel?"

$\mathcal{F}$OURTEEN

TO AVOID CHARLES I went out the back gate. I looked to see whether the car Ike had seen earlier had returned: it hadn't. The night was so damp that it was cold without actually being cold. The sky's black lid was unrelieved by moon or stars. Even during Carnival Week the sidewalks at this end of the Quarter were empty. No one took a nocturnal pleasure stroll here anymore. That is, unless he had some specific pleasure in mind as his destination. Heading toward Rampart, I felt as if I'd sneaked out after curfew. Even so, I took my time.

It was nine-thirty when I reached the auditorium. Rows of limousines were parked by the side entrance. Inside the building the "Triumphal March" from *Aïda* resounded. That meant not only that the ball had begun but that the queen and her court were being presented. I showed my admit card at the door and entered the circular hallway. The hall was nearly empty; everyone was inside the theater either taking part in or watching the presentation. I was late, but I knew the drill and knew also that no one cared much if I ignored it. I waited in the hall until I heard the orchestra strike up the first dance. Just as I approached one of the doors into the theater, someone tapped me on the shoulder from behind.

It was a masker in a spangled cream-colored satin suit. He

lifted his mask with exaggerated care, just high enough to reveal a tentative grin. "It's Jason Bradford," he said. "After tomorrow you might not want to admit you know me."

"What happens tomorrow?"

"The shit hits the fan."

"You've seen Shushan, then."

"He has an appointment with Dad in the morning."

"Does your father know what's up?"

"I don't know exactly what Shushan said to him, but Dad's inside already, tanked to the gills. He'll have a whopping hangover tomorrow."

"Do you want to hit him when he's down?"

"He's always hungover, especially at this time of year. That means he'll be belligerent and vulnerable."

"What have you and Shushan decided?"

"I told him to go the limit if he has to. Dad may not be able to pay me back, but I'm not letting him steal another penny."

"Remember what I said, Jason. Some things may not be worth tearing a family apart for."

"It has to be this way. We'll do everything we can to keep it out of court, but Dad's not rational and he's not used to having his actions questioned, least of all by me."

"Are you still living at home?"

"I can stay at Jamie Carere's apartment as long as I have to. I moved some of my things there today."

"Let me know what happens, Jason."

"I will. Thanks again for putting me in touch with Shushan. He makes more sense than I'm used to."

Left alone, I turned and opened the door to the theater, only to be confronted by Douglas Hobson. Panting from his exertions on the dance floor, he spoke the inevitable refrain: "Let's find a drink."

"So soon?"

"Reason not the need."

"I was just going inside to do my duty."

"First show me where the maskers dress. Your cousin Haynesworth told me to go there when I got thirsty."

"You've already had enough of the ball?"

"It's like church. A little goes a long way."

"And Grandmother?"

"She's gabbing away in the front row with the other ex-royals. She had enough foresight to put a flask in her bag for when she visits the ladies' room."

I led Douglas around to a wide doorway behind the auditorium, partly obscured by what looked to be hospital screens. The cavernous room inside held chairs, benches, lockers, and bar stations. Small groups of maskers, refugees from the dance floor, stood drinking from plastic cups. Some had lifted their masks back over their heads. Others had simply cut the eye and mouth holes bigger to facilitate talking, drinking, and smoking: the ragged shapes of these openings made the maskers look like gaping gargoyles, especially when their double chins were visible below the masks. The room stank of whiskey and sweat, like a distillery that had once been a gymnasium.

"Before you go," Douglas said, after a waiter had poured him a stiff bourbon, "I should tell you straight out that Julia has you much on her mind."

"She's been talking to you, too? Well, please, Douglas, no lectures—and not one word about the Berensons."

"Berenson? I haven't heard that name since I left here twenty years ago. There was a time when I could have written a book on the old man." He shook his head. "Julia didn't say anything about the Berensons. Why would she? She just thinks you've been feeling restless lately. I take it she meant in your job."

"I'm surprised she's noticed."

"Julia's led a conventional life but she's too canny to miss much."

"I know she's canny."

"I think she secretly prefers the Hobsons to the Haynesworths. We have our fair share of mavericks."

"Such as you?"

"I'm just a hack journalist. I don't know whether that makes me a maverick. Twice divorced: both wives said I was too much in love with my own voice. Two sons, both grown and living out West. When I finish my years at the *Constitution* I'll probably move back here."

I smiled. "In spite of the decadence?"

"Because of it. One plus to an unregenerate place like this, it's always known how to say fuck you to the rest of the world. Tell me, though. Is Julia right or wrong about the job issue?"

"I wonder why you ask."

"Only because, years back, I waited too long in one job before finding myself another."

"She's right, of course. It's not the law; I like the law. It's something else."

"Your cousin's firm?"

"Yes."

"Too constrictive?"

"That's both euphemistic and accurate."

"So why stay?"

"I've been wondering. But listen, Douglas, this isn't the time to talk careers, much as I'd like to. I'm going to make an appearance inside, then head out."

"I may see you inside." He lifted his glass. "Then again I may not. But I will see that Julia gets home from the Queen's Supper."

I opened the door to the theater expecting a floodlit space. Instead, I stepped into a submarine world of differing light and blue, shafts of light falling from above through an undulating blue-green canopy washed with gold, blue yielding to green, gold to silver, beneath which dancers swirled like sea creatures on the floor of an enchanted lagoon.

Beyond the dance floor the thrones of the king and queen shone opalescent as seashells against a backdrop, itself shifting as sunlight through water, of ropes of pearls, clusters of coral, a brilliance of gold coins that seemed to sink only to rise again, as if governed by a tidal force.

The queen, crown of pearls catching the light, was on her throne holding court. The other throne was empty. Where was the king, dim Rudolph Carere? Doubtless he had withdrawn, but only after the third dance, to the inner sanctum of the King's Room, where he and his confreres would find goblets of champagne or whatever else might briefly slake their unquenchable thirsts.

In this strange world of underwater images, recognizable faces floated into view, then disappeared: Spencer with his mask up, braying on the dance floor with the strong-jawed blonde named Lou; Aunt Bessie teaching the fox-trot to one of the queen's pages; small Cousin Emily, diminished again by her dress, talking with her mother, large Diana, probably anticipating her own moment of regal glory two nights away; and Jamie Carere in a curious winged costume that glistened like fish scales and made me wonder what special role he had played in relation to his father's king.

And there, among the dancers, was Grandmother. The military bearing of her masked partner told me it was Charles. I made my way through the crowd and tapped him on the shoulder. "May I?"

Grandmother's face lighted up. "Harry. You're here."

"We missed you, Harry. You're becoming exclusive." Charles spoke without lifting his mask. The eye holes revealed nothing; the mouth was a slit.

"Don't try to make him feel guilty, Charles. That's such an awful old person's trick to play on the young." Grandmother turned to me. "Look around, Harry. Can you believe how this cavern's been transformed?"

"Where are we?"

" 'Full fathom five.' " She handed me her folded program. "The tableau, lovely really, was based on that song in *The Tempest:* the one about a drowned man who undergoes a sea change into something rich and strange. The only false note," she added, keeping a straight face, "was Rudolph. He wasn't quite right as Prospero."

"You can't see Rudolph as a master magician?" Charles's voice was dryly noncommittal.

"Perhaps as one who's renounced his magic. Physically, he would have made a much better Caliban."

A woman's voice spoke from behind me: "Mrs. Hobson, hello." Someone took my arm, pulled it slightly, said, "Harry, I decided to meet you here," and I turned to see Elizabeth.

Even in this tricky light her face, her eyes shone, and whatever she wore, some supple dark column of a dress, seemed barely to contain her radiant vitality.

"Grandmother, you know Elizabeth. Charles, this is Elizabeth Bennett, if you haven't met before."

Charles dipped his masked face in a silent curt nod, then abruptly turned and walked away.

"Who on earth was that?" Elizabeth said.

"Kin," I said.

"A rather rude man, child, whom I always took to be otherwise." Grandmother stared at Charles's back as he receded into the crowd. "Pay him no mind." She held out a small velvet box. "Here's something I want you to have, that I hope you'll accept. It's a favor that man just gave me for being queen of this ball so long ago."

"But I couldn't."

"He gave it to me, so now it's mine to give. Open it."

In the satin-lined box was a gold pin whose shape suggested a marine creature with a diamond-and-emerald-flecked tail.

"It's beautiful, Mrs. Hobson. But I can't accept it."

"Why not? I'm too old to wear such a charming frivolity. You should have it. Don't feel that you have to put it on now, though. On you, less is more."

Grandmother's eyes held Elizabeth's. Elizabeth said, "Thank you. If you want me to have it, I'll accept. I love it. I'll remember when and how it was given. Harry, this is your dance with your grandmother. I'll get my coat and meet you in the hall."

Strong as I knew she still was, Grandmother was so slender she seemed almost weightless when we danced. "How I used to love to dance with your grandfather. He always said he hated to dance. That was absurd. He danced perfectly, as he did so many other things." For a moment she looked eighteen, then her face shifted, drooped. "That young woman needs you, doesn't she? I wonder how much."

"She needs someone, Grandmother. I'm not sure it's me."

A hand touched my shoulder and I yielded Grandmother to the embrace of a potbellied masker.

"Ashton Willard, I don't have to ask who this is," Grandmother said. "I'd recognize you anywhere, even in disguise," and off they spun.

The circular hallway was now populated by maskers and women in ball gowns, desperately smoking cigarettes. A green-and-gold sea horse with a prominent snout, who must have taken part in the tableau, separated himself from a group near the door and lumbered unsteadily over to where I stood.

"Preston. Harry Preston. Howya doin', old buddy?"

If I had struck a match too close to his snout it might have ignited his breath.

When he saw my blank stare he lifted his mask to reveal the puffy facsimile of a face I remembered from law school. "It's me, Harry. Don't you remember your classmate Ned?"

"Ned! Howya doin'?"

"Good, real good." With his right hand he pumped mine; dark brown whiskey sloshed from the paper cup in his left. He shoved his sweating face forward and dropped his voice to a conspiratorial whisper. "Now come on, Harry. Gimme the lowdown on the high ups."

"Lowdown?"

He winked. "The lowdown on the high ups."

"Sorry, Ned. I don't get around much anymore."

Elizabeth came into view behind Ned's right shoulder. She was wearing a full-length gold evening cloak, with a hood pulled up over her black hair. In the lighted rotunda she shimmered like a Byzantine icon.

Moving rapidly as if with a fixed purpose she brushed past Ned and inserted her arm under mine. With her free hand she pulled my face down and planted a kiss firmly on my mouth.

"Harry." Her smile was brightly artificial. "All set to go?"

Ned peered into Elizabeth's face, then into mine; his tongue found the empty space in his cheek.

"What's that you said, buddy? Don't get around much anymore?" Without waiting for the reply, which in any case I couldn't have given him, he headed back toward the group he had left. They had stopped talking and were staring at us.

As we left the building, I said, "I thought I was meeting you at the Trade Winds. And by the way, what was that little show you just put on?"

"The show was for *their* benefit. The rest I'll explain in the car."

FIFTEEN

A SILVER GRAY Mercedes was waiting at the corner. The driver was a yellow-thatched young man who looked like a college student and whom Elizabeth introduced as Sam Wilkins.

In order to get to the Trade Winds, Sam had to traverse the Quarter. The last float of the Neptune Parade had long since disappeared into the night, but the never-say-die crowds of pedestrians on Bourbon and Royal still impeded our progress. Mostly they were young people about Sam's age who carried beer cans or outsized glasses from Pat O'Brien's, filled with the neon-pink brew known as a Hurricane. One Hurricane shook your foundations; the second swept you away. Street cleaners were shoving broken glass into the gutters.

"Here's what happened," Elizabeth said. "After our lunch, in spite of that scene with Jack, I felt so much better that I decided to reenter the land of the living. To use the term loosely. I'm talking about the Neptune Ball. I know the girl who was queen: Sally Montrose. Since I was coming downtown anyway, and since I knew you would be there, I thought what the hell. I went home when Jack was still at work, got the car and some more clothes. The hotel found me Sam, and he's been a lifesaver. I wanted to see what it was like to go to one of these functions alone. It's odd, Harry. For better or worse I'm the same person I always was, but now that my name's Bennett, not Berenson, I get sent this sort of invitation. Tonight proved easier than I dreamed it could be. I sailed in, tried to look smashing, danced twice, and found you. And your grandmother," she said. "How generous she was." She drew back her cloak. "I did put the pin on, after all."

We had reached Decatur and turned toward Jackson Square. This area was bathed in an orange phosphorescent glow that seemed to suffuse even the sky. A gust of air carried the smell of coffee from the Tchoupitoulas docks. The street was patchworked with cartons and rotted lettuces, discards from the open-air market. At the square, in the cold illumination of floodlights, the bleached façade of the cathedral and the statue of the general, frozen for eternity astride his horse, repudiated everything beyond the periphery of the light.

The Trade Winds was the only nightclub in its block. This was no recommendation. The building that housed it was squeezed like an unwelcome stranger between two sagging structures with a wanly commercial air. On either side of these buildings garbage-littered alleys plunged rearward to invisible conclusions. The Trade Winds announced itself discreetly, at least. A pockmarked stucco archway framed its entrance. Embedded in the stucco were diminutive neon letters spelling the name of the bar. By way of atmosphere, the *T* in "Trade" was shaped like a palm tree. Above the sign a wrought-iron balcony fronted windows curtained heavily as if for a blackout.

Sam pulled up and we got out. As we did, a middle-aged couple emerged, reeling slightly, from the entrance of the bar. She was as overweight as he looked underfed. On his lapel he wore a red, white, and blue plastic tag that said "Cleveland or Bust."

The woman tittered. "Some place. Nothing like that back home."

"They'd pass an ordinance."

"Come on, Elizabeth," I said. "Let's get this over with."

There was nothing special about the Trade Winds' layout.

We entered a room that was a smoke-filled tunnel. Artificial palm trees sprouted here and there. White-clothed tables lined one sidewall, a polished wooden bar ran the length of the other. At our end of the room, near the door, a tiny, wizened black woman was playing the piano and singing in an expressive croak.

> *My mama told me a thing*
> *Before she ran away.*
> *Said if I be a good little girl*
> *She'd put my hair in curl.*
> *I wouldn't give you none of my jelly roll,*
> *I wouldn't give you piece of cake—*
> *Not to save your soul.*

She sang as if impervious to the fact that she was not the main feature of the place. Judging from the customers' faces, the waiters were the main feature. They were young hustler-types who wore G-strings and stoned expressions and drifted between the tables like tray-carrying sleepwalkers. The surprising thing was not that most of the customers were men but how many tables held conventional-looking couples or women in groups of three and four. A redheaded woman at a table near us reached out and snapped the waistband of her waiter as he was taking the order; then she fell back in her chair, laughing raucously.

As Elizabeth stood in the entrance, shining in her golden cloak, a number of heads swiveled in her direction, took in what they wanted to take in, then swiveled back to their original positions.

We sat down at one of the tables. A waiter materialized. In a face clear as a child's, his eyes were so dilated that they were mostly pupil.

"Just tell Mr. Famiglietti that Mrs. Bennett's waiting for him."

When the waiter left, Elizabeth said, "It's hard to believe that a dump like this could be a step up in the world for Famiglietti. But if you'd seen the Gin Mill, you'd know that it is. In those days, Greek sailors were the house specialty."

If she was telling me something about herself, neither her face nor her tone revealed it.

"Here's Famiglietti," she whispered.

"Lizzie, I thought you were coming alone. If you needed an escort I could have supplied one."

The voice was a drawling nasal purr. It belonged to a heavyset man in his fifties with a spherical acne-scarred face, combed-back black hair, and a pug nose with a small crater in its tip. Considering his place of business, he was oddly dressed in a pin-striped banker's suit that could have been worn by a member of the Jackson Club, except that it was too well tailored. Even his inconsistently fastidious diction seemed to be fighting a losing battle with his origins, whatever they were.

Elizabeth gave him a level look but didn't smile. "Mr. Preston's a lawyer, Rico. I didn't know you supplied legal aid."

"A lawyer. I'm disappointed in you, Lizzie. I thought we were going to have a private chat about old times." He faced me. "I don't want to seem rude, Mr. Preston." He held out a hand that was pudgy and damp. "A lawyer's presence makes everything so official. Above all, I wanted this to be an informal talk."

"So does Elizabeth. Let's go some place where we can be more informal."

"By all means. My office is out back."

We followed him through a beaded curtain behind the bar into a dimly lit passage, scarcely larger than a vestibule, that smelled of urine and disinfectant. When Famiglietti turned to a door on his left I stepped forward and opened the shuttered door facing me. "Not that way," Famiglietti said, but I had already glimpsed what lay beyond: a second hallway like that of a dormitory, lined on both sides with doors and ending in obscurity. "Sorry," I said.

Famiglietti eyed me as he stepped aside to usher us into his office. At first it seemed a different world, in keeping with the clothes that he wore. Carpeted in deep red, it contained leather wing chairs and a flat-topped mahogany desk. But maybe it wasn't such a different world, after all. When he closed the door I noticed that the room smelled of the passage we had just left.

Famiglietti motioned us to chairs, then sat down behind his desk. "Now what's Lizzie been telling you, Mr. Preston? I hope there's been no misunderstanding."

"I hope there has. In any case, I'd rather let you and Elizabeth do the talking. At first."

There was a knock on the door. The nearly naked waiter who had greeted us in the bar came in and set a tray with small glasses and a cognac bottle on the desk. Except for a dull purple bruise on his neck and another on his left shoulder, his nacreous skin was untouched by time or experience; his face was unmarked by thought. I wondered whether he was even ten years older than Ike. Exposed as he was, in that curious costume that was less protective than a diaper, he looked like a child whose innocence was his best defense. I didn't believe that for a second.

"Anything else, Mr. Rico?"

"Not just now, Henry. Go strut your stuff."

When the door closed, Famiglietti turned to Elizabeth. "I thought we trusted each other, Lizzie. The way you've handled this makes me feel sad."

" 'Trust?' I don't know you well enough to trust you, Rico. Or maybe I knew you too well, once. And don't call me Lizzie."

"But you *can* trust me, Elizabeth. Old friends are the best. How long have you known Mr. Preston?"

"Long enough to tell him about your phone call."

"What about it?"

"That you pressured me to use influence that I just don't have."

"I merely asked you to do me a favor for old times' sake."

"Rico, if I had any say you could buy that building tomorrow."

"I believe you. But you will have."

"Have what?"

"A say. Quite soon, from what I hear."

"What do you hear?"

"Your grandfather's a very sick man."

She glared at him fiercely. "Grandad's had several strokes. He's been ill for years. But I can't imagine him dead."

"Others can. And you're his only heir."

"Grandmother's alive."

"She doesn't count. She never has. You told me that yourself years ago."

"I still don't see—"

"You're not an easy person, Elizabeth. You don't roll with the punches. Look at the way you've handled this business. None of this was necessary. You've wasted Mr. Preston's valuable time."

"I told him about the pictures, too, Rico."

"Ah, the pictures." He removed an envelope from a desk drawer and placed it on the blotter in front of him. "I was rummaging through my memory book the other day and stumbled on these. Would you care to have a look, Mr. Preston?"

"Rico!"

I said, "No. As far as I'm concerned, they belong to Elizabeth."

"Not quite. Let's just say our Elizabeth was a willing subject in a group portrait. As to ownership, well, you're a lawyer, Mr. Preston. I don't have to explain it to you." His smugly insinuating tone was as subtle as a brick in the head.

"No, but speaking of ownership, I'd like to clear up a few things. For example, why did you let Elizabeth think you owned this place?"

Elizabeth looked at me. So did Famiglietti, silently. Finally he said, "I never said I owned it."

"Elizabeth, I had Esther run a check on this building at the assessor's office. Seems it belongs to an outfit called Harlow Properties. Famiglietti leases it."

"So what?" he said.

"You told Elizabeth you wanted to expand your operation. What you really want is to be able to control it. If what goes on here were known, you might not have any operation."

He shrugged. "Skin. Boys. Around here that doesn't rate as a misdemeanor. I pay who and what I have to."

"I'm sure you do. But the management at Harlow Properties seems to think this place is nothing more than an old-fashioned piano bar.''

"What are you getting at?''

"Just this. Harlow Properties is a legal fiction. The actual owners of this building are a well-known family named O'Donnell. Irish Catholics who made money in the grocery business at the turn of the century and bought up property in the Quarter. Only a renegade O'Donnell would show up in a place like this, and then he wouldn't want it known. One of the younger O'Donnells is a priest. Another you may know as Tricia Macready: councilwoman for District A, mother of five, daily communicant at Holy Name, active fighter against crime uptown *and* downtown. You get the picture. One call to her office and you'd be peddling ass on the street. Worse yet, Councilwoman Macready might choose to make an example of you. Some of those kids out front look like minors to me.''

Famiglietti sat motionless in his chair like a pockmarked Buddha. Then he said, "Elizabeth, Elizabeth. That's what I meant when I said you didn't roll with the punches. There's no need for you or Mr. Preston to get so hot and bothered. All I wanted was a simple exchange of favors. Remember, I did you a lot of favors once.''

"Favors. The best favor you could have done would've been to turn me away from your door.''

"You were so determined even then, Elizabeth, that I couldn't deny you anything. I'm sure Mr. Preston understands the problem.'' He flicked his glance in my direction. "Maybe you dolled yourself up tonight to remind me you were slumming. Time was when you felt at home in my place. You made friends, connections. A lot of them passed in the night, it's true, but I've stayed put. And believe it or not, I am your friend. I'll prove it to you.'' He picked up the envelope and tore it in half. "The pieces are yours to get rid of. I've got no negatives.''

Elizabeth didn't move or speak.

"But I forgot. Maybe you don't care about the pictures after all. Then let's see. How can I prove I'm a friend you can trust?'' He paused self-consciously. "I know. I'll tell you about a visit I had last week. This character with a rat face came sniffing around here. I've seen him around. Name's Shapiro. Private cop who didn't play it careful and lost his license. Know what he wanted to talk about? You.''

"Me?"

Famiglietti nodded. "He was digging for information about your activities, past and present. He was pretty picky about the kind of stuff he wanted, too. Wanted to know whether you'd been involved in anything—well, not quite legal. And he wasn't talking about traffic tickets.''

"Not legal?"

"Elizabeth, you forget that a lot of habits people like you pick up and take for granted, they fall into the category of not legal. I don't want to cause trouble between you and your lawyer friend. Lawyers don't want to be told more than they have to know, so I won't go into details. But you don't need total recall to catch my meaning.''

"What did you tell him?"

"Not one thing."

"Of course not. If you had, you would have compromised yourself.''

"Not true. You made a lot of connections here, some of them may have helped you pick up habits, but you can't pin that rap on me. My traffic's different.''

Elizabeth said to me, "Harry, what does this mean? It has to be Jack. But why?''

"Let's hear Mr. Famiglietti out. I want to know what this Shapiro character was offering in return for information.''

"He didn't offer anything, not exactly. But he knew about the building next door.''

I said, "Assuming you had something to tell him, why didn't you?''

"I'm Elizabeth's friend."

When he saw my skeptical look he said, "I'll tell you, Mr. Preston. I didn't like the feel of this. This character, he wasn't operating on his own. One thing I know about this kinda situation is you got to choose sides. Well, our friend Lizzie''—he spoke as if she weren't in the room—"she's been a loser in her day, but even when she's losing she looks like a winner. When Grandaddy goes she's going to be a winner for sure. If I have to wait to expand my operation, so what? I place my money on the lady.''

He seemed suddenly overwhelmed by his own generosity of spirit. Or possibly his venal vision of her future activated cheap sentiment. In any case, something prompted a tear to roll down his scarred right cheek. An acne pit held it briefly in suspension.

Elizabeth said simply, ''Thank you, Rico. What you've told me matters.''

''If you hadn't come in tonight dressed to kill and toting a lawyer,'' he said, ''I wouldn't have acted the way I did. I never meant to do anything with those pictures. My point is, this guy who was sniffing around and whoever he's working for, they know you're going to be a winner, like I do. But they want you to stay a loser.''

$\mathcal{S}$IXTEEN

IN THE CAR, Sam was reading a paperback book with the help of a small pocket flashlight. I gave him my address, and as we headed toward Barracks, Elizabeth said, "I'm scared, Harry."

"I know."

"The hounds of hell are hot in pursuit."

"Meaning?"

"The past. What Rico said back there was true. I've never worried much about things I've done—certainly never about legal consequences. Or almost never, and then not for long. I took it for granted that the only piper I might have to pay was in my own psyche. With the help of modern science," she said, "if psychiatry is a science, I've become pretty good at scraping away traces of shame: the way a surgeon uses his knife to scrape for cancer. When all else has failed I've told myself: Elizabeth, at least you can say you've done everything once. The truth is, though, I've done too many things more than once."

"Well, who hasn't? Look, Elizabeth, I'm not in the market for revelations. But we've reached the point where you'd better level with me if you want my advice. Just tell me what I need to know. Remember: decent lawyers, like analysts, don't talk."

"I know you won't talk, Harry. Rest easy. I haven't done murder—not yet." She smiled to herself. "I guess I have been trying to have it both ways. I do need advice, God knows, but I also want you to think well of me. Which only proves that the surgeon's knife hasn't quite done its job."

"You'd be surprised how tolerant I can be."

"I'm not so sure. I think you're something of a prig."

"That's the second time you've called me that. You make it sound like 'prick.' "

"Don't get mad. I know you're conventional. That's why I need you, Harry. You're such a prig and oh so conventional."

"Hold on, Elizabeth, we're here."

She sat up, dazed, and pulled her hood over her head. Drawing apart, we assumed formal attitudes.

"Can you come in?" I said loudly.

"Well, that would be fine. But won't we disturb Ike?"

"Ike's at Grandmother's. Sam, what about it? Can you wait?"

"Hell, I'm being paid."

"What'll you drink?"

"Beer, if you have it."

"A couple of beers."

I led Elizabeth upstairs and took Sam his beers. He was standing inside the courtyard.

"Sorry about that," I said.

"Forget it. Money's money. I'm just tired of sitting in the car, Mr. Preston. I'll wait here."

Elizabeth was stretched out on the bed, wrapped in her golden cloak. Her dress and underwear lay crumpled on the floor. Fear, or something else, had made her eyes dazzled, dazzling.

"We should talk. But I don't want to, Harry, not now."

"Neither do I." My heart was pounding in my penis.

Outside, commotion flared. A muffled yell, the thump of flesh against metal. Rapid footsteps, a car gunning, tires squealing.

Sam's voice called: "Mr. Preston. Hey, up there."

I pulled my pants back on and ran downstairs. Sam was

sitting on the flagstones, rubbing his head. The wooden gates stood open.

"What the hell?" I helped him up. He sank back down. "Jesus," he said.

"But what happened?"

"This guy."

"What guy?"

"This guy. I was just sitting here, sitting on the fender of your car when I heard the gate latch rattle. Then the gate opened a little bit. Then all the way. This guy was standing there. He didn't see me but when he finally stepped inside I said, 'Hey.' I guess that was stupid, but I thought he might be a friend of yours. Anyways, next I knew he charged me like an elephant, popped me on the head, picked me up and threw me against the car. Then he ran. Ow." He rubbed his head again.

"You all right? Want me to call a doctor?"

"I'm okay."

"This guy. What did he look like?"

"I couldn't see. A moose, an elephant."

"Maybe we should go upstairs." When I turned, Elizabeth was standing at the foot of the stairwell.

I said, "Somebody—"

"I heard." She hugged her metallic cloak to her as if it were armor. "If Sam's all right I want to go home. I mean the hotel."

"Whoever this character was, Elizabeth, he's gone."

"I don't care." Her face and lips were colorless; her eyes seemed to have receded into her skull. "Nowhere's safe. Not anymore. But at least there're people at the hotel—lots of people."

"I'm not people?"

"You don't understand. I want to be surrounded by people, anonymous people, but I need to be alone, too. I've got to think. If Jack's behind this—"

"This man was just some prowler, Elizabeth. Ike saw someone hanging around yesterday; this is probably the same man."

"Yesterday?" Her eyes stared. "Harry, forgive me. I've

got to go. I've got to think. Sam, are you well enough to drive?"

"Yeah, sure. I'm okay."

I placed my hands on Elizabeth's shoulders. "At least let me ride with you to the hotel."

"Of course." But she was past caring whether I accompanied her or not; she had already found her way to an isolated place inside herself and it was more to herself than to me that she spoke when she let her head fall back against the car seat and whispered, "Dr. Jasper gave me an assignment once. He taped a session and told me to listen to the tape. It was supposed to make what I said more real to me, but it did the opposite. I sounded so practiced, so rehearsed to my own ears that I might have been an actress in a play. But listen. It's not all bullshit. I really do know some things other people don't."

"What things, Elizabeth?"

"Listen. Imagine a dinner party given by one of Jack's uptown friends. The dining room glitters. Twenty coats of red lacquer on the walls. A king's ransom of Scalamandre silk at the windows. Venetian mirrors, Georgian silver, and a rosewood table that reflects candle flames and the crystal chandelier overhead. My dinner partner drones on—about last night's party or the newest restaurant, about salmon fishing in Alaska or raising llamas in Slidell. I nod and smile but I'm not really there. I'm already long gone."

"Where are you?"

"In another world. A world most people would be afraid of, but not me. He made it safe. Then something happened."

"What kind of world?"

"The first people who came thought those black streams were dead. They aren't dead. The current's there, it shifts back and forth even if you can't see it. He taught me that. If you follow a bayou on foot, it's like being pulled toward the center of a whirlpool. One leads to the lagoon. That's where egrets come back in March to mate and nest. You hear them far away, then the cry gets louder, sadder. White flocks move across the sky. I know other things, too."

"What?"

"Alligators swallow water rats whole. At night they roar

like lions. If you shine a flashlight into the dark you can see their yellow eyes shining.''

We pulled up in front of the hotel. Elizabeth opened the door before the doorman had a chance to. ''Alligators don't blink,'' she said. She stepped from the car without looking back and disappeared into the lobby.

Sam and I scarcely spoke as he drove me back downtown. In my apartment I found Elizabeth's bra on the bedroom floor. I kicked it under the bed, took off my clothes a second time, and got between the sheets. Then I lay awake, listening.

$\mathcal{S}$EVENTEEN

I HAD BARELY sat down at my desk the next morning when the first telephone call of the day came through. It might as well have been the last.

"Harry." It was Elizabeth's voice, but so faint that she seemed to be speaking from the far end of a tunnel.

"Elizabeth? What's wrong?"

Silence. Then she said in the same collapsed whisper: "Harry, get over here. Now. Quick."

"What's wrong, Elizabeth? Where are you?"

"Home."

"You mean the hotel?"

"No. Home. Philip Street."

"What are you doing there? I thought—"

"Harry. Please come. Now. Something's happened."

"Elizabeth, I have a life to lead. I've got meetings with two clients—"

"Harry, I need you. Please come." Then the phone went dead.

I sat stewing. I cursed myself for having gotten mixed up with someone as neurotic and demanding as this. I said out loud, "Sorry, not this time." Then I reached for the telephone book, looked up the Philip Street number, and dialed it. I let it ring twenty times before hanging up. I looked at the directory again and memorized the address. Grabbing my coat, I went out to Esther's desk. "Something's come up. You'll have to cancel my first appointment."

"That's Erskine. What'll I tell him?"

"Tell him it's an emergency. A family emergency."

"But that was—"

"Mrs. Bennett. Just tell him that. I'll let you know about the rest of the day."

I drove too fast up St. Charles toward the Garden District. The low ceiling of clouds had finally lifted to reveal blue sky and a day that burned with piercing New England clarity. Only the dull subtropical green of the live oaks and the azaleas seemed anomalous. That, and the debris from the previous night's parade, the Dixie cups and food wrappers and collapsed beer cans, that littered the Avenue from Lee Circle to beyond where I turned off onto First.

On the sidewalk in front of the cottage three carefully clipped crape myrtles stood at attention. The cottage itself was narrow—no more than fifty feet wide, including the strip of side yard—but deep. Originally designed for modest living, with a modestly columned front porch, it now glittered in the sunlight like a gift-wrapped package. It was painted the color of an overripe cantaloupe; its columns were white and its shutters creosote green. A low fence of black iron palings separated it from the sidewalk. Narrow though the property was, the fence had two gates. One led to the front door. The other was a double gate opening into a brick walk, bordered by raised beds of camellias, that had perhaps served as a driveway. I peered down the length of the walk, which was deeply shaded by oaks and magnolias. This was the place, all right. In front of the hedge at the far end, just as Elizabeth had described it, a gray army tank crouched like an animal in its lair.

I went to the front door and rang the bell. When no one answered I banged the brass knocker several times. The third time, the door swung open.

Stepping inside, I felt illicit—as if I were reading someone else's mail, or worse. The entrance hall, a small square of space carved from what had been a front parlor, was entirely walled with mirrors. In the light pouring in from behind me, my reflected face had a hot, angry look. I slammed the door.

I called Elizabeth's name but expected no answer and received none.

The living room to my left was some thirty feet long and furnished largely with antiques. But it contained, in addition, comfortable-looking sofas and armchairs; the place wasn't quite as formal as Elizabeth had implied. The rug was a faded, almost bleached Oriental. The red in it was brick red. An asymmetrical stain of deeper, more purple red, glowed dully in the far right-hand corner. I knelt to touch it. It was wet. I jumped back.

Beyond the living room, and separated from it only by an archway, the dining room gleamed with silver and mahogany. An open door to the right of the sideboard showed a hall, at the end of which I could see a square of sunlight and the aquamarine shimmer of a swimming pool.

A thin trail of red traversed the polished floor of the dining room and pursued its erratic, ribbonlike course down the white runner that carpeted the rear hall. I followed it, mesmerized.

The sliding glass door that terminated the hall was open to the day. I walked through it onto a brick patio that contained a pool almost as large as itself. A red-streaked white bath towel lay bunched on the bricks. In the sunlight the pool shone the same brilliant blue as the sky. Jets of water pumping into it from the side faintly agitated its surface.

In the center of the pool, well below the surface but clearly visible, a man's naked body—a lean brown body bisected by a strip of whiter flesh—floated facedown, gyrating gently and with supreme languor, as if drifting on a current that had no place to go.

$\mathcal{E}$IGHTEEN

FOR WHAT MAY have been minutes I stood stupidly on the terrace, eyes smarting from the glare and fastened on the thing in the pool. All the events of the preceding days had hurled me toward this conclusion that now seemed unreasonably inevitable.

On the bricks near the blood-smeared towel lay a pole with a net on the end, the kind used for collecting leaves from a pool. I took the pole, leaned out over the water, and with the netted end caught the man's shoulder and pulled him toward me. I might have been trawling for a rare aquatic specimen. The pressure of the pole momentarily pushed the body further underwater, where it turned over once with a flash of black pubic hair before lazily resuming its original position. By this time I could reach his ankles. I knew, with a furious certainty that would have brooked no denial, that he was past feeling anything, but some queasy concern for his face and genitalia prompted me to turn him on his back again before hauling him up over the pool's edge onto the terrace.

I needn't have worried about his face. It was so battered that it was almost—but not quite—unrecognizable. His eyes seemed locked in a ferociously lewd wink. One, its white gone purple-red, protruded from its socket and gazed blindly at the bright winter day; the other was buried between twin mounds of puffy, discolored flesh. I did not bother to feel for his pulse.

I went inside, found a telephone in the kitchen, and called the emergency police number. Then I quickly made a tour of the house. The bedrooms, like the living room, were undisturbed, but the small study to the right of the dining room looked as if it had been vandalized. Desk drawers had been emptied and thrown on the floor; the desk itself was overturned. More riveting than anything else, though, were the bizarre costumes and objects that had been pulled from the wall of closets at one end of the room, and which covered the floor in multicolored, grotesque profusion. Some of these—an iridescent cloak made of blue-black feathers, a shattered lamp with a deceptively parchmentlike shade—I recognized from Elizabeth's descriptions. Others, skirts and what looked like pieces of underwear made of brightly-dyed lace or silk, almost beggared description. In the midst of a litter of European-looking handguns was an implement shaped like a rough-veined penis with an electrical cord attached to it.

I went to the front door and opened it. I could hear a siren approaching from the avenue—the pulsating yowl that signifies urban catastrophe. The door of the house across the street opened, and a black woman in a white uniform stepped onto the porch. Two small children, both girls, followed her. She shoved them back inside. Then she stood with one hand on her hip, coolly assessing me as the police car pulled up. A young patrolman with a pudgy, bland face got out and sauntered over to where I stood by the gate.

"You the one who called in?"

"Yes."

I led him through the house to the body by the pool. He whistled faintly, then knelt and brushed a spider from the dead man's forehead. He turned to me. "This how you found him?"

"He was in the pool. I pulled him out."

"Maybe you shouldna done that."

"It seemed the right thing at the time."

He eyed me indifferently. He took a notebook from his

pocket and wrote something in it. "You better give me your name and address," he said, and I did.

"You a friend of his?" he asked casually, indicating the body with his thumb.

"Not really."

"Well, just take it easy until Captain Lanaux gets here."

"Charlie Lanaux?"

"Yeah. Know him?"

"I know him."

After that, he didn't ask for any more information, and I didn't offer it. Together we went back through the house to wait out front.

Nineteen

FROM THE LOOK of recognition he gave me when he arrived, I could tell I was lucky to have gotten Lanaux and that he knew it, too. He was no run-of-the-mill New Orleans cop who was in the game simply to throw his weight around: far from it. Beneath his heavy brows his eyes were intelligent and shrewdly humorous. He was ambitious, too. The previous winter he had been one of my students in a night course in tax law that I had taught at the university. He was a little older than I, but having taught him gave me the advantage I needed in the present situation: he had worked hard in the course and received the top grade.

At his suggestion, I sat in the living room and waited while he supervised the procedural ritual attending the discovery of a corpse. Ann's death had made me familiar with that ritual. Men came and went; flashguns flashed. After what seemed an interminable period, Lanaux returned and sat on the coffee table facing me; when it creaked alarmingly under his weight, he jumped up and moved to a side chair. Elegant and fragile, it creaked, too.

"Now tell me what you know, Mr. Preston."

I had had time—he had given me time—to decide what I would and wouldn't say. I stated briefly what I was doing there: that Mrs. Bennett, the dead man's wife, had consulted me informally on legal business and that I had received an emergency call from her that morning.

"Did she say what kind of emergency?"

"No."

"Since when do lawyers make house calls? Since the medics gave them up?"

"I almost didn't make this one. It would have been easier if I hadn't."

"Got any ideas where she is?"

I shook my head. I had decided, maybe unwisely, not to mention that she had been staying at the Pontchartrain.

"Think she did this?" His tone was casual.

I hoped mine was. "If you want an informal opinion, I'd say no."

"Then why'd she vacate?"

"Panic, maybe? Your guess is as good as mine. For all I know, she may be in some danger herself." It occurred to me that this was in fact a possibility. Though I didn't mention it, the incident at Grandmother's the night before swooped back and settled in my head. I could no longer refuse to take it seriously.

"What kind of danger?"

"I don't know."

He went on questioning me, laconically but thoroughly, and I kept my answers minimal. When he asked me about the Bennetts' marriage I said I had heard rumors but that I didn't know the Bennetts well enough to confirm or deny them. Lanaux didn't look as if he believed me, and I would have respected him less if he had. But he didn't press me. After all, he was studying to be a lawyer.

A thin man wearing glasses and an impersonal, academic expression came from the back of the house and stood by Lanaux's chair.

"Captain?"

Lanaux turned to him.

"His skull's been fractured. Compound fracture penetrating through the frontal bone into the calvarium. Could have been done with a sap or a piece of pipe, though there doesn't seem to be any sign of the weapon. The blow depressed the roof of the orbit, causing one proptosed eye. But we can't tell yet whether the fracture killed him. We'll have to check for water in the lungs."

"Thanks. Call the coroner if you haven't already."

The man nodded and left the room. Lanaux said to me, "Well, I guess that's all for now. You want to split?"

"Sure. I thought I might be a suspect."

"Not as yet. Just don't go far. We'll need you as a material witness." He observed me closely. "I'm going to put out a call for the Bennett woman. You haven't told me much, and I don't know how much more you know than you've told. Do her and me a favor, though. If she gets in touch with you, get her to turn herself in. This doesn't look like a woman's crime—not that you can tell nowadays—but it'll go easier for her if she doesn't try to dodge us. Oh, something else. Know anything about her family? She local, or what?"

I told him who her mother was, what she did and where she lived. Then I told him who her grandfather was.

"Not so good," he said. "The papers'll have a field day with this unless she turns up."

"They will anyway," I said.

TWENTY

OUT FRONT THE street was now lined with official-looking cars. Sunlight danced prismatically on their highly polished hoods. Two middle-aged women, probably neighbors, were being held at a distance by the young patrolman who had first answered my call. Otherwise, the neighborhood seemed eerily quiet and undisturbed, as if murder were an everyday occurrence or in too bad taste to be noticed. As I headed for my car, the black maid reappeared on the porch of the house across the street. Small, thin, gimlet-eyed, she stood facing the street like a sentinel. I walked toward her, keeping my eyes on hers. At first I thought she might withdraw, but she remained frozen, hand once again on her hip, returning my gaze but without expression.

"May I speak with you a moment?"

"Who you I should speak with you?"

"My name's Preston. I'm a lawyer and a friend of Mrs. Bennett."

"What's going on over there?"

"You'll find out soon enough. The police will be questioning everybody in the neighborhood. But I'd like to ask you a few questions myself."

"Miz Bennett, she in trouble?"

"Maybe, maybe not. Her husband's been killed."

"Jesus." She repeated this twice. Then she said: "Miz Bennett wouldn't do nothing like that."

"No one said she did."

"Miz Bennett a nice lady. Mr. Bennett, he not so nice. He holler at Miz Bennett all the time."

"Well, he's stopped hollering for good."

I didn't want to talk about Bennett. Whatever he had been, he was a dead man now. "What I want to know is, did you see Mrs. Bennett leave her house this morning?"

"What if I did?"

"Look, I'm not trying to make trouble for Mrs. Bennett. I want to help her. But I need to know what car she was driving when she left here."

"Her own car," she relented.

"The Mercedes?"

She shrugged.

"Silver gray?"

"That's it."

"Did you see anyone else go in or out of the Bennetts' house this morning?"

"I don't get here till eight."

"But did you see anyone?"

"I never saw nobody."

"Any strange cars?"

She reflected. "Beat-up old dark-blue car at the end of the block. It was there when I got here. Gone when I come out to sweep the porch."

"Then what?"

"Miz Bennett drive up. She wave when she see me. She always wave and call out: Hey, Mary! Mr. Bennett, he different. He never give nobody time of day. Not even Pearl."

"Pearl?"

"She the girl who cleans for the Bennetts. She tell me plenty of things."

"Did Mrs. Bennett speak to you again when she left?"

"I was inside."

"But you did see her?"

She sighed. "You sure you a friend of Miz Bennett's?"

"I told you I want to help her."

She was silent for a moment. Then she said slowly, "Last

I saw her, she look like she need some help."

"What do you mean?"

"She come running outa that house like it was on fire. She trip and nearly fall. Then she jump in the car and drive off."

"Thank you, Mary."

"You her friend, you find her and tell her what Mary said. Tell her anything I can do for her, just ask Mary."

Heading back downtown on St. Charles, I pulled up to the curb across from the Pontchartrain Hotel. No out-of-town tourist, looking at its unobtrusively awninged façade, could have guessed that behind the hotel crouched block after block of the city's most ramshackle tenements. The building wore its respectability like armor. It was partly residential: rich women moved here when their husbands died and their children left home; sometimes they retained their servants to keep them company. But discreet though the hotel was, I knew that by the end of the day, when the late papers hit the stands, some employee would report that Elizabeth had been staying there if the police had not already discovered it on their own. Any questions I chose to ask at the front desk would also be reported and would inevitably find their way to Lanaux. I didn't want that to happen. I didn't want to give him a reason not to trust me.

I got out of the car, crossed the avenue, and went round to the side of the hotel. Its small garage was open to the day. I didn't see an attendant, but I wasn't looking for one. I saw what I had come to find out. In the far corner, three cars from the wall, was Elizabeth's silver gray Mercedes.

I recrossed the Avenue and called the hotel from a drugstore. I asked for Mrs. Bennett's room.

After a pause the operator said, "Sorry, sir, there's no answer."

That didn't surprise me. "Did she check out?"

"Not officially."

"Connect me with the garage, please."

The attendant's voice was sluggish and unsuspicious. When I told him I was looking for Mrs. Bennett he said, "Her car's here but she ain't. She left here in it this morning, but then she came back and had me call Hertz for a rent-a-car. She took a cab to their place. Ain't you the same party as called before?''

I said I wasn't the same party.

TWENTY-ONE

IT WAS AFTER twelve when I got to the office. Esther was standing by her desk, back to me, struggling to get into a lime-green woolen overcoat that seemed too small for her. She had a fake fur hat on her head.

"You forget it's the tropics out there," I said.

"Oh, Mr. Preston!" She turned around, flustered. "I'm glad to see you. It's my lunch hour but ever since you raced out of here this morning I been sitting on tenterhooks wondering what that phone call was all about."

"I don't want to talk about it, Esther. Not now."

"Oh." Her mouth formed a perfect circle. Her penciled eyebrows met in the middle. "You in a bad mood or something?"

"Something."

"Well, speaking of Mrs. Bennett," she said, and maybe after all we had been, "you got a long-distance call a few minutes ago from some woman who says she's Mrs. Bennett's mother but calls herself Miss Ames. How could that be? I mean, 'Miss' and all?"

"It's complicated. What did she want?"

"She's arriving in town this afternoon and says she's got to meet with you. Says five-thirty's the best time for her.

She's staying with some people named Montrose—anyhow, it's all in this note I was leaving you."

I took the slip of paper she handed me. "When you get back from lunch, Esther, call the Montrose house and say I'll be there."

She nodded.

"Then call Grandmother. Remind her it's her day to pick Ike up but to wait for his call from school. Ask her to give him dinner. I won't be home until late."

She looked at me questioningly.

I said, by way of an answer, "I don't want to talk to Grandmother just now. The truth is, Esther, I'm in no mood to talk to anyone." But I knew I would have to talk to Charles.

"Oh." She peered up at me through her glasses. "You sure you all right, Mr. Preston?"

"I'm all right."

As I turned to enter my office, she said, "One more thing, Mr. Preston. A taxi driver delivered a manila envelope for you after you left this morning. I put it on your desk."

"Thanks, Esther. For everything."

Brilliant noonday sunlight poured through the window wall in my office. Outside, bridges, rooftops, streets—all had sharp edges that glittered. I sat at the desk. My hand-printed name on the manila envelope confronted me. There was no return address.

I tore the envelope open. Inside, unaccompanied by a covering letter, written in ink on the stationery of the Pontchartrain Hotel and dated the night before, was Elizabeth's will.

I, Elizabeth Berenson Bennett, sane and in good health, revoke all former wills and now make my last will and testament.

All property transferred to me in trust by my grandfather, Saul Davidov Berenson, and anything else I may own when I die, I leave to my psychiatrist, Dr. Raymond Jasper, and I request that he use this inheritance to support research into the problems of emotionally disturbed children. I name my lawyer, Harry Preston, as executor of this bequest.

To my husband, John Henry Bennett, I leave nothing what-soever. He is no longer my husband.

To my mother, Eleanor Ames, I leave nothing whatsoever. She was never a mother.

The will was signed and witnessed by two women—Mary Castor and Elvire Washington—whose names I didn't rec-ognize. Their addresses were the Pontchartrain Hotel. Whether they were residents or employees I had no way of knowing.

I reread the will several times. It might have been subject to attack, had Elizabeth died and Bennett been alive to chal-lenge it, but it was certainly a will: one that demanded an eye for an eye. It told me that I had glimpsed only the surface of an emotional history whose bitterness went deeper than I could fathom. Each time I reread it, excitement mounted in my head and chest. I felt like an actor in a play, unsure not only of his lines but of what the next act, or scene, might bring. I didn't even know who the author was. Elizabeth had had a hand in writing the piece, but the total conception—if there was one, and if it was her own—eluded me. The will was simply her latest contribution, a fragment in the design.

TWENTY-TWO

IN THE CENTURY-OLD Turkish bath on an upper floor of
the Jackson Club, gusts of steam eddied and swirled. The
air, what there was of it, was thick and wet. The discolored
tiled walls sweated like the walls of a tomb; fat drops of
water eased from the ceiling, then plopped to the floor. The
thin light had the unnatural yellowish tint of sunlight seeping
through storm clouds. Wrapped in a heavy towel the size of
a small rug, I sat on a marble bench next to Cousin Charles
who, similarly swathed, resembled the sculpted likeness of
one of the more ascetic Roman senators. My face dripped
like the walls, and I had trouble breathing, but when the
steam receded and my cousin swam into focus I could see
that he thrived in this hothouse atmosphere. His pale, almost
hairless skin glowed as if what little moisture remained in it
had been activated by the rain-forest heat. This was not the
place I would have chosen for our conversation, but then I
had had no choice in the matter. It was where I had finally
tracked him down.

"There's no point in saying," he said, "that I gave you
fair warning. The point, Harry, is for you to sever your connection with all this as swiftly and efficiently as you can."

"I can't do that, Charles."

"Why not?"

130

"Obligation."

His sigh was scarcely distinguishable from the hissing of the steam.

"What about your obligation to the firm? Or to your family?"

"Are you talking about bad publicity?"

"Yes and no. I can keep your name out of the papers, of course. If it's not too late to keep it out. But what I can't stop is word-of-mouth. In this city, or that segment of it that you inhabit, word-of-mouth's more insidious than the most sensational headline."

"Aren't you exaggerating?"

"Maybe. Whatever else, this cancels your possible involvement in any messy divorce proceeding. But when the Berenson woman turns up, if she does turn up, she may try to involve you in her affairs in some other way."

"How? Elizabeth doesn't seem much interested in her financial affairs," I said disingenuously, "and as far as I know, or at least for the moment, they're being handled by your Mr. McIntyre."

"My Mr. McIntyre?"

"That's a manner of speaking. You told me you knew him in the old days."

"Never very well, I assure you," he said dryly. "From time to time, Harry, we all have clients whose—well, whose sense of probity isn't what it should be. But at least we're dealing with the more familiar forms of dishonesty and venality—tax evasion, fraudulent invasions of trust funds, acrimonious divorce settlements." In the strange light, I saw him smile ironically. "Have I told you, for instance, about this Bringier mess? Stop me if I have. Young Bringier—well, he's fifty-five, that seems young to me—went broke in real-estate development and had to declare bankruptcy. At the same time, his mother was dying of cancer. In her will, quite naturally, she had left everything to him, her only child. It amounted to millions. The problem was, he didn't want his creditors to claim the inheritance. So he went to the old woman on her deathbed and persuaded her to change her will, leaving her estate in trust to his children with himself as trustee. Now we might accuse Bringier of bad taste—that deathbed business and so on—but what he did was simply a matter of prudence. More than one creditor would like to file suit against him, of course, but they haven't a legal leg to stand on." He grimaced. "That's the sort of thing I meant when I spoke of familiar forms of venality. But who knows what McIntyre's been involved in, working for Berenson?"

"You make Berenson sound like a mafioso."

"Well, there've been rumors," he said. "Listen, Harry, you've already learned, the hard way, what can happen when you allow yourself to get pulled into a situation without knowing what that situation will entail. Now's the time to accept your place in the world. I've often observed," he added surprisingly, "how difficult it can be to grow up without a father."

"I had a father, Charles. I was seventeen when he died."

"I meant a father you could rely on."

"I loved my father."

"Love is cheaper than respect; it doesn't have to be earned." Then he said, and I could tell from the lilt in his voice that he was quoting, " 'There are few people whom I love, and still fewer of whom I think well. The more I see of the world, the more am I dissatisfied with it; and every day confirms my belief in the inconsistency of all human characters, and of the little dependence that can be placed on the appearance of either merit or sense.' Or something like that." He coughed self-consciously. "But let that pass. I suppose our generation was schooled by rote."

I didn't care how his generation had been schooled. I said, "I respected my father, Charles."

"Did you? Well, your father was a very attractive man. He had great gifts: good looks, intelligence and wit, a true sense of gaiety that's very rare in a man. I recognized that: I don't possess it myself. I clearly remember when he appeared on the scene. He had roomed with the Vergne boy at Harvard, and after they graduated he came here to be in Vergne's wedding. He met your mother on a sailing excursion. Julia was there; so was I. Your parents were young, they were beautiful, they were golden. At least, everyone said they were golden; everyone spoke of them as if they should be viewed through a filter. I tried to see them that way, through the haze of romanticism. I really tried. But what I saw were two good-looking, careless young people drenched in sun, whiskey, and adoration. They frolicked and frisked and sniffed each other like puppies. But need we romanticize puppies?''

I said nothing.

''In any case,'' he went on, ''when your father met your mother on that visit, she fell head over heels for him. Why not? He was a charming man and one of the brightest I've ever known. But to say he was feckless—I hope you'll forgive me—would be a polite understatement. Surely that must have been obvious to you when you were growing up.''

''Feckless isn't a word I would use to describe my father.''

''No? Well, probably not, Harry, because loyalty is one of your greatest virtues. But he married too young. Then he served in the Navy. His record was admirable, but when he left the Navy he dissipated his inheritance, such as it was, by traveling around the world with your mother. I'm sure they had fun—they were famous for having fun—but then your mother got pregnant with you and they had to settle down. Or try to settle down. He went into publishing, switched to advertising, switched to teaching, tried to write poetry. And all the while your parents ran with a fashionable crowd, or several fashionable crowds—and I use 'fashionable' in its most pejorative sense—that drank ruinously. In the end, the drinking was what it came down to. When your father died, all he left was an insurance policy.''

By this time I could hardly breathe. ''It was something,'' I said.

''Yes. Enough to send you to Harvard and allow your mother to continue her ruinous habits.''

''Leave Mother and Father out of this, Charles.'' I shoved my face closer to his: in the fog his eyes looked like empty sockets. ''Just what are you trying to get at, anyway?''

Something in my voice made him draw back so sharply his head struck the sweating tiles. Then the door of the steam room swung open. Steam billowed into the outer area. A beefy black man dressed in terry cloth shorts entered and said, ''More Perrier, Mr. Haynesworth?''

''Thank you.''

"What would you like, Mr. Preston?"

"A double bourbon."

Cousin Charles shifted his head slightly in my direction. He had regained his composure. "Bourbon?" he said. "In a Turkish bath?"

"Why not? It's as good a place as any to get drunk."

"Do you want to get drunk?"

"Maybe ruinous habits run in the family."

But I didn't want to get drunk. I didn't even want a drink. When the attendant returned with it I left it untouched on the bench beside me. I said, "Charles, you talk as if money is all a father can, or should, give."

"What else is there?"

"If you can ask that question, you wouldn't understand my answer."

"Tell me anyway."

"Apart from love? Well, in the case of my own father, you said it yourself. Intelligence, wit, a sense of gaiety. He showed me what those were. With other fathers the answer would differ. What any father can give has to be valued on its own terms."

"You haven't felt the lack of money?"

"Charles, I do make a living."

"Yes, well, of course. My point is that you could make an even better living than you do. You're a fine lawyer, Harry. But except in the case of this Berenson woman, you've tended to be rather particular about the clients you're willing to work with."

"I've handled cases I didn't want to handle."

"But not many, and not important ones."

"The more important the case, the more offensive the client—if the client's offensive to begin with. You know, you seem to be doing a turnabout, Charles. After all, wasn't that your main complaint against Berenson? Ethics, politics, morality, and all that?"

He looked at me intently. "You do have some of your father's sharpness, Harry. I sometimes forget that because you also have the gift of silence." He sat up rigidly. "Anyhow, I did mean what I said the other day. About Julia's and my having your interests at heart."

"I'm sure that you did."

"So at least tell me that you'll consider what I've said. After all," he added, "you don't want to go on being a junior partner forever."

"Count on it, Charles. I'll definitely consider what you've said."

TWENTY-THREE

PORTRAITS OF THE Jackson Club's former presidents lined the wall of the curved stairwell that led down to the entrance hall. Bearded or clean-shaven, depending on the era in which they had lived, these men were a stiff-necked crew. Several were my progenitors: I could never remember how many, no matter how often Charles reminded me. The masks of pompous rectitude they presented to posterity made them generally indistinguishable from their companions on the wall. As I came down the stairs, I stopped in front of the single exception.

This was my great-great-grandfather Hobson, who stared at me insouciantly from his gilded frame. He had a beard, but it wasn't patriarchal. He was Victorian, but his eyebrows and hat were tilted at rakish angles that declared war on repression. His stance wasn't erect: standing, he managed to lounge, hands halfway in his pockets. He had written a book on the Civil War that, when it was reissued in this century, had prompted *The New York Times* to call him the most literate general of the Confederacy, though that might have been their way of damning him with praise. But at that moment I wasn't interested in his literacy. I had once tried to read the book and been lulled by its Augustan cadences. I didn't think I would be lulled by him. I wanted him to step from his frame and speak to me man to man. What I needed were the laughter and shrewdness this man in the portrait was capable of. Charles might have said I wanted my father—my feckless father—and doubtless he would have been right. Father would have understood about Elizabeth. He might even have gone wild over her.

"Harry? That is you up there, isn't it?"

The raspy voice was familiar. I turned to face a living relative, my out-of-town cousin who stood at the foot of the staircase.

"Douglas, this is the last place I'd expect to see you."

"I stay here when I'm in town."

"I didn't know you were a member."

"Nonresident: much more affordable. But it shouldn't surprise you that I'm a member. We share that ancestor on the wall."

"I don't think of the Jackson Club as a haven for mavericks."

"What about our ancestor? Or you, for that matter?"

"I have a way to go yet."

"I'm not so sure."

I came down the stairs. "Douglas, you may be able to give me some help. Something you said at the ball last night—that once you could have written a book about old man Berenson. Was that true?"

"Odd that you should ask. I'm just back from lunch with some of my former cronies at the *Picayune*. A story's going out about Berenson's granddaughter. Seems her husband—"

"I know about that."

"If I were still a reporter this might be when I said: you wouldn't hold out on me, would you?"

"No, I wouldn't. But right now, I'm the one who needs information, Douglas, and I need it quick." The grandfather clock next to the manager's desk told me my meeting with Elizabeth's mother would be in less than an hour. "What can you tell me about Berenson?"

"What do you need to know?"

"Details about background and career."

"That's easy. I once wrote Berenson's obit when I worked at the *Picayune*."

"His obit?"

"Berenson's more national than local. When a man's as well known as he is, or was, the newspapers always have an obituary ready to roll."

"That seems indecent, somehow."

"The price of fame."

"But how much can you remember? I need specifics."

"My memory gets going with a drink."

"Jesus, Douglas, can't anything get done around here without a drink?"

"Pardon an old man's weakness."

We both laughed.

"Actually," he said, "if my memory fails, I have files upstairs that would probably more than satisfy your need for specificity. When I moved to Atlanta twenty years ago the club let me store some boxes in the attic annex for safe-keeping. I never bothered to send for them."

"Attic annex?"

"There's a kind of dormitory space, mainly for members who get too drunk to go home, but nonresidents can use it too. The club doesn't publicize it because they don't want people to stay any length of time. I think they let me be because once, as a joke, I told the then-president that I was going to write an article on the history of that annex. Would you believe that a hundred and thirty years ago it was the upper story of Banks's Arcade? That's where slaves from Virginia and North Carolina were put on the auction block. Walt Whitman describes planters lounging at the bar while their neighbors bought themselves rich in blacks. Strange what stays with you: 'Etty, thirty years, an excellent cook and washer, fully guaranteed excepting sometimes drinks'— Whitman cites that advertisement in his journal. But I'm going on, as usual. I can tell from your face you really are in a rush. Which means I won't have time to go upstairs and rummage in my files."

"It would be quicker to get you that drink."

A few minutes later we were seated in the front library, exactly where Charles and I had sat when we discussed Berenson the day before, and the same waiter named Welman brought Douglas his bourbon and water.

"What you should know at the start," Douglas said, "is that Berenson appeared on the scene, the local scene that is, trailing clouds of personal myth that had already been well established. Ordinarily, when you discuss such a figure facts scarcely matter because they've been obscured by layers of apocrypha, but in Berenson's case the facts are fairly well documented and contain their ready-made mythical element. In his heyday, Berenson was profiled in *Time, Life, Fortune,* and God knows how many other periodicals that don't even exist anymore. Early in his career he subverted a State Department treaty with Central America because it would have interfered with his personal profit making; a decade later, he was one of Roosevelt's economic advisers. When he decided to make this city his home base it was chiefly a matter of geographical convenience. He was just as at home at the Ritz in Boston or the Dorchester in London or, for that matter, in jungles south of the border. Maybe he never had close friends, but he was equally at ease with peasants and presidents.

"When folks here talk about him, though, and over the years they've talked a lot, they try to cut him down to their size. They puff themselves up by claiming that Berenson never got over being rejected by the local power brokers. When they talk about having kept him out of clubs like this one and how it stung him, they reduce him to the scale of their own snobberies. Berenson was conceived on a larger scale—a more *generous* scale—than these characters even conceive of.

"He changed over the years, his vision of things grew as he himself did. I interviewed him twice, you know, many years apart, and I could see how he had grown. But he was never, not even early on, mean spirited or small minded."

"What about when he assumed control of International Fruit and ousted the board?"

"That was necessity—enlightened necessity. Oh, I don't say he didn't feel a rush of righteous revenge: he was too human not to. But let me come back to that." He sipped his drink and thought a moment.

"In a sense, except that he wasn't so insufferably noble, Berenson could have been one of Horatio Alger's heroes. He had something in common with Gatsby, too, they would have been of an age, though Berenson was never given to romantic delusions. Both were the sons of farmers, but whereas Gatsby came from—where was it in the Midwest? Nebraska?—Berenson was born outside of Aughstów, Poland, in the last decade of the last century. He was sent to the States at twelve or so to live with an aunt in Mississippi and in his teens began working the docks in Mobile, buying ripe bananas that had to be sold fast before they rotted. That's how he started—speculating in ripes—and by the time he was twenty he'd banked more than $90,000 and was ready to head into the major league.''

I could have told time according to Welman's caretaking rituals in the club. As on the day before, he now entered and crossed the room to turn on lamps. Suddenly the antique rug glowed like a jewel. Light and shadow suffused the vaulted ceiling with its wedding-cake medallions, magnifying its height and gathering up, as in a net, the panoramic details of the story Douglas told. Above that ceiling, in a humid chamber, Charles lay like a corpse on a long narrow table while a black masseur oiled and pummeled his flesh, preparing it for reentry into the social world; above and beyond him, in an obscure attic annex, ghosts of slaves stared impassively from a ghostly auction block; in the curved, descending stairwell, men who had owned those slaves or others, men like the ancestor Douglas and I shared, gazed out from their blackening portraits—these formed the silent audience for Douglas's tale. It was fitting that the spirit of the man whom this club had excluded fifty years before should now invade the silence surrounding us. If nothing else, the narrative celebrated an entrepreneurial drive that had pursued its own path of progress, reinventing itself to serve an always broadening vision that could not, finally, have been contained by a room such as this or by the city whose inner sanctum this was.

''Berenson never denied his modest beginnings,'' Douglas said, ''and maybe that's why the first phase of his career only emphasized the next phase, the one in which he became known as Jonah who swallowed the whale.'' It wasn't only

the distance of time that gave this part of Douglas's account
the ring of a boy's adventure story; adventure was its subject.
During the next quarter hour I realized Douglas was no hack
journalist. He invested the immigrant's rise with his own
energy as he told me how, in 1919, Berenson had shipped
out to Panama on a salvaged tramp steamer and begun buying land on the Bayano River—first five, then ten thousand
acres—with money he frenziedly borrowed in New Orleans,
Mobile, and New York. How, when the Panamanian government refused him railroad concessions, he had sailed back to
New Orleans and teamed up with exiled Panamanian President Manuel Sanchez, supplied him with money and guns
and incited the revolution that returned Sanchez to power.
How he then began banana growing on a grander scale—
increasing acreage, building railroads, acquiring a fleet of
steamers; developing new methods of irrigation, scientific
pruning, and soil enrichment. He had learned Spanish
quickly, he could get through the jungle by mule or on foot,
and even the natives liked to deal with "El Jefe," because
they knew he could be trusted. When success brought him
into competition with already-established companies like
United and International, he finally sold out to International
in 1927 for 300,000 shares of its stock. Those shares were
worth $30 million. He became International's major stock-
holder.

Douglas's face glowed from bourbon and the pleasure he
took in all he had filed away in memory. He shared this
storyteller's zeal with Grandmother, though the details that
delighted her tended toward the strictly personal. They
shared another quality: both saw the world, or its inhabitants,
as divided not between the good and the bad but between
the expansive and the niggardly spirited. "Here's the most
curious point in Berenson's history," Douglas said, leaning
forward with narrowed eyes and dropping his voice like a
conspirator. "Out of some perverse blindness, International's
directors continued to treat him like a little guy they had
bought out. Of course, his management style had been completely different from theirs. He had lived in the tropics and
pioneered practices that became standards for the industry.

International's managers were like absentee landlords: they just pulled in the money and spent their lives in New Orleans restaurants and clubs like this one. Most of them had never been to the tropics and didn't know much more about bananas than whether or not they liked them sliced on their morning cereal.

"I once asked him how he felt about being regarded as the little guy even though he was International's major stockholder. He just smiled—his humor was sly and sharp—and said the little guy had fun poking the giant's knee with his little shovel."

"You really liked Berenson, didn't you?"

"More than that, and it had nothing to do with approval or disapproval. He had that quality really big men sometimes share, of being absolutely private and accessible at the same time. Only a fool, or a pack of fools, could have discounted him." He snorted. "I guess that's what those guys who ran International were."

"So what's your version of this coup that he pulled?"

"Well, it's a fact that Berenson's stock had declined ninety percent. At some board meeting in the early thirties he presented his detailed assessment of the company's mismanagement. The chairman, a character named Freret, said, 'Sorry, Mr. Berenson, we can't understand a word you say.' Berenson pulled a stack of proxies from his briefcase and set them on the table. 'If these need translation,' he said very clearly, 'you'd better call your legal interpreters.' That was a mannerly way of saying fuck you, though Berenson was fully capable of having said that as well. The upshot was that he ousted most of the board and became Managing Director in Charge of Operations. Under his control the stock rose rapidly once again."

"In the Depression?"

"My boy, everyone went ape over bananas back then. And this was when Berenson moved into his next phase, which I can only call philanthropic."

"I never thought of Berenson as a philanthropist."

"A cynic might say: well, that's the American way— make your pile any which way you can, then start to dabble in good works. In Berenson's case the cynic would be wrong.

Berenson had been known for generosity and enlightened business practices all along. Sure, it was a form of colonialism, but it was his way of acknowledging his debt, and his competitors thought it was lunatic. He housed his Central American employees free and paid them three times as much as local employers. He funded schools and hospitals and archeological expeditions. In this country he gave away millions, often in secret, sometimes to back progressive causes even though I suspect he was fundamentally conservative. He actively supported the New Deal, for instance. He used money and influence to fight Huey Long's machine—''

''Long? I thought they worked hand in glove.''

''Berenson would never have supported a demagogue, as far as I know. His opposition to Long was the one thing he had in common with the old guard here, though his reasons were essentially different. He saw what was happening in Germany and Italy. That was why he believed so strongly in education and poured so much money into it. He established schools of Central American studies and endowed chairs at Tulane, Harvard, and Yale. Locally, he underwrote the symphony and gave the major donation that opened the Child Guidance Clinic. Then there was that vast estate of his, Berenson Island, over between Covington and Slidell. In the forties and fifties he spent a fortune establishing bird and wildlife sanctuaries on the Island, just as he had done in Panama, and then opened them to the public. But why go on? You can see that Berenson's philanthropy was more than skin deep.''

''Oil, you've left that out. Didn't they strike oil on Berenson's estate?''

''I did leave oil out. That happened in the last twenty years, since I left New Orleans and stopped keeping up with Berenson's career. But I read somewhere, maybe in *Fortune,* that oil put him in the stratosphere. Apparently they discovered important plays on the Island, on the western edge of what's known as the Tuscaloosa Trend. But even without oil, Berenson was one of the richest men in the country for decades.''

''Enough, Douglas.'' I sank back into the chair. My head

was clogged with the furiously churning flotsam of fact and rumor. "No, wait. What about his family?"

"Berenson never talked about family. He was much too reticent for that. He had a son—something happened to him after I left here, I can't remember what—and that grand-daughter. I take it she's the cause of your interest."

I nodded.

"Have I helped you, Harry? Have I answered your questions?"

"I'm not sure what my questions were. But yes, you've answered some and raised others."

He drained his drink. "Will you do me a favor?"

"What's that?"

"As I told you, my sons live out West. But we could always talk freely when they were growing up, except when I bored them with my long-windedness. You and I can talk freely, too, I think. When you've got time, I hope you'll tell me your side of the story. Even if you have to call me in Atlanta."

"Douglas, when I know it, I will tell you my side of the story."

TWENTY-FOUR

THE MONTROSE HOUSE was on Third Street, not five blocks from Elizabeth's but in scale and conception distantly removed from it. An ivory-colored mansion with neoclassical columns, it had been added to over the generations so that its rear end was now a rectilinear tunnel hitched to an imposingly authentic façade. A canvas awning extended from the columns to the sidewalk. In the formal garden to the right of the house, a green-and-white-striped canvas tent shone in the fading sunlight like a medieval pavilion. Both the awning and the tent were in the process of being disassembled by a team of black workers.

When I saw these emblems of the Carnival I made the connection: a girl named Montrose, whom Elizabeth knew, had been Queen of Neptune the night before.

The handsome maid who opened the door looked as exhausted as her starched uniform was fresh. Before she could mouth the obligatory welcome, a young woman darted from the room on the right and interposed herself between the black woman and me.

"Thanks, Jessie, I'll get it."

The young woman's eyes were trellised with red and carried purple shadows under them. Otherwise, they were pale blue and intelligent, like Ike's but not as round or as large.

Her skin had the tautness of youth and was so translucent that I could see muscles and veins at work under it. The ash-blond hair that fell straight to her shoulders was the only limp thing about her. She wore faded jeans and a thin white sweater that emphasized her narrow back and full breasts. She had white woolen socks on, but no shoes.

"Mr. Preston." She held out a hand and shook mine vigorously. "I'm Sally Montrose."

"Elizabeth's friend."

Her bright face brightened even more. "She mentioned me? I'm glad. Because I understand she's why you're here."

"She is. Actually, I'm here to see her mother. Mrs. Berenson. Or I guess I should say Miss Ames."

"Confusing, isn't it? It's confused Elizabeth, too." We were still standing in the front hall. She looked behind her, as if expecting someone momentarily to appear. "Miss Ames is upstairs, on the telephone, as usual. If you're willing to be ten minutes late for your appointment with her, we can talk in the study. When she sees you she may say you're late, but if I told her you were here now she'd keep you waiting at least that long. Maybe that means we'll have twenty minutes." Again, she looked over her shoulder. "I'm only worried about my family. We had a production here last night, as you can see, and they're holding a hangover party out back. My married sister and her husband and her son are all here, downing gin, eating red beans, and rehashing the great event."

"You were queen of that ball."

"Queen for a day." She smiled crookedly, with as much cynicism as someone young and obviously not cynical could muster.

From the rear of the house came a blast of noise so hellishly loud that it was not, at first, recognizable as music. Abruptly its volume sank, and the pulsating rhythm, if not the words, of "If Ever I Cease to Love" became intelligible.

Through the doorway on my right I could see half of a long parquet-floored room lighted by a mammoth chandelier that depended from the ceiling like a transparent Christmas tree. The room glowed deep amber. Its furniture—old wood and brocade—had been pushed against the walls. At the front end of the room, near the hall where Sally and I stood, a wiry, gray-haired black man was positioning a rolled carpet for unrolling. Suddenly, with an infernal whoop, a fat boy-child of six or seven shot into view on roller skates and headed straight toward the black man. The black man stood holding his ground and the rug stoically as if to block an expected assault. At the last moment the child veered to the right, whinnying hysterically, and crashed into a tea table. The impact sent it spinning toward the floor.

Before it struck, the black man had dropped the rug and caught the spinning circle of mahogany by its pedestal; he held it firmly with his right hand and with his left pressed the top to his chest. The way he cradled it, it might have been human. His face was noncommittal and resigned.

The child righted himself. "I'm gonna get you next time, Sam," he shrieked gleefully, then sped on his skates out of sight toward the far end of the room. His skates left tracks in the polished parquet.

A burst of approving adult laughter greeted his return.

"I think you've got the picture," Sally said. "That's my nephew and godchild, and the idea of spending the rest of my life buying him birthday presents and being polite to him at family gatherings makes me wonder—well, what else life has in store."

"A lot, from the look of you."

"You sound as if you mean that. Thanks." She motioned to a door on my left. "That's the study. We can talk in there."

The study's disproportionately high ceiling made it seem smaller than it was: that, and the chandelier that looked like the misplaced twin of the one in the larger room. A mahogany breakfront and two recessed bookcases held polished leather volumes that might have been read but probably hadn't been: at least not since they had taken up residence at the Montroses'.

Sally laughed. "I can tell what you're thinking."

"Am I that transparent?"

"I don't know about you. But that look of critical appraisal sure was."

"I might be wrong."

"True. But in this case, unfortunately not. Dad collects first editions, and, Lord, does he make a fuss over them, but I've never seen him pick one up in an idle moment. Anyway," she said, dropping onto the leather sofa that faced the fireplace, "please tell me about this awful mess Elizabeth's in. Oh!" She jumped up again. "I didn't offer you a drink."

"That can wait."

"Then tell me what's going on. All I know is what I've heard on television. Elizabeth's mother arrived this afternoon, but I've hardly seen her. She's been in her room, locked up with that woman she travels with, and when the phone rings—it's been going ever since she got here—she gets it on the first ring." She hesitated. "Maybe I should warn you first. Mama and I think there may be something wrong with Miss Ames. I mean that she's sick in some way. She's on medication, but we don't know why. I think it's emotional—she has a history of emotional problems—but Mama thinks it could be physical this time. She says Miss Ames may be wearing a wig, which might mean she's been having chemotherapy, but her hair's always looked like a wig to me, it's so perfectly in place."

"Why's she staying here?"

"She and Mama knew each other when she was married to Mr. Berenson. Since then, whenever she comes to New Orleans she arrives with scarcely a moment's notice and uses this house as her headquarters. I guess she and Mama are friends, of a sort, but I get the impression that she stays here largely as a matter of convenience. Central location, maid service—the works."

"The works here include a lot more than maid service."

"I see your point. And yes, Miss Ames is like that. She behaves like royalty. I mean, she takes everything supremely for granted."

"How did you and Elizabeth become friends? She's older than you."

"Seven or eight years." She reflected a moment. "She was my sister's classmate. They used to take me riding up at the Audubon stables, then Ellen lost interest in riding and Elizabeth and I started going alone. I think I'm a better friend of Elizabeth's now than Ellen ever was," she said. Her voice changed as she turned to face me. "Mr. Preston, what *is* going on, and how can I help?"

I started to ask her to call me Harry—she wasn't *that* much younger than I—but then, looking at her, decided not to. Then I thought again. "Call me Harry," I said. "I don't really know what's going on myself, Sally. I'm a lawyer, and Elizabeth consulted me informally about some things that had been bothering her. If you want to help, tell me more about her family. Whatever happened to her father?"

She said simply, "Of all the awful hands she was dealt, that was the worst. She idolized him. He took her everywhere with him, on fishing trips, when he made the rounds of his father's estate, everywhere. He was a country boy at heart: he only went to Harvard Business School to please his father. He never cared about the old man's millions. Mama says he was a radical, but that might just mean he was rebellious in a quiet sort of way. He wanted his father to turn most of that enormous place near Covington into a bird and wildlife sanctuary, but then they found oil and that put an end to his dreams. And then—"

"My dear Sally," a fluty voice interrupted from the doorway behind us, "gossiping as usual? Really, you'd do well to conquer this shop-girl habit of using other people's lives as the basis for your adolescent embroiderings. It doesn't become you, you know."

Sally's eyes widened. I stood up and turned to greet the figure who had entered the room without our noticing and whose voice now shifted into high gear.

"Sally, I do think it's rather naughty of you to appropriate my guest as your own without even announcing his arrival. Of course, now that I see how relatively young Mr. Preston is, and so forth, I'm consoled to realize that your lapse in manners didn't signify a total lapse in taste."

She smiled with practiced ease, but the eyes above the smile were as cold as a Gila monster's and her voice, crystalline in its total self-absorption, moved relentlessly on: "I would think, Sally dear, that with all this party going and gallivanting you might by this time have acquired a following of eligible young men without having to try to turn Mr. Preston's business call into a social call. After all, acquiring eligible young men is the frantic business of your life now-adays, isn't it? Or do I misunderstand the intent of these tribal rituals you're caught up in? Because it is just possible that I do misunderstand. Boston, it's true, has its own tradition of coming out, but when I was your age I was far too busy studying languages and literature to pay much heed to such goings-on. But then, when all's said and done, I suppose I was something of a bluestocking.''

Seizing her first opportunity Sally stood up and said, "I'm sorry, Miss Ames. Really, I—''

Miss Ames crossed the room and, placing her hand on Sally's shoulder in what might have passed for an affectionate gesture, turned her around and firmly propelled her toward the door.

"Never mind, dear. I'm getting old but my work's with the young and I'm constantly being reminded how thoughtless youth can be. Now run along to your family. They're holding some sort of raucous celebration in the back room, and I know they require the presence of the golden girl. Do give my apologies for not joining in. I hope they'll understand. I just don't think it would be quite seemly, do you, on the day my son-in-law's been murdered and my daughter has vanished just one step ahead of the police?''

Sally glanced in my direction. Then she averted her face and hurried from the room.

Miss Ames turned and gave me an evaluative stare that began with my forehead and ended at my crotch. Then she said unexpectedly, "Now what can I do for you, Mr. Preston?''

She was a woman of perhaps fifty-five, of medium height with slender bones and a prominent bosom made more so by her staunchly erect posture. Her auburn hair was totally free of gray and worn in the time-honored fashion of her class: drawn up and back from her forehead so that it framed her face like a helmet. If she wore makeup it wasn't visible; her eyes were light, of no discernible shade, and her skin and lips seemed oddly devoid of color, as if they had been bled pale. Her woolen suit was as expensively unobtrusive as a uniform. Physically, I would not have taken her to be Elizabeth's mother. Although in her own way she was an imposing presence, she had force but no dash.

"I'm sorry, Miss Ames. I thought it was you who wanted to see me."

She blinked. "Well," she said, exhaling the word with a disapproving lilt, "of course it was I who called you, but I was only trying to anticipate my daughter's wishes. I assumed that as her lawyer you might naturally need to ask me some questions."

"Who told you I was Elizabeth's lawyer?"

"I can't possibly remember. It seems to be common knowledge. Like so much else in this city."

"Meaning?"

"Meaning that people have eyes and ears, Mr. Preston. Especially in a city like this one that hasn't a concern in its pretty little head except what to serve at the next meal and who is doing what to whom: when, where, and how, if not why."

"Please explain."

"Meaning that you can't possibly expect to create a public spectacle in a restaurant like Galatoire's, a place thick with people who traffic in the worst kinds of gossip—" here she drew breath, then raced breathlessly on—"and then again in the lobby of the Municipal Auditorium, without its being noised abroad far and near."

"How could you know this stuff?"

"What does that signify? I tell you these things as a friend, Mr. Preston, because however innocent such activities may be, at least from your point of view, and I have no real doubt about your innocence, if not about that of my daughter—I tell you these things because you should know that you are surrounded by people who feel absolutely compelled to place the most damaging construction on the most trivial peccadillo. You did, after all, discover Jack Bennett's poor body."

"Yes."

"Well, when the police initiate their inquiries, as I'm sure they already have, and learn the sorts of things I've learned without any desire to learn them, don't you think they'll start making connections? Even if those connections are, as connections tend to be, misleading if not totally erroneous?"

"I see your point."

"And that's why I thought you might want to see me during my brief visit. Because I won't, I can't be here for any length of time. The Trustees and the Admissions Committee have decided that Ames Academy has to broaden the base, so to speak, of its constituency, and actually I was already on the road, trying to drum up business in the hinterlands, when this awful piece of news found its way to me. But Elizabeth has always had an infallible sense of timing." Abruptly she cocked her head. "By the way, Mr. Preston, from your accent I detect that you're not a native of this city, or that you were at least educated elsewhere. Am I correct?"

I nodded in amazement.

"May I ask what schools you attended? As an educator, such matters concern me."

"Andover and Harvard."

"Ah. Good. Then we have something in common. I went to Radcliffe. So, for that matter, did Elizabeth, though of course she didn't graduate. But I suppose she told you."

"She mentioned it. We had other issues to discuss."

"And so do we. Doubtless you want information, if only about Elizabeth's deplorable history."

I sat down on the sofa, settled back, and held her eyes with mine. I counted to five. "I'm not sure that I do," I said.

"Come now. Lawyers are in the business of collecting information."

"We have to consider the source."

She blinked, then trilled a laugh. "How scrupulous you are, Mr. Preston. You must have acquired your idealism in the East—certainly not in New Orleans. In any case, Elizabeth has always resented any show of concern from me, she regards it as interference, but if I can help you be of greater help to her, I'll rest easier." She paused. "But where to begin? Ah yes, I'll begin by telling you what it was like when I first married Saul Berenson and came South as a bride, so sheltered and inexperienced that I couldn't possibly have known what lay in store for me in this—"

"Excuse me, Miss Ames. Naturally I want to hear what you have to say, but are you sure—"

"That it's relevant? Of course it's relevant. In order to understand what Elizabeth is, you need to understand what she is not. You've glimpsed only one side of her heritage, and though it may be the showy side, the pushy, aggressive, and flamboyant side, there are still those in the world who might consider it to be the lesser side of the two.''

As her voice rose in intensity, two bright spots of color appeared in her cheeks. That voice held me in its grip. I was trapped by vocal cords, muscles, larynx, and the deranged energy charging through them. The red walls of this room with their inlay of gilded leather volumes closed in on me. What Miss Ames made me feel jarred me. Only the necessity of hearing her out kept me from bolting.

"Don't misunderstand me, Mr. Preston. I'm not denigrating the value of money, even when it's new money acquired God knows how. Oh no. Jews aren't the only ones with a sense of property. We Yankees have it too, never more so than when we find ourselves adrift in the world with nothing that we can call our own except the intellectual and moral traditions that we drank in at our parents' sweet knees, and that when we were young we foolishly thought were all we needed to conquer the world.'' A look of bewilderment swept briefly over her face. Then she drew herself up sharply. "But I was telling you what it was like when I first came South as a bride. I had met Saul when he was at Harvard Business School and I was doing graduate work at Radcliffe. Maybe it was the nearsighted romanticism of youth, maybe it was the way Saul looked—so Semitically black: whatever it was, he seemed like someone from another world, a foreign prince out of a fairy tale. But he was a dreamer, Mr. Preston, as I was too at the time, I suppose. It was the dreamer in him that made him want to go live in the country in the first place, on that godforsaken tract of his father's across the Lake. We lived in New Orleans only briefly, you see. Maybe if we had stayed here things would have been different. After all, I'm not totally immune to the frivolous charms of this place.''

"But you didn't live here. You went to the country.''

"We went to live in the country. And can you imagine what it was like for an inexperienced Boston bluestocking to live in the wilds of Louisiana while all day her husband tramped the woods and swamps with a gun in one hand and a book in the other? I was so green and inexperienced that I was six months pregnant before I even knew what was happening—young people were more innocent then, you'll forgive me for saying so—and the next I knew I had an infant picking at my breast when all I wanted was to sleep, sleep forever or until someone woke me up and transported me back to reality.''

There was a perfunctory knock on the door. It then opened to admit a short, stocky woman of indeterminate age who announced: ''Eleanor, sorry to interrupt, but the other two chaps are here. McIntyre and Jasper. They say they can't wait much longer.''

The woman had forgettable features and a brown Prince Valiant bob. Her accent was, unlike that of Miss Ames, authentically British, but it was North Country with a whining undertone built into it. She wore a short-sleeved knitted sweater with an alligator emblem, a plaid skirt, and new oxfords.

''Edwina,'' Miss Ames said, ''if I can't delegate authority to you, then to whom can I delegate it? You tell those two 'chaps,' as you vulgarly choose to call them, that I'll be with them in a minute.''

''If you say so, Eleanor. But remember to take your pill.'' She closed the door without further ceremony.

''My pill? Who does that woman think she is? My duenna?'' Miss Ames faced me again. ''But where were those pills when I needed them? In the old days we had to rely on the power of our poor, abused minds to draw their own merciful blanks, and that's just what happened after Elizabeth was born. I kept wondering: where are those infants of yesteryear, those lace-wrapped bundles trundled in to be seen and fussed over but not to be heard? All day long I was forced to hear that child's importunate squeals, as if she never could get enough of whatever I offered, and when I offered it she would shake her head and squeal all the more. And that's the point, Mr. Preston. In due time I offered Elizabeth the world, when I had the world to offer her, and she rejected it out of her own willful perversity.''

''I thought you were separated. I thought there was this matter of custody.''

"Let's not speak of custody, please. Custody implies some form of imprisonment, and what has that to do with human ties? But we were separated, yes. You must understand, Mr. Preston, that my husband had almost no money in his own right, not even an insurance policy, and that in any case the circumstances of his death were such—well, the circumstances were such as to turn the issue of inheritance into an impenetrable snarl. I found myself in the position of having to depend on the droppings, the crumbs from the table of a man who had always resented me. Why? Because I embodied, if I may say so, certain qualities and traditions which were closed to him forever in spite of his wealth. Even today, Mr. Preston, some things like manners and background cannot be bought in a department store, and my father-in-law could never bring himself to accept this unalterable fact."

"Miss Ames, I don't mean to be rude. But it's nearly six-thirty, you've got people waiting, and I really don't see—"

"Of course you don't, Mr. Preston. How could you possibly see until I've finished my story? I was speaking of the mysterious ways in which the Lord reveals His beneficence to those He has taken under His wing. Of course, after Saul's death I felt He had abandoned me, but then I learned that a deathblow can be a life blow to some. That's what Emily Dickinson wrote, and I'm living proof of the truth of her sentiments."

"I'm sorry, I—"

"Through his lawyers my father-in-law let me know that if I chose to take my daughter and return to Boston I would be depriving her of the material advantages that he alone could provide."

"State exactly what you mean. Did he threaten to deny her an inheritance?"

"His implication was clear. In the end I forced myself for Elizabeth's sake to take the long-term, not the short-term, view."

"You gave up custody of your child."

"They *took* custody, if you insist on using that word! What choice did I have in the matter if my daughter's future was at stake? Of course, I couldn't foresee, at the time, the success that God had mapped out for me. I mean personal success of the kind that sustains you when human ties seem to fall by the wayside. I didn't know that any more than I knew that Elizabeth would finally reject what I had worked so hard to achieve. The decision I made then, I made for my daughter's sake.''

''Then you received nothing from—''

''I told you, Mr. Preston, that I'm concerned with my daughter's welfare. That's why I've gone out of my way, at this most inconvenient of possible moments, to come here and try to do the right thing once again. So let's proceed to the business at hand.''

''What business?''

Ignoring my question, she went to the door and opened it. ''Edwina,'' she said, ''please show the gentlemen in.''

TWENTY-FIVE

THE TWO MEN who entered seemed to have nothing in common except a look of irritation at having been kept waiting by Miss Ames. In fact, they moved instinctively to opposite sides of the doorway as if to emphasize that in no sense did they constitute a pair. The one introduced as McIntyre must have been nearly the age of Cousin Charles but, like him, looked younger than he was. Tall and extremely thin, he nevertheless had a paunch of good living that rested like a small melon on top of his belt buckle. He had a long, weather-beaten, comfortably cynical face and eyes that had been reduced to slits by their fleshy overhang. Dressed in checked tweeds and a string tie, he carried an initialed leather briefcase that was as shiny and pristine as the volumes on the Montroses' bookshelves and might, from the importance with which he wielded it, have been an emblem of office.

Dr. Jasper was middle aged, short, overweight, and intense. He had restless black eyes and a bushy black mustache. His nondescript suit looked as if he had slept in it.

Miss Ames's manner was no longer agitated. Resuming her air of authority, she motioned Dr. Jasper and me to the sofa in front of the fireplace and Mr. McIntyre to the chair facing us. She remained standing, however, perhaps to emphasize that she could, when she chose, be taller than any man in the room.

She then addressed the woman who stood by the door. "Edwina, since we'll be leaving early tomorrow morning, I think this might be the moment for you to go pack."

Edwina scowled under her bangs. "But Eleanor, you still haven't taken your pill."

"Edwina." Miss Ames spoke the name in a tone so freighted with purpose that it achieved it. When the door closed, she said to Mr. McIntyre, "My daughter's welfare brings us together once again, I see, but this time I hope not on opposite sides of the table. In fact, when these gentlemen understand the issues involved, I have no doubt that we'll all be in amicable accord."

Dr. Jasper looked at me and I at him: I felt at once that we could be allies. Then we both turned to Mr. McIntyre who, confronted by our twin stares of noncomprehension, began talking in a drawl so elongated that it might have been a form of mockery: even, perhaps, of self-mockery. I remembered that he was from Mississippi.

"Son," he said to me, "I want to avoid hard feelings. I know you and the good doctor got Miss Elizabeth's interests at heart, but so do we all. Let's try to get together. No point getting riled and het up. It just don't set well with me, wasting energy getting riled."

He sat with his briefcase upright on his knees and his two hands placed firmly on its handle. Above it his smile was broad and blandly benevolent.

"I can't rightly say," he said, "that I would have chosen this moment to bring the matter to a head. Not when Miss Elizabeth is in such deep trouble."

"The moment chose us," Miss Ames interjected.

Letting this pass, Mr. McIntyre said, "You two gentlemen need to recognize that I'm here strictly in my fiduciary capacity as a trustee of the Berenson estate. Naturally that means that certain discretionary powers have already been conferred on me. They have to be in the case of inter vivos trusts. But long as the old man is alive, and God willing that'll be a good while, he's calling the shots. He always has."

Miss Ames winced. Then she stepped back out of the circle of light created by the chandelier and remained for some time, still standing, in shadow.

Dr. Jasper said, "Hold on, please. Maybe as a lawyer Mr. Preston knows what you're getting at, but I sure don't."

"Doc, I know how you feel. I'm from the country, I'm used to plain speaking, and us lawyers and doctors do have a problem with gobbledegook. I'll try to speak plainly." He paused, brow furrowed. "It all goes back to when Miss Elizabeth was just a bitty thing and her grandaddy decided to set up some trusts in her name. We all know that Mr. Berenson is a man of—well, a mighty rich man, so I won't try to pretend tax considerations weren't in his head. They were. But some of these trusts are irrevocable in nature, and in those cases Mr. Berenson was motivated by considerations that made tax considerations of secondary importance. I'm speaking of his desire," he paused heavily, "at least at that time, to make Miss Elizabeth financially independent in her own right."

"Just how independent is she?" I asked.

"Hold on." Mr. McIntyre raised his hand. "I assumed you were familiar with Miss Elizabeth's financial situation."

Instinct told me that I had made a tactical error. "To some degree I am," I said. "But our business so far has been of another nature."

"I see. That puts a different light on things." He let his eyelids droop. "Course it doesn't surprise me much that Miss Elizabeth didn't fill you in on her situation. That girl. I called her up, I remember, on her twenty-first birthday and told her I thought we should have a heart-to-heart talk about her financial future. I mean the future her grandaddy was generous enough to map out. Know what that child said to me? Said, 'Uncle Mac, far as I'm concerned it's easy come, easy go. Long as I keep getting my check, I'll be happy to go right on not knowing the difference between a stock and a bond.' And every time since then that I've tried to offer her instruction, well, she's had other fish to fry." He peered solemnly at Dr. Jasper and me. "Boys, I'll say it plain. That attitude grieved me. It hit me right where it hurt: in my fiduciary capacity. 'Cause some people might consider that attitude downright irresponsible.''

"And others," Dr. Jasper put in, "might see that a manner of speaking isn't always the best index to the speaker's true feelings."

"It's my turn to ask what something means," Mr. McIntyre said. "Remember, I'm a plain speaker."

"We all want to be plain speakers, Mr. McIntyre, but sometimes circumstances prevent it. Take me, for example. I'm reduced to speaking in generalities because, like you, I'm here in a fiduciary capacity."

"Fiduciary?"

"I need hardly tell you that the relationship between doctor and patient is, or should be, one based on trust. Without wanting to sound pompous, I take that trust to be irrevocable. Where Elizabeth is concerned, that means I can't discuss what her possible feelings and motives might be, or might once have been. But I don't think it would be violating her trust to point out that her flippancy, about money among other things, is often defensive. It's no secret that she's had a lot of problems.''

Mr. McIntyre leaned forward. "Doc, now we understand each other. Because that's what we're really here to discuss: Miss Elizabeth's problems. You see, for some time now Miss Elizabeth's troubles have been preying on her grandaddy's mind. For one thing, that husband. I don't think I'm violating my client's trust," he said, looking at the doctor, "when I tell you Mr. Berenson never really cottoned to that young man. Oh, Bennett seemed nice enough at first, I guess. And Mr. Berenson threw Elizabeth and him a wingding of a wedding; after all, he wanted her to be settled and happy. But soon as the candles were blown out on the wedding cake, that young fella showed his true colors. He began ringing the old man up at home, pestering him about business and legal matters that weren't no concern of his at all. Wasn't long before Mr. Berenson just stopped taking those calls. He told me, 'Mac, it's a fine line that separates ambition from greed, but that boy has stepped over the line. He wasn't satisfied with the wedding cake I bought him. Now he wants a piece of my pie.' " Mr. McIntyre stared down at the still erect handle of his briefcase. "However. That young soul has gone to meet his Maker, and it's no point speaking ill of the dead. We got to worry about the here and now."

I said: "Mr. McIntyre, I've been worrying about the here and now for an hour. I've been here that long and I still don't know what for. I don't think Dr. Jasper does either. You and Miss Ames are taking a long time getting to the point."

"Calm down, son. We've gotten to the point, even if you don't see it. The point is Miss Elizabeth's troubles and the way they weigh on her grandaddy's health."

"Just what is the state of his health?"

Mr. McIntyre's tired eyes circled the room and came to rest on the table in front of the sofa.

"See that bowl on that table?"

All our eyes followed his. In the center of the table was a crystal bowl filled with glass or crystal balls that reflected the light of the chandelier overhead and were as iridescent and fragile as soap bubbles.

Mr. McIntyre raised one finger solemnly. "He can see, he can think, he can talk. But the state of his health is as delicate as any one of those balls in that bowl. If we could have kept him from knowing what happened this morning, we would have. I make no apology: his health comes before truth. But we had to tell him before he caught it on the evening news. You understand. There's no keeping that man from his news."

"How did he react?"

"The way anyone reacts when someone they love lets them down."

"You mean he assumes Elizabeth was involved in Bennett's murder?"

"Not the way you mean it. But she married Bennett in the first place, didn't she?"

"What exactly does Mr. Berenson propose to do?"

Mr. McIntyre's look became more veiled than ever. "After what's happened," he said, "the old man doesn't rightly think Miss Elizabeth can take care of herself. Not to speak of the property she's come into."

Dr. Jasper sat forward on the sofa.

"Good God, man. Am I to understand you rightly? Here the woman's disappeared, no one knows what the hell's happened to her, and you're saying—"

"I haven't said anything yet."

"You're implying that her grandfather—"

"Wants to have her interdicted. Wants her declared a legal incompetent."

It was Miss Ames who spoke. Stepping once again into the circle of light, she crossed to where the doctor was sitting and planted herself firmly in front of him.

"My former father-in-law and I have agreed on few things, but this happens to be one of them. All we want is to provide for Elizabeth's welfare in such a way that we won't have to tear our hair and beat our breasts every time she gets involved in one of her sordid messes."

Dr. Jasper stared at the woman in front of him as if she were a rare and fantastic species of animal that he had just encountered, for the first time, in a zoo.

"Declaring someone legally incompetent," he said in a measured tone, "is the next thing to having that person committed. In fact, one often necessitates the other. And if you don't mind my saying so, Miss Ames, that hardly seems appropriate or even possible in the present case. Elizabeth has never been more—"

"More what? Capable of running her own life? You may be Elizabeth's psychiatrist, Dr. Jasper, but you'll forgive me for pointing out that she has a history of antisocial behavior that cannot be denied. Behavior whose sole purpose has been to smash every law of decency and propriety."

"Maternity has its laws, too," Dr. Jasper observed mildly. "But those laws are broken every day."

"What is that supposed to mean?"

"Only that the kind of behavior you've described has its sources."

"Don't speak to me of sources. I'm interested in truth. I've been bearing the brunt of it since Elizabeth was a child."

Dr. Jasper said nothing. He held himself absolutely still and let his face go opaque. His thoughts and feelings seemed to be standing at attention. I sensed that he felt as I had: it was pointless to try to reason with a self-absorption as total as Miss Ames's.

"Do you know," she said now, "that Elizabeth was barely fourteen when she launched the career of promiscuity that she has pursued ever since? Do you know how I found out? Because her—I can't call them lovers, whatever you call them would sometimes turn up on my doorstep in Boston. Greek sailors, itinerant seamen that she had picked up in bars and even on the dock itself, for all I know. When she had finished her dirty games with them she would give them my name and address and tell them to look me up whenever they got to Boston. Why do you think she did that, doctor? What other possible motive than the crazy desire to spit in her mother's face?"

Dr. Jasper wore his imperturbability like armor. "What other reasons can you think of, Miss Ames?"

Ignoring this, she went on. "But Elizabeth's sexual escapades have been the least of it. When she was eighteen I put my professional reputation on the line to get her into Radcliffe. Of course she had never exhibited the least trace of academic discipline, but some of her test scores, I recall the Otis in particular, showed exceptional promise. I thought that finally I could guide her toward those intellectual pleasures that are, in the final analysis, the only pleasures that sustain you in this long—" She halted in midsentence. She seemed for a moment to have lost the thread. Then she shuddered, drew herself up once again, and said, "But it was all a fantasy. She failed all her courses that first term. She didn't even take her examinations. When I demanded some sort of rational explanation, she shrugged and said, 'I guess I wasn't cut out to be a Harvard man.' Naturally she was afraid to tell me the real reason. The real reason I had to learn from the proctor on the floor of her dormitory who called me on the telephone to tell me what my own daughter couldn't bring herself to admit. Do you know what that was, Doctor? Has Elizabeth ever told you about this episode from her past?"

Dr. Jasper shrugged slightly and remained silent.

"Even now, I can't bring myself to speak of this without feeling outrage and mortification. Of course I had noticed the symptoms. The signs of physical deterioration and mental withdrawal, the evasive stare and the foggy mind. But it never occurred to me that Elizabeth was using her grandfather's money''—her eyes caught Mr. McIntyre's—''to finance an addiction to heroin. In my wildest imaginings that, I assure you, had not occurred to me.''

Dr. Jasper said quietly, ''That was nearly ten years ago.''

''Come now. An alcoholic may stop drinking but he remains an alcoholic. Can you tell me, in any case, that Elizabeth no longer uses drugs?''

''She is not addicted to heroin.''

''That doesn't answer my question. But let's stick with the past just a little bit longer. When I received that call from her proctor at Radcliffe I canceled all my meetings, went home, and took to my bed. But I didn't stay in bed long, I assure you. I couldn't allow myself the luxury of withdrawal, not that time. I got up, drove to Radcliffe, yanked Elizabeth out of her dormitory, and pulled her downstairs and into the automobile. I can still remember where I was parked: the corner of Shepard Street and Garden. I avoid that corner to this day. I said: 'Show me your arms. Show me that it isn't true.' She didn't say or do anything. She just sat there like some Oriental idol. It was February, she had on a long-sleeved sweater, and by the time I was through that sweater was ripped to shreds. But I had proved my point. In any case, she never bothered to deny it.''

Miss Ames took one step forward like a soldier about to march into battle. ''Then I did what I had to do, Doctor Jasper. I had her committed to McLean's.''

''Miss Ames, are you sure that's quite accurate? Are you sure Elizabeth didn't commit herself?''

''That's a technicality. She committed herself only because she knew I would if she didn't.''

''Technicalities can be important.''

''I won't quibble with you. I want to finish what I have to say. I nearly am finished. It was when she was in McLean's, and she was there for months, that Elizabeth began tormenting me with stories of her descent into a moral underworld. Most of these stories I'll spare you. I'm interested only in those episodes out of her past that bear on the present issue. I mean the issue of her ability to manage her own life, which includes the inheritance that her grandfather prematurely made available to her.''

She turned to Mr. McIntyre. ''Years ago I swore to myself never to tell this to anyone. But things have gone too far. What happened this morning proves that Elizabeth's criminal behavior—''

''Criminal?'' Mr. McIntyre's exhausted eyes came awake. He held his briefcase tighter than ever.

Dr. Jasper stood up. ''Miss Ames, I don't know what you intend to say. But please stop and reflect before you say it.''

''Reflect? I've had years to reflect, I didn't even believe her when she first told me. But then I forced myself to go to the library and pull out the back issues of the *Globe* and what I read convinced me that Elizabeth was not indulging in some malicious fabrication. She was telling the truth. Because she knew things about the robbery that weren't even reported in the newspaper, details that not only confirmed those reports but went further.''

''Robbery?'' Mr. McIntyre said. ''What robbery?''

''When she was at Radcliffe, she and two men, men who were addicts like herself, robbed a Charlestown bank at gunpoint and got away with it.''

Having remained silent for too long, I now had a crazy impulse to laugh. ''Miss Ames, that's absurd. Why would Elizabeth get involved in a robbery?''

She turned toward me. ''Money wasn't the issue, don't you see? Oh, maybe they thought it was in the planning stage, but after they did what they did, they never spent a penny. They were too scared to. That's why nothing was ever traced back to them. One of those two men had a father who was in international finance. Somehow, this young man, this friend of Elizabeth's, arranged to have the money smuggled out of the country and into a Swiss bank account. As far as I know, it remains there to this day. Because they didn't really do it for money. That's the point. They did it to prove that they were above, below, or beyond all those laws that other people—''

Suddenly Miss Ames began to cough. She clapped a hand over her mouth, but her body heaved and shook in a paroxysm. Her face turned red, then purple. I stood up and grabbed her wrists.

"You wouldn't bring this to a court of law, Miss Ames. If it's true, Elizabeth would—"

She coughed again, violently, and fell back from me. If I had let go of her wrists she would have collapsed rearward into the fireplace. Dr. Jasper and Mr. McIntyre jumped up to support her from behind. They sat her down in an armchair. She coughed, thrashed, and lay still. Then, eyes gone to flat discs, she peered up at me. Instinct made her grab for the last word.

"Be put where she belongs," she rasped hoarsely.

Some law of restraint snapped in my head. "You've proved your point, Miss Ames. You've proved how painful a mother's love can be."

Just outside the door there was a scuffling noise and a clap of loud laughter. A voice I recognized as Sally's said, "No, Dad. Don't go in there. Not now, please." Then the door flew open and a masked apparition danced into the room. His arms embraced an invisible partner and his hips swiveled in a modified grind. He was a schizophrenic apparition. Above his conventional costume of navy blazer, regimental striped tie, and gray flannels leered the papier-mâché semblance of a satyr's lewd countenance. Bloodshot eyes gleamed beneath Mephistophelean brows and above fleshy pouches that proclaimed a lifetime devoted to pleasure; fat purple lips were bared to reveal a hot-pink tongue that lolled like a phallus in the first stage of tumescence. This figure gyrated over to where Miss Ames, dazed and glassy-eyed, still half reclined in her chair, and stopped squarely in her line of vision. He thrust his rear end backward, extended his arms in mocking invitation, and abruptly burst into song:

> *Way down yonder in New Orleeens,*
> *That's the land of the dreamy dreams—*

Then he leaned toward Miss Ames and scooped her from her chair. "Eleanor, what the hell's going on in here? Are you holding a goddam summit conference?" Impeded by the mask, his voice was a muffled alcoholic shout. "For Chrissake, girl, this is the week before Mardi Gras. Pack up your troubles! You may have to act respectable in front of all those pluckable virgins you play nursemaid to in Boston, but you're not in Boston now and I can remember one night twenty-five years ago when you and I danced until dawn—!"

"Howard, please act your age." Still dazed and visibly weak, Miss Ames struggled feebly to free herself, but Mr. Montrose only tightened his embrace.

"Goddammit," he roared, "I am acting my age. And when I look at you, what do I see? Banked fires! So let loose, woman, you're no spring chicken and this old rooster wants to make hay while the sun still shines." His tone was drunken, good-humored, and mocking all at once. "And don't you worry about that Elizabeth of yours. That girl's an A-number-one survivor. She'll show up fit as a fiddle and raring to go. You should've seen her at that ball last night. She looked like a million dollars. It's no wonder that poor excuse of a husband turned up dead as a doornail. Why, there wasn't a man at that ball who—"

"Dad, please. Please. You've said far too much already. Can't you see Miss Ames isn't well?"

Sally had been standing in the door throughout her father's performance. Now the conviction in her voice abruptly punctured the afflatus of his mood. He set Miss Ames down in her chair. His shoulders sagged. "Aw, what the hell," he said. "It was only a joke, Eleanor," and he lurched past Sally into the hall.

"I'm terribly sorry, Miss Ames. Dad's been up late every night this week and it's taking its toll. He didn't mean to offend. I'll call Miss Stockton to help you upstairs."

Miss Ames said nothing. From the look on her face, she might have stared into the last circle of hell and been blasted by what she had seen there. When Miss Stockton appeared, she said automatically, "I'm perfectly capable of taking care of myself, Edwina," but she allowed herself to be led away without a backward look, like a patient or a prisoner.

The room was silent. Then Dr. Jasper said to Mr. Mc-Intyre: "This meeting seems to be over. I can't say it was a pleasant experience, but it did prove illuminating."

"It sure did."

"Probably we don't mean the same thing, though. I only meant that psychiatrists rarely get such an opportunity to compare their patients' versions of reality with"—he hesitated—"what passes for objective reality."

"What's your verdict?"

"Oh, I'm withholding judgment. Until all the evidence is in." The doctor gave me a comic wink in full view of Mr. McIntyre.

The two men did not shake hands. As he turned to leave, Dr. Jasper said to me, "I know you understand my hesitancy in discussing a patient. I also know we're both worried about Elizabeth. If you think I can be of help to you and to her, please feel free to call me."

"I'll do that, Doctor."

Sally showed the doctor out. Left alone with me, Mr. McIntyre said genially, "I got to get going, too. But I'd like a few words with you first, Mr. Preston, if you'd be so kind."

"And when you two have finished your business, maybe Mr. Preston would stay to have that drink I promised him." Sally had reentered the room. I hoped that her artificial brightness was for Mr. McIntyre's benefit, not mine.

"Sure. Where'll I find you?"

"Outside. I'm still not in the mood for family celebrations."

When the door closed behind her, Mr. McIntyre eyed me narrowly. "Are you with Mr. Berenson or against him, son?"

"I have my own client to think of." In saying this I accepted, if only publicly, the role others kept forcing me into.

"Mr. Berenson just wants to protect Miss Elizabeth's interests and his own interests at the same time."

"I'm not sure the two coincide."

"Mr. Berenson's sure. And once he decides how to proceed, he doesn't look back."

"Even in the case of irrevocable trusts?"

"That's different. Years had to pass before he saw that he might have made a mistake in wanting Miss Elizabeth to be independent."

I didn't believe that. All that I had learned about Berenson contradicted this sudden shift in viewpoint. But his weakened state was possibly so severe that he was taking advice he would have earlier rejected.

"Well, he's making another mistake if he tries to have her interdicted," I said. "And frankly, if you let him think it's advisable or even possible, you're not giving him sound counsel. It's a half-assed idea. Whatever Elizabeth's history may be, she's not a mental incompetent."

"What about that story Miss Ames told?"

"Which one? She told a lot of stories."

"That robbery business."

I said with more conviction than I felt: "That was a lot of crap. Miss Ames is obviously not rational on the subject of Elizabeth. And by the way: just what's in all this for Miss Ames?"

"I told you. She's worried about that girl, with good reason."

"Nothing else?"

Mr. McIntyre sidestepped this. "You think Miss Ames made up that robbery story?" he said.

"No, but I think Elizabeth probably did."

"Hopheads have done stranger things than rob banks when they didn't need the money."

"Even if the story is true, you'd have a hard time proving it. And if you could prove it, then what? Criminality doesn't constitute incompetence. Besides, does your boss want his granddaughter in jail?"

"She may end up there yet."

We eyed each other.

"The point is," he said slowly, "we don't really know what that girl's been up to, or what she's up to now. I heard tell she tried to kill herself more than once."

"Are you sorry she didn't succeed?"

"I didn't say that, son. But in the event of her death Mr. Berenson's interests would be taken care of."

"How?"

"Most of what he set up for her would revert to the Berenson estate."

"Most but not all? What about property that's hers free and clear?"

"Far as I know, the only valid will she ever made was one I helped her with six years ago. It's still in the safe at my office."

"And you were careful to protect Mr. Berenson's interests?"

"Naturally. Miss Elizabeth was only too happy to oblige. She didn't even make a move to change that will after she got married." He chuckled. "I'll bet that husband of hers kept after her about it, though."

I decided to play my wild card. "Louisiana recognizes olographic wills, Mr. McIntyre. We both know that."

He stared at me a full ten seconds before he said: "So?"

"I have a very recent will of Elizabeth's down at my office."

"Do you now?"

"Uh-huh. It's handwritten, but it's signed, dated, and even witnessed. No court of law would reject it."

"Mr. Berenson might be interested to know how she's disposed of his property."

"His?"

He sighed. "I don't suppose you'd care to discuss the nature of that will. In general terms, I mean. I merely ask on behalf of my client."

"And on my client's behalf I have to refuse."

A telephone by the sofa rang twice. Elsewhere in the house someone caught it on the second ring. As if in response to a signal, Mr. McIntyre retrieved his briefcase from where he had left it by the fireplace and said, "Well, I'll be getting along. When I make my report to the old man I'll have to say nothing's been settled. Then again, Rome wasn't built in a day. These things have a way of working themselves out."

"I'd like to talk to Mr. Berenson myself. Would he be willing to see me?"

"I can't say that he would. Then again, I can't say he wouldn't."

"How should I take that?"

"Just as it's meant. Son, Mr. Berenson has nearly reached the end of a long life. He's tired. I don't know that he ever liked people much. He was never one of the boys, if you catch my meaning. Since his last stroke, he just lives out his

days in his room. Far as I know, the only people he sees are
the doctor, Miss Taylor, Mrs. Berenson and me. Miss Elizabeth used to drop by sometimes to read to him, but she
stopped that a while ago. You would've thought it was the
least she could do, but then I guess young people are naturally selfish. Anyway, I'll mention to him that you'd like to
make his acquaintance, and who knows? Everything depends
on his mood.''

   ''What if I call the house?''

   ''No harm in trying. Like I say, everything depends on his
mood.''

$\mathscr{T}$WENTY-SIX

I SAW MCINTYRE to his car, then went around to the side of the house looking for Sally. She was nowhere in sight. Since my arrival, night had descended and the green-and-white-striped tent had vanished from the garden. Spectral light spilled from a tall window at the rear of the house, illuminating beds of camellia bushes and the gnarled roots of a massive live oak. Through this window I could see the ghostly figures of the Montrose family gathered around a television set, watching what must have been a videotape of the previous evening's ball. In full regalia, Sally stood in the center of the screen, smiling beatifically and waving a wand.

Lights bloomed suddenly in the windows of the second floor. A woman's voice called out. The light in the living room flashed on, then the porch light above the front door. When the door opened, Sally appeared on the gallery.

"Sally. Over here."

She ran down the stairs, hugging a down jacket close to her body. Her eyes were black holes in a dead-white face.

"Do you have a car?"

"Yes."

"Then let's get out of here. Now. Please."

"What's happened?"

She shook her head. "I can't talk here. Where's your car?"

Inside the car she stared straight ahead and breathed deeply and slowly several times. She said, "I'm all right now. I really am. But Harry, it's so awful, grotesque. Why today of all days?"

"Just tell me what's going on."

"Were you inside when the phone rang?"

"Five or ten minutes ago, yes."

"That call was for Miss Ames."

My heart jumped. "Elizabeth?"

"No. I wish to God it had been, except now I'm so afraid—" She stopped herself. "It was from the sheriff's office in Comfort."

"Where's that?"

"It's a nothing town near Berenson Island. That's what they call Mr. Berenson's country place, but it's not an island, not really. It's just surrounded by swamp." She turned to me. "Harry, we've got to find Elizabeth now. We can't let her hear about this—"

"You're not making sense. Calm down and tell it to me slowly."

"I'll try. Last week they started drilling some new wells on Berenson Island. The wells are in a swamp or bayou: that's all I know. Yesterday the drilling crew came on some bones underwater. Human bones."

"Whose?"

"There's been no official identification. The sheriff called Mr. Berenson's house here in New Orleans, but when he explained his business, they wouldn't put him through to the old man. They said his health couldn't take it. That's why the sheriff tracked down Miss Ames."

"Why Miss Ames?"

"What that drilling crew found—the sheriff thinks it might be Elizabeth's father. Unfortunately, Miss Ames is in no condition to help anybody with anything. She doesn't want any part of this, either. Right now, she's in a state of collapse upstairs. But Miss Stockton told Mama they still plan to catch the morning flight back to Boston."

"Sally, before this evening, just what was the story on Elizabeth's father?"

"I started to tell you earlier. People talk about Saul Berenson as if he died a perfectly natural death, but the truth is no one ever knew what happened to him. He was a moody man, and Dad says he was dead set against this business of drilling for oil on his father's land. Anyway, one day when Elizabeth was about eight he just disappeared. Vanished without a word. That's what made it so awful for Elizabeth. When she was growing up, she kept hoping that someday he would reappear. Of course there must have been talk about suicide, and maybe at some point he was declared officially dead, but until this—"

"What made the sheriff think these bones might be Berenson?"

"Because he was last seen on the Island. The man who's sheriff now was on the police force in Comfort then. He remembered how they searched the woods and so on."

"So if it's Elizabeth's father, he did commit suicide after all."

"Not necessarily. Apparently there's damage to the skull. Whether or not this is Elizabeth's father, he might have been murdered."

$\mathcal{T}$WENTY-SEVEN

WHILE SALLY AND I sat in the car, a pounding of drums began in the distance, like the signal for a native uprising. Above us, streetlights made golden discs inside magnolia leaves. People started milling in the street, most of them headed toward St. Charles Avenue. Parents carried small children on their shoulders; older children, some wearing Frankenstein or Dracula masks, formed their own clusters; middle-aged residents of the neighborhood stood chatting on the sidewalks with drinks in their hands. When a little girl wearing a fright wig stuck her head in at the window, Sally jumped. "Life goes on," she said, "and that means a parade. I can't even invite you back into the house. In there, the Lord of Misrule reigns."

"This crowd will pass soon."

"Harry, I can't believe Elizabeth had anything to do with Jack Bennett's death. But then why would she vanish the way she did?"

"Fear."

"Of what?"

"I don't know. I'm not sure Elizabeth does, either, but I could be wrong. You talk about her honesty, Sally, but the truth is she's more outspoken than honest. She may know something that she hasn't told anyone."

"Do you think she has cause to be afraid?"

"Anyone with a family like that has plenty to be afraid of. Her mother and her grandfather want her locked up, or the next thing to it." I told her what had happened at the meeting earlier that evening.

"I can't believe it," Sally said. "Miss Ames, maybe. But Elizabeth and her grandfather have always been close, in their own way. At least she thought they were."

"Maybe she had to believe that."

"Elizabeth's not very good at fooling herself."

"Sally, you've known her so much longer than I have. Can you think of a place she would go to hide out?"

"Only one place. I haven't mentioned it because it seems so obvious. I'm talking about Berenson Island."

"With all that oil drilling it must be crawling with people."

"You don't understand. It's enormous: thousands of acres. The sections that have been leased to the oil company are just one small part of the whole. Or they were when I was there four years ago."

"You've been there?"

"With Elizabeth. It's strange. She loves that place, but she hates it, too. She almost never goes there. The day she asked me to go with her was an exception. And she wanted company because she was afraid to go alone."

"Why?"

"She didn't spell it out, but she was afraid. All she said was that some questions had come up in her meetings with Dr. Jasper, and she wanted to 'check things out,' as she put it. 'I need to make a journey into the past,' she said, 'but not alone. Alone, I might not make it back.' You know the way Elizabeth talks. But when I saw the Island, I knew why she wanted someone with her."

"What's it like?"

"Growing up in New Orleans, you forget what's all around you out there. There was the main house, of course, a big sort of lodge, and some outbuildings, but it didn't look as if anyone had been there for years; it was like a ghost town. Beyond those buildings, there was just wilderness."

"How long would it take to drive there?"

"Less than two hours."

"Sally, Elizabeth must know she can't stay on the road if she wants to avoid the police. If she did go to the Island, she could almost have gotten there by the time the call went out on her this morning."

"There's something else. If Elizabeth wants to hide, she wouldn't have to stay at the main house. She told me her father had built a cabin, somewhere in the woods, that he went to when he wanted to be alone. Sometimes he took Elizabeth with him; it was like camping out. She started to take me to see it, but then she got cold feet. I was relieved. I had already seen enough."

"Do you remember how to get to the Island?"

"There's a marked turnoff from the main road."

"Would you go with me?"

"When?"

"Tomorrow morning. Early. I have to take my son to school, but after that I could probably rearrange my schedule."

"I have a schedule, too," she said. "Remember: it's Carnival Week."

"Well, what about it?"

"All right. I'm supposed to go to a luncheon, but I'll cancel it." She smiled. "Lord, I hope Mama doesn't find out."

TWENTY-EIGHT

MY HEAD WAS still filled with our whisperings when, after the parade had passed, I drove downtown and parked the car on Barracks Street. From Bourbon Street two blocks away came the sounds of drunken laughter and of bottles breaking. Our street was as quiet as usual. It was empty, too, except for a man standing by a parked car at the end of the block. I noticed him, but that was all. There was a gay bar over on Chartres: men cruised the area often, looking for pickups. When I put my key in the lock of the green wooden gate, I heard a car door slam. I looked over my shoulder. The man was still standing in the street. I entered Grandmother's courtyard. Someone grabbed me from behind in a bear hug that pinned my arms to my sides. A second figure moved from the shadows and hit me on the head with something heavy but resilient. A piece of cloth that felt like a towel was clamped over my face. When I fought to free myself, the man pinning me tightened his embrace until I heaved for breath. I kicked outward and up, connected, heard a muffled yelp, and received a blow on the mouth that sank my teeth into my lower lip. Then someone forced me into a kneeling position and, from the front, shoved steel between my legs and up under my scrotum.

"It's what you think, fucker. Ever been butt-fucked by a

bullet?'' The voice was a nasal jeer. It was not a voice that I had heard before. Holding my right shoulder, the speaker pressed his face so close to mine that I could smell his acrid breath through the towel. The man who held me from behind laughed softly in my ear.

''So where is it?''

''Where's what?''

'' 'Where's what?' '' the jeering voice echoed. ''Hear that? This fucker said 'Where's what?' ''

''Wowee!''

''The letter, asshole. Better yet, the girl and the letter.''

''What letter?''

''The fucker says 'What letter.' '' He shoved the gun upward. ''Listen, asshole, you don't know me. If you're lucky you never will. But I know who you been running with and you moving outa your league. You shoulda stayed home with your boy and the old lady. Fact, let's get your boy out here now. Maybe that'll remind you what letter.''

''Get the boy. Get the boy.'' The giggle sounded again in my ear.

''Somebody up there likes you, asshole. That's why our friend's staying out by the car this time. But I got a lot of leeway. That boya yours. How old's he? Eight or nine? You saw him spread-eagled, you saw me doing to him what I'm doing to you,'' he moved the gun between my legs, ''how long'd you hold out? So where's the letter?''

The rage I felt was impotent but so murderous that it exploded in my chest. ''Mother-fucking bastard. I may not know you, but from now on I'll recognize your smell.''

He clamped his hand over my mouth and shoved the gun upward.

''Christ, get down. Lights!''

It was the giggler who spoke that time. Then, from a distance, Grandmother's voice called, ''What's going on out there? Is that you, Harry?''

The hand closed tighter on my mouth.

''If it's not Harry, then get out of here, whoever you are. I'm an old woman but I've got a rifle and I know how to use it.''

''Shit!''

A straight-armed shove sent me backwards. My head collided with concrete. Lights flashed on, then off.

My return was slow. I heard a voice but did not, at first, recognize it as Grandmother's. "Harry, can you understand me?"

I could, but when I tried to answer no sound came. For a moment I thought I had been in a car crash. My head throbbed like an irregular pulse. So did my anus.

"Ike. Where's Ike?"

The cloth had been removed from my head. When I opened my eyes, Grandmother's face came slowly into focus close to mine, framed by the nimbus cast by the carriage lamp directly above her.

"Ike's the point, Harry. I've got to tell you about Ike. Can you stand up? If I help you, can you walk?"

Her thin right arm went under mine and with amazing tensile strength, lifted me to my feet. My legs buckled.

"Walk, Harry. We've got to get inside. No, not your place—the stairs are too steep. My house."

Inside the kitchen she got me to a chair, soaked a towel in water at the sink, and pressed it to my mouth. She half filled a glass with bourbon. "Drink this." I did. The whiskey stung my cut lip so sharply that I jumped. The pain, or the whiskey, cleared my head.

Grandmother stood before me in her black-and-white housecoat. Her left cheek twitched, and her dark eyes shone with something beyond apprehension.

"Do you need a doctor?"

"I don't think so."

"Then stay here. Drink that. I'm going back outside for the gun."

She returned with a .22 rifle that she deposited in the center of the kitchen table.

"Where the hell did that come from?"

"You forget I used to go hunting with your grandfather. All his guns are in the back room upstairs."

"Loaded?"

"I keep this one loaded."

"You would have used it, too, wouldn't you?" I remembered everything then: the men, questions that made no sense, crazy threats, and Grandmother's voice penetrating the darkness and putting an end to it all.

"Of course." She looked at me steadily. "I've never admitted this to anyone, Harry. Since Ann was killed I've wanted— No. Some part of me has wanted a reason to use this gun. One of the worst things about Ann's death was what it taught me I could feel."

"I know. I've felt the same way. Go easy, Grandmother. If you had fired that gun tonight you might have hit me."

"Give me credit for some sense," she said. "But where on earth have you been, Harry? I've tried to get you since five o'clock, but when I called your office Esther had already left and no one knew where you were. I've been frantic. Now this—" She made a helpless gesture that took in both the gun on the table and me, or my condition. "I couldn't call the police because I was afraid to. I won't now unless you say I can."

"Why'd you want to call the police?"

"About Ike."

"Ike?" I grabbed her arm. "What about Ike? Isn't he upstairs asleep?"

"Do you think that boy of yours would have slept through all this? No, Harry. Ike's not upstairs. He's with her."

"Who?"

"Elizabeth Berenson."

"That's not possible!"

"So you think. When he didn't call by four-thirty, I called the school. They said this, this woman"—her face twisted with fury "—had come by the school during second period this morning, pulled Ike out of class, and taken him off with her."

"How could they let him go?"

"Because they *knew* her! She had gone to school there too, and it never occurred to anyone that she wasn't telling the truth."

"The truth about what?"

"She said she was doing you a favor, that there was some sort of emergency and you had asked her to pick Ike up. When the secretary told me that, I didn't know what to say. Of course they hadn't heard anything about young Bennett's death, not at the time I called, and I hadn't either. I had to hear that on the news, and can you imagine my panic since then? As it was, when I talked to the school I simply tried to smooth things over. For your sake, Harry, I assure you. Not for hers. If that had been Elizabeth Berenson in the courtyard tonight, so help me I might have shot her dead.''

She grabbed my right hand in both of hers and started kneading my knuckles. She peered intently into my face. "Look at me, Harry. I'm an old woman who's led a long, frivolous life. I won't defend or excuse it because it needs no excuse. It's what I am. But I'm not quite as frivolous as I may seem. I do believe in some things, though it doesn't seem right to talk about them. Honor and honesty, for example. Loyalty. And tradition, even when I see that the tradition is empty. More than anything, I guess I want some order in life, maybe just the illusion of order, because what goes on out there is chaos. I knew that before today. I knew that long before Ann died. If I'm superficial, if I care too much about appearances, it's because that's what order is: appearances. There's no real order, Harry. I'm not fool enough to think there is. So I hang on to what I can." She pressed her fingertips into my knuckles and the palm of my hand in a gesture both harsh and caressing.

"I'm telling you this," she said, "because I want you to know what you and Ike mean to me. I failed with your mother. I don't find that easy to admit, but I did fail even though I can't see how or why. Of course her drinking was a kind of suicide, just as you've said. I haven't wanted to admit that, either, because you seem to dwell on it so. Now that I've admitted it, I'll say how much I care that your life and Ike's turn out all right. You're a good father and a good man, but you don't always see things clearly. Oh, you have a sharp enough eye, but sometimes it has a mighty big mote in it. You didn't see the risks when Ann went to work at Charity and you didn't see them again when you got mixed up with this Berenson girl."

She had often kissed me in a perfunctory way but now she bent forward and very carefully pressed her lips to my forehead.

"This is a time when we both have to see things clear,"

she said. "Tell me the truth. Those men out there weren't just trying to mug you, were they?"

"No."

"It had to do with Elizabeth Berenson, didn't it?"

"Yes."

"Are you in love with her?"

"It didn't get that far. And now this."

"Do you know where she is?"

"Maybe."

"Now that she has Ike, do you want me to call the police?"

"I'm surprised you didn't call them earlier."

"Would you have wanted me to?"

"I don't think so."

"That's why I didn't. What I want doesn't really matter. Ike's your son, and you have to decide."

"Then I don't want to call them. Not yet."

"You still trust this girl?"

"I've never trusted her. Not in the usual sense."

"What other sense is there?"

"I can't explain. I won't forgive her for doing this—I couldn't—but I think Ike may be safe."

"With someone who's crazy?"

"There's crazy and crazy."

"I want to be charitable. I just don't understand."

"I'm not crazy, Grandmother. But you said my eye has a mighty big mote in it. So does yours."

"So?"

"I'm not sure Elizabeth's has."

TWENTY-NINE

I SPENT THAT night at Grandmother's house, in Mother's old room. Through the balconied window I could see the glare of the lights we had left on in the courtyard. The outsized rosewood bed I lay in was a relic from one of the Haynesworth plantations up the River Road, when the Haynesworths had had plantations. Lying in it, unable to sleep, I could stare down at the silhouette of the fantastically carved footboard and feel that I was floating in a baroque boat. But not alone. That boat was manned by a crew of ghosts.

I willed the roar in my head to subside and tried to think clearly. What had Elizabeth told Ike that had persuaded him to go with her? Whatever she was capable of, I didn't think her capable of the cruelty necessary to tell him that something had happened to Grandmother or me. Also, Ike could spot a fraud at twenty paces. Elizabeth was a mystery, but she wasn't a fraud. Ike had sensed that from the start. I saw again the intensity of his blue stare when it had fastened on her for the first time. She had become a mystery to be plumbed. When he had asked me to tell him what she was like, I hadn't been able to tell him much; what little I had learned wasn't repeatable. He hadn't pressed me—clear evidence of his tact. But the fervor of his laser-gaze had shown me that she had already taken up residence in his imagination and that he would be pleased to have her remain there on a long-term lease.

It was possible that he had left school with Elizabeth that morning simply because he had felt like it. Maybe he had wanted to learn for himself how she operated. Since Ann's death, his sense of adventure had been circumscribed by a caution born of fear. On Sunday, something had made him afraid of the man he had seen on the street. But since Ike must have gone with Elizabeth willingly, that meant he was not afraid of her. I forced myself to trust his instincts. One problem with being the parent of a child as astute as Ike was that he arrived at his judgments by a logic that didn't always coincide with my own. The fact that these judgments so often proved right was an unsettling truth that I had not quite learned to accept.

I got up shortly before dawn. There was a light on in Grandmother's room. She was sitting up in bed with a leather-bound book propped open on her lap. She wore a lace bed jacket and an editor's green eyeshade. "Well," she said, "I won't pretend that I've gotten any sleep."

"I don't want to alarm you further, but I have a favor to ask. Will you give me a gun to take with me today?"

I should have known that that wouldn't faze her. "Of course," she said. She reached under the sheet on the far side of the bed and withdrew the .22 rifle.

"Grandmother, what an unlikely bedmate."

"At my age, comfort is all you ask from a bedmate. Even if it's cold comfort."

"You keep that. Give me one of Grandfather's guns."

"Do you think those men will come back?"

"No. If they do, please don't use them for target practice. Call the police. Still, I'd feel safer if you kept the .22 and gave me something else."

"I'll see what there is."

She led me into a rear bedroom that all during my childhood I had thought of as the junk room. It was filled with crates of moldy books, old steamer trunks pasted with exotic labels, and furniture in need of repair or beyond it. In the bleak gray light the room had a sepulchral air. A glass-doored cabinet in the far left corner of the room held a col-

lection of rifles and shotguns. The only handgun I could find
was an unwieldy .45 revolver on the bottom shelf. I picked
it up and held it.

"You know, I used to play with this gun when I came
here during the summer. I put caps in it."

"Harry, don't tell me that. It makes me wonder what Ike's
up to when he explores this house."

"Does he even know about this room?"

"He's your son, isn't he? There isn't a corner of this mau-
soleum that he hasn't inspected."

I looked at the .45. "This isn't handy, but it's better than
nothing."

"I'll see if I can find you some bullets," she said, then
rummaged in a drawer and produced a faded green cardboard
box with Remington printed on it in orange letters. I wondered how long those bullets had been in that drawer. She
presented them to me with a slight ceremonial bow, as if she
were a matriarch sending a son off to war. Some such notion
may have been in her head—she was a great reader—but I
only felt like a fool. I hadn't fired a gun since summer camp
twenty years before; and I had never fired a .45 revolver.

Grandmother looked at me as if she could read my
thoughts. Sometimes she could. So could Ike. "If you want
to hit your target," she said, "cock it first. Otherwise it's
hell to shoot." She took my hand. "Stay and have breakfast.
Leona will be here in an hour."

"I couldn't face Leona this morning. When she learns
about Ike she'll go wild."

She smiled crookedly. "You're a funny sort of coward,
aren't you? Leona scares you more than those men last
night."

"Those men scared me. They still do. My stomach feels
as if something's been chewing on it. But guilt scares me
more."

"Guilt?"

"Leona's brand of loyalty has reduced the relationships in
her life to a very few. And she views those in irreducible
terms."

"So do I. So do you."

"Not anymore."

THIRTY

WHEN I CROSSED to my apartment the courtyard was filled with early morning mist that floated, motionless, seven feet above the ground like a canopy of spider webs draped from the tops of banana trees and of twisted sweet olives. The mist stirred when I opened the door to the stairwell; a vaporous tendril pursued me part of the way up the stairs as I kicked the door shut behind me.

I went to the kitchen, where I made myself a pot of coffee and scrambled some eggs. When my stomach said no to the eggs, I threw them back in the pan and cooked them until they were stiff and dry. That way I got them down.

I looked at the clock. It was six-fifteen.

The door to Ike's room was partly ajar. Without wanting to, I opened it wide. Leona, I could see, had been in to clean the day before. The room contained none of Ike's smell. It was unbearably free of his clutter. No jeans or Jockey shorts littered the floor. The bed was made. Ike's books were piled neatly on his pint-sized desk next to a tall stack of Dungeons and Dragons character sheets. Holding a silver basketball in each gargantuan mitt, George "Iceman" Gervin grinned at me from a poster on the wall. I turned away.

Taking the coffeepot with me, I went into the living room, sat at my desk, and wrote out the checks for the telephone and electric bills. I usually had Esther pay the bills from my office: doing it myself, on that particular morning, gave me the illusion of being in control of my life. Then, in spite of the early hour, I called Dr. Jasper.

I left my name with his answering service and went into the bathroom to shower and shave. When the doctor returned the call, I was examining my cut lip and the lump on my forehead in the mirror of the medicine cabinet. There was more than professional concern in Jasper's voice when he asked whether I had heard from Elizabeth.

"No. But there's an off chance I know where she is."

"Where?"

"Sally Montrose thinks she might be at Berenson Island."

He deliberated. "It is possible," he said. "But her associations with that place are loaded."

"There's another thing, Doctor. Wherever Elizabeth is, my son, Ike, is with her."

"Your son?" His tone registered the absolute bewilderment that I still felt.

"My nine-year-old son. He and Elizabeth had never even met, not really. For whatever reasons, she went to his school yesterday, sometime after Bennett was murdered, and persuaded the school to let Ike go off with her. And he went, presumably of his own accord. I don't know why I'm telling you this now," I said, "except that I'm ready to jump out of my skin and, since you must know Elizabeth as well as anyone, or better, maybe you could give me some kind of assurance that Ike's safe with her."

The anxiety in my own voice made me pause. It was the voice of a stranger—someone hanging on by his fingernails.

"Sorry," I said.

"Don't be. Let's see if we can make some sense of this. Please understand, though, that I haven't even seen Elizabeth since she met you—when was it? Just a few days ago?"

"Saturday night."

"Since Saturday I've talked to her only once. She called on Sunday to cancel her Monday morning appointment. She sounded keyed up, on the verge of making decisions we had been talking about for some time. She mentioned that she had met a man she trusted, a lawyer, and that she wanted to see him first thing on Monday, before her resolve might weaken. That's why she broke her appointment with me. It's true,'' he said dryly, ''that in one sense she was rejecting me in your favor, but I took it as an encouraging sign. After all, there's only a limited amount a psychiatrist can do to help a patient with the more practical aspects of life. *Real* life, so called.''

I remembered Elizabeth's having said the same thing. For a moment I had the eerie sensation of hearing her speak now, like a ventriloquist, through him. Even the faintly mocking tone was the same. I wondered what he would say if he knew that in her will Elizabeth had yoked him and me in a tie that bound. This triggered another thought: what if he already knew the contents of that will? What if he had in some way, if only by suggestion, dictated its terms?

These thoughts led nowhere. Or rather, they could have led anywhere—into the mazelike intricacies of endless suspicion. Was there, in fact, a minotaur at the core of the maze? Or was there only more intricacy—complication piled upon complication—intricacy that curled back on itself and that had no solution? Was that the maze, that the minotaur? If so, to confront it head-on would be to confront the rarest monster of all.

''The truth is, Mr. Preston,'' the doctor was saying, ''I don't know enough about the situation to offer any sort of explanation, even if I felt free to offer it. You say Elizabeth and your son—Ike, is it?—don't know each other. Is there anything about Ike that might have caught Elizabeth's attention, made her identify with him in—''

''He didn't catch her attention, Doctor. She caught his.''

''Did he say why?''

''I think she looked—well, different. Exciting.''

''She is that.''

''But Elizabeth knew nothing about Ike, nothing except—''

''Except what?''

''That his mother is dead. Still,'' I went on, struggling to express an idea that I couldn't fully formulate, ''she doesn't even know how Ann died.''

''Would that matter?''

"My wife was a psychiatric social worker. She was killed by one of her patients, a Charity Hospital patient who turned up at our house."

Silence. Then, "I'm not sure what you're getting at, Mr. Preston."

"I'm not either. I'm not sure I am getting at anything. I'm just stumbling in the dark. I can't say what made me mention Ann, except that I was thinking of Elizabeth's own situation. I mean her parents. A mother who wasn't there, and who isn't a mother anyhow. A father who—"

"Who what?"

"Hasn't Elizabeth spoken about her father?"

"Of course. What were you going to say?"

"If Elizabeth is at the Island, if she is there with Ike, then she's sitting on an emotional powder keg."

"That would be true whether or not your son was there."

"Yes, but I'm talking about what I learned last night at the Montroses' after you left. An oil-drilling crew has turned up the remains of someone who might have been murdered, someone who could be Elizabeth's father."

"Christ. Elizabeth was with her father at the Island the day he disappeared."

"What does that mean!"

"Hold on, Preston. I have to think." Finally he said, "Look, there's no point in our trying to second-guess a situation as bizarre as this."

"But what about Ike?"

"If Elizabeth is acting something out, if that's why she has your son, we can't know what it is. Have you called the police?"

"No."

"Why not?"

"Instinct."

"Then follow that instinct. Go to the Island, find Elizabeth and Ike, if you can. Whatever else, Elizabeth shouldn't learn about her father, if it is her father, from the newspapers or television. Maybe you shouldn't even tell her right away if you do find her."

"Why shouldn't I tell her? What are you suggesting?"

"I'm not suggesting anything."

"Doctor, just what is Elizabeth capable of?"

"What is anyone capable of?"

"That's no answer. Miss Ames says Elizabeth is capable of anything."

"Maybe Miss Ames is, too. Maybe we all are. It just depends on the pressure point."

THIRTY-ONE

IN THE BACK of the hall closet I found a stained canvas bag big enough to hold my jeans, a heavy wool sweater, a windbreaker, a pair of old hiking boots I hadn't worn in years—there was nowhere to hike to—the revolver, and the box of cartridges. Before putting the gun into the bag, I sat down on the hall floor, removed the oily rag the .45 was wrapped in, and examined it. It showed no sign of rust. Its single black eye had the power to mesmerize. There was a sliding catch on the left side of the pistol. When I pulled this catch back, the cylinder swung out of the frame and downward on a hinge. I took three cartridges from the box and inserted them into the cylinder, spun it so that an empty chamber was in line with the firing pin, and returned the cylinder to its original position. Any fool, it seemed, could load this gun. The length of its barrel still struck me as unwieldy, but when I raised the pistol to take aim at the small mirror above the hall table, it seemed to move on its own and point instinctively at the target. Apparently, any fool could use this gun. I wrapped it again in the rag and placed it at the bottom of the carryall.

Then I called Sally. It was only seven-fifteen but she answered the phone on the first ring. Elsewhere in the house someone picked up another receiver and a woman's sleepy, irritable voice said, "Yes?" but Sally said, "I've got it, Mama. It's for me," and a click told us that Mama had rung off.

"Some things have happened since we talked last night, Sally. You may want to back out of today. In fact, you probably should."

I told her what had happened. At several points while I talked she responded with an audible intake of breath. When I had finished, she said, "Elizabeth would never do such a thing without good reason. There has to be a good reason."

Her confidence in Elizabeth seemed so misplaced that I couldn't bring myself to comment on it. I said, "Well? What's the decision?"

"Of course I'll come. This doesn't change anything."

"I probably shouldn't let you come. I'm thinking of those men. I could find Berenson Island myself."

"I want to come."

I wanted her with me. It was as selfishly simple as that. I said, "Do you have a car?"

"I can always get the station wagon."

"I don't want to take my car today. I'm sure those men know it too well."

"I understand."

"What I want you to do is this. My office is in the Poydras Building. Behind that building is a parking complex. The crossover between the two buildings is on the fifth floor. Meet me there at nine-thirty, as close to the crossover as possible. You can't miss it, and you won't have to worry about a parking space. Just take one of the reserved spaces. That's where I park, and at least one space will be empty."

"I'll be there."

A plan was forming in my head. In fact, it had begun to take shape, without my knowing it, the day before. Now its first aim was to get Ike back safely, as quickly as possible. The fury I felt toward Elizabeth was such that her own dilemma had receded into the background. Yet I knew, or sensed, that for the time being her problems and mine were inseparable.

When I put on my dark gray lawyer's uniform I might have been getting into a Mardi Gras costume. Looking in the mirror, I felt no connection with the young executive type who stared back. In any other city the strained look in my eyes and the circles under them would have been taken for the signs of anxiety they were, but this was Carnival Week in New Orleans and black circles were de rigueur.

I called a cab. Instead of giving my address on Barracks I gave Grandmother's on Esplanade. Carrying the canvas bag, I went out to wait at the front gate. The mist had lifted. The boy astride a dolphin who crested the fountain in the center of the lawn saluted a sky that threatened rather than promised rain. Black clouds hung poised as if for combat.

The front gate was nine feet high, made of intricate grill-work, and set into the brick wall that faced the street. Although the gate could be opened by anyone who wanted to get out, it was permanently locked to anyone outside who did not have a key. Grandmother admitted guests by pushing a button in the front hall. The absurdity of these precautionary measures struck me as I stood waiting for the cab. The brick wall was itself only six feet high, and two sections of the grillwork that surmounted it and achieved the height of the gate had been removed for repair work. Anybody could scale that wall. For that matter, anyone who knew the trick could open the ancient wooden gates of the Barracks Street courtyard simply by applying his shoulder and pressing hard—gently at first, then with greater insistency—three times. Antiquity had given the gates an elasticity that Grandmother and I often joked about. Last night had proved, though, that it was no joking matter.

When the cab drew up, I got into it in record time. I gave the black driver my office address, sank back on the seat, heaved a sigh equal to one of Grandmother's, and felt the roar begin to mount again in my head. When the driver turned right on Royal I asked: "Anyone behind us? I don't want to turn around to look."

He didn't ask why. "Only car behind us is a red Caddie."

I didn't think that was the one to worry about.

"Wait now. Nuther car plowing down on that red one like crazy."

"What kind?"

"Can't tell. Old. Black or dark blue."

My heart plummeted. I didn't see what those men could gain by following me to my office. If there were only two of them, even three—I remembered the man standing by the parked car on Barracks, the sound of his door slamming as if to signal my arrival—they couldn't expect to stake out an office building with as many entrances and exits as ours. My firm's offices took up the whole of the twenty-second floor. There was an elevator hall in the center but it was used only by members of the firm, clients, and deliverymen. Anyone waiting around in that small area would be instantly noticed. Also, without being familiar with the plan of the building these men couldn't know about the fifth floor crossover to the parking complex. In any case, since I had left my car behind, it seemed unlikely that they would keep the garage under surveillance.

I paid the driver while we were still moving. When he pulled up, I made for the lobby of the building without looking back.

At that hour—it was still before eight—the twenty-second floor was nearly deserted except for an eager recent law graduate doing research in the library. Esther wouldn't arrive until nine. I was glad of the breathing space. In my office I closed the curtains of the window wall. It was not a morning for heights or distant vistas. Close quarters might keep me from coming unstrung.

The manila envelope containing Elizabeth's will was still on my desk. I buried it under some papers in the top drawer.

I spent the next hour on the phone, leaving messages to cancel the day's appointments. When I heard the sound of coffee cups and drawling chatter in the hall, I opened the door. Esther looked up from her typewriter.

"Mr. Preston! You here mighty early this morning."

"I have to leave town on business, just for the day, and I wanted to map things out."

"I got hold of Erskine yesterday, like you asked, and put him off till next week."

"It's lucky things are so slow this time of year. I still haven't gotten used to the fact that Carnival Week means time out in New Orleans. Erskine probably thought I was nursing a hangover."

"Erskine knows better than that, Mr. Preston. He knows you're a clean-living young man with a little boy to take care of."

Her tone was serious, motherly even, but "clean living" was not a label that I desired or had earned except by default. "Is that what people really think of me, Esther?"

"They sure do. And when that Ike of yours comes into this office there isn't a secretary whose heart doesn't melt."

"Ike would be pleased to hear it. Still, I don't much like being regarded as a plaster saint. You know, twice this week somebody's called me a prig, and it's stuck in my craw."

Her face went hot pink. "Now Mr. Preston, who'd call you a thing like that? For shame."

Had she misunderstood what I said? Possibly the word sounded slightly obscene, as it had to me when Elizabeth used it. She took refuge in her coffee cup while I flipped through yesterday's mail. Then she glanced up again. "I meant to ask you, Mr. Preston. Was that right what I heard on TV?"

"What was that?"

"About Mrs. Bennett's husband."

"He was murdered, if that's what you mean."

"They said the police were trying to locate Mrs. Bennett."

"I guess they are."

"The way they talked, they made it seem kind of strange that she's missing." She set her cup down and focused her gaze on the typewriter. "Don't want to speak out of turn, Mr. Preston, but don't you think you should give the police a call?"

"About what?"

"About seeing Mrs. Bennett yesterday morning."

"I didn't see her."

"But after she phoned, you—"

"I know. But I didn't see her after all. I only talked to her on the phone, and I've already reported that to the police, Esther, like the clean-living solid citizen that I am."

"Mr. Preston, I didn't mean—" She blushed again. "I only meant it was kind of peculiar, her calling. The timing and all."

"I agree. It was mighty peculiar."

I went back into my office. There was no point in disillusioning Esther, no point in saying that I had reported to the police only what I had felt compelled to report. It was best to have her remain an ardent supporter who wore her heart, like her curiosity, on her sleeve.

It was nearly nine-fifteen. I was preparing to leave the office when Esther buzzed me on the intercom.

"Mr. Haynesworth would like you to stop by his office, Mr. Preston."

"Damn. Can't you put him off?"

"Don't see how. I told him you were leaving but he knows you haven't left yet."

Charles's office was the largest in the firm. In itself that wasn't saying much, but its mode of decoration made it seem larger than it was. The mode was antique and austere. The leather sofa and side chairs were obligatory, but what the visitor saw, first and last, were Charles's desk and the portrait on the wall behind it. The desk was an elegant leather-topped eighteenth-century writing table whose surface was scrupulously bare except for a massive crystal inkwell with a silver stopper. The portrait was not of Charles—that would have been too grossly self-serving—but rather of his paternal grandfather, whose plantation had been burned by Butler during the Civil War. Though less official, the portrait resembled those on the wall of the Jackson Club. The subject had his grandson's gaunt features, a neatly trimmed beard, and a glance aimed unflinchingly at posterity.

Charles was standing behind the desk when I came in. He walked around to where I stood. In a gesture that was, for him, unusually demonstrative, he put his hand on my shoulder and kneaded my collarbone twice. He smelled, almost undetectably, of bay rum.

"Esther says you're about to hit the road."

"A business matter across the Lake. It shouldn't take long."

"I hope it's nothing to do with the Berenson woman."

"Nothing at all," I said, looking him straight in the eye.

"I wondered whether you had heard from her."

"Not a word."

"If you do, you will tell her to turn herself in, won't you?"

"Of course."

"I've been thinking, Harry, about our talk yesterday. I rarely regret the things I say, but perhaps I sounded"—he scrutinized me—"well, somewhat harsh when I spoke of your parents."

"Forget it."

"No hard feelings?"

"None." I looked at the grandfather clock in the corner of the room. It was nine-twenty.

As if he had noticed where my glance was directed, he smiled and said, "I guess you want to be on your way. Know when you'll get back?"

"Late afternoon, I suppose."

"But you haven't forgotten about this evening."

"This evening?"

"Tonight's the Atlantis Ball."

My mind gyrated. "Of course it is. Emily's going to be queen."

"As captain of the ball, it means a lot to me to have family there. I know Emily will be crushed if you don't show up. At the very least, come to the Queen's Supper after the ball." He peered at me intently. "I can count on you, can't I?"

Charles's tone conveyed its usual latent sense of threat. I was beyond caring. My lies had come so easily that I knew with a bracing, liberating clarity that I would not go on working for this man.

I was still smiling when I said, "Charles, I'll be there if I possibly can."

Back in my office, I felt that I had been running in place. I grabbed the canvas bag and headed past Esther toward the elevator.

"Oh, Mr. Preston," she said. "I forgot to tell you Ike called yesterday when you weren't in the office."

I turned around very slowly. "Oh? What did he want?"

"Didn't say. But whatever it was, you've seen him since then and I guess he's already told you."

"What time did he call?"

"After I got back from lunch."

"Any message?"

"No message. Just said he'd see you later on."

"That was all?"

"Mr. Preston, you look kind of funny. You been looking funny since yesterday. Must be that Bennett business. You sure you shouldn't cancel everything and go home?"

"I'm sure. So long, Esther."

Head thrumming, I moved past the long row of secretarial desks, past the switchboard operator's closed-off room, through the reception lobby, and into the outer hall. A janitor was sweeping the floor. Otherwise, the hall was empty. When I boarded the elevator there was only one other occupant, a man I recognized as an accountant who worked on the floor above mine. The elevator stopped in its descent at the twenty-first floor. The doors opened. Facing me, in the hall, was a wiry middle-aged man. In his thin, sallow face sharp eyes shone like a ferret's. He wore a greasy suit and a felt hat of indeterminate color. His eyes met mine for an instant, then flicked away. Boarding the elevator, he took up a position behind me. That was when I recognized his smell. I could feel his eyes boring into the back of my head. I didn't allow myself to glance in either of the small round mirrors above the elevator doors. The doors slid shut again. We descended. I had pressed the fifth floor button for the connecting walkway to the parking complex. But when the elevator stopped there I didn't get out. Scarcely breathing, I counted the seconds that we hung suspended in space before resuming our descent. Fifteen. We stopped once more before reaching ground level. Again I timed our stop's duration: the same as before. If the elevator was programmed to wait this long at each floor, then the wait would, I reckoned, be somewhat longer in the lobby. But although I had ridden this elevator thousands of times through the years, I could not have said how much longer that wait would be.

When the passengers filed into the lobby, I filed with them. Just outside the elevator I halted. Counting the seconds, I leaned down and began to rummage through the canvas bag as if checking its contents for something I might have forgotten. The ferret-eyed man brushed past me and stopped on the periphery of my vision. Head down and still counting, I fastened my eyes on his cheap, scuffed shoes. I shifted my gaze to the elevator door. Fourteen, fifteen, sixteen, seventeen: I couldn't wait any longer. As the doors closed I stepped through them and wheeled around. I had a split-second's satisfaction of staring into a face contorted in angry disbelief. Then the face disappeared, like an image on a screen.

In the parking complex a tank-sized Ford station wagon more than filled one of the reserved spaces. Behind the wheel, Sally waved when she saw me. I didn't wave back. I just ran.

When I slid in next to her, "Christ, am I glad to see you," I said.

"What's happened?"

"Those men last night."

"What about them?"

"They're in the building. At least one of them is. When I came down in the elevator he was waiting on the floor below mine. He must have kept pushing the down button, watching who was in each elevator as it stopped. I think I lost him but let's get out of here. Quick."

Footsteps clattered on concrete. Looking up, I saw a long-armed short man racing toward us down the ramp. He raised his arms as if signaling us to wait.

In reply to that signal Sally gunned the engine, jerked the steering wheel to the left, and with tires shrieking plunged hard and fast down the spiraling descent. A high-pitched whine echoed through the building and my head. When we reached the ticket window I leaned across Sally and handed the attendant my card. "Let's go," I shouted under my breath. "Go!"

"Get down, Harry. A man's out there on the sidewalk. He's staring at us."

I ducked. "What's he look like?"

"Big and ugly."

"What's he doing?"

"I don't know whether he saw you, but he's standing in the middle of the sidewalk. As if to block whatever comes out or at least slow it down."

"Can you see if traffic's coming?"

"Yes."

"When it's clear, hit the accelerator and don't stop."

"I can't run over him!"

"Just do it. Tell me when it's clear."

"It's clear."

"Then go!"

I kept my eyes on her profile as she floored the gas pedal. Unblinking, she stared straight ahead as the wagon shot forward. From where I crouched, it seemed to sail freely through space, then come to ground with a riveting crunch. Rubber screamed as Sally veered left, and I was thrown up against the door.

"That man moved, Harry. Did he move!" She laughed loud and hard. "I guess you can come up for air now."

I came up. "I can see why you and Elizabeth are friends," I said.

PART TWO

Asylum

THIRTY-TWO

FROM THE OVERPASS, in that morning's eerie apocalyptic light, the Superdome resembled a monstrous spacecraft that had just crashed in the center of the city. We sped past it and through sleazy suburbs on roadways that finally funneled us onto the Pontchartrain Causeway, a ribbon of concrete that stretched far as the eye could see as it bisected an expanse of water the same gunmetal gray as the sky.

Sally and I had switched places. For a time we rode in silence. The adrenaline pumping through my system might have enabled me to carry a packed trunk from a burning house but, as it was, only urged my foot on the gas pedal dangerously close to the floorboard. My thoughts were in a state of agitated suspension. What was Sally thinking? Her profile gave no sign. Her skin was porcelain but the profile was strong: blunt nose, assertive chin. A pale brown eyebrow extended halfway to her ear. She wore a suede jacket and gray slacks, and her blond hair, no longer limp, gleamed as if it had just been washed. She looked new and shiny, like a freshly minted coin.

She spoke first.

"I know what you must be feeling, Harry. I wish I could say something to make it better."

"I wish you could, too."

"We'll find Elizabeth and Ike. I know we will."

"At the moment, I'm not interested in Elizabeth. I want my son."

"Elizabeth acts on impulse, but there's always logic at work behind that impulse. Even if she herself doesn't know what it is."

"I've had it with her inscrutable logic."

My voice sounded even surlier than I felt. Not being given to idle chatter, she fell silent again before asking, "Those men back there—do you think they'll try to follow us?"

"I haven't seen any sign of them."

"Anyway, what could they do in broad daylight?"

"I don't have faith in broad daylight."

After Elizabeth, Sally seemed young and uncomplicated. But appealing as her youth was, it depressed me. It made me feel prematurely old. I wasn't old. In fact, I was young, too. But some of the things that had happened over the years, and in the last few days, made the age difference between us seem insurmountable, like an invisible wall. Was that wall self-pity? If so, I wanted to smash through it and be done.

"You can do something, Sally. Help me keep my mind occupied. Tell me anything—tell me how you spend your days."

"That won't keep your mind occupied," she said with a laugh.

"Why not?"

"You heard what Miss Ames said. All I do is party-go and gallivant."

"You don't seem the type."

"Oh, I can be nitwit frivolous," she said lightly. "Sometimes I have to work at it, that's all."

"It can't be a full-time job."

"In New Orleans? Listen, Harry. Lots of the girls I know wake up at noon, swallow a Coke and a couple of aspirins, race off to the dressmaker's to have their queen's costume fitted, then head for that day's luncheon. Afterwards, they race home to wash their hair, have a drink or smoke a joint, or both. Finally, when the sun goes down they climb into their ball gowns and go spinning off into the night. The next day, they start all over again."

"Isn't that a waste of time and energy? Not to say money?"

"Of course it is." She dropped her bantering tone. "And I'll be honest with you. It isn't quite like that for me. I do go to Tulane, I do get my work done, and I bide my time."

"For what?"

"My parents don't know it yet, in fact almost no one knows except the teachers who wrote my recommendations, but I'm skipping town next year. I've applied to Harvard, Stanford, Yale, a couple of other places. Harvard's where I want to go. In spite of Elizabeth's experience there, and certainly in spite of Miss Ames's proximity." She laughed again. It was a good laugh—simple and straightforward. "I just might get accepted. Wait and see."

"I don't doubt that you will. But why didn't you apply two years ago?"

"I could say because my parents wanted me to stay home and make this debut, and that would be true but only up to a point. Awful as it is to admit, I know that when I was queen of that ball on Monday, Dad regarded it as the crowning glory of his career. That dress I wore the other night: can you believe it cost twenty thousand dollars? Dad didn't tell me—he wouldn't. I learned from the dressmaker. When I put that dress on, I nearly threw up. It was obscene."

I listened and watched her face as she laid out the plan for her future that was equal parts declaration of independence and simple bookkeeping: she'd done her duty, now she was presenting a bill to her father. There was more than simple determination in her voice. Obviously she had made these plans long ago and expected to carry them through, with or without her father's support. Her faith in herself, in her friend Elizabeth, and in a world where plans wouldn't go awry made her seem even younger than before. Then she surprised me.

"I've been wanting to ask you something, Harry, and I don't know how to ask it except straight out. Are you just Elizabeth's lawyer? Or are you her lover, too?"

"Why do you want to know that?"

"I'm not sure."

"Well, I'm not really her lawyer. I've let people believe

I am because I didn't want her out on a limb, all alone. As
for the other . . ."

I hesitated. She laughed.

"Never mind. Let's just say you're not a disinterested
party."

"Honestly, Sally, at this point I don't know what Elizabeth
is to me. Or I to her."

She said abruptly, "You know, Harry, Elizabeth did me a
big favor once. She pulled me out of a slump, I guess it was
four years ago, and I've never been quite the same since."

"Tell me about it."

"I shouldn't. I don't know you well enough yet."

"Then don't."

"I want to, really. I want you to know exactly what Elizabeth did for me and why I have confidence in her no matter
what crazy circumstances she gets caught up in." She sat
silent for a moment. "Well, here goes. All this happened
when I was sixteen and fell in love with absolutely the wrong
man. He was wrong not just because he was twice my age,
which he was, or because he was married to one of my cousins, which he was, but because of him, the kind of person
he is. He lived in the Quarter. He was an artist, or he called
himself that, specializing in portraits of young women. When
he asked me to pose for a portrait, I was stupidly flattered,
as only a young girl can be."

"What happened?"

"Here's how it was. Mother got all fired up about the
portrait—having her daughter painted seemed so fashiona-
bly old-fashioned. She would drive me downtown in the
afternoons and drop me off at his studio in the Pontalba,
just as she would if I had been taking piano lessons. It was
May, already hot and steamy, but the studio wasn't air-
conditioned. He said he didn't like air-conditioning. He
said New Orleans weather inspired him. Can you believe
it? He said he liked the sound of ceiling fans turning overhead. I bought it all. What happened was that my brain
emptied and the hot, sticky weather poured in. Oh, he
knew what he was doing. But I didn't. I didn't have a
clue. Does that seem strange?"

"Not really."

"Posing for a portrait, you become so self-involved. All the while he kept flattering me, telling me how much he loved the curve of my cheekbone, the two freckles on my forehead, and so on. Seeing myself through his eyes made him seem, somehow, all the more attractive to me. Oh yes, he was very good looking, and still is, even though he's begun to go to seed, get paunchy and jowly, the way so many New Orleans men do at an early age. Not that you have, Harry. That's one of the first things I noticed about you."

My face got hot.

"Well, that's how it was that hot and steamy May. One afternoon he suggested we smoke some dope. I already felt half stoned, so I thought: why not? The dope smoking was how it started, the sex came later. It wasn't long before I was absolutely dependent on him, more than I have been on anyone else before or since. During this period, when he and his wife came to dinner, Mother would sometimes seat him next to me at table. And when she would ask us, as she always did, how the portrait was going, he would have his hand on me under the damask tablecloth while he answered her questions with an absolutely straight face." She paused. When I turned to look at her, she was looking at me. "You really listen, don't you?" she said.

"Sometimes. When I'm interested." I wondered whether she noticed my vague discomfort. Maybe she did, because she said, "Are you sure you want me to go on?"

"Absolutely sure," I said despite my qualms.

"Well, that was how it began. Here's how it ended. During that previous winter, I had often gone riding with Elizabeth. We had stopped, though, when the weather got too hot: I hadn't seen her in about two months. Then one Saturday she called and asked me to come swimming. She was already living in the cottage on Philip but this was before she was married and the place hadn't been fixed up yet. In fact, it was a shambles. The living room was filled with the packing crates Elizabeth used for furniture, and her clothes, those clothes that some women would kill for, were all over the place, unpressed and probably not very clean. Elizabeth is funny that way. She has more style than any woman I know but neatness is something she can't be bothered with.

I remember how her clothes looked that day because the way I was brought up—everything folded neatly with tissue paper or hung up on cloth-covered hangers—made all this mess seem disturbing and somehow exciting.''

I shifted my weight in the driver's seat.

''Well, Elizabeth took one look at me and knew something was wrong. I had never really confided in her before, she was older and seemed so sophisticated, but it only took a few of her kind words to make me spill the whole ugly story. I didn't mention the man's name, though. He was married, and I thought it was wrong to screw and tell.

''Elizabeth listened to my outpourings with a sort of ferocious concentration. She didn't say a word until I was through. Then she stood up, took me by the arm, and led me out to the pool. Lord, I remember that day. As bright as yesterday. It was June by this time, and so hot you could have fried an egg on the terrace. Elizabeth told me to get into the pool. I had my bathing suit on under my clothes, so I did what she said. I felt like a sleepwalker. She disappeared into the house.

''I remember so many details of that day. When Elizabeth came back she handed me a drink made of gin, ice, and lime juice. She hadn't put much sugar in it, and I can still feel how it stung going down.

''Then she knelt by the pool and said it was time for a catechism lesson. 'Catechism?' I asked. 'Yes. Question and answer. Question number one: when this man kisses you for the first time during those steamy afternoon sessions, does he tickle your earlobe with his tongue and then insert it, oh so slowly and wetly and firmly, into your ear?' I was dumb struck. 'And then,' she said, 'as an introduction to the second phase, does he—?' But there's no need to go on, Harry. All you need know is that Elizabeth described with malicious accuracy every detail of how that man made love to me. In fact, she even included details of how I responded to him. I was horrified, but when she had finished I managed to ask, 'How could you know these things? How?' 'Guess,' she said.

''When I didn't reply, she said, 'Sally, that man you're bedding down with has a notorious penchant for young girls.

Since I've known him he's tampered with enough jailbait to staff a whorehouse in Tangiers.'

"When I said, 'But Elizabeth, he says he loves me,' she laughed so explosively it was a slap in the face. 'They always, always do,' she said, 'when they tamper with jailbait.'

"In that moment I hated her, Harry. It was as if she had taken my heart and torn it into two pieces.

"When she saw the look on my face she said, 'He's not worth it, Sally. I wasn't his first and you won't be his last.'

"I got out of the pool without looking at her, pulled on my clothes, and went home. I felt destroyed. I thought: what a crude bitch. I swore to myself that I wouldn't see her again.

"But of course, after that, it wasn't ever the same, with him. Not ever. Elizabeth had said to keep my eyes open, and I did. That meant not smoking dope. That meant not being so pliable. And he didn't like me the new way. In fact, he didn't know how to handle me. It was all finished when the portrait was finished, and you can believe he finished that in quick time. Mama has it hanging above the mantel in her bedroom; and don't I look the dewy virgin.

"One day, about a month later, I woke up with a clear head. Elizabeth loves champagne, so I went out, bought two bottles of Veuve Clicquot, took them to her house and banged on the door. When she opened the door she smiled and said, 'I hoped you would come back.' Then she threw her arms around me. Then, in all that mess, she found a silver ice bucket and chilled the champagne. We drank both bottles. We sat in the living room on packing crates, and Elizabeth made me laugh—laugh hard at things I had never laughed at before. I won't tell you what those things were. They seemed awful then and still do. Once you laugh like that, you're not the same afterwards. Do you know what I mean?''

"I think so."

"Harry, people say that even your best friends won't tell you. I learned from Elizabeth that it's your best friends who will.''

Sally was quiet again. But she had certainly kept my thoughts occupied, long enough for us to have crossed the Lake.

THIRTY-THREE

THE CAUSEWAY FED onto a concrete highway that was a landlocked extension of the bridge. Tall pines and occasional suburban villas sped past. For miles on end we were in sole possession of the road. It seemed almost suspiciously empty.

"There's the Covington exit," Sally said. "It can't be much farther."

It wasn't. We left the highway and towering pines for a two-lane blacktop that wound south and westward through marshland. Here and there, in the marshes and the onyx-black ponds that punctuated them, oil pumps rose and fell with the motion of dinosaurs grazing. The damp air, so thick it felt palpable, was saturated with the rotting stink of sulphur gas. At some point the blacktop began to run parallel to a bayou, a cluster of buildings crested in the distance, and then we turned right to cross a bridge that deposited us in a settlement like no other I had ever seen.

"So this is Comfort," I said. It was more question than statement.

"Well, it used to be," Sally said. She looked around with distaste. "Last time I was here oil was here, too, but this was still a sleepy Louisiana village. Now it looks like a boomtown."

Or something. Vestiges of that village were still visible in the fishermen's houses, some of them not much more than jerry-built shacks on stilts, that stretched along the bayou to our right. Beyond these, at the end of town, we could see a row of new toy houses, identical except in color, that looked to be made of plywood and plastic. Interspersed with neo-classical and rococo buildings along the main street were concrete and glass-brick one-story structures: liquor stores, pizzerias, all-night groceries, and bars. The center of town, if it still had a center, appeared to be marked by a white-steepled church with an oil derrick and a slush pit in its side yard.

People milled in the streets, but few were women and few had the look of locals. Most were rangy men with the sun-bleached hair and squinting eyes of transplanted cowboys. In front of the church, a paunchy gray-uniformed policeman stood with an unbuttoned holster on his hip. If he was directing traffic, the traffic was human. As we drove past, his eyes followed us.

Beyond the cemetery at the end of town we came on a part-stucco, part-wood rectangle that looked like any other small truck-stop café. On the glass door, beneath the sign saying IDA'S, the words "Home Cooking" had been painted with flames shooting from the letters.

"Wait! Stop here," Sally said.

"What the hell for?"

"I've got an idea. It'll only take a minute."

"Christ, lunch can wait, Sally."

"No, it's not that. It's something else."

I braked the car. She got out and vanished into the restaurant. In five minutes she reappeared with a broad smile on her face.

"It's just as I thought," she said. "Come on inside. There's someone I want you to meet."

Miss Ida Breaux was a swarthy, middle-aged woman with black hair piled in curls on top of her head. Standing by the cash register, she looked dressed for action. Her stockings were rolled down below the knees and her multipocketed apron was full of pencils and small plastic menus.

"Miss Ida," Sally said, "this is my friend Mr. Preston.

Go ahead and tell him about that order you got yesterday and who came to pick it up.''

"Well." Miss Ida inhaled deeply as a prelude to her recitation. "Like I was telling this young lady, we do pretty good business but not too much of it is takeout. You know how it is. The kind of food we serve, man wants to sit down in the middle of the day, drink his beer, enjoy his lunch in peace. We don't do too much business with the new folks: I mean the oil crews they ship in from Texas and Oklahoma. They like their food fast. Burgers and Popeye chicken. But Ida's was here before they came, and God willing it'll see them go. You understand. We serve real Louisiana food to old regulars. We got the gumbo, the duck and dirty rice, the stuffed eggplant. We got the shrimp Creole. We got the crawfish bisque, crawfish étouffée, boiled crawfish, fried crawfish—''

"Tell him about the order you got yesterday," Sally interrupted, as gently as she could.

"That order. Well, long about eleven-thirty yesterday morning some woman called in and asked us to pack her up food to go. We were real glad to oblige, but she must've been planning some party. She ordered a gallon of gumbo, two quarts of the Creole and the étouffée—that's two quarts each—a whole mess of boiled shrimp, four orders of eggplant—''

"Now tell who picked it up.''

"About a half hour after that phone call, a little boy with the biggest blue eyes walked in the door, came over to the counter, and I said, 'Can I help you, sonny?' and he said, 'I've come to pick up the order for Preston.' ''

"Preston?''

Miss Ida did a double take. "Now that's a real coincidence—that little boy's name's the same as yours. You kin?''

"Could be.''

"We had packed everything up in cartons while it was nice and hot, but there was so much of it that little boy couldn't carry the whole load. When I offered to send someone with him out to the car, he said no, he'd make two trips, and that's just what he did do. Now what kind of parents you think'd let a sweet boy like that come in and have to carry all their food out to the car by himself?''

''I wonder.''

''Well,'' Miss Ida said, looking at Sally and then at me, ''you folks want to sit down and order? Tell you what's special today—the gumbo. We got us in some oysters with real big bellies.''

Sally looked at me. She was radiant. Clearly she was proud of the gift she had presented to me. But knowing where Elizabeth and Ike were was one thing. Knowing what Elizabeth was up to, or what her emotional state might be, was another.

I said: ''We're here. We might as well eat. Let's have two bowls of that gumbo.''

We sat down. Our knees brushed under the oil-clothed table. Sally smiled at me. On a jukebox somewhere in the background, to an incongruous disco beat, a raspy male voice chanted the single directive, ''Sucka dem heads and squeeza dem tips.''

I felt, for the moment, like a randy adolescent. There were worse ways to feel.

''That's the crawfish song,'' Sally said. ''In case you were wondering.''

Miss Ida served the gumbo herself. More stew than soup, smoky and dark as mud, it smelled of the saltwater marshlands that border the Gulf. In the middle of the bowl was a domed island of steamed rice. I had more appetite than I would have thought possible. Miss Ida hadn't been joking about the bellies on those oysters.

$\mathcal{T}$HIRTY-FOUR

SOUTH OF COMFORT the road plunged again through marshland, then crossed a second bridge over a second bayou. Beyond the bridge a wood-and-glass tollhouse marked the entrance to Berenson Island. The tollhouse was empty. A handwritten card posted on the window read "Closed to the Public" but nothing blocked the road. I drove past. A half mile further on we left the marsh and entered another world. Live oaks, bamboo, palmettos, and magnolias crowded each other in a jigsaw jungle that pressed in on both sides of the road. In the dull light the trees cast no shadows.

Two signs marked a fork in the road. The sign on the right said: BERENSON BOTANICAL GARDENS. In order to read the smaller print beneath that caption I had to get out of the car.

Four hundred acres of trees and flowering plants that represent botanical samplings from all over the globe. Varieties include thousand-year-old Himalayan evergreens; scarlet Mountain of the Moon daisies from equatorial Africa; Indian crape myrtle; Grecian hemlock and wormwood hedges; water gardens of Egyptian lotus; purple Chinese finger bananas; Japanese dwarf wisteria; jujube trees; Brazilian rubber plants; flowering acacia; black oranges from the province of Hunan; Philippine ginger lilies; ten thousand camellia bushes in five hundred varieties; Iris gardens; thirty thousand azaleas; winter-blooming Mongolian plum.

On the support frame below this sign a newer placard had been mounted; it said, in raised gold letters against a black background:

Aetna Oil is privileged to share with the Berenson family the responsibility for preserving this testament to the manifold wonders of God's work on Earth. We will not abuse this privilege.

—Rudolph Carere, President, Aetna Oil.

I snorted when I read this last piece of puffery then said to Sally through the car window, "Wheels within wheels. Berenson may be a pariah, but Aetna Oil doesn't mind taking the credit for some of his ecological good works. This Carere character is married to my cousin Diana."

"I know the daughter, Emily. In fact I'm supposed to go to a supper being given for her tonight."

"So am I. But at this point it isn't high on my list of priorities."

The sign marking the left side of the fork read: PRIVATE ROAD. KEEP OUT. Situated in a clearing in the woods, in the middle of the V formed by the road's divergence, was a small white frame house fronted by a screened-in porch. The screen had been blackened by age and mildew, but behind it I could make out the figure of a man dressed in white. The man had to be black. Since I could see neither his face nor his hands, his white clothes seemed to be standing at attention on their own, like the clothes of an invisible man.

"The Berensons' lodge is to the left," Sally said. "Can't we just drive on?"

As if in answer to that question the door of the screen porch opened and the man stepped into view. He was small and delicately made. He was also very old. The skin covering his high cheekbones had gone eggplant-purple with age. He wore a starched white shirt and white linen trousers, and in his right hand he carried a double-barreled shotgun. But he was holding the gun in a mannerly way, aimed, temporarily, at the ground. I walked over to where he stood. He did not raise the gun.

"Who you looking for?" he said.

"Mr. Berenson's granddaughter."

"Miz Elizabeth?"

"That's her. Did she come through here yesterday with a little boy?"

"Can't say she did. Then again," he added reflectively, "can't say she didn't."

"Can't say or won't?"

"They come to the same thing. What you want with Miz Elizabeth?"

"The little boy with her is my son."

Still holding the gun in his right hand, with his left he shaded his eyes against a nonexistent sun.

"Can't see too good no more. Anybody in that car with you?"

"Yes. A friend of Elizabeth's."

"Why don't you two come onto the porch and sit awhile? I got some things to say."

"We're in a hurry."

"Lots of folks in a hurry. But they don't always get no-where."

I wasn't in the mood for folk wisdom, but the way he held himself and the gun gave him all the authority he needed. Sally got out of the car.

On the porch, he motioned us to a wicker settee that crunched when we sat on it. Besides the settee, the porch contained a wooden rocker, a wicker table, and two wicker side chairs, all spotlessly clean and bleached bone white by sun and rain. He settled in the rocker with the gun resting, as if weightless, across his knees. Then he took a pair of rimless spectacles from the pocket of his shirt and carefully fitted them on. The lenses magnified his eyeballs so that they seemed to exist, disembodied, somewhat in advance of his small, well-shaped skull.

"Don't see many folks around here no more," he said conversationally. "Except for the ones that come through on the oil trucks. But those folks don't stop—not so's I can talk to them, anyway."

Sally said: "I remember you from the time I was here with Elizabeth four years ago. You're Mr. Foster, aren't you?"

He nodded. "Miz Elizabeth used to come here when she was a girl but she don't come no more. How long ago you say that was?"

"Four years."

"I seem to remember that time. But I can't rightly say I remember you."

"Have you lived here on the Island long?"

"All my life. But it wasn't called an island till Mr. Berenson took it over. Bayou La Chute circles it on three sides, cypress swamp on the fourth. Guess you can call it an island," he said. "People do. But that's stretching it some."

I wanted to get out of there, but Mr. Foster's manner chided my impatience. He settled back in his rocker as if we had all the time in the world. And as long he had that shotgun resting across his knees, he controlled the clock. His magnified eyeballs fastened on my face, shifted lazily to Sally's, then returned to mine and rested there. He was silent. But since he'd said he had things to say, I asked him the first question that came to mind.

"How'd Mr. Berenson come by this land?"

"Bought it," he said after a pause.

"I mean who owned it before him?"

"Depends what you mean. You mean right before Mr. Berenson, or before that?"

"Whichever. Both." I had no idea what this was about or where we were going, but he seemed satisfied, as if something was finally falling into place.

"Well, Choctaws had it first. Then the early settlers, I guess they got it in land grants. Then Southern Lumber bought it—that was around 1890."

"And Berenson?"

"That would be a story. More than one story." He rocked gently back and forth as if to jog his memory, but I didn't think his memory needed jogging.

"Southern Lumber went bust. My daddy worked for that company. He took care of the main building—it wasn't much more'n a couple of shacks strung together in a row. They let

us build this house on their land. My daddy built it by hand
with the help of some kin from over near town. When Mr.
Berenson bought the land he decided to let us stay on.''

"Did Southern Lumber sell out to Mr. Berenson?''

"I wouldn't say that. Not exactly.''

I smiled at him. "What would you say, Mr. Foster?''

He saw that I was trying to adjust to his rhythm. He
smiled, too, very slightly. "This was back in the thirties, the
hard times. But I guess Mr. Berenson never really suffered
hard times. When everyone else was going hungry, he was
scouting around for land to buy. Lots of land. One day one
of his men come by to look over the place. He liked it, too.
He liked it mighty fine.''

"But Berenson didn't buy it?''

"Not straight off. Not directly.''

"Explain.''

"Well, my brother Leon worked in the courthouse in
Comfort. See, Southern Lumber had been taken over by the
court. It had passed into—''

"Receivership?''

"That's it. That's the word. Then Mr. Berenson's man
come scouting around. As I say, he liked the place. But then
something happened.''

"What happened?''

"Quicker than you could say quick this land was bought
up. Some city folks bought it up. Some city folks from New
Orlyuns.''

"Who were they?''

"City folks.''

"Then what?''

He rocked to and fro. His body quivered slightly in a
soundless chuckle. "Not two months later those men sold
out to Mr. Berenson. I guess they couldn't hold on to the
place. Leon said they made a mighty big profit, though.
Mighty big.''

I was beginning to get a purchase on what he was trying
to say to me. "Did you ever tell Mr. Berenson any of this?''

His free-floating eyes settled on my forehead. "Now why
would I do that, son?''

"If somebody who worked for him used inside knowledge

to cheat him—well, that's something he might want to know.''

''Never was no way of telling what Mr. Berenson knew or didn't know. He always played his cards real close to his chest. But it wouldn't surprise me none if he had a pretty good idea some of his own people made money when this land changed hands. Wouldn't surprise me at all.''

''Why do you say that, Mr. Foster?''

''I remember the first time I saw that man. He was a big man, tall man in those days. Like you. But people do shrink some when they get old. Look at me. I never was what you'd call tall but I wasn't a runt neither, not back then. Anyhow, tall's what Mr. Berenson was. Everyone say: he a big cat, that one. Course they meant more'n one thing when they said that. They wasn't far wrong.''

''Why do you say—''

''Hold on. I'm getting there. He come by here one day before he bought the place, come right up to the door and said who he was real plain, then asked if he could sit a spell. If I recall, he sat just about where you sitting now. Might even've been that very same seat.''

His dilated pupils gleamed. On this porch, in this clearing in a jungle, I could feel the past pressing in on me. My skin went cold, as if I had just come to in a roomful of ghosts.

''That day, he said he had a proposition to make. Said I could stay on in this house—my daddy's house, but Daddy was years dead by then—if I would look out for his place when he wasn't here. He said he needed somebody who knew the land and had a feel for it, that he was just a stranger stepping in and he'd heard tell we been living on this land long as people could remember.''

''That still doesn't explain—''

''Hold on still. It was early spring, about a month later'n now. Reason I know is we saw two of those white birds fly over on their way to the pond. Course this was way back, when we had only a few of those birds left on the Island. Back before Mr. Berenson built that safe place for the birds. That sanctuary.'' He abruptly sat forward and peered at me. ''You seen that sanctuary yet? No, guess not. You never been here before. Maybe this young lady has.''

"Yes. Elizabeth took me there. It was early spring, and the egrets were just coming back from wherever they go in the winter."

"South America. Back before Mr. Berenson, those birds were leaving this place. Now we got thousands. Thousands and thousands. How that happened would be a story in itself. You might like to hear that story."

I knew he would tell it whether I wanted to hear it or not. For him, stories interlocked and commented on each other. All I could do was try to hold on to the point of departure—a day when Mr. Berenson had sat on this porch and told him things I wanted to hear now—while Mr. Foster spun his narrative web.

"Well, before Mr. Berenson took over, only a few of those white birds were left in the marshes. Did you know those birds called a fancy price? People used to put their feathers in fancy hats for women. Back then, lot of hunting and killing had been going on. But Mr. Berenson put a stop to all that. He got himself an idea how to save those birds. He took some men from round here—I was one of them—and we went tramping through the swamps and came back with ten of those white birds. Babies. Chicks. Then Mr. Berenson, he put those chicks in a bamboo cage we made out on a platform in the pond, and he raised them by hand. I mean he fed them himself with tadpoles and minnows and shrimps. Those little birds got used to that man. After all, he was their daddy.

"So when fall came, they began to shiver, but they didn't fly away. They wanted to stay. But Mr. Berenson, he had other ideas. He said he wasn't raising no house birds. He wanted those birds to fly away like all the other birds around here, then come back on their own. Know what he did? He locked those birds out of that bamboo cage. Still they stayed on. Then he broke that cage into pieces, but those birds just went into the trees around the pond. Every day Mr. Berenson went there to see had they left. And one day they had. When he went out to the pond that morning, those birds had flown clear away at last, just like he meant them to all along.

"Come spring, when the other birds flew back, Mr. Berenson kept an eye out for those ten white birds he had raised.

And sure enough, day came when he spotted eight of those ten on the branches of some trees by the pond. When those eight had eggs, he took the eggs and gave them to some other birds to hatch and raise. That made those white birds make more eggs, and more eggs still. See, he had it in mind to make those white birds breed. It all came about just as he planned. Those white birds flew away in the fall, just like they was meant to, but next spring they came back again: twenty-four of them that time, and each year more and more came back. This was a safe place. They knew that. They knew they'd be taken care of. And they was—first by Mr. Berenson, then by young Mr. Saul. Now we got thousands and thousands. Come back here in a month and you'll see those birds fly back. It is a sight. Don't you think so, young miss?''

Sally nodded.

I said: ''I like that story, Mr. Foster. I like the way you tell it. But let's go back to the day—''

''I'm getting there, son. Just give me time. Like I said, the day he asked me to stay on, Mr. Berenson was sitting just about where you are now. Then we saw those two white birds pass by overhead. That was when he looked at me and said something strange. Mighty strange. Said: 'Foster, when you catch one of your own men with his hand in the till, there might just be a reason to let him get by with it.' I said: 'Do tell.' He said: 'Yes sir, if he's a God-fearing Christian sonofabitch, and you let him steal just a little, it might put him right where you want him. Under your thumb.'

''Now I wouldn't have argued with Mr. Berenson,'' Foster said, ''not then or any other day. He wasn't a man I'd argue with. But all these years I been thinking to myself: you might just be wrong about that, Mr. Berenson. You a mighty smart man but that time you could've made yourself a mistake. 'Cause if you let people steal from you once, they might go on stealing. Maybe not right away. Maybe not even soon. But some day, when they think they can get by with it again, that's when they might make their move.''

''Mr. Foster,'' I said, hoping to move this to a conclusion, ''what do you mean?''

Instead of answering me directly—that wasn't his way—

he said: "Lot of changes going on around here, son. Lot of changes. You take this drilling for oil. It started back in the forties, just a couple wildcat operations in that patch of marshland the other side of town. Then it creep over this side of town, right up to the edge of Mr. Berenson's land. Mr. Berenson, he held off long as he could, but that was when young Mr. Saul was still alive. That boy sure did keep after his father about keeping this place clean. That's how he put it: 'clean.' " He paused. When he spoke again, I thought at first that his mind had slipped out of focus.

"You say you ain't seen our bird sanctuary yet?"

"Not yet."

"Well, nothing much there this time of year but a big empty platform in the pond, but in a month that platform'll be filled with those white birds again. Least it should be. Unless this new drilling scares those birds away."

"Is the drilling near the sanctuary?"

"Not too near. But not too far, neither. It's in the swamp the other side of the pond. If the wind's right I can hear that drilling right here on this porch. It do make a powerful loud noise." He paused again. "I did think it kinda funny," he said, "when they started drilling so near to that bird pond, but I guess they know what they're doing."

"What's funny about it?"

"That territory back there was young Mr. Saul's territory. I heard his daddy say more than once that was one spot he'd swore to keep clean. The truth is, Mr. Berenson hasn't come here much in the last twenty years, not since young Mr. Saul been gone. It was like he blamed this place for whatever it was happened to that boy. Not that they ever knew what did happen, you understand."

The way his disembodied eyes fastened on mine I couldn't tell whether he was testing me or simply hadn't received the latest report from whatever news network he was tapped into.

He sighed heavily. "Well, they do say money gets money. With young Mr. Saul gone so long, I guess his daddy just gave in."

"Gave in? Who to?"

"Why, to that lawyer of his. That Mr. McIntyre. That man always after Mr. Berenson to let the oil company do more

drilling, more drilling. I guess Mr. Berenson being so old
and all—we pretty near the same age—maybe he just gave
in at last. You know," he said, looking up at me slyly, "I
seen a lot of Mr. McIntyre lately. Yes sir, he drives past in
that big white car of his without even slowing down to wave.
I guess he's got important business to tend to. But he hasn't
changed much in forty-five years—not since he first came
round here scouting out this land for Mr. Berenson."

I sat forward. "Let me ask you, Mr. Foster. Just why are
you telling me all this?"

"You seem like a knowledgeable young fella."

"No other reason?"

"Well," he said, almost in a whisper, "Miz Elizabeth said
you was a lawyer. She said you might be coming this way."

"When did she say that?"

"Yesterday. When she stopped by here with that little boy
of yours."

"Can you tell us where they are?"

From the pocket of his starched white shirt he pulled a
key. When he leaned slightly forward to hand it to me he
misjudged the distance and nearly fell from his chair. I
caught him by the arms. His bones felt as light and brittle as
kindling.

"Set me back just so, if you please. Thank you kindly,
young man."

Then he handed me the key.

"This is to the main house," he said, still in the same
hushed whisper. "Near the chimneypiece in the big room
you'll see a map of the Island. Miz Elizabeth and your boy,
they're at the place marked Saul's cabin—that would be
young Mr. Saul—over near that pond those birds come back
to. Those white birds I spoke of before."

THIRTY-FIVE

THE GRAVEL ROAD curved through a forest of bamboo, took a final turn, and emerged into a broad cleared area surrounded by woods. On the right, across an expanse of lawn interrupted by thick rounded clusters of hydrangea bushes, was a series of buildings that appeared to have been constructed according to the dictates of convenience rather than of any comprehensive scheme. The main house was a large two-story wooden structure painted dull ocher. A deep verandah ran along its front; the rear addition had railed galleries above and below. Beyond, as we approached on the gravel drive, I could see several low outbuildings and a double-doored barnlike structure.

"Is that the garage?"

"I don't remember. It might be."

I parked the car in front of the double doors and got out. When I pulled at the right-hand door it swung outward, the hinges shrieking. Confronting me almost at chest level, like astounded eyes, were the headlights of a massive automobile that in the gloom had the look of a hearse. When I went round to one side, I saw it was a black Packard sedan dating back to the thirties. It seemed to have been designed for a race of giants.

To the left of the Packard, and grotesquely dwarfed by its

scale and grandeur, was a shiny blue Honda Accord. The keys were in the ignition.

I went back to the station wagon. "Her car's here," I said. "I'm pulling yours in next to it. With those oil people around, the less attention we attract, the better."

The lodge had the desolate look of a house long untenanted. Two small panes were missing from the fanlight above the front door. The verandah steps creaked and sagged as we mounted them. In this subtropical climate where everything rotted fast, wood was the first to go. I opened the door with the key Foster had given me, and a blast of musty air struck me in the face.

Lightning flashed. It was followed, seconds later, by a rolling clap of thunder that might have emanated from a dragon's bowels. Then the black skies opened and enormous raindrops crashed like tin cans on the roof of the porch.

"Christ, let's get inside."

The hall was dark as a cave. I set my canvas bag on the floor and found a light switch. When I flipped it on, nothing happened. "The electricity must be shut off. Let's see if we can find some candles."

A door to the right opened into an oversized room filled with the white-sheeted shapes of oversized furniture. When I pulled back the curtains at one of the windows, a cloud of powdery dust descended. In the scant illumination I located a pair of hurricane lamps on the baronial mantelpiece at one end of the room. I took a lamp down and set it on the hearth.

"Matches?"

"I don't smoke."

"Neither do I."

"Let there be light—and there was none."

Competing as it did with the thunder and rain, our nervous laughter seemed a feeble defense against ghosts. We talked in hushed voices as if someone might be listening.

"I'm going after them."

"We can't. Not in this rain."

"I've waited too long already. Stay here."

I went out to the hall and stripped off my tie, suit, and shoes. I was pulling my other clothes from the canvas bag when Sally appeared in the doorway of the living room. "Harry, what on earth . . . ?"

"Just changing clothes."

"Sorry," she said, and withdrew.

I unwrapped the pistol and shoved it into the pocket of my windbreaker. Then I dressed, folded my business clothes, and put them in the bag. Carrying my boots, I went back to the living room. Sally was standing by the window. Rain streamed down the panes behind her.

"A minute ago," she said, "when you left the room so abruptly, I thought you were leaving me here alone. That's why I came after you."

"I wouldn't have gone off like that, Sally. I'm staying long enough to get you settled somewhere safe. Upstairs, preferably."

"I'm not going with you?"

"I want to do this alone."

I was prepared for an argument, but something in my voice seemed to convince her.

"You won't be long?"

"I don't know how far the cabin is. Let's find that map."

The map was exactly where Foster had said it would be. It wasn't a professional job. The size of a large print, it had been painstakingly executed by someone who had painted small pictures to represent the places named on it. I located where we were: Berenson Lodge, marked by a meticulously exact representation of the exterior of the house as seen from the front. A little to the southwest, at what seemed no great distance from the lodge if the map's scale could be trusted, was the roughly circular outline of a pond, in the center of which was the drawing of a platform filled with nesting birds.

"Here's the cabin," Sally said, placing her finger on the map at a point not far from the pond.

"But according to this, there's no way to get there except on the bayou."

"That's true. The dock's at the end of a path leading from the lodge. See where it's marked? The day I came with Elizabeth she took me that far before she got cold feet."

"Any skiffs? Canoes?"

"All I saw was a kind of shed by the dock."

I studied the map for a few minutes, memorizing the location of the cabin in relation to the lodge, the bayou, and the pond. When I turned back to Sally she was staring at me. But since the light, what there was of it, was behind her I couldn't quite read the expression on her face.

"Please reconsider," she said. "Let me go with you."

"No, Sally. Ever since I met Elizabeth people have been trying to explain her to me. To warn me away from her or try to defend her. There's quite a lineup on the negative side, especially if you include Miss Ames. Miss Ames may be emotional, but the evidence she presented was highly specific. On the other side there's you. And a black woman who works across from Elizabeth on Philip Street. And Jasper, her doctor."

"What about Foster? What about Ike?"

"He's only nine years old, " I said, and in saying that felt I had betrayed him.

"Children know," she said, rubbing it in.

"Maybe. I want to do this my way."

"I won't argue with you, Harry. But I still think you're wrong."

I took her arm. "Let's find that room upstairs for you to wait in."

"Elizabeth showed me her room. I know where it is."

In the hall I grabbed the canvas bag with my things in it and followed Sally upstairs to Elizabeth's room. The room had that forlorn air peculiar to rooms in summer houses when they are visited off season. The white wicker furniture and straw matting, the brass bedstead, dulled now and spotted with mildew, the organdy bed cover and ruffled curtains at the window—surprisingly and conventionally girlish—these now seemed the debris of summer dreams. If Elizabeth had ever been allowed such dreams, or had allowed them to herself. Above the dressing table, a collection of unframed photographs had been mounted on the wall. Most of these appeared to be of her father and grandfather: big, dark men both. I studied a close-up of her father. What Sally had said was true: his eyes looked bruised and wistful. Judging from these photographs, Elizabeth had inherited the hawklike eyes of her grandfather.

"What are the empty spaces?" I asked Sally. "Looks like some pictures have been torn off the wall."

"Those must have been of Miss Ames."

THIRTY-SIX

SEATED IN THE stern of an aluminum canoe that I'd found in the shed, I pushed away from the dock with the paddle. The rain had stopped. The black and fuming bayou was so narrow a stream—no more than thirty feet across at this point—that I scarcely expected to feel any current. But before I put my paddle into the water, the canoe was seized by a sluggish and complicated force that swung it out toward midstream. Not willing to be controlled by it, I started to paddle.

With the ceasing of rain, the mass of clouds had begun to disassemble. Lines of light now slanted through treetops, touching the water at intervals and revealing vistas of layered undergrowth on the banks and beyond. Fields of palmettos and arrowhead ferns formed the forest's lower level, the palmettos spreading fanlike leaves above scaly trunks and the giant splayed fingers of exposed roots. At the bayou's edge stood rows of live oaks whose limbs created a dripping, moss-laden canopy overhead. At one point I had to steer to the left in order to avoid a massive branch that had collapsed into the stream. The current pulled moss forward from the branch so that it floated in the black water like the hair of a drowning woman.

Nothing stirred along the banks. Only the dip and swirl of

the paddle agitated the stillness of this world. That, and the
urgency that impelled me forward with a greater force than
the current's.

The oaks gradually gave way to water hickory, locust, and
a strangling web of vines. At a turn in the bayou the stream
opened into a swamp almost entirely taken over by bald cypress. The swamp looked blasted. Mossy beards depended
from swollen tree trunks. The water seemed more transparent
here; or perhaps it was merely that below the surface and
striving toward it I could see a fantastic submarine jungle
the same bleached gray as the moss. Crooked knees of dead
cypresses rose above the water. Two buzzards squatted on
the naked tops of trees. A piece of bark dropped to the water
not far from the canoe. It floated where it fell, without moving.

On the far side of the swamp there was a break in the wall
of cypresses. I steered toward it. This was where the bayou
recommenced. As I swung around the first turn I saw, on the
left, a small landing dock similar to the one back by the
lodge. An aluminum canoe, heavy with rain and half submerged in the water, was tied to one post. I back watered
my canoe, docked it, and secured it alongside its mate.

A path led away from the dock through deep woods. The
woods were cold, black, and impersonal but the path promised a destination. Then, at a bend in the trail, I came on the
cabin. Made of native pine with the bark on it, it had screen
porches in front and back and a corrugated tin roof. There
was no sign of Elizabeth or Ike, but from inside I could hear
rock music playing. The singer shouted angrily for love and
satisfaction.

The living room with its exposed beams was surprisingly
cheerful and almost hot. In the wood-burning stove a fire
shone. The room was furnished with comfortable chairs, Indian rugs, and chintz curtains; only a trace of mustiness remained in the air. Beyond the living room was a primitive
kitchen. On a pine trestle table were the remains of Miss
Ida's takeout order—cardboard cartons, stained paper plates
and napkins, and Coke bottles. In the midst of this litter a
Monopoly game had been set up; some pink-and-white
bills—small change—had fallen to the floor. A half-empty

bottle of Wild Turkey stood next to the sink, alongside a portable radio. The rock singer was escalating his furious demands. I switched him off.

"Ike," I said loudly. I repeated his name more loudly still. There was no answer.

I went back to the living room. It was the wrong moment to see the gun: a 12-bore shotgun propped against the wall behind the wood-burning stove. The anxiety I had been trying to keep in check detonated inside my head. I charged from the house and chased the path deeper into the woods. The air was heavy with pine and decay.

The trail diverged. On the right a worn footpath led again to the bayou, some thirty yards ahead. Two small spots of bright yellow exploded against the gloom. It had to be them. Two people in yellow slickers seated by the water's edge. Nearly shoulder to shoulder, they might have been fishing.

"Ike!"

At the sound of my shout the smaller of the two figures started, turned, jumped up, and hurtled toward me like a yellow cannonball that had been fired through the tree-lined alley.

"Dad." He threw his arms around my waist in an embrace that knocked the wind out of me. I cradled his head to my stomach. "Elizabeth was right," he said. "She said you would come."

"Did she?"

Elizabeth was standing now, facing us, but still at the water's edge. At that distance I could not see her face.

"Are you all right?" I said to Ike.

"Sure I'm all right. I'm fine."

"Why didn't you call me?"

"I tried."

"But you didn't leave a message."

"Elizabeth said not to. She said no one but you should know where we were."

"But unless you left word, how could I know?"

"Well, you found us, didn't you?"

His logic was irrefutable.

"I need to talk to Elizabeth," I said.

"But don't be mad."

I didn't reply. With my arm too tightly around him, I steered him toward where the figure in the yellow slicker stood waiting.

"Hello, Harry," Elizabeth said. She started to extend a hand but let it fall by her side when she saw my face. I stood at a safe distance from her.

"Hello, Elizabeth. Ike said you knew I'd come."

"I hoped so."

The vivid slicker did even more for her than her shimmering golden cloak. Above it her face, with its strong jaw and high cheekbones, had a kind of brutal distinction. Her hair was a thick black tangle. Her eyes burned, but she held herself absolutely still.

"Let's go back to the cabin," I said.

She nodded and walked on, leaving me behind with Ike. The way she held her shoulders did not suggest an attitude of contrition.

"Did you ever see a place like this, Dad? What about that swamp back there? Elizabeth and I went canoeing there this morning before it rained. And what about that rain? When it hit the tin roof it sounded like an avalanche."

"I'll bet it did."

"Elizabeth's dad used to bring her here. He taught her how to fish and shoot. She was going to teach me how to use the shotgun but she couldn't find any shells."

"I don't want you playing with guns," I said, feeling the weight of the pistol in my windbreaker.

"I wouldn't have been playing. I would have been learning."

"I stand corrected."

Ike lowered his voice. "Elizabeth thinks you're great, Dad. She said she knew she could trust you the first time she met you."

"Did she?"

"She's great, too. She knows all about things boys like: things like shooting and cheating at Monopoly. We let each other cheat. It was more fun that way. It made the game go quicker."

"Just a gal who's one of the guys."

Having caught my tone, he turned to read my face.

"Something like that," he said, and was silent.

When we neared the cabin I took his arm. "Ike, I need to talk to Elizabeth alone."

"Okay."

"What will you do?"

"Take a walk. Go down by the dock."

"I promise I won't be long."

"Okay, Dad." He turned to Elizabeth, who was standing by the door of the porch. "See you, Elizabeth."

"See you, Ike." She raised her hand in a small salute. Clearly my arrival had interrupted their intimacy.

When Ike disappeared around the bend in the trail, I said to Elizabeth: "Get inside." My voice was barely controlled.

In the living room I grabbed her from behind by the shoulders and swung her around. My arm came back, ready to hit her across the face, hard. She didn't flinch; she looked almost expectant. That look checked me.

"Go ahead and get it out of your system."

I let my arm fall. "I don't think I would like myself much."

"Then read this." Under the slicker she dug into the pocket of her jeans and withdrew a small envelope, which she handed to me.

The message was printed in capital letters on Pontchartrain Hotel notepaper. It said, "Give us the letter or Preston's boy will pay."

"When did you get this?"

"Yesterday. It was left for me at the hotel desk."

"After Jack was murdered?"

"Then he is dead."

"You didn't know that?"

"I guessed it. I didn't see his body, if that's what you mean. I never got past the blood in the dining room. And I deliberately haven't listened to the news."

"Elizabeth, I need to get this straight. Tell me what happened yesterday morning. Tell me why you went to Philip Street."

"Jack called me."

"At the hotel?"

"Yes."

"How did he know you were there?"

"It wasn't hard to figure. I had gone there before, when he pulled one of his rages."

"What did he say?"

"He said he had to talk to me. He said the way things stood between us didn't count. This was strictly business."

"Did he say what kind?"

"No."

"So you went."

"With misgivings. I wanted to tell him I was definitely getting a divorce. Since he had phoned, it seemed as good a time as any."

"What time did he phone?"

"About seven-thirty. I didn't get there until a little before nine."

"Then what?"

"The front door wasn't locked. I went in and saw the blood. That's when I called you. Then I panicked. I couldn't stay alone in that house, so I drove back to the hotel."

"Having set me up?"

"Don't say that. I never intended to run away. Really I didn't. But when I got to the hotel the desk clerk handed this to me," she gestured to the piece of paper in my hand. "He said it had just been left for me."

"Did he say who by?"

"Just some man. I couldn't have missed him by more than a few minutes. I don't want to think about it."

"What about the will?"

"I had written it the night before. You know how desperate I was when I left your apartment. I thought making a will would at least give me some control over . . ." She gestured with her hands, palms upward. "Anyway, I remembered the will as I was leaving the Pontchartrain yesterday. I asked the desk clerk to have it delivered to you."

"What did you do then?"

"I acted completely on instinct. You may find that hard to believe, but it's true. Whenever I'm in a tough situation, I always do what instinct tells me."

"Why didn't you call the police?"

"I can't answer that question, not rationally. I simply don't trust the police."

"Have you had many dealings with them?"

She looked at me intently. "No, of course not," she said. "I suppose it's just that they represent a kind of law I don't have much faith in." She laughed. "Even if you do."

"Nevertheless, you've felt free to use me as much as it's suited your purposes."

"If you insist on putting it that way." She hesitated. "I don't know whether I can make you understand this. I don't have much faith in the law, Harry, but I do have faith in you."

"Am I supposed to be flattered?"

"I wouldn't try to flatter you. Not now, anyway. The night I met you I had arrived at a point in my life when I knew I would have to start playing by other people's rules. Those rules included the law. After all, I had decided to divorce Jack."

"You don't need a divorce now."

"I couldn't have known what would happen."

"You could have made it happen."

She shook her head slowly. "You can't think I killed Jack. You can't think me capable of that."

"I don't know what you're capable of."

"I said to you once that I hadn't killed anyone. I was joking, but it still happens to be true."

"Let's go back to yesterday. When the desk clerk gave you that message—what then?"

"I told you. That's when instinct took over. I knew I had to get to a safe place, fast, and I had to take Ike with me. I had the desk clerk call your office but you had already left. Well, if someone was trying to get at me through Ike, I didn't want to be responsible for what might happen to him. I wanted to make it *not* happen. So I rented a car and drove uptown to his school. The secretary recognized me. Mary Broussard, the same secretary who was there when I graduated eleven years ago. Mary used to cover for me sometimes when I skipped school. She would say Miss Taylor had called in to report me sick."

"You have friends in high places."

"I've always had friends, when I've chosen to have them. Anyway, I told her—"

"I know what you told her. Grandmother filled me in on that bunch of crap. Can you imagine what we felt? You talk about panic—what about ours?"

Her eyes widened. It was clear that, to a large extent, she could remain unaware of other people's feelings when it was convenient to be unaware. To be reminded ruffled her, but only slightly.

"I want to know about Ike," I said. "I want to know what you told him."

"You may not believe this—I keep saying that, don't I?— but I told him the truth. Without details. I didn't even know the details. I said I was in trouble, that someone had threatened him in order to frighten me, and that I was going to take him to a safe place until the trouble was over. I said you were trying to make it be over."

"I see. You conned him by turning me into some kind of hero. Mr. Fixit."

"He and I have had a good time, for what that's worth."

"It's worth exactly nothing. I've had a rotten time. So has Grandmother. Why didn't you call?"

"I let Ike call once, from a gas station. When we got to the Island, the phones in the lodge had been disconnected, and there's never been a phone in this cabin. Besides, if you want to know the truth, I was afraid to call."

"That's dime-store paranoia."

"I have every reason to be afraid. If Jack was dead—and I was pretty sure he was—I figured they'd want me dead too."

I couldn't argue with her on that score. I had the feeling she was right.

"Elizabeth, what letter do those people want?"

"I have no idea."

"Think, then. Jack may have been killed for that letter."

"Maybe so. But I don't know anything about it."

She baffled me, stirred my anger. I could hear the strained patience in my voice when I said, "Then we'll have to be systematic. Tell me what you do with old letters."

"What does anyone do? Throw them away."

"Haven't you ever kept any letters? From anyone?"

"I'm not sentimental about letters."

"What about letters from your father?"

"Father never wrote me any. As far as I can remember, the only mail he ever sent me was a picture postcard from Panama, when he went there on some business for Grandad."

"What did you do with it?"

She hesitated. "You're right," she said. "I didn't throw it away."

"Where is it?"

"In the bank box, I think."

"What did it say?"

"Nothing more consequential than 'Wish you were here.' "

"Are there any other letters in that bank box?"

She sat down in a chair by the wood stove. I could see that she was letting herself take the issue seriously. After a pause she said slowly, "Only one I can think of."

"Who from?"

"Grandad."

"Tell me what it said."

"I told you I wasn't sentimental about letters. As usual, I spoke without thinking. I am sentimental about this one."

"Why?"

She got up, turned from me, and walked over to a window. She said, "That question stirs up a lot of memories. I feel shivery, the way I do when I talk to Dr. Jasper."

"I'm not your psychiatrist."

"But you do ask loaded questions."

"It was a simple question."

"Simple questions carry the heaviest freight. Like 'Why?' "

"Tell me."

She inhaled deeply. "Grandad sent me that letter on my eighteenth birthday. I was at Radcliffe. It was my first term there, but I was already coming apart at the seams. In spite of that, I remember exactly where I was sitting when I read the letter. On a sofa in front of the fireplace in Bertram Hall.

When I started to cry, I went into the bathroom and finished reading it there.''

"Why did you cry?''

"That question again! 'Why?' I cried because it was the first letter like that I had ever received from him, or from anyone else for that matter. And the last, as it's turned out. I told you once that Grandad and I were close in a distant kind of way. This letter wasn't distant. At least part of it wasn't. I need to explain that. Actually, it was two letters. One, the longest part, was something that I never read all the way through. It was the other letter that mattered. For one thing, it was handwritten. Coming from Grandad, you'd better believe that meant something!

"The letter started out 'My dearest Elizabeth.' Well, he had never called me that before. On that day, in the mood I was in, that salutation by itself would have been enough to make me cry. He went on to say— Do you know, Harry, that I could quote most of that letter verbatim? But I'll spare both of us that; I think I would break down all over again. What he said was that my having gone off to college had made him realize how much it had meant, over the years, to have me growing up in his house, especially with Father gone. He said I truly was Father's daughter—you can guess how that got to me. Then he praised my beauty, my intelligence, my strength of character. God! Strength? For him to write that to me when I was coming apart seemed the cruelest of ironies, but he wasn't being ironic. Then he said that on the occasion of my birthday he wanted me to know he was doing for me what he had failed to do for Father: he was making me independent. Of course, he meant financially—''

"Elizabeth, you told me you didn't know any details about the trusts your grandfather set up for you.''

"I don't, really, but it was all there in that document he enclosed with his letter. To me, the letter was the important thing.''

"Didn't you look at the document?''

"I told you. I never finished it. I just flipped through it, but it all seemed so technical.''

"Can't you remember anything?''

"Only the part about Berenson Island. He summarized that

part in his own letter. You see, it had to do with Father—''

''What about the Island?''

''Grandad wrote that he intended the Island to go to me because Father—''

''All of it?''

She frowned. ''No, but most of it. The rest would belong to the Berenson Foundation.''

''What else do you remember?''

''He said he had established a trust. An irrevocable trust. The part of the Island designated for me would become mine when I'm thirty, or sooner in the event of his death.''

''Do you remember what areas your share would include?''

''The part Father considered his own domain. That would be all this around here—the cabin, the land along the bayou, back to the bird sanctuary and beyond that, too. It's a strange thing, Harry. Until yesterday, until I came here with Ike, Grandad's giving me so much of the Island didn't mean much to me. I loved it when I was young, when I came here with Father, but after what happened to him I hated it. Then yesterday, when I needed a place to hide, this was the first, the only place I could think of. Being here with Ike, doing with him things Father and I used to do, has made some of the hatefulness go away.''

I said quietly, ''You were here with your father the day he disappeared.''

She nodded. ''I was only eight. Afterwards I suppose I was asked a lot of questions but I don't remember them. Since then, I've never talked about it to anyone except Dr. Jasper, and then only once.''

''Can you tell me now?''

''I think so. Is it important?''

''It may be.''

''Then I'll try. There really isn't that much to tell. It's just that one minute Father was here and the next he was gone.'' She began pacing the room. ''You see, Mother always stayed at our cottage over by the lodge. Father and I usually did, too, but sometimes we would come spend the night in this cabin. Father called it 'getting away from it all.' 'Let's go get away from it all,' he would say, and I would shout 'Let's

do!' He made it into a sort of game, the way he did so many
things. I've often wondered what 'away from it all' meant
to him. I mean, whether he meant Mother''—she laughed
shortly—''or something more abstract. But it's dangerous to
second-guess the dead.''

"Go on.''

''We came here late in the afternoon and spent the night.
What I remember is what happened the next morning. Or
maybe it was still night: I think it was dark. He said he had
heard a noise and was going outside to see what it was. The
last thing he said was, 'Just lie there, honey, and stay absolutely quiet. Go back to sleep if you can. But whatever you
do, just stay here and stay quiet.' Then he left the bedroom
and closed the door behind him. I heard the screen door slam.
That was the last I saw of him. I didn't even tell him good-
bye.'' Her voice broke. ''That was the last time I saw him,''
she said, ''and nothing's ever been the same for me since.''

I said: ''There are two things I have to tell you, Elizabeth.
This isn't the best time, but I do have to tell you. The first
concerns your father. An oil crew here on the Island has
found the remains of a man who may have been murdered.
That man could be your father.''

I had steeled myself to expect a violent reaction. But Elizabeth only looked at me steadily for a time. Then she said:
''I knew Father was murdered. I've always known it.''

''How did you know?''

''The only alternative was suicide.'' She corrected herself:
''I mean the only alternative was that he had committed suicide. Of course, people who plan to commit suicide do very
strange things. They straighten their desks and go to the hair-
dresser's. They go to lunch at Galatoire's''—she smiled—
''and enjoy every mouthful. They even keep their psychiatric
appointments and speak calmly of their own despair. But
through the years the one thing I've held on to, the thing
that I've known, is that Father would never have left me
alone in this cabin, not if he could have prevented it. I trusted
him absolutely. I still do.''

I was silent.

''I've often thought about this,'' she said. ''I've often
thought that when he told me to stay quietly in bed he was

trying to protect me. I've wondered about that noise he heard outside, about what he thought he might have heard. Because when he left me, it was as if he was going toward something unknown and wanted to keep me safely uninvolved. Of course," she added, "as the years have proved, that's not been possible. Because now someone wants me dead, too. I know that, Harry, just as I've known from the start that Father was murdered."

"Elizabeth, I have to go back a minute. To that letter your grandfather wrote you. You say it's in your bank box. Did Jack know about that letter?"

"I never told him about it, no. I haven't thought about it in years." Then she stopped herself. "Wait, though. Right after we were married, Jack started pestering me about putting that bank box in both our names. Finally, this year, I gave in. It didn't mean anything to me, after all. I don't keep anything there except a few pieces of jewelry and some old stock certificates."

"And that letter."

"Yes, but why would Jack—?"

"Elizabeth, listen to me. In that letter, did your grandfather mention the restrictions he had placed on the oil drilling here at the Island? Can you remember?"

"Yes. That was one of his main points. He said there was a lot of pressure on him to expand the operation and that by setting land aside in my name, and in Father's memory, he wanted to end the issue once and for all."

"What are your views about the drilling?"

"I don't have any views."

"Why not?"

"As I said, I haven't been to the Island in years. Well, I did come here once, but even that was four years ago. Until yesterday, I had no real interest in coming here again."

"And now?"

"You keep pressing me! If you insist, I suppose my views would be like Father's. Maybe not so adamant, but more or less the same. After all," she said lightly, "it isn't as if I need the money."

"Elizabeth, there's one more thing I have to tell you. I

don't quite know how to put it. I think your grandfather may have had second thoughts—''

"About what? Have you seen him?"

"About giving you so much financial independence."

"I don't understand."

"Apparently he's authorized McIntyre to start an inquiry into the issue of your legal competence."

"Competence?"

"If a court judged you incompetent for psychiatric reasons, then someone would have to be appointed to handle your affairs."

I could see from the stricken look on her face that she had taken it in. "But is that possible?" she asked.

"I told McIntyre the idea was absurd. But it does mean your grandfather—"

"No." She came over to where I stood. Her face was contorted. She raised a clenched fist. For a moment I thought she would hit me, but she only brought her fist down in a sweeping gesture. "No!" she said again, shouting the word this time.

"No what?" I said quietly.

"Grandad would never, not ever, try to do that to me."

"But it's possible that he has tried."

"You don't understand. I said Father was someone I trusted absolutely. Well, in a different way Grandad is too. He meant it when he said he wanted me to be independent. I know he wouldn't go back on his word." She grabbed both my arms. "Take me back to New Orleans, Harry. I'll go to the police. I'll do whatever you say. But first I have to see Grandad."

Outside the house, Ike yelled.

When I ran to the porch I saw him racing toward us on the path that led from the dock. "Dad!" His face was white, wild-eyed. I was out the door in time to catch him when he stumbled and fell.

"There's a man," he said. "A man back there on the bayou."

"What man?"

"He was too far away to tell. But he's heading this way."

I held Ike's shoulders to calm him. "Just tell me what you saw."

"This man. In a canoe like ours."

"Exactly where was he?"

"Making the turn back by the swamp."

"Did he see you?"

"I don't think so."

"Was he alone?"

"Yes."

I thought: And so is Sally. The ground rocked under my feet. I said to Elizabeth, "We've got to get back to the lodge. We have to get Sally out of there."

"Sally?"

"Your friend Sally Montrose. I left her there alone."

"But—"

"No questions. Just tell me: is there another way to the lodge?"

"Only the bayou."

"Any way to the dock except the path?"

"Through the woods."

"That's it, then."

In order to stay out of sight of the path we had to head deep into the woods and then circle back toward the dock. Elizabeth led the way. We kept our heads down, but pine branches tore our faces and vines caught our feet. Gripping Ike's hand, I pulled him along with me. I was breathing hard when Elizabeth stopped, turned, and said, "We've gone far enough. Now we cut left." When I saw a break in the black-green wall of woods ahead of us, I said, "Quiet. Go slow. We don't even know if he's docked yet." I moved in front of Elizabeth. "Stay back with Ike."

I shoved my right hand into my pocket and felt the gun. As I moved forward, the path and the dock gradually came into view. Looking to the left, toward the cabin, I saw no one. But instead of the two canoes that had been fastened to the dock there was now only one, tied to the other post. If I had had any doubts about our visitor's intentions, that single canoe dispelled them.

"Now!" I called in a hushed shout, and Elizabeth and Ike

moved forward through the undergrowth. The noise they made crashed in my ears.

"He must have sent the other canoes downstream," I said. "Well, we're leaving him stranded. Elizabeth, get in first. Ike, stay in the center of the canoe. I'll shove off."

Elizabeth moved expertly and lightly toward the rear, but when Ike climbed in after her the canoe rocked dangerously. As he turned to face me, I was steadying the canoe with my back to the path. All I saw was the fear in his eyes when he lifted his arm to point.

"There he is, Dad. He sees us and he's running."

Ike's fear held mine in check. I did not look back. I untied the rope and threw it into the water. In a single movement I stepped into the canoe and with my left foot shoved away from the dock. The canoe rocked again under my unsteady weight. My eyes caught Elizabeth's.

"Paddle," I said. "Back water."

Half crouching as we moved rearward into the stream, I turned to see for the first time what it was that charged toward us down the trail from the cabin. Head lowered and hunched in on himself, holding in his right hand something black and metallic—but it didn't look like a gun—the man seemed propelled by a force that was greater, or less, than human. Without faltering when he reached the end of the dock he hurled himself at us through the air and crashed with the weight of a boulder into the pitch-black water. The waves nearly capsized us.

When he came up for air, the first thing I saw was that his left hand held the rope fastened to the bow of our canoe. The second thing I saw was his face.

"That's him," Ike said behind me. "The man outside our house last Sunday."

Against the black water his face stood out like something hacked from granite by an unskilled sculptor. His eye sockets looked small and empty above a nose that had been smashed flat by too many fights. Thick lips drawn back from his teeth in a grimace, he shook water from his head violently, like a dog, and spat twice with his tongue.

I could not tell how tall he was, but his massive head and shoulders rose above the water's surface as he pulled the canoe toward him by the rope. His feet must have been planted firmly in the muck at the bottom of the bayou.

When I took the gun from the pocket of my windbreaker, nothing in his face showed that he saw it. He just kept on pulling, with the ferocious concentration of an animal.

Behind me, Elizabeth said in a cold furious voice: "Do it, Harry. Don't think. Just do it."

But it was Ike's voice, when he said, "Do it, Dad," that decided me. With my right thumb I cocked the hammer. Then, holding the gun in both hands, I raised it high, brought it down, aimed, and pulled the trigger. The hammer clicked on an empty chamber.

He heard that click. He looked up, saw the gun and my face above it. We were so close that I could have leaned forward and touched him without straining. Our eyes met in a split second of communion before I saw his right hand, his free hand, rise from the water still gripping that piece of black iron. Without cocking the hammer this time, I pulled the trigger.

Thrown backwards against Ike's knees, I struggled to right myself and the heaving canoe as the explosion rocketed down the waterway. In front of me I could see the man thrashing on his back in the water, arms flailing furiously, but when I felt the canoe seized again by a force that wasn't the current's I knew he still held the rope. He was using it to pull himself upright.

I waited until I saw his face rise spluttering and choking from the bayou. The bullet had torn away part of his left cheek and ear, and blood streamed from the wound into the agitated water. He was gasping savagely for breath, mouth open, when I cocked the hammer, aimed, and fired again.

For a moment his face registered nothing but a freezing unbelief. Then howling, blood pouring from his mouth like the vomit of some terrible water animal, he subsided at last below the water's black surface. Even dying, he held fast to the rope as if bent on dragging us down with him. I untied the rope from the canoe and threw it into the water. It sank, too.

When I turned, Elizabeth was leaning forward and embracing Ike from behind. Her head of tangled black hair was positioned on his shoulder as if to shield him from what had happened, but one of his ice-blue eyes was still visible and staring at me. It told me he was seeing his father for the first time.

He moved away from Elizabeth and bent toward me. "You had to do it, Dad." That was all he said but it was the only absolution that could have counted.

THIRTY-SEVEN

WE GROUNDED THE canoe downstream from the dock near the lodge and left it hidden in a thicket of reeds. The bayou's late afternoon silence was profound, but the two shots I had fired still echoed in my head.

I said to Elizabeth: "Where's the garage from here?"

"This way."

The wide doors of the garage stood open. Elizabeth's rented car and Sally's station wagon were exactly where we had left them, miraculously intact. At the very least I had expected slashed tires. Even the keys were still in the ignition of Elizabeth's car. "They're too sure of themselves. Elizabeth, I want you and Ike to get in the wagon and stay there. Here're the keys. I'll go find Sally."

"What if—"

"Don't say it. Those men travel together. The one who came after us—I think he was used for special errands. The other two must be around here. Sally would have heard them drive up. I'm counting on that. And I have the gun."

I didn't say that there was only one bullet left in it and that, like a fool, I'd left the box of cartridges in my canvas bag in Elizabeth's room.

"I'll find her. When you see us coming, start the engine

and move out fast. Ike, you get in the backseat, stay down, and do just as Elizabeth says.''

He nodded.

''Elizabeth, if you hear commotion from the main house, leave then. Don't wait for us. Whatever happens, I want you to get Ike safely back to Grandmother's and call the police. The man you want is Captain Lanaux.'' I spelled his name for her. ''Got that?''

''Harry, we're not leaving you and Sally here.''

''If you have to, do it. We still have your car.''

About fifty feet from the lodge I moved off the driveway into undergrowth. Keeping down, I headed toward the back of the house. A faint light shone in a rear window that could have been the kitchen's. Someone had lighted a candle: someone who had a match. There was too much open space between me and the window for me safely to get to it and look in. I would have been a fool to try.

Circling behind the house, I finally came to the expanse of lawn broken by rounded masses of hydrangeas that Sally and I had skirted when we arrived. This area was bordered, on my left and straight ahead, by the entrance road that became the driveway; and on the other two sides by the lodge and the grove of woods behind it where I then stood. Across the lawn I recognized the dark blue sedan in the parking area near the front porch. I studied the house as if to read its secrets. In the dull light, shadowed by the overhang of the first- and second-story galleries, the tall windows were blank. I scanned the upper gallery, trying to determine where Elizabeth's room might be.

Something—a huddled mass, a dark shape—stirred on the gallery. Afraid that I was too visible, I moved back into the undergrowth. I saw the shape was Sally.

I stepped forward just long enough to catch her attention and signal her to get back and stay quiet. Then I flattened myself on the grass and, keeping close to the foundations of the house, pulled myself on my elbows to the middle of the rear wing.

''Sally, can you hear me?''

''Yes.''

''We've got to get you down from there. Elizabeth and

Ike are waiting in the garage. Can you jump?''

"It's too high.''

"Listen. Climb over the railing and gradually let yourself down. Hold onto the edge of the porch.''

She quickly and nimbly did as I said. Knowing I would be visible to anyone in the house who might look from a window, I stood and reached up to grab her legs. Even straining, I could barely touch the soles of her shoes.

"Let go and drop straight,'' I said, and without hesitating or looking down, she did.

I had made a circle of my arms to catch her as she fell. When I closed them around her body in a fierce embrace, the impact of her weight knocked me backwards onto the grass, where my head hit the ground and I lay flattened with her body on top of me.

"Are you all right?'' she said, rolling away from me.

"Once I get my breath.''

It was an absurd moment and we both knew it.

"Make for the garage,'' I said. "Whatever happens, don't stop.''

Instinct made me take the revolver from my pocket. As we ran past the front of the house the door opened and a hatted figure stepped onto the verandah. I never knew whether he saw us or not. Scarcely aiming, I raised the pistol and fired. The man disappeared backwards into the house.

Above the sound of my heartbeat I heard a dull roar, the screeching and scraping of tires gouging through gravel, and then the station wagon shot around the bend in the drive. Ike threw the rear door open, and with the wagon still moving, Sally and I fell into the car. That left Elizabeth alone in the driver's seat, where she had always wanted to be.

Elizabeth floored the accelerator and the car lurched forward, sending a shower of gravel into the air behind us. Once again, as when Sally had driven from the parking garage that morning, I marveled at the force of the wagon's momentum once it got going, the sense that force conveyed of its having an unbreakable will of its own. As we roared past the open front door of the lodge, it occurred to me that I might have killed two men that day, but I forgot that when I saw the running figure who emerged from the rear of the house and raced not toward us but through the hydrangea bushes on the lawn that separated the lodge from the entrance road.

I registered these facts: the runner was the long-armed short man who had chased Sally and me down the ramp of the garage; he had a gun; he was trying to reach the entrance road before we did.

Elizabeth had seen him. Her hands gripped the wheel so tightly that her knuckles turned white. She had no choice but to follow the curve of the driveway as it led to the entrance road. If she had tried to forge a diagonal path across the lawn she would have risked crashing into those clustered bushes behind which I had already lost sight of the runner.

As the entrance road rushed toward us, Elizabeth said "Hold on" and demonstrated her own technique for taking a sharp turn. She went into it full speed, swung the wheel to the right for one second, then shifted sharply to the left. The weaving motion spun us around the curve, but the wagon's rear end shimmied and rocked as if bent on pursuing a direction of its own.

The runner had already reached the road and was blocking it forty yards ahead. Lifting his gun in both hands, he pointed it straight at the windshield of the car.

"Get down," I yelled, throwing Sally and Ike forward onto the floor of the backseat as a bullet popped through the windshield and sent glass pellets over our heads.

Even if that bullet had gone through the windshield on the driver's side and crashed into Elizabeth's skull, she would probably have found it in herself to do what she did next. Her face was hidden from me, but the look in her eyes when I glimpsed them in the rearview mirror was demonic. She was racing toward liberation. She knew that this was her chance to let rage explode. The short man with the gun must have sensed that he was outmatched; he threw himself off the road to escape the oncoming machine. It wasn't enough to save him.

In the few seconds since she had come out of the turn Elizabeth had hit seventy. To keep going straight was the safest, the only thing to do. But with a quick shift of the steering wheel she left the road and plowed over the figure who, his back to us, was scrambling to get away. Metal met bone with a whump as the man disappeared beneath the wheels, then the three of us in the rear were thrown to the left when Elizabeth veered the wagon back onto the road and headed out of Berenson Island.

Elizabeth's body trembled as she sank back into the driver's seat. She inhaled enormously. "Well," she said, "I did it."

Did what? I thought. Murder? Maybe now she could truly say that she had done everything once. If not more than once.

Sally and Ike were huddled in the right-hand corner of the backseat, clinging to each other as if afraid of being swept away. Their astonished faces might have been staring straight ahead into the eye of a hurricane.

As Foster's frame house curved into view, Elizabeth began the process of braking the car.

"Keep going, Elizabeth. There's another man back there. I shot at him but he may come after us."

"Foster would never have let those men get through if he could have prevented it. If he's hurt, we'll have to take him with us."

"Then stay here. I'll go."

It didn't take long to see what had to be seen. Foster lay, facedown, on the floor of the porch just inside the screen door. He seemed to have been hurled there like a bunch of old rags. Blood streaked the wall and floor. Whoever struck the blow had spent more force than was necessary to smash the fragile shell of bone that had been his skull. I looked around for his shotgun. I didn't see it. There was no time to search.

At the car, I said: "There's nothing we can do but get out of here—fast."

Elizabeth hit the steering wheel with her closed fist. Then tears welled from her lower lids as if her violent gesture had agitated a brimming cup. I had never seen her cry before.

"Do you want me to drive?" I said.

"No."

"Then move."

We left the Island. As we crossed the bayou I looked back, but all I saw was a road, empty in twilight, that disappeared into jungle.

$\mathcal{T}$HIRTY-EIGHT

"TELL ME WHAT happened after I left you, Sally."

"You should have let me go with you."

"Maybe, but we had a bad time, too. You were able to take care of yourself."

"When I heard a car on the gravel I looked out Elizabeth's window. The car pulled up in front of the house. I couldn't see who was in it. It was the men who were after you this morning, wasn't it?"

"Yes. Did they break into the house?"

"I didn't hear anything. They must have had a key."

"Go on," I said.

"I knew there was nowhere I could hide if they searched the house carefully. So I did the obvious thing. I went out onto the gallery, closed the window behind me, and sat down between two windows where no one could see me from inside. I took your bag with me too, so they wouldn't know anyone had been there. I'm afraid it's still back on the gallery."

"Forget it. Did they come upstairs?"

"If they did, I didn't hear them. At some point I realized they weren't looking for anyone in the house. I felt safer after that."

Then we were passing through Comfort. It was dark by

now. The flames on Miss Ida's "Home Cooking" sign burned brightly and the bars and fast-food joints on Main Street were doing a booming business. I told Elizabeth to drive slowly. A tank-sized wagon with a bullet hole in the windshield, chauffeured by a woman who looked like a mythological figure, was enough to attract attention without taking chances. As it turned out, the policeman had left his post near the church, and no one gave us a second glance.

When Elizabeth reached the road that wound through marshland toward the main highway, we picked up speed again. Once, car lights appeared out of the blackness and seemed to head straight for us. Elizabeth veered to the right as the car went past. I recognized the driver as our lights caught his face. It was McIntyre. He didn't glance our way. Like Elizabeth, he drove with grim-faced concentration.

I said to Sally: "You're right. Those men didn't expect to find anyone in the lodge. They knew, or thought they knew, where we were. One of those men came after us. Probably the hulk you saw on the sidewalk at the garage. I shot him."

"How could they know you were at the cabin?"

From the driver's seat, Elizabeth said: "It has to be some-one close to the family. I've always known that."

"Like McIntyre?" I said. "That was him we just passed on the road. He could have been on his way to the Island."

"But if he knew—"

"That's the question. If he was behind what went on to-day, the Island should be the last place he would head for."

At a pay telephone just before the causeway I had Eliza-beth stop so that I could put a call through to Grandmother. I told her Ike was safe and that we were on our way home. I didn't tell her that we would be making another stop first.

When I went back to the car I got in next to Elizabeth. "We'd better talk," I said.

Her thoughts were elsewhere. "I'm glad I did what I did back there," she said.

"You were glad even before you knew Foster was dead."

She gave me a slow sidelong glance.

"I keep learning more and more about you, Elizabeth. That doesn't mean I understand you. You deliberately ran that man down. He was trying to get out of the way. He had his back to you. The tire marks will show that—so will the position of his body. That kind of evidence is going to be hard to explain.''

''Explain?''

''Do you really think we can leave all this behind us? Just like that? We're going to have to account for it. All of it.''

''What about the man you shot?''

''Him too.''

''These weren't men, Harry. They were *things* that wanted us dead. At least they wanted me dead.''

''Maybe. They murdered Foster. And you've got a bullet hole in the windshield to support your view. But the fact remains that you drove this car off the road to run a man down.''

''In cold blood? Is that what you mean?''

I said nothing.

''Well, it's true. I do know what 'in cold blood' means. Back there, when I did what I did, I was all alone. No, not alone. The car was there too, but the car was me; and the man on the road wasn't just himself, he was everything and everyone I wanted to get back at. You're right. I am glad I did it. I would do it again.''

''I'm sure you would.''

''You sound so smug. That man you shot in the bayou—wouldn't you do it again?''

''It may not have been quite the same thing.''

''That's not an answer. I have no doubt that my conscience is made of cruder stuff than yours. But I'll tell you this, Harry. I couldn't see your face when you pulled that trigger. Maybe you didn't feel the satisfaction I felt—that sense of getting back. But I wouldn't bet on it.''

''Anyway,'' I said, ''we're in this together now.''

''We have been from the start.''

PART THREE

Something Rich
and Strange

MEDIA PLAY #8138
SOUTH HILLS MALL POUGHKEEPSIE, NY
PHONE 298-7353

```
                8138 00007 31117      04/27/02
SALE                         946      04:16 PM


02113413              MR SMITH WASHINGTON
  DEPT #9                                14.99
05088414              HOUSESITTER
  DEPT #9                                 5.99


                      SUBTOTAL           20.98
      20.98           TAX   7.250%        1.52
                      TOTAL            $22.50
XXXXXXXXXXXXX3625     VISA               22.50
AUTH CODE 131672
```

JOIN REPLAY OUR CUSTOMER REWARD PROGRAM
SEE ANY ASSOCIATE FOR DETAILS!

RETURN POLICY: All returns are subject to management approval • We accept returns for 30 days • All cash refunds require a valid register receipt • Open or defective product exchanged for identical item only • Manufacturer's repair or exchange warranty applies to electronics, video game and computer hardware, and musical instruments • Refunds for purchases made by check are subject to verification of funds

RETURN POLICY: All returns are subject to management approval • We accept returns for 30 days • All cash refunds require a valid register receipt • Open or defective product exchanged for identical item only • Manufacturer's repair or exchange warranty applies to electronics, video game and computer hardware, and musical instruments • Refunds for purchases made by check are subject to verification of funds

THIRTY-NINE

THE BERENSON HOUSE on Walnut Street was adjacent to the park and several blocks from the university. Fronted by a wall made of polished gray stone, the house was set farther back from the street than its neighbors and dwarfed them. Leaving Ike with Sally in the car, Elizabeth and I got out and went to the gate. The gate was iron, like Grandmother's, but spearlike black spikes replaced ornamental grillwork: this was a security gate that frankly proclaimed its purpose. Through it I could see what looked like a fortress hewn from granite. Although there were trees and bushes on either side of the house, its dimensions demanded terraces and parks and a half mile of gravel driveway. The dimly illuminated front door was protected by outer doors made, like the gate, of iron bars, and was framed by a portico resting on Corinthian columns that seemed to have been grafted onto the building as an afterthought. The purpose may have been decorative but served only to underscore the basic intentions of the house, which were to conceal and exclude.

"Do you have a key to the gate?" I asked Elizabeth.

"Not with me. We'll have to ring the bell."

"Wait. I'm going in first. You stay to one side where you can't be seen, but don't let the gate shut behind me. I want you to be able to come in when I call you."

"But—"

"Just do this my way," I said, meaning it, and rang the bell.

After a minute or so, the gate swung inward on its spring and a tall, black-haired, swarthy-faced young man wearing black trousers and a white jacket appeared on the front step. He waited in silence as I approached, the kind of silence meant to remind visitors that they were intruders from the outer world. The glance he flicked over my muddy jeans and pullover was the same he would have given a tramp.

"I'm Mrs. Bennett's lawyer. I want to see Mr. Berenson."

"Not possible," he said, with some sort of accent that I couldn't place.

"My business concerns his granddaughter."

"Not possible."

"Isn't he worried about her?"

"Miss Elizabeth not welcome here."

"Oh? Since when?"

"Since the doctor say Mr. Berenson need peace. Rest and peace. Say he no can be disturbed."

"He'll have peace enough later on. Right now, I'm going to see him."

I started to push past him, but he blocked the way.

"No enter," he said.

A female figure materialized in the doorway behind him. She was almost as tall as he—six feet or slightly over—and so thin her limbs seemed to have been fashioned from pipe cleaners. She had red hair going to gray, sharp birdlike features and eyes, and faintly freckled skin pale enough never to have seen the sun. The bulky tweed suit she wore did nothing to conceal her body's skeletal angularity. "That will do, José. I'll speak to the gentleman."

"But orders say—"

"That will do." The inflections of her high-pitched British voice conveyed familiarity with various forms of hysteria and in this instance carried a sharp-edged threat. "I've told you repeatedly that your rudeness to strangers will not be tolerated. If you can't manage to be civil I'll send you packing back where you came from. Considering what's waiting for you there," she added mysteriously, "I shouldn't think you would like that very much, would you?'' She turned to me and said loudly as José disappeared into the hall, "Now won't you come this way, please, Mr.—?''

"Preston."

"Mr. Preston. I'm Miss Taylor. We can talk more privately inside."

I thought of Elizabeth behind me at the gate, but there seemed, at the moment, little choice but to do as Miss Taylor said.

She led me into a square two-story hallway, roughly the size of a small auditorium, that had been scaled to overwhelm rather than to receive. Dark except for the light granted by a single wall fixture, its floor was almost entirely covered by an Oriental in the deeper shades of blue and maroon. Against the walls were teak chairs and standing lamps of a sort I had never seen before. The arms and legs of the chairs were carved in barbaric animal shapes, and the lamps looked like totem figures confiscated from some Pacific island—totem figures with fringed hats on. These were not chairs to sit in, lamps to read by. A monumental carved hat rack positioned in the curve of the stairwell looked like a leafless tree in dead winter.

Miss Taylor led me into a sitting room to the right of the hall. It was filled with tufted brown velvet chairs and more fringed lamps. In one of the chairs rested a basket of knitting. The lamp next to that chair was turned on, but its pool of light had a niggardly circumference. As if the presence of an outsider made her suddenly see the room for the mole's lair it was, Miss Taylor extravagantly pulled the cords of two other lamps. Now the room was bordered by three pools of light that served only to emphasize the larger pool of blackness that remained at the center.

"Please sit down, Mr. Preston. Did I hear you correctly outside? Did you say you were Elizabeth's lawyer?"

"Yes."

"Then how do your propose to handle this sordid affair?"

"Which affair? I'm not a criminal lawyer, if that's what you mean, and as far as I know Elizabeth's no criminal."

Shooting me a veiled look, she said, "Then why have you come? Surely you didn't expect to find her here."

PREFACE

This book discusses the assumptions, ideas, and techniques of Dryden's major poetry, including not only his nondramatic work but also his plays, as represented by *All for Love*, and his translations, as represented by *Fables*. Until recently much the most fruitful modern study of Dryden had been of his ideas, but in the past few years we have seen the development of critical study as well. It is my belief that Dryden may be further understood by combining the scholarly and critical enterprises. Only by so doing can it be shown that his thought possesses a unity by virtue of its characteristic expression in poetry, and that his poetry is informed by consistent themes. To put it differently, and more exactly, Dryden is what is usually called a Christian humanist and at the same time a historical progressivist and a modern. It is this interplay that accounts for much of the creative force of his work. When he speaks of "The dance of planets round the radiant sun," it is clear that his assumptions are Copernican but that the concept given life is indebted to the outmoded if attractive notion of the music of the spheres. Similarly, his two religious poems bespeak an unusual force of personal commitment at the same time that their public expression implies full engagement with his age. Given such considerations, the historical sequence of his career, the absence of most biographical information, and the difficulty of many of his poems, the problem of discussion is one of finding a point to begin.

I have assumed that the poems themselves are the proper objects to study, even while recognizing that attention to their assumptions about such matters as their intellectual positions and the relation of the author to his audience must necessarily determine the way the poems are regarded. Part One of the book is, therefore, concerned with "Public and Private Experience," the literary and human assumptions that necessarily determine our regard of the poems. This point of departure is the more necessary because present-day conceptions of poetry are largely determined by quite different assumptions as to the poet's privacy, revulsion if not alienation from society, and recourse to a lonely integrity. Such assumptions would have made little sense to Dryden, who is not a Waste-lander, a Romantic, or a Metaphysical poet. Most of his poetry is radically public and engaged, which is to say that it is personal in commitment rather than private in exploration. The first chapter deals with Dryden's formulation of a public style in *Annus Mirabilis* and other early poems, the second with the tension of public and private experience in *All for Love* and other plays. Since the one is the first important poem in the language to be conceived in historical terms that seem modern, and the other is often said to be the last high tragedy, they deserve examination in their own right. If it is difficult to weld initial discussion of public modes with critical analysis, I must ask the reader's patience for the first chapter and hope that thereafter he will find that the discussion has successfully merged analysis of specific poems and treatment of larger topics. I hope that I have shown that Dryden himself succeeded in achieving an inner relation of ideas, structure, and figurative language in *Annus Mirabilis* and *All for Love*.

In Part Two, "Metaphor and Theme," such inner relations are major concerns in examination of *MacFlecknoe*, *Absalom and Achitophel*, *The Hind and the Panther*, and other poems of the decade from 1678 to 1688, in which his powers found their first full expression outside the theatre. In each of these major works, there is a tendency to dissolve plot, or replace its function, with a dynamism of ideas and striking metaphorical conceptions. Their success as poems is shown to involve an interplay between personal feeling on important matters, public commitment, what may well be called configurations of metaphor, and ideas both of his own and earlier times. The last chapter of Part Two is concerned with a lesser poem, *Eleonora*, in which the absence of personal feeling is a crucial flaw in a poem of considerable formal and historical interest. Its fundamental flaw, as well as its residual virtues, illuminate by contrast Dryden's characteristic success and reveal the greatest danger to his poetic styles. Part Three, "Themes and Variations," explores Dryden's fusion of idea and figurative language, of poetic assumption and structure, in the many variations represented by his lyric poems and the *Fables*. The lyrics vary greatly in significance. Yet together they show, as do other features of his career, how much he is a part of his own century and how little the first poet of the next. The *Fables*, which is chiefly comprised of works much altered in translation, affords an excellent opportunity to review his career and to examine with close literary con-

trol what is characteristic in his poetry. In brief, my aim is to place
Dryden firmly in his own, the seventeenth century, and to bring him
into view by our century through critical interpretation.

It will be plain from this forecast that the discussion is more representative than comprehensive of Dryden's career. Poems other than
those named are indeed repeatedly considered but, with the exception
of *Eleonora*, I have kept to the fore Dryden's greatest and most characteristic poems. Such an examination reveals, as I think a more comprehensive survey would only confirm, that from the beginning to the end
of his career his thought was in theology close to that of Aquinas and
Hooker, in politics compounded of belief in regal divine right and the
rectitude of the Clarendon Settlement—that his thought is so conservative in cast that it antedates in numerous particulars the ideas of many
of his predecessors in the century. His creation of larger metaphorical
structures is indeed original, but from the time of his conversion to
Catholicism it is possible to see an isolation from his age and a turning to
poetic as well as intellectual resources harking back to the middle ages
as well as to classical writers. What makes such a conservative poet modern, and what I think to be of special interest, is his sense of history based
upon a degree of relativism and a strong faith in man's capacity for
progress in time. It is possible to say of much of his poetry that it is historical, whatever its clear or confusing generic status, and in poems not
themselves historical in materials, the temporal treatment often provides
a strong historical undercurrent. Against such modernity must, however,
be set his faith in the power of human achievement to rise above the
stream of time to an immortality of fame, and his belief in the ultimate
transcendence of such eternal concerns as religious faith and eschatology.
It is this complex of conservativism and modernity, of idea and metaphor,
of personal commitment and public engagement, and of the orders of
time, immortality, and eternity that at once accounts for the very best
in Dryden and is the proper index of his achievement. Readers will be
aware that I have made no attempt to conceal my admiration for his
poetry or to conceal its difficulty, its faults of unevenness, or its most
serious limitation, an over-intellectualized response to human experience.
I think that the unevenness must be regretted but may be readily forgiven. Each reader will need to weigh for himself the limitation against
the greatness. And upon returning to Dryden's poems, each will discover
that, however detailed my discussion, I have rather primed Dryden's

pump than exhausted his poetic springs. Even if it were possible for me, it would be undesirable to pre-empt the pleasure other readers have in discovering much else in his writing. As he said himself, "The last verse . . . is not yet sufficiently explicated." There seems little likelihood that it ever will be.

E. M.

Los Angeles
January, 1965

ACKNOWLEDGMENTS

The decade and a half in which Dryden has commanded my interest has been assisted in more ways than a faulty memory can recall. To this extent neither the Notes nor the Bibliography do my predecessors justice. Certainly I have met only kindness from those I have approached for help. I have some debts of long standing, and it grieves me that my work on other subjects in recent years has prevented me from acknowledging those to two of my colleagues in the California edition of Dryden —Edward Hooker and John Harrington Smith—before death took them. It is a pleasure, therefore, to record yet older debts, to the teaching of Samuel H. Monk and Robert E. Moore at the University of Minnesota. There are more recent obligations. Like many before me, I must salute with gratitude the courteous help of librarians, particularly that given me by my friends at the Clark Library, by the staff of the Huntington Library, and by the staff of the British Museum. There were a number of readers at the British Museum who came to my aid: Paul Olson of the University of Nebraska was particularly helpful on medieval and typological matters; Phillip Harth of Northwestern University, who is preparing a book on the development of Dryden's religious thought, was of steady assistance; and Robert Elliott of The University of California, San Diego, suggested some points of value concerning *Absalom and Achitophel*. My stay in England also put me under obligation to Alan H. Roper, then of Queens' College, Cambridge, and now a colleague, whose own interest in Dryden led us to long, stimulating and, to me, profitable discussions. R. P. C. Mutter of the University of Sussex has assisted the development of this book in ways academic and convivial. Others, at the University of California, Los Angeles, have assisted me. M. E. Novak has made valuable comments on *All for Love*, Philip Levine has corrected my translations from Latin, and Hugh G. Dick has advised me on astrology. My greatest continuing debt in the study of Dryden is, however, to H. T. Swedenberg, whose knowledge and time I have unabashedly drawn upon. I am grateful for both, and for his tolerant hearing of interpretations sometimes at variance with his own. I must also thank my wife for her patience, especially through the trying English winter of 1962-63, when our children were often ill.

The editors of *Philological Quarterly* and *Studies in English Literature* have graciously permitted the use, in scattered pages of this book, of material they had originally published.

I owe acknowledgments of gratitude to some corporate bodies: to my University for sabbatical leave and to its Committee on Research for steady support, as also to the American Council of Learned Societies for a fellowship enabling me to work in London. I am grateful to the Houghton Mifflin Company for its kind permission to use the text of George R. Noyes for the poems and the text of George H. Nettleton and Arthur E. Case in their *Major British Dramatists* for *All for Love*. To the Trustees of the British Museum, to The Regents of the University of California, and to the Trustees of the Huntington Library, I am indebted for kind permission to use in this book the reproductions of pictures and other material in their collections.

I wish finally to thank three people to whom I am deeply indebted for the final form of this book. Mr. E. T. Webb took time from his study of Shelley at Wadham College to assist, with great care, in the reading of proof. Miss Jeanette Dearborn has once again given all manner of help that her position on our staff for the edition of Dryden does not require. And I also appreciate the aid I have received from Mrs. Dorothy Wikelund, who edited the book with the care of an ideal reader. If hereafter the book receives such close scrutiny by others, Mrs. Wikelund will have smoothed their path, and mine.

THE NOTES

Notes explaining or enlarging upon matters in the text have been asterisked and placed at the bottoms of pages. Notes offering citations or providing references are numbered and placed at the back of the book. The line numbers of quoted materials normally follow the passages. It is hoped that this procedure will make possible a full and continuous narrative and yet provide thorough scholarly documentation.

ABBREVIATIONS

Where appropriate, the titles to which abbreviations refer are cited in more detail in the Bibliography. When not specified, Dryden is the author.

Absalom: Absalom and Achitophel
Ann. Mir.: Annus Mirabilis
Arendt, *The Human Condition:* Hannah Arendt, *The Human Condition*
Baker, *Wars of Truth:* Herschel Baker, *The Wars of Truth*
BNYPL: Bulletin of the New York Public Library
Congreve: To My Dear Friend Mr. Congreve
ELH: ELH, A Journal of English Literary History
Exomologesis: Hugh-Paulin de Cressy, *Exomologesis*
Franzius, *Historia:* Wolfgang Franzius, *Historia Animalium Sacra*
Franzius, *History:* Wolfgang Franzius, *The History of Brutes*
Hind: The Hind and the Panther
HLQ: Huntington Library Quarterly
Hoffman: Arthur W. Hoffman, *John Dryden's Imagery*
Honor'd Kinsman: To My Honor'd Kinsman, John Driden, of Chesterton
JEGP: Journal of English and Germanic Philology
Johnson, *Lives:* Samuel Johnson, *Lives of the English Poets,* ed.
    G. B. Hill, 3 vols.
Killigrew: To the Pious Memory of the Accomplish'd Young Lady,
    Mrs. Anne Killigrew . . . An Ode
Kinsley: *The Poems of John Dryden,* ed. James Kinsley, 4 vols.
MLN: Modern Language Notes
MP: Modern Philology
Noyes: *The Poetical Works of Dryden,* ed. George R. Noyes, rev. ed.
Ogilby: John Ogilby, The Fables of Æsop [and]
    Æsopics
Oldham: To the Memory of Mr. Oldham
Ormond: To Her Grace the Duchess of Ormond
Par. Lost: John Milton, *Paradise Lost*
Par. Regained: John Milton, *Paradise Regained*
PMLA: Publications of the Modern Language Association (America)
PQ: Philological Quarterly
Purcell: An Ode on the Death of Mr. Henry Purcell
Rel. Laici: Religio Laici; Or, a Layman's Faith

Scott-Saintsbury: *The Works of John Dryden,* ed. Walter Scott and George Saintsbury, 18 vols.

Song: A Song for St. Cecilia's Day

SP: Studies in Philology

Ward, *Letters: The Letters of John Dryden,* ed. Charles E. Ward

Watson: John Dryden, *Of Dramatic Poesy and Other Critical Essays,* ed. George Watson, 2 vols.

Works: The California edition of *The Works of John Dryden,* ed. Edward N. Hooker, H. T. Swedenberg, Jr., *et al.*

Dryden's Poetry

Public and Private Experience

PART ONE

Personality and Public Experience:
Annus Mirabilis

CHAPTER I

> *The public realm [has the] power to gather [people] together, to relate*
> *and separate them . . . It is the publicity of the public realm which can*
> *absorb and make shine through the centuries what men may want to*
> *save from the natural ruin of time.*
> —Hannah Arendt, *The Human Condition.*

The virtues of Dryden's poetry have never been thought to include intimacy. That which is prized in life for belonging only to oneself, that which is too delicate for prose to express unashamedly, and that which seems universal to all men though each values it alone must be sought in other poets. Dr. Johnson admitted that "Dryden's was not one of the *gentle bosoms.*" Wordsworth thought him rather coarse. Arnold a classic of our *prose.* In accounting for poetry which does or does not explore the intimate, we have come to think in terms of a private-public distinction. The private manifestly deals with matters absent from most of Dryden's poetry. We have come to regard the public as that dealing with what men share, with that differentiating but not isolating them, with inherited values, with men and women in a civilized context. The public-private polarity has sometimes been discussed as well in terms of esthetic distance. The public poet is said to share the values of an audience close to him while surveying experience from a distance, the private to turn his back upon the world he shares with others while more closely approaching his subject. Some subjects and genres have seemed more appropriate to one mode than the other. Passion and the lyrical are better expressed by private, as thought and the epic are better celebrated in public poetry.

These distinctions have proved too useful to be discarded. But in an-

swering some questions they pose others. They lead us with good logic
to identify Dryden with the eighteenth century but fail to put him with
better reason in his own. They do not account for the considerable variety of public (or private) poetry, nor much assist us in differentiating
its kinds and qualities. How do we distinguish between Dryden's various
public styles? His first known poem, the overwrought and underfelt
elegy on Hastings, holds *public* and generic assumptions like those of
the ode on Anne Killigrew.[1] Metaphysical, or Clevelandish as it is, it has
none of the *personal* force of the Killigrew *Ode*, of "To the Memory
of Mr. Oldham," or of *To My Dear Friend, Mr. Congreve*. All four are
poems on writers. And if the last three are to be sure more wholly public,
they are also more wholly personal, whether the personality be that of
the one lamented or of Dryden himself. Whether public or private, the
question is not one of emotions but of their nature: from either we expect artistic and personal convictions. The *Heroic Stanzas* on Cromwell,
yet another of Dryden's epicedes, reveals him in the process of discovering with first success the norms of public poetry that he subsequently
gave greater flexibility, grace, and profundity. He has discovered, and
overexploited, the utility of the first person plural pronoun in public
poetry.

> By his command we boldly cross'd the line,
>   And bravely fought where southern stars arise;
> We trac'd the far-fetch'd gold unto the mine,
>   And that which brib'd our fathers made our prize. (121-24)

The lines show as well his fixing upon those active verbs and that rhetorical direction of his thought which come to mark his style. In his
treatment of Cromwell he makes some attempt, more memorable than
successful, to accommodate the personal with the public.

> His grandeur he deriv'd from heav'n alone;
>   For he was great ere fortune made him so:
> And wars, like mists that rise against the sun,
>   Made him but greater seem, not greater grow. (21-24)

Perhaps he was aware of two more general features of the *Heroic Stanzas* which were to be crucial in his later practice. Death gives the public
poet a problem no less difficult than, though different from, the private.

In the poem on Hastings he thrice essayed tears such as mortals weep, and each time he merely spoke. In the *Heroic Stanzas* and almost always thereafter in elegies he chose wisely to speak of triumph, to celebrate achievement.

> His ashes in a peaceful urn shall rest;
>   His name a great example stands, to show
> How strangely high endeavors may be blest,
>   Where piety and valor jointly go. (145-48)

Mourning may be no less available to public poetry than celebration, but it did not arouse John Dryden to a heat. Why this is so is implied in the second general feature by which the poem excels the verses on Hastings, its concept of time. Cromwell's great actions were, of course, taken in time. They are made triumphant, however, by rising above the human and temporal in imagery suggestive of endurance or transcendence.

> Peace was the prize of all his toils and care,
>   Which war had banish'd, and did now restore:
> Bologna's walls thus mounted in the air,
>   To seat themselves more surely than before. (61-64)

The result of these innovations is a marked advance in clarity, force, and grace. The murmuring, however intellectual, of the poem on Hastings has become a recognizable music. There is a purity and wholeness to the *Heroic Stanzas* that Dryden was not to achieve again on a comparable scale till *MacFlecknoe*. But the music is for the treble voice, and the gains are achieved in part by rejecting possible complexities. Although less successful as total poems, *Astraea Redux* and "To His Sacred Majesty" demonstrate some of the means by which he acquired that deeper resonance. The titles themselves suggest the classical and biblical elements found in both poems. What Dryden seems to grope for and repeatedly to find and lose, is a way of adapting these two central sources of value in Christian humanism to a lively public poetry. Certainly the Virgilianisms of *Astraea Redux* sound more deeply than comparable passages in the poem on Cromwell.

> And now Time's whiter series is begun,
> Which in soft centuries shall smoothly run:

> Those clouds that overcast your morn shall fly,
> Dispell'd to farthest corners of the sky. (292-95)

The classical and simple English senses of *whiter* play their changes in the four lines. Yet the attempt to join the classical to contemporary experience is of ambiguous success.

> O happy age! O times like those alone
> By fate reserv'd for great Augustus' throne!
> When the joint growth of arms and arts foreshew
> The world a monarch, and that monarch *you*. (320-23)

These lines closing the poem have a real weight in recalling such Virgilian phrases as *O fortunati, quorum iam mœnia surgunt*, and more specially the passages prophetic of Augustus in the *Æneid* (see Dryden's *Æneis*, VI, 1073-92). But somehow that weight has not come over to Dryden's English to one's complete satisfaction. The absence of imagery (apart from the allusion) is unfortunate at the end of the poem. There is simply a certain awkwardness, because although the quatrain movement of *Heroic Stanzas* is still felt in the two poems on Charles II, with it there are larger, weightier motions of mind and style that are not yet wholly natural. The opening lines of "To His Sacred Majesty" show as much.

> In that wild deluge where the world was drown'd,
> When life and sin one common tomb had found,
> The first small prospect of a rising hill
> With various notes of joy the ark did fill:

The first two lines are big with promise of *Absalom and Achitophel*. The next two collapse into a variation of the quatrain rhythm of *Heroic Stanzas*, weakened by that expletive *did*.

Dryden had discovered but not yet seized the opportunity to be great. He is still uncertain of the relation between the experience of his day and that of the biblical or classical pasts. Past and present are sometimes treated as if equally historical, sometimes as if metaphorical in relation. Sometimes they seem lacking in àny purpose except provision of high-astounding terms. Such diffidences are representative of larger uncertainties: neither poem is clearly defined as a panegyric, as a narrative of historical events, or as a picture of heroic endeavor. Each is all, but none. Such uncertainties provide the major possibilities for his later achievement, but in his first triumph of forging a public poetry of force and clarity, he failed to make its elements cohere. So many forms of poetic coherence were offering themselves to him that it was time, and he found time, for that reflection which at last brought him full command of his powers and the ability to shape his alternatives into varied yet satisfyingly whole works. The first of these was *Annus Mirabilis*.

When the poem appeared early in 1667, Dryden was in his thirty-sixth year and best known for four plays, three of which had won acclaim. Another three were soon to appear. The plague of 1665 had sent him to Charlton in the country, the seat of his Catholic brother-in-law, the Earl of Berkshire, who afforded him the opportunity for reflection. He took it in the manner in which he most excelled, working out his ideas in terms of his personal needs, in poetry and in "the other harmony of prose" for the *Essay of Dramatic Poesy*. The *Essay* reveals Dryden deeper in literary controversy than he was ever to allow himself to be taken again, and yet more dignified than he was ever again to attempt to be in prose. Plays, prose, and poetry prove 1666 to have been Dryden's own year of wonders, and the works in all three forms show a confidence born of awareness of achievement. *Annus Mirabilis* and its accompanying "Account of the Poem" define what he had been seeking since the *Heroic Stanzas* and what were to be some of the major characteristics of his nondramatic verse. Like not a few of his critical prefaces, the "Account" seems to have been written on the counter of his poetic shop, where at his ease he convinces us that the high value he sets on his works is just. He does so partly by anticipating our first question about the poem, that of its unity. The answer comes to us in a distinction between historical and epic poetry.

> I have called my poem *historical*, not *epic*, though both the actions and the actors are as much heroic as any poem can contain. But since the action is not properly one, nor that accomplished in the last successes, I have judged [epic] too bold a title for a few stanzas, which are little more in number than a single Iliad, or the longest of the Æneids.[2]

Plainly, this rather transforms than answers our question. We are willing to alter our expectations of the poem, but we still wish to know whether it is unified. Dryden knew the answer to be that the poem lacks formal unity of action. Partly in the interests of unity, partly for political reasons,* and partly because it could not be overcome by heroic action, he had omitted sustained treatment of the great plague of 1665. English heroism in the naval war with the Dutch and the efforts to quell the great fire of London were at once historical and capable of epic treatment. To argue that they were therefore unified in the poem required shifting to new grounds.

Near the end of the "Account"[3] he attacks the problem in a breathtakingly rapid review of Renaissance critical ideas. Taking poetic language as his subject—the mimetic *verba* of the reality or natural *res*—he concerns himself with the ways in which certain genres or sub-genres are mimetic of nature.

> Such descriptions or images, well wrought, which I promise not for mine, are, as I have said, the adequate delight of heroic poesy; for they beget admiration, which is its proper object . . . for the [epic] shows nature beautified.

The Ciceronian *admiratio* which Italian critics had used to gloss and extend the Horatian *dulce*, or pleasure, as an end of poetry is in characteristic Drydenian fashion set as the primary end of literature, above the *utile* and *docere*, the profit and teaching. There is little new in this, unless it be the emphasis and the approach through figurative language. Yet it is the approach which leads him to distinctions of utmost significance to his subsequent poetic career.

> But though the same images serve equally for the epic poesy, and for the historic and panegyric, which are branches of it, yet a several sort of sculpture is to be used in them.

It is difficult to believe that panegyric and historical poetry are necessarily branches of the epic genre. Yet in the public poetry which Dryden had been fashioning since the *Heroic Stanzas*, the relations between the three are valid. They are also remarkably prescient for his subsequent career.

---

* See *Works*, I, 258-59, on the extent to which the anti-court party regarded the plague and fire as divine punishment for royal sins, and concerning other political aspects of the poem.

He was later to write numerous poems whose claims to purity of subject or genre are as slight as those to unity are assured. Repeatedly their cohering conception is to be found in the historic, while the epic and panegyric are ever close at hand, whether in their proper or their inverted forms of mock-heroic and satire. Whether in narrative or metaphor, or both together, the historical provides the center upon which his poetry turns, even as variations of the other two provide those precessions and epicycles which the old astronomy allowed to maintain its explanations of order and the music of the spheres. The basic historical harmony, with its accompanying chime of epic and panegyric, will be recurred to in ensuing discussions. But it had a special appropriateness in 1667 when the greatest epic in the language and Cowley's ode *To the Royal Society* followed *Annus Mirabilis* into print. *Paradise Lost* is as centrally epic and as incidentally historical (in the older Augustinian teleological assumptions) and as panegyric as Cowley's ode is panegyric, with historic metaphors and occasional epic sweep. Dryden's poem alone is radically historical in the modern and in the poetic senses he defines. Yet it parallels the heroic narrative of *Paradise Lost* in its actions and in its groundings through allusion or emulation in classical epics. Similarly, its apostrophes to the Royal Society and London, like the praise of the king and lesser heroic figures, employ the resources of panegyric.

I have said in Dryden's words and my own that *Annus Mirabilis* lacks full unity of action. It remains to be shown that it possesses unity of poetic language and effect, as also that there is structural control of the two major parts. The first matter is essentially one of style. In this respect the evaluation of the poem has been remarkably consistent, apart from details. Bounding in its energy, the poem soars at times towards the heavens and plunges at times to earth in hideous combustion. It is not clear that in 1666 Dryden always distinguished between grand soaring and noisy falling, but in exaggerated form the unevenness, as in so much better else, *Annus Mirabilis* forecasts his whole career. The crystalline candle-snuffer with which God "hoods the flames" of the fire (1121-24) may not be much minded by those whose tastes are formed by the seventeenth century, but none dare admire it. Such sins are venial, if too frequent in the poem, because they are those of commission and overplus. More serious are the occasional obscure passages. Obscurity is a peril to Dryden's style because for him emotion impels or accompanies thought but seldom exists apart from it. His very complexities, more-

over are of a kind that must be seen clearly if they are to constitute
poetic riches.

> And tho' by tempests of the prize bereft,
>> In heaven's inclemency some ease we find:
> Our foes we vanquish'd by our valor left,
>> And only yielded to the seas and wind. (117-20)

The first line is slack enough. The third and fourth have gone wholly
out of control. Dryden's style so puts into action the resources of English
syntax that when, as here, we must parse for him the alarm bell sounds.

The latter portion of the poem dealing with the fire has been admired
so long that, with admission of unevenness and excess, a quotation from
its conclusion will be sufficient to demonstrate that force of language
which gives the poem its unity of effect. The vision is of London renewed after the rigors of war and fire.

> Before, she like some shepherdess did show,
>> Who sate to bathe her by a river's side;
> Not answering to her fame, but rude and low,
>> Nor taught the beauteous arts of modern pride.
>
> Now, like a maiden queen, she will behold,
>> From her high turrets, hourly suitors come:
> The East with incense, and the West with gold,
>> Will stand, like suppliants, to receive her doom.
>
> The silver Thames, her own domestic flood,
>> Shall bear her vessels like a sweeping train;
> And often wind, (as of his mistress proud,)
>> With longing eyes to meet her face again. (1181-92)

The mastery of complex details of metaphor and fact is as evident as the
majesty of an imagination stirred by hopeful visions of peace. Familiarity, not analysis, is what is required. The less often admired prior
action of the poem, dealing with the naval war, calls for analysis to
reveal the rendering of public and personal experience into a design
satisfying in its fullness of deeply felt life. The account of the war with
the Dutch has indeed often been given over as an episodic loss redeemed
to some extent by striking passages. In reclaiming the first half of the
poem from its undeserved obloquy, I shall not put in hazard a certain

case by claiming it perfect. It is enough to show the poem's merits as true poetry satisfactorily unified.

Dryden's subject in the first part, as in the whole, is the public one of his world, which is to say himself in it. His involvement is clear in the personal attestation of the tone and of isolated explicit passages: "So have I seen some fearful hare maintain / A course, till tir'd before the dog she lay . . ." (521-22). The narrative intrusion is softened by allusion to the communal experience of the hunt. More commonly personality is created by presentation of historical characters who sometimes speak of themselves. As night falls, the Duke of Albemarle contemplates his certain death in the battle to come.

> Amidst these toils succeeds the balmy night;
>   Now hissing waters the quench'd guns restore;
> And weary waves, withdrawing from the fight,
>   Lie lull'd and panting on the silent shore.
>
> The moon shone clear on the becalmed flood,
>   Where, while her beams like glittering silver play,
> Upon the deck our careful general stood,
>   And deeply mus'd on the succeeding day.
>
> "That happy sun," said he, "will rise again,
>   Who twice victorious did our navy see;
> And I alone must view him rise in vain,
>   Without one ray of all his star for me . . ." (389-400)

The scene opens with what seems an insistence upon silence and cessation. It is a "silent shore" that the waves withdraw to. Yet such phrases as "amidst these toils" and the serpentine "hissing waters" are significant as indicating subjects or even characters. It is they who "the quench'd guns restore." The sea is a kind of bestial, neuter element, but alive. The next stanza introduces the moon with "her beams," while "That happy sun" is even more fully rendered as a human being: it is happy because it "will rise again," and because in other years it "twice victorious did our navy see." Against this life in the inanimate world (whose scale of increasingly sentient personified being the passage follows), Albemarle reflects upon his own approaching death: "I alone must view him rise in vain, / Without one ray of all his star for me" (399-400). Such animation seems calculated to heighten the pathos, as though it is a kind of ironic sympathetic fallacy. Albemarle's courage and his tragedy are *personal* matters, felt most deeply when withdrawn for the moment from the world. Rather than supply human witnesses to increase the pathos of the scene, and tempt a sentimentality he invariably avoids, Dryden supplies his doomed hero with a society for the event—a mysterious world, inexorable but discoverable, full of death and yet of a continuing life in precisely those realms which we regard at other times to be lifeless. We know from our own experience of similar events that our environment takes on such an almost surrealistic vitality at our moments of great suffering. But there is no grandeur in suffering alone, whether the grandeur be that of the theatre or the epic. It is the sense of man before an audience, freed from the accidentals of private life to assume a full personal character in his world that makes historical poetry, or poetry imbued with history possible. Dryden brings that collectively public and personal experience into poetry and makes it convincing, true. His esthetic distance is that of a man looking with other men upon events seen less minutely than in private poetry. It is no less specific, but specific about larger and less intimate matters.

Something of the range of experience in this world, and much of the manner of observing it, can be understood from the opening stanzas of the poem.

In thriving arts long time had Holland grown,
    Crouching at home and cruel when abroad;
Scarce leaving us the means to claim our own;
    Our king they courted, and our merchants aw'd.

Trade, which like blood should circularly flow,
    Stopp'd in their channels, found its freedom lost:
Thither the wealth of all the world did go,
    And seem'd but shipwrack'd on so base a coast.

For them alone the heav'ns had kindly heat;
    In eastern quarries ripening precious dew:
For them the Idumæan balm did sweat,
    And in hot Ceylon spicy forests grew.

The sun but seem'd the lab'rer of their year;
    Each waxing moon supplied her wat'ry store,
To swell those tides, which from the line did bear
    Their brim-full vessels to the Belgian shore.

> Thus mighty in her ships stood Carthage long,
>   And swept the riches of the world from far;
> Yet stoop'd to Rome, less wealthy, but more strong;
>   And this may prove our second Punic war. (1-20)

The background of tension over trade (those "thriving arts") is followed in the next stanza by a theory of trade illustrated in part by a marine image. The third and fourth stanzas develop the low images mingling topography and personality for the Dutch in the first two stanzas into an explicit subject of Netherlandish luxury, which has its own imagery from recent scientific speculation about the formation of precious stones and the action of tides. There are also highly exotic suggestions leading to the avowed distinction between Holland/Carthage and Rome/ England. This judgment in the appeal to classical history had been implicit in the secondary meaning of the opening phrase, "In thriving *arts*." In twenty lines Dryden has touched upon a number of subjects in rapidly changing imagery. The movement of the lines alters with the sense: "Trade, which like blood should circularly flow, / Stopp'd in their channels, found its freedom lost" is appropriate but differently so from lines but two stanzas later which are of the kind usually thought "poetic": "The sun but seem'd the lab'rer of their year; / Each waxing moon supplied her wat'ry store." The differences of movement are partly to be found in the contrast between the phrasing of the rhythmic units. Yet the two rhythmic movements are part of one style and one view of the world. They both make wholly clear what is theirs, what ours, and what is shared. They flow forward between their banks of rhyme to the same end, to show the inevitability of struggle and its cause in trade. Trade is part of external nature and related to human nature by the image of blood, because it is the life-stream of the nations involved, as also in the same or other senses, of their "arts" and power.

Dryden had ended the fifth stanza by saying, "this may prove our second Punic war." Such a speculation develops the temporal and more-or-less historical note sounded throughout the preceding lines into what is intelligibly historical in the allusion. There is also an assumption of recognition, of an audience that knew and cared about the past and found in Rome a *locus* of value. Now in a succession of lines he exploits the opening review of the *casus belli* with a generalization, a picture of

the opposed nations, a condemnation of Louis XIV, and attention to
Charles II:

> And this may prove our second Punic war.
> What peace can be, where both to one pretend?
> . . . .
> Behold two nations then, ingag'd so far
> . . . .
> See how [France] feeds [the Spaniard] with delays
> . . . .
> This saw our king. (20-21, 25, 29, 37)

In these selections from eighteen lines there is a rapid although slight
change of tone which is mirrored in the changing modes of syntax; a
conditional, an interrogative, two imperatives, and a declarative. The
voice we hear is close with its "*our* second Punic war"; more distant in
its generalized question; close to us—and how distant from the scene
pointed to—with the request to "Behold" the nations of Europe; and
once more close with "our king." A choice of esthetic distance capable
of such rapid modulation, a tone that will admit complex attitudes toward the principles of human motivations to war (in 21-24), and an
imagination that gives a rapid historical review of Europe on the brink
of fighting create poetry at once clear and rich in subtle effects. The
style performs in subtle ways—

> Each waxing moon supplied her wat'ry store,
> To swell those tides, which from the line did bear
> Their brim-full vessels to the Belgian˜shore. (14-16)

The implications of "brim-full vessels" are full in logical and paralogical
meanings that take us back to the personified moon supplying a watery
store, back to the sun who is also a laborer, yet farther back to the
tropic moisture of the third stanza, and to that flow of wealth in the
second stanza which is ceaseless until it is unfortunately stopped in the
shipwreck of those vessels, the full stoppage of the blood of trade.

It is not possible in Dryden or other poets to judge the extent to which
such metaphorical felicities are inspired in the true poet or are effected
by the craftsman. What is unmistakable in Dryden is the personality
behind the style—the driving mind and the public voice, at once en-

thusiastic and urbane. It is also a humane sensibility that can give us that rare thing, a sympathetic English reflection upon the Dutch—those sailors who have sailed within sight of home only to be captured or killed by their opponents.

> Go, mortals, now, and vex yourselves in vain
>   For wealth, which so uncertainly must come:
> When what was brought so far, and with such pain,
>   Was only kept to lose it nearer home.
>
> The son, who twice three months on th' ocean toss'd,
>   Prepar'd to tell what he had pass'd before,
> Now sees in English ships the Holland coast,
>   And parents' arms in vain stretch'd from the shore.
>
> This careful husband had been long away,
>   Whom his chaste wife and little children mourn;
> Who on their fingers learn'd to tell the day
>   On which their father promis'd to return.
>
> Such are the proud designs of humankind,
>   And so we suffer shipwreck everywhere!
> Alas, what port can such a pilot find,
>   Who in the night of fate must blindly steer!   (125-40)

Our first impression is of the vitality of an energetic style. The first line of a quatrain surges toward the second, the third towards the fourth, cutting across the rhyme patterns and keeping the stanza on the move. The intellectual drive behind the style is like nothing else in English poetry. "By him we were taught," as Dr. Johnson said, "to think naturally and express forcibly."

As usual with Dryden at his best, thematic order is another aspect of intellectual movement. His is a careful sequence: from *mortals*, to *son* and *parents*, to the family, and back to *humankind*. Two stanzas of generalization enclose two of illustration. It is a typical instance of a passage with its local government, energetic movement within it, and connections both minor and important with the whole poem. Yet what is most significant is the humane conception from which the passage begins, the aim with which it ends. "So *we* suffer shipwreck everywhere." It is a condition of life, the position of all men, "who in the night of fate must blindly steer." The imagery grows unobtrusively from the maritime context: the metaphor rises from the experience and helps judge it. The thought—expressed equally by generalization, figurative language, situation, and less specifiable overtones of rhythm— qualifies the nationalistic distinctions drawn elsewhere in the poem by assuming a world in which the inscrutable, ironic, and tragic direction of things is common to all men. It is not therefore less specific. The sequence of *humankind . . . we . . . such a pilot* shows how the poet participates in the general, in the collective public whole which he addresses with characteristic ease, and in the individual for whom acting as a tragic *pilot* is the counterpart of the poet's speaking as *we* in these lines. The poet as much as the Dutch is the Palinurus of this passage, mourned by an Æneas whose continuing voyage is the same hazardous life. One does not quote Dryden's "so we suffer shipwreck everywhere" as one does Gray's wonderful sentence, "The paths of glory lead but to the grave." In Dryden, the line (however striking in itself) belongs to a larger whole, and that whole to yet a larger. Here is perhaps one explanation of why Dryden has remained so high in the favor of those who could not explain why.

What the people of the Netherlands share with those of Dryden's islands is a world of tragic potential, a possibility of triumph but in a life precarious amid such disasters as war and fire. The two actions of the poem are, therefore, whole in their view of life, to which danger is a common element in varying experience. Naval war and fire are international and national perils. The national peril had been overcome by the time Dryden wrote his poem, as he shows in its second half. The threat of the first was not lifted till 1688, when the two countries were joined in the persons of William and Mary. It was manifestly a structural concern that led Dryden to treat the fire second, making its quelling imply ultimate victory in the naval war. The threat of disaster, with the promise of continuing life, enters the poem at its beginning with the attribution of life to inanimate things and to theories of trade. The threat is real. It is inherent in war, a major theme of the poem finding expression in the personal experience of Albemarle. Yet there is a contrary theme absorbing the threat: the heroic elements give life. The epic aspect of the history provides means to achieve immortality, to absorb the past and conceive the future. If trade is lifelike in flowing like blood, life is like trade in being a voyage.

> Such are the proud designs of humankind,
> And so we suffer shipwreck everywhere! (137-38)

The war is an attempt to set the blood flowing again. No doubt this old political and economic notion is as suspect today as bleeding for illness. But the theme is sound. War, the realm of valor and honor, is in itself wholly unattractive: "But war, severely, like itself, appears" (208); and it is the English whose cannons are called "murdering guns" (219). From the outset the poem's values are in suspension. Does war suggest the positive values of heroism or is it a wretched business? The answer, very fully developed, is that it is both.

The Dutch are historically fortunate: "For them the Idumæan balm did sweat." Even the stuffs of trade have life, but life involves danger, as Charles II knows:

> His gen'rous mind the fair ideas drew
>   Of fame and honor, which in dangers lay;
> Where wealth, like fruit on precipices, grew,
>   Not to be gather'd but by birds of prey. (41-44)

Much of the rest of the account of the war develops the paradoxical relation between life and death in the epic terms of reference, between the valor that saves and creates but cannot save itself. We need not turn the pages of *The Golden Bough* to understand what psychological depths Dryden is plumbing.

> But since it was decreed, auspicious king,
>   In Britain's right that thou shouldst wed the main,
> Heav'n, as a gage, would cast some precious thing,
>   And therefore doom'd that Lawson should be slain.
>
> Lawson amongst the foremost met his fate,
>   Whom sea-green Sirens from the rocks lament:
> Thus as an off'ring for the Grecian state,
>   He first was kill'd who first to battle went. (77-84)

The mythical, almost primitive, sacrifice is obviously related to the theme, and is rendered complex in its celebration by lamenting sirens, traditionally sea-green (and life-green) upon their destructive rocks. Dryden also introduces, but does not yet develop, the myth of royal marriage to the sea.

The most often quoted lines of the poem are probably those describing "The Attempt at Berghen." The famous conceits seem merely wittily brilliant unless they are related to the themes being developed. The rich fecundity of trade, the involvement with death of man's highest capacities in life now emerge together in a blaze of imagery. *These* Dutch and *those* English are compared.

> These fight like husbands, but like lovers those:
>   These fain would keep, and those more fain enjoy;
> And to such height their frantic passion grows,
>   That what both love, both hazard to destroy.

The lines (109-12) convey the irrationality, even the folly of war. The Dutch husbands here prepare for those captured later (125-40), and it is by no means certain that the brisk lovers are wholly to be preferred to them. The Dutch are not for Dryden quite the men the English are, but they are men. We need only compare both the husband Dutch and the lover English with "threat'ning France, plac'd like a painted Jove" and its king, "That *eunuch* guardian of rich Holland's trade" (155, 157). In them there is neither fecundity nor valor, only intrigue and treachery. The Dutch and English by comparison, really live and, in so doing, really die. This is less tragedy or irony than epic sorrow and epic exaltation. The experience possesses an eerie beauty.

> Amidst whole heaps of spices lights a ball,
>   And now their odors arm'd against them fly:
> Some preciously by shatter'd porc'lain fall,
>   And some by aromatic splinters die. (113-16)

There is an irony in such a situation, and a larger tragedy in the all-too-animated nature of the lifeless sea, as when a Dutch ship goes down:

> The wild waves master'd him and suck'd him in,
>   And smiling eddies dimpled on the main. (375-76)

But the irony and the tragedy are part of the full epic awareness, of a Homeric view of war. The Dutch come to battle "To reap the harvest their ripe ears did yield" (446). Nothing could be more natural than such an expectation, or than the "sheets of lightning [which] blast the standing field" (448).

Valor is equally double in its implications. It is perfectly obvious that Dryden praises heroism and thinks the English braver than the Dutch. Once so necessary a thing is said, however, it must be added that there are complexities like those in Albemarle's soliloquy quoted earlier. All the marine and celestial elements are alive; it would be difficult to say whether it is therefore appropriate or ironic that he should conclude of his own fate: " 'The sea's a tomb that's proper for the brave' " (404). More obviously remarkable is the scene of valor rendered impotent by its own potency in action in the scene of Prince Rupert's broadside battle with two Dutch ships.

> Already batter'd, by his lee they lay;
>   In vain upon the passing winds they call:
> The passing winds thro' their torn canvas play,
>   And flagging sails on heartless sailors fall.
>
> Their open'd sides receive a gloomy light,
>   Dreadful as day let in to shades below;
> Without, grim Death rides barefac'd in their sight,
>   And urges ent'ring billows as they flow.
>
> When one dire shot, the last they could supply,
>   Close by the board the prince's mainmast bore:
> All three now, helpless, by each other lie,
>   And this offends not, and those fear no more. (509-20)

The effort of valor leads only to immobility, and the potency so lost is transferred by the active verbs to the almost animated wind, sails, and billows. The mixed attitude toward war is wonderfully conveyed by such a line as, "And flagging sails on heartless sailors fall." The characteristic alliteration creates the special effect of sail-less sailors, which is a microcosmic expression of the tone and implications of the passage. Less obviously, the spectre has its meanings: "grim Death rides barefac'd in their sight" because the winding sheet about the emblematic figure has dropped, leaving him barefaced—that is, the bare yardarms of the ships lead the men to expect death from the waves rolling into the holes made by the cannon shot. Similarly, the "shades" below deck provide a Dantesque underworld; the men beholding them there are understandably terrified by the unnatural light streaming, just before the billows, into their ships' open sides. Such details are very meaningful, but they are to be understood only in terms of the larger purposes of the poem.

The vitality of the sailors' environment and of their actions (though these may earn them only death) is stressed throughout the first six hundred lines of the poem by recurrent natural images, similes, and metaphors. Trees and flowers, bees, fish, birds, and lions, and many kinds of inanimate things heightened into life are a marked feature of the poem, giving an unusual vitality, both to the environment of heroism and its companion, death. When such details become similes in Dryden, it is because similes more than metaphors direct their imagistic vehicles to a clearly intended tenor.

> As in a drought the thirsty creatures cry,
>   And gape upon the gather'd clouds for rain;
> And first the martlet meets it in the sky,
>   And with wet wings joys all the feather'd train.
>
> With such glad hearts did our despairing men
>   Salute th' appearance of the prince's fleet;
> And each ambitiously would claim the ken
>   That with first eyes did distant safety meet. (437-44)

The simile directs our attention by its explicitness, and having directed us leaves us to discover. As the martlet, a kind of swallow—a bird who traditionally foretold the weather—first *meets* the rain, so the sailor highest in the masts "with first eyes did distant safety *meet*." The identical verb strengthens the comparison. Yet another nautical significance is implied, as a triplet from *The Hind and the Panther* on the hesitant Swallows makes clear:

> Nor need they fear the dampness of the sky
> Should flag their wings, and hinder them to fly,
> 'T was only water thrown on sails too dry.[4]

That such similes have the sanction of epic practice seems less important than their ability to function figuratively in ways different from strict metaphor. Different modes of comparison serve different ends.

Following the first six hundred lines the poem enters a new movement which, with other elements, will eventually resolve the seeming paradox that life and death should be so involved with each other. The *Loyal London,* a ship fitted by the city, but also a symbol of the city itself, is first described (601-16). The passage has the effect of conveying a lull in the battle and of a digression in subject. In both respects it moves naturally into the next two subjects dealt with, the "Digression concerning shipping and navigation" (617-56) and the "Apostrophe to the Royal Society" (657-64). It is curious that these digressive sections should advance the poem so considerably, whereas the return to the battle (665-788) provides the weakest part of the poem. The last episode of the naval war is sung in lines stirring and brisk, but the themes developed earlier in the poem, the expectations that have been aroused in us, are largely ignored.

> Thousands were there in darker fame that dwell,
>   Whose deeds some nobler poem shall adorn;
> And tho' to me unknown, they, sure, fought well,
>   Whom Rupert led, and who were British born. (701-04)

That's all very fine, but at this distance in time one can scarcely throw his cap into the air. Dryden's least generous comment on *Paradise Lost* may be turned back upon him: his *Annus Mirabilis* "is admirable; but am I therefore bound to maintain that there are no flats amongst his elevations, when 'tis evident he creeps along sometimes for above an hundred lines together?"[5]

Dryden surges off his plateau of mere narrative gusto as soon as he draws upon history (789-832). England's sufferings are due to the assistance she lent France and Holland against Spain when that nation "Hatch'd up rebellion to destroy her king" (792). The rebellion against a divinely ordained monarchy led to the strengthening of France and Holland; now their power rises swiftly to "dominion" over the seas and English shipping.

> In fortune's empire blindly thus we go,
>   And wander after pathless destiny;
> Whose dark resorts since prudence cannot know,
>   In vain it would provide for what shall be. (797-800)

This is the historical application of the personal shipwrecking we read of earlier. With the historical application of the tragedy of heroism, we begin to understand the providential, moral laws at work:

> Our fathers bent their baneful industry
>   To check a monarchy that slowly grew;
> But did not France or Holland's fate foresee,
>   Whose rising pow'r to swift dominion flew. (793-96)

The tragedy of the heroism is that it should have been unnecessary.
Just as the alternative to such "baneful industry" is loyalty to a providential order, the alternative to tragic heroism (in another sense of the
complementary value) is the heroism of the humane arts. The three
related digressions (601-64) are, therefore, the thematic center of the
poem, presenting us with positive values, the alternative, and the future,
to contrast with the actual past and present. I wish to return to these
stanzas after discussing further the structural inner relations of the
poem.

   The explanation of the cause of English suffering is followed by a
section (801-32) on English triumph at sea, and in particular on the
"Burning of the fleet in the Vlie by Sir Robert Holmes." This action,
historical as it is, is itself an easy transition to the "Transit to the Fire
of London" (833 ff.). Thus, as so often with Dryden, the first section
gives an imagistic preparation (in fire) for what is more explicitly
or more formally a characteristic of a following section. As the account of the naval war had ended with the thematic explanation, so the
account of the fire begins with it, still more closely unifying the two
halves of the poem:

> Yet London, empress of the northern clime,
>   By an high fate thou greatly didst expire:
> Great as the world's, which at the death of time
>   Must fall, and rise a nobler frame by fire.
>
> As when some dire usurper Heav'n provides
>   To scourge his country with a lawless sway,
> His birth perhaps some petty village hides,
>   And sets his cradle out of fortune's way,
>
> Till fully ripe his swelling fate breaks out . . .
>   . . . .
>
> Such was the rise of this prodigious fire,
>   Which, in mean buildings first obscurely bred,
> From thence did soon to open streets aspire,
>   And straight to palaces and temples spread. (845-53, 857-60)

Others have described the relevance of these lines to contemporary predictions of divine vengeance or of the end of the world, and have related them to Dryden's political ideas.[6] It is enough to see that the theme of insurrectionary fire as a national purgation for political rebellion had already been dwelt upon in the other terms of England's guilt for hatching rebellion in Spain. The naval war in its tragic sides is a punishment for English error abroad, the fire for domestic sin. The double cause and effect are telescoped, however; foreign sins produce the tragedy of war; but that war will end in English triumph; therefore, the fire is the ostensible result of foreign sins, and is a purgative force *like* that provided by a divinely sent usurper. In fact, what is meant is that the fire is the punishment for allowing the usurpation of English sovereignty. The "dire usurper" is of course Cromwell. Dryden buries, or expresses, the true thematic cause in metaphor in order ultimately to allow for the triumph of human endeavor that is possible if men work harmoniously in a stable society rather than rebelliously in anarchy. Ostensibly and truly about war and destruction, in which positive elements are to be found amid tragedy, the poem is also and most profoundly concerned with the achievements possible in peace.

The integration of the poem is to be found even in details of imagistic handling. The fire is treated with animation as great as or greater than the sea and sky are in the first portion of the poem.

> In this deep quiet, from what source unknown,
>   Those seeds of fire their fatal birth disclose;
> And first, few scatt'ring sparks about were blown,
>   Big with the flames that to our ruin rose.
>
> Then, in some close-pent room it crept along,
>   And, smould'ring as it went, in silence fed;
> Till th' infant monster, with devouring strong,
>   Walk'd boldly upright with exalted head. (865-72)

The genesis of the fire resembles Lucretian descriptions of obscure forms of birth from seeds or atoms, whether in clouds or other elements. The generation is less important than its presentation, however. Here we have one of those metaphors in Dryden that is very nearly impossible to define. (The animation goes up the scale of being and is developed in complex detail.) It is extended metaphor, too natural to be a conceit, too clear to be symbolism, and too sporadic to be allegory. It is some manner of analogy or controlled metaphor of a kind we find yet more complexly developed in *MacFlecknoe* and *Absalom and Achitophel.* (See Chapters III and IV.) It is significant that the life of the monster fire brings death. This almost causal sequence of the life of the rebellious fire producing death differs from the vitality of valor involving tragic fatality in the naval war, but the resemblance is important to the poem. There, death was less an effect of the cause, heroic life, than a tragic accompaniment. That was partly because such heroic activities as defense of the nation seem in themselves more laudable, and partly because the war was not wholly due to English sins. The fire produces not so much a number of individual tragedies—although there is again attention to families caught up in the disaster—as a single frightening tragedy of the endangered city and, by extension, the nation. This difference, and the extent to which London is the microcosm of the country, can best be appreciated in a stanza of political nightmare highly admired by both Dr. Johnson and Sir Walter Scott.

> The ghosts of traitors from the Bridge descend,
>   With bold fanatic specters to rejoice;
> About the fire into a dance they bend,
>   And sing their sabbath notes with feeble voice. (889-92)

Towards the end of the first half of the poem there had been numerous prefigurings (the word seems uncommonly exact) for such spectres: barefaced grim Death, for example. What Dryden has done is to take his animating and humanizing imagery a step further by moving from the primarily natural in the earlier part of the poem to the supernatural in treating the fire.

The solution of such movement is, therefore, a supernatural one that leads back to the natural, and in the plot a quelling of the fire that leads back to assurance of naval victory. The furious naval battles have had their respite in the section, "His Majesty repairs the Fleet" (565-600). The parallel passage in the supernatural terms of the second half of the poem is the "King's Prayer" (1045-80). In one of those accurate and therefore doubly happy strokes that mark his fusion of history and metaphor, Dryden gathers together both halves of the poem in the last line of the King's prayer and in the first destination assigned by God to the assisting angel:

"And let not foreign foes oppress thy land."

Th' Eternal heard, and from the heav'nly choir
  Chose out the cherub with the flaming sword;
And bade him swiftly drive th' approaching fire
  From where our naval magazins were stor'd. (1080-84)

The close of the prayer relates of course to the as yet unfinished war
with Holland. The divine assent to the royal prayer is marked the more
clearly by the angel's protecting, first of all, the naval stores in the
Tower, the means of national defense. Contemporary accounts show
that the sparing of powder by the fire at this moment in the war was
thought providential.[7] Today it is the overtones of the passage that
seem more happy. There is an obvious justice in the choice of "the
cherub with the flaming sword," since it was only by fighting fire with
fire (and firelanes) that there was any hope of stopping the blaze
sweeping through London. The greater significance lies, however, in
the fact that the angel chosen is St. Michael, one of the patron saints
of England, as Dryden makes clear in this allusion to Cowley.[8] It was
also Michael who led Adam and Eve from Paradise according to the
stories Milton's *Paradise Lost* was to make forever familiar later in the
year. The flaming sword had similarly been the traditional bar to the
return to Eden; now it rescues man in answer to the King's prayer. The
implications swell rapidly. The King's prayer is an allusion to both
David's prayer, which is followed by success over his enemies, in 2
Samuel, vii-viii, and to the famous prayer attributed to Charles I in
Eikon Basilike, the great royalist propaganda triumph of the century.
Now, Charles I is the martyr king; David is a type of Christ; London
is saved by royal/divine grace. Rebellion is therefore akin to original
sin, and royal grace is Christ-like in saving the nation from the punishment due it in justice. From this point it is possible to look forward to
triumph. The quelling of the fire, and rebellion, enable us to envisage
London as a new Eden, paradise of those arts which, in their ideal state
or perversion, have been a major subject of the poem from the first
stanza.

The close of the poem describes London in terms of its rebuilding,
so that the vision has its basis in reality. The terms of the vision have
already been prefigured in the crucial digressive, middle sections of
the poem. The *Loyal London* is more than a ship given as a present to

the royal navy—it is the "loyal city" (614) itself, combining the
marine imagery, the humanizing imagery, and imagery suggestive of
transformation in fire.

> The goodly London in her gallant trim,
>   (The Phœnix daughter of the vanish'd old,)
> Like a rich bride does to the ocean swim,
>   And on her shadow rides in floating gold.
>
> Her flag aloft, spread ruffling to the wind,
>   And sanguine streamers seem the flood to fire:
> The weaver, charm'd with what his loom design'd,
>   Goes on to sea, and knows not to retire. . . .
>
> This martial present, piously design'd,
>   The loyal city give their best-lov'd king . . . (601-08; 613-14)

The passage reveals much of the whole of the poem by suggesting
elements elsewhere in it. The *martial* ship, the *loyal city*, the *sanguine*
image, the *fire*, the *Phœnix* transformation, art and trade in the *weaver*,
and the *bride* all echo and re-echo important elements in the poem. The
image of the bride, for example, fulfills the decree of fate that Charles
would "wed the main" (78).

In another passage, the city is "London, empress of the northern
clime" (845), and by the close of the poem the images of *bride* and
empress have coalesced into "a maiden queen" (1185), to whom "hourly
suitors come" bearing the gifts of trade. By rendering Charles into a
divine figure granting the people grace, Dryden allows himself to treat
the city as the more immediate subject of the closing stanzas of the
poem. Dryden even grants her a "new-deified" state of her own (1178),
because the nation is as important a subject of the poem as the king:

> . . . peaceful kings, o'er martial people set,
>   Each other's poise and counterbalance are. (47-48)

There is no doubt that Dryden's convictions are ultimately royalist.
The first half of the poem is by extension concerned with the king's
valor and honor—his brother James and cousin Rupert are captains
in the royal navy. But the first part also concerns trade and the arts,
and the second finds its focus in the sufferings and loyalty of the city.
Both externally (in the war) and internally (in the fire and plague) the

threatened nation is saved by the king, but what is to be saved is represented by London as a symbol.

Since such matters are set, like the action, in a recent past illuminated by comparisons with the remoter past, the poem is clearly what Dryden thought it to be, a historical poem. It deals with two major historical events ripe with tragic possibilities, and sets them within a vision of ideal polity, an ideal historical plan that stretches not only towards a successful conclusion to the threat but also to a glorious future in peace and creative effort. The positive aspect of the history, the ideal plan, is therefore to be found in the "Digression concerning shipping and navigation" and the closely related subsequent "Apostrophe to the Royal Society." The digression and the apostrophe comprise a progress piece, the *translatio studii*, or history of the development of the arts. The arts are, it must be stressed, those of peace: trade, science, discovery; and the words that celebrate them, poetry. Because martial arts are also a subject of the poem (dominating the historical past and present), and because the war is naval, Dryden chooses as his focus for the progress piece the maritime arts. He traces the development of boats from an analogy with fish, to logs, to more complex vessels; he relates the invention of "coin and first commèrce" and the modern compass; and he is led at last to a vision of a politically unified world in which trade and science benefit all men (617 ff.).*

> Instructed ships shall sail to quick commerce,
>> By which remotest regions are allied;
> Which makes one city of the universe;
>> Where some may gain, and all may be supplied.
>
> Then, we upon our globe's last verge shall go,
>> And view the ocean leaning on the sky:
> From thence our rolling neighbors we shall know,
>> And on the lunar world securely pry. (649-56)

* In the seventeenth century, *commerce* was one of the numerous words of similar derivation given an accent upon the root syllable. The compass image which follows is significant. Apart from its appropriateness to this progress piece it was, with printing and gunpowder, one of the three stock examples of modern superiority over the ancients. Dryden is not a simple progressivist, but he does not believe in historical decay. The image of the "ocean leaning on the sky" has sometimes been reprobated by those who do not see in it that visual phenomenon of the ocean's seeming to tilt upwards when viewed from a height at or behind the shoreline. Guyomar's famous speech on the arrival of the Spanish in the second scene of *The Indian Emperour*, like many other passages, shows Dryden consistently to have imagined such an upward sweep from the land-mass into the sky or supernal realms.

It is such visions of human possibility that give lasting satisfaction in Dryden's poetry. The royalist and other assumptions from which he starts have interest still, but it is the generous humanity that moves us.

Like many of the progress pieces Dryden was to write subsequently, this possesses a view of human achievement in the past and a sense of potentiality in his own time which are, for all their idealism, admissible as history. It also possesses a transcendent conclusion that cannot be called historical, because it lies in the future, and is rather an expression of faith in divine providence and human endeavor. Shipbuilding has led to navigation and science; these lead to a vision of the world as a single harmonious city-state free from want; and from the world we are in the last stanza gradually edged off into the larger universe. Having explored the "last verge" of "our globe's" landmass, and having unified the nations of it, man will find other elements to be civilized. The great desert of the ocean will be seen and explored—the verbs in succession are *view, know, pry*, showing the degree of understanding easily possible in each case. Vision, or seeing, implies knowledge, even without the explicit verb. There is sublimity in the breathless sweep; the conceit of knowledge as spatial exploration moves us rapidly to land's end, then off across the sea upwards into the heavens, where we see and know our neighbor planets, and are able to examine the moon.

It is necessary to stress that the emphasis upon action makes it a symbol of achieving knowledge, since Dryden's scientific interests (and later his religious faith) are susceptible to misinterpretation. It is clear that he has had the Royal Society patriotically in mind throughout the progress piece:

> But what so long in vain, and yet unknown,
>   By poor mankind's benighted wit is sought,
> Shall in this age to Britain first be shown,
>   And hence be to admiring nations taught. (641-44)

The essential thing is that the stanza emphasizes knowledge: it is knowledge "yet unknown," sought by man's "wit," "shown" to England, and "taught" to other nations.* Dryden is perfectly aware of

---

* The theme had been introduced in parody in the first two lines: the "thriving arts" of the Dutch are those of handicraft and trade as well as of cunning practices. It is not always pointed out that both Charles II and James II were ardent supporters of trade, among other arts of peace and war.

the benefits technology and science and trade confer upon man ("some may gain, and all may be supplied"), but his emphasis is with good reason upon knowledge rather than upon what Bacon termed "commodity," or than upon discovery as exercise of the will in action. The reason is involved in the next two stanzas on the Royal Society.

> This I foretell from your auspicious care,
>   Who great in search of God and Nature grow;
> Who best your wise Creator's praise declare,
>   Since best to praise his works is best to know.
>
> O truly Royal! who behold the law
>   And rule of beings in your Maker's mind;
> And thence, like limbecs, rich ideas draw,
>   To fit the level'd use of humankind. (657-64)

Such phrases as *wise Creator*, or *Maker's mind* and the successive rhyme-words—*care, grow, declare, know, law, mind*, (ideas) *draw*, (human) *kind*—seem almost remorseless in their insistence upon human knowing and upon God's wisdom.

Dryden is emphatic because he is affirming his belief in a certain kind of God and in a certain kind of science. The God is not the Deistic God of natural religion, because for him the object of such knowledge is transcendent: "the law / And rule of beings in your Maker's mind." Similarly, although science should "fit the level'd use of humankind," it should not be merely a democratic utilitarianism in the human sphere, but *truly Royal*, with its object the magnification of the King of kings. Finally, the line, "Since best to praise his works is best to know," has precisely the opposite meaning from what similar sayings were to have in the mouths of the Deists.* Praising a transcendent God for his works is the best *knowledge* man can show. Faith is the only means of apprehending God Himself, or rather of entering into the realm of grace (which is later depicted in the King's prayer), God's Providence, and the restoration of paradise. Dryden's point of view is that of the main orthodoxy of Christian humanism from patristic, medieval, and earlier Renaissance times.[9] There are other consequences to be drawn from Dryden's belief, and as usual he draws them.

---

* English Deism was not yet born in 1667 as an express, named belief. I use the term for the attitudes leading up to the explicit expression of Charles Blount. The ideas date back to Lord Herbert of Cherbury and before.

The Royal Society, as he conceives it should be, is *truly Royal*. It is so because it confirms a view of society, a monarchic society both in respect to earthly kings and to the King of kings. The Royal law is the ethical expression of reason.[10] Although neither is here explored at length, his political beliefs are entwined with his religious, and in a form that he was to hold consistently throughout his life. It can be seen that his praise of the Royal Society implies a good deal more than meets the eye immediately. His panegyric always lauds the object of praise, but by the standard of what it should be, not necessarily of what it actually is. Like his satire, the praise creates something more glorious than the thing itself. It does so by reference to a widely ranging yet unified set of beliefs and ideas. Dryden's was not a sensibility to recoil from an imperfect world. Nor was it one to despair over the actions of men, who might be made sound and whole by faith. The divisive private alternatives are rejected in favor of a unified public view. What is important, then, is that the reason he possessed a comprehensive view of different creditable human activities, and could look upon the future with such moving hope, is that he thought and felt from those assured, tested principles which had given Christian culture its foundation. He is more orthodox and less classical than Milton, more capable of treating the excitement of the new science in ways that absorb it into his own beliefs, the *Weltanschauung* of Christian humanism. One reason this is so is shown in his "Account" of the poem: he is a historical poet who looked upon the world, or imitated "nature," by means of metaphor; another is that he, along with Milton, has discovered, or rather made great, the public mode of poetry.

Dryden's discovery of the personality of public poetry in *Annus Mirabilis* involves, then, certain metaphorical strategies he later exploited more fully, a firm control over poetic structure and development, a humanistic view of man in his world, and an imagination fired by history. So few details of his life are known that we can scarcely speculate upon the motives impelling him to the first three. It does, however, seem possible to say something of his historical motives. Simply put, it seems most likely that his absorption with past and present grows from his concern—in hope and fear—with the future.

This impulse to history could be studied with some care by attention to the role played in his writing by *fate* and related words (e.g., *fatal*, *fated*, *fate's*). There are almost eight hundred usages in his nondramatic poems alone.* If the twenty-eight plays and the prose were added, the number would be prodigious. Some have sought to explain this concern by reference to Dryden's Puritan background or his supposed Hobbism. But since his thought from the beginning to the end of his extant writings is neither Puritan nor Hobbesian—of course he does have characters who espouse such views—these explanations are misleading. As the many usages of the words denoting fate in his translations of Virgil show, the concept is closer to that of classical thought. But there is also an emotional impulse. Towards the end of his life he wrote to Walsh: "fate without an epithet, is always taken in the ill sence. *Kind* added, changes that signification. (Fati valet hora benigni.)"[11] Even more significant is his interest in astrology, which is expressed somewhat ambiguously—that is, without certain commitment to it—throughout his career and which is clearly expressed in a late letter to his sons.

> Towards the latter end of this Moneth, September, Charles will begin to recover his perfect health, according to his Nativity, wch casting it my self, I am sure is true, & all things hetherto have happend accordingly to the very time that I predicted them: I hope at the same time to recover more health according to my Age.**

There were many of his contemporaries, including scientists, who believed in judicial astrology, and its importance to Dryden himself is therefore easy to overestimate. Coupled with his conservative fears of disorder and anarchy, however, and related to his apparent desire to assure the state of the future either in lasting architectural images or in others transcending the temporal flow,[12] there is some evidence at least of a psychological compulsion to deal with events in time and to reduce them to something even more assuring than intelligibility. For such reasons, his interest in history includes much more than that which today

* The statistics come from my count of words listed in the *Concordance*, which does not include the plays or prose. Dryden's reversion to this interest late in life is discussed in Ch. VIII.

** Ward, *Letters*, pp. 93-94. In the *Hind* (III, 471-72; 1765-66), the Martin is said to be "In superstition silly to excess, / And casting schemes by planetary guess." Since in view of Dryden's numerous astrological images (e.g., *Annus. Mir.*, 1161-68; *Killigrew*, 39-43), it seems unlikely his belief in astrology dates after the *Hind*, the apparent contradiction must indicate a distinction between casting a medical horoscope for an individual and mere "guess" about the effect of heavenly bodies upon public events. The widespread use of astrology by Lilly and other practitioners during the Commonwealth had rendered highly suspect the "casting schemes by planetary guess," though other forms remained respectable.

is thought of as the historical province, the mere record of time. He is
also much concerned by those sublime moments at the beginning of
things, when the direction of history is set, and at the end, when the
necessary human failures in history are corrected by eternity. The notes
of *Dies Irae* and a vision of the last day mark parts of *Annus Mirabilis*
as well as later poems.

> Yet London, empress of the northern clime,
>   By an high fate thou greatly didst expire:
> Great as the world's, which at the death of time
>   Must fall, and rise a nobler frame by fire. (845-48)

Dryden cites Ovid in the margin; classical fate and Christian belief are
harmonious in his thought. Another instance shows a more Christian
(and conceited) version, introduced with a phrase like the Virgilian
Nox erat.

> Night came, but without darkness or repose,
>   A dismal picture of the gen'ral doom;
> Where souls distracted, when the trumpet blows,
>   And half unready with their bodies come. (1013-16)

Sometimes history leads Dryden to considerations of fate or fortune
in the poetry (whether or not fate be the original cause for considering
history), as in that passage describing England's guilt in fomenting rebellion against the lawful Spanish monarch, Philip II.

> Our fathers bent their baneful industry
>   To check a monarchy that slowly grew;
> But did not France or Holland's fate foresee,
>   Whose rising pow'r to swift dominion flew.
>
> In fortune's empire blindly thus we go,
>   And wander after pathless destiny;
> Whose dark resorts since prudence cannot know,
>   In vain it would provide for what shall be. (793-800)

Had Dryden so written twenty years later of the Catholic Philip II,
his motives might have been severely reprehended by those who do
not see that throughout his career, whether he is an Anglican or a
Catholic, what he opposes—voluntaristic anarchy—remains as constant
as what he affirms, a providential but not temporally teleological history

based upon wisdom and grace. Action is necessary, but it is ill-judged when it is fruitless wandering, an attempt to scrutinize with the reason what can only be affirmed by faith and obedience.

If motives like these are, as they seem, springs of Dryden's concern with history, it must also be added that there is some alteration in them during the four decades of Dryden's literary life. As the years pass, the concerns suggested in *Annus Mirabilis* by words such as *fate, destiny*, and *fortune* come to play a lesser, though by no means insignificant, part. The shift can best be conveyed in terms of his most deeply held convictions, from faith in a gracious God whose essence is wisdom to faith in a wise God whose most meaningful gift to man is grace. The change enables Dryden to accept more and to still any abiding uncertainty over the future. The change can be represented in part by attention to words like *fate* and its variations, which in *Annus Mirabilis* appear on the average of once in sixty-four lines. By *Absalom and Achitophel* (where the grace of the king as an analogue of divinity is much more evident), it is once in every 103. By *The Hind and the Panther* (in which grace is one of the most crucial concepts), it is once in every 152 lines. Of course the nature of these usages is also important, but I think from general impression that the usages reflect the same diminishing preoccupation with the potentially ominous nature of the future. No doubt it is possible to evaluate both the original state and its alteration differently; however, it seems likely that what is purely irrational in Dryden's motives provides him with some of his poetic power. There is no emotion like fear, however controlled, to rouse a man to his depths. In looking back "with a wise affright" over the two revolutions that had already occurred in the century and in regarding some of the wilder activities of his contemporaries—they must have seemed even wilder then than they do to us now—he had good reason to trust to his own powers, to hold to a conservatism to which he was naturally inclined, and to question the future. Yet in his century many were obsessed by the future; the end of the world was constantly being heralded, and even the most sensible people appear to have had misgivings about what might happen in 1666, which had the number of the Beast.

The obsessions and hopes of Dryden's troubled century led other men as well to one of its great discoveries, that the very times in which they lived were as much part of history as the glories of Greece and Rome. Cleveland in his political satires appears to have been the first to have found poetic expression for the awareness, but his Puritan opponents made the lesson unforgettable in prose and action. If the typical royalist appeal was to right reason dressed in tradition, ritual, and myth, the Puritan's was to the finger of God writing in human history. The Restoration political verses that found their way into volumes of *Poems on Affairs of State* show that the lesson had been learnt, not only that the present is a historical order of time, but also that it may be compared to segments of the past.[13]

Dryden's historical sense is, therefore, neither unique nor first in time. But his is the first great poetic achievement embodying that sense and making it a norm of poetic eminence. He is the first really important English poet to bring contemporary history into poetry. So far is this the case that many of his greatest poems treat happenings not yet at their end. Such was the task he set himself in treating the naval war with Holland in *Annus Mirabilis*. And such the labor with the political events treated in *The Medal, Absalom and Achitophel,* and *The Hind and the Panther*. What enabled him to treat inchoate contemporary experience with assurance, what gave him the power to shape it into orderly structures, what furnished him with resources of metaphor, and what gave him immutable standards with which to imbue his writings was an older religious and royalist way of thought. The tradition, ritual, and myth of Christian humanism in its Renaissance royalist formulations provided him no less with the means of poetry than with faith in a divinely ordered world. In some respects, as in the belief in historical relativism and in historical progress shown in the digression on shipping, he is more radically modern than Milton. In such others as his typologies of kingship, his enduring optimistic faith in divine Providence, and his conception of the divine essence as reason or wisdom, his beliefs antedate those of Milton and of his major contemporaries.

Dryden could not have foreseen the ways in which his later poems would dramatize the interplay in his thought between event and belief, between the modern and the old. Yet like the later works, *Annus Mirabilis* extols the triumph of public achievement wrought from personal and even national tragedy and celebrates the temporal in such a fashion that history is taken to a transcendent order above time. His earlier poems had moved with lesser or greater ease between these poles. It was essential that the paradoxes be resolved into a larger harmony. With all its faults, *Annus Mirabilis* achieves just that, and it does so by defining its purposes in terms that were to be basic to much of his subsequent poetry. *Annus Mirabilis* is a historical poem in narrative method, in subject, and in assumption. To this constellation of basic historical features are added the heroic and the panegyric, as he suggests in his "Account" of the poem. As everyone knows, all historical writing is in a sense dialectical, the past being directed toward the initial conceptions of it. For Dryden, history is the narrative of great events, epic in grandeur and revelatory of men deserving praise. Such optimism was to be closely tested in the public and personal crises of the seventies and eighties. Panegyric would turn to satire and epic grandeur to ironic posture, shifts accompanied and expressed by radical changes in technique. But the poetry would remain at root historical, the very satire would usually take forms of praise, and the epic aspirations would continue to be posed as a norm. With *Annus Mirabilis*, Dryden had discovered his New World of poetry.

Since the world he discovered is one with an ethos differing in some respects from that we have come to value in other seventeenth century poets, some readers may be likely to feel that what is simply different in Dryden is somehow deficient. There are some things his poetry does not do. It does not show thought felt as immediately as the odor of a rose, as has been strikingly claimed for some poetic styles earlier in the century. It embodies a kind of thought requiring more protracted consideration. But it is no less personal or fraught with feeling than more intimate kinds of poetry. The destinies of nations, and the place of personal tragedy or achievement in them, the overcoming of impending disaster by reasoned human action, and the faith in man's capacity to improve his civilization in the frame of its supporting values are subjects no less charged with feeling now than three centuries ago. It can only be our expectations of poetic expression that have changed. We expect to see our poets alone. Mr. Dryden seems always to be in company. We expect the poetic scene to be indoors or otherwise intimate and isolated. His is almost invariably out-of-doors, which is usually to say in sight of men and women. This is true even of his love poems, where the pastoral mitigates the English weather as best it may. The scenes are personal but not often private; they are rich with feeling but, in the non-dramatic poems at least, not intimate or tender. It may even be that the emotions conveyed are commonly, so to speak, thinking feelings. Dryden knew, however, that there are some emotions that cannot be thought, that there are those reasons of the heart which, his contemporary Pascal said, the reason did not know.

Drama of the Will: *All for Love*

CHAPTER II

> *What is the race of humankind your care*
> *Beyond what all his fellow creatures are? . . .*
> *Nay, worse than other beasts is our estate;*
> *Them, to pursue their pleasures, you create;*
> *We, bound by harder laws, must curb our will,*
> *And your commands, not our desires, fulfil.*
> > —Palamon to the "Eternal deities,"
> > *Palamon and Arcite,* I.

In *Annus Mirabilis* Dryden had succeeded in creating a public world and the means of expressing it. That world is one fashioned of the ideals of Christian humanism, imbued with history, public beyond merely private concerns, and affirmative of life for its potential. That world is the very one well lost in *All for Love: Or, The World Well Lost* (1678). It is lost with some regrets but triumphantly. What is gained is another world fashioned of the ideals of pagan passion, affirmative of an ecstatic moment above time, private in its exclusion of the larger world, and laudatory of gain in death. The two worlds seem as incompatible as might be; yet both are parts of the larger world of his poetry, and both are aspects of his values as a man. To the extent that they are contraries, they represent conflicting motives in the man, and themes that found expression in different genres.

The opposite pole to Dryden's public poetry is love poetry. Although he wrote a number of love lyrics, mostly songs for plays, that affirm the passions of private individuals, no one has ever taken them as the overflowings of his heart. The intimacy and ecstasy of private poetry at its intensest are absent, in part because the private individuals are dramatic fictions in the situations of plays, in part because the songs have a public audience.

> You charm'd me not with that fair face,
>   Tho' it was all divine:
> To be another's is the grace
>   That makes me wish you mine.
>
> The gods and Fortune take their part,
>   Who like young monarchs fight,
> And boldly dare invade that heart
>   Which is another's right.[1]

The private address is qualified by the awareness of others implied in the generalizing second stanza, and the public world is conveyed by the religious diction and political metaphor.

If Dryden's plays show similar qualifications of the private motive, the matter is a highly complex one. The drama is a represented genre, sharing at once in the private world of its characters and in the public of its audience. To the extent that the mode of his plays is private, his is a drama of the human will challenging the standards expressed in *Annus Mirabilis*. To the extent that it is public, the larger movements of his plays, like those of his poetic career, challenge and at last harmonize the will with other forces. In practice, the distinctions are not so easily drawn, and two extremes must be avoided. The common, and I think mistaken, notion that the claims of passion and will had no appeal to Dryden is one whose testing must await consideration of the development of *All for Love*. The contrary idea, known better to the pages of scholarly journals than to popular opinion, that because his characters espouse strongly voluntarist behavior Dryden is therefore a Hobbist, a Puritan, or libertin has been fully answered by the scholarly essays of John A. Winterbottom.[2]

Some twenty-eight plays make up Dryden's dramatic canon, a few of them falling outside generalizations that may be made about the majority. Among the lot there are such diverse forms as tragedy, comedy, tragi-comedy, the heroic play, and opera or masque. Although such variety precludes a characterization at once simple and adequate, we may say that the major subjects of most of the plays are related in some fashion to those Dryden thought proper to the heroic play: "Love and Valour ought to be the subject of it."[3] The love is usually that known in the century as heroical love, the passion overriding the limits that might bound it.[4] Usually caught at first sight, it overturns reason and charges the will to seek its object, whatever the cost. "Valour" is similarly unbridled in its claims, and is often less a legitimate search for public trust than an exercise of its own pleasure. Dryden declared his grand fire-eater Almanzor to be descended from Achilles, through Tasso's Rinaldo and Calprenède's Artaban.[5] It has been suggested that such a character is a type of the Herculean hero owed to remote antiquity through Roman drama and such earlier Renaissance types as Marlowe's Tamburlaine.[6] Whatever his ancestry on one side or the other, Almanzor is—in love and valor—as voluntaristic a creature as ever lived on fire and words. Coextensive with his will, he resembles such other of Dryden's own characters as "little" Maximin, the tyrant of *Tyrannic Love*. The chief protagonists in the comedies match wills and words, usually brandishing challenges at the conventions of sexual behavior in the century.

At their worst, such characters will huff and puff. At their best, they are borne by the currents of their passionate wills. They are the very kinds of person who were to rouse Dryden to his one angry poem, *The Medal*, where he says sarcastically of the crowd,

> Pow'r is thy essence, wit thy attribute!
> Nor faith nor reason make thee at a stay,
> Thou leap'st o'er all eternal truths in thy Pindaric way! . . .
> Ah, what is man, when his own wish prevails!
> How rash, how swift to plunge himself in ill;
> Proud of his pow'r, and boundless in his will! (92-94; 132-34)

The passage ironically parodies Dryden's own belief that God's essence is reason, His will but an attribute, and that man's reason should in correspondence control his will. The same assumptions underlie the plays, although their expression is so greatly complicated that Dryden the critic does not always seem to get those matters straight.

His description of *All for Love* in the Preface is not of a play in which the claim of passion is accepted. Speaking of the various writers who had dramatized the story of Antony and Cleopatra, he writes:

> I doubt not but the same motive has prevailed with all of us in this attempt: I mean the excellency of the moral. For the chief persons represented were famous patterns of unlawful love; and their end accordingly was unfortunate. . . . I have therefore steered the middle course [between perfect and wicked characters]; and have drawn the character of Antony as favourably as Plutarch, Appian, and Dion

Cassius would give me leave: the like I have observed in Cleopatra. That which is wanting to work up the pity to a greater height was not afforded me by the story; for the crimes of love which they both committed were not occasioned by any necessity, or fatal ignorance, but were wholly voluntary; since our passions are, or ought to be, within our power.[7]

The description of the play is inaccurate. It accords with the sort of tragedy that Thomas Rymer might have written.* Or, alternatively, Dryden has described what he might have written in a historical poem expressive of his public values. His Preface speaks a public, his play a private, language. He recognized as much himself twenty-three years later, when he raised the very same issue of characterization in the play.

... my characters of Anthony and Cleopatra, though they are favourable to them, have nothing of outrageous panegyric. Their passions were their own, and such as were given them by history; only the deformities of them were cast into shadows, that they might be objects of compassion; whereas if I had chosen a noon-day light for them, somewhat must have been [revealed] which would rather have moved our hatred than our pity.[8]

This is very much more to the point: it speaks of the play we have read. It distinguishes between the "shadows" of private treatment and the "noon-day light" of public knowledge. In effect, the shadows obscure the public world, allowing private experience and the private motives of passion to make their claim. The "noon-day light" is that of the Preface to *All for Love*. There is no doubt that the actions of Antony, unshadowed and open to public view would rouse us into the shock we would feel if similar "crimes" had been committed by an Alexander in Egypt or a MacArthur in Japan. But it is precisely the scope given to private desires that distinguishes the world of the play from that of *Annus Mirabilis*. In writing of the similar proclivities of Charles II in *Absalom and Achitophel*, Dryden was sorely pressed to admit them without arousing condemnation. Only the brilliant wit of the opening lines and the biblical metaphor were to save that day.

So natural is it for all men to invoke separately the one standard of

---

* Rymer, who had just published his *Tragedies of the Last Age* (1678), was clearly on Dryden's mind, though the fact is not of prime significance, as it is to the Preface to *Troilus and Cressida* (1679).

shadows or the other of noonday light, that we are scarcely conscious of
any contradiction. Dryden seems to have been no exception. His
Antony dismisses normative "nature" and the public "world" in frequent
grand gestures.

> Die! rather let me perish: loosened nature
> Leap from its hinges! Sink the props of heav'n,
> And fall the skies to crush the nether world!
> My eyes, my soul, my all!—   [*Embraces Cleopatra.*
> VENTIDIUS. And what's this toy,
> In balance with your fortune, honor, fame?
> ANTONY. What is't, Ventidius?—it outweighs 'em all. (II, 424-29)

The private claim is accepted: "*My* eyes, *my* soul, *my* all!" But Dryden
would not be himself if he failed to recognize, or in some manner to
accommodate, the public as well. The exchange echoes an earlier
speech by Ventidius, who is given to the imagery of scales and the
public judgment it implies.

> Behold, you pow'rs,
> To whom [Antony] you have intrusted humankind;
> See Europe, Afric, Asia, put in balance,
> And all weighed down by one light, worthless woman!
> I think the gods are Antonies,* and give,
> Like prodigals, this nether world away
> To none but wasteful hands. (I, 369-75)

Antony as well as Ventidius is aware of the "nether world" of public
values, and Ventidius as well as Antony of a realm of private values at
once transcendent and destructive of rival claims. As the two speeches
together suggest, the play works out the claims of both in its imagery
and structure. These aspects of poetry are important to every poet, but
they are of special weight in Dryden's writing, where repeatedly diverse interests—old and new, public and private, temporal and eternal,
or literal and figurative—are given, or seek, harmonious expression by
their embodiment in careful structures grounded in figurative language.
Examination of these matters in *All for Love* should reveal the nature
of the drama. It also helps explain the cast of values in most of his

---

* "Antonies" refers both to Antony himself, so wantonly generous, and to the
blockheads of Restoration slang: see the Prologue, 15.

plays and Dryden's artistic maturation leading to the great nondramatic poetry of the 1680's.

All for Love opens with ambiguous expression of alternatives—of the public, historical, and ethical values—and of the death-creation of passion. The famous opening speech by the Egyptian priest, Serapion, sets the possibilities in a way characteristic of Dryden's imagistic handling.

> Portents and prodigies are grown so frequent,
> That they have lost their name. Our fruitful Nile
> Flowed ere the wonted season, with a torrent
> So unexpected, and so wondrous fierce,
> That the wild deluge overtook the haste
> Ev'n of the hinds that watched it: men and beasts
> Were borne above the tops of trees, that grew
> On th' utmost margin of the water-mark.
> Then, with so swift an ebb the flood drove backward,
> It slipt from underneath the scaly herd:
> Here monstrous phocæ panted on the shore;
> Forsaken dolphins there, with their broad tails,
> Lay lashing the departing waves: hard by 'em,
> Sea-horses flound'ring in the slimy mud,
> Tossed up their heads, and dashed the ooze about 'em. (I, 1-15)

The initial line is one of those tragic portents our older playwrights use for poetic convenience; the next seven, concluding the first sentence, relate the rise of the Nile in its forward motion, as the second seven and another sentence its fall and backward motion. We begin with a "fruitful Nile"; we end with "slimy mud" and "ooze." A later appreciation of Cleopatra by Antony realizes the first alternative.

> There's no satiety of love in thee;
> Enjoyed, thou still art new; perpetual spring
> Is in thy arms; the ripened fruit but falls,
> And blossoms rise to fill its empty place;
> And I grow rich by giving. (III, 24-28)

His reply to Ventidius, welcoming the fall of "loosened nature" upon "the nether world" realizes the second alternative. The general air of threat in Serapion's speech is part of the tragic tone, but it foretells even such imagistic steps along the way as Antony's declaration to Ventidius at the close of the first act:

> thou and I,
> Like Time and Death, marching before our troops,
> May taste fate to 'em; mow 'em out a passage,
> And, ent'ring where the foremost squadrons yield,
> Begin the noble harvest of the field. (449-53)

Serapion's descriptions of the Nile naturally suggest the usual idea of fertile creation, but his emphasis upon the monstrous implies destruction as well. The paradox is temporarily resolved at the end of the first act by turning the imagery of a "fruitful Nile" into that of "the noble harvest of the field." Antony has revived his *honestas*, his personal and public integrity. Ventidius is the agent, having, as we say, called upon all that is best in Antony. The public resolution of the first act has also been foreshadowed in the emphasis given Serapion's first speech by his second. In this he recalls the portents within the temple's

> iron wicket, that defends the vault,
> Where the long race of Ptolemies is laid . . .
> From out each monument, in order placed,
> An armed ghost [starts] up . . .
> . . . a lamentable voice
> Cried, "Egypt is no more!" My blood ran back. (21-28)

The realms invoked are those of history, discipline, religion, and art. They are conveyed by the temple, which is girded in iron, the sanctuary of Egyptian history, and the monuments *in order placed*. The blood runs backward, like the Nile. The issues are such that they could be resolved in a number of ways. In the first act, they are treated as public values for the larger part, and the balance is that of Ventidius' scales. As Egypt or the Nile falls, Rome and "intrusted humankind" rise in the triumph of normal human experience heightened and glorified, or guaranteed, by the hero's honor, *honestas*.

The first act also concerns the past and present. Antony's analysis of the past, in the imagery he employs, speaks for itself in terms of the imagery we have been following.

> I have lost my reason, have disgraced
> The name of soldier, with inglorious ease.
> In the full vintage of my flowing honors,
> Sat still, and saw it pressed by other hands.
> Fortune came smiling to my youth, and wooed it,

And purple greatness met my ripened years.
When first I came to empire, I was borne
On tides of people, crowding to my triumphs. (293-300)

This is the public response to the disturbance of the public realm by
merely private affairs. It would be a foolish person who argued that
great men cannot be destroyed in such fashion. Yet the imagery of flowing, of wines, of the regal purple, and of tides combine both halves of
Serapion's initial speech in a Roman version whose values are public,
but whose expression suggests a powerful undertow in an opposed direction. Similarly, Ventidius speaks of Antony's past in Roman terms employing the imagery of creativity. The difference between his speech
and Antony's is that his figures and diction are completely harmonious
with the public values they espouse:

> you, ere love misled your wand'ring eyes,
> Were sure the chief and best of human race,
> Framed in the very pride and boast of nature;
> So perfect, that the gods, who formed you, wondered
> At their own skill, and cried, "A lucky hit
> Has mended our design." Their envy hindered,
> Else you had been immortal, and a pattern,
> When heav'n would work for ostentation sake,
> To copy out again. (403-11)

It is this version, of creation in the immortal terms proper to classical
gods and according to the *perfect*, the *design*, and the *pattern*, that represents the main current of the first act. Such an assessment of Antony's
past is a Roman assessment and, confirmed as it is by the structure of the
play, is a very real alternative for those eyes of Antony, wandering in
error to Cleopatra and private delights. The imagery makes us feel we
know the values. These are powerfully reinforced by the scene of
reconciled *amicitia*—by the resolution in heroic friendship of the quarrel between Antony and Ventidius, itself strengthened by the precedents
in Homer and in *Julius Caesar*. By the second act, it has become necessary to return to Egypt, for Cleopatra to enter, her values much in doubt.

   Her first words offer a passive, defenseless version of Antony's inability to comprehend his proper sphere of action: "What shall I do,
or whither shall I turn?" Her complaints voice a pathos from which
she soon recovers. Antony had berated himself: "I have lost my reason,

have disgraced / The name of soldier, with inglorious ease" (I, 293-94).
When the issue of reason is raised again by Iras, "Call reason to assist
you," Cleopatra justifies herself for intensity of feeling in language that
gives a new aspect to the imagery of motion at the opening of the play.

> I have none,
> And none would have: my love's a noble madness,
> Which shows the cause deserved it. Moderate sorrow
> Fits vulgar love, and for a vulgar man:
> But I have loved with such transcendent passion,
> I soared, at first, quite out of reason's view,
> And now am lost above it. (II, 16-22)

Here in the transcendent soaring of passion, with a logic of causes known
only to the heart, is the origin of a triumph "out of reason's view" with
which the play will leave us. Cleopatra's opposition to the public claims
of Ventidius is clear, in fact too simply clear to satisfy Dryden. Most of
the second act takes as its thematic and imagistic business the qualifying,
countering, and even parodying of Cleopatra's claim. It begins with Iras
telling Cleopatra to forget about it: "Let it be past with you: / Forget
him, madam." Cleopatra shakes her head.

> Never, never, Iras.
> He once was mine; and once, though now 'tis gone,
> Leaves a faint image of possession still. (29-31)

Her love soars—it cannot march in public myth as the resolutions of
Antony and Ventidius do at the end of the first act. The soaring is that
of "transcendent passion," but its base is a physical one like that of the
beasts in the Nile. Antony offers such a version in reproaching Cleopatra
with their past love.

> I loved you still, and took your weak excuses,
> Took you into my bosom, stained by Cæsar,
> And not half mine: I went to Egypt with you,
> And hid me from the bus'ness of the world,
> Shut out enquiring nations from my sight,
> To give whole years to you. (275-80)

"Shut out enquiring nations from my sight" is the public version of
"Quite out of reason's view." But Antony, whose birthday this last day
of his life is, has introduced time as a consideration. He continues:

> How I loved,
> Witness, ye days and nights, and all your hours,
> That danced away with down upon your feet,
> As all your bus'ness were to count my passion!
> One day passed by, and nothing saw but love;
> Another came, and still 'twas only love:
> The suns were wearied out with looking on,
> And I untired with loving. (281-88)

These lines must be treated with some care. One of their purposes is to show in their "poetry" the extent of Antony's love still, for all he may say. But more importantly, they convey a languor, a timelessness of time, sterile in a deadening ceaselessness, a static dance. And yet this treatment of time, too, will be absorbed into the final affirmation.

The reproach of shared love is always cruelest, but Antony's emotions lead him to mistake in his rhetoric. He has chosen to emphasize the sterility of their time together by parodying the imagistic strains of ripeness and fruitfulness.

> When I beheld you first, it was in Egypt,
> Ere Cæsar saw your eyes; you gave me love,
> And were too young to know it; that I settled
> Your father in his throne, was for your sake;
> I left th' acknowledgment for time to ripen.
> Cæsar stepped in, and with a greedy hand
> Plucked the green fruit, ere the first blush of red,
> Yet cleaving to the bough. (262-69)

In rhythm and diction and imagery, the passage conveys Antony's intention marvelously, but it also shows how his reproaches can betray him. Once his imagination is committed too far to re-creating memory and passion, even in parody, the physicality and over-ripeness will begin to seem glorious in their very decadence.

> While within your arms I lay,
> The world fell mould'ring from my hands each hour,
> And left me scarce a grasp (I thank your love for't). (295-97)

Cleopatra need do little more now than speak to reclaim him. However ironic his intention and bitter his tone, he has too feelingly recalled the past.

> Give, you gods,
> Give to your boy, your Cæsar,
> This rattle of a globe to play withal,
> This gewgaw world, and put him cheaply off:
> I'll not be pleased with less than Cleopatra.
> CLEOPATRA. She['s] wholly yours. My heart's so full of joy,
> That I shall do some wild extravagance
> Of love, in public. (442-49)

Antony in his image of payment, and Cleopatra in hers of defiance, could not more clearly reject the "world." "Some wild extravagance / Of love, in public" expresses it perfectly. Antony's lines closing the act seem to suggest that he believes he has found a way to accommodate his military resolution to his love—a belief his own and Cleopatra's words have just shown to be impossible in any workable terms. Yet the phrasing is exact and moves us forward to the last images of the play:

> How I long for night!
> That both the sweets of mutual love may try,
> And once triúmph o'er Cæsar [ere] we die. (459-61)

The gods must have attended his remarks, because Antony gets exactly what he asks for, if not what he intends. The interval between the second and third acts is that of his triumphant battle. Dryden was inspired to have it follow that speech of Antony just quoted rather than that to Ventidius closing the first act. His victory is now entangled in his love: the tragic web is woven by its prey. In order to make a tragedy out of human disaster, Dryden has needed to conceive characters and issues of unusual scope. His style is, then, crucial to the experience molded in the play, and some consideration of it will lead to a firmer understanding of the final affirmations of the play. There are a number of passages like Antony's "rattle of a globe" speech. In the first act he had questioned,

> Why was I raised the meteor of the world,
> Hung in the skies, and blazing as I travelled,
> Till all my fires were spent; and then cast downward
> To be trod out by Cæsar? (I, 206-09)

And yet, "How I long for night!" The imagery of light, time, and worlds echoes throughout the play with each echo taking on a new meaning. Such imagery is of uncommon scope, as in Antony's remarks upon Octavius.

> He would live, like a lamp, to the last wink,
> And crawl upon the utmost verge of life. . . .
> Fool that I was, upon my eagle's wings
> I bore this wren, till I was tired with soaring,
> And now he mounts above me.
> Good heav'ns, is this—is this the man who braves me?
> Who bids my age make way, drives me before him,
> To the world's ridge, and sweeps me off like rubbish?
>
> (II, 129-30; 138-43)

The imagistic relations of this to other passages in the first two acts is clear. The image of the lamp, even in itself, is splendid, especially as its "last wink" is followed by the "utmost verge." The eagle of the Roman legions is similarly well fused with the Æsopian fable of the Eagle and the Wren.

Many readers find such imagery highly pleasing for its stylistic resemblance to Shakespeare's. There are resemblances, which should not be surprising, but it is equally true that one does not get very far comparing other writers to Shakespeare at his greatest. Dryden is best appreciated for himself. As is his structure, so is his style reined in tightly. A phrase like, "her darling mischief, her chief engine" (I, 191) possesses that exploration of the range of disciplined English syntax which was to become a stylistic basis of Pope's greatness. Often the discipline conceals the imagistic conceits in clarity.

> A foolish dream,
> Bred from the fumes of indigested feasts,
> And holy luxury. (I, 37-39)

The ironic parallelism gives a complexity to the direction taken by the alliteration; the sexual image, emphasized by the initial stress upon *Bred*, is rather felt than observed. There is a special kind of wit in this, the same that plays over the four chief words of "cooler hours, and morning counsels" (I, 104). The larger design is made up of numerous closely woven details.

The stylistic span of the play is from the simple to the complex; it ranges from poetry of a high order to one excruciating passage. In the third act, Ventidius looses Antony's children by Octavia upon him, saying,

> Was ever sight so moving?—Emperor!
> DOLABELLA. Friend!
> OCTAVIA. Husband!
> BOTH CHILDREN. Father!
> ANTONY. I am vanquished; take me. (III, 362-63)

It is a painful, even ridiculous tableau, a morality play of the public world exerting its series of claims upon Antony, but so baldly that it is positively good manners on Antony's part to give in with as little delay as possible. The public tone is much to be preferred in so simple a sentence as Ventidius' "I have not wept this forty year" (I, 263), which carries its proper emotion. At times the style has a sinuous winding through repetitions and patterned rhythms that recalls Milton.

> Set out before your doors
> The images of all your sleeping fathers,
> With laurels crowned; with laurels wreathe your posts,
> And strow with flow'rs the pavement; let the priests
> Do present sacrifice; pour out the wine,
> And call the gods to join with you in gladness. (I, 144-49)

At other moments, a passage seems, like many in *Annus Mirabilis*, to be a microcosm of the imagery running through the play as we have followed it in the first two acts. Such a passage is Antony's "But I have lost my reason" speech (I, 293-300). Again, also as in *Annus Mirabilis*, often the imagery of a passage anticipates major imagistic or thematic motifs that subsequently come into the play. A fine example, which sets into the motion the theme of manliness and its ruin, can be found in the first act.

> Does the mute sacrifice upbraid the priest?
> He knows him not his executioner.
> Oh, she has decked his ruin with her love,
> Led him in golden bands to gaudy slaughter,
> And made perdition pleasing; she has left him
> The blank of what he was;
> I tell thee, eunuch, she has quite unmanned him.
> Can any Roman see, and know him now,
> Thus altered from the lord of half mankind,

Unbent, unsinewed, made a woman's toy,
Shrunk from the vast extent of all his honors,
And cramped within a corner of the world?
O Antony!
Thou bravest soldier, and thou best of friends!
Bounteous as nature; next to nature's God! (168-82)

Antony excels in such manliness but, according to Ventidius, the exercise of his virility with Cleopatra has unmanned him. It is easy to see what he means, yet difficult to understand how Antony, and Dryden, are going to show the hero a man among men as well as with one woman. The style creates a complex of alternatives requiring resolution and so is congruent with the structure and thematic development of the play.

The beginning of the third act offers a solution in imagery of language, of the stage, and of myth. For much of the third and fourth acts, especially in their middle sections, the imagery of the stage will dominate. That is, what we see on the stage or imagine visually in reading becomes at times imagistically more important than the language. The transition in the first thirty lines of the scene is splendid. To represent his hero and heroine Dryden recalls the song of Mars and Venus in the *Odyssey;* and Rome and Egypt, enemies for two acts, are joined in full, if not lasting, harmony. The degree to which this masque evokes the preceding two acts can be more easily declared than demonstrated. We may posit a few images, however, and compare them with the opening lines of the third act.

[He] leaves a faint image of possession still. (II, 31)

While within your arms I lay. (II, 295)

I shall blush to death (I, 269)

The conqu'ring soldier, red with unfelt wounds. (I, 275)

. . . .

At one door enter Cleopatra, Charmion, Iras, *and* Alexas, *a train of Egyptians: at the other,* Antony *and Romans. The entrance on both sides is prepared by music, the trumpets first sounding on* Antony's *part, then answered by timbrels, etc., on* Cleopatra's. Charmion *and* Iras *hold a laurel wreath betwixt them. A dance of Egyptians. After the ceremony,* Cleopatra *crowns* Antony.

ANTONY. I thought how those white arms would fold me in,
And strain me close, and melt me into love;
So pleased with that sweet image, I sprung forwards,
And added all my strength to every blow.
CLEOPATRA. Come to me, come, my soldier, to my arms!
You've been too long away from my embraces;
But, when I have you fast, and all my own,
With broken murmurs, and with amorous sighs,
I'll say, you were unkind, and punish you,
And mark you red with many an eager kiss.
ANTONY. My brighter Venus!
CLEOPATRA. O my greater Mars!
ANTONY. Thou join'st us well, my love!
Suppose me come from the Phlegræan plains,
Where gasping giants lay, cleft by my sword,
And mountain-tops pared off each other blow,
To bury those I slew. Receive me, goddess!
Let Cæsar spread his subtile nets, like Vulcan;
In thy embraces I would be beheld
By heav'n and earth at once;
And make their envy what they meant their sport.
Let those who took us blush; I would love on
With awful state, regardless of their frowns,
As their superior god. (S. D. and 1-23)

It is no small part of the dramatic irony of the play that Antony has unknowingly summed up the preceding two acts while consciously describing a present earned by his actions in the immediate past. But the "awful state" he predicts (cf. V, 505 ff.) is one that must be earned before our eyes and suffered through. Only so will this lovely myth come to life.

Acts III and IV bring this about largely through dramatic imagery. The language itself does not cease to be imagistic, but the crucial imagistic role is dramatic or theatrical, consisting as it does of images made by actors in action. The Restoration playhouse was ideally suited for such visual imagery. Although the exact nature of the theatres of Shakespeare's day is in dispute, surviving inventories show that it was in some sense symbolic but that it also made use of such rude, realistic devices as a flowery bank, a view of Rome, and a "machine" for seemingly true decapitation. The Restoration stage is not symbolic in the same way. It maintains some of the emblematic features of Jacobean masque, but for the most part develops a stage idiom in a ground intermediate between symbol and realism. Audiences had to imagine less (Hieronimo does not bite out his tongue any more), but they had to see more—both with the eyes and the understanding. Such visual effects cannot of course be regarded apart from the language of the play: *All for Love* is not a dumb show. But it is a carefully created play. Although the evidence for this is to be found for the looking, a letter from Dryden to Walsh in 1693, written about his last play, *Love Triumphant*, shows how concerned he was with the purely theatrical aspects of drama.

> I have plotted it all; & written two Acts of it. This morning I had their chief Comedian whom they call Solon, with me; to consult with him concerning his own Character; & truly I thinke he has the best Understanding of any man in the Playhouse.[9]

As usual, Dryden anticipates the shift to visual imagery in *All for Love* by means of a striking instance, the stage ceremony opening Act III.

The pageantry at the beginning of the third act is, then, a masque marking a turning point in the play, both in the action and the kind of language of drama employed. It is the play's climax insofar as all that follows is a turning away from this triumph (in both the private and public realms) through action and myth. As a step forward towards the tragic triumph, however, it is the first of three tableaux, and the first as well of a number of closely knit scenes of wishful hopes and of an ever-growing illusion that leads Antony in the end to clear-sighted truth. The beginning of the third act naturally grows immediately from the close of the second in the mythic reconciliation between Antony and Cleopatra. No sooner is the myth created, however, than we find a visual image repeated from the first act. Once again Ventidius enters, standing apart in the chill glow of Roman armor. There stands the surrogate of Roman Antony. As in the first act, the Egyptian Antony is awed by the "virtue" of his other self and wishes to flee. Nothing makes clearer the ill success of the masque of Mars and Venus in harmonizing Antony's two worlds: we observe that the myth was devised by Cleopatra. Rome, which is to say the public, ethical, and historical sides of human experience, must perforce challenge the strange pact Antony tries to make between Rome and Egypt, between war and love. In under a hundred lines later, Dolabella enters for the first time, a Roman fresh from Cæsar's camp but with the graces of Antony. From this point, the alternatives which had seemed so simple—Cleopatra or Ventidius, the private or the public world—become increasingly qualified by each other. The imagery Antony uses to greet his younger friend seems familiar enough to us.

> Thou hast what's left of me;
> For I am now so sunk from what I was,
> Thou find'st me at my lowest water-mark.
> The rivers that ran in, and raised my fortunes,
> Are all dried up, or take another course.
> What I have left is from my native spring;
> I've still a heart that swells, in scorn of fate,
> And lifts me to my banks. (127-34)

The imagery of the opening of the play has been rephrased in reverse form.

Antony senses in Dolabella, who resembles him in many more ways than Ventidius does, a more dangerous version of his native world than the older general. Without knowing why, but with strong subconscious compulsion, he justifies himself by sharing with Dolabella the memory of his first sight of Cleopatra. The vision rises from Antony's reproach of his younger friend to an implicit self-justification.

> Her galley down the silver Cydnos rowed,
> The tackling silk, the streamers waved with gold;
> The gentle winds were lodged in purple sails;
> Her nymphs, like Nereids, round her couch were placed,
> Where she, another sea-born Venus, lay. (162-66)

"My brighter Venus! O my brighter Mars!" Antony may well chide his friend for finding in Cleopatra an appeal he feels even more strongly.

> She lay, and leant her cheek upon her hand,
> And cast a look so languishingly sweet,
> As if, secure of all beholders' hearts,
> Neglecting, she could take 'em: boys, like Cupids,
> Stood fanning with their painted wings the winds
> That played about her face: but if she smiled,
> A darting glory seemed to blaze abroad,
> That men's desiring eyes were never wearied,
> But hung upon the object. To soft flutes
> The silver oars kept time; and while they played,
> The hearing gave new pleasure to the sight,

And both to thought. 'Twas heaven, or somewhat more . . .
Then, Dolabella, where was then thy soul?
Was not thy fury quite disarmed with wonder?
Didst thou not shrink behind me from those eyes,
And whisper in my ear, "Oh, tell her not
That I accused her with my brother's death?" (168-87)

The lush passage, with its undertone of niggardly eroticism, takes in
neither Dolabella nor Ventidius—although it is instrumental in having
Dolabella fall to Cleopatra's pretended blandishments in the next act.
For the moment, he urges home to Antony the values of the public
world.

But yet the loss was private that I made;
'Twas but myself I lost: I lost no legions;
I had no world to lose, no people's love. (199-201)

These are some of the clearest distinctions in the play. Here we begin
to see the wellsprings of Antony's tragedy—his public grandeur has de-
prived him of the opportunity to obtain private pleasure. Dolabella has
lost himself; Antony has lost a self that desires a private as well as a
"people's love."

What follows is presented in more vivid stage imagery than linguistic.
Ventidius is out and back in a moment (III, 238) with Antony's wife
and two daughters. Rome plays its three female characters against the
three Egyptian. Growing desperate, Antony strives repeatedly and
unsuccessfully to bring back the reality shown by Ventidius into manageable symbols—in particular to Octavius—so that it may seem his
enemy. Octavia's appeal is generous, warm, noble, and in fact possessed
of every grace. But Antony feels no passion; he tells her with honesty
and a new insight into himself,

Octavia, I have heard you, and must praise
The greatness of your soul;
But cannot yield to what you have proposed;
For I can ne'er be conquered but by love;
And you do all for duty. (313-17)

Rome has still to exert its claims; these come in the act's second tableau,
which is again one of relationships, in the passage quoted earlier as the
stylistic nadir of the play.

Dryden has another surprise in the wings. *"Enter* ALEXAS *hastily"*
(372 S. D.). Now Egypt comes to exert its attraction, and just as the
ambassadresses of the public realm had been those who might excite
personal feeling, so now the viceroy of passion is the eunuch.

> ALEXAS. The queen, my mistress, sir, and yours—
> ANTONY. 'Tis past.— . . .
> . . . .
> VENTIDIUS.There's news for you; run, my officious eunuch,
> Be sure to be the first; haste forward;
> Haste, my dear eunuch, haste! (373-78)

What follows is remarkable. Dryden clears the stage for the traditional
soliloquy of the villain, but the effect is to humanize Alexas, to give him
humanity and passions that we are made to feel. He becomes for himself
a potential statesman and lover, a might-have-been Antony, now that
the real one has left the stage, and he speaks of Ventidius with considerable insight.

> This downright fighting fool, this thick-skulled hero,
> This blunt, unthinking instrument of death,
> With plain dull virtue has outgone my wit.
> Pleasure forsook my earliest infancy;
> The luxury of others robbed my cradle,
> And ravished thence the promise of a man.
> Cast out from nature, disinherited
> Of what her meanest children claim by kind,
> Yet greatness kept me from contempt: that's gone.
> Had Cleopatra followed my advice,
> Then he had been betrayed who now forsakes.
> She dies for love; but she has known its joys:
> God, is this just, that I, who know no joys,
> Must die, because she loves? (379-92)

The depth of understanding makes this one of the great humane passages
of the play. Antony has created his tragedy; Alexas has his inflicted on
him. This solitary anguish yields to yet a third pageant in this act, the
encounter between Cleopatra and Octavia. Once again it is a matter of
relationship, as wife and mistress exert their claims and credentials to
each other rather than to their usual object, Antony. Skirting comedy
as it does, the encounter releases our tensions with the abuse. We think
Octavia to be right, and sympathize with Cleopatra. Although matters

are not decided in this scene, Cleopatra wins the word-engagement and loses the battle. She who had been described in imagery of eternal fruitfulness now speaks of herself in terms altering the endurance to death and the mature fertility to childhood. Egypt is again sinking.

> My sight grows dim, and every object dances,
> And swims before me, in the maze of death.
> My spirits, while they were opposed, kept up;
> They could not sink beneath a rival's scorn . . .
> Lead me, my Charmion; nay, your hand too, Iras:
> My grief has weight enough to sink you both.
> Conduct me to some solitary chamber,
> And draw the curtains round;
> Then leave me to myself, to take alone
> My fill of grief.
>   There I till death will his unkindness weep;
>   As harmless infants moan themselves asleep. (470-73; 477-84)

The act is a triumph (with one accompanying blemish in the language) of stage metaphors and of a nearly total shifting in roles through three pageants dealing with relationships. We feel the need for the ironies to clear and for the "complexities of mire and blood" to simplify.

Instead of filling the need, the fourth act heightens it. Antony wishes Dolabella to be his ambassador to Cleopatra to bid her farewell, which is of a piece with his earlier trying to accuse Dolabella of loving Cleopatra. The responsibility is properly his own. As he leaves Dolabella with his charge, Antony has four exits in about fifteen lines (IV, 26-42), on each entry trying to soften the blow for Cleopatra. Now Roman Dolabella is left to make the traditional soliloquy of the hero's surrogate. The resemblance is not to Shakespeare's Enobarbus, but to Alexas, for Roman Dolabella is even more of a would-be Antony. The imagery is that of the chamber and childhood with which Cleopatra had ended the preceding act.

> Men are but children of a larger growth;
> Our appetites as apt to change as theirs,
> And full as craving too, and full as vain;
> And yet the soul, shut up in her dark room,
> Viewing so clear abroad, at home sees nothing;
> But, like a mole in earth, busy and blind,
> Works all her folly up, and casts it outward

To the world's open view: thus I discovered,
And blamed the love of ruined Antony;
Yet wish that I were he, to be so ruined. (43-52)

Curiously, Antony seems better matched against the ruin spoken of by
Dolabella than against the unsexed tragedy of Alexas.

What follows is a rapid succession of intrigue and pretense, whose
effect is to ennoble Antony's consideration and even his softness by
making it plain-dealing. Ventidius enters after Dolabella's soliloquy,
again unseen, and very like Alexas in the opening scene of the play. He
has designs of getting Dolabella in love with Cleopatra, so to rouse
Antony's anger against them for their betrayal. Alexas has the same
scheme, but with the opposite motive of arousing Antony's jealous concern. Cleopatra, dizzy on her sinking ground, yields to the counsel, perhaps because it has so much of death in it. Alexas urges:

Believe me; try
To make him jealous; jealousy is like
A polished glass held to the lips when life's in doubt:
If there be breath, 'twill catch the damp, and show it. (70-73)

Cleopatra protests. Adversity has made her regard herself in new terms,
terms which make us come to see that Alexas' condition, Dolabella's
dilemma, and her role are alike in being examples of what is tragic and
inscrutable in the roles men find they must play.

Nature meant me
A wife, a silly, harmless, household dove,
Fond without art, and kind without deceit;
But Fortune, that has made a mistress of me,
[Has] thrust me out to the wide world, unfurnished
Of falsehood to be happy. (91-96)

This is what she says before acting a falsehood, and it is in any event too
simple a picture of herself. She will not rise to true tragic dimensions till
she learns to act, nor Antony till he can no longer act. We are given a
courtship scene that involves pretense on all sides, and the self-pretense
of all concerned.

Cleopatra cannot sustain the role of coquette through the abuse Dolabella reports Antony to have thundered at her. (He betrays the condi-

tions of his charge in every way.) As she sinks, Dolabella recovers himself and calls upon his absent friend in Cleopatra's imagery of childhood.

> My friend, my friend!
> What endless treasure hast thou thrown away,
> And scattered, like an infant, in the ocean,
> Vast sums of wealth, which none can gather thence! (204-07)

She responds with Roman imagery. She is

> Like one who wanders through long barren wilds,
> And yet foreknows no hospitable inn
> Is near to succor hunger, eats his fill,
> Before his painful march. (210-13)

Ventidius brings in Octavia to see Dolabella take her hand as a pledge of their truth to Antony and his abortive love for her. The watching eyes think it a new affair for Cleopatra. The delusions of the characters grow apace, and in that growth begin to give the play a clarity of ironic outline that is taking us steadily on to an end. Ventidius' remarks on Cleopatra and her dangers are parallel to the soliloquies of Alexas and Dolabella. What we learn about him is that no little part of his hatred for her grows from jealousy of her rivalry for Antony's affection, and indeed from her claim upon his own.

> I pity Dolabella; but she's dangerous:
> Her eyes have pow'r beyond Thessalian charms
> To draw the moon from heav'n; for eloquence,
> The sea-green Sirens taught her voice their flatt'ry;
> And, while she speaks, night steals upon the day,
> Unmarked of those that hear. Then she's so charming,
> Age buds at sight of her, and swells to youth:
> The holy priests gaze on her when she smiles;
> And with heaved hands, forgetting gravity,
> They bless her wanton eyes: even I, who hate her,
> With a malignant joy behold such beauty;
> And, while I curse, desire it. (233-44)

The revelations of such depths and alterations in the characters suggest a time span of many years in the scheme of the play. In fact, we have moved simply from early morning to afternoon of the same day.

In truth, the play's unity of time is artificial, and anyone could be forgiven for presuming that several days go by in the action. Somewhat
differently, unity of place seems to be strictly adhered to—but it also
seems to make no difference, to be so natural as to be unimportant. It is
the unity of action which we all know to be the important thing, and
in which Dryden took pride, and which in the third and fourth acts
achieves special importance.

The unity of the action—and included in that is not only the direction
of details to a single end but a sense of that end towards which all moves
—contrasts with the growing confusion and delusion from which the
characters suffer. As we come to understand them better in the fourth
act, they understand each other less. Similarly, in the rest of this act and
in much of the last we begin to understand the nature of the tragedy
and its destination, while the characters find the action is getting out of
their control. The scene of Alexas' entry (IV, 319 S. D., ff.) is a masterpiece of clear confusion, cross-purposes, self-deluded intrigue, and
ironic confidence. Ventidius catches sight of him, thinks (wrongly)
that Alexas does not wish to be seen, and calls him in. Alexas begins a
mock-humble series of addresses couched in a marvelously oriental
vagueness and flattery, at last getting round to the suggestion that Cleopatra (full of measured consideration for everybody's feelings in this
difficult matter) has decided she might as well fall in love with Dolabella.
Only the self-deluded could believe such a tale. Ventidius is so very
pleased ("On, sweet eunuch; my dear half-man, proceed," 376), thinking quite wrongly that now Antony will be cured. Antony, who alone
has no plans working under cover, is also taken in. His protestations
upset Octavia, and while Alexas is delighted to find himself thrust out
by the jealous emperor, she leaves voluntarily, never to see Antony
again. Antony has a soliloquy which shows him, like Cleopatra, reduced
to simplicity. The speech (431-40) echoes Dolabella's descriptions of
Cleopatra, rephrasing his imagery of the transparent soul (IV, 202-03)
and applying to her (205-06) the river/marine imagery so prominent in
the play. It is now Antony's turn to misconstrue the situation and everyone involved in it. Confident, but wrong, that he now for the first time
clearly sees himself and the world, he indulges in self-pity. At this stage,
Dryden brings back once more the linguistically complex imagery that
he had for the most part foregone in the latter half of Act III and the
first two-thirds of Act IV. Such construction is very typical of his art:

a change in imagery prefigures a change in other matters. For although the action has not yet started its tragic rise, the imagery of scope and complex values that alone can make suffering positive is introduced while the characters are continuing to fall into dismal confusion. It is notable that the self-delusions and the complexity of intrigue in this portion of the play employ like, say, *Othello* and *King Lear*, a manipulation of plot and characters, of motive and action, that seems more the stuff of comedy than tragedy, as it is usually conceived. Like them, too, it is concerned with seeing, that is, understanding, both passion and the world in which men find themselves.

The return of the imagery of language to a dominant role in the play re-introduces the imagery of ripeness, which now comes to achieve prime importance. Antony reproaches Cleopatra and Dolabella:

> you have ripened sin,
> To such a monstrous growth, 'twill pose the gods
> To find an equal torture. Two, two such!—
> Oh, there's no farther name, two such!—to me,
> To me, who locked my soul within your breasts,
> Had no desires, no joys, no life, but you;
> When half the globe was mine, I gave it you
> In dowry with my heart; I had no use,
> No fruit of all, but you: a friend and mistress
> Was what the world could give. O Cleopatra!
> O Dolabella! how could you betray
> This tender heart, which with an infant fondness
> Lay lulled betwixt your bosoms, and there slept,
> Secure of injured faith? (478-91)

The image of infancy is remarkably developed here. Antony treats his heart as the child of the bosoms of Dolabella and Cleopatra, lying innocently asleep between them while they plan adultery. This is indeed to ripen sin, if it be true. Cleopatra admits to her degree of guilt and so starts the action upwards—and gives the imagery of flood one of its last expressions.

> Ah, what will not a woman do, who loves!
> What means will she refuse, to keep that heart
> Where all her joys are placed? 'Twas I encouraged,
> 'Twas I blew up the fire that scorched his soul,
> To make you jealous, and by that regain you.

> But all in vain; I could not counterfeit.
> In spite of all the dams my love broke o'er,
> And drowned my heart again. Fate took th' occasion;
> And thus one minute's feigning has destroyed
> My whole life's truth. (513-22)

The act concludes with Antony trying, still unsuccessfully, to control his world by telling Cleopatra and Dolabella how they must all live. His last speech (586-97) shows him giving orders more out of habit than desire, as much out of weariness as self-pity. Only death can lie ahead, death renewed into life by feeling expressed in language, by the knowledge of truth, and by some symbol that will both contain and express the experiences endured.

The last act opens with a new kind of question being asked— and the wrong answer given. Charmion exclaims,

> Be juster, heav'n: such virtue punished thus,
> Will make us think that chance rules all above,
> And shuffles, with a random hand, the lots,
> Which man is forced to draw. (V, 1-4)

To Dryden this is obviously irrational fatalism. In its psychological import it is also a gesture towards death, as is shown in a moment by a stage image, Cleopatra's gesture of suicide. She is restrained, and in her reproaches of Alexas for his central guilt, and in his reply, we get the last changes rung upon the imagery of the waters, if not upon that of motion accompanying it.

>   Thou, thou, villain,
> Has[t] pushed my boat to open sea; to prove,
> At my sad cost, if thou canst steer it back.
> It cannot be; I'm lost too far; I'm ruined! (32-35)

Alexas accepts the imagery but would correct its application.

> Suppose some shipwracked seaman near the shore,
> Dropping and faint, with climbing up the cliff,
> If, from above, some charitable hand
> Pull him to safety, hazarding himself
> To draw the other's weight; would he look back,
> And curse him for his pains? The case is yours;
> But one step more, and you have gained the height. (39-45)

To this Cleopatra's reply is "Sunk, never more to rise" (47), a judgment confirmed too soon by news that the Egyptian fleet has gone over to Octavius, that Antony's cause with Egypt is doomed. (The handling of this, the second military action reported in the play, leaves Cleopatra absolved of the guilt attributed to her in some versions of the story.) Significantly, it is Serapion who brings the news, using her word, *sunk* (one of the play's many variants on Latinate meanings of *ruin*), and recalling his second speech at the beginning of the play.

> Egypt has been; our latest hour is come:
> The queen of nations, from her ancient seat,
> Is sunk for ever in the dark abyss:
> Time has unrolled her glories to the last,
> And now closed up the volume. (71-5)

As the play moves closer towards its affirmation of passion, the public realm, now of Egypt, is introduced. Indeed we are beginning to see what is to a considerable extent a reversal of roles. The most attractive Romans become attractive in their private selves, the Egyptians most attractive in their public dignity. The reversal is not whole; perhaps it is not half. But it establishes that balance of experience which the action and the characters have been seeking. This opening scene of the last act cannot be left without reference to the second, and again sympathetic, villain's soliloquy of Alexas.

> O that I less could fear to lose this being,
> Which, like a snowball in my coward hand,
> The more 'tis grasped, the faster melts away.
> Poor reason! what a wretched aid art thou!
> For still, in spite of thee,
> These two long lovers, soul and body, dread
> Their final separation. (131-37)

It is ignominious of him to wish to save himself "No matter what becomes of Cleopatra," but his talk of these "two long lovers" inevitably calls to mind the central love theme of the play.

The next scene, between Antony and Ventidius, is one of Dryden's microcosmic views of the play which yet moves the whole forward. Beginning (149-56) with the imagery of Serapion's opening speech, they go through the will to do battle that had come from their resolved

friendship at the end of the first act. Next, first Ventidius and then
Antony take over the imagery of transcendence Cleopatra had introduced at the beginning of the second act.

> Now you shall see I love you. Not a word
> Of chiding more. By my few hours of life,
> I am so pleased with this brave Roman fate,
> That I would not be Cæsar, to outlive you.
> When we put off this flesh, and mount together,
> I shall be shown to all th' ethereal crowd,—
> "Lo, this is he who died with Antony!"
> ANTONY. Who knows but we may pierce through all their troops,
> And reach my veterans yet? 'Tis worth the tempting,
> T' o'erleap this gulf of fate,
> And leave our wond'ring destinies behind. (178-88)

That what is expressed here is personal cannot be doubted. The spirit
seems Roman and, we might think, therefore public. There is no reason
why the public values cannot be personal, but the emphasis upon the
emotional strength of *amicitia*—"Now you shall see I love you"— suggests private values as well. Ventidius is saying after all that he loves
Antony so much that he will die for him. We can only say that the
public and private are beginning to lose some of their distinctions. It is a
characteristic bit of management on Dryden's part to have Ventidius
make his declaration just as Alexas is on his way to give Antony the
(false) news that Cleopatra has taken her life out of love for him.

   This lesser irony is as nothing to the handling of Antony's approach
to death. Dryden still refuses to allow him adequate insight into himself
or his world. Unwilling to give Alexas a chance to tell the (false) news
he brings, Antony assumes that Cleopatra is untrue and his life meaningless. Time comes to be a major consideration now that there is so little
of it.

>   ... my whole life
> Has been a golden dream of love and friendship.
> But, now I wake ...
>   Ingrateful woman!
> Who followed me, but as the swallow summer,
> Hatching her young ones in my kindly beams,
> Singing her flatt'ries to my morning wake;
> But, now my winter comes, she spreads her wings,
> And seeks the spring of Cæsar. (204-13)

Upon allowing Alexas at last to tell him that Cleopatra has committed suicide Antony's thoughts tend at once to the same act. Alexas leaves pleased with himself if anxious—"But, oh! the Romans! / Fate comes too fast upon my wit, / Hunts me too hard" (254-56). Antony is simply exhausted in public will—"I will not fight: there's no more work for war"—but the exhaustion brings a reconciliation. "The bus'ness of my angry hours is done" (261-62). The decision made, his emotions are all with Cleopatra. What reason could not decide and action not achieve has been managed by the lie of Cleopatra's death. The price he pays for a clear mind is the sacrifice, over a lie, of half the world. He thinks of Octavius.

> 'Tis time the world
> Should have a lord, and know whom to obey.
> We two have kept its homage in suspense,
> And bent the globe, on whose each side we trod,
> Till it was dinted inwards. Let him walk
> Alone upon't; I'm weary of my part.
> My torch is out; and the world stands before me
> Like a black desart at th' approach of night:
> I'll lay me down, and stray no farther on. (280-88)

When he extracts from Ventidius a promise to kill him but finds that his friend has slain himself instead, Antony falls on his own sword and is mortally wounded though not at once killed.

His earlier hope of resolving the contradictions and dilemmas that faced him had been vain because he was unwilling to face up to the truth of a world governed, not by Charmion's celestial lottery, but by men's own freedom of action, and also to the related truth that such freedom is assured and rendered intelligible only by laws of human affairs. Antony had tried to be emperor at the courts of both arms and love. Unlike Æneas, who gave up most of his private desires and so succeeded in the public world, Antony wished to accommodate his military valor to the myth of Mars and have his Venus, too. The play shows that it is impossible to sustain such a life. That it is possible to live it in delusion for a moment, upon condition of dying, it also shows —in the vision at the beginning of the third act, as again truly at the end of the play. The tragic irony that he founds his truth on the basis of Alexas' lie is transcended by the merger, in death, of the private and public values. The Roman death in suicide which saves the soldier's

honor is invoked—as he falls on the field of love. There is therefore no
need of further adjustment or bickering when Cleopatra hurries in to
reassure him, and then to vow her own death. Calm and reconciled for
the first time on this long last day of his life, he can reassure her.

> But grieve not, while thou stay'st[,]
> My last disastrous times:
> Think we have had a clear and glorious day,
> And heav'n did kindly to delay the storm,
> Just till our close of ev'ning. Ten years' love,
> And not a moment lost, but all improved
> To th' utmost joys,—what ages have we lived!
> And now to die each other's; and, so dying,
> While hand in hand we walk in groves below,
> Whole troops of lovers' ghosts shall flock about us,
> And all the train be ours. (387-97)

Just as the play's unity of time is a formal symbol of a man's adult life,
so Antony has had "a clear and glorious day" and yet has lived "ages."
Living, then to die, and then to live below forever; dying for love, they
shall lead a lovers' army of "troops."

Cleopatra completes the harmony of values. She becomes a Roman—
"I have not loved a Roman not to know / What should become his wife"
(412-13), and with the marriage returns the myth of Venus and Mars,
and religion. She dresses with "pomp and royalty"

> As when I saw him first, on Cydnos' bank,
> All sparkling, like a goddess: so adorned,
> I'll find him once again . . .
> For I must conquer Cæsar too, like him,
> And win my share o' th' world.—Hail, you dear relics
> Of my immortal love!
> Oh, let no impious hand remove you hence. (457, 459-61, 465-68)

The imagery of the fruitful yet destructive Nile with which the play
opens, like the imagery of ripeness and of death that develops from it,
receives one last brilliant expression in language as well as in dramatic
imagery when Iras hands Cleopatra the basket with the serpent: "Underneath the fruit / The aspic lies" (471-72). By themselves the six words
are simple enough, but at the end they carry much of the weight of the
play's configuration of experience. Charmion and Iras die with her, and

it is left, with great artistic propriety, for Serapion to close, as he had begun the play, with the choral voice.

> See how the lovers sit in state together,
> As they were giving laws to half mankind!
> Th' impression of a smile, left in her face,
> Shows she died pleased with him for whom she lived,
> And went to charm him in another world.
> Cæsar's just ent'ring: grief has now no leisure.
> Secure that villain [Alexas], as our pledge of safety,
> To grace th' imperial triumph.—Sleep, blest pair,
> Secure from human chance, long ages out,
> While all the storms of fate fly o'er your tomb;
>   And fame to late posterity shall tell,
>   No lovers lived so great, or died so well. (508-19)

The march of Roman feet leaves grief no leisure. We are reminded at the moment of the lovers' triumph of their defeat, for unlike some earlier dramatists, Dryden does not dissolve all into a mist. The nature of his art, here as elsewhere, depends upon seeing clearly even when that requires the admission of dissident elements or mixed feelings. It would be difficult to demonstrate that clarity better than in the exactness of Serapion's observation that the lovers sit, "As they were giving laws to *half* mankind," to half of that complex of public and private values that makes up our lives and sometimes divides them. But which half is it?

Octavius, Rome, and all that is as it were near at hand offstage cannot break their "spousals," "a tie too strong / For Roman laws to break." By the same token, however, there is the other half of mankind whose laws have proved too strong for them. They have lost the world, or rather one world. There is no doubt of that. And yet they have equally certainly won. Ventidius has not been converted to their love, but he has shared with them their resolution of conflicting claims at the price of tragedy. Looking back over the play, we see that the resolution has grown from the contradictory decisions of the first two acts, from the delusions of the third and the fourth acts, and from a deceit that no longer matters in the fifth. We also see how other seemingly contradictory elements have been accommodated to each other—"ages" within a single day, imagery of great scope rendered very nearly intimate, and even to some extent the private with the public. The imagery ennobles the action, but also gives it a manageable proportion, what one would call tenderness if it were not accompanied by something like irony. Antony's speech—

> Give to your boy, your Cæsar,
> This rattle of a globe to play withal,
> This gewgaw world—

shows how the scope is encompassed in little, in that which is manageable (II, 443-45). Antony's first speech in the play suggests as much.

> Why was I raised the meteor of the world,
> Hung in the skies, and blazing as I travelled,
> Till all my fires were spent; and then cast downward
> To be trod out by Cæsar? (206-09)

But for its change from agony to assurance, a speech of his in the last act suggests much the same.

>   I'm weary of my part.
> My torch is out; and the world stands before me
> Like a black desart at th' approach of night. (285-87)

The large lodges in the small, energy in extinction, day in night.

> Think we have had a clear and glorious day,
> And heav'n did kindly to delay the storm,
> Just till our close of ev'ning. (389-91)

The gain is loss, their day ends well only with the dark. And so the Roman feet march in to claim a different triumph.

The fact of tragedy is plain; the loss it represents is quietly conveyed. But what kind of tragedy has occurred? What has been finally affirmed?* If the world lost is the public one in a "noon-day light" of vitality, continuity, and achievement, it is because in imagery as well as in other respects the play leads to the dark. The tragic gain accrues from an identification with this dark, this death of that creative yet doubtful love. Most of the imagery of the play can be referred to the

---

* The second question was put to me by my students in a seminar at Osaka University in 1961. To them I owe the genesis of this chapter and much else for which I am grateful.

central integration of love and death. In this Dryden presents a version
of one of the most abiding images of human experience, one that in
Western literature may be called Romantic in view of its most characteristic expression in the medieval romances.* (There are of course
religious and patriotic analogies, but even in such Latin phrases as *amor
patriae* or *dulce est pro patria mori* we sense the analogy to two comparable features of experience.)

The sense of the relatedness of death and love is to be found throughout the literature of the century, whether in the familiar quibble upon
"death" and "dying" or in the emotional climaxes of the Jacobean and
Caroline stage. The Aspatias who seek death at the hands of those
Amintors who do not return their love are not always credible creatures,
but their motives have a genuine basis in psychological truth. Although
in expressing the same truth so well in *All for Love* Dryden was to be
more essentially the "Romantic" dramatist than in any other important
play, Romantic elements have been discovered in more plays than this.
The usual reasons for speaking of his plays as Romantic have been their
sources in romances and their cultural primitivism. To read Dryden's
prefaces is sufficient to demonstrate his familiarity with the Scuderys
and the Calprenèdes. Cultural primitivism, that fascination with another,
simpler civilization contemporary with one's own, marks a number of
his plays, especially those situated in the New World. Significantly, it is
Dryden who, in *The Conquest of Granada*, gave the language the phrase,
the Noble Savage. These are matters in which it is difficult to speak
briefly without claiming too much. Certainly, in the century there is
much at Versailles or London that could not be termed Romantic in
any sense, and Dryden is often to be found putting what is sentimental
coin in other writers to calculated use.

Yet Noyes was very perceptive in speaking of "Romantic tragedy" in
the Restoration and in deriving it from Beaumont and Fletcher, the
French romances, and the romantic epics of Tasso, Ariosto, and Spenser.
"It would be hard," he observed, "to frame a definition of romanticism

---

* In his article cited in note 4 above, Osborn clearly distinguishes in the
heroic plays between an "irrational *heroical* love" and "true rational love." The
difficulty of applying the distinction to such characters as Cleopatra and Octavia
lends support to those (including Osborn) who hold this play to be something
other than pure heroic tragedy. The best general discussion of the nature of the
play (though I disagree with parts of it) is that of Moody E. Prior, *The Language
of Tragedy* (New York, 1947).

that should include *Marmion* and exclude *The Conquest of Granada*."
He felt that this side of Dryden was "a distorted survival of medieval
romance" and that it had "no future before" it.[10] But in that he judged
hastily. Dryden's plays indeed had little influence, since there is no
actable tragedy and little comedy to be found fifty years after his death.
But they assisted in a continuity of thought, as did also his similar images
of experience in another genre, the narrative poetry of *Fables*, which did
in fact have influence upon the nineteenth century.

The important fact is that in such historical senses some of Dryden's
plays have a character that can conveniently be termed Romantic. More
importantly some of them, notably *All for Love*, identify and affirm
two kinds of experience that will seldom be found identified, much less
affirmed, in his other writing. Clearly, the special esthetic conditions of
drama (as also of lyric, as dealt with in a later chapter) provided Dryden
with the opportunity to explore new kinds and images of experience.
Certainly without the "Romantic" identification in *All for Love* the
play could not exist. There is nothing whatsoever in the play to show
that death is a punishment of the two lovers; on the contrary, it brings
their final and most exalted union. That fact is not controverted but
modified by the presence in the play of a contrary image identifying
the public world with life. This public image is not as significant to the
play as the Romantic, but it is of great importance to a full view of it,
and to our sense of the consistency of Dryden's interests. To pose the
matter in terms of dramatic choice, Antony is faced with the alternatives
of a vital public honor he has tired of and a mortal private desire which
is insatiable.* It is a question of will, of choice, of the extent to which—
in the old faculty psychology—the will is directed by passion or reason.
Yet, partly to make the lovers' triumph the magnificent thing it is, and
perhaps partly as well to avoid a total commitment to the passionate
will, Dryden makes the vital public honor and the mortal private desire
accommodate themselves to each other part way by exchanging some
of their values. What in the great nondramatic poems is a force of personal and even private feeling energizing a public mode, is in this play

---

* In his *Herculean Hero*, Waith persuasively defines the conflict as one between
public and private aspects of our honor (see, e. g., pp. 76 and 155). Such a distinction seems to me to fail to see that one's public honor is the most highly
valued *personal* distinction, while one's private desire is equally capable of transcendence; and it seems incapable of making sense of a line like "Why, love does
all that's noble here below."

the private dignified by the public. This larger motion of the play is one factor in its claim to be Dryden's greatest, but it is typical of the motions of most of his plays. In all the will is to be seen choosing rightly or wrongly a private or public course, whether for a testing time or, with the finality of tragedy, choosing culpably, nobly, or in tragic ignorance of its true range of choice.

The special acclaim given *All for Love* may make it seem that the play is an exception in its affirmations and in the kind of human drama it presents. Such an attitude can only be countered by attention, however brief, to others of the plays. The reader, whether of them or of criticism in the last century and a half, will soon discover that *All for Love* is not the exception it is commonly thought to be. Scott and others have advanced good reasons for considering *Don Sebastian* to be Dryden's greatest play, and other titles have a way of making their way into criticism, if seldom with claims of superiority to *All for Love*. If Dryden's version of the story of the famous lovers has some special claim as the center of quality in his dramatic work, it is not, like *Annus Mirabilis* in the public realm, his first success in fashioning the other world of private will in his writing. Fifteen plays had preceded it, and twelve were to follow. Even granting the success which the earlier fifteen had brought him, it is not easy to explain why he should wish to treat a subject in which our greatest poet should have anticipated him. He knew that "Shakespeare's magic could not copied be; / Within that circle none durst walk but he."[11] The only explanation to make full sense is one that covers his other plays as well: that he felt a personal attraction to a kind of human experience not readily seen in most of his nondramatic work. Perhaps something must be granted to what he says in the Preface to *All for Love;* perhaps attempts by other writers than Shakespeare gave him "the confidence to try myself in this bow of Ulysses amongst the crowd of suitors."[12] But he was not given to courting the failure the allusion implies to be inevitable and total. He later claimed it as the only play he had written for himself, and whether that be true or not, it is difficult not to believe—in the context of nearly thirty plays—that his own heart to some measure sanctioned the lovers' rejection of the "world" for passion. It is evident to anyone that he devoted much of his genius and his feeling to such tragedies as *Aureng-Zebe, Don Sebastian, Cleomenes,* and even *Oedipus.* It seems equally evident that for all his lament of his saturnine humor he enjoyed laugh-

ing at, or even mingling with, the absurdities of man as he revealed them
to be in *Marriage A-la-Mode*, in *Amphitryon*, and even in so mindless a
jeu d'esprit as *Sir Martin Mar-All*.

What is at issue is not the high opinion of Dryden's plays that my
remarks imply but his own attitude toward them. The protests that all
but one were given to the public, like his doubts of comic gifts, are
often quoted as if they ended the matter. I think them defensive comments betraying uneasiness. The bulk of the evidence, after all, is on the
other side. His single essay in what Dr. Johnson termed elaborate
criticism is the *Essay of Dramatic Poesy*. His plays were accompanied
into print with prefaces of theoretical or practical criticism, or both,
designed in no small part to justify his dramatic work. Except for the
"Account" prefixed to *Annus Mirabilis,* almost all his prose criticisms
are in fact joined either to plays, to translations, or to collections.
MacFlecknoe is a gay satire, if there ever was one to come from a saturnine disposition, of a playwright who had offended his standards of
drama as much as of personal behavior and political principle. Unless we
are prepared to think Dryden alone an exception to normal ways of
assessing human nature or to literary rules of evidence, we must conclude that his plays, and the kinds of experience they treat, were of
great emotional importance to him. It may well be that he felt something akin to embarrassment or guilt over them, perhaps for their
occasional though much exaggerated indecency, perhaps for the rant of
some of the heroic plays, or perhaps for the unevenness resulting from
too hasty work. Beyond such reasons, however, there was a better one.
In the plays, he challenged with will and passion what his faith and
reason supported. It is as though the absence of critical prefaces to his
nondramatic works showed that they needed no apologia to the world
and himself, while his plays required the best efforts of justification,
whether literary or personal.

If so, it is a fine irony that he should feel the need to justify to the
world plays whose values come closer to those of that world from his
birth to the present than do the values of his nondramatic works. The
affirmation of passion, the preoccupation with boundless will, the opposition of private interest to public care, and the exaltation of the
moment over history and eternity as he understood them, are harmonious with the voluntarism of most writers of his generation and
since. It is further ironic that his plays violate his own "rationalist" or

"realist" position less than he had reason to fear. The limiting of conscious will by the irrational passion of heroical love and the opposition
to love by the code of honorable behavior afforded some small but
significant qualification. His conscience should have been yet more
assuaged by the larger movements of his plays, from freeing to limiting
the will, or from attacking public values to absorbing them. That such
qualifications of the voluntaristic concerns of his plays did not quiet his
doubts testifies to the power of will, passion, and the irrational in a man
whom other emotions and the force of his mind bore in an opposed
direction. It was not until these but barely subdued ideas could be
translated into the emotional force of religious faith, love of his sons,
and the secure admiration of his contemporaries that he gained full
composure.

His greatest play after *All for Love* and after his conversion is *Don
Sebastian* (1690), and it shows the extent to which he has at last understood himself. Sebastian describes his beloved Almeyda, who, only
later he learns, is his sister, as one "Strong in her passion, impotent of
reason."[13] And even the embittered Dorax can say, "Why, love does all
that's noble here below."[14] The claim of the heart is heard and set into
its place alongside the public values in a larger whole. Upon learning of
his incest, he has a parting scene with Almeyda, an experience once again
rousing his love and with it the will to break "laws divine and human."
But the reason judges, and will submits.

> One moment longer
> And I should break through laws divine and human,
> And think them cobwebs spread for little man,
> Which all the bulky herd of nature breaks.
> The vigorous young world was ignorant
> Of these restrictions; 'tis decrepit now;
> Not more devout, but more decayed, and cold.—
> All this is impious, therefore we must part.[15]

The speech is very like the passage quoted from *Palamon and Arcite* as
the epigraph to this chapter. Palamon in his suffering also questions the
constitution of things, protesting man's tragic place in it. Like Palamon,
Sebastian challenges all that Dryden's public world held firm, giving
rise to a sense of tragedy and of the blind night of fate in which men
steer like that of *Annus Mirabilis*, but more wholly realized. Only, the

sense has been absorbed, even while being allowed fuller expression, by a Stoic acceptance of suffering. *Lacrimae volvuntur inanes*, the Virgilian sense of the tearful nature of experience is harmonized with the greater sense that the natural human protest must yield to acceptance of the nature of things. The tragedy, like its resolution, is heightened by the fact that the suffering originates not in the willful actions of Sebastian and Almeyda but in their father's adultery and concealment of their relationship. Caught like Oedipus in a tragic web woven by forces beyond his power of will, Sebastian naturally rebels. But with implicit faith and in affirmation of "laws human and divine" he accepts a world in which will and such laws break man's heart in their clash.

In other plays, the drama of the will undergoes different, although kindred motions. The play in which "will" is most often mentioned is *Tyrannic Love* (pub. 1670), with its ranting Maximin totally voluntaristic and its composed St. Catharine wholly true to reasoned faith. The play moves very simply from the dominance of the one to that of the other. In *The Indian Emperour* (pub. 1667), *Secret Love* (pub. 1668), and other heroic plays, the major good characters learn to alter the private will of their desires to a will choosing the public value of a "heroic" world. In the comedies, the "gay couples" move from an initial "perfect balance, in which the absurdity of the antimatrimonial mode is so delightfully heightened" to "another perfect balance, as the facts of basic human nature weigh the [antimatrimonial] mode and find it wanting."[16] Whether married or seeking, such characters in the comedies willfully hunt out the fruits forbidden them by public convention and, just before burning their fingers, come to terms with the public world, usually by accepting its most important social expression, marriage. The force of the public world is not usually given the full expression of *Marriage A-la-Mode* (1673), where it is conveyed in what may best be called a serious sub-plot. Nor is there always in the tragedies, as there is in *Don Sebastian*, a comic subplot ridiculing the indulgences of private will. Yet in plays of all kinds there is a form of reconciliation managing by insight, acceptance, or yielding to bring into "perfect balance" a tragic or comic action of the human will. So much are these motions basic to Dryden's plays that it is difficult to find that conflict between a prevailing libertinism in most of the play and a final acceptance of convention which makes the tone of some Restoration comedies so difficult to assess. In his best plays, the reconciliation mingles the two worlds of private will and public reason or with opened eyes affirms the disparity between them.

In like fashion, the course of Dryden's dramatic career shows an increasing degree of protest and of awareness of the chasm between will and reason, even while leading to a higher reconciliation. The development from *The Indian Emperour* to *All for Love* and to *Don Sebastian* shows that he gradually found means of absorbing his own contrary motives in that blind tragedy, or comedy, of human life he had glimpsed as the fate of others in *Annus Mirabilis*. Similarly, his nondramatic poetry after his conversion affirmed in faith a faculty superior to reason and yet harmonious with it. Until that time he argued the reasons of the heart most eloquently in his plays and felt in his poetry outside the theatre the emotions of hope for a world meaningful in its rationality. In the plays we often find, whether in imagery of language, of action, or of both, that ages-old identification of love and death, the world of shadows and private desires. In works other than the plays, in their imagery and tone, we usually find a very different identification of meaningful action and civilized life, of the noonday world of light and personal achievement in a public arena. It may seem, then, that Dryden has two literary worlds, the dramatic and the nondramatic. Yet for all their concern with private shadows the plays finally submit to light, and for all their bright publicity the nondramatic poems take form in the obscure private reaches of Dryden's personality, whether his concern be with fate as in *Annus Mirabilis*, with that which causes bristling anger as in *The Medal*, or the salvation of his soul as in *Religio Laici* and *The Hind and the Panther*. For in both his dramatic and nondramatic works there is but one man responding, attempting to define his interests by exploring the limits of his forms and by searching for a "perfect balance" that could be struck in the writing only to the extent that it held between Dryden's inner needs and the values he could discover in his world.

Metaphors and Themes

PART TWO

Metaphor and Values: *MacFlecknoe*

CHAPTER III

Neither is it true that this fineness of raillery is offensive. A witty man is tickled while he is hurt in this manner, and a fool feels it not.
—Discourse Concerning Satire.

Sure [Dryden] goes a little too far in calling me the dullest, and has no more reason for that than for giving me the Irish name of Mack, when he knows I never saw Ireland till I was three-and-twenty years old, and was there but four months.
—Shadwell's reaction to MacFlecknoe

Although *MacFlecknoe* is not Dryden's greatest poem, it is his gayest. In it laughter rules, a monarch over "all the realms of Nonsense absolute." The raillery creates that which it seems utterly to destroy, and the deadly stroke is scarcely felt. There had been satire in English before, but none quite like this. Dryden might have applied to earlier English satirists the words of Horace: *Et Græcis intacti carminis auctor.* Evidently his first satire, it appears to have sprung partly from obscure personal differences, partly from a sense of outrage over the mindless, artless literature of the seventies and particularly the drama, in which he had acquired his fame. He must have known it to be the liveliest work he had written and his most unified apart from his plays. Yet, for whatever reason, he was slow to release it for printing. More or less finished by 1678, when John Oldham set down part of it in his copybook, *MacFlecknoe* was not published with Dryden's approval till 1684.* Congreve appears to have been right in saying he was not vin-

---

* The fact that *MacFlecknoe* grows from a wider literary situation than its identification with Shadwell suggests is shown by George McFadden in his excellent "Elkanah Settle and the Genesis of *MacFlecknoe*," PQ, XLIII (1964), 55-72. His evidence strongly supports the belief that the poem was written in 1678. Basing his discussion upon as yet unpublished material of David Vieth,

dictive, and the highly personal quality of the poem—for Dryden
himself as well as for poor Shadwell—seems to have restrained him
from publication. Although little can be said about the poem before
publication, it is clearly a continuation of his dramatic criticism into a
form of poetry so assured that it seems almost inevitable that satire
should be of its kind. The somewhat idealistic and grave heroic world
of *Annus Mirabilis* has gained in urban bustle by accepting laughter.

If he had not known it before, *Paradise Lost* would have shown
Dryden that the values of public poetry could be presented in a middle
esthetic distance suggestive of a timeless generality of truth. As frequently in later poems, the opening lines of *MacFlecknoe* begin with
the neutral public mode.

> All human things are subject to decay,
> And when fate summons, monarchs must obey.
> This Flecknoe found, who, like Augustus, young
> Was call'd to empire, and had govern'd long;
> In prose and verse, was own'd, without dispute,
> Thro' all the realms of *Nonsense*, absolute. (1-6)

We meet with a sober orotundity which the implications of the second
couplet alter, since to couple Flecknoe with Augustus is to appeal to a
public that shares with the poet a knowledge of both. The third couplet
reveals the moral, classical gold to have been applied over English
lead. The poem shows even more the result of Dryden's experience
as a dramatist. It reads like a narrated representation of a climactic
scene from a play, re-creating the kind of confrontation of two men
that so pleased Dryden in the first act of *All for Love*, and the scene
is laid with great care. The attention to costumes, properties, scenes,
and machines also suggests the stage. This is no accident, for although
the narrative allows for introduction, comment, and looking into the
past, and although it is not dramatic in the strict sense, it is about a
dramatist and dramatic principles; it is full of monologue; and it is
theatrical in conception. The stage may be said provisionally to furnish
the poem with a general, unifying metaphor: it deals with what is acted

George deForest Lord suggests that "Dryden probably wrote *MacFlecknoe* . . .
between July 1676 and December 1677" (*Poems on Affairs of State*, I [New Haven,
1963], 376-78). The argument is complex, plausible, and unconvincing. The poem
first appeared, apparently unauthorized, in 1682.

but not real. All that is done by King Flecknoe or by MacFlecknoe is but an imitation of reality. This is generally true of art, as everyone has been taught, but bad art is merely acted and wholly false, as part of the coronation ceremony shows. The true emblems of kingship remain untarnished, but Flecknoe's are shown to be wholly degraded.

> In his sinister hand, instead of ball,
> He plac'd a mighty mug of potent ale;
> *Love's Kingdom* to his right he did convey,
> At once his scepter, and his rule of sway. (120-23)

The opening lines are a kind of prologue to the first episode of the poem, which gets under way with the first of King Flecknoe's speeches (13-59). The choice of Shadwell as successor to the ruling monarch of Nonsense is announced and explained. The show is on. The king speaks longer than a character in a play would be allowed to, longer than is logically necessary. It is our first experience of his garrulity, but we can hardly begrudge an old man the pride he expresses in his son. Four lines of narrative *continuo* follow the speech, and with the next section of the poem (64-93) the scene is laid. The abdication speech is preceded by a kind of cinematic panning of the throngs flocking to the event—"Rous'd by report of Fame, the nations meet" (96)—and by introduction of the two principals upon the regal stage before us. The ceremony is followed by the abdication speech (139-210), a wonderful harangue in praise of the newly crowned prince. On and on he goes, bestowing encomium after encomium "Full on the filial dulness." Their nature is established by the invocation:

> "Heavens bless my son, from Ireland let him reign
> To far Barbadoes on the western main." (139-40)

We observe Dryden's characteristic exactitude. From Ireland as a symbol of folly and ignorance to the Barbadoes with their suggestion of barbarity that great realm extends—and in between mile after tedious mile of nothing. The poem ends with seven lines of appropriate anti-climax (211-217): the "yet declaiming" old king is sent down a "trap" by two of his son's men. So anxious is Shadwell to inherit the kingdom of Nonsense that he interrupts even the unceasing praise of his father Flecknoe.

The image of the theatre is clear even in the plot, if one can call a single episode by that name. It is strengthened by numerous details, things not metaphorical in themselves but collectively so. Dryden's larger metaphors are commonly of this kind, growing almost imperceptibly and wholly naturally even to the alerted reader. Everything seems to refer to drama and to the theatre, once one decides them to be the basis of the poem. The scene of the coronation is that of the "Nursery," a place for training actors and actresses made necessary after the Roundheads had interrupted the English drama. It is located near the Barbican, now in ruin.

> From its old ruins brothel-houses rise,
> Scenes of lewd loves, and of polluted joys. (70-71)

To most men then living, this scene could be compared with only one event, the triumphal English coronation of Charles II upon his return. Dryden's details can best be understood, and their metaphorical suggestions of decaying sham made clearest, by comparison with the emblematic arches erected in honor of Charles. (See Plate I.) The scene in *MacFlecknoe* is theatrical.

> Near these a Nursery erects its head,
> Where queens are form'd, and future heroes bred;
> Where unfledg'd actors learn to laugh and cry,
> Where infant punks their tender voices try. (74-77)

The play upon queens/queans and upon heroes/stage heroes (the second meaning is one of Dryden's introductions into the language), like the distortion of true human feelings involved in learning to act, make it seem that we have been taken upon a distasteful visit behind the scenes of a disgusting play. The theatrical metaphor is further amplified by the constant reference to earlier and contemporary dramatists, as well

---

PLATE I   *The Return of Monarchy.* From John Ogilby, *The Relation of his Majestie's Entertainment* (1661). The emblems of royalty and the progress of Charles II to his English coronation are adapted in *MacFlecknoe*. Reproduced by permission of the Trustees of the British Museum.

The RETURN of MONARCHY

The First Triumphall Arch, Erected in Leaden hall street near Lime street, for ye Entertainment of our Gratious Soveraigne Charles ye Second, in his Passage through ye City of London, to his Coronation Aprill ye 22th 1661. Composed by Iohn Ogilby Esq, and performed at ye Charge of the City of London, by their Artificers.   Sold by Wm Morgan, near ye blew Bear in Ludgate street.   Price 6 d as to the selection of absurd details of language or stagecraft from Shadwell's own plays, with which Dryden was clearly very familiar.

What I have provisionally called a theatrical metaphor is the basis of the poem in the sense that it accounts for the kinds or sources of details repeatedly introduced. The same metaphor can also be treated as an ironic means of presenting positive values. Shadwell is praised either for qualities that he does not possess but which are admirable, or for qualities that we see are contemptible and that can be referred to the positive values opposite to them. The theatrical metaphor is useful for the transparency of its irony. We are never left doubting what attitude to take, nor with the fear that there is no course open at all. It is extraordinary that *MacFlecknoe* bases its effects on praise, upon ceaseless magnification. With the exception of some details to act as signposts for those unwary readers who might otherwise miss the employment of irony, or to amuse with anticlimax, the poem is filled with magnification. Some satirists recur constantly to the base, the petty, or the small. What English satirist other than Dryden does not? This, too, is an advantage of the theatrical metaphor: the pretended greatness of Shadwell may be but pretended, but it shows that greatness is possible in human life.

Because of the running irony of the poem, its positive values are only implied, either through simple inversion (we translate praise of nonsense into praise of meaningfulness) or complex inversion. By complex inversion I mean only that when Shadwell is praised for "majesty" we must translate by inversion to see that he is lacking in dignity and greatness, and by a re-inversion that these qualities are yet to be found in other men. Most often the two are combined—Shadwell is for example praised for "thoughtless majesty"—and they are repeatedly combined with allusions that aid in expressing the positive values of the poem.

> But let no alien [Sedley] interpose . . .
> . . . .
> Nor let false friends seduce thy mind to fame,
> By arrogating Jonson's hostile name.
> Let father Flecknoe fire thy mind with praise,
> And uncle Ogleby thy envy raise.
> Thou art my blood, where Jonson has no part. (163; 171-75)

One needs little knowledge of the literature of the seventeenth century, nor of Shadwell's pretensions to friendship with Sedley or his assumption that he was the heir to Jonson, to see that Sedley and Jonson are clear standards by which Flecknoe and Ogilby are dismissed. Yet to know these things increases one's satisfaction, just as the fourth and fifth lines quoted take on greater humor and meaning when one hears their Virgilian echo: " Et pater Æneas et avunculus excitet Hector." This allusion is but one of many Virgilian echoes in the poem. Such allusions in themselves are not satiric. In his verse epistle to Congreve, Dryden similarly compares his friend to such older English dramatists as Fletcher and Jonson (20-25), to such contemporaries as Etherege, Southerne, and Wycherley (28-30), and to Romans like Scipio (35-38).[1] There is even in the *Congreve* (37-38) a closely similar use made of Hannibal as a threat to Roman civilization (*MacFlecknoe*, 112-13). Whether such allusions are satiric or not depends upon their employment and their application. The tonal control is a crucial matter, and Dryden gains his with explicit or hidden comparisons. These vary in subtlety and depth considerably, but whatever their nature, all are metaphors.

The naturalness with which comparisons came to Dryden's mind is evident in his literary criticism. Without his critical force of comparison Dryden would not have become our first great literary critic; equally, without metaphor, he would not be the poet he is. The analogy between his critical prose and his poetry is not exact, however, for in the poetry there is a constant working between the two elements compared. There is assimilation as well as differentiation. Shadwell is not merely dismissed by comparison to Jonson, he is dismissed as a man of the same kind. He may be dull, but he is a poet. Not that being granted "poet" would much compensate for being dubbed so dull. Surely the fact is that although here Shadwell's reputation is forever to be tarnished by Dryden's ironic praise, still his reputation is ensured. The same is not true of Dryden's portrait of Shadwell as Og in *Absalom and Achitophel*, Part II.

> Now stop your noses, readers, all and some, ⎫
> For here's a tun of midnight work to come,   ⎬
> Og, from a treason-tavern rolling home . . . . ⎭
> A double noose thou on thy neck dost pull,
> For writing treason, and for writing dull;
> To die for faction is a common evil,
> But to be hang'd for nonsense is the devil:

Hadst thou the glories of thy king express'd,
Thy praises had been satire at the best;
But thou in clumsy verse, unlick'd, unpointed,
Hast shamefully defied the Lord's anointed:
I will not rake the dunghill of thy crimes,
For who would read thy life that reads thy rhymes? (457-59; 496-505)

As in his panegyrics, so in *MacFlecknoe*, he has constant reference to what Maynard Mack has well termed Dryden's realm of supernal order. *MacFlecknoe* testifies implicitly to the enjoyment he felt in looking at contemporary London, in its dinginess and gilt as well as in its majesty and gold. It testifies equally to his assurance of abiding ideals and values to which lesser realities might be referred with ease. In such references he was to find a basis of metaphor, and in the interplay between the two the power and movement of most of his work.

Shadwell's fate in *MacFlecknoe* is, therefore, not so much to be annihilated as to be made an unwitting symbol of values for which he is given only ironic credit. Like Pope's Betty, he is praised for labors not his own, and in addition for his own labors in ways that show how foolish they are. Although these are chiefly his plays, he had enough other artistic pretensions to show that a major subject of the poem is art. The subject has obvious connections with the unifying metaphor of the theatre, and there are less obvious connections as well. Because the theatrical metaphor conveys the sham sides of Shadwell's art, it suggests that which is not true art. And that which is not true is unnatural, because art is the mirror of nature or, as Dryden put it in the progress piece in *Annus Mirabilis*, is "nature's handmaid." What true nature and true art have in common is quite simply truth; what misrepresented nature and witless art have in common is non-sense, unreality. These subjects are developed both singly and separately. Singing (209-10) is but one of the arts assimilated into the larger subject. We encounter as well lute-playing (43-48), dancing (53-54), architecture (64-82), rhetoric (165), word-games (203-08), and several skilled trades. Each of these is debased by Shadwell's art—his fumbling pretense to the reality and his degrading expression of his motives in his attempts. Nature is for the most part less explicitly treated, although the very first argument adduced by Flecknoe for Shadwell's right to the throne shows how a debased view of nature is made a vehicle of censure and a concomitant of art.

... " 'Tis resolv'd; for nature pleads, that he
Should only rule, who most resembles me.
Sh------ alone my perfect image bears,
Mature in dulness from his tender years." (13-16)

Only by recalling that the rule is over a realm of artistic meaningless-
ness do we see that in this passage nature and art are related. The
relation is clearer in later passages, now of paternal advice.

"But let no alien [Sedley] interpose,
To lard with wit thy hungry *Epsom* prose.
And when false flowers of rhetoric thou wouldst cull,
Trust nature, do not labor to be dull." (163-66)

"False flowers of rhetoric" is an obvious if inspired combination of art
and nature in their debased non-sense form. The next line, full as it is
of tenderest parental solicitude, is beyond appreciation. Both this and a
later passage suggest that the "nature" of Shadwell's art is unnatural:
" 'Like mine, thy gentle numbers feebly creep; / Thy tragic Muse gives
smiles, thy comic sleep' " (197-98). We need no dissertation on the many
important meanings attached to "art" and "nature" in the century to
understand the effect of such lines.

The withering gaiety of these and similar passages has long been
regarded as a hallmark of Dryden's lighter satiric style. There is a
paradox in the gaiety of a poem about a dull writer, and in the energy
of a style creating an enduring image of nullity. The stylistic texture
of the poem needs some attention if one is to understand how it is
possible for the subject of art to become a metaphor. Abstractions are
capable of expressing many important poetic effects, but they are not
often to be found in Dryden's highly particular style. He draws upon
active verbs, evaluative adjectives, and nouns specifying details with an
imagistic potential. He avoids the copula, which is used only some ten
times in the 172 lines of the poem, and in the middle of the poem there
is a stretch of about 140 lines from which it is altogether absent. The
copula is often avoided by appositive constructions, especially in the
second lines of couplets, a syntactical device which allows for the
rigor of what may be called definition without a loss of activity.
Sometimes, as in the line, "And lambent dulness play'd around his
face" (111), the adjective makes an image of an abstraction. At other

moments the adjective itself is an abstract, evaluative epithet which achieves metaphorical status by its connection with nouns.

> In thy felonious heart tho' venom lies,
> It does but touch thy Irish pen, and dies. (201-2)

The euphony joins *felonious* and *venom* in imagery, and the parallelism thus augmented of *felonious heart* and *Irish pen* translates *Irish* into metaphor.

The more or less generalized language of the opening couplet is a yet better example of the relation between diction and certain unusual figures in Dryden's poetry.

> All human things are subject to decay,
> And when fate summons, monarchs must obey.

No one would wish to part with such lines. Their ponderous, portentous aphorism is just right. Equally, no one would argue that they are strikingly imagistic. The lack of strong images and the presence of an abstraction, *fate*, gives us what may most accurately be described as a generalized language neither typical nor rare in Dryden's style. The lines are not abstract, but general, and general in such a way that they manage numerous particulars, bring them together, relate them, and in the association produce something that can only be called metaphor. The second line, with its summons of fate, underlies the whole poem. In it Flecknoe finds his reasons for abdication. In it is implied the nature of such rulers or writers as his son, MacFlecknoe, and himself. It is a basis of his long speeches, and his ridiculous exit gives a final, almost literal, demonstration of the truth of the line. Regarded quite another way, this line is the element which allows for the comparison between Flecknoe and Augustus. To call such a function metaphorical is to extend the application of the term, since it may seem more strictly to be the basis for the metaphorical function than the metaphor itself. Yet, if it be asked what is meant by *fate, fate summons, monarchs,* and *monarchs must obey,* the only reply outside of a prose gloss that is poetically meaningless (King Flecknoe must abdicate when required to) is that language is used to represent other things, that implicit comparisons are involved. The metaphorical functioning is, then, not to be understood in the autonomous line but in its relationships through ideas, repetitions, and associations with numerous other elements in the poem.

The first line has the same function, although since it is amplified by highly particular images, its metaphorical function is more readily followed. In writing that "All human things are subject to *decay*," Dryden has at the outset introduced a concept (and weak image) that governs the nature of much of the imagery in the poem. It develops and relates the themes of art and nature by showing their degradation in Flecknoe and Shadwell. It is in the nature of merely human things that they should decay, as the Arion passage (43-50) shows in its concluding couplet.

> About thy boat the little fishes throng,
> As at the morning toast that floats along.

Charmed by his music, great fish had saved Arion's life. In Shadwell's case, it is not superlative music but the city's garbage (Shadwell's music) that attracts "the little fishes." Similarly, decay of architectural as well as moral kinds makes the Barbican area repulsive. The decay is general and symbolic in a carnage, ghostliness, and filth attendant upon MacFlecknoe's royal progress to coronation.

> No Persian carpets spread th' imperial way,
> But scatter'd limbs of mangled poets lay;
> From dusty shops neglected authors come,
> Martyrs of pies, and relics of the bum. (98-101)

The famous wit of the last line illustrates the decay in more ways than one. But it lacks the imaginative power of the line before it, which converts dead books into live spectres.

Successive passages in such fashion develop the generalized opening. But "human things" include art as well as nature, as the last quotation has brilliantly implied, and as is made clear by one of the most scathing lines of the poem—Flecknoe's bland question to his son, " 'What share have we in nature, or in art?' " (176). Shadwell emerges as little more than a gross nullity, a human "thing" lacking in that vital creativity which is to Dryden the common property of nature and art. The *decay* is opposed to creativity. If even the natural venom of his heart dies when it touches his artistic pen, then he is beyond hope. There is indeed an air of unreality hanging over the whole scene, as if it were some theatre in which sleazy actors in a yet sleazier setting had been fixed by a sudden volcano for a later century to rediscover. Yet paradoxically there is the shadow of life—"From dusty shops neglected authors come" (100). And there is somehow an element of danger as well as of magic in what is basically bizarre: "Amidst this monument of vanish'd minds" (82). The utter sterility, the decay of the artist to the last extremity is conveyed by a happy device. Two couplets report Mac-Flecknoe's taking the coronation oath. But throughout the poem he does not speak a word. Flecknoe has been a meaningless writer. His son—also a writer—goes a step further and becomes wordless. He thinks no thoughts. He is stirred by no feelings. His only actions are to sit (108) and swear (114). Not even Samuel Beckett has created so vegetative a hero. It is characters from one of his plays who send the "yet declaiming" Flecknoe down the trapdoor (211-17). For a moment of music-making on the Thames (in the past) he is granted a creativity, even a pregnancy.

> Swell'd with the pride of thy celestial charge;
> And big with hymn, commander of a host. (40-41)

Yet it turns out that this was after all an early mistake. Flecknoe sets his son right with later advice:

> "Success let others teach, learn thou from me
> Pangs without birth, and fruitless industry." (147-48)

In such a passage there is a coalescence of the themes that nature and art are creative, but that the Flecknoe line is merely human, decayed, sham, hollow of art, and dispirited of nature. When it is recalled that all of this damning indictment is presented as praise in a clearly detailed situation of a coronation, it is perfectly obvious that here is a new kind of metaphor and a new kind of control in English satire.

The nature of the control is too readily misunderstood in terms merely of the manipulation of the heroic couplet. That is rather a symptom than control itself. The real force ordering the poem is the control of Dryden's imagination over himself, over his object of satire, and over his world. It is all the more forceful for being assumed naturally. One need only compare the repose, assurance, and calm of the narrator of *MacFlecknoe* with that in almost any other satire in English to become aware of a fullness of conviction. He is sure of himself and therefore all the more capable of criticizing others. Assurance does not require the weapons of uncertainty. The criticism is voiced through praise, however ironic, and through constant magnification in metaphor. Dryden avoids the usual technique of belittling and chooses as his central human situation one of the most natural passions, certainly one of the strongest of his own life, paternal love. He is also supremely confident of his world and the values that shape it. He takes us to unpleasant places and introduces us to the unsavory aspects of art, because both are in the world. Yet they too take on in his imagination a magic and a scale of size or time that make them attractive and a credit to our human nature. The opening comparison of Flecknoe with Augustus is just such a case. Only a poet sure of himself would risk it; only a poet sure of his object and his world would choose it in this tone. Such matters seem clear and simple enough till we try to question the functioning of the metaphors. Why, after all, is Flecknoe not like Augustus? Why is Shadwell not properly compared to Arion, Ascanius, or Ben Jonson? Are not "*all* human things . . . subject to decay?"

The questions are really like those of the relation between fate and history in *Annus Mirabilis*. (*Fate* summons in the line after "All human things are subject to decay," and is linked by assonance to *decay*.) The sense of *decay* and what it symbolizes is felt and real. There is a danger, or Dryden would not have been drawn into satire for the first time. The assurance with which that danger is met and disposed of reveals the answer to the questions raised. Such strong positive values are invoked, so supernal a realm appealed to against the merely *human*, that the decay is dealt with. The question is how. The method is obviously that of inversion in the "mock heroic," if the term may be applied beyond its strict generic meaning to include as well ironic versions of pane-gyric, of coronation, and of religion. While the burlesque disproves Shadwell's claims, the double nature of the irony emphasizes the truth of the values mocked in him. The numerous allusions to writers other and greater than Shadwell, with the momentary suffusions of elevated tone in the style, comprise the true heroic—which is to say, epic—basis of the poem and two of the principal means by which Dryden effects the mock heroic. In both the most exact and the most superficial senses, however, the poem is remote from the heroic. Strictly speaking, the poem lacks epic narrative, action of an elevated kind. Superficially, there are none of the epic trappings so beautifully draped by Pope in *The Rape of the Lock*. Even the darkly pessimistic *Dunciad* relies much more on the familiar epic devices than *MacFlecknoe*, and it develops a greater epic action. The action of *MacFlecknoe* is more verbal and imagistic than strictly active. It does depict a royal progress, but the emphasis is upon the speeches at a coronation. Dryden's plays show, if proof be necessary, that he could develop the most complex plots if he found his purposes served by doing so, but in *MacFlecknoe* he creates a mock encomium of Shadwell for being a dull writer. He does not attempt to deal with subjects as important in themselves as the excursions into Spain of Edward the Black Prince, or King Arthur's conquest of the Saxons.[2] Talk of the mock heroic should not obscure the simple truth that the poem is a satire.

The satiric style is careful and much more closely organized than it seems at first—the organization of passages with repeated or developed initial words (72-78, 149-64, for example) is a single symptom. Yet there is a deliberate roughness. If there is not that "harsh cadence of a rugged line" for which Dryden found it necessary to excuse Oldham, there is also not the smoothness of *All for Love*. The style has the roughness of a gentleman in the country, but it is extremely flexible. It mimes now this, now that author (including Shadwell) with great skill, but without creating that steady, harmonious pressure the epic requires. It gives the illusion of action and has great vitality. Otherwise it is more lyric than epic within the range of satiric possibility.

If the positive values are not invoked by inverting the epic, they do come out of what is clear in the poem: that there is a great deal of theatrical talk (along with other reference to music, architecture, epic, and dance) to describe a coronation. Or, to phrase this differently, as we have seen, an important subject of the poem is art—especially literature, and more particularly drama—which is expressed in the pervasive imagery of a coronation. Since imagery of one kind is employed to express meanings of another, the imagistic function is of course metaphorical.

> This Flecknoe found, who, like Augustus, young
> Was call'd to empire, and had govern'd long;
> In prose and verse, was own'd, without dispute,
> Thro' all the realms of *Nonsense*, absolute. (3-6)

It is perfectly clear from these familiar lines that the empire is that of
letters, that the succession is one of title to being the dullest writer in
Christendom. Dryden recurs constantly to the monarchy-literature
metaphor, often varying the local image, but sustaining and developing
the metaphor. As with the theatrical metaphor (which is in reality one
part of the larger metaphor of literature or art), so the metaphor of
monarchy grows from intermittent details into a figure informing the
whole. Some of these details can be noted in order to show the way in
which monarchy is made to fuse with other elements in the poem.

> This aged prince [of *Nonsense*] . . . (7)
> . . . .
> To settle the succession of the State (10)
> . . . .
>   which of all his sons was fit
> To reign (11-12)
> . . . .
>   he
> Should only rule, who most resembles me (13-14)
> . . . .
>   thoughtless majesty;
> Thoughtless as monarch oaks that shade the plain,
> And, spread in solemn state, supinely reign. (26-28)

By such means the metaphor of monarchy is unobtrusively established
in the first thirty lines—here by a phrase, there by an image like that
of the oak. It is typical of Dryden that when he chooses such an image
from the old scale of nature and correspondences, as the oak of royalty,
he should give it independent historical life by the ironic suggestion of
that tree in which Charles II found safety at Boscobel.

After the first thirty lines the imagery of monarchy is allowed to
develop more freely. Flecknoe gives his son the Bible of the realm of
Nonsense, his own play, *Love's Kingdom*.

> *Love's Kingdom* to his right he did convey,
> At once his scepter, and his rule of sway;
> Whose righteous lore the prince had practic'd young,
> And from whose loins recorded *Psyche* sprung. (122-25)

In four lines, what is put into the prince's hand is spoken of in a number
of complex ways—every unit of the sense approaches the meaning of

Love's Kingdom differently. It is a sceptre held in the hand in a travesty
of a coronation. It is the realm he is supposed to rule over—the kingdom of love, romantic drama. It is *righteous lore*, the Bible of idiotic
dullness. The *prince* had practiced love, or had what we presume to be
unattractive affairs, while young. That being true, the soul of the prince
(his Psyche) was begotten by him in his "practice" upon *Love's Kingdom;* and since *loins* is pronounced identically with *lines*, the literary
application makes it all the clearer that (to paraphrase *Absalom and
Achitophel*) there has been an incestuous, displeasing rape upon the
crown.

Without awareness of its metaphorical function, we might see on
close reading that a literary work called *Love's Kingdom* is a symbol
of rule in the ceremony of coronation. What we would be unable to
see is that what is true of this detail is true throughout the poem in the
sense that monarchy and literature are metaphors for each other. Only
such a technique accounts for the way in which the different meanings
of this passage develop. This metaphorical interchange, this reciprocity
of roles of metaphorical tenor and vehicle, is probably unique (as a
characteristic method) to Dryden. To speak of such figurative language in terms of the mock heroic, or the Augustan metaphor, or the
metaphor of tone—all descriptions with some degree of currency—is
not to help very much. The problem is to know what to call a metaphor
that functions in so many different ways at once—as a phrase, as an
image, as a local metaphor, as a local subject, as part of a larger metaphor. Since Dryden was to develop the technique used in *MacFlecknoe*
in the very different ways of *Absalom and Achitophel*, the *Song for St.
Cecilia's Day*, and *The Hind and the Panther*, we have a considerable
interest in understanding what is involved even if we end with no single
satisfactory term.

A single term seems to me difficult to discover because the emphasis
in these four poems is so different. In his excellent book, *John Dryden's
Imagery*, Arthur W. Hoffman provides us with numerous phrases and
acute insights.

> The whole pattern . . . of allusion (p. 16)—the more tacit sort of refer-
> ence (p. 16)—this network of systematic analogy (p. 25). Every simile
> is potentially valuative as well as definitive (p. 26). Analogy can be a
> way of talking about two realms at once (p. 29)—conventional
> similes and metaphors are enriched by their repetitions; they become

major junction points of a network of analogy (p. 30). There are also cases . . . in which images occurring within a single poem and not necessarily standing in any close syntactical relationship interact and affect one another (p. 44). There is, in other words, a kind of action in the imagery, and the major contrasting images are the termini of that action (p. 46)—the . . . effects of multiple analogy (p. 47).

Each of these phrases or sentences is acute. But what are we to call the whole? The phrase "controlling metaphors" will perhaps do, since it suggests I believe a largeness and continuousness of function that is crucial to Dryden's use. For such metaphors there is no single source such as the heroic. The pastoral is as possible, or the biblical. To the extent that the controlling metaphors of *MacFlecknoe* express and lend coherence to a body of thought, they are clearly related to what has been called myth.* Yet Dryden shows in *The Medal* and *Religio Laici* that a coherent body of traditional thought does not require metaphors of this kind to control it, and he is equally capable of creating myths of another sort that do not involve traditional thought of this kind. The Venus-Mars meeting of Cleopatra and Antony at the beginning of the third act of *All for Love* shows as much.

If we may speak, then, of controlling metaphors, we must add also that they control by being interchangeable. And they are reciprocal not only with each other, but with yet a third metaphor of the same kind, the religious. Vaguely biblical phrases appear throughout the poem— "from whose loins," for example, in the passage on Flecknoe's play, *Love's Kingdom* (122-25). We are reminded that that play is the Bible as well as the sceptre of the coronation, the holy book "Whose righteous lore the prince had practic'd young." And what is suggested in particular is the New Testament of Love rather than the Old of Law. In this passage the religious metaphor—it functions for literature and monarchy and they for it—is subdued almost to the point of burial. The religious metaphor is indeed the least obvious of the three, because it is most often conveyed through allusion. Yet it is plain enough, as a couple of passages show.

---

* In *Dryden and the Conservative Myth* (New Haven, 1961), Bernard N. Schilling terms myth the body of conservative ideas and assumptions drawn upon by Dryden in *Absalom and Achitophel*. As various traditional kinds of integrated thought are being found by students of Dryden's writing it is perhaps inevitable that they should attempt to characterize these wholes.

The king himself the sacred unction made,
As king by office, and as priest by trade. (118-19)

The diction suggests the metaphor, but the allusions develop it. Flecknoe is "king by office"—the kingdom, we know, is literature. He is also
priest by trade—he was said to be a Roman Catholic priest.* Dryden
refers to the unction still used at English coronations and modelled, like
his passage, on the biblical precedent, the anointing of Saul by Samuel.
The second passage does not explicitly concern monarchy.

> . . . Bruce and Longvil had a trap prepar'd,
> And down they sent the yet declaiming bard.
> Sinking he left his drugget robe behind,
> Borne upwards by a subterranean wind.
> The mantle fell to the young prophet's part,
> With double portion of his father's art. (212-17)

Once again there is a biblical allusion, of course to Elijah's assumption
into heaven and to Elisha's inheriting his mantle (2 Kings, ii). This
awesome incident is rendered ridiculous by the expedient of recalling
Shadwell's stage management in the *Virtuoso*, Act III. The awe rendered
to absurdity is changed yet further into irony when we recognize the
allusion to Cowley's poem on the death of Crashaw, which concludes:

> Hail, *Bard Triumphant!* and some care bestow
> On *us*, the *Poets Militant* Below! . . .
>   . . . .
> Thou from low earth in nobler *Flames* didst rise,
> And like *Elijah*, mount *Alive* the skies.
> *Elisha*-like (but with a wish much less,
> More fit thy *Greatness*, and my *Littleness*)
> Lo here I beg (I whom thou once didst prove
> So humble to *Esteem*, so Good to *Love*)
> Not that thy *Spirit* might on me *Doubled* be,
> I ask but *Half* thy mighty *Spirit* for Me.
> And when my *Muse* soars with so strong a *Wing*,
> 'T will learn of things *Divine*, and first of *Thee* to sing. (59-60; 65-74)

---

* Marvell saw Flecknoe in Rome during the interregnum and wrote a satire,
Flecknoe, an English Priest at Rome (see Noyes, p. 967, l. 3 n). The poem seems
to have fixed Flecknoe as an archetype. In *MacFlecknoe* the allusion fits into a
series of Roman and Virgilian references in 108-38, a humorous example of the
kind of local government often to be found in Dryden's style.

Elijah rising and Shadwell's own Sir Formal sinking, Crashaw and proud King Flecknoe merge on the one side, just as Elisha and Bruce and Longvil, Cowley and MacFlecknoe-Shadwell do on the other. Elisha-Cowley receives the mantle from above with but half of Elijah-Crashaw's art. Our young, wordless prince, Elisha-MacFlecknoe, is much luckier, two times more the artist than Elijah-Flecknoe, twice as dull, four times curst to Cowley's blessing.

The three metaphors are three subjects capable of becoming figures for each other while remaining important in their own right as subjects. These two conditions of the metaphorical potential of the poem, and of Dryden's natural tendency to integrate his poetry closely, allow for a very great deal of intensity of organization.

> Heywood and Shirley were but types of thee,
> Thou last great prophet of tautology.
> Even I, a dunce of more renown than they,
> Was sent before but to prepare thy way;
> And, coarsely clad in Norwich drugget, came
> To teach the nations in thy greater name. (29-34)

Here is the drugget robe of the end of the poem. Here is also talk of *types*. The *last great prophet* in the Bible is of course Christ, of whom there were several Old Testament *types* (Adam, David, and others). Here Flecknoe is a John the Baptist, making his son a Christ, or rather anti-Christ. Since the earlier "types" are dramatists, literature enters into the religious context: and since the passage argues MacFlecknoe's fitness to succeed his father, monarchy is also involved, as the biblical *nations* may perhaps suggest. But which is the dominant subject: does the passage concern literature metaphorically or religion and monarchy properly? Do not Heywood and Shirley get swallowed up by the religious intensity of the succeeding lines? And so also do we not have the coronation in mind all the time? The three metaphors are very nearly fused, as again in another passage where religion enters through allusion.

> The hoary prince in majesty appear'd,
> High on a throne of his own labors rear'd. (106-07)

The notion of the workingman king, who either chooses or has necessity to build his own throne, is partly dependent upon the "topical" allusion to the fact that some of Flecknoe's works were published only at his own expense ("his own labors"). Much more of our comprehension of the religious element depends upon our recollection of Milton.

> High on a Throne of Royal State, which far
> Outshone the wealth of *Ormus* and of *Ind*
> . . . .
> Satan exalted sat. (*Par. Lost*, II, 1-5)

The allusion shows us how little the two major characters of the poem can pretend to any of the values suggested by the words *monarchy, art,* and *religion.* We need no special knowledge of Dryden's own views to guess that these are values of permanent importance to him.

It is true, however, that allusion requires sharing knowledge with the poet if the allusion is to function as allusion. Without such a recognition, we may enjoy more or less of a work, but we miss something. Dryden gives something to every reader. There is a meaning at once obtainable, but there are also others less obvious. The architectural succession of meanings, the further harmonies, proceed farther and yet farther on. It is possible to read Dryden in ignorance of some things that are essential to any full understanding of a work, as it is not with some other writers whose difficulties are immediate. With their poems our understanding is apt to be contingent upon facing up to them at once. Dryden is often not least complex when he appears simple, as at the end of the coronation scene.

> Th' admiring throng loud acclamations make,
> And omens of his future empire take.
> The sire then shook the honors of his head,
> And from his brows damps of oblivion shed
> Full on the filial dulness: long he stood,
> Repelling from his breast the raging god;   } (132-38)
> At length burst out in this prophetic mood . . .

Apart from an exaggerated elevation, a grandiose and jesting foolishness, that have led people to speak of the poem as a burlesque, there is little overt reason in these lines to give many readers a second thought. But with our attention drawn to the passage, we see that it does not seem very clear. The test is always, why should Dryden have said this? "Honors of his head" is a clear Virgilianism. Indeed, the whole picture is that of the ancient diviner. The primary allusion of the passage is to Virgil's description of the Sybil in *Æneid*, VI. The allusion helps explain the noise at the coronation and the word *omens*. As Dryden later translated the passage,

> Thus, from the dark recess, the Sibyl spoke, ⎱
> And the resisting air the thunder broke; ⎰
> The cave rebellow'd, and the temple shook. ⎰
> Th' ambiguous god, who rul'd her lab'ring breast, ⎱
> In these mysterious words his mind express'd; ⎰
> Some truths reveal'd, in terms involv'd the rest. ⎰
> At length her fury fell, her foaming ceas'd,
> And, ebbing in her soul, the god decreas'd. (*Æneis*, VI, 147-54)

And with this passage is recalled the earlier possession by the god, of Helenus who, in the third *Æneid* prophesies (as the Sybil does not) of the future reign. (See *Æneis*, III, 480-591). But another allusion altogether is involved, as the phrasing shows.

> He said, and on his Son with Rays direct
> Shone full; hee all his Father full exprest
> Ineffably into his face receiv'd,
> And thus the filial Godhead unswerving spake. (*Par. Lost*, VI, 719-22)

The scene in Paradise and in the Barbican is obviously the same, and obviously different. Dryden has in fact caught the Miltonic rhythm exactly,

> And from his brows damps of oblivion shed
> Full on the filial dulness. (135-36)

This is not the rhythm of Milton's passage, which could have been too easily replayed, but of Milton, as we know him. The result of the Virgilian and Miltonic complex is to imbue the already sufficiently complex controlling metaphors with a depth that they do not superficially possess. That depth strengthens the metaphors by extending the religious to classical and Christian forms, the monarchic to the rule of Æneas and of Christ, and the literary to embrace the *Æneid* and *Paradise Lost*. The depth is therefore also evaluative. The invocation of such *loci* of value is a way of dismissing the pretensions of Flecknoe and Son. But the light of significance in a passage like this is clearly a reflection of our resources.[3]

The allusions to Virgil and to Milton fuse into a whole. The three controlling metaphors—art (or literature), monarchy, and religion— similarly exchange their roles throughout the poem as subjects, figures, and values. This is not to say that we are unable to make distinctions between the dominant functions of the controlling metaphors. The metaphor of art is particularly important as a subject, because the satire focuses chiefly upon literature. The metaphor of monarchy is particularly important for structure, since it governs the situation and the plot. The metaphor of religion is particularly important for evalua- tion, because it controls our response to the elements introduced into the poem. All the same, Dryden obviously feels monarchy and art to be important values. By the same token, each crucial point in the action of the poem is governed by literary suggestions or allusions, so that litera- ture in addition to monarchy is crucial to the structure. Used as they are for equivalents of each other as well as for such other functions as subject, structure, and evaluation, the metaphors play a role so central to the poem that one can scarcely imagine a poet who conceives of poetry in more figurative terms. It would be difficult to decide whether, in the end, *MacFlecknoe* is finally simple or finally complex. The whole is so entire, so integrated, that one's mind can embrace it at once. Yet the articulation of that whole is minutely and ceaselessly significant.

One source of the humor of the poem is to be found in the ironic failure of the metaphors to do what they seem to boast of. Flecknoe is no Elijah, and the particular stage trick taken from one of Shadwell's plays is not biblical. At each juncture the point of the metaphor de- pends upon its not working. The tenor is never quite what the vehicle would have it to be: Shadwell is not Ascanius or Christ. Or, to speak in other terms, the irony itself is metaphorical. The terms of praise of Flecknoe and Shadwell are those dealing with art, religion, and mon- archy; the very demonstration that Flecknoe is no monarch, no prophet, and (therefore) no poet, is ironic, because he is praised all along for being these things. The effect of praise is to elevate even what is ridiculed in such a way that the satire of *MacFlecknoe* enlarges both our world and that of its victim, giving a kind of mythical existence to Thomas Shadwell. In fact, the poem is really not much more about him than about the nonentities of any age. Shadwell was not a representative, enduring nonentity until Dryden in this poem hollowed him out and painted him in gilt. Perhaps his complaint to Dryden that he had very little experience of Ireland is not as foolish as it seems. What else could he say? He could not very well complain that he was not Christ, Ascanius, Elisha, and the rest. The ironic functioning of the metaphors has, then, both the satiric function of ridiculing the object, and also the function of finding a way to introduce positive values. Dryden is able to look upon a world in decay and call it good. He means it is bad; but he also means that it is good, because to call it good shows how far it can be made a symbol of what its appearance denies. He believes in what his praise of Flecknoe and Shadwell makes them fail to represent.

Dryden redeems the irony of *MacFlecknoe* in two quite different ways. One is phenomenal. The realism of the London scene in the poem gives us an immediate satisfaction. We are convinced that, however much distortion there may be incidental to art and satire, what is distorted is basically real. Such realism or truth can be regarded either in terms of detail, or in terms of the objects singled out for ridicule, or in Dryden's grasp of the abiding human relevance of the kinds of phenomena he deals with. This realism does not equal in force that of Pope and Swift. The drawing-room in *The Rape of the Lock* or the London of the *Dunciad*, or Lilliput or Brobdingnag each has a greater immediate reality and a stronger sense that its folly is a universal, enduring condition of human life. Relatively we sense a certain remoteness in Dryden's satire. There is never too much of his personality in his satire, as there is with Pope and Swift. But by comparison there is too little in terms of his involvement with the objects of satire.

The second means of redeeming irony—by faith in the metaphors, even though they may be ironic—is Dryden's great strength. It is no doubt significant that he of our great poets was most given to panegyric. It is certainly significant that his panegyric is for values imperfectly represented by the people praised. We cannot believe Flecknoe to be Æneas or Shadwell Ascanius any more than we can believe Belinda to be Eve or religion a coat quarreled over (as Swift shows it in his *Tale of a Tub*). In each case the metaphors work ironically. There is, however, a difference of the first magnitude: Dryden does believe in religion, art, and monarchy, as Pope does not believe that Edenic innocence is possible in his world. Further, the heroic metaphor of *The Rape of the Lock* may suggest an abiding value in a world of change, but if there is any scope for heroic action, neither this poem nor the *Dunciad* reveals it. Swift's *Tale of a Tub* shows greater degeneration in the value attached to the central metaphor. One can believe in a religion, but not in a coat. In saying this, I do not imply that Swift lacks imagination. All three writers are as imaginative as any three others in English. I do mean that in Dryden's poetry there is an assurance of an integrated world in which the various elements have a harmony that may be affirmed. We believe with Dryden in his metaphors, because his values carry conviction even in irony. In fact, as so often in Dryden there is in *MacFlecknoe* a kind of overspill of value from the metaphors to the object incapable of sustaining them. To a limited degree the metaphors not only pretend to praise Shadwell but even actually do so, because throughout the tone is panegyrical of the values. If it is true that his insufficiency cannot contaminate values that are more real and vital than he, it is also true that he benefits as well as suffers from comparison with that which is so much greater than himself.

It would seem a difficult question indeed to decide which has the greater force in Dryden's poem, poetic "truth," the real, or the ideal world. Much of *MacFlecknoe* is proof of the nonexistence of Shadwell —"What share have we in nature, or in art?" And yet the very proof of nonexistence establishes the fact that Shadwell exists for all time. Similarly, the timeless values of art, religion, and monarchy are brought into time and questioned by being applied to Shadwell and other actualities. They pass the test with ease but look different after it. This exchange of qualities between the two terms of the metaphor is only partial in *MacFlecknoe*. It will be nearly whole in *Absalom and Achitophel*. Behind such questions and such shadings of metaphor there is that question of tone which is always the most difficult to sort out for Dryden, as for Chaucer. Some of the people Dryden praised were John Oldham, Anne Killigrew, Charles II, James II, Congreve, Purcell, and the Duchess of Ormond. Some he ridiculed were Shadwell, Buckingham, Shaftesbury, Elkanah Settle, and Gilbert Burnet. For either set, a world is created that is at once partial as far as the accuracy of relation between the actual historical person and his portrait is concerned, and larger in terms of the way in which he is made to represent something timelessly true. In part the creation is a matter of metaphor, and in part it is a matter of tone. Since in Dryden's satire the irony is a governor of metaphor, it becomes nearly impossible to separate the two.

In his satiric poems and satiric passages (in poems not in themselves satires) we find a number of very different worlds conveyed by this mingled tone and metaphor. How different are the two following passages in their tone.

> A beardless chief, a rebel, ere a man:
> (So young his hatred to his prince began.)
> Next this, (how wildly will ambition steer!)
> A vermin wriggling in th' usurper's ear.
> Bart'ring his venal wit for sums of gold,
> He cast himself into the saintlike mold;
> Groan'd, sigh'd, and pray'd, while godliness was gain,
> The loudest bagpipe of the squeaking train.

. . . .

> A fiery soul, which, working out its way,⎫
> Fretted the pigmy body to decay,   ⎬
> And o'er-inform'd the tenement of clay.   ⎭
> A daring pilot in extremity;
> Pleas'd with the danger, when the waves went high,
> He sought the storms; but, for a calm unfit,
> Would steer too nigh the sands, to boast his wit.
> Great wits are sure to madness near allied,
> And thin partitions do their bounds divide;
> Else why should he, with wealth and honor blest,
> Refuse his age the needful hours of rest?
> Punish a body which he could not please;
> Bankrupt of life, yet prodigal of ease?

The tone of the second is far more elevated than that of the first. For one thing, the first (as is unusual with Dryden) uses images rendering a person small (*vermin, bagpipe*), while the second is enlarging. The first concentrates on the development of a seditious career, the second upon the distraction and perversion of great powers. And the style of the first is a close-bitten, angry style, whereas the second is more reflective and sad. Yet the two passages of course describe the same person, Shaftesbury. The point is that they do not create the same character. Achitophel is not the same as the unnamed "chief" of *The Medal*.* The

---

* The passages are from *The Medal*, 28-35, and *Absalom*, 156-68. In both he is on occasion Satanic, in *Absalom* majestic though in ruin, in *The Medal* of cloven hoof and dirty.

passage quoted from *Absalom and Achitophel* may not show as much
in any specifiable way, but we are aware of the effect of the biblical
metaphor. Here then are two satiric possibilities, distinguished in themselves by tone and style and in the poems from which they have been
taken by the presence or absence of something like the controlling
metaphors of *MacFlecknoe*.

Dryden's seriousness in *Absalom and Achitophel* and *The Medal* does
not preclude wit. It does omit the robust humor, however, that we
can find in his description of two poets unworthy of the name. The
first is Elkanah Settle (Goldsmith later wondered how much could be
expected of a person with so unpropitious a name), who,

> tho' without knowing how or why,
> Made still a blund'ring kind of melody;
> Spurr'd boldly on, and dash'd thro' thick and thin,
> Thro' sense and nonsense, never out nor in;
> Free from all meaning, whether good or bad,
> And, in one word, heroically mad . . .
>
> . . . .
>
> If he call rogue and rascal from a garret,
> He means you no more mischief than a parrot;
> The words for friend and foe alike were made,
> To fetter 'em in verse is all his trade.
> For almonds he'll cry whore to his own mother;
> And call young Absalom King David's brother.
> Let him be gallows-free by my consent,
> And nothing suffer, since he nothing meant.
>   (*Absalom and Achitophel*, II, 412-17; 425-32)

The surprising thing about this rollicking satire is its good humor,
since it is very difficult to specify just where the writer's sympathy
lies. I think it probably is to be found in an assumption: Settle is such
a nonentity that if he can accomplish anything at all he deserves credit.
What would be evil in an ordinary person is really a pretty good show
for a numbskull like him. Such sympathy obviously is of a kind the
recipient would willingly be spared, but it is sympathy of a kind. The
last advice of Flecknoe to his princely heir is somewhat similar.

> "Thy genius calls thee not to purchase fame
> In keen iambics, but mild anagram.
> Leave writing plays, and choose for thy command

Some peaceful province in acrostic land.
There thou may'st wings display and altars raise,
And torture one poor word ten thousand ways.
Or, if thou wouldst thy diff'rent talents suit,
Set thy own songs, and sing them to thy lute." (203-10)

Here the style is more elevated, the tone much more complex. The attitude of indulgence shown by Flecknoe is one of course at variance with the actual tenor of his advice. He is saying, Don't do anything; at least try nothing of importance. The last couplet is especially barbed, in that it represents the height of paternal pride and Dryden's own sense of another climax, a means of doubling the literary inanity by putting it to music of similarly ideal vacancy. Yet the last five lines quoted have an air of magic, of a kind of fairyland—of an "acrostic land" that Alice might find beyond the looking glass. Dryden creates a world which is perfect in its macabre kind. Industry leads to the assumption of misguided divinity, penal torture, and the joys of discordant music. (Since it is a *province* for *command*, the metaphor of monarchy is also present.) Shadwell like Settle, is being blest with an imaginative endowment which no man would desire, but it cannot be doubted that he has been transferred to another world, where he lives another existence, and where he is seen by the light of the imagination rather than the light of day. There is something about the free play of the imagination which is in itself creative and positive.

The laughter in *MacFlecknoe* is withering precisely because it does not seem to set out to be cruel. Dryden's attitude is truly Olympian in that after showing his full understanding of the faults or virtues of Flecknoe and Shadwell, without malice and in complete good humor, he laughs and engages our laughter at them. We do not scorn Shadwell. What is better and more final, we understand him and laugh at him. We wish him well, in acrostic land. It may be argued that all this is especially deliberate on Dryden's part, the very most sophisticated kind of satire, which damns with tainted praise. There is something in this, but it is not the effect we get from the poetry. *The Medal* is quite different, half unsure whether man can represent, positively or even ironically, the values so effortlessly supported in *MacFlecknoe*. Rather, I think we must say that Dryden's satire is especially effective in *MacFlecknoe* and in his passages of *Absalom and Achitophel*, Part II, because it is the response of a man who likes his world and the people in it, even though they cannot measure up to adequate standards. No other English satirist has a passage like his on this world's false stage and its foolish or evil human actors.

> Near these a Nursery erects its head,
> Where queens are form'd, and future heroes bred;
> Where unfledg'd actors learn to laugh and cry, ⎫
> Where infant punks their tender voices try, ⎬
> And little Maximins the gods defy. ⎭   (74-78)

The world of the Nursery is an immoral, decaying Lilliput. It is the world of the *Song for St. Cecilia's Day*, "This crumbling pageant" (60). Although the creation of this little world is like that of the acrostic land later in the poem, what is so special about it is its final, climactic line: "little Maximins the gods defy." Little man, imagining himself great, defies the gods. The pun is very nice, and the application to Shadwell and Flecknoe as they are presented in a poem where they are measured by standards of religion is clear: their efforts to support such values are really a form of defiance. But Maximin is no character from a Shadwell play; he is Dryden's own ranting hero from *Tyrannic Love*. The climax of the scene of decay in London and decay in nature comes with this self-criticism. The little Maximin rants on as ever in defiance of the gods, still aspiring to kingdoms. It is the joke of an exceedingly capacious mind upon itself, a joke of a kind that only a man wholly assured of himself and his standards can bear to make. (More such self-raillery will be found in his translation of Juvenal, *Satire I*, 122.) It also shows the degree to which the poem itself has transformed Shadwell from a real person into an artistic creation. The frame of reference in time and space of *MacFlecknoe* is enormous, and all is imagined: there never was in fact such a coronation or such a writer. The important thing for Dryden is, however, that there will always be a form of human government to which one gives allegiance in order to preserve social opportunity and order. There will always be writers whose words endure beyond decay. And there will always be a realm to which man will wish to give the assent of his faith. People like Shadwell may question these realms of value, but the values themselves answer back in such a way that the questioner is transformed.

The indirect affirmation of such values in satire can only be effected by transformation. The workings of the transforming process can best be understood by reference to recent views of utopian literature, the very reverse of satire. As recent writers have shown, the motive force of utopian writing is at least in part satiric.[4] An ideal world is created precisely because the real is so inadequate. The ideal is a constant satiric judgment upon the real, the more pronounced the more specific it becomes in social detail. Something like the reverse is true of Dryden's satire. The positive norms of the sourest satirist can be understood in a moment by inverting the specific folly or vice attacked into its opposite virtue. But *MacFlecknoe* is not sour, and its method rises above these truisms. Its major positive values—art, monarchy, and religion—rise unobtrusively as subject metaphors into an ideal architecture of values from the debris that seems about to stifle them. If we do not think of Dryden as a utopian, it is because he is too conscious of the reality about him. If the utopian writer sometimes retreats to his ideals, Dryden advances with a seemingly unconscious superiority upon the foolish or vicious. It is just such a sense of engagement as well as appreciation of style that led him to prefer Juvenal for his majesty over smiling Horace and rough Persius. There is a similar majesty, if in shirt-sleeves, about *MacFlecknoe*, which secures its transformation of all that is inadequate through metaphor. The metaphors, with the assured values they imply, make an imaginary moment forever real by bringing to bear upon them the lasting standards of the poem. It would take a more ideal order of time used as a fable to bring about the utopianism manqué in his later works. In their way, *Absalom and Achitophel* and *The Hind and the Panther* provide differing versions of such idealism, the one in a poem concerning two historical periods at once, the other in a fable whose conditions are at once timeless and historical. Both resemble *MacFlecknoe* in employing controlling metaphors. It seems appropriate that both have satiric passages, enough Attic salt to preserve their author's ripened values.

Metaphorical History: *Absalom and Achitophel*

CHAPTER IV

> [*History*] *helps us to judge of what will happen, by shewing us the like revolutions of former times. For mankind being the same in all ages, agitated by the same passions, and moved to action by the same interests, nothing can come to pass but some precedent of the like nature has already been produced, so that having the causes before our eyes, we cannot easily be deceived in the effects, if we have judgment enough but to draw the parallel.*
>
> —*Life of Plutarch.*

Absalom and Achitophel (1681) is commonly thought Dryden's greatest, most characteristic work. If the commendation is deserved, Dryden earned it by using to advantage certain inherent disadvantages of the subject of the poem. One of the most troublesome of these was the fact that the events treated had not yet reached their conclusion. The crisis over efforts to exclude Charles' brother James from the succession, the Popish Plot, and the challenge by Shaftesbury and Monmouth to Charles, to the Stuart line, and to the Clarendon settlement were continuing events, big with threat of civil war. The constitutional issues, like their accompanying political passions, were not overcome even by 1688. Dryden's first attempt to mold the flux of history into shapely artistic wholes was of course *Annus Mirabilis. Absalom and Achitophel* followed after fourteen years. The subsequent file is a long one. *The Medal* (1682), *The Second Part of Absalom and Achitophel* (1682), *The Duke of Guise* (1682), the translation of Maimbourg's *History of the League* (1684) with its Preface to the king and Postscript, *Threnodia Augustalis* (1685), *The Hind and the Panther* (1687), *Britannia Rediviva* (1688), and numerous other works in sum or in part essay the difficult feat. They reveal a persistent impulse to arrest and to assess the flow of history, which betrays a degree of engagement with politics, at once personal and literary, common to Dryden's generation and to those immediately preceding and following it. Milton and Cleveland, Butler and Marvell, Pope and Swift share Dryden's involvement. In certain forms of literary intensity as also in time, Dryden is at the center of this period, just as his lifetime spans the three major revolutions which inspired such engagement.

What distinguishes Dryden from the others is his treatment of the momentous happenings, especially of the eighties, in a variety of literary forms and, even more, his persistently historical view of contemporary events. If I have been correct in interpreting his concern with fate in *Annus Mirabilis* as an expression of conservative fear of undesirable change in the future, his appreciation of history in his *Life of Plutarch* (1683) gives explanation why he should turn to the historical past for light and assurance. It "helps us to judge of what will happen, by shewing us the like revolutions [changes] of former times." The causes of human action remaining in his view constant throughout history, "we cannot easily be deceived in the effects, if we have judgment enough but to draw the parallel."[1] The historical parallel he judged best for the events of 1680 and 1681 was of course that of the plot against King David by Absalom and Achitophel in 2 Samuel. What such a parallel implies, if it can be properly drawn, is that the historical sequence—a metaphor—taken from the Bible will foretell the outcome of the present secular sequence. Certainly the metaphorical biblical sequence is as true, as real, as the "antic sights and pageantry" of contemporary England. It had a claim to be thought truer. It was not only complete but also divinely revealed, giving it the force of God's judgment to evaluate subsequent events, "if we have judgment enough but to draw the parallel."

That Dryden drew the parallel he did was natural in that he had ample precedent.* But it was not inevitable. He draws other parallels in works following soon after *Absalom and Achitophel*. *The Medal*, *The Duke of Guise* in which he assisted Lee, and the translation of the *History of*

---

* As earlier writers had treated Charles I as David, so had Dryden Charles II in the prayer scene of *Annus Mirabilis* (1045-80). Earlier uses of the story in 2 Samuel for political purposes are treated by R. F. Jones, "The Originality of *Absalom and Achitophel, MLN*, XLVI (1931), 211-18; and by Bernard N. Schilling, *Dryden and the Conservative Myth* (New Haven, 1961).

the League, with his remarkable Postscript, all employ analogies other than the biblical. Those drawn in the later works—whether poem, play, or political prose—are to segments of secular history. Among Shaftesbury's papers had been found a proposal for an Association assertedly to protect the Protestant religion, the king, and the rights of subjects. Although not in his handwriting, the papers provided the Crown with the basis for a charge of high treason (later dismissed by a Whig jury, occasioning the striking of a triumphant medal and provoking Dryden's *Medal*). The Whig justification took the form of an analogy to the Association in Elizabeth's reign to avenge her death upon all Catholics. Robert Ferguson, "the Plotter," argues so in his *No-Protestant Plot: or the pretended conspiracy of Protestants against the King and Government discovered to be a conspiracy of the Papists against the King and his Protestant Subjects* (in parts, 1681, 1682). Dryden rejected the parallel, but not the drawing of parallels, in the Epistle to the Whigs prefixed to *The Medal.*

> In the mean time, you would fain be nibbling at a parallel betwixt this [Whig] Association and that in the time of Queen Elizabeth. But there is this small difference betwixt them, that the ends of the one are directly opposite to the other—

one being designed to support, the other to undermine the throne. Earlier in the Epistle Dryden had drawn what he regarded as the proper analogies for Shaftesbury's Association:

> the third part of your *No-Protestant Plot* is much of it stolen from your dead author's pamphlet, call'd *The Growth of Popery;* as manifestly as Milton's *Defense of the English People* is from Buchanan, *De Jure Regni apud Scotos;* or your first [Solemn League and] Covenant and new [Whig] Association from the Holy League of the French Guisards. (Noyes, p. 127)

The same double parallel is invoked more concisely in the opening lines of the Prologue to *The Duke of Guise:*

> Our play's a parallel: the Holy League
> Begot our Cov'nant; Guisards got the Whig.

Both the French and Elizabethan aspects of the parallel are dealt with at length in the Postscript to the *History of the League.*

The analogies to earlier English history are not wholly ignored in *Absalom and Achitophel*. The last line but one, "Once more the godlike David was restor'd," implies that Whig agitation is paralleled by the events leading up to, during, and after the Civil War of the century. It is even possible that the parallels with events in Elizabeth's time and the Ligue's plot against Henri III were in his mind as he wrote the poem. It is all the more possible because, as J. H. M. Salmon shows in his excellent study, *The French Religious Wars in English Political Thought* (Oxford, 1959), the analogy was recurred to by political writers and historians from early in the century. It is one of the ironies coloring shifting politics in the century that the anti royalist, anti-Catholic writers of England should borrow arguments from the monarchomach writers, many of them Jesuits, who provided the philosophical grounds for rebellion against a king sympathetic to the Protestant cause in France. Dryden was not the last person to observe irony and ambiguous metaphors. For the purposes of his new poem, a biblical parallel would obviously enable him to steer a surer course through events variously interpreted in his day.

His choice of a "parallel" from sacred history was unquestionably his major poetic decision. It gave his Tory treatment of contemporary events a seemingly divine sanction unavailable to other analogies, and enabled him to suggest an outcome to matters still very much undecided. The choice was one of a metaphor controlling far more explicitly than those of *MacFlecknoe* the actions, characters, and meaning of his poem. The nature of that control depended upon a further decision, whether the metaphor should be cast in the imagery and allusions typical of *Annus Mirabilis*, in the reciprocally functioning metaphors of *Mac-Flecknoe*, or in terms of some new principle. He chose novelty. He chose to describe contemporary experience as if it were unvaryingly biblical. As a result there is very little indeed in the poem that cannot be read as an expansion of 2 Samuel. One could do worse than read *Absalom and Achitophel* as a biblical poem, and one would find it difficult to prove, on the evidence of the poem *in vacuo*, that it concerns anything other than the biblical story. The metaphorical vehicle of biblical history has swallowed up the metaphorical tenor of Restoration history. Like nature, however, readers abhor vacuums, and we know from the epistle "To the Reader" and the evidence of history that a contemporary tenor is conveyed by the biblical vehicle.

If we could read the poem as it was read on that mid-November day of 1681 when it first appeared, we would approach it with the tense excitement that men feel when the threat of civil war is in the air. Words and names that might mean several things on other occasions would now mean but one. But we cannot read as if we were Dryden's contemporaries, and at our distance in time we are less involved in the events themselves than in their poetic expression, especially in the workings of the metaphor, difficult as they are to describe. It is not easy to designate the metaphor, whether as parallel, analogy, allegory, or what. For the fact is that to Dryden and his age, and to the workings of the poem, the vehicle has a greater truth than the tenor. Even today we accept the biblical analogy as something less partisan than Dryden's picture by it of Restoration history. Believing as he did that monarchy was divinely ordained, the imperfect demonstration of that truth by his account of the happenings he witnessed very nearly makes Restoration history a metaphor or type of the biblical.[2] As in *MacFlecknoe*, so in this poem, there is an exchange of metaphorical roles, except that now the exchange is between the explicit and sustained pole of metaphorical vehicle and an implicit but sustained pole of metaphorical tenor.

The problem of describing such workings is that of showing the metaphorical relation of the two histories to each other. Regarded as conventional allegory, the poem seems at times to dwell upon one or the other historical sequence, or upon something not relatable precisely to either and yet not irrelevant. Dr. Johnson recognized this, in his way,[3] but did not see that the fact implies an equal weight of biblical and English history, or quite grasp the issue of relationship. In his *John Dryden's Imagery*, Arthur W. Hoffman presents a much more discerning examination, postulating the two sides of the metaphor, or the two historical sequences, as part of a larger and other poetic whole.

> The poem . . . is neither Jewish history nor English history but a *tertium quid*, an action somewhere between or above both histories and commenting on both. The imagery is *relevant* to both histories, but the images are designed and made *appropriate* in terms of the *tertium quid*, the fundamental action of the poem. There are instances where particulars of English history are related to particulars of Jewish history without resort to imagery; in these cases the action of the poem is simply not given a symbolic embodiment. The symbolic embodiment, the action in the imagery, rises above and dominates the whole mass of the particulars of both histories, but without appearing

concretely in significant relation to each particular as it occurs. An occasional connection between Jewish history and English history with no image of God or Satan or Eden or Hell or Heaven can be accepted because the multiplicity of such connections *accompanied by* such images adequately establishes the general symbolic action; in the same way, a connection that specifically involves one but not both histories with the symbolic pattern can be accepted because the multiplicity of triple connections has adequately related both histories to the general symbolic action. In cases of the former type, historical parallels are prominent and the symbolic action distant; in cases of the latter type, the symbolic action is dominant. The former is more occupied with history and the latter more with value. The office performed by the imagery ... is to provide an emblem of and residence for value (pp. 80-81).

It is difficult not to believe that Hoffman has got at the heart of the matter. It is also difficult to locate "the fundamental action of the poem" and "the symbolic embodiment" in a *tertium quid* unless that be precisely in the two aspects of the metaphor functioning, now together, now separately and, when separately, sometimes implying a tenor in the other and sometimes providing only a general presumption of metaphor.

There are moments, as Hoffman suggests, when Dryden includes details from the one that have no historical equivalent in the other: the reference to aristocratic support of colleges (872) is not biblical, and that to David's gift for sacred song (197) does not apply to Charles. It may be that the long-sought-for topical significance of Absalom's guilt for Amnon's murder (39) is an instance of a biblical detail without a Restoration equivalent. Such instances resemble others in *MacFlecknoe* when the metaphor endows the actuality with a meaning it did not possess in historical fact. In *Absalom and Achitophel* we often discover the tenor and the vehicle exchanging their functions, or one of the two basic histories filling out details appropriate to, but lacking in, the other.

There are other passages in which imagery and metaphor are employed, but not the controlling metaphor of the poem. The famous passage on government (753-810) mentions *Israel* at the beginning (753) and refers to *our ark* towards the end (804). In between there are such details as *cov'nant* (767), *Adam* (771), and *Sanhedrins* (787) to suggest a biblical metaphor. Yet the metaphors may be said to coast along through this passage in neutral gear, since although *Adam* and *Sanhedrins* are certainly biblical, they refer, as Hoffman points out, to biblical times other than David's. Such passages, where the metaphor is suspended but yet potential, present but not functioning, seem no more to require a doctrine of the *tertium quid*, than the metaphorical pretense that Flecknoe is a king in *MacFlecknoe* needs to be sustained in every line. In fact almost all allegories have passages in which the metaphor is not only suspended but broken. In *The Hind and the Panther* Dryden develops this technique of suspension yet further by giving passages which are wholly governed by fable, some in which the fable is suspended but not clearly violated, and others where the fable is deliberately broken for shorter or longer passages. In *Absalom and Achitophel* the metaphor may coast, but it never stops; biblical history may at one moment explain something not known (that is, not actually present) in English, or English may so expand the biblical.

Each of these histories is in itself amplified by reference or comparison to earlier segments of history. Rebellion against royal authority in the Restoration is compared with rebellion earlier in the century. "The general cry, / 'Religion, commonwealth, and liberty,' " takes us back to another historical period, but to a period English rather than biblical. Much more obviously, there are numerous amplifications of events in the reign of David by reference to the earlier rebellions of Satan (273 and elsewhere), of Adam (51), and of Israel against Moses and Aaron (66 and elsewhere).

What requires some effort to appreciate is not that Satan's rebellion against God could be a metaphor both for that of Absalom and Achitophel against David, and of Monmouth and Shaftesbury against Charles II, but that the commonwealth rebellion of English history can be a metaphor for that of David's reign. Yet so it is, because such royalist comparisons had long since become types, as Dryden was to show often in *The Hind and the Panther* (see I, 182-89 for treatment of the rebellious Presbyterian Wolf as a type manifested in early Jewish history).

Whether we consider the metaphorical functioning of *Absalom and Achitophel* to be that of a parallel, an analogy, or an allegory, the metaphor is remarkable for three things. It is "closed" to an almost unbelievable extent: the biblical air is maintained throughout, with only one revealing blink of the eyes (130-33). Denying himself the convenience of allegorical abstractions, Dryden gives no "key." If it be allegory, it is more tightly shut than other modern English allegories. The two other important features of the metaphor seem quite incompatible with this.

That a closed metaphor should all the same exchange the roles of its tenor and vehicle, and that it should at times coast along with neither functioning in more than presumption is a situation in theory all but impossible. Since Dryden's practice is of this kind, however, and since it is so assured, it is natural to suppose that something so complicated did not spring fully grown from his own mind. He could hardly have found it in earlier literary practice or in the kinds of historical parallel-drawing discussed by Salmon in his *French Religious Wars in English Political Thought*. Treating sacred history metaphorically, he naturally enough turned for examples of his special "reading" of it to traditional glosses on Holy Scriptures. St. Augustine had drawn comparisons between the corrupt earthly city (he had Rome in mind) and the City of God, but his theory of historical movement was one of decay not shared by Dryden.

The change to belief in the possibility of progress, which Dryden himself held, seems to me in part a delayed effect of the Reformation. However much it was argued that the Reformers were returning to the primitive purity of the Church, the fact was that they were trying to improve upon the Church of Rome. The idea received emphasis in the agitation of the English Civil War, when pleas were made repeatedly for a "more thorough" Reformation, a second to improve yet further upon the first. In addition, the translation of the Bible into the vernacular tongues and the encouragement to read and apply it to daily experience allowed a great new source for comparison with secular life. As the theologians, whether Protestant or Catholic, recognized, there was at the heart of the debate over faith and of almost every other theological dispute the question of interpretation, which is to say the understanding and application, of the Bible.

Dryden's understanding of these issues is amply shown by *Religio Laici* and *The Hind and the Panther*. To show how the understanding relates to his metaphorical handling in *Absalom and Achitophel*, we can follow the interpretations of a typical earlier Anglican divine. About a century before Dryden's poem, one of the important Elizabethan controversialists, William Whitaker, had wrestled with the problem "Concerning the Interpretation of Scripture."[4] His argument begins in typical fashion with reference to the "Protestant" Father, St. Augustine. Augustine had distinguished four kinds of interpretation in *de Utilitate Credendi* (cap. 3). They are: the *historic* (also termed grammatical or literal), which concerns what was done and what was not; the *ætiolog-*

ical, which shows why something was done or said; the *analogical,* which involves the explanation of or agreement between the two Testaments; and the *allegorical,* which concerns those things to be taken *per figuram* rather than *per literam.* These are distinctions that do not remain clear for long in the modern mind, and they had their rivals. Origen and others added mystical senses of interpretation; the middle ages developed the *moraliter,* which dealt with matters ecclesiastical and the fate of the Church; the Jesuit Cardinal Bellarmine "divides all these senses into two species: the historic or literal, and the mystic or spiritual." Whitaker's solution is one commonly recurred to by Anglicans. For although, he admits, there are different modes of interpretation, there is only one *literal* sense. That is to say that at any one time the letter of scripture possesses only one sense that is meant (and clearly meant) although the mode employed at the time may be historic, anagogical, or whatever. He also speaks of another kind of interpretation which is not so much religious as secular in its application. Indeed he takes us to *Absalom and Achitophel* when he speaks of tropology, which

> is nothing more than an ethical treatment of scripture, when we collect from the scriptures what is suitable to direct our lives and form our minds, and hath a place in common life . . . Christ hath used this mode of interpretation, Matth. xii, 41, 42, where he accommodates to the case of the Jews then present the repentance of the Ninevites immediately upon hearing Jonah, and the long journey of the Queen of Sheba to Solomon.

It is not necessary to assume that Dryden had read Whitaker. He could have found similar ideas less concisely stated by Richard Hooker, whom he had read, and like ideas in Augustine, other Fathers, Bellarmine, Stapleton, and numerous additional writers concerned with the problem of interpreting the Bible. The tradition of applying biblical to secular history had in any case grown steadily in the century and had had some poetic expressions. The importance to him of tropological "accommodation" lies in its usefulness in bringing to bear a weight of truth from biblical experience to the experience of his own day. The Word was not only Revealed but revelatory. What was required to make the possibility an actuality was a literary tradition or an inclination that was basically historical. Earlier men had worked at the one, and his own character provided the other. He had shown in *Annus Mirabilis* how recent events might be adapted to the quasi-epic genre of history, and in *MacFlecknoe* he had proved that he could create a mythological historical moment. In *Absalom and Achitophel* he made two major historical sequences, one biblical, one secular, progress simultaneously through a tropology presumed to be continuous.

The result was a unique metaphor, though one growing from the metaphorical success of *MacFlecknoe* and tending toward the fable of *The Hind and the Panther*. But it was not a solution to all his poetic problems. There remained the difficulties of getting into the metaphor and of giving it articulation in something like a plot. Both require analysis. Both are in large measure structural problems, *Annus Mirabilis* over again, but with difficulties added by the metaphor. The entrance into the metaphor is of course the opening of the poem, where we find the central figure, the king, who is at once Charles II and David. It was not enough that the Stuarts had been given David as a prototype or that the metaphor would work with ease once set in motion. Dryden had to take cognizance of the personal character of Charles II before he could compare him in his political and religious character to David. Or, to use the centuries-old distinctions lasting into Dryden's day, he needed to account as well for the king's body natural as for his body politic.[5] Dryden was as aware as any man that the royal body natural had gained notoriety. He also knew that David possessed the same fondness for women. His solution of the problem was open recognition of it in a way that would get it wittily over at once.

It is altogether natural, therefore, that the opening lines should come to us with no suggestion whether English or biblical history is being related.

> In pious times, ere priestcraft did begin,
> Before polygamy was made a sin;
> When man on many multiplied his kind,
> Ere one to one was cursedly confin'd;
> When nature prompted, and no law denied
> Promiscuous use of concubine and bride;
> Then Israel's monarch after Heaven's own heart,
> His vigorous warmth did variously impart
> To wives and slaves; and, wide as his command,
> Scatter'd his Maker's image thro' the land.

The first six lines are devoid of imagery. Yet I wish to show that they are metaphorical in themselves and by implication invoke both David and Charles II. From the first line there is a metaphor in the identification of *pious times* with a series of times parallel in their prescription of sexual liberty. The presence of metaphor might be debated if sexual liberty had been proscribed rather than permitted, because then our usual notions of *pious* would require no adjustment. What were those *pious times?* They were times before priests entered into their guilds; they were times before polygamy was thought sinful; they were times before man had to stifle nature's promptings; and so on. They were blessed ages, those pious times, and seemingly long ago. Beneath the passage lies just this notion of a blessed past with a special kind of freedom, allowing *pious* to have its usual meaning and also those imposed upon it here. Dryden has constructed these six lines with even greater care than usual, dividing them into units of growing length and enforcing logical connections by alliterations that show ideas now to be related, now opposed.

The syntactic framework, or the natural English rhetoric of the lines, can be set forth to show the way it functions in counterpoint to the heroic couplet. I shall break the lines into their units, stress words of temporal significance, and indicate important alliteration with capital letters.

> *In* Pious times:
> *ere* Priestcraft did begin
> *before* Polygamy was made a sin
> *when* Man on Many Multiplied his kind
> *ere* One to One was Cursedly Confin'd
> *when* nature Prompted and no law denied Promiscuous use of
> concubine and bride

Each unit begins with a temporal preposition or adverb, advancing in units of increasing length. The alliteration of *pious / priest-* follows the usual connotations only to deny them wittily by the somewhat ambiguous *-craft* and to equate *pious* rather with *polygamy*. The succeeding couplet is built upon the antithesis reflected in the first of its lines by the alliteration of *man, many, multiplied*—words of increasing length. The next, opposed line is rigorously balanced by *one / one . . . cursedly / confin'd*. The third couplet makes up one unit of a brilliant subdued double parallelism with contrast of ideas:

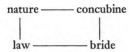

Such use of the couplet anticipates Pope, who more often than Dryden uses it for such effects, though never more skillfully than Dryden here. With Dryden we have as always further questions to deal with. Is this general language, though metaphorical in its internal relations, related to the historical sequences we know the rest of the poem employs? In a poem of this title, and with talk of sexual license, it seems to me impossible for anyone not to assume at the outset that David is "Israel's monarch." (Dryden mentions David several lines later, but it seems plain that he is not so much relinquishing information in a teasing fashion as giving the reader the pleasure of savoring the slow revelation.) And David is after all mentioned in the epistle To the Reader. The problem is rather to show that Charles II is also meant. The fact that he is not mentioned in the opening lines is not very significant, considering that he is not mentioned anywhere else. Yet, given the common David-Charles analogy, Dryden's real problem lay in rising above cliché. He did this by grappling at the outset with the characteristic in the life of David and Charles most open to question. They are wittily praised for what "Nature prompted."

Those who had some special knowledge of divinity and of English court life under Charles had special reason to relish the opening lines. Dryden was not the first to treat the king's fondness for women. In his "History of *Insipids:* A Lampoon, 1676," Rochester had written:

> Our *Romish* Bondage breaker *Harry*,
> Espoused half a dozen Wives,
> *Charles* only one resolv'd to marry,
> And other Men's he never *swives*,
> Yet hath he Sons and Daughters more,
> Than e're had *Harry* by threescore.

The comparison with Henry VIII is like that of Dryden's with David, and in each case the tone is mixed. Since Rochester chooses to make no more than a passing conceit of the comparison, his tone is very different. There is one respect, however, in which Rochester and Dryden are thinking in common terms. Rochester associates sexual license with other kinds of freedom—that from Roman Catholic *Bondage*. It would appear that Charles brought off what the Puritans failed to, a more godly, thorough Reformation. Dryden's lines are also about this ironic greater freedom, which he places in the past. The era referred to is primarily that of David-Charles, but a more exact reading would show that we would have to place those *pious times* before the reign of David as well as Charles. Dryden well knew that *priestcraft* dated at least back to the time of the rebellion by Korah against Aaron, or even to the worship of the golden calf (see 49-50). What Dryden did was refer to a time that never really existed except in the daydreams of masculine desires. He created an imaginary age that could account for the faults of Charles II (or David) in such a way that almost made them seem virtues.

He did so by manipulating a certain view of history, a view which was at once orthodox and capable of suspiciously heterodox individual interpretation. It is the doctrine of Christian liberty, the view that Christ freed man from the earlier rigor of the Law. In the *Irenicum, A Weapon-Salve for the Churches Wounds: or the Divine Right of Particular Forms of Church Government*, Edward Stillingfleet treats the issue of Christian liberty as one crucial to the important problem of reconciling the various Protestant sects after the divisive upheavals of mid-century. Christ came with a historical design:

> to ease Men of their former Burdens, and not to lay on more; the Duties he required were no other but such as were necessary and withal very just and reasonable. He that came to take away the insupportable Yoke of *Jewish Ceremonies*, certainly did never intend to Gall the Necks of his Disciples with another instead of it.[6]

Stillingfleet is clear about the primary condition of "Christian liberty," which

> is, that nothing be imposed as necessary, but what is clearly revealed in the word of God . . . whatever is imposed as necessary, doth immediately bind conscience. And whatever binds mens consciences with an opinion of the necessity of it, doth immediately destroy that Christian liberty which men are necessarily bound to stand fast in, and not be intangled with any yoke of bondage. Not only the yoke of Jewish Ceremonies but whatever yoke pincheth, and galls as that did, with an opinion of the necessity of doing the thing commanded by any but the word of God [is that] Which the Apostle calls *Dogmatizing* . . . the commandments and doctrines of men. And such

he calls a snare, . . . which was making an indifferent thing as *Cœlibate*, necessary.[7]

It would be difficult to say whether Dryden extends or overturns Stillingfleet. Celibacy is not demanded of the clergy by the New Testament, Stillingfleet says, so that in imposing it the Roman Church merely re-imposes the Jewish yoke. But the New Testament also does not stipulate monogamy. In some strict sense of this kind of latitudinarian history, Charles is therefore only exercising his Christian liberty in scattering "his Maker's image thro' the land." Dryden and Charles himself must have taken particular pleasure in an argument turning sectarian ideas back upon the sects. Yet to speak in these terms is to turn not only the usual conception of where Christian liberty should be applied quite awry, but also Dryden's time scheme upside down. The blessed past of the first six lines is a remote past, and even if David is a type of Christ and of Charles (as *vice versa*), he would still be suffering from that unsupportable "Yoke of *Jewish Ceremonies*." Of course both polygamy and concubinage were practiced in ancient Israel. Then why is there not an even greater freedom under the covenant of Grace? Dryden quite simply turns these issues inside out and back again until we neither know nor care what period is being talked about. The whole complex mixture is suspended in an ironic solution.

An amusing and certain connection can be made between these ideas and Charles. When in 1662 the question of his lack of an heir came up, there was a considerable debate whether his marriage with sterile Queen Katherine might be annulled; whether a divorce on the grounds of infertility was permissible; and even whether polygamy was legal under ecclesiastical law. In a document he chose to suppress during his lifetime, that irresistible rogue Gilbert Burnet argued both that barrenness was just cause for divorce and that polygamy was more than lawful. His title, "Two Cases of Conscience," recalls the key word in discussions of Christian liberty like that of Stillingfleet. Of the second case he writes:

Before the Flood, we find *Lamech* a POLYGAMIST: such were *Abraham* and *Jacob* after it . . . this *Polygamy* was practiced, without either Allowance or Controul, as the natural Right of Mankind; neither is it anywhere marked among the *Blemishes* of the Patriarchs; David's Wives (and Store of them he had) are termed by the Prophet, *God's Gift to him:* Yea, *Polygamy* was made, in some Cases, a *Duty* by

> *Moses's* Law . . . I see nothing so strong *against* POLYGAMY as to
> balance the great and visible Hazards, that hang over so many Thou-
> sands, if it not be *Allowed*.[8]

Few readers would have known of this debate among the advisers to
Charles, but it was for those few that Dryden provided a special wit. If
there is only one English poet who might choose to deal with royal
proclivities in such fashion, there is also only one English monarch who
could say, unlike Victoria, "We are amused."

Yet another strand of thought of which Dryden makes use in the
same independent way is what has come to be called in recent times
libertinism, but which in Dryden's day was associated with Epicurus.[9]
If in the pattern of Christian liberty rearranged, "no law denied" the
regal pleasures of the bed, so is it also true that neo-Epicurean "nature
prompted" the gratification of the senses. The sexual overtones of this
were set forth by Dryden's friend Dr. Walter Charleton in a curious
work combining eroticism and philosophy, *The Ephesian Matron*.[10]
The story shows the Matron interrupting her vigil over her husband's
corpse to satisfy a fancy she takes for a passing soldier. Her behavior
had led Charleton to characterize her religion in advance.

> As for her *Religion*, . . . I should take her to be of old *Epicurus's*
> Faith, following the simple dictates of *mother-Nature*, and living by
> the plain rule of her own *Inclinations;* as holding it a contradiction, *to
> be born under one Law, and to another Bound*.[11]

The resemblance of all this to Stillingfleet and Burnet is obvious, even
if the language varies a bit here and there. It would be no great distortion
of what Burnet says to translate "conscience" as he uses it into "mother-
Nature." If we do so, our range of reference for the opening lines is
complete, as another look at them would show, and the look would now
reveal how clearly Charles II, as well as David, is meant. But we have
come upon the threshold of much of the poem as well. It is not just
Charleton who speaks of Nature and Law in these terms. Dryden does
also in the opening six lines. The *Libertins* or neo-Epicureans commonly
went on (as Rochester and Etherege show) to make nature a law to
itself. Dryden is quite happy to play with the terms in their neo-
Epicurean sense in the opening lines. Thereafter, however, he alters
them to their usual meanings in his poetry.

Nature is the sphere over which reason has proper sway, and law is the ethical expression of reason. Law also encompasses liberty in the seventeenth-century sense of legal, customary, and stipulated rights (e.g., the "freedom" of the city). What Dryden does is to use this important complex of ideas in an unorthodox way at the beginning of the poem and change almost at once thereafter to the traditional conceptions. It is as though he felt that honesty required him to get the worst over at once in a poem centering upon Charles or David. But he obviously enjoys his blandly wicked wit and manages to present the worst as something unusually admirable. The tone is impossible to describe, because it turns upon Dryden's attitude toward Charles, David, and a whole complex of ideas. If we think merely of the king, we see that if the lines give us metaphors redounding to his credit, then he is damned with very sly praise. If they are diminishing figures pretending to glorification, then matters are even stranger in a poem designed to praise the king, which repeatedly (as here) imputes godlike qualities to him. Who comes off the better, the promiscuous English king, or David with his "Store" of wives and with no compunction about gaining Bathsheba, even sending her husband off to be killed in battle? But then Charles has not been mentioned, and will not be. We know without being told, and we are told in a way we can scarcely describe. The irony of these lines is at once catalytic to meaning and solvent of any attempt at analysis.

The opening lines do not wholly contradict the treatment of ideas of nature later in the poem, however. Prompted by *nature, after Heav'n's own heart*, the king *scatter'd his Maker's image thro' the land*. The last phrase shows how much the king can be regarded as a type of God the Father, creating like Him, after his own image, and indeed after His image. The Idea of God is, if imperfectly, represented in the king in the terms of biblical-political typology that the Stuarts retained from the middle ages, and merged with the Renaissance theory of the absolute monarch. David is as much the symbol of such thought as the biblical *Mene Tekel* was to the antiroyalists. There is also perhaps a residual neo-Platonism in the typology, as the passage on Achitophel's monstrous fertility implies. He is "Bankrupt of life, yet prodigal of ease," and must be contrasted with the fertile David of the opening lines.

> And all to leave what with his toil he won,
> To that unfeather'd two-legg'd thing, a son;

> Got, while his soul did huddled notions try;
> And born a shapeless lump, like anarchy. (169-72)

The absurd definition of man attributed to Plato, *implumis bipes*, is recast to show the *unnatural* fatherhood of a man who has wasted his life on destructive activities. Because the soul is in chaos, its result is worse than nothing, an *anarchy* that takes Dryden from Achitophel the private person to the public figure. The king's natural promiscuity is infinitely preferable to this perversion of nature.

The king is also given his promiscuity at a time when *no law denied* it. Both he and Achitophel are prompted by nature to beget children. The king serves ends sanctioned by the law (in Dryden's sleight of hand) but Achitophel perverts nature by lawlessness. Dryden recurs to this element of willful perversion repeatedly, showing that Achitophel first corrupted his own nature.

> A fiery soul, which, working out its way,
> Fretted the pigmy body to decay,
> And o'er-inform'd the tenement of clay. . . .
>
> . . . .
> O . . . had the rankness of the soil been freed
> From cockle, that oppress'd the noble seed. (156-58, 192-95)

Achitophel is called *wise;* he is one of the *great wits* of his day. But he is introduced with the epic epithet, *false*. He is false to his nature, his gifts, and to the ethical expression of reason and nature, law. "The statesman we abhor, but praise the judge" (187). When, in a double sense, Achitophel followed the law, he deserved praise. Now that he perverts his legal gifts to illegal efforts to overturn the monarch and introduce anarchy, he is abhorrent. There is a comparison for such a person, just as the comparison for the king is God.

> But wild Ambition loves to slide, not stand,
> And Fortune's ice prefers to Virtue's land.
> Achitophel, grown weary to possess
> A lawful fame, and lazy happiness,
> Disdain'd the golden fruit to gather free,
> And lent the crowd his arm to shake the tree. (198-203)

The last two lines show Achitophel to be another Satan. Too haughty to enjoy the *golden* blessings of Heaven given freely by a gracious God,

Lucifer falls; then he attempts to seduce the *crowd* as Satan did. The tree image develops out of that of fruit, telescoping the celestial and earthly rebellions in which Satan took part. In this passage, and in others where the allusions are specifically Miltonic (e.g., 373-74), Achitophel becomes the antagonist of God. The earthly and divine types of kings and rebels lend the poem and the histories it treats an eternal pattern.[12]

The mind of Achitophel is both his greatest strength and, perverted, his motive to ruinous sin.[13] The nature of his sin, as the Satanic analogy shows, is pride—in wisdom, wit, intelligence. Absalom, too, is a type of pride, but in his physical beauty. A writer on humility earlier in the century sets forth the two. Concluding a prayer in his Preface, he says that pride

> is abominable to see in them that have it through opinion of their own excellent beauty, so as had *Absalom*, whom thou [God] sufferedst to be hanged up by the hair of which he was so proud . . . It is obvious to see in them who are opinionated of their own wisdome, as was manifested in *Achitophel*, whom thou sufferedst to become his own executioner because his counsell was not followed. . . . how must I fall short of *Absalom* in beauty . . . in Wisdome of *Achitophel*.[14]

Now it is a very nice question to know where to stop in speaking of typologies and biblical symbolism. Without sufficient care, we who try to recover them from old books are apt to become more medieval than the schoolmen. May we really say that in using these typologies Dryden predicts a similar end to Shaftesbury and Monmouth? He raises the question of their future in his epistle To the Reader (Noyes, p. 109). Of Shaftesbury-Achitophel he says,

> I have not so much as an uncharitable wish against Achitophel, but am content to be accus'd of a good-natur'd error, and to hope with Origen, that the Devil himself may at last be sav'd. For which reason, in this poem [*sic*], *he is neither brought to set his house in order, nor to dispose of his person afterwards as he in wisdom shall think fit.**

---

* The portion I have italicized after "in this poem" paraphrases 2 Samuel. xvii. 23: "And when Achitophel saw that his counsel was not followed, he saddled his ass, arose, and gat him home to his house, to his city, and put his household in order, and hanged himself, and died . . ."

Irony could scarcely be blander or more devastating. Of Absalom he says,

> Were I the inventor, who am only the historian, I should certainly conclude the piece with the reconcilement of Absalom to David. And who knows but this may come to pass?

Who indeed? We need only check the original story in 2 Samuel, where the "Inventor" does conclude the piece. In the course of the penultimate paragraph of the dedicatory epistle, Dryden has claimed the role of "the historian," compared Shaftesbury with Satan, suggested that we should consider the ends to the lives of Absalom and Achitophel, and hinted that they are the same as in the Bible.

Obviously what is involved is more than just allegory, analogy, or metaphor, call it what we will. The metaphor itself is amplified by metaphor. Instead of using biblical materials as just the stuffs of his poem, Dryden uses them also for getting other effects through traditional associations and typologies, and through allusion. We are asked to remember more of the story than is actually presented. In this sense, the poem's ending is forecast from the beginning, and the last few lines (1026-31) only realize a probability. If nature is perverted, the Law, justice, will be satisfied, and the story will end as it ended in the Bible. Yet, as Dryden says in the last sentence of his paragraph on Absalom and Achitophel in the dedicatory epistle, "God is infinitely merciful; and his vice-gerent is only not so, because he is not infinite." Perhaps all will end well. It is a theoretical possibility, if we follow Origen in the belief that the Devil, implicitly, identified with Shaftesbury, may at last himself be saved. But David's speech (modelled on that of Charles to the Oxford Parliament sitting in March, 1681), in effect withdraws grace (or mercy) and takes out the sword of Law.

> "Thus long have I, by native mercy sway'd,
> My wrongs dissembled, my revenge delay'd:
> So willing to forgive th' offending age . . .
>
> . . . .
>
> Must I at length the sword of justice draw?
> O curst effects of necessary law!
> How ill my fear they by my mercy scan!
> Beware the fury of a patient man.
> Law they require, let Law then shew her face;

They could not be content to look on Grace,
Her hinder parts, but with a daring eye
To tempt the terror of her front and die." (939-41; 1002-09)

The place of Law and its relation to Grace could not be more emphatic.
The king's opponents were pleading for their rights under the law. He
counters by saying that they should have been content with what they
had been allowed as a *Grace*, and he invokes the full power residing in
the throne as the ultimate source of sovereignty and executive authority.
With this a new age begins:

Once more the godlike David was restor'd,
And willing nations knew their lawful lord. (1030-31)

The outcome of the rebellion is shown here and is wholly implied by
David's speech. We see that both passages follow the outlines of the
story in 2 Samuel, even to the suddenness of the change in the situation.

The speech of the king reveals the truth; as Bernard N. Schilling remarked: "The poem is in fact about Charles II and his kingly office." As
he also observed, the basis of the poem is its movement from the witty
opening passage to the grave conclusion.

For David as Charles II, the first ten lines show him as he in fact was,
a very faulty human being. The last lines show him as he was supposed
to be, a majestic ruler restoring divine order to his realm, like God
bringing order to the world. The poem moves from the man to the
king, from the real to the ideal, and the human to the divine order.[15]

Matters are not quite that simple. The two bodies of the king were
thought to possess a mystical relationship. Also, the poem concerns not
just Charles', but David's "kingly office" with a typological relation
between the two. Even the "real" beginning is wittily given a quality
of the ideal. But the general movement is certainly as Schilling describes
it. The beginning will seem to most of us a more brilliant achievement
than the ending, but the latter possesses greater thematic importance.
Like not a little else in the poem, it differs from our expectations. The
winding-up of the story is sudden, though less so than that of the biblical
story. What is important and probably less evident than in the opening
lines is that the king is at once Charles and David.

The resemblance between the speech in the poem and Charles' address

3

Confilium quærunt quo poßint vincere Regem,   Dißipat illorum cepta nefanda Deus.   2 Sam. 17.

to the Oxford Parliament makes clear the force of the metaphorical tenor. The force of the biblical vehicle in these lines can best be known by attention to older conceptions of David resisting the rebellion. Plate II shows him in dress suggestive of his various roles in tradition and in Dryden's poem. There are some Jewish trappings. There is a Roman cast to the armor suggestive of epic qualities. There is a European crown on his head, indicative of his type as an earthly king. And the grouping of the figures suggests his type as a Christ figure. (There is also Achitophel hanged on his rope and the tree that brought Absalom his death.) The Jewish, epic, royal, and sacred elements are developed throughout the poem, and are present at the end, always in reference to the king. The ending modifies the elements somewhat. Rebellion forces the king to give up his Davidic role as a type of Christ, of God the Son expressive of divine Grace. He turns reluctantly to his role as a type of God the Father, the King of kings, invoking that justice which is the ethical expression of His essential wisdom. Abstractly considered, it is earthly justice typifying the perfect justice of God that completes the poem by correcting injustice. Whether considered abstractly in thematic terms or more concretely in terms of character, the ending resolves the issues and closes the poem's slight action.

As in Dryden's other poems written about continuing events, the historical outcome of the sequence of English history is not recounted, for the good reason that it lies in the future. But as in the other poems, it is dealt with. It is predicted. The last line reveals the nature of the resolution: "And willing nations *knew* their lawful lord." The past tense involves both aspects of the metaphor in differing ways. It is the narrative past tense for the biblical story and the prophetic past tense for the English.

PLATE II   *The Plot Against King David and its Quelling.* "They seek counsel by which they may be able to conquer the King; God routs their abominable plots." David is shown with crown and "sword of justice," others with mixed Roman and oriental costumes suggestive of Dryden's fusion of the heroic and the biblical. From an interleaved Bible in the British Museum (C. 7. d. 16, Vol. II). Reproduced by permission of the Trustees of the British Museum.

Metaphors, typologies, and certain other traditional conceptions assist Dryden in transforming the largely natural king of the opening
lines into the largely sacred king of the closing. But the transformation
itself is effected by the poem's structure, which is almost as unusual for
a seeming narrative poem as are the beginning and ending, and which
requires our attention as the second aspect of Dryden's working out of
his metaphorical history. The first sixteen lines introduce the king and
make the point about all his "concubines"—that "No true succession
could their seed attend" (16).[16] With the very next line begins a passage
(17-44) on Absalom which is only less ironic than that on David. He is
praised unstintingly, till the time comes to stint. It is the king who is
first blamed: "What faults he had, . . . his father could not, or he would
not see." Thereafter Absalom is severely questioned while the air of
praise is maintained. He has done things "which the law forebore," and
in spite of a "specious name" given to his action, he has murdered his
half-brother, Amnon. The first section of the poem ends blandly.

> Thus prais'd and lov'd the noble youth remain'd,
> While David, undisturb'd, in Sion reign'd.
> But life can never be sincerely blest;
> Heav'n punishes the bad, and proves the best. (41-44)

The fiction of the blessed past, of an idyll, is maintained through this
first section. All is well, and Absalom is praised and loved, as long as
David reigns undisturbed. What happens thereafter is conveyed by the
next couplet. We know who the best is, and we have some clear misgivings about who may be the bad.

Apart from its remarkable complexity of tone, the opening comprises
a conventional beginning. The temporal adverbs and prepositions remind us of the opening of *The Canterbury Tales*, and to some extent
the tone is that of Once Upon a Time. Yet as we have seen, the tone is
far more complex, and no one can really feel that this is a conventional
opening. What follows is, however, the most conventional part of the
poem (45-149). It is the historical exposition, combining an account of
the past with an introduction of the third character of the poem—the
populace.

> The Jews, a headstrong, moody, murm'ring race,
> As ever tried th' extent and stretch of grace . . . (45-46)

David's speech is already anticipated.

This section is remarkable for two symptoms of Dryden's ease and control. Even so early we see his skill with the biblical metaphor. The passage on "the Jews" is a dazzling demonstration of complete ease in relating biblical and English history together or separately. It is also remarkable for the alteration in tone. Its beginning is grim: these are people "No king could govern, nor no God could please," who "thought that all but savages were slaves." But it soon takes on a strange gaiety. Beware the laughter of a serious man. The Jebusites (Catholics, especially Jesuits) are introduced in a reprehensible, disgusting passage on transubstantiation (118 ff.), from which Dryden recovers to say of them:

> Their busy teachers mingled with the Jews,
> And rak'd for converts even the court and stews:
> Which Hebrew priests the more unkindly took,
> Because the fleece accompanies the flock.
> Some thought they God's anointed meant to slay
> By guns, invented since full many a day:
> Our author swears it not; but who can know
> How far the Devil and Jebusites may go? (126-33)

The whole of the passage has the important function of making some important adjustments through laughter. The Catholics get little sympathy, but they are exonerated from any serious plot against the king. The English are shown to be generally greedy. But the chief function is to render the poet impartial: that collocation, "even the court and stews," is a very remarkable one for a royalist poem like this. Similarly, the poet detaches himself as an artist by using an anachronism to break, for the only time in the whole poem, the biblical metaphor. Those are witty Catholic guns in Israel. Dryden insists that he is reserving judgment on many matters. From such laughter we move to full seriousness in the account of the rising of the feverish faction of rebellion after the Plot. The final lines of the section (144-49) rise in tone, invoking the analogy between the rebels and Satan. We are ready for Achitophel.

The famous description of him (150-207) is introduced by that epic epithet dominating all we are shown of him: *false*. He is false to his own great gifts, to his nature, to his role in society as a judge, to his king, and to God. It is this falseness which will seek to persuade Absalom that he is eligible for "true succession." It is this falseness which is opposed to the royal truth. Given the character of the poem, we regard this character of Achitophel to be a natural one, and its place in the structure of the poem to be proper. We would further expect it to be accompanied by a comparable description of the king or at least of the other characters in the poem. The king is not described in a set "character," however, because Dryden counts on the metaphor of biblical history to keep the king a strong figure of a known and felt kind alive throughout the poem. His personal and public character is stressed repeatedly in details revealing a person different from that ambiguous figure of the opening lines, keeping him steadily before us but never starkly so. As for the other characters, I think that we are not surprised to move from the introduction of Achitophel directly to his temptation of Absalom. (Certainly not if we think of the confronted pair in *MacFlecknoe* or of the Antony-Ventidius scenes in *All for Love*.) But we are surprised to discover later that *after* the action is past we are introduced to the other rebels (543-681) and to the "short file" of loyalists (817-913). We shall need to examine Dryden's reasons for these and other unusual movements after a consideration of the section of the poem dealing with its only sustained sequence of action, Achitophel's temptation of Absalom.

The successful temptation is brought about in two very long speeches by Achitophel (230-302 and 373-476), with Absalom's weakening reply between (303-72). These speeches, like the summary of what they led to thereafter (477-542), are presented in straightforward narrative. Yet the action narrated is almost entirely that which neither Dryden nor anyone else can truly recount—the workings of Shaftesbury upon Monmouth. What Dryden presents as the actual plot or action of the poem is something whose details are impossible for a historian then or now to recover. Literary narrative is made to replace historical fact. What he has done is employ the biblical metaphor, recall the temptation scenes of *Paradise Lost* and *Paradise Regained*, and give a sense of action which is really no more than the expression of the motives and characters of Absalom and Achitophel. They are condemned by what they say or do in such a way as to reveal what they are. Dryden could only have assumed that he knew what they were, and but guess what had been done. These facts give one reason why he delays the introduction of the many personalities on both sides. They would have externalized the action, in fact made it action so much in the usual sense that David's concluding speech would have been anticlimactic unless accompanied by a narrated action. We also see from Dryden's handling how generally helpful to him the biblical metaphor is. The fact that he describes not only English history, but with it biblical, enables him to convey a conviction of action and of historicity. Since presumably this all happened before, it is clearly capable of happening again: as he said in the *Life of Plutarch*, "nothing can come to pass but some precedent of the like nature has already been produc'd." Moreover, the amplifications of the biblical metaphor of 2 Samuel by allusion to Milton's epics and their development of Christian tradition of yet earlier events does give by analogy a powerful sense of action.

Achitophel's first speech begins by recalling the temptation of the kingdoms in *Paradise Regained*. By analogy, Achitophel is Satan, Absalom Christ.

> "Auspicious prince, at whose nativity
> Some royal planet rul'd the southern sky;
> Thy longing country's darling and desire;
> Their cloudy pillar and their guardian fire:
> Their second Moses, whose extended wand
> Divides the seas, and shews the promis'd land;
> Whose dawning day in every distant age
> Has exercis'd the sacred prophets' rage:
> The people's pray'r, the glad diviners' theme,
> The young men's vision, and the old men's dream!
> Thee, Savior, thee, the nation's vows confess,
> And, never satisfied with seeing, bless." (230-41)

It is a remarkable paragraph, merging details attendant upon the birth of Christ, the Old Testament type (Moses), prophecy, and other biblical echoes, till climactically Absalom is called *Savior*. There is in this first speech very little echo of *Paradise Lost*. However, a false analogy *is* drawn by Achitophel for the king, who

> "like the Prince of Angels, from his height
> Comes tumbling downward with diminish'd light." (273-74)

This analogy will not do, except to reveal the Satanic attempt of Achitophel to attribute his own role to the king. More importantly, it asks us to consider what role the king does play in this analogy.

To ask the question is to answer it and to reveal Dryden's handling of the metaphor. By showing Absalom to be a false Christ, David is shown to be a true type of God the Father. Once more the strange music of that extraordinary opening passage is heard. We are reminded, by Achitophel's pretense that Absalom is the Messiah and David is Lucifer, that David is in fact a type of Christ. The effect of Achitophel's first temptation is to establish David yet more firmly as an analogy to God the Father and to intimate the more usual typology of Christ. The balance suggests the extent to which the God of Law will assert Himself instead of the God of Grace. If Achitophel's falseness is clearly revealed in the passage, Absalom's reply must similarly characterize David and himself.

He begins by saying that he has no "pretense . . . To take up arms for public liberty" (315-16). He has none because he is ineligible to rule. He also has none because

> "My father governs with unquestion'd right;
> The faith's defender, and mankind's delight;
> Good, gracious, just . . ." (317-19)

More than that:

> "Were he a tyrant, who, by lawless might
> Oppress'd the Jews, and rais'd the Jebusite,
> Well might I mourn; but nature's holy bands
> Would curb my spirits and restrain my hands." (337-40)

This certainly means that a son is obligated to honor his father. It also means, according to Bodinian and Erastian theory, that the only action men can take against a tyrant is passive resistance. In any event, David is not a tyrant. What shifts Absalom from this acknowledgment (and characterization of the king) is the thought of David's brother. Of course David's brothers do not enter into the biblical account. The biblical metaphor suddenly turns, as it were, from stained glass pictures to clear glass transparency. It is James who is meant, the crisis over the Bill of Exclusion that is recalled. It is as if Absalom is good enough to restrain

his ambition when he thinks of his father, but not if he thinks enviously
of those he imagines to be his rivals: the "lawful issue" or "the *collat'ral*
line, where that shall end" (351-52). It is typical of Dryden's handling
of Absalom that he should present him with seeming favor (not that any
careful reader could possibly be taken in) and yet by numerous means
make clear his strongest objections.

> "Why am I scanted by a niggard birth?
> My soul disclaims the kindred of her earth;
> And, made for empire, whispers me within,
> 'Desire of greatness is a godlike sin.'" (369-72)

We are meant to recall the passages in the character of Achitophel that
deal with his soul.

> A fiery soul, which, working out its way, ⎫
> Fretted the pigmy body to decay, ⎬
> And o'er-informed the tenement of clay . . . . ⎭
>
> . . . .
>   that unfeather'd two-legg'd thing, a son;
> Got, while his soul did huddled notions try;
> And born a shapeless lump, like anarchy. (156-58, 170-72)

The relation to Achitophel needs no stress. Less obviously, by hearkening to the corrupt, seductive arguments of Achitophel, Absalom is taking
a new father.

The consideration of David and of Absalom's relation to him in
Achitophel's second speech combines for its effect with the Miltonic
introduction.

> Him staggering so when hell's dire agent found,
> While fainting Virtue scarce maintain'd her ground,
> He pours fresh forces in, and thus replies . . . (373-75)

We have moved from the temptation of Christ (and a general allusion
to *Paradise Regained*) in the first speech to the temptation of Eve (and
recollection of *Paradise Lost*) in the second. To be sure, the comparison
of Absalom with Christ revealed itself to be wrong, but there is still a
falling-off in his role, a degeneration. The remarkable thing is that this
degeneration can be spoken of in terms of a metaphor from early Hebrew history (as the Fall, rewritten in Christian legend and expressed

by Milton) which is used to amplify the story of David, which is in turn
a metaphorical vehicle to describe Charles II and his rule. It should be
clear that much of what we understand from the temptation scene has
no connection whatsoever with this further play of metaphor, and that
there are other biblical metaphors—of Noah (302) or of Jacob and
Esau (436)—that slip casually in and out. These other biblical metaphors
assist in providing an illusion of action to the narrative of temptation—
which is in fact historically unclear in both 2 Samuel and the Restoration. So lively is the drama of temptation and so useful is the controlling
biblical metaphor, that this unhistorical action seems the most historical,
or real, in the poem. At this stage *Absalom and Achitophel* is almost half
over, and the two chief opponents of the king are self-exposed. Self-
exposure has been given a greater illusion of action than simple condemnation could ever have done. It does not, however, satisfy the feeling
we have that some sort of action is required to overcome the threat to
Charles. In this need, and in Dryden's novel means of fulfilling it, we
have the explanation for the unusual construction of the poem.

It is ultimately impossible to know why he did not adapt his materials
to show the king or his forces in triumph over the rebels, making the
poem heroic in plot as well as in tone. But if the king had been shown
to act in such usual human fashion, the forces of the rebels would have
had to be shown in actual civil war. I cannot believe that Dryden wanted
even to admit to such a possibility. Certainly he would not wish to
encourage it. However this may be, we can understand why he has
arranged the rest of the poem as he has. After establishing Absalom's
agreement to act as a figurehead for Achitophel, he deals with the rest
of the rebel party and their actions. The first party are of "the best":

> Who thought the pow'r of monarchy too much;
> Mistaken men, and patriots in their hearts;
> Not wicked, but seduc'd by impious arts. (496-98)

Soon thereafter the villains come on amain. The Presbyterians, or rather
the Levites, are treated in a significant way. They

> Resum'd their cant, and with a zealous cry
> Pursued their old belov'd Theocracy:
> Where Sanhedrin and priest enslav'd the nation,
> And justified their spoils by inspiration:
> For who so fit for reign as Aaron's race,
> If once dominion they could found in grace? (521-26)

Here we have the voluntarist, Calvinist perversion of grace, just as Shaftesbury and Monmouth show perversion of nature and the law. With the character of Zimri, the section of characters of named rebels begins (543-681). Although there will be few people who will not find this one of the high points of the poem, we must not overlook in our appreciation how skilfully Dryden is shifting our attention and expectations.

Much of what is said in these brilliant characterizations has in reality no proper connection with the plot against David. We are introduced to rebels, but their folly and knavery are only partially that of rebellion. If Dryden is careful not to stray from his subject, he is equally careful to shift its emphasis from a possible resolution in events to a resolution in personalities. With these characters, coming as they do after and not before the temptation scenes, there is no longer any need to have the poem culminate in action of the usual kind, which might only put ideas in certain rebellious heads.*

The illusion of matters being worked out, and the actuality in the redefined terms, are created in the remaining sections of the poem. Absalom's second speech (698-722), not in answer to Achitophel's second of temptation but itself a parallel temptation of the people, with the accompanying description of his and Achitophel's actions, is indeed the closest the poem comes to narration of the actions of the rebels against the authority of the king, whether in Jewish history or English. Absalom now casts himself in a role very like that given him in Achitophel's first speech, as Christ. He offers himself as a sacrifice, although not so much to the necessary demands of eternal justice as to the tyranny (700-712) and caprice (713-22) of his father. The analogy is made explicit by the crowd's treatment of "their young Messiah" (728). The action is, however, described as a preliminary test by Achitophel of the probabilities of success and of the prudence of undertaking a real rebellion (741-44). Still, some sort of answering action on the king's part would be necessary if the next section (751-810) did not decisively set the issues of the poem in terms of principles.

---

* Although I cannot remember that Dryden ever names Bacon, the character of Zimri seems to echo "Of the Greatness of Kingdoms and Estates," Ellis, Spedding, Heath ed., *The Works of Francis Bacon*, 7 vols. (1857), VI, 444-52: "there will be found a great many that can fiddle very cunningly, but yet are so far from being able to make a small state great, as . . . to bring a great and flourishing estate to ruin and decay," etc. (p. 445). The 1612 ed. of the essay holds elements yet closer to Dryden's character of Zimri, and still others apply to Achitophel.

This passage on government rejects both Hobbesian notions of government by power and the idea of a king ruling without those laws that guarantee a people's rights (759-64). Having fixed to this extent the upper limits of the sovereignty of the throne, Dryden next limits the sovereignty of the people and the legislature in a rejection of republican theory (765-94). The passage closes with a plea for order and continuity in human affairs (795-810).

To readers today, Dryden's views are more moving for their personal conviction than for their details. Few of us are committed royalists. But the views do emphasize in ways we can understand the conservative case for adhering to a system that works well, and allow by implication for more than is expressly stated. By discussing monarchy, and considering its limitations, Dryden allows the inference that there may be some rational discussion and difference of opinion on the subject. We are reminded that "the best" of the party opposed to the king "thought the pow'r of monarchy too much." Further, to deny the people and the legislature the central and ultimate authority which they claim in their dangerous exaggeration is in effect to admit that in fact they have a share in government, however much less that may be in Dryden's view than in the Whigs'. Finally, there is a slight but important change in this passage from talk of the *law* elsewhere in the poem to mention of *laws*. The change is from a conception of legal principles ordained in the divine and human constitution of the world to legal enactments, the English constitution as opposed to those of other countries. What these views imply is stated explicitly in the poem to his *Honour'd Kinsman, John Driden* (see Chapter VIII).

The emphasis of the two poems is of course different. Men feel and think differently, especially if they are conservative in temperament, when there is a present danger of civil war, as there was in the years considered in *Absalom and Achitophel*. It is important to see Dryden's principles of government in the light of that threat, as also in relation to their larger conception, the Clarendon Settlement, which gave the throne and parliament nearly equal powers. In this constitutional theory, the power of the king was thought greater in executive and military matters, the parliament's in financial affairs, and both organs of power were thought to be ruled by those laws of the realm which make up the Constitution and guide governmental practice. By urging in *Absalom and Achitophel* that prudence restrains men from touching "our ark,"

Dryden emphasizes his conservatism. In the later poem his theory is shown more nearly in its entirety.

The passage on government is both meaningful and personal. In its positive doctrine and in its tone—"What shall we think!"—we are reminded of parliamentary debate, of Halifax during the Exclusion crisis, or of Burke on later occasions. Having translated the action of Absalom corrupted into a matter of political and historical principles, Dryden at last introduces an equal number of good men to set against the chief rebels (811-913). This "short file" of good men is well praised. If the poetry given them lacks the intensity of that describing the major rebels, and it does, the description of them is like that of the earlier characters in going beyond matters purely political to others which help make up a picture of Dryden's ideal of the aristocracy. It sets limits to support of the throne, saying with truth of Barzillai-Ormond that "The court he practic'd, not the courtier's art" (825). Similarly the support of poetry (827 f.) and of learning (869 ff.) is regarded as a duty of the aristocracy.

The "small but faithful band" of loyal royalists lacks the vitality of the plotters, perhaps because in literature villainy is always more interesting than virtue. It is also true that Dryden could not afford to make the loyalists too strong. To do so would weaken in advance the impact of David's speech. Having, as it were, the loyal royalists confront the rebels across the passage of governmental principle, and having on either side of the tableau an equal number of men (though not an equal strength), it is necessary that one further personality resolve the action of the poem. The king speaks with the voice of God the Father (937-38), a role for which (as we have seen) there has been preparation from almost the opening of the poem. Like Achitophel he is capable of invoking analogies from earlier Jewish history.

> "Kings are the public pillars of the State,
> Born to sustain and prop the nation's weight;
> If my young Samson will pretend a call
> To shake the column, let him share the fall." (953-56)

We recall the architectural image of the passage on government (801 ff.), note the stress upon *born* and its contrast with *pretend a call*. In such small details (the alliteration might also be examined), Dryden maintains the large distinctions of his poem. The king's differentiation between Law and Grace, his reluctant drawing of the sword of justice, and the confirmation of his act by God (1026-27), dispel every threat of danger. A new age is introduced: "Henceforth a series of new time began" (1028). The poem closes as it began, with emphasis upon another age.

Such a description of the functional ordering of the poem answers, I think, questions about Dryden's reasons for emphasizing what he does. At the same time, it raises other questions, in particular that of the relation between such a structure and historical sequence. Unquestionably the stress of the unusual form of the poem and the striking characterizations is so strong that the historical narrative of the poem can be lost sight of. Yet it has a simple chronological line, one moreover which is Dryden's favorite temporal basis for his poems. We begin with the blessed past, long, long ago. (It is of course also the present, but we need not sort out again the complexities of the opening.) Then we are shown the situation giving birth to the plot against the king: an indulgent father on the throne, a handsome and wild son. About them seethes the giddy, innately inconstant and treacherous populace. The action leaps forward with the introduction of Achitophel, who sees that the "people easy to rebel" may be shaped to his ends. Seeking a "chief," he chooses Absalom. A time of parrying follows: Achitophel urges, Absalom says he cannot be disloyal to his father. But his words show how he weakens, and the narration of Achitophel's further urgings is tantamount to description of the actual development of the plot. That is, Dryden in the biblical plot has Achitophel propose a course of action against David that describes Shaftesbury's maneuvers against Charles.

By presenting matters in such terms he achieves a dramatic effect like that of Satan's temptation of the kingdoms in *Paradise Regained*, with the epic effects of Satan's temptation of Eve in *Paradise Lost*. He also conveys the progress of the plot without allowing the plotters to seem to pose a real threat of civil war. He then returns to the public at large, as before the temptation, giving the illusion of a turbulence growing with the passing of time, although nothing is said about a chronological progression. The portraits of the rebel "chiefs" follow, interrupting the forward temporal movement; it can scarcely be said that the passage gives even a sense of the spreading of rebellion.

It is a digression which leads us to condemn the plotters. After these portraits, even Absalom will be seen to have lost his personal attractiveness (he has never had any other), and David seem more and more to be needed. The need grows in the description of Absalom's forsaking the court, and with his speech. He now seeks to corrupt others as Achitophel has corrupted him. The passage on government once again interrupts the temporal development, interpreting with political theory the importance of the issues involved. The interruption of chronological development continues with the presentation of the characters of the loyalists. In the interval between this description and David's speech the time scheme resumes. In effect, the king is warned and his speech to quell the danger is evoked.

It may seem that the chronological narrative of the first half of the poem yields to unhistorical description in the second. What it yields to are, however, merely other aspects of history, as history was conceived in Dryden's day, and indeed as it has been practiced by the narrative historians in classical and modern times. Two years after the publication of *Absalom and Achitophel*, Dryden wrote of such matters in his *Life of Plutarch*.

> History is principally divided into these three species: *commentaries* or *annals; history* properly so called; and *biographia*, or the lives of particular men. Commentaries or annals are . . . naked history; or the plain relation of matter of fact, according to the succession of time, divested of all the other ornaments. The springs and motives of actions are not here sought, unless they offer themselves, and are open to every man's discernment.

Plainly *Absalom and Achitophel* does not belong to the historical genre of annals, or commentaries. The better analogy is with "history, properly so called," which

> may be described by the addition of those parts which are not required to annals: and therefore there is little farther to be said concerning it: only that the dignity and gravity of style is here necessary. That the guesses of secret causes inducing to the actions be drawn at least from the most probable circumstances . . .

One such addition to the barer form of annals is Dryden's passage on government. Another is what passes between Absalom and Achitophel. Yet another is that of the historical characters introduced. Such characters are common to narrative history, and equally commonly interrupt the narrative flow. The best analogy for Dryden's two sets of characters is to be found in *Paradise Lost,* where the chief fallen angels are introduced in historical characters and are, like Dryden's rebels, so introduced as to be condemned. There is also an analogy to be found between such historical characters and *biographia,* or biography, as Dryden later translates it, giving the language another new word. This genre is "the history of particular men's lives"; and although it is both inferior in dignity and more confined in action than the other two forms, yet "in pleasure and instruction it equals and even excels both of them."[17] Continuing, he emphasizes the ethical, didactic possibilities of biography to an extent one doubts he really believed or that we can concur in. But it is true that in *Absalom and Achitophel* the characters or portraits lead us to pass judgment upon both the individuals portrayed and the causes they represent. What such conceptions of the alternative forms of historical writing show us is that in his poem Dryden draws upon "history, properly so called" for the main narrative line and upon "biography" for evaluation. The possibilities are so taken advantage of that we can discern beneath the functional structure of the parts of the poem a historical narration that insists upon the truth of what is said.

The two parts of the poem which least fit into such legitimate conceptions of history are the opening and close of the poem. The opening collapses past and present, good and ill. Insofar as it is part of the historical plan, it deals with a golden age in the remote past. Such beginnings are only less common in Dryden's poetry than transcendent endings. David's speech is less plausible historically than in terms of the functional structure of the poem. Its effect is to create another golden age. We are reminded by the speech and its prediction of the similar ending Dryden was to give *The Medal.*

> Thus inborn broils the factions would ingage, ⎫
> Or wars of exil'd heirs, or foreign rage,   ⎬
> Till halting vengeance overtook our age;   ⎭
> And our wild labors wearied into rest,
> Reclin'd us on a rightful monarch's breast. (318-22)

Both because the happy outcome is born in the last couplet and because the poem is Dryden's most questioning, least sure of human values, the prediction (also in the prophetic past tense) is less convincing. David's speech carries conviction for several reasons: it resolves the theme of

law and grace; it is longer and develops its own logic; it has been prepared for by Dryden's handling of the structure of the poem; and the
poem itself is more assured than *The Medal*. Shaftesbury-Achitophel is
obviously a far greater threat in his way than Shadwell-MacFlecknoe in
his. The enlarging metaphors of *Absalom and Achitophel* are not
humorously ironic. But from the poem's very beginning, we are assured
that everything is under complete control, as we are not in that remarkable outburst which begins *The Medal:*

> Of all our antic sights and pageantry,
> Which English idiots run in crowds to see . . .

I can understand why many people should esteem so highly the almost
fearsome energy of the satiric style of *The Medal*, because I admire it,
too. But I am also reassured to find that in his contribution to Nahum
Tate's *Absalom and Achitophel*, Part II, the smile has returned to
Dryden's face.

It may seem strange that nothing in this discussion has suggested that
Absalom and Achitophel is a satire. The reason is that I do not think it
a satire, although some fifth of the poem is undoubtedly satiric in cast.
Absalom and Achitophel is rather partisan history, as Dryden conceived
history to be in his *Life of Plutarch* and in the Account prefixed to
Annus Mirabilis. We should recall that in the Account of the earlier
poem he said the historical and the panegyric are branches of the epic.
Allowing for satire as the obverse of panegyric, as *MacFlecknoe* itself
proves, this constellation of generic qualities is precisely that of *Absalom
and Achitophel*, with a focus upon history in the central metaphor of
the poem. Dryden does, after all, claim the role of "historian" in the
epistle to the reader. If only the full constellation of genres and the
central emphasis be allowed, it does not much matter whether the descriptive term chosen for the poem be satire, political poem, biblical
allegory, epyllion, mock heroic, or other of the terms with some currency.[18] But if so much is accepted, as I believe it must be, then it seems
to me that to describe it as a historical poem does fuller justice to its
range of qualities and to its metaphor.

The one feature of the poem which appears to deny the historical
label is the slighting of narration. It may seem a strange history in which
so little happens, and in this respect it differs markedly from *Annus*

Mirabilis and from the plays with their carefully developed plots. Yet it is precisely this that is to be remarked of the poems Dryden published during the eighties: in them the normal functions of plot are replaced by other poetic features. It is equally remarkable that the major lyrics of the eighties and nineties are made to accommodate temporal or historical sequences; as also that the two major enterprises of translation to which Dryden devoted his talents late in life—the *Virgil* (1697) and the *Fables* (1700)—feature poetic narrative. His *Æneis* at least was in major part a substitute for the epic he had hoped to write.

Plainly it was neither disinclination nor inability that led him to dispense with narrative to the extent that he does in *MacFlecknoe, Absalom and Achitophel, The Medal, Religio Laici,* and *The Hind and the Panther.* Rather, it was a choice of other means for ends other than those served by usual forms of narration. The means employed in *MacFlecknoe* are those chiefly of a quasi-static metaphorical development of a situation or incipient plot. The action possible is transformed by the metaphors into an interplay of personalities and values. In *Absalom and Achitophel,* one function of the biblical metaphor is to imply a more straightforwardly chronological narrative and indeed a greater degree of narrative in the English tenor than the poem's structure in fact allows. Allusions to other biblical episodes and to such narrative poems as Milton's two epics heighten the illusion of action. The real action, if that is not too strong a term, is to be found in the interplay of the two terms of the metaphor. *The Medal* possesses even less action, real or illusory; and in the sense of plot, *Religio Laici* has no action at all.

The fact that *Religio Laici* is also the least metaphorical assists us to understand that one of Dryden's purposes in dispensing with plot is to make possible a poetry in which ideas take the place of characters, their development the place of plot. Such thematic "action" is one major alternative, as metaphorical "action" is the other. *Religio Laici* is an instance of Dryden's using but the former. *Absalom and Achitophel* is an instance of the use of both. In the most complex poem of them all, *The Hind and the Panther,* he manipulates his two kinds of action, thematic and metaphorical, in almost dizzying alternation and combination.

The passage on government in *Absalom and Achitophel,* and the whole of *Religio Laici,* suggest the motives which led Dryden to such unusual alterations of narrative poetry. He was impelled by more than a desire to exploit new forms of metaphor, by more than an interest in developing themes. Most simply, the national political crises of the eighties, and his personal religious crisis in the middle of the decade, required that attention to the meaning of events be given priority over the events themselves. All these poems, however public they are, possess an intense personal drive to discover what is meaningful to John Dryden. The drive accounts for the partisan historiography of *Absalom and Achitophel* and the uncharacteristic anger of *The Medal*.

He had, as it were, committed himself as a royalist, a progressivist in history, and a Christian humanist in *Annus Mirabilis;* but it was not till *MacFlecknoe* that he became fully engaged. Even apart from the passage on government, there are moments in *Absalom and Achitophel* when the narrator emerges before us. (See lines 132, 187, 832.) The epistle "To the Reader" is yet more personal. These are symptoms of a degree of personal engagement that even the closed metaphor could not keep out. Similarly his criticism of Charles' indulgence to Monmouth or of his dependence upon Louis XIV tell strongly of a free mind shaping historical materials so that they express personal needs. The extent to which these needs are reflected by his novel poetic conceptions is, however, best shown in his religious poetry. Four lines from *Religio Laici* testify to the personal force behind the major poems of the eighties.

> If others in the same glass better see,
> 'T is for themselves they look, but not for me:
> For MY salvation must its doom receive,
> Not from what OTHERS but what *I* believe. (301-04)

Faith and Fable in *The Hind and the Panther*

CHAPTER V

> *What may this mean? Language of Man pronounc't*
> *By Tongue of Brute, and human sense exprest?*
> — *Paradise Lost*, IX: 553-54.

> *Let none think that these things were written only to relate a historical truth or without any typical reference to anything else; or contrariwise, that there were no such things really acted, but that it is all allegorical; or that whatsoever it is, it is of no use, nor includes any prophetical meaning concerning the Church.*
> — *The City of God*, XV. 27.

The Hind and the Panther is the most difficult of Dryden's poems. Readers have commonly been entangled by biographical fact (how much simpler it would be if he had moved from Rome to Canterbury) and by a metaphor that seems to paint a confused landscape of beasts changing into men, and which allows "one beast [to] counsel another to rest her faith upon a pope and council."[1] From the time of Montague and Prior's *Hind and the Panther Transvers'd*, some readers have laughed and some have been disturbed. Yet others have thought it Dryden's greatest work. W. D. Christie called it his "most imaginative" poem.[2] And in our own day, F. T. Prince has said that although it is "more than usually difficult," it is central to our judgment of Dryden.

> The ineffectiveness of much modern criticism lies in not having given this massive poem its proper place. Dryden can never be seen clearly without the evidence of this poem, and of "Religio Laici," which is an ante-chamber leading to it. Without these two pieces his thought will seem incomplete, when it is in truth firmly built. . . . I should be surprised if anyone who could appreciate Dryden's verse

at all were not forced to recognize here the extraordinary mastery with which he has ranged from plain statement to exalted rhetoric, from shrewd satire to the glimmering, ambiguous fantastic beast-and-forest pictures òf the later poem. . . . [His style] can only be fully appreciated as a personal version of the mixed style created by the Elizabethans, the mixture consisting, as in Spenser and Shakespeare, in the vocabulary, the tone, the interplay of rhetoric and simplicity.[3]

Those who find greatness in the poem, or who feel it to be Dryden's greatest work, seem like F. T. Prince to be "forced to recognize" its stylistic achievement. Like all his longer poems, it has a very large number of lines that appear striking when removed from their context. They may be noteworthy for wit, for imagery, for aphorism, or for simple beauty, as lines selected from a hundred-line passage chosen at random will show.[4]

So much of rancor in so mild a kind.

. . . .

The Passive Church had struck the foremost blow.

. . . .

But Int'rest will not trust, tho' God should plight his word.

. . . .

. . . Chanticleer the white, of clergy kind.

. . . .

. . . a deadly shibboleth . . .

. . . .

And which was worse (if any worse could be).

. . . .

. . . drunk with fumes of popular applause.

. . . .

For those whom God to ruin has design'd,
He fits for fate, and first destroys their mind.

. . . .

And veil'd their false advice with zealous fear.

. . . .

For fools are double fools, endeav'ring to be wise.

.   .   .   .

One, more mature in folly than the rest.

.   .   .   .

. . . desp'rate cures must be to desp'rate ills applied.

.   .   .   .

Give up our forms, and we shall soon be friends.

.   .   .   .

More learn'd than honest, more a wit than learn'd.

.   .   .   .

The most unlucky parasite alive.

Yet such lines, or the really moving passages of the poem, or any consideration of style alone, evade the most important questions. How can the poem be seen whole? What is Dryden's "crowning *ethos*?"[5] To answer such questions it seems wisest to put aside for the moment with a willing suspension of dismay the fearful spectacle of beasts debating divinity. We may start with a simple description of the poem, one that amplification and development can correct where necessary later.

The Hind and the Panther possesses a discontinuous allegory making use of a slight plot concerning the encounter of the Catholic Hind with the Anglican Panther. They are shown in nocturnal conversation, at supper in the Hind's retreat, and in conversation before slumber. The poem is divided into three parts, of which the third is almost exactly equal in length to the first two together. The first deals chiefly with the past, the second with the present, the third with the future. Each part has a personal or confessional passage of uncommon interest. Each is made up, to a considerable extent, from materials developed out of the arguments advanced by Catholic and Anglican writers in the heated religious controversy during the reign of James II.

Part One opens with a description of the timeless Hind, the Catholic Church, "immortal and unchang'd" (1-34). The other animals, symbols of what Dryden had come to regard as schismatic heresies, are introduced in typological progress pieces and characters (I, 35-510). These are twice interrupted, first to give Dryden's own confession of faith, no doubt the most famous passage of the poem (I, 62-149), and later to plead for religious toleration in a passage (I, 236-307) including one of Dryden's several accounts of the creation. Part I closes with the meeting of the Hind and the Panther (I, 511-72). Their talk throughout Part II is not plainly allegorical in presentation, and often the element of beast fable is conveyed only through allusion. The personal section of this part appears towards the end (1226-34; II, 654-62) in a section marked *poëta loquitur*, and deals with a spectacular celestial omen of the royal victory over Monmouth at the Battle of Sedgemoor. Although couched in a clear and witty narrative of argument, which rises at times to great beauty, the somewhat technical theological issues of Part II will probably lead most modern readers to place it below the first and third in interest. Part III begins with an apology for the fable form (1295-1309; III, 1-15) and moves on to discussion between the Hind and the Panther (1310-1720; III, 16-426), now of the social and political implications of the religious stands taken earlier by the two debaters. The personal section justifies conversion and reprehends pride (1529-91; III, 235-97). Then the Panther relates a fable of the Swallows (1721-1932; III, 427-638), foretelling the destruction of English Catholics. More discussion (1933-2199; III, 639-905) is followed by the Hind's fable of the Pigeons (2200-2582; III, 906-1288), which gives another version of the future of England. The poem ends with a brief last apostrophe to the Hind (2583-92; III, 1289-98).

I. FABLE

Since to many readers that aspect of the poem which should be one of its readiest claims to interest today—the fable—is most disturbing or controversial, we must begin by facing up to two questions. What is to be made of a fable that shifts its metaphorical terms? What explanation can there be for Dryden, of all people, adopting a fable of this kind? The first question is logically part of the second. In practice, however, I think that readers are more apt to be put off by a line like "The lady of the spotted muff began" than comforted in being told that there is a noble tradition of discontinuous allegory. The poem seems to collapse when one or the other of the two elements of the fable—the beast metaphor or the religious significance—suddenly seems inconsistent. This inconsistency is what Montague and Prior parodied in *The Hind and the Panther Transvers'd,* and this inconsistency is what catches every reader's attention. It does so because it is of fundamental importance: the relation between fable and meaning is as significant to *The Hind and the Panther* as to *Absalom and Achitophel.* We are concerned with what seems a basic absurdity, because the absurdity is there. Is it under control? It might have been thought that the author of *MacFlecknoe,* of the opening lines of *Absalom and Achitophel,* of many comedies, and of numerous witty prologues and epilogues would be one uncommonly aware of the uses of absurdity. Has not his sensibility somehow got dissociated by critics unable to believe that Dryden might jest on serious occasions and at his work as it proceeds? A sense of humor is not among the things Dryden was required to give up at conversion. Such passages are, in short, to be enjoyed for their absurdity and especially, as so often with our poet, for the added point given to what has (in its very absurdity) a special claim to attention. One potential of the fable is a wit founded upon absurdity. (There is much more to it than that, but the element of absurdity must be dealt with first.)

In Part II, the Hind and the Panther are at one point arguing over the Eucharist, the Hind accusing her spotted friend of equivocation in holding there to be in the sacrament a Real Presence of Christ, though "only after an heavenly and spiritual manner" (Anglican Article XXVIII). The Panther has just said, in part, that the Hind was lucky to escape so well the hunt of the Philistines (the Whigs in the Popish Plot).

> "As I remember," said the *sober* Hind,
> "Those toils were for your own dear self design'd,
> As well as me; and with the selfsame *throw,*
> To catch the *quarry* and the *vermin* too:
> (Forgive the sland'rous tongues that call'd you so.)
> Howe'er you take it now, *the common cry*
> Then *ran you down* for your rank loyalty.
> Besides, in Popery they thought you nurs'd,
> (As evil tongues will ever speak the worst,)
> Because some forms, and ceremonies some
> You kept, and stood in the main question dumb.
> *Dumb you were born indeed;* but, thinking long,
> The Test it seems at last has loos'd your tongue. . . .
>
> . . . .
>
> I freely grant you spoke to save your life,
> For then *you lay beneath the butcher's knife.*
> Long time you fought, redoubled batt'ry bore,

But, after all, against yourself you swore:
Your former self; for ev'ry hour *your form*
Is chopp'd and chang'd, like winds before a storm.
Thus fear and int'rest will prevail with some;
For all have not the gift of martyrdom."
    The Panther grinn'd at this, and thus replied . . .

This is surely a fair sample of mixed fable, divinity, and history from the most theological section of the poem (590-602, 624-31; II, 18-30, 52-60). Yet there is a delightful irony throughout. The Hind is *sober*. She is plain milk-white to the Panther's gay parti-color. She is also serious minded, whereas the Panther is most amiable for her witty giddiness and unecclesiastical passions. The Hind has just had "a sober draught" (I, 534), while the Panther's luxury is insisted upon throughout the poem. Through much of the first part of the passage the Hind develops imagery of the hunt (*throw, quarry, vermin, common cry, ran you down*—see *O. E. D.*). There is a nice irony in such imagery being applied by the Hind, the animal of the two to be hunted, to the Panther, which was an animal often used for the hunt, though not as its object. The Panther was born dumb indeed, like the Hind, whose tongue it may be noted is loosened, by whatever stimulus, to speak about five words to the Panther's one. The Anglican Panther did lie earlier "beneath the butcher's knife"—but it is in England deer that are more often "chopp'd and chang'd" in form for eating. Finally, of the phrases italicized, one of the choicest is the Hind's wickedly bland confession, "For all have not the gift of martyrdom." *The Panther grinn'd at this.* How could anyone imagine Dryden's not smiling and expecting us to smile? And yet we have moved along from hunted beasts to the Test Laws to the Real Presence and to martyrdom.

    Whatever Dryden's faults, naïveté is not among them. Yet what delicacy and feline exactitude there is in the portrait of the Panther astonished by the Hind's ascetic cell.

    The silent stranger stood amaz'd to see
    Contempt of wealth, and wilful poverty;
    And, tho' ill habits are not soon controll'd,
    A while suspended her desire of gold;
    But civilly drew in her sharpen'd paws,   ⎫
    Not violating hospitable laws,   ⎬
    And pacified her tail, and lick'd her frothy jaws. ⎭
                                    (1286-92; II, 714-20)

This is imagination of the airiest kind. The sequence of "suspended her desire of gold; / But civilly drew in her sharpen'd paws" is especially witty—but *only* upon our acceptance of Dryden's deliberate intent to play upon the Panther as beast and the Panther as a church of men. The closing triplet, whose last line is stressed (as so often) yet further by the alexandrine length, is above comment. Yet those who are familiar with the poem will not be surprised that these effects should be accompanied by an allusion to *Paradise Lost*, IV, 114-357, especially 183-93. There Milton compares Satan arriving in Paradise to a wolf and a thief, with special application to "Church lewd hirelings," and in 119-23, where the description of Satan shows that he "each perturbation smooth'd." No gloss is necessary to show the interpenetration of wit and serious judgment, imagination and evaluation. Such allusions may or may not register with us upon a casual reading. One would have thought, however, that the wit would be plain enough.

Unlike many of the other beasts in the poem, the Hind and the Panther are feminine. Dryden does enjoy playing upon the fact. The Panther is a "well-bred civil beast" (I, 569). How any poet, much less Dryden, could call her so without a humorous intention needs a kind of explanation that will not soon be invented. This civil beast is, to the Hind, "more a gentlewoman than the rest" (I, 570), and elegant in the height of Restoration fashion with her "spotted muff" (I, 572). The Hind is not one to invite just anyone to sup, but she does ask the Panther, who, though angry at the restraints placed upon her (she would like to devour the Hind), drinks some water "And with a lenten salad [cools] her blood" (1321; III, 27). The austere diet has been prepared for by numerous comparisons of Anglican luxury to Catholic austerity. It involves as well the contemporary debate over the merits of Roman fasting. Yet surely we are meant to see an inseparable wit and seriousness. We do not expect vegetarianism of a carnivorous beast like a Panther, but we do expect clergymen to lead temperate lives. Metaphorical vehicle and tenor are wittily separated—until we realize that there is also the problem of whether we can expect this Panther, the Anglican Church, to eat a lenten salad, to live a modest life. Can we or can we not? Where does the vehicle, where the tenor end?* There is no reason to fear enjoyment of the beast fable of the poem.

* Dryden's deliberate play with metaphor may be compared with Spenser's in *Mother Hubberds Tale* (which Dryden says—1300 ff., III, 6 ff.—was a model), where a male lion is used to represent Queen Elizabeth. Dryden silently corrects the sex to female in his allusion.

The more difficult problems posed by the fable are those of how Dryden came to use the discontinuous typological allegory, and what he sought to express by it. In seeking to solve these problems, I think we shall come upon some of the most interesting aspects of the poem. What we need to account for first is the kind or quality of metaphor Dryden fashioned. The discontinuousness involves both the clear interruption of the metaphor and, as we have seen, either sudden or sliding changes from vehicle (beast) to tenor (church, man). There are other matters involved. We are interested in the fusion of fable, typology, and allusion —whether in a passing reference or in sustained metaphor. And we would like to know what special fitness a beast fable may be thought to have for a religious poem. No matter what aspect of imagery or meta- phor in the poem be studied, we are at once brought up against the beast fable. Since there is nothing else quite like it in English poetry, we may safely say it is original. It is also original in the sense that neither many of Dryden's contemporaries nor, it seems, later critics have pene- trated what he calls "this mysterious writ." What Dr. Johnson says of certain allusions and passages is even truer of the fable. "Some of the facts to which allusions are made are now become obscure, and perhaps there may be many satirical passages little understood."[6]

The nature of Dryden's larger metaphors is a major concern of this book. If we consider that in *Absalom and Achitophel* he created an allegorical metaphor more wholly closed and continuous than any in English works since medieval times, one can at least assume a deliberate purpose in his choice of the most open and discontinuous metaphor for *The Hind and the Panther*. As in *MacFlecknoe*, there is even more in this poem of what may be called a continuous supposition of metaphor. In the satire the supposition was founded upon coalescence of disparate images into coherent metaphors. In the religious poem it is founded upon types, or symbols.

The supposition, obvious though it may seem, violated (or continued) as it often is by Dryden's witty movement back and forth from fable to simple relation, is essential to the movement and meaning of the poem. One symptom of this potential is the considerable number of passages as to which one really cannot judge whether they are allegorical, fab- ulous, or not; and of passages where it is impossible to say that the allegorical fable begins or ends at a given line. Here we find that the "coasting" of metaphor which appears upon a few occasions in *Absalom and Achitophel* has become a common technique. The whole description of the Panther (I, 327-527) shows just how imperceptibly the narrative glides in and out of the basic metaphor, or fable, of the poem. In Part II, the metaphorical supposition created by Part I is fulfilled chiefly at the beginning and end, although either through obvious or allusive detail, even the middle section keeps the fable alive.[7] By the time one has reached the fables of the Swallows and the Pigeons in Part III, one has discovered that the metaphorical supposition has become a condition of one's attitude, of one's terms of viewing the poem. To speak more specifically, we accept without surprise the fact that animals in the fable—the Panther and the Hind—should tell fables of their own. (Dryden of course makes sure that we move down the scale of nature to birds.) And so accustomed are we to such fable, that we assume that the Panther and the Hind will find other beast images to represent those very churches and beliefs that they themselves represent elsewhere in the poem. It should be plain that Dryden has created not only a new but also a most flexible metaphorical convention.

The convention was not created *ex nihilo*. Rather, as one would expect when Dryden creates a new kind of metaphor for a religious poem, it is created from religious sources. The most obvious analogue and source for discontinuous metaphor is the tradition of biblical exegesis, with its reading now purely *per literam*, now *moraliter*, now *allegorice*, and most often together. That parabolic reading which was called the *moraliter* is devoted (unlike, for example, the *allegorice*) to metaphorical explication of the significance of the text for *ecclesia*, the Church and its affairs. The important thing about the *moraliter* gloss is that it is discontinuous and capable of mingling with the other readings. The formal source for such parabolic readings is the Vulgate in editions amplified by the *Glossa Ordinaria* and commentary (*postillae*) by Nicholas de Lira and others, editions of which continued to be published in the seventeenth century. Whether Dryden owned such an edition is at once incapable of proof and unimportant.* The habit of so reading the Bible, and the specific readings themselves, were spread broadcast by other kinds of writing. Among them are certain kinds of handbooks, like those of the English Catholic, Thomas Stapleton—*Promptuarium Morale in Evan-*

---

* Dryden's college, Trinity at Cambridge, has such editions. His play upon *cathedra* (e.g., *miter'd seats . . . David's bench*, 2027; III, 733) and other such details show an acquaintance with the Bible in the Vulgate. There are also numerous instances showing his knowledge of *moraliter* readings, whatever his source of knowledge.

gelica Dominicalia and *Promptuarium Catholicum*—which provide running, intermittent allegorical interpretations of the scriptural story.[8] The most obvious source of all was the Bible, which often in the Old Testament is given Christian or allegorical heads (notably in the Canticles), which were themselves explicated in *moraliter* fashion by sermons.* Whatever the exact source, Dryden's detailed knowledge of the actual typological glosses demonstrates beyond question his familiarity with the technique.[9]

The habit of mind underlying the allegorizing of scriptures is related to that which made possible the analogy of biblical to English history in *Absalom and Achitophel*. It differs in its origin, which is biblical exegesis, and therefore in its assumptions. We may look again at St. Augustine's remark, which is concerned with exegesis and which follows his interpretation of Noah's ark as a figure "in every respect" of Christ and the Church.

> Let none think that these things were written [in the Bible] only to relate a historical truth or without any typical reference to anything else; or contrariwise, that there were no such things really acted, but that it is all allegorical; or that whatsoever it is, it is of no use, nor includes any prophetical meaning concerning the Church.[10]

Not only the *locus classicus* for the theory of parabolic reading of scriptures, this passage was elaborated on by medieval allegorizers of pagan classical writers. Augustine's ideas became a crucial matter after the Reformation, since those who held that the Bible alone (and not the tradition of the Church) was the proper "rule of faith" raised in an acute form the problem of what the Bible meant. No serious theologian could deny that a figurative reading was at times necessary. All agreed that the Old Testament prophets foretold the birth of Christ. St. Paul himself referred to the new Adam, Christ. Indeed, the Canticles could be admitted to the canon only by adapting the late Hebrew reading of it as an allegory of God's love for Israel into an allegory of Christ's love for His Church. No one supposed that such meanings were continuous. Everyone except the mystics would probably have thought with St.

---

* There are a number of beast allegories in Restoration sermons. In a late Anglican example, "A Sermon Preached . . . Before His Highness the Prince of Orange" in 20 January, 1688/9, Simon Patrick glosses Isaiah, xi. 6 ("the Wolf shall also dwell with the Lamb," etc.) so that the animals are sects of Jews, Gentiles, Christians, and also types of men.

Augustine that the "historical truth" was continual if not continuous and "typical reference" intermittent and yet potential (as in *The Hind and the Panther*) throughout. The debate arose chiefly over sorting out passages, especially in the New Testament, interpreting them, and applying them. Such issues are to be found alive today in debates whether translators should render certain Hebrew words as "virgin" or "young woman," "redeemer" or "vindicator."

The old tradition of scriptural exegesis had been designed in its *moraliter* gloss not only to explain the text but also to show the nature, vicissitudes, and ultimate triumph of *vera ecclesia, sponsa Christi*. The relevance of such a purpose to Dryden's poem needs no stress. Important as it is, this tradition did not alone afford him with the means of his fable. There were other elements, old and new, which went into the composition of his figurative language. One literary and intellectual tradition of a considerable indirect importance lent a special sanction to the use of beasts in imaginative writing touching upon social affairs. In his useful and curious book, *The Happy Beast in French Thought of the Seventeenth Century* (Baltimore, 1933), George Boas gave this tradition its name, theriophily, the love of wild animals. He shows that although beasts had had their advocates in antiquity, the sceptical writings of Montaigne—and in particular the somewhat misinterpreted *Apology for Raymond Sebond*—combined with the Italian genre of the paradox to give theriophily its late sixteenth- and early seventeenth-century impetus. From *pensée* and *jeu d'espirit*, theriophilist writings developed into a thoroughgoing primitivistic position, holding that beasts are better off than man either for lacking the curse of reason or, contrariwise, for possessing it with a greater naturalness than man. Descartes, Pascal, and Bossuet as well as more conservative writers opposed theriophily. But satirists with varying degrees of serious intent found it useful to their purposes. Fontenelle, Boileau and, notably, La Fontaine in beast fables used the theriophilist assumptions. These became sufficiently a part of the libertin thought that crossed the channel to appear openly in Rochester's masterpiece, the "Satyr Against Mankind," and covertly in the beast imagery of Etherege and Wycherley. Dryden rejects theriophilist thought quite explicitly in his passage on the creation of beasts and man.[11] What he rejects should be made wholly clear. It is the complex of theriophily, libertin thought, and the underlying scepticism. The basis of the rejection, apart from common sense, is that of orthodox Christianity and humanism. His own comparisons of man to beasts are founded on quite other premises. But theriophily had stimulated contemporary interest in them, and it is no doubt true that the rejection of a certain kind of thought entails some degree of negative influence.*

Another element contributing to Dryden's fable is the emblem, with which he was demonstrably acquainted. He speaks more than once of the "Holland emblem" (e.g., 2350; III, 1056). The early elegy on Hastings, like the "wings and altars" passage in *MacFlecknoe*, shows his awareness of differing literary adaptations of the form. He had read Quarles carefully.[12] For him the truly significant aspect of emblem writing in the latter part of the century is not so much the deterioration that can be found in the old styles[13] as new developments in the form. These are chiefly of two kinds. The first, the emergence of a more social and even political suggestiveness, has an obvious relation to the literature of the age. The second, the alteration of the simultaneity of disparate parts in the traditional emblem into something approaching coherent description, if not narrative, is a basic and important change in the concept of the emblem. Such changes make it adaptable to extended description and poetic narrative with historical interests. One can say that the emblem has moved away from the epigram towards the fable.

These developments can be seen as early as the *Emblemata Sacra* of "B. H." (? Amsterdam, 1631), which combines a high quality of engraving with Dutch poetry, scriptural glosses, and a development of historical, classical, and naturalist glosses. Often the result is close to the beast fable. Parallel developments occur later in England. The continuity and popularity of a genre something between emblem and fable can be seen in the crude work, *The Fables of Young Æsop* (4th ed., London, 1700). In spite of its title and the expectations perhaps aroused by its date, it has simple emblematic pictures, verses of narrative on numerous subjects, and passages of "The Morals." The religious and political fable developing from such and other sources reaches the height of its popularity well after Dryden. By far the greatest works to show kinship with this literary subtradition are Dryden's poem and those two works by his "cousin Swift," *A Tale of a Tub* and *Gulliver's Travels*.

* There are of course many other theories, and practices, involving comparisons of beasts to men. Africa, Eastern Asia, and Europe as well show them. Most of these are, however, animistic survivals unlike the sophisticated primitivism of the theriophilists.

The most pertinent metaphorical material came to Dryden from a genre involved in all the literary or intellectual traditions mentioned. Dryden as much as says that his poem is a beast fable.

> Much malice mingled with a little wit,
> Perhaps, may censure this mysterious writ;
> Because the Muse has peopled Caledon
> With Panthers, Bears, and Wolves, and beasts unknown,
> As if we were not stock'd with monsters of our own.
> Let Æsop answer, who has set to view
> Such kinds as Greece and Phrygia never knew;
> And Mother Hubbard, in her homely dress,
> Has sharply blam'd a British Lioness,
> That queen, whose feast the factious rabble keep,
> Expos'd obscenely naked and asleep.
> Led by those great examples, may not I
> The wanted organs of their words supply?
> If men transact like brutes, 't is equal then
> For brutes to claim the privilege of men. (1295-1309; III, 1-15)

This is an important and characteristic passage. Dryden's awareness of what he is doing in handling his metaphor, and the purposefulness with which he breaks it is apparent in the statement that he has *peopled* an imaginary Britain with *beasts*. A little later there is a fine example of just this. Spenser, he says, criticizes a British *Lioness*. From his own use of the royal animal for kings and queens earlier in the poem, we need no gloss. But he provides it: the *Lioness* is *that queen* discovered *naked* and asleep—in order to satirize the *factious rabble* which celebrated "Queen Bess's Night," November 17th, with pope-burnings. (Spenser shows not a queen so discovered, or indeed even a lioness, but a lion; there seems a deliberate effort to discourage identification with Elizabeth.) Dryden's last two lines are his closest approach to theriophily, even though they constitute a rejection of it. Of course the chief significance of the passage lies in his announcing to the world that Spenser's poem and Æsopian fable are important sources to him. The two have some characteristics in common. In both, the beast fable is developed to unusual narrative lengths. It is given a high degree of social and political implication. It mingles animals and men. And it possesses that curious form of glossed metaphorical significance, the "moral." Many of the editions of Æsop are also adorned with "sculptures," pictures only slightly emblematic, but enough so to show that the emblem and the beast fable have been acting upon each other.

The *general* relation between Spenser's poem and Æsopian lore on the one hand and Dryden's poem on the other is clear enough. More particularly it is difficult to make any significant connection, even in the handling of allegory, between Spenser's and Dryden's poem.* Dryden's debts to the Æsopian fable are another matter. There are many casual allusions to fables, in one instance to three fables within ten lines.[14] Such local allusions cannot be said to have a crucial importance to the poem, except for contributing to the general supposition of fable. There are other debts. Most obviously there are connections in the fables of the Swallows and the Pigeons which, we shall see, are adapted from Æsop, and in the slight plot of Dryden's poem as a whole. The meeting and debating of beasts is not new in *The Hind and the Panther*.

In the Epilogue to *Albion and Albanius* Dryden had referred to the work as "our Æsop's fable." The implication seems to be that of allegory, although it is difficult to see how the term applies better to that work than, say, to *The Duke of Guise* or *Absalom and Achitophel*. That "Æsop's fable" had been spoken in mid-1685, and it seems likely enough that even so casual a reference echoes some thought about using Æsopian lore more seriously than contemporary practitioners had succeeded in doing. Like everyone's, his knowledge of Æsop was probably miscellaneous and eclectic. He seems to have read Phædrus who, like him, gives apologies for the fable form.[15] And it seems *prima facie* certain that he knew the major collection of Æsop published in his day, La Fontaine's *Fables Choisies* (1st ed., 1668).

The most significant by far, however, is the retelling of Æsop by John Ogilby, *The Fables of Æsop Paraphras'd in Verse*.[16] This was printed in a sumptuous folio for a so-called second edition in 1668, favored with pictures, and augmented (in some bindings) by what Ogilby called *Æsopics*, very free and sometimes very lengthy imitations of the Æsopian tale in narrative verse. His versions of the fables proper are lengthened, decorated with learned glosses, and commonly political or social in emphasis. Master of the Revels and an ingenious projector,[17] Ogilby had clearly sensed the possibilities in the fable for entertainment

---

* Spenser also employed a beast fable to social and moral ends, but his technique is somewhat confused, and since there were precedents nearer to hand, Dryden must have sought to invoke Spenser's authority rather than his example.

and even for serious reflection. It was left to Dryden to transcend the discovery with his learning and genius. Ogilby's verse is halting, his mind clever but lacking in real comprehensiveness and power. Yet in some respects his long "Æsopic" version of "Androcleus: or, the Roman Slave" (*Æsopics*, 1668, pp. 129-95) is more like *The Hind and the Panther* than Spenser's *Mother Hubberds Tale*. The picture (see Plate III) taken from the book shows Androcleus among animals in human attire, and with "real" dogs. One could not find a better graphic equivalent of Dryden's fable.

One further element enters into Dryden's fable, serving as an important source of materials: the natural histories or sacred zoögraphies. In some respects the latter type is the most important of all. Sacred zoögraphy mingles some small careful observation with a great deal of the fabulous, and biblical references to beasts with typology. Like the fable, this sacred version of natural history has its origin in antiquity, most notably in Aristotle and the elder Pliny. By the seventeenth century, the scientific and other accretions upon classical zoölogy had swelled enormously with that strange lore which is commonly attributed to the middle ages but which seems in fact as much a part of Renaissance excess as anything. It would not be possible to enumerate all the writers on natural history that Dryden might have read,[18] but there are certain characteristics in these writings highly pertinent to his poem. The best secular rationale for natural history is probably to be found in one of the most familiar of English zoölogies, Edward Topsell's *History of Four-Footed Beasts:* "many and most excellent rules for publick and private affairs, both for preserving a good conscience, and avoiding an evill danger, are gathered from Beasts."[19] Yet it is the timelessness of natural history as opposed to the temporal flux of human affairs that evokes his highest praise.

PLATE III   *Androcleus at Banquet with the Beasts.* From John Ogilby, *Æsopics* (1668). The mingling of Androcleus, beasts graced with human dress and speech, and real dogs gives visual expression of Dryden's fable in *The Hind and the Panther*. Reproduced by permission of The Huntington Library, San Marino, California.

An Sect 6

> This History [of beasts] is to be preferred before the Chronicles and
> Records of all ages made by Men, because the events and accidents of
> the time past, are peradventure such things as shall never again come
> in use; but this [history of beasts] sheweth that Chronicle which was
> made by God himself, every living Beast being a word, every Kind
> being a sentence, and all of them together a large History.[20]

Topsell's words are important for their seeming confusion: history is
really static in its truth, because it is divinely ordered. The details—the
"word" or "sentence"—of natural history can be observed, as human
history, which is static in its flux, cannot. Moreover, there is an implied
single history, the divine, which is mirrored by both the natural and the
human. Dryden's view of history is far more modern than this, as earlier
poems have shown. Where Topsell assumes an analogy (word, sentence,
history) and, as it were, a literal identification or correspondence, Dryden develops metaphors that allow for difference as well as likeness. It
must also be said that in his text Topsell fails to develop his historical
conception. Nor, although he alludes in the Preface to the "holy uses"
of "beasts" in scripture (sig. A6ᵛ) does he develop them in his discussion
of the animals. It is the properties of animals, linguistic considerations,
and medicinal uses that most interest him.

It appears that Dryden knew Topsell, or at least the line of natural
historians he represents. When Dryden writes that the Wolf "could not
howl; the Hind had seen him first" (I, 552), he uses one of Topsell's
alternatives: "if a Wolf first see a man, the man is silent, and cannot
speak, but if the man see the Wolf, the Wolf is silent and cannot cry."[21]
There are other such signs, but for *The Hind and the Panther* Topsell's
is not the most important zoögraphy. That work is by Wolfgang Franz,
or Frantse, or Franzius, *Historia Animalium Sacra*, published in Wittenberg in 1612 and in such other editions as *Animalium Historia Sacra* at
Amsterdam in 1653.[22] The section on quadrupeds was translated into
English by "N. W.," *The History of Brutes* (London, 1670). A fuller
version of the original title will indicate Franzius' purpose and the nature
of the book's importance to Dryden. *Historia Animalium Sacra. In qva
Plerorumque Animalium Praecipuae Proprietates in Gratiam Studio-
sorum Theologiæ & Ministrorum Verbi ad usum εἰκονολογικὸν breviter
accommodantur.* (A Sacred History of Animals. In which the Salient
Characteristics of Many Animals Are Briefly Adapted for Iconological
Purposes to Serve Students of Theology and Ministers of the Word.)

Franzius' book differs from those of Topsell and other natural historians in being exactly what its title indicates, a sacred zoögraphy. His iconological purposes are fulfilled, moreover, in a way that Topsell's suggestive comparisons of human and natural history are not. Being no historian of ideas, I can only speculate about some of the differences between Topsell, Franzius, and Dryden. It may be that to Topsell such comparisons between the human and natural and divine histories are assumed as data, or a fixed scheme that needs no inquiry. Certainly they go undeveloped. To Franzius the iconological features of animals seem to be ideas of faith, or matters capable of parabolic adaptation in teaching ideas of faith. It should be pointed out that Franzius is at once Lutheran and an inheritor of Christian teaching from pre-Reformation days. To him, the beasts manifest God's will. Dryden seems to me to look upon the ideas and details of Franzius as symbols of divine providence, not as facts of a quite verifiable kind. The details may or may not be true, but they testify to God's wisdom. He seems to seek to

> behold the law
> And rule of beings in [his] Maker's mind;
> And thence, like limbecs, rich ideas draw

for expression in poetry. It is not the case that Dryden turned his attention backwards in time only after his conversion. There is in his poetry some typological imagery of beasts from *Annus Mirabilis* forward. It is true, however, that such typologies fitted in with other materials to form the best expression of his Catholic faith. The details Franzius gives and their sacred application are also important. In his "Lectori Pio," Franzius gives the traditional arguments for figurative interpretation of the Bible and indicates the proper methods of employing it. He paraphrases St. Thomas Aquinas:

> That which in one place of the scriptures is conveyed metaphorically in others is set forth more explicitly. You have the guidance of the most holy Fathers themselves; the matter is touched upon in the following passage by Jerome in his commentary on Matthew xviii [with the parable of the unforgiving servant]: what listeners cannot grasp through simple precept they can through analogy and examples.*

---

* "Quæ in uno loco traduntur scripturæ sub metaphoris, in aliis locis expressius exponuntur. Habes manuductionem ipsorum sanct[i]ssimorum patrum, Et hunc per-

I find it worthy of some stress that such ways of thinking, which are commonly considered medieval today, originate in late classical times, and are here embodied in a Latin treatise by a Lutheran and thence conveyed in poetry by a late seventeenth-century English Catholic.

Dryden's selectiveness in what he takes from Franzius follows the tradition of use of typologies. Had free selection of details been impossible, it is doubtful that he could have written his poem in anything resembling its actual kind. No one could accuse this kind of thought of lacking alternatives. Almost every last animal has both good and evil typologies; each signifies virtues to be emulated and weaknesses to be avoided. The typologies of the Hind (or Hart), for example, are generally but not entirely good. Franzius calls the animal "timerous" and "in some sense . . . stupid." Dryden plays somewhat upon both of these. By the standards of those who are not of Christ's true Church, the Hind *should* fear, but: "She feared no danger, for she knew no sin" (I, 4. See also 1310-13; III, 16-19). The Panther is "amaz'd," that is, astonished beyond comprehension—by the Hind's "Contempt of wealth, and wilful poverty" (1286-87; II, 714-15). This is the Pauline Christian foolishness as opposed to the Panther's worldly wisdom. Not only does Dryden so adapt typologies; he commonly omits many of the alternatives and frequently finds reason to add to the types. The symbolic whiteness of the Hind ensures against the wrong responses. The choice of the Wolf as an emblem of qualities Dryden particularly detested and feared can partly be explained by its special typological status among animals. As Franzius says, "he hath no qualities that do deserve any commendation."[23]

Without question it is the metaphorical potential of the sacred *zoographia* (as Franzius calls it) rather than its wealth of alternative detail that makes it the most significant element in Dryden's fable. Dryden's treatment of the Fox shows how the sacred zoögraphy could be employed so as to furnish him now with important traditional comparisons, and now with free symbols.

---

tinet illud Hieronymi in caput *18*. Matthæi: quod per simplex præceptum teneri ab auditoribus non potest, per similitudinem exemplaque habetur" sig. c8r–c8v. It should be noted that although a Lutheran, Franzius finds no difficulty in accepting assumptions, procedures, and indeed individual entries of the *Glossa Ordinaria*, which is the *manuductionem* referred to.

With greater guile
False Reynard fed on consecrated spoil:
The graceless beast by Athanasius first
Was chas'd from Nice; then, by Socinus nurs'd,
His impious race their blasphemy renew'd,
And nature's King thro' nature's optics view'd. (I, 52-57)

Franzius says of the beast:

> there are three things which I observe in the Fox: it is a very crafty
> and subtle, and it is a cruel and gluttonous Creature. . . . some of the
> Holy *Fathers* understand by these little *Foxes* [of Canticles ii. 15,
> "*Take us the little Foxes which spoyl the Vines*"] Hereticks that lay
> waste and destroy the Vineyard, that is the *Church* . . . And as Foxes
> by their craftiness do great mischief to Vines and Gardens, so the
> *Church* never suffereth more than from subtility of arguments . . .
> and as the *Fox*, if he be necessitated to it by hunger, will seem to be
> tame, so do these deceivers seem to imitate the true Church; an
> eminent instance of this we have in Ecclesiastical History, of *Arrius*—

whose deceitful behavior at the Council of Nicæa is described.[24]

The connection between this and Dryden's character of the Fox does
not require comment, but certain aspects of his treatment do call for
analysis. He treats the Fox in a historical progress piece from Arius in
the fourth century to Socinus in the sixteenth and on to "new swarming
sects." But the whole couplet needs quotation.

New swarming sects to this obliquely tend,
Hence they began, and here they all will end. (I, 60-61)

In these few lines we have the two basic assumptions upon which the
structure and the figurative language of the poem are based: the historical assumption that things develop in time, and the religious
assumption of timeless truth. The working out of these two seemingly
contradictory elements is peculiarly Drydenian and so complex a matter
that its consideration must be deferred.

Dryden's Fox and his other animals, however, may be looked upon as
types whose attributes develop in time and history, while their essences
remain the same. The craft and gluttony of the Fox become in the poem
a guileful feeding upon "consecrated spoil"—that is, when those who
deny the divinity of Christ (and also when those who do not believe in

transubstantiation) take the sacrament, they feed upon the Body of Christ in the Host as if it were just so much bread. Pretend to orthodoxy though they may, those who deny a transcendent, incarnate deity are heretics of the most essential kind. As the passage of confession which follows shows in its emphasis upon the sacrament, the Anglican Church is associated with this heresy, because in eucharistic doctrine it is a "new swarming sect" denying Christ in this particular. Early in the English Reformation there had been those who believed in a nearly Roman Real Presence, but by Dryden's time the issue of transubstantiation had come to be one of the outstanding differences between Rome and Canterbury, a difference indicated still today in such a phrase as "the Roman communion." The governing theological terms used in the description of the Fox must be observed: he is "the *graceless* beast" and his is an "impious race" which looks upon "*nature's King* through *nature's* optics."

The meaning of each of the lengthy fables in Part III of the poem depends to an appreciable extent upon sacred typology. The Panther's fable of the Swallows, one of Dryden's most notable tonal successes, shows how he adapted Franzius and other sources. The fable has a very urgent, and therefore somewhat veiled, topical allegory concerning the disputes among English Catholics—between on the one hand the views of James II and his rash advisers and on the other those of the moderates, including Dryden, but more specially the old landed Catholic nobility and gentry.* As a part of this, there is criticism in allegory of the rash actions of the Court party in Irish affairs. To state matters so shows how Dryden has used the Panther's fable to express his own criticisms and indeed his fears for the future. However, he has her tell the story with malice and with an obvious satisfaction in cruelty: the Catholics will all be killed (see 1916-30; III, 622-38). Cruelty is one of the chief typologies of the Panther. Even her beauty, which Dryden seems to insist upon with such gallantry in the poem, is a lure for other animals. As Franzius in his *History* says (with some confusion of gender):

> It is very crafty and subtle, and hath a very deformed head, insomuch that it frightens all other Creatures . . . but the rest of her body

* Sir Walter Scott was the first to explicate this aspect of the fable in any detail. Like much else in his edition, the explication marks a new beginning in our understanding of Dryden, although there were inevitably some errors.

is very beautiful and comely . . . it is observed that she is most cruel**
to any beautiful creature; thus, *Jer. 5. 6. The Wolf of the Evenings
shall spoyl them and the* Leopards *shall watch over their Cities, every
one that goeth out shall be torn in pieces.* . . . Of all Creatures the
Panther hath a most fragrant and pleasant smell, by which means he
draweth other Creatures to him, and so maketh a prey of them. (p. 63)

Dryden opposed religious persecution and criticized Louis XIV for his
actions against the Huguenots (he is the "prince of tyranny," 1974;
III, 680), and no doubt found it agreeable to think of that great and sensible man then pope, Innocent XI, and to forget Roman persecutions
of earlier times. But the accounts by the Quakers of their sufferings and
the almost pathetic joy with which the Sects greeted James's Declaration
for Liberty of Conscience show that there was some reason to represent
in the Panther the Church by Law Established.

The plot of the fable of the Swallows is adopted from Ogilby's
Æsop's Fables, XL, "The Parliament of Birds," where the Swallow and
the Linnet (whom Dryden makes a Martin) offer contrary advice. The
Swallow tells of their recent defeat of such predators as Eagles, Kites,
and "Monarch-hating" birds as the background for their own prosperity
as milder birds. But now a new danger has arisen. Man has grown linen,
which the birds must destroy if they do not wish to be captured by it
when it is woven into nets. The Linnet ("Linseed was his Food") argues
that man need cause them no fear, and speaks ironically of such as the
Swallow, "Who now from Churches Lunatick have brought / Revelations, both for Life and Doctrine taught." Disagreement ensues, the
Swallow foresees disaster and makes a pact with Man, who "grants him
Chimneys for his stately Nest, / For which his Song must calm Man's
troubled Breast."[25]

In his adaptation Dryden also has the Panther introduce man at the
end of the fable—as the destroyer of the Catholic Swallows. The difference between the two versions is something between allusion and
adaptation. Dryden clearly wishes that the Catholic party would make
a moderate settlement with English Protestantism in the manner of
Ogilby's Swallow, and thereby avoid destruction.[26] It is manifestly

---

** Dryden touches upon the element of cruelty several times. And both in Part I
and Part III (following the Panther's fable of the Swallows) he dwells upon the
evil of religious persecution, as elsewhere upon the "sanguinary laws" against
Catholics and Dissenters.

skillful of him to cast his criticism of James's policy in terms which suggest Anglican cruelty. He has it both ways. The Panther's character of the Martin, that is, of James's foolhardy adviser, Father Petre (or Petres), is amusing, just, and grim. But there is more to the fable than this. Franzius has a good deal to say about the Swallow. On the basis of Psalm 74. 3—"Yea the sparrow hath found a house, and the swallow a nest for herself, where she may lay her young, even thine altars"—the Swallow had become an emblem of the faithful. (Alluding to Jeremiah, viii. 7, Franzius contrasts the Swallow type with the Jews in idolatry.) In addition, since the wintering of swallows was not understood until the nineteenth century (cf. 1744-46; III, 450-52), their seeming death in the winter and resurrection in the spring made them a symbol of Christian resurrection. The hope that this offers English Catholics at the end of the Panther's fable is clear in spite of her cruel wishes.[27]

Moreover, there are typological suggestions (of which the Panther is unaware) that the anxiety of the Catholic Swallow will be her salvation. "As the Swallow is said to flee a collapsing structure, so the Church should regard the instability of temporal things, that it not be crushed by its own self-aggrandizement."* As this remark shows, the most important typological meaning of the Swallow for Dryden is that she is (with the dove and the lamb) one of the types of the true Church. Franzius draws numerous comparisons to illustrate this typology. One brief comparison is of special relevance to Dryden's fable: "As the Swallow lies hidden in winter, so the Church endures in persecutions."** In other words, the Panther's tale possesses a central irony of which she is not aware. Her "malice" leads her to tell a tale whose typology confirms the fact that the Catholic is the true Church—even the foolish and rash Martin is at least a member of it. More than this, the Panther's forecast of death in winter is, after all, neither surprising nor too much to be feared. What appears to be a wintry death comes to the Church again and again. Persecutions are numerous, and yet she is sustained. The typology from sacred zoögraphy and the outcome of Ogilby's fable combine to convey a meaning not otherwise ascertainable in the fable. Surely only Dryden, and he only at this point in his career, could create a fable of Swallows, told by a Panther, warning James and the rash

---

* "*Sicut* hirundo ruinosas ædes fugere 'dicitur: ita Ecclesia temporalium rerum instabilitatem consideret, ne ipsius studio opprimatur." Franzius, *Historia*, p. 523.

** "*Sicut* [hirundo] hyeme latet: ita Ecclesia in persecutionibus tolerat." Franzius, *Historia*, p. 523. Cf. Dryden, 1731-38, 1916-18; III, 437-44, 622-24. The winter scene suggests persecution and death; the typology holds the promise of rebirth.

Catholics, showing Anglican cruelty, and making the Panther in her very "malice" confirm that the Catholic is the true Church, which will always endure.

The Hind responds with her own forecast of the future of religion in England. Although simpler in tone and allegory than the Panther's, hers of the Pigeons is more complex in character and event. The source of the plot is once again Æsopian, Ogilby's "Of the Doves and the Hawks" (Fab. XX). In this fable, the Doves have enjoyed a long peace. Attacked now by the Kites, finding the battle "hot," they "call a Councel," which decides to engage the Hawk to defeat the Kites. After their victory, however, the Hawks turn upon the Doves and devour large numbers of them. In the Hind's retelling, the Hawk becomes the Buzzard, who is described as a "theologue" and a "prince" (2441, 2435; III, 1147, 1141). As Dryden's description and the background provided by Ogilby's story both show, the Buzzard is not only an emblem of Gilbert Burnet (as Sir Walter Scott clearly saw), but also of William of Orange, Burnet's patron abroad.* The fable from Æsop therefore forewarns the Anglican hierarchy against seeking aid from a Latitudinarian like Burnet and a foreign prince like William. Ogilby's Moral:

> *Effeminate Nations to long Peace inur'd,*
> *Are by Auxiliaries ill secur'd:*
> *Who e'r prove Victors, they shall be the Prize.*

The possibility of at least partial destruction of the Established Church underlies the fable of the Hind, both because of the Æsopian tale and because of analogy with the apparent forecast in the Panther's tale.

The actual outcome of the Hind's fable is somewhat different. There are more and different characters. There are many kinds of birds that live upon the estate of a "plain good man" (James II). The agitation of the Pigeons and the Buzzard is dealt with when this man, or king, or God, pronounces a "doom" assigning each group of birds its rights (2522-49; III, 1228-55). This is James's Declaration for Liberty of Conscience, or Declaration of Indulgence (4 April 1687). The difference between this "just" pronouncement and the traditional outcome of the fable is the difference between what the Anglicans can hope for from James and what they should fear from Burnet/William. The prediction proved reasonably accurate for those Anglican divines who refused

---

* "God save King Buzzard!" is but one of many details inapplicable to Burnet but very pertinent to William.

allegiance to William and Mary and so lost their positions. But if the nonjuring Pigeons suffered, many others proved Dryden's forecast wrong in their prosperity.

There are a number of such changes from the version given by Ogilby. One of them, by no means the least important, is Dryden's distinction between what in Ogilby are interchangeable terms, Dove and Pigeon. From their first appearance as "a sort of Doves" (2240; III, 946) it is clear that the Pigeons are not really Doves. In fact, as Dryden has the Hind say towards the end, the Pigeon is a "pretended Dove" (2550; III, 1256). Although the Pigeon is very like the Dove zoölogically, it is a different bird. Similarly, pretend as it may, the Anglican is not the true Church. It is a "pretended Dove," because in the old typology the true is *columba mea*. It is the Catholic Church which is that Dove, the *sponsa Christi*.[28] Since, however, to introduce both Pigeons and Doves into his fable would have risked blurring the outlines of his plot, Dryden introduces another type for the true Church. The Catholics are the "poor domestic poultry" of the "plain good man." In particular, the Catholic clergy is represented by the Cock, and the sisterhood by "sister Partlet." The identification of the Cock with the priest is ancient and even pagan. It was made Christian all the more easily because of the bird's warning "St. Peter of his fall." The fact that the Cock is a type at once of vigilance and of libidinousness permits Dryden some characteristic mischief. Franzius presents the typologies.

> This animal is most vigilant . . . And this vigilance of the Cock ought to be commended especially to ministers of the Word. . . . As then the Cock announces that the sun will rise, and calls men forth to their works, so ought the minister of the Word to announce the imminent coming of the last day, and awaken men to repentance . . . He has a very hot nature . . . and because his seed is abundant, he is therefore most libidinous, and one of him suffices for many hens. Although all other animals are enervated and debilitated by venery, and so all are depressed after venery, only the Cock crows after coitus . . .*

* *"Vigilantissimum hoc est* animal . . . Et hæc vigilantia galli inprimis ministris verbi debet esse commendata. . . . Ut enim gallus prænuntiat ortum solis, & evocat homines ad operas, ita minister verbi debet prænunciare adventum ultimi diei, & homines exsuscitare ad poenitentiam . . . *Naturam habet* calidissimam . . . & quia semine est plenus, idcirco est libidonisissimus, & unus sufficit multis gallinis. Cumque reliqua animalia omnia Venere enerventur & debilitentur, & sic omnia post Venerem contristentur, ipse solus gallus cantat post coitum. . . ." *Historia*, pp. 406-07, 405. Franzius of course amplifies the usual Gospel reference ("gallus Petrum monet de suo lapsu," etc.), p. 407.

These remarks must be compared with the attitude of "Our pamper'd Pigeons" (the Anglican clergy) who were caused much grief

> to see so nigh their hall
> The bird that warn'd St. Peter of his fall;
> That he should raise his miter'd crest on high,
> And clap his wings, and call his family
> To sacred rites.

The Anglicans are upset that the vigilant Roman priests were allowed into England after the accession of James. It is not the principle but the inconvenience of it. For, as the passage continues, the Cock *will*

> vex th' ethereal pow'rs
> With midnight matins at uncivil hours:
> Nay more, his quiet neighbors should molest,
> Just in the sweetness of their morning rest.
>   Beast of a bird, supinely when he might
> Lie snug and sleep, to rise before the light!
> What if his dull forefathers us'd that cry,
> Could he not let a bad example die?

What a beast of a bird it must be to sleep supine! Dryden obviously has fun with his fable. The idea of a Hind telling a story about supine birds to a Panther has a wonderful imaginative charm, and a significance augmented by the appropriateness of its details.

Dryden of course does not feel obligated to like priests as a class just for the mere accident that they are Catholic. The passage concludes:

> Good sense in sacred worship would appear
> So to begin, as they might end the year.
> Such feats in former times had wrought the falls
> Of crowing Chanticleers in cloister'd walls.
> Expell'd for this, and for their lands, they fled;   ⎫
> And sister Partlet, with her hooded head,   ⎬
> Was hooted hence, because she would not pray abed. ⎭
> The way to win the restiff world to God,
> Was to lay by the disciplining rod,
> Unnatural fasts, and foreign forms of pray'r:
> Religion frights us with a mien severe.
> 'T is prudence to reform her into ease,
> And put her in undress to make her pleas. (2299-2325; III, 1005-1031)

These doctrines of the Pigeons show their luxury in the gayest way. To end the year (i.e., in March, also Lent) as it was begun (in the new calendar, with the revels of New Year's and Twelfth Night) is good Anglican doctrine. The austerities are rather bad form. It appears at first that "such feats" as ascetic practices were the cause of expulsion of the Catholic clergy. But it is plain that the subdued sexual metaphor is in reality developing that other typology of the Cock—libidinousness. The libidinous *falls* of the monks are one cause for expulsion. Anglican greed for their wealth is another. The nuns are expelled because they "would not pray abed." This is no doubt what it pretends to be, a reference to ascetic vigils in convents. But as the diction in lines 2323-24 (III, 1030-31) insinuates, the nun would be agreeable to Canterbury if only it were possible—speaking to be sure of her religion—to "put her in undress." Dryden typically criticizes the Roman priests, acknowledging the pre-Reformation corruption in the monasteries, but yet makes them seem at least less hypocritical than the Anglican clergy. The issue is really settled by the couplet concluding the passage; the Pigeons feel that:

> A lively faith will bear aloft the mind,
> And leave the luggage of good works behind.

This plays upon the thought of two of the Anglican Articles,* and suggests that, whatever the Pigeons say, they envy the "feats" of the monasteries, and are willing to outdo the monks in anything. To their minds, it is not what one does, but what one believes. In such fashion, by following the thought-processes of the Anglican Pigeon, Dryden shifts the charge of libidinousness from the Roman Cock to the Anglican priests. The Pigeons are "these *jolly* birds" (2285; III, 991).** As the stigma shifts, it is the typology of vigilance that is left for the Roman priest. Dryden has so constructed the passage that it shows the superiority of Roman faith while leading the Anglican Pigeons to reject the Roman doctrine of good works.

* Cf. Anglican Articles XI and XII: "That we are justified by faith only is a most wholesome doctrine" (XI); "Albeit that Good Works . . . cannot put away our sins . . . yet are they pleasing and acceptable to God in Christ, and do spring out necessarily of a true and *lively Faith*" (XII; my italics). The article was framed with the special intent of correcting what was thought Catholic error.

** *Jolly* means "Amorous; amatory; wanton; lustful" (*OED*). The epithet is used more than once; cf. "jolly Luther," I, 380 ff.

As perhaps this passage has already suggested, the Hind's fable of the Pigeons has been formed in part from elements in the Nun's Priest's Tale. Chaucer's "povre widwe, somedeel stape in age" is altered to the "plain good man" (2200; III, 906), but the frame is similar. The introduction of Chanticleer and Partlet is but one of several borrowed details. The climactic image of the bees is yet another (2579-80; III, 1285-86). More importantly, Dryden's fable is seriously concerned with developing the "moralite" of Chaucer's tale: the dangers of treason and flattery. In Dryden's translation of "The Cock and the Fox" we read:

> In this plain fable you th' effect may see
> Of negligence and fond credulity;
> And learn besides of flatt'rers to beware,
> Then most pernicious when they speak too fair.
> The cock and fox the fool and knave imply;
> The truth is moral, tho' the tale a lie.
> Who spoke in parables, I dare not say;⎫
> But sure he knew it was a pleasing way, ⎬
> Sound sense, by plain example, to convey. ⎭
> And in a heathen author we may find,⎫
> That pleasure with instruction should be join'd; ⎬
> So take the corn, and leave the chaff behind. ⎭ (810-21)

Although the typology of the Cock and its reference to the Roman clergy suggests an identification between Chaucer's hero and heroine and Dryden's Roman clergy and nuns, it is rather the Anglican Pigeon who is the negligent and credulous "fool," the Buzzard who is the flattering "knave." Dryden is warning the Anglican bishops against Burnet and William. Such adaptation is characteristic, just as is the expansion of Chaucer's conclusion to the Nun's Priest's Tale with the introduction of new biblical and classical elements. It is also typical of Dryden's personal conception of English Christian humanism that it should discover and bring to renewed life typologies such as those of the Cock which have only recently been discovered in Chaucer's own tale.[29]

Dryden's conclusion differs from Chaucer's because the theme of his fable has immediate historical applications as well as the more general, abstract *moralite* of Chaucer's. Instead of the wonderful Chaucerian commotion, Dryden provides the King/God figure of the end of *Absalom and Achitophel* to bring order and happiness by his pronouncement. That order is the order of law, "a doom," the Declaration for

Liberty of Conscience. But it is *grace* rather than *law* which Dryden emphasizes here (2523, 2541; III, 1229, 1247), for the good reason that—theology apart—in his declaration James was exercising royal prerogative to an extent that was legally doubtful.* Dryden's tone is therefore very different from Chaucer's.

> Here ends the reign of this pretended Dove; ⎫
> All prophecies accomplish'd from above,   ⎬
> For Shiloh comes the scepter to remove.   ⎭
> Reduc'd from her imperial high abode,
> Like Dionysius to a private rod,
> The Passive Church, that with pretended grace ⎫
> Did her distinctive mark in duty place,   ⎬
> Now touch'd, reviles her Maker to his face.   ⎭
>
>   (2550-57; III, 1256-63)

The concinnity of the passage is manifest in the encasement of a couplet by triplets and the successive extension of syntactical units. The regal imagery unifying the passage is also obvious. The allusions are tantamount to rapid-fire conceits. As almost always in Dryden, the general prose meaning is clear, as is the poetic if we read carefully. The "pretended Dove," the Anglican Pigeon and not the true, Catholic Church, has its supremacy ended.** The passage speaks of prophecies and is one itself, forecasting the reduction of the importance of the Anglican Church. It is compared to Dionysius the Younger, tyrant of Syracuse (B. C. 377-43) who, after expulsion by Timoleon, was reduced to keeping school at Corinth. The Anglican tyranny and the new role are set forth in the "private rod," which is partly contrasted with the "sceptre" removed by Shiloh in the most crucial allusion in the passage. The echo is of Genesis xlix (especially 8-10), in which Jacob blesses his sons and, in Christian glosses, prophesies of Christ.

> Judah is a lion's whelp; from the prey, my son, thou art gone up: he
> stooped down, he couched as a lion, and as an old lion; who shall

---

* God created man with "Reason to rule, but mercy to forgive; / The first is law, the last prerogative" (I, 261-62). The analogy is of course with God, whose laws proceed from reason (his essence being wisdom), but whose treatment of men with mercy and forgiveness proceeds from Grace.

** The many religious and political particulars connected with *reign* and the predictions made here need not be adduced to show that a realignment is predicted. The details of the passages will be glossed in *Works*, III.

rouse him up? The sceptre shall not part from Judah, nor a lawgiver
from between his feet, until Shiloh come; and unto him shall the
gathering of the people be.

Judah is the synagogue (the symbol of Judaism and Old Testament
worship), Shiloh, Christ and His Church; Judah is the tyranny of the
old Law, Shiloh the grace of the new. It would seem that Judah, the
"lion's whelp," is also Monmouth, who had crowned himself in the west
the year before and was defeated at Sedgemoor. The Judah of the
passage is therefore secular as well as ecclesiastical (the Anglican
Church), while Shiloh is James and Roman Catholicism. "This pretended Dove" has no truth and only a "pretended grace"; the true Dove
has both. (The placement of the two phrases in the passage is indicative
of Dryden's structural care.) The allusive irony runs yet deeper. The
Anglican hierarchy, which took pride in its loyalty to the throne and
espoused passive obedience even to a tyrannical king, the same bishops
that had criticized Catholics for the Jesuitical "deposing doctrine," are
made "passive" as a censure. The alliteration drives the irony home—
"The Passive Church, that with Pretended grace." In those excited days
midway in the reign of James II, she is "touch'd" for her metal of duty
and found false. Since the betrayal is of her "Maker," it may also be the
case that the Shiloh/Rome/Christ/James metaphors invoke the Judah
/Monmouth/Canterbury metaphors to include Judas and his betrayal.
The blessing of Jacob was commonly dated by Christian historians at
B. C. 1689.

The allusion to Shiloh and other details in the passage show that the
imagery of the poem is not always typological. Yet the images usually
catch hold of the dominant typologies, fable, and allegory in some
fashion or other. Biblical allusions and parallels abound throughout the
poem. They usually relate to the larger metaphors by suggesting the
traditional *moraliter* readings. Next to the Bible, Milton and Virgil are
most often the sources of allusion. The comparison, in allusion, of the
Panther astonished by the Hind's asceticism (1286-94; II, 714-20) to
Milton's Satan (*Par. Lost*, IV, 114-357) has already been examined. The
role of Virgil's *Georgics* is difficult to estimate. There are a few undoubted echoes, but more often one feels that verbal details are less
important than the kinds of details and cast of thought. The changes of
the weather in the fable of the Swallows seem particularly Virgilian.

What one means, if one's impressions can ever be set forth logically, is that Dryden follows Virgil through the *Georgics* with delight and the same gentlemanly knowledge of the sky, field, and fold. Dryden's poem is certainly the better for his taking a real as well as humorous joy in the actualities of his beasts. His descriptions are exact. The Panther's "glowing eyeballs glitt'ring in the dark" (795; II, 223) give both a well-observed image of a feline creature and the typology for a predator. The Wolf of "th' Helvetian kind, / Who near the Leman Lake his consort *lin'd*" (I, 178-79) "covers" her in exact beast terms and in a locality allowing for a play on "Leman." But it is the nature of a number of elevated passages (e.g., 1221-34; II, 649-62) that seems most like the *Georgics*.

If Virgil's rural poetry suits Dryden's fable, his epic suits his symbolism and theme. It is no surprise to find that he has drawn upon the religious elements of Æneids III and VI, or parts of I, since these are suggested by the epigraphs to the poem: "Antiquam exquirite matrem . . . Et vera, incessu, patuit dea." The second, "The true goddess was revealed by her stately movement" (*Æneid*, I, 405), is recalled more than once in the poem, at no time more dramatically than at the climax, the Hind's revelation of herself as the true Church (970; II, 398), where it combines with words of Christ. The first, "Seek your ancient mother" (*Æneid*, III, 96), is suggestive of the specific denominational emphasis of the poem. The differences between the Hind and the Panther as mothers are repeatedly dwelt upon. What the poem and its epigraphs urge is no more than what Dryden had done in his conversion.

Yet it is allusion to other parts of the *Æneid* that seems most effective. A very obvious allusion (in 2060-74; III, 766-80) shows the characteristic practice. The Panther is speaking. She rejects the Hind's offer of reconciliation: "Methinks such terms of proffer'd peace you bring, / As once Æneas to th' Italian king." The Panther insists that the land is hers "by long possession"; that the Hind's claim, like that of Æneas, to "an ancient pedigree" is wrong; and that the Hind is demanding a "Lavinia" and bringing her "exil'd gods . . . those household poppits." It is a careful allusion to a passage in *Æneid*, VII (see *Æneis*, VII, 290 ff.). Regarded another way, the Panther's usual witty protest insinuates the charge in contemporary Protestant polemics that the Roman Church is guilty of idolatry in its veneration of relics and images. Yet the chief force of her allusions merely underlines her error. One need only recall or reread the Virgilian passages to see how wholly she rejects her own claim. As the Trojan civilization is superior to the Italian (i.e., Anglican), so it is Catholicism that is destined by fate to triumph.

This passage is but part of a larger that is unified by legal imagery— of court, title, contract, and law. The larger passage (1969-2193; III, 675-899) comprises almost the whole of the section of debate separating the two fables in Part III. To be sure, the heated discussion of the Test Acts and related matters there makes such imagery natural, but naturalness is the normal reason for Dryden to choose a certain kind of figurative language. There is also the larger reason for the choice, and one which accounts for the use of legal language elsewhere in the poem. For Dryden the central issue between the two churches is one of authority. Of the many claimants, which is the true Church? Dryden considers only two, Canterbury and Rome, with any seriousness and feels that the true one is known by looking upon her stately features. Again and again the language becomes legal, because the thinking is in part legalistic. As in political and social affairs, so in religion, Dryden and most people in his day felt that a Judge was required to settle controversies. It is no accident that the poem is resolved by a righteous "doom" (2527; III, 1233). Nor that in another thirty lines (2557; III, 1263) "the plain good man" has become the Heavenly King imaged in His earthly surrogate. But the central feature of the religious beliefs can best be typified in the ending by the way in which the "Church by Law Established" is not only shown to be founded on inadequate law, but also is necessarily rejected in favor of the Church of Grace. The diction, imagery, metaphors, allusions, and typologies that assist in making up the complex of fable in the poem are after all of interest not only in themselves. They are a poetic means to express Dryden's religious and political faith.

II. FAITH

In his dedicatory epistle, "To the Reader," Dryden speaks of "the matters, either religious or civil, which are handled in" his poem. These are matters which the men of his century found the utmost difficulty in separating. There were probably few men who would not have thought it dangerous to attempt a distinction that would not allow consideration of the one in relation to the other. Certainly he had no

wish to do so. The readiest description of his "civil" beliefs is his own
in the Postscript to *The History of the League*, whose first four pages
contain several assertions of principle.

1. "Government . . . is of divine Authority."
2. Power is "deriv'd from God."
3. "A King at his Coronation, swears to govern his subjects by the
   Laws of the Land"; his subjects swear "Allegiance and Fidelity."
4. However, "the failure of the People is punishable by the King,
   that of the King is only punishable by the King of Kings."
5. Subjects give up for themselves and their sons "their power without a capacity of resumption." (A comparison to the doctrine of
   original sin follows.)
6. The English hereditary monarchy is "naturally poiz'd by . . .
   municipal Laws, with equal benefit of Prince and People."
7. The King governs "by explicit Laws"; where laws are lacking he
   has prerogative.
8. Men must bear with an evil king in passive obedience, till he is
   punished by God, who also punishes usurpers.*

Since the Postscript is a piece of polemic against the Whigs, Dryden
has presented his royalist theory more harshly than in *Absalom and
Achitophel* and the poem to his *Honour'd Kinsman, John Driden*. But
these eight principles present a reasonably fair and considered statement
of his beliefs. The persistent religious elements in his "civic" thought
reveal a position like that of the Gallican clergy and of the English
Catholic controversialists from early in the century through the reign
of James II.** But these same principles were those of Erastian, Tory
Anglicanism in his day. Dryden's change from Canterbury to Rome
involved no change in political principle and, it may be added, a
conversion was not in theory necessary to hold to these ideas.

---

* "Postscript," pp. 1-5. The emblematic frontispiece shows hands in the clouds
granting a king of Caroline features a crown in a beam of light in which is the motto:
"*PER ME REGES REGNANT.*" Similarly Dryden's epigraph for his translation
is "Neque enim libertas gratior ulla est / Quam sub Rege Pio." Dryden's stand for
royal divine right was of course official Anglican (and Gallican) doctrine, because
it guaranteed the superiority of the crown in temporal matters to the papacy.

** Dryden's stand is incompatible with the ultramontane "deposing doctrine" of
Cardinal Bellarmine and others who fashioned the monarchomach theory. They
held only the Church or the Pope to possess divine commission, and argued that
heretical princes forfeited obedience. In the tangled situation of the century, Dry-
den's stand is that of the Gallican clergy but against the French state under Louis
XIV; the same as that of the English Cardinal Howard (a relative of his wife) and
Pope Innocent XI, who was prejudiced against Jesuits, angered by the actions of
James II, and worked as an ally of Protestant countries in foreign affairs.

The reign of James II was a time, however, when theory was put to severe test, with much of the Anglican hierarchy deserting the political analogues of its religious principles. Everyone with Erastian and royalist beliefs faced a crisis of conscience, just as those who lived on were to face another with the accession of William and Mary. *The Hind and the Panther* suggests that in the political extremities of those days, Dryden's royalism led him to a "political" conversion—that is, the logic of his political views took him to Rome, which alone of the religions in divided Christendom could show a title like that of a hereditary monarch. The desire for as assured an authority in religious as in civic matters led him to conversion. This, and remaining a Catholic after 1688, made up one consistent stand in those times when consistency was not easy. Another was the Erastian position, which made life so difficult for some Anglican bishops devoted to the throne but fearful of James, and which lost them their sees or lesser places in 1688 when their consciences forbade them to swear allegiance to William and Mary while James and his son were alive. There were other consistent stands among dissenters and republicans. And there were many men whose only consistency was their own interest, or timidity. In judging any of them, we are well advised to look into our own lives and opinions before giving sentence.

It is the case that Dryden's poems show less change in his political ideas than his religious, and that the religious change can be represented by *Religio Laici* and *The Hind and the Panther*. The two poems possess many of the same terms of intellectual and religious reference. They argue for the most part against the same religious errors. But it is also true that no one reading *Religio Laici* showed suspicion that its author was destined in a few years to become a Roman Catholic.* And no one knew how sorely all royalists were to be tested in the same period. Dryden's position in both poems shares a central English Christian humanism. What is Anglican and patriotic humanism in one poem is Catholic and patriotic humanism in the next. The difference is not great in intellectual terms. But it was of course enormous in social and other

---

* The attribution by Louis I. Bredvold in his *Intellectual Milieu of John Dryden* (Ann Arbor, 1934; 1956) to *Religio Laici* of a proto-Catholic fideism and scepticism, and the attribution of these to Catholic thought generally in the century has been rigorously challenged. (See n. 32, below.) Donald R. Benson "Theology and Politics in Dryden's Conversion," *SEL*, IV (1964) has argued Dryden not to be a philosophical fideist but an ecclesiastical fideist, appealing to "experience and history." Dryden so appeals, but my own study and that of others has shown fideism of whatever kind less relevant than the issues actually debated in the age.

considerations in his day. There is, moreover, a great difference in certain important aspects of the poetic expression of faith. *Religio Laici* is not only Anglican, traditional, and personal. It is also without fable, and it progresses from initial imagery to nearly bare statement.[30] *The Hind and the Panther* is Catholic, moderate in certain crucial doctrines, and personal. In addition it is conceived in fable and rich in imagery, even in its relatively bare second part. These poetic differences reflect the social and literary differences in Dryden's conversion.

Dryden's basic religious ideas are set forth early in the poem. His central premise is of a supernatural deity (I, 62-69) whose essence is wisdom (rather than will) and who governs His creatures according to a rational plan (I, 255-60). Since God is transcendent, and religious faith necessarily supernatural in object and inspiration, private reason must submit to faith (I, 62-63). To give man a rational, unerring director to faith, God has appointed His Church as guide (I, 64-71). The ethical expression of divine reason (or wisdom) is law, and of divine love grace (or mercy). God has created man like Himself in possessing these attributes (I, 255-62). The only alternative possibilities which Dryden considers seriously are represented by the Fox, whose heresy is the denial of the supernaturalism of religion; by the Wolf, whose heresy is voluntarism, the belief that God's essence is will rather than wisdom; and by the Anglican church, which is almost true but increasingly corrupted by Fox-like naturalism (in the Latitudinarians) and Wolf-like voluntarism (in accommodation with Presbyterianism). Nothing is said or implied in the poem about fideism or scepticism.

The essential difference between Dryden's Anglican and his Catholic stand—and that which is accounted for by his conversion—is the answer to the question of what is a rational faith. (Numerous subordinate questions are of course involved.) Formerly the Anglican compromise —embodying the sum of the Written Word, Patristic tradition, and episcopal government—had seemed sufficient. Now it is essential to have a guide, an unerring authority, possessor of the Oral Word of tradition and interpreter of the Written Word of Scripture. The crucial point is whether the rule of faith is the Church interpreting the Written by the Oral Word, as Dryden the Catholic believed; or whether it was the Written Word, clear enough in essentials to human reason guided by the Church, as he had earlier believed. The old position, established in the second half of *Religio Laici* is skillfully demolished in Part II of

The Hind and the Panther. The certainly vulnerable Anglican compromise is exposed with remorseless, although commonly only implicit, analysis. Most of the vulnerable aspects of Catholicism, and especially the late medieval corruption, are silently ignored.[31]

Part I of the poem expresses Dryden's ideas both negatively and positively. The negative expression comes in the characters of the heretical beasts. The first of these to get extended discussion is that typified by the Fox. A passage quoted earlier can now be shown in the light of its religious emphasis to have a fuller meaning.

> The graceless beast by Athanasius first
> Was chas'd from Nice; then, by Socinus nurs'd,
> His impious race their blasphemy renew'd,
> And nature's King thro' nature's optics view'd. (I, 54-57)

Nothing could be clearer than the superiority of *grace* to *nature*— or of the monarchic government of the realm of grace to some as yet unspecified alternative. *Grace* is probably the most crucial term in the poem, whether in the political or religious sense made possible and nearly exchangeable by the divine-earthly king analogy.* *Nature's optics* (now man sees but through a glass darkly) means reason, which is created for understanding nature, not its Creator. As this passage implies, and as the famous *confessio* which follows (I, 62-149) shows, "private reason" is insufficient to comprehend a supernatural God:

> Thy throne is darkness in th' abyss of light,
> A blaze of glory that forbids the sight.**

The supernatural, transcendent matters Dryden turns to are the mysteries of the Church: the Trinity (I, 79), Incarnation (I, 80-84), and particularly the Sacrifice in the Mass—the communion of transubstantiated elements (I, 85-137). In one of his wittiest couplets Dryden later compares Roman to Anglican conceptions of this sacrament:

> The lit'ral sense is hard to flesh and blood,
> But nonsense never can be understood. (I, 428-29)

---

* *Grace*, or variants, are used twenty-seven times in the poem. *Mercy, kindness,* and *forgiveness* are related words.

** I, 66-67. The imagery recalls the opening lines of *Rel. Laici.* It should be noted that in that poem the attack upon natural religion, represented by Deism, is also related to a *confessio*, which it follows rather than precedes. Cf. *Rel. Laici* 1-41 and I, 62-149 here; 42-211 there with I, 52-61 here.

Since the *confessio* has long been thought to have special importance to any judgment of Dryden's religious views, it is necessary that it be assessed accurately. It does more than stress grace and supernatural religion. It establishes what is in effect an ascending hierarchy of human faculties—sense, reason, and faith. There is no doubt of the relative importance of each. Nor is there of the competence of each in its sphere: "For what my senses can themselves perceive, / I need no revelation to believe" (I, 91-92). Some have held that the superior place given faith shows Dryden is motivated by a personal fideism or a seventeenth-century scepticism, either or both of which led him to "abuse" reason. (The same has been said of the opening lines of *Religio Laici*.) The fact is that Dryden's hierarchy is that of the so-called realist or rationalist orthodoxy of Aquinas and Hooker.

> Wherefore seeing that God hath endued us with sense, to the end that we might perceive such things as this present life doth need; and with reason, lest that which sense cannot reach unto, being both now and also in regard of a future state hereafter necessary to be known, should lie obscure; finally, with the heavenly support of prophetical revelation [grasped of course by faith], which doth open those hidden mysteries that reason could never have been able to find out, or to have known the necessity of them unto our everlasting good: use we the precious gifts of God unto his glory and honour that gave them, seeking by all means to know what the will of our God is.[32]

So Hooker wrote, in terms like Dryden's, affirming the providence of God with an optimistic view of man's capacities. The same optimism will be found in Dryden's creation passage and elsewhere in the poem. It will be found as early as *Annus Mirabilis* (1667) and as late as *Fables* (1700). The same hierarchy of faculties will be found, moreover, in seventeenth-century English Catholic writings. The *confessio* is not a proclamation of doubt, fideism, or scepticism. If it has been taken as such, the error results from the failure to see how thoroughly his writings counter the growing voluntarism of the century, how almost uniquely among its great literary figures he espouses the rationalist orthodoxy of pre-Reformation times and of the Anglican tradition of Hooker. The *confessio* reveals a major sense in which he is a humanist. Its affirmation of faith reveals a major sense in which he is a Christian.

The *confessio* is followed by the lengthy character of the Wolf (I, 152-235), described in terms of predestination (I, 165), sexuality

(I, 179, etc.), wildness (I, 194 ff.), rebellion (I, 211 ff., etc.) and zeal (I, 228). Although unspecified, the common element is voluntarism. Whereas the Fox had been a *graceless beast* because he had mistakenly regarded God as scrutable to the unassisted natural reason and therefore untranscendent, the Wolf mistakes the nature of the transcendence: "Never was so deform'd a beast of grace" (I, 162). The Wolf's heresy is especially dangerous for its parallel of the orthodox "rationalist" or "realist" position taken by Dryden. The heresy also rests its belief upon transcendence: in grace expressed through divine will rather than divine wisdom.[33] To Dryden, the Calvinist God decreeing predestination by fiat of his Will is a debased Deity. That God is put in a position like Zeus's: "God, like the tyrant of the skies, is plac'd." And those who so misconstrue His grace and rational essence are certain to allow themselves the same unbridled anarchic voluntarism in secular matters: "And kings, like slaves, beneath the crowd debas'd." The two assertions are halves of a couplet (I, 219-20). The parallelism suggests an analogy, the analogy a theory of government as well as religion. Just as the Fox's naturalism had been rejected by the affirmation of supernaturalism in the *confessio*, so now is the Wolf's voluntarism rejected by a passage (I, 236-307) pleading for tolerance and subordination of the will to reason. It shows that the ethical expression of reason is law and of grace (or mercy) forgiveness rather than the Calvinists' angry punishment by a just God of men utterly depraved. It is one of the great passages in Dryden, one whose vision of the dignity of man and of the benevolence of God, whose plea for tolerance is unparalleled in the poetry of the century.

> But ah! some pity e'en to brutes is due:
> Their native walks, methinks, they might enjoy,
> Curb'd of their native malice to destroy.
> Of all the tyrannies on humankind,
> The worst is that which persecutes the mind.
> Let us but weigh at what offense we strike;
> 'T is but because we cannot think alike.
> In punishing of this, we overthrow
> The laws of nations and of nature too.
> Beasts are the subjects of tyrannic sway,
> Where still the stronger on the weaker prey;
> Man only of a softer mold is made,
> Not for his fellows' ruin, but their aid:

Created kind, beneficent, and free,
The noble image of the Deity.
      One portion of informing fire was giv'n
To brutes, th' inferior family of heav'n:
The smith divine, as with a careless beat,
Struck out the mute creation at a heat;
But, when arriv'd at last to human race,
The Godhead took a deep consid'ring space;
And, to distinguish man from all the rest,
Unlock'd the sacred treasures of his breast;
And mercy mix'd with reason did impart,
One to his head, the other to his heart:
Reason to rule, but mercy to forgive;
The first is law, the last prerogative. (I, 236-62)

The passage shows how much Dryden's fable assists him. Strictly
speaking, the first paragraph is illogical: it begins by urging pity and
freedom of conscience for beasts (i.e. those who believe differently,
especially the Dissenters) and soon is dropped to distinguish between
man and beasts. The metaphor is used and broken. This is because
Dryden is arguing for a view of man that is especially humane, and
opposing it to a view that treats him as a beast. At the same time, his
humane view permits him to ask for "pity" and freedom for those
whose ideas are so to speak bestial. It maintains the distinction which
is at once important to Dryden and the refutation of the Wolf's heresy;
yet it is itself an example of man's reason making distinctions which
his mercy can yet transcend. Having established the double nature of
the metaphor, he turns to the differences between men and beasts,
utterly rejecting the theriophilists. The beasts are given will but not
reason, and they are created by a single casual act of the will. Their
creator is "The smith divine." Man's creator is "the Godhead," who
considers—thinks, reasons—and gives man as the qualities to distinguish
him from the beasts His own two highest: reason and mercy. It is essential to consider this elevated passage with the *confessio*, and that
with this, lest Dryden be misjudged. That insists upon faith and supernaturalism, this upon reason and grace. The two affirmations are parts of
a whole, and the whole receives now the stress of that, now of this, depending upon whether the nature of the challenge to the whole is that
of naturalism or of voluntarism.

      The passage has other elements of interest. It is one of Dryden's
creation pieces—and leads, it may be noted, into a progress piece of

human history in respect to tolerance and persecution. Its assumptions are sturdily Aristotelian, holding that man is a being given to social activity and capable of speech. In Dryden's distinction, "Man only of a softer mold is made, / Not for his fellows' ruin, but their aid." The beasts are the *mute creation*, man implicitly gifted with words of the best kind in "Reason to rule, but mercy to forgive." The view of man dismisses Hobbes, who did not think him to be "Created kind, beneficent, and free." It should also be stressed that the passage was written before James's Declaration for Liberty of Conscience.[34] Consistent in thought, dignified in its concept of man, noble in its tolerance, and imaginative in its account of the creation, this passage deserves as close attention as the seemingly more personal *confessio*.

The extent to which Dryden's affirmation of faith in the *confessio* and of reason in the creation passage are to be judged as parts of a whole can be seen by the way in which the heretical forces of the Fox and the Wolf are joined (I, 190-234). As this is the collective opposition to Dryden's orthodoxy, so his collective orthodoxy includes faith, reason, and sense in a hierarchy, with grace rendering them into a harmonious whole. The creation myth is especially significant in its emphasis. It might have led to preoccupation with the will of God, as it does in Calvinist thought and, I think, in most modern conceptions. The voluntarist view is natural to the most extended Renaissance poetic treatment of the creation, Du Bartas' *Divine Weekes and Works* (trans. Joshua Sylvester, 1605, etc.), because he was a Huguenot, a French Calvinist. If it is hard to give an account of the creation which does not emphasize the will of God, then Dryden has deliberately entered enemy territory, as he has also in adapting the mechanistic conception of nature—as a metaphor for beasts alone. The orthodoxy of Aquinas and Hooker—and of Dryden from *Annus Mirabilis* forward—emerges triumphant, and the benign ethical implications of that orthodoxy are for once in its long history recognized. One such implication is the necessity for tolerance. The others are equally plain but not systematically treated. Faith is the basis of action: "Good life be now my task: my doubts are done" (I, 78). Action, not an inner light, is the test of a real faith (1515-28, 1573-99; III, 218-34, 281-305). Man is created *kind*, with the numerous meanings possible to the century; he is created *free*, to do good or ill; and in the mediate of those two terms, he is created *beneficent*.

The further denominational and specifically Roman Catholic emphases of this general view take us into the complexities of religious controversy in the century. Dryden's position is that of moderate English Catholicism, itself a branch of moderate Gallican Catholicism. With but one exception, Dryden takes the most moderate possible stand on the controverted issues. Religion being what it is, "how can finite grasp infinity?" Religious controversy is somewhat less than infinite, and religious positions like any other are seldom wholly consistent. There are some seeming paradoxes. Divine authority permits human freedom. To Dryden, the Church is "an unerring guide" (I, 65), "my director" (I, 70). The necessity for such an authoritative, infallible guide is argued extensively in Part II. Yet man is "free, / the noble image of the Deity" (I, 249-50). And although man might be thought to have lost some freedom because of the tyranny resulting from the Fall (I, 274-83), Christ, Pope Innocent XI, and James II display that mercy which qualifies the law and precludes persecution (I, 284-90). We are reminded that "Of all the tyrannies on humankind, / The worst is that which persecutes the mind" (I, 239-40). Even freedom is conceived in rational rather than voluntaristic terms, and it is perhaps in this that the paradox is resolved.

The problem of the relation between faith and reason is one that has exercised Christianity from patristic to modern times. It certainly was an issue in the seventeenth century, as also one which has confused many of our guides to the intellectual history of the age. Dryden's "change in faith" between *Religio Laici* and *The Hind and the Panther* has a double meaning. The question is which branch of Anglican faith he gave up for which kind of Catholic. One can say generally only that he moved from an Anglican eclectic, commonsensical, personal idea of a rational faith to a Catholic traditional, moderate, personal idea of a rational faith. The issue is now, as the issue was then: what is meant by a rational faith? The tone and emphases, as well as the intellectual position, of moderate English Catholicism at that time can best be conveyed by quotation from Hugh-Paulin de Cressy's *Exomologesis* (Paris, 1653). Like Dryden a convert from high Anglicanism, Cressy, too, had felt impelled to give an explanation of his conversion. Although antedating the reign of James II, *Exomologesis* is the clearest model for Dryden's poem. In Section Two, Chapter XXXVIII, *"Of the use of Reason in Faith,"* Cressy writes:

Now I only speak of a *rationall* and well grounded faith, not such an one, as with which many ignorant or interested persons assent, that is, rather with their wills and passions, than their reason or understanding. . . . *Beliefe* therefore in generall is an assent of the understanding to any thing related to us. (p. 305)

Two concepts of the rational are involved. One is of the reasonableness of the *grounds* of faith (Cressy has of course the testimony of the historical Church in mind) and what may be called the psychology of assent: a rational (not a voluntarist) faith is that in which the assent is of the reason, not of the will or passions. Cressy has yet to grasp the nettle of rational faith in a supernatural religion, however. This he does in sentences that may be compared with Dryden's poetry.

Belief *supernaturall* is, when the prime relator is supernaturall, and also when the object is supernaturall: I might add, and which is begotten in the soul by a *supernaturall vertue* (but that is not debated here [with the Protestant controversialist, once converted to Catholicism, Chillingworth]).

> man is to believe
> Beyond what sense and reason can conceive,
> And for mysterious things of faith rely
> On the proponent, Heav'n's authority. (I, 118-21)

. . . .

Discourse of reason [i.e., rational thought] may, and ordinarily does precede belief; but belief it self is not discourse, but a simple assent of the understanding.

> If then our faith we for our guide admit,
> Vain is the farther search of human wit;
> As, when the building gains a surer stay,
> We take th' unuseful scaffolding away.
> Reason by sense no more can understand;
> The game is play'd into another hand [i.e., faith's]. (I, 122-27)

. . . .

Therefore though faith be an act of the reason [in assent], yet it is not said to be resolved into reason, though produced by it [in acceptance of the most rational grounds of authority], but into authority.

The whole of Dryden's *confessio* develops this idea.[35] And the harmonious relation of the hierarchy of human faculties which Dryden develops in the two crucial passages of Part I is clearly set forth in Cressy's conclusion.

> The use of reason antecedent to faith, and [the] act of the understanding, in assenting to a thing revealed for the authority of God the revealer, do not prejudice neither the supernaturallness, nor certainty of Faith; because the same things have place in any revelation, though made immediately by God; for it is with my senses that I receive the thing revealed, and convey it to my understanding; it is with my understanding that I assent to it, and the reason why I assent to it is, because it is most reasonable to believe God, yet none of these things diminish either the supernaturallity, or absolute certainty of this belief.[36]

Cressy's and Dryden's concern with "Heav'n's authority" distinguish their stand within Christian humanism from that of, say, Hooker. It is a question of the Rule of Faith, that subject with which the second half of *Religio Laici* and much of the first two parts (especially the second) of *The Hind and the Panther* are concerned. The Anglican view was essentially:

> that the Scriptures, tho' not everywhere
> Free from corruption, or intire, or clear,
> Are uncorrupt, sufficient, clear, intire,
> In all things which our needful faith require. (*Rel. Laici*, 297-300).

Moreover, "The things we must believe are few and plain" (*Religio Laici*, 432). The operative words are *sufficient* and *clear* (or *plain*). Yet in warding off various Dissenting ideas about private interpretation, the Anglican Church necessarily took refuge in "what unsuspected ancients say" (*Religio Laici*, 436)—that is, in the tradition of the Church. Similarly, there were some in the Anglican fold, chiefly those who sought accommodation with some of the sects or with the new philosophy, who held that private reason was also admissible as a component in the rule of faith. These—the Deists of *Religio Laici* and the "Sons of Latitude" in *The Hind and the Panther*—incur Dryden's censure as latter-day manifestations of nonsupernaturalists. They are children of the Socinian Fox. When pressed on the right by Catholicism, the Church of England was apt to respond in the direction of private reason interpreting the Written Word as the rule of faith; when pressed on the left by dissenting sects, it responded with the necessity of pure tradition and episcopal government. The total view is a very English compromise, workable, noble, and illogical. Dryden was satisfied with it in *Religio Laici*, although to hindsight there are a few signs it is possible to interpret as unrest. The strength of his attack upon the Deists and the Sects far exceeds that upon the Catholics. Perhaps it is more significant that he should twice, and quite unnecessarily, offer to submit his belief, if errant, to "my own Mother Church" and "our Church" (*Religio Laici*, 319 and especially 445 ff.).* To Dryden the Catholic, the submission was all the more necessary because the Anglican compromise seemed muddled rather than workable.

The rejection of Anglican doctrine is half the function of the argument of Part II. The other half is the identification and description of the true authority, the proper rule of faith. It is of course the Catholic Church. (In a sense other denominations are described in Part I, while the full character of the Roman Church is given in II). In Cressy's words, the "guide" to a Catholic's faith

> is *infallible*, or rather speaking in his guides language, that *she ha's authority to direct him*. This is true, but not all that is true; for he judges of his way too, namely that that way and rule, by which, and in which, his guide sets him and directs him is manifest. And he judges of this more rationally, than a *Protestant* can, because the same that God appointed to be *his guide* [the Church], *is both entrusted with this rule and an explainer of it likewise to him, having not only words, but sense delivered to her*.[37]

The concluding, italicized clauses of Cressy's summary raise without really answering any more clearly than the Anglicans did two questions that Dryden found it necessary to get clear before his "doubts" were "done." The Panther's challenge to the Hind to speak upon one of the points is wonderful.

> "But, shunning long disputes, I fain would see
> That wondrous wight Infallibility.

* Contrast Anglican Article XX, which concludes: "Wherefore, although the Church be a witness and a keeper of holy Writ, yet, as it ought not to decree anything against the same, so besides the same ought it not to enforce anything to be believed for necessity of salvation."

Is he from heav'n, this mighty champion, come,
Or lodg'd below in subterranean Rome?
First, seat him somewhere, and derive his race,
Or else conclude that nothing has no place." (636-41; II, 64-69)

The Hind is forced to hem and haw, for the good reason that there was at the time no authoritative Roman decision whether infallibility resided: (1) in the Pope; (2) in General Councils; (3) in the Pope and General Councils; or (4) in the Pope, General Councils, and "diffusive" Church. Dryden had the choice in writing his poem of avoiding the issue, which in conscience he could not, or of slurring it, which he rejected, or of choosing from one of the four theories. He presents them all and characteristically chooses the most moderate. He rejects the first two for being too narrow, and the fourth as being too broad to mean anything. So, "That wondrous wight Infallibility" is to be found in the "Pope and gen'ral councils": "Both lawful, both combin'd: what one decrees/ By numerous votes, the other ratifies" (653-55; II, 82-84). One cannot resist drawing the analogy, although it is not wholly exact, of his description of the English polity in King and Parliament, in *To My Honour'd Kinsman*, 171-94. Both descriptions give nearly equal weight to the executive and legislative functions, while making both subject to law.

The moderation of Dryden's choice for the locus of infallibility does not characterize his answer to the other question raised by Cressy's remarks—that of the relation of the Church to the Bible, of God's revelation in the Oral and in the Written Word. What is involved is the basic position on what constitutes the rule of faith, the Bible or tradition, the written or the oral catechesis. The two extreme positions were held by some Catholics and some Protestants. Reacting against an authoritative Church that reserved the right to interpret the Bible for itself, some reformed denominations held that only the Bible in itself was the proper rule of faith. All that is in it is true; anything not in it is either false or unnecessary to salvation. To many who held this position, the question of how the Bible was to be read—the crucial theological issue of the century—was decided by the inspiration of the Holy Ghost in each man's heart. Bunyan showed how moving and decent such a faith might be.

At the other extreme, some Catholics held that the oral catechesis preceded the written—that Christ and the Apostles taught before writing;

that much that was divinely inspired came not through writing to separate churches in apostolic times, but through teaching within the early
church; that the teaching was handed down in purity from age to age;
and that, in any case, without the Church to interpret, the Bible either
was just so many written characters on the page or the prey of every
unlettered zealot. The Anglicans in theory adhered to the former, in
practice approached, at some considerable distance, toward the latter.
Cressy is somewhat to the right of Canterbury: "the same that God
hath appointed to be his [the Catholic's] judge, is both entrusted with
this rule, and an explainer of it likewise to him, having not only words,
but sense delivered to her." But he does not define "this rule" as the
written or the oral word, which is the disputed point. Dryden un-
equivocally insists upon the priority of oral catechesis, the obscurity of
the written, the necessity for a Church interpreter without which the
Bible is "mute," and of a "living guide" or infallible judge of the meaning of God's revelation. The importance as well as the difficulty of the
issue can hardly be exaggerated. The Council of Trent had wrestled
with it and decided very nearly in the terms Cressy uses—that is, it gave
a decision more of words than of ideas. Some notion of the continuing
difficulty of the question can be gauged by the fact that it was raised
as one of the central issues in the second Vatican Council, called by
John XXIII and reconvoked by Paul VI.

Dryden's stand is not eccentric, but it is extreme. And it is English.
From Elizabethan times English Catholics had tended to hold to the
radical Catholic position of the priority and, more importantly, the
superiority of the Oral Word.[38] Yet Dryden knew the alternatives. He
could have chosen to compromise, obscure, or completely ignore the
issue. That he did not, and that in this one instance he chose an extreme
position is quite simply due to the fact that without this fuller authority
Rome could not have attracted him from Canterbury. It was this assurance of belonging to Christ's Church, which could not err though
its popes might be sinful, and against which not even the gates of Hell
might prevail, that positively drew men like Dryden to it. Negatively,
the Protestant denominations presented a clear alternative to the
Catholic in the sectarian insistence wholly upon the Word illuminated
by the inner light, and in the mixed alternative of Anglicanism. Dryden
found in the first alternative a kind of logic that might be admitted as
logic (822 ff.; II, 250 ff.) and in the Anglican eclecticism only confusion

(719-868; II, 147-296). His personality could only reject the anarchy of private interpretation, and find repellent anything suggestive of muddle. The issue had to be solved. To one like myself, a "son" of "the bloody Bear, an *Independent* Beast," it is evident that there is in the logic of Dryden's decision an emotional satisfaction and calm of mind not so easily to be found in the ferment and lonely freedom of Protestantism. What is important is conviction.

> So when of old th' Almighty Father sate
> In council, to redeem our ruin'd state,
> Millions of millions, at a distance round,
> Silent the sacred consistory crown'd,
> To hear what mercy mix'd with justice could propound;
> All prompt, with eager pity, to fulfil
> The full extent of their Creator's will:
> But when the stern conditions were declar'd,
> A mournful whisper thro' the host was heard,
> And the whole hierarchy, with heads hung down,
> Submissively declin'd the pond'rous proffer'd crown.
> Then, not till then, th' eternal Son from high
> Rose in the strength of all the Deity;
> Stood forth t' accept the terms, and underwent
> A weight which all the frame of heav'n had bent,
> Nor he himself could bear, but as omnipotent.
> Now, to remove the least remaining doubt,
> That ev'n the blear-ey'd sects may find her out,
> Behold what heav'nly rays adorn her brows,
> What from his wardrobe her belov'd allows
> To deck the wedding day of his unspotted spouse.
> Behold what marks of majesty she brings;
> Richer than ancient heirs of Eastern kings:
> Her right hand holds the scepter and the keys,
> To shew whom she commands, and who obeys;
> With these to bind, or set the sinner free,
> With that t' assert spiritual royalty. (1071-97; II, 499-525)

This is mythmaking of a grand order. There is another elevated passage on the catholicity of the Catholic Church.

> Thus one, thus pure, behold her largely spread,
> Like the fair ocean from her mother-bed;
> From east to west triumphantly she rides,
> All shores are water'd by her wealthy tides:

The gospel-sound diffus'd from pole to pole,
Where winds can carry, and where waves can roll;
The selfsame doctrine of the sacred page
Convey'd to ev'ry clime, in ev'ry age. (1120-27; II, 548-55)

Here it is a vision combining great spatial and temporal sweep with specific ideas about missionary activities that is moving. Such lines should be compared with the beautiful lines that open *Religio Laici*.

Dim as the borrow'd beams of moon and stars
To lonely, weary, wand'ring travelers,
Is Reason to the soul; and, as on high
Those rolling fires discover but the sky,
Not light us here, so Reason's glimmering ray ⎫
Was lent, not to assure our doubtful way, ⎬
But guide us upward to a better day. ⎭
And as those nightly tapers disappear,
When day's bright lord ascends our hemisphere;
So pale grows Reason at Religion's sight;
So dies, and so dissolves in supernatural light. (1-11)

The difference between the tentative cadences and deep plangency of these lines and the triumphant grandeur of the vision of the Church in the passages from *The Hind and the Panther* may scarcely be ignored. I think that each speaks to real religious moods. I think it also the case that the tone of the later poem is the more assured. His odyssey over, a man has found his spiritual home. It turns out to be a palace.

The issue of the unity and authority of the Church, which is treated in Part II, is central to an understanding of the poem and its author, then, in showing how his conversion, his religious position, and his transformed faith depend upon the cornerstone of the authority of the church. This is but one of the many issues controverted in the day, however. If it is almost always true that we have little notion of the terms in which men of a certain time in the past regarded the important issues of the day, the religious controversy in the reign of James II is a remarkable exception. The Anglican divines who were living through those excited years kept a running bibliography of works written either by their side, or by both sides. The first, by William Claget, is dated "May 7, 1686"; William Wake's "Continuation" appeared in 1688; and Edward Gee's "Catalogue" in 1689. The fourth and last was put together by Francis Peck in 1735.[39] The significant thing about

the bibliographies is their chapter titles. Chapter VIII—"Of the Discourses Written on Occasion of the Conference Between Father Andrew
Poulton and Dr. Thomas Tennison"—names but one of the several
"conferences" of debating opponents which together suggest the basis
for the plot of *The Hind and the Panther*. Chapter XVIII, "Of the Discourses Written of the Unity, Authority, and Infallibility of the
Church," characterizes the major cluster of issues in Part II. In fact of
the topics in the thirty-nine chapters (the number does seem accidental),
there are but few which Dryden does not incorporate in his poem. He
followed the religious debate in his day and contributed to it. There
is no need here to document his awareness of the issues and of the
writers. It need only be said that the bibliography shows factually what
Dryden's poetry shows imaginatively—the full learning, the comprehensive breadth, and the complex conviction of his poem.

III. FAITH AND FABLE

Dryden's religious ideas are expressed in the fable he employs. Moreover, as is shown by the order of the passages on the Fox, the *confessio*,
the Wolf, and the creation, the ideas are in part determined by the
very structure of the poem. It is no new thing to discover structure,
metaphor, and significance so much a part of each other in his poetry.
It is now time to try to draw these matters together for *The Hind and
the Panther*. Parts I and II are obviously parallel to the two halves of
Religio Laici. Affirmative passages apart, it is the business of the first
section of each poem primarily to reject heresies; and of the second
primarily to affirm belief while distinguishing it from errors. *The Hind
and the Panther* is, however, written on much the greater scale and with
a very much richer poetic conception.

We may begin by touching upon some of the structural characteristics of the poem. The Hind is envisioned at the beginning and the end.
The presence of what is in effect a confessional or affirmative passage in
each part (64 ff., 1226 ff., and 1529 ff.; I, 64 ff., II, 654 ff., III, 235 ff.)
is one of many devices to keep the poem informed with the strength
of personal conviction. The introduction of the Panther only after the
sectarian beasts is not merely climactic in Part I. More fundamentally,
it adversely affects our opinion of her. As the Wolf was worse than the
Fox, the Panther is fiercest of all. If there be any doubt, the repeated

emphasis upon her sexual relations with the Wolf is a strong reminder. In particular there is one passage (I, 351-60) which parallels and alludes to the extraordinary relations between Milton's Satan, Sin, and Death in *Paradise Lost*, II. There need not be any doubt, however. For as the Wolf is more dangerous than the Fox because he represents grace "deform'd," and also as he and the Fox are then shown in their combined relationship and rejected by the creation-toleration passage, so too is the Panther a step further toward the Catholic Church; so too is she associated with the Wolf; and so too is she rejected. The rejection comes in Part II, which is structurally parallel to the *confessio* and creation-toleration passages of I. In itself, Part II is a controlled piece of steady tonal elevation. The patterning of Part III is clearer in the parallel sections of debate followed by parallel sections of fables. In rude form, the poem spends 572 lines introducing heresies and combating two of the major ones by affirmation of a humanistic faith; 720 lines combating the Anglican heresy and affirming Catholic orthodoxy; and 1298 lines showing the relation of religious to "civic" matters and the significance of both for the future.

It can be seen, therefore, that it is a considerable oversimplification to characterize the temporal orders of the successive parts as past, present, and future. There are many exceptions. All the same, we can see that the particular emphases of the parts follow this plan. And in it, with its modifications, we can discern Dryden's conception of history and the role of the fable. Part I deals with the past in the important sense of providing the histories of the major heresies which Dryden sees threatening England. These are chiefly the heresies represented by the Anabaptist Boar, the Fox, the Wolf, and the Panther. How far this is true can be judged by the verb tenses Dryden employs. The dominant tense is the past—sometimes the historical past tense, sometimes the narrative past. It becomes impossible really to distinguish them. But having run through the development of the heresy, the account turns at last to the present tense. Sometimes the progress piece of heresy ends with the future, as with the now familiar Fox (I, 52-61). Even the *confessio* follows the temporal pattern, because it leads from erring youth and manhood to repentant maturity. Even the creation-toleration passage follows such a historical scheme, although more complexly, since it involves beneficent creation, sin, and regeneration in the Church (the analogy is with the *confessio*, rather than with

Milton's picture of a world in decay). Even indeed the opening portrait
of the Hind is in the narrative past tense, yielding in the last couplet
(I, 33-34) to the present for a timeless generalization, which itself
yields to the past until the end of the history of the Fox.

   Part II deals with the present in the sense that it introduces the largest
number of religious issues controverted in the day. It is in fact a
mirror of the debate over theological matters in progress even as
Dryden was writing his poem. It also contains a good deal else from the
past. The dialogue sign-words ("said the Hind") are of course in the
narrative past tense. But the verb tenses within the dialogue are largely
those of the present—whether simple present or present perfect—even
where we might expect the past.

> "True," said the Panther, "I shall ne'er deny
> My brethren may be sav'd as well as I:
> Tho' Huguenots contemn our ordination,
> Succession, ministerial vocation;
> And Luther, more mistaking what he read,
> Misjoins [sic] the sacred body with the bread:
> Yet, *lady*, still remember I maintain,
> The word in needful points is only plain." (709-16; II, 137-44)

Towards the end of Part II there is a growing suggestion of futurity.

> Despair at our foundations then to strike,
> Till you can prove your faith apóstolic. (1184-85; II, 612-13)
> . . . .
> If such a one you find, let truth prevail. (1194; II, 622)
> . . . .
> Then think but well of him, and half your work is done. (1210; II, 638)
> . . . .
> Discern'd a change of weather in the skies. (1239; II, 667)
> . . . .
> So might these walls, with your fair presence blest,
> Become your dwelling place of everlasting rest. (1273-74; II, 701-02)

   The last quotation is from the Hind's invitation to reconciliation with
Rome. Part III follows with some superficial hope that this might come
about. If the hope has been taken for probability, it is shown otherwise
when the "civic" matters join the religious. These civic matters are
events of the recent past, chiefly political events since the Restoration.
Foremost among them are the Test Acts and the Exclusion Bill, events

of the decade preceding the poem. This past, which is really contemporary happening, repeatedly yields to the present by concern with the actions of either side at the moment. And we are led to implications for the future.

> But then, perhaps, the wicked world would think
> The Wolf design'd to eat as well as drink. (1423-24; III, 129-30)

A question of motive implies future intentions. Similarly, the Huguenots fleeing France might be expected to come in even greater numbers if the conditions were to become more favorable.

> More vacant pulpits would more converts make. (1476; III, 182)

And, as for the Catholics,

> For what they have, their God and king they bless,
> And hope they should not murmur, had they less. (1537-38; III, 243-44)

The two fables of the Swallows and the Pigeons are of course most simply Anglican threats and Catholic hopes for the future. The whole temporal progress of the poem can most easily be represented by the first and last couplets of the poem.

> A milk-white Hind, immortal and unchang'd,
> Fed on the lawns, and in the forest rang'd.
> . . . .
> Ten thousand angels on her slumbers wait,
> With glorious visions of her future state.

The pattern of past, present, and future in the three parts must be qualified, but it is the governing pattern of the poem's movement and development. It is from one or the other of these normal temporal orders that the transcendental departs. It is to them that it returns, as it must in a work concerning man and his institutions. The eternal is the object of faith, but the object of study is history. The historical pattern, the sequence from past to future, is in one way or another a salient characteristic of most of Dryden's most serious poetry. If it be said that we would hardly expect a seventeenth-century poet to move like a surrealist from the future to the past, it may be replied that in

Dryden's case the pattern is one of movement, of concern with historical subjects and events, of examination of the relations between past and present, and in short one possessing a historical nature. Milton's most analogous passage is of course that of the pageant of history in "decay" shown to Adam in the last two books of *Paradise Lost*. The temporal pattern of the rest of Milton's poem, or (for example) of Donne's *Anniversaries*, or of works other than Dryden's, shows that his differ by employing a temporal pattern that is used for historical purposes. Even, as in *Absalom and Achitophel*, where the functional structure of the parts employs atemporal means, Dryden takes care to set forth an underlying temporal sequence between the beginning in the ancient past and the ending with the future triumph. Having insisted upon such basic matters, I must add that in *The Hind and the Panther* matters are more complicated. The Hind is "immortal and unchang'd," as we are told in the first line. From the outset Dryden sets before us an order beyond history in which things are not subject to mutation. The problem of approach to such realms is an enduring human concern. It is also a poetic test. Dryden asks in his *confessio*, "How can finite grasp infinity?" The answer is that it cannot, but that religious faith can overcome the gap by accepting it as well as what lies dimly beyond, as in the case of transubstantiation.

> Good life be now my task: my doubts are done:
> (What more could fright my faith, than three in one?)
> Can I believe eternal God could lie
> Disguis'd in mortal mold and infancy? ⎫
> That the great Maker of the world could die? ⎬
> And after that trust my imperfect sense, ⎭
> Which calls in question his omnipotence?
> Can I my reason to my faith compel,
> And shall my sight, and touch, and taste rebel?   (I, 78-86)

Poetry as well as faith has its means in certain kinds of figurative language (as well as other resources). By choosing to cast over his poem what may be called by analogy to electromagnetism, a metaphorical field of fable, Dryden merges the historical motion and emphasis of his poem with a static, timeless, and transcendent symbolism. Since this is easy enough to say, more difficult to analyze, we may begin with a simple example. The first verse paragraph deals with the Hind, "immortal and unchang'd." She need fear no death, not so much because some zoölogies gave her a life of 3,600 years, but because her whiteness symbolizes a purity proof against death (I, 3-4). "Not so her young" (I, 9) There is a distinction made between the Church and its believers. The one extends through all time; the others live inevitably in a moment of time. In such a distinction we find Dryden's simplest means of treating the eternal and the historical together. Dryden is naturally led to the analogy with Israel (I, 19-20), chosen by God, all too mortal in the sufferings of its individual believers, but promised enduring survival as a people.

The characters of the major heretical beasts show very clearly how typology and fable have been commingled with history. Having been our example before of typologies, the Fox will serve now to show how history is involved.

> With greater guile
> False Reynard fed on consecrated spoil:
> The graceless beast by Athanasius first
> Was chas'd from Nice; then, by Socinus nurs'd,
> His impious race their blasphemy renew'd,
> And nature's King thro' nature's optics view'd.
> Revers'd, they view'd him lessen'd to their eye,
> Nor in an infant could a God descry:
> New swarming sects to this obliquely tend,
> Hence they began, and here they all will end. (I, 52-61)

The passage is a progress piece, one of Dryden's commonest methods of dealing with history. Fast-paced though it is, the account begins in the fourth century when, at the council of Nicæa, Athanasius and other fathers fought the Arian heresy. Next Socinus in the sixteenth century renewed the "blasphemy," reversing (that is perverting, but the image of God's sudden smallness as *an infant* is also involved) "nature's optics," reason. His conclusion deals with his own century.* The last two lines

---

* I have said that the account begins with the Council of Nicæa. Actually, as 52-53 suggest and as 150-51 make clearer, the first type of the Fox was Satan, not Arius. This example illustrates the way in which the typological and historical complexities are augmented by those of allusion. Also involved is the common Catholic accusation in the day that the Anglican position is tantamount to Socinianism, suggested at the close of this passage. Discourse III of Woodhead's *Rational Account* is perhaps the wittiest and deadliest of such polemic against the Anglican position.

shift the verb tense to the generalizing present and to the future. Yet this future is governed by the typology into a recurrent pattern. If the heresy, the typological Fox, can be seen at various historical moments and even achieves a new personality, as it were, according to the stage of the historical sequence at which it appears, then the pattern of origin and destiny in history is inevitable: "Hence they began, and here they *all* will end," no matter how "obliquely" various historical accidents may lead the progress to be.

The same combination of history and typological symbolism is yet more skillfully developed in the character of the Wolf. This is, however, so complicated in detail that only a few general remarks seem necessary.* The type so dominates the character that even the historical sequence is interrupted and upset. In under twenty lines (I, 170-87) we are shifted in sequence from Anglo-Saxon times, to the spread of Calvinism among the Huguenots, back to "Wycliffe," to "Zuinglius," to Calvin, and back to the "Sanhedrin" of Israel, and back yet farther to the earlier period of Moses. There are alternatively possible reasons for this extraordinary sequence. For one thing, Dryden is concerned with origins as much as with developments. He wishes to stress the possibility of the birth or return in any age of the voluntaristic heresy symbolized by the Wolf. It is also highly likely that Dryden—to whom the manifestations of this heresy seemed most dangerous of all of the "ills in Church and State"—was so emotionally involved in the elements represented by the type that the historical emphasis became less important. We observe, and feel in reading, that the Fox and Wolf achieve through their mingled typology and history a far greater force than that of any of the other heretical beasts except the Panther. More than this, it can be seen both by what they essentially represent—*graceless* naturalism and a voluntarism that deforms grace—and by Dryden's strength of feeling that the other beasts are for the most part absorbed into their typologies.

In some ways the most admirably handled of these mergers of typology and history are the two fables of Part III. Each narrates a sequence

---

* The complexities of the account of the Wolf are such that they need separate analysis; see "The Wolf's Progress in *The Hind and the Panther*," *BNYPL*, LXVII (1963), 512-16. But the chief point to be made is that while maintaining the air and to some extent the practice of the progress piece, Dryden stresses the typologies of voluntarism to the point that the historical progress is interrupted, suggesting thereby the danger at all times of an outburst of heresy.

of events that in itself, in its prophetic emphasis, and in its metaphorical tenor represents historical matters. In fact, the narrative of these fables is the most sustained ordinary narrative in the poem, and the introductory debates in this Part between the Hind and the Panther are more properly "civic" and historical than any other part of the poem. It is typical of Dryden at his most mature that he should treat that segment of history which seems most historical by its very nature—the past—most typologically; and that that portion of history, the future, which is of an altogether questionably historical nature should be given the most thorough-going historical treatment. Of course the terms of the history in the two fables are typological as elsewhere in the poem. But the balance has shifted completely from that of the poem's opening. In fact, we can see a change come over the poem with the passage on creation and toleration (I, 236 ff.) and the passage on the Panther (I, 327 ff.), with which historical elements become somewhat stronger.

The effect of the whole poem is difficult to describe on balance, since it is in a sense as mixed as the temporal states at the beginning of *Absalom and Achitophel*. But I believe that it can best be described as a historical structure infused and controlled by typological elements suggestive both of matters beyond history and of areas in which history is not the proper mode of regarding human experience. I do not think it to be typology with historical suffusions. Both in this general emphasis of the poem and in such parts as the fables of the Swallows and of the Pigeons, we can see that the technique of discontinuous fable or allegory has in its very conception a possibility denied to other kinds. It can reap the advantages of both history in its narration and of the eternal in its typological symbolism. Ordinary metaphor, or even the closed "parallel" of *Absalom and Achitophel,* can render the details of one historical sequence true in themselves and true as well of other historical moments that resemble it generally. The infusion of typology into historical pattern, like the breaking of fable (with yet the supposition of return) to deal with matters not fabulous, enables Dryden in *The Hind and the Panther* to treat not only such historical moments as the Exclusion crisis and not only parallel historical moments like those of the possible times of emergence of Wolfish voluntarism in the past. Over and above these it can suggest timeless truth and errors, and even allow Dryden to be most historical in emphasis when he presents fables of birds told by animals, themselves fabulous, and with details highly typological.

Comparably, in Dryden's poetry history alone is capable of leading us to exalted visions of the past or of the future, as in *Annus Mirabilis* and, to take a less familiar example, in the opening and concluding lines of the witty poem to Roscommon. Without metaphor, Dryden can convey the exaltation he feels only by stress upon a hope inherent in sequence—the idea of progress in historical succession. If there is any single term for this combined technique of discontinuous allegory and history it is surely fable, which is capable at once of chronological development in sequence and of typological symbolism. If there is any one word for Dryden's motive force in using the fable it is faith, a belief at once in the "finite" and in "infinity," in historical time and in eternity harmonized in a single vision.

Without such harmony there would be a dualistic conception of time, and indeed the harmony is to some extent founded upon distinctions that may be dualistic. (The matter is treated in Chapter VII.) But there is still another order of time, which is in a sense that of a middle ground between time and eternity, and which lies also between history and typology. This is the realm of that which is supposed to exist throughout all time but not eternally. It is that of the immortal.[40] Only by understanding distinctions between the historical, that belonging to a given period; and the immortal, which lasts through time; and the eternal, which stretches far beyond time, shall we understand certain aspects of Dryden's poetry, as some excerpts will show.

> A milk-white Hind, immortal and unchang'd,
> Fed on the lawns, and in the forest rang'd;
> Without unspotted, innocent within,
> She fear'd no danger, for she knew no sin.
> Yet had she oft been chas'd with horns and hounds
> And Scythian shafts; and many wingèd wounds
> Aim'd at her heart; was often forc'd to fly,
> And doom'd to death, tho' fated not to die.
>   Not so her young; for their unequal line
> Was hero's make, half human, half divine . . . (I, 1-10)
>   . . . .
> Ten thousand angels on her slumbers wait,
> With glorious visions of her future state. (2591-92; III, 1297-98)

One distinction clear in these lines is that between the Church, which is "immortal," everlasting in time, and the mortal Roman Catholics that make up the Church from age to age. The fate of the Church is well expressed in that conceit, "doom'd to death, tho' fated not to die." Her enemies take actions to doom her to destruction, but God has decreed she shall not be destroyed. The difference between her and "her young" (which is not wholly clear in I, 9-10) is the difference between the immortal and the mortal:

> With grief and gladness mix'd, their mother view'd
> Her martyr'd offspring, and *their race renew'd;*
> *Their corps to perish, but their kind to last,*
> *So much the deathless plant the dying fruit surpass'd.* (I, 21-24)

The italicized clauses dwell upon the distinction. If the Hind be "fated not to die," then what is "her future state?" It is of course that in eternity, when at time's end the eternal souls rise to be judged, when the betrothed Church at last marries Christ. The lengthy passage (1071 ff.; II, 499 ff.) on the Church already quoted is an excellent illustration showing her relation at once to the eternal, to the immortal, and to the mortal. God has assembled the heavenly host "to redeem our ruin'd state." God and his angels exist of course in eternity; mortality such as we know it is the result of the Fall. Between the eternal and the mortal there are two connections. One is Christ, who, though "th' eternal Son," is involved through His incarnation in a universe of time, the only one in which a pluperfect tense has meaning. The second connection is that of the Church, an institution of mortal men but immortal itself and hopeful of eternal life. It is typical of Dryden's handling that the mingling of eternity and mortality should be portrayed in the narrative past tense to suggest history; and that the marriage of the Church to Christ, which is an event to take place in the future, and so bring together the immortal and the eternal (as well as the mortal "sects," 1088) is related in the present tense immediately following the other past tense. The effect would seem to be an accommodation of the eternal and future to the historical, or to something giving the effect of the historical. The eternal has been brought to happen before the eyes of such fallible mortals as the "sects" and the reader.

Dryden's treatment of mortality, immortality, and eternity varies greatly in his poetry. What seems to me common to all instances is the way in which he seeks always to find some historical pattern in which to locate the particular temporal mode or modes and metaphors that he deals with. This is very much the same thing as saying that although we might expect him to treat history only in reference to the mortal, he treats it with equal assurance in relation to the immortal and to the eternal. The heroic plays and the tragedies commonly deal with very mortal characters—whose actions and aspirations are governed by values determined in terms of immortality. Such values spring from motives that have all but died from our lives in the last two centuries. They are involved in ideas such as the powers of poetry to render someone immortal, or of ethical concepts like honor, *honestas*.

> The task and potential greatness of mortals [in this view] lie in the ability to produce things—works and deeds and words—which would deserve to be and, at least to a degree, are at home in everlastingness. . . . By their capacity for the immortal deed, . . . men, their individual mortality notwithstanding, attain an immortality of their own and prove themselves to be of a "divine" nature.[41]

In *All for Love*, we are taken a step further, and it is that additional movement that helps give the play its "Romantic" image. Antony at last turns his back upon the mortal-immortal world of public life in which he had shown his capacity for "immortal deed" to a world in which the moment mingles with eternity. This is not set forward quite as clearly as it might be, at least not by Antony. It is rather the function of the imagery and the concluding speeches by Cleopatra and Serapion. Yet other handlings are to be found in the lyric poems (treated here in Chapter VII). The significant thing is that all three temporal orders are in some way related to what we consider history, that the logic of time includes three kinds of discriminations of mode, and that the three are yet interrelated.

It would be difficult to specify the most poetic aspects of Dryden's unusual sense of such temporal orders. His sense of that which is mortal furnishes him with particulars of place and personality, of values, and of metaphors. His particularity is surely due to his discovery of history in the modern sense of actual, even nearly contemporaneous, events with mortal actors. The immortal order is the most difficult to re-imagine today. When Shakespeare writes in his sonnets about how his poetry will confer immortality or when a character in one of Dryden's heroic plays speaks about honor, we are apt to feel that the poetic blood has run thin. Yet the prominence of such considerations makes public poetry possible, and sets the highest kind of ideal and value for the *individual himself*. Immortality rather than mortality alone, and certainly in distinction to eternity, is the conception that allows for tragedy in its reality of loss and triumph, just as it makes the fullest sense of such a couplet as—

> Of these the false Achitophel was first;
> A name to all succeeding ages curst.

Achitophel possesses, that is, immortality. He is immortal in his infamy as also in his celebration in poetry. Yet it is the fact that in his non-dramatic poetry (and his plays to some extent) Dryden was able to admit the eternal and to celebrate it which distinguishes him from other poets to whom he is often compared. It is this, surely, that led Dr. Johnson to call his genius not only acute and comprehensive, not indeed only argumentative, but sublime.[42]

What renders his thought at once coherent and difficult is his integration of the three temporal modes. Almost invariably his progress pieces end in one of two ways: with an image more enduring than those previously used, and therefore suggestive of immortality; or with imagery transcendent and therefore suggestive of eternity. Architectural imagery may follow that of cultivation, as in the poems to Roscommon and to Congreve. Or the temporal may be dissolved in the eternal, as in the *Song for St. Cecilia's Day* or the poem to Purcell. Invariably the direction is to the higher order. Historical progress is possible; great achievements whether of action or art, move out of the realm of mortality into that of immortality. They last, and so the individual lasts in the collective human memory. The possibility of such achievement, such immortality, is the basis of many of his poems of praise. It is also the basis of one highly significant aspect of his metaphor, specifically of his allusion.

Allusion can be made only to that which is "everlasting" by virtue of its value and its liveliness in the minds of the poet's readers. Otherwise what he intends as allusion might become merely a borrowing and sometimes a mystification. It is natural, therefore, for poets to allude to some familiar and established classic rather than to new works untried by time. What is unusual about some of Dryden's allusions is their reference to great achievements by a contemporary writer. Within a decade or so after *Paradise Lost* had been published Dryden was alluding to it in

MacFlecknoe. He alluded to it steadily thereafter and, once *Paradise Regained* appeared, he used it in *Absalom and Achitophel.* What this unusual practice implies is the same as that suggested by the climactic architectural imagery in progress pieces: a deep faith in the capacity of man in Dryden's own time, or after, to achieve immortality. Without this lively faith, his satire and praise would lose their nerve. Without it his optimism, his belief in the meaning of an ordered world, and his energy would be lost.

There is little question that such faith accounts for much that is attractive and affirmative in Dryden's poetry. But it is only fair to ask, which is the truly historical subject, the mortal or the immortal? Surely modern historians would answer that history concerns the mortal. It is Barbican in decay, it is Shaftesbury seeking to alter the constitution of English political life, it is the Tory triumph after the Rye House Plot. To the extent that Dryden's appreciation of such events in ordinary time is governed by an evaluative faith in man's capacities to achieve immortality and rise above time, and to the extent that both mortality and immortality are finally governed by the eternal eschatology he shares with earlier poets, it is necessary to say his history is not that of our day. Yet it is not only a strict sense of history which determines our response to human events. Our enduring preoccupation with great men and women assumes an interest in something beyond a full knowledge of what actually happened and the way it happened. It assumes an element of idealization of human behavior and human capacity for good or ill. Such idealism enables us to respond with human and poetic consent to the poetry of Dryden and other earlier writers even when their conceptions of history are not our own.

For all its momentous events, the decade of the eighties shows the maturation of Dryden's poetry. In this, the high noon of his career, his faith emerged the stronger for the tests it underwent. *The Medal,* the Postscript to *The History of the League,* and his parts of *The Duke of Guise* show how challenging the tests were. *MacFlecknoe, Absalom and Achitophel, The Hind and the Panther,* and a number of his major lyrics show how he rose above the trial. The achievement of the eighties also reveals a degree of personal engagement with the subjects treated in his poetry that was necessary to give his writing, however public, a full integrity. Whether such personal force was the anger of *The Medal* or the faith of *The Hind and the Panther* it was an essential part of his poetry if its metaphors and themes were to carry conviction for him and for us. The most skillfully handled of metaphors and the noblest of themes are in themselves inadequate for poetic success, at least in his styles. Dryden sometimes falters, out of what seems carelessness, leaving behind that unevenness remarked upon by Dr. Johnson. And he sometimes also fails, to varying degrees—significantly, at those moments when he is unable to involve himself personally with his subject. We can best understand his success with metaphor and theme by attention to a poem like *Eleonora*, in which the full assurance of his artistic powers fails him because he could not convince himself, or us, that he felt what he wrote.

Metaphorical Transport as Surrogate for Feeling: *Eleonora*

CHAPTER VI

> *Let me add, and hope to be believ'd, that the excellency of the subject contributed much to the happiness of the execution; and that the weight of thirty years was taken off me, while I was writing. . . . The reader will easily observe, that I was transported by the multitude and variety of my similitudes.*
>
> —Epistle Dedicatory to *Eleonora.*

Dryden claims in the epistle dedicatory to the Earl of Abingdon that he wrote *Eleonora* with a "double strength" as priest of Apollo: "for I have really felt it [inspiration] on this occasion" (Noyes, pp. 269-270). It is this surge of inspiration and feeling, he says, that led to his transport, by metaphor, in the poem. We can believe that there are many "similitudes," because we can see them. But we cannot believe that he felt the loss of Eleonora deeply, because he does not make us feel it deeply. Yet the poem retains an interest, both for its demonstration by default of the importance of feeling in Dryden's poetry and for those artistic sides of the poem, other than emotional integrity, which are worthy of admiration. *Eleonora* has a wealth of echoes, chiefly of Donne and the Bible, so ordered as to develop a complex theme. The echoes of Donne are especially remarkable at this late stage in Dryden's career. Coming when they do, they give some reason for the statement that, while writing, the weight of thirty years was taken off him, since that interval takes him back in his career to the poem "To My Lord Chancellor" (1662), his last to employ the late Metaphysical wit that he had inherited from Donne through that "darling of my youth," Cowley. In writing *Eleonora* Dryden substituted something like a revisit to his own early career for an engagement with the life of the

Countess of Abingdon. The substitution cannot fail to interest those curious about Dryden's development or desirous of comparing his late recasting of Donne with the original article.

For the fact is, as many must have noticed, that throughout *Eleonora* he echoes Donne's *Anniversaries* and their pendant "Funerall Elegie." He echoes other poems by Donne as well and claims to "have follow'd his footsteps in the design of his panegyric; which was to raise an emulation in the living, to copy out the example of the dead" (Noyes, p. 270). The extent to which Donne's poems constitute a panegyric upon Elizabeth Drury was questioned in his own time and has been much debated in ours. There can be no question that Dryden aimed at panegyric, or that he levied upon Donne, although the success of the one and the scale of the other may be subject to debate. In the nature of things, echoes that seem clear to one pair of literary ears may seem to another but similar phrasing on a common topic. Unquestionably, however, most of the borrowings are from the more eulogistic passages of the *Anniversaries*, and some similarities are beyond dispute. When Dryden writes, "If looking up to God, or down to us, / Thou find'st that any way be pervious" (*Eleonora*, 342-43), it is manifest that he had read Donne's "If looking up to God; or downe to us, / Thou finde that any way is pervious" (*Obsequies to the Lord Harrington*, 5-6). And, although no specific echo seems involved, no one would question the occasional Donnean cadence of such a line as "Thus fix'd she Virtue's image, that's her own" (*Eleonora*, 230). There seem to me more than fifteen clear echoes from Donne's three poems on Elizabeth Drury with a few from other poems.[1] A few examples will illustrate the nature of Dryden's use of "the greatest wit, tho' not the greatest poet of our nation" (Noyes, p. 270) and show the way toward his metaphorical development of his theme.

> Thus Heav'n, tho' all-sufficient, shows a thrift
> In his economy, and bounds his gift:
> Creating, for our day, one single *light;*
> And his reflection too supplies the *night.*
> Perhaps a thousand other worlds, that lie
> Remote from us, and latent in the sky,
> Are lighten'd by his beams, and kindly nurs'd;
> Of which our earthly dunghill is the worst. (*Eleonora*, 75-82)

*   *   *

> . . . yet in this last long *night*,
> Her Ghost doth walke; that is, a glimmering *light*,
> A faint weake love of vertue, and of good,
> Reflects from her, on them which understood
> Her worth; and though she have shut in all day,
> The twilight of her memory doth stay;
> Which, from the carcasse of the old world, free,
> Creates a new world, and new creatures bee
> Produc'd: the matter and the stuffe of this,
> Her vertue, and the forme our practice is. (*I Ann.* 69-78)[2]

Dryden's debt, which includes rhyme words, is evident; so is it evident that his style possesses greater clarity and rhetorical balance. Some echoes are indeed yet closer.

> As in perfumes compos'd with art and cost,
> 'T is hard to say what scent is uppermost;
> Nor this part musk or civet can we call,
> Or amber, but a rich result of all. (*Eleonora*, 154-57)

*   *   *

> But as in Mithridate, or just perfumes,
> Where all good things being met, no one presumes
> To governe, or to triumph on the rest,
> Only because all were, no part was best. (*II Ann.*, 127-30)

Yet even here, Dryden's greater interest in logic—in science, one may say—leads him to work out the details with greater clarity. Another example, showing his use of an unusual image from Donne, will make clear the specific way in which at times he drew upon his great predecessor. The subject is the manner of death of Eleonora and of Elizabeth Drury.

> As precious gums are not for lasting fire—
> They but perfume the temple, and expire:
> So was she soon exhal'd, and vanish'd hence;
> A short sweet odor, of a vast expense. (*Eleonora*, 301-304)

*   *   *

> But like a Lampe of Balsamum, desir'd
> Rather t' adorne, then last, she soone expir'd. (*A Funerall Elegie*,
> 73-74)

Dryden's expansion again shows his greater interest in the actual details of what he describes; and the expression of the interest involves greater clarity, more rigorous logic in the comparison. It also shows his stronger sense of decorum, for he is not content that the woman he praises should be made to seem merely an adornment—she must be made to seem something inherently and richly precious if praise is to be praise.

The three examples just given show that Dryden draws upon both *Anniversaries* and upon the *Funerall Elegie* as well, as if to him the three poems were parts of a larger poem, a panegyric on the dead young woman, "Mrs. Drury." In other words, Dryden's poem is modelled not so much upon any one of Donne's three as upon a generic conception of the group. As with *Absalom and Achitophel*, which is even more closely modelled on its chief "historical" source, *Eleonora* is conceived of by a mind habituated to thinking in terms of a pattern of allusion. (The question of the possibility of allusion to Donne in the Restoration must be set aside for the moment.) Donne's "elegies" are treated as panegyrics, the genre Dryden himself names as that of *Eleonora*. The distinction between elegy and panegyric in Dryden's mind is, like much else there, by no means easy to ascertain. Such another elegy as the poem, "On the Death of a Very Young Gentleman," shows perhaps his distinction.[3] It praises the dead man, but in himself as it were, not raising him by comparisons with monarchs or in other amplifying metaphors. Similarly, "On the Death of Amyntas," with its subtitle, "A Pastoral Elegy," shows yet another kind of generic distinction.[4] *Eleonora* and Donne's poems are therefore to be placed with the Anne Killigrew *Ode* and *Threnodia Augustalis:* for Dryden these are panegyrics requiring a "multitude and variety of . . . similitudes." He has followed Donne in using the couplet, but the style he associates with the panegyric is more exalted in a lyric way: "for the whole poem, tho' written in that which they call heroic verse, is of the Pindaric nature, as well in the thought as the expression."[5]

Although such considerations may seem remote from Dryden's bor-rowings, they explain the nature of his echoes of Donne. All close echoes conform to a pattern. To understand it, we must recall Louis Martz's analysis of the structure of the *Anniversaries* in his *Poetry of Meditation* (New Haven, 1954). Showing how Donne drew upon forms of Catholic meditation, he analyzes the structure of the *First Anniversary* into an Introduction, Conclusion, and five main sections, each of which consists of a Meditation, Eulogy, and Refrain with Moral

(Martz, pp. 222-23). He shows the *Second Anniversary* to have a similar, though shorter, Introduction, and Conclusion, and seven main sections, all of which have a Meditation and Eulogy, although the first has also a Refrain and Moral, and the second a Moral (Martz, p. 237). For readers today, if not for Ben Jonson and Dryden, it is the Meditations that are most interesting. Dryden must have found the loathing of decay a subject uneconomically combined with eulogies. At all events, it is significant that his undoubted echoes of Donne are to sections other than the lamentatory sections of Meditation—that is, Dryden echoes the more laudatory Introduction, Conclusion, or Eulogies. *The Second Anniversary* is tonally more consistent, enabling Dryden on one occasion to find appropriate material in a Meditation (*Eleonora*, 90-96; II *Ann.*, 417-24). His other close borrowings are from the eulogistic sections of the *Second Anniversary* or from the *Funerall Elegie* which, indeed, is a eulogy throughout. It would be difficult to say whether instinct or design led him to borrow from Donne's eulogistic passages. But clearly it is in these sections that he found his common bond with Donne as a panegyric poet. Much the same point can be made of those passages in which he shows but a less certain, or more general debt to Donne, although talk of "general" borrowing must proceed with greater tact. There are, to my mind, a dozen such instances.[6] In one Dryden speaks of the way in which those in want came to Eleonora for succor and charity.

> As to some holy house th' afflicted *came*,
> The hunger-starv'd, the naked and the *lame*. (*Eleonora*, 46-47)

*　　*　　*

> But shee, in whom to such maturity
> Vertue was growne, past growth, that it must die;
> She, from whose influence all Impressions *came*,
> But, by Receivers impotencies, *lame*. (*I Ann.*, 413-16)

Donne's expression is crabbed but a certain resemblance and the use of the same rhyme words suggests that Dryden may have had Donne in mind. Yet his debt is but small in any case: the context of his couplet shows that he has not the *Anniversaries*, but the New Testament chiefly in view.

Another instance shows the use of an idea close to that in a passage from the *Second Anniversary*, though in very different language.

So she was all a sweet, whose ev'ry part,
In due proportion mix'd, proclaim'd the Maker's art.

(Eleonora, 158-59)

*   *   *

Shee whose Complexion was so even made,
That which of her Ingredients should invade
The other three, no Feare, no Art could guesse:
So far were all remov'd from more or lesse. (*II Ann.*, 123-26)

Although Dryden is speaking of parts, or virtues (see l. 160), and
Donne of the four humours, there seems to be a general debt; and all the
more so, since the two couplets that precede this from *Eleonora* are a
close echo of the two that follow Donne's passage quoted here. But it
would be too much to claim anything more than a general debt of
ideas, and those not exactly the same.

The two "general" borrowings are like all the rest of the twelve but
one, in using eulogistic passages from Donne or in using ideas that might
easily be rendered into praise. But there is one passage differing from
all the rest of Dryden's borrowings, close or distant: in the Epistle
Dedicatory (Noyes, p. 271), Dryden presents one of those comments
on the opinions and criticisms of him by his contemporaries that often
appear in his prefaces and dedications. This one has an odd ring for a
dedication as devoted to compliment as this: "They say, my talent is
satire: if it be so, 'tis a fruitful age, and there is an extraordinary crop
to gather." The intrusion of personality and the criticism of the age here
find a curious though powerful expression at almost the very end of the
poem (ll. 359-70).

> Let this suffice: nor thou, great saint, refuse
> This humble tribute of no vulgar Muse;
> Who, not by cares, or wants, or age depress'd,
> Stems a wild deluge with a dauntless breast;
> And dares to sing thy praises in a clime
> Where vice triumphs, and virtue is a crime;
> Where ev'n to draw the picture of thy mind
> Is satire on the most of humankind:
> Take it, while yet 't is praise; before my rage,
> Unsafely just, break loose on this bad age;
> So bad, that thou thyself hadst no defense
> From vice, but barely by departing hence.

In this passage alone Dryden echoes something of the tone and the general idea that inform the Meditations of the *First Anniversary*. Donne had so built his poem on the contrast between a world in decay and the "Idea" of a virtuous woman that sometimes the artistic balance is lost. Dryden's passage, too, coming near the close of his panegyric sounds odd, though like Donne's meditative sections it is meant to justify the extremity of eulogy elsewhere. With this one exception, then, his "general" borrowings from Donne's poems on Elizabeth Drury are also those of passages from eulogistic sections of the poems or, exceptionally, of materials from Meditations that might yet be rendered into praise.

Another aspect of the resemblances between *Eleonora* and the *Anniversaries* is easily named but analyzed only with some difficulty. Dryden's concept of Eleonora as a "pattern"—which had been the working title of the poem (see Noyes, p. 270)—clearly relates to Donne's concept of Elizabeth Drury as an "Idea." Dryden as much as attributes the same purpose to Donne (Noyes, p. 270) and, when in lines 174-75 he refers to Eleonora as a *pattern* of virtue, he echoes the thought of two eulogistic passages in the *Anniversaries* (I *Ann.*, 227-29; II *Ann.*, 306-307). Donne's word is not pattern, but "example," and it may be that Dryden was aware of the last line of "The Canonization"—"A patterne of your love"—since he, too, is speaking of a "saint." The intellectual common ground of the two poets is Platonism, or neo-Platonism. This is, however, probably the philosophical subject most in need of investigation for Dryden. The problem is too large to discuss in a comparison of Donne and Dryden, but it can be seen easily enough that the two poets held to some manner of Platonism as a basis for certain ideal aspects of their metaphors, although in both the Platonism was highly modified by other kinds of thought—kinds, indeed, that are often discordant with Platonism. Of these differences, only one need be developed. In the *Anniversaries* Donne found his Platonism to be some small grounds for hope and emulation of the Idea of a virtue in Elizabeth Drury; but given the context in which the Platonism appears, it was in practice grounds for a greater anxiety and despair. Dryden, on the other hand, picked up as it were the firm world view in his conversion to Catholicism that Donne had lost; and Dryden's faith was buttressed by his other assurances in the stability and harmony he could perceive in his world.

These differences in attitude are reflected by the structural schemes employed by the poets. Both what is disposed in these poems and the methods of disposition are similar enough for comparison, and different enough to reveal the art of their authors. *Eleonora* is of a length comparable to the *Anniversaries*, its 376 lines being some seventy fewer than the first of Donne's poems and some 150 fewer than the second. Like Donne, Dryden begins with a labelled introduction and ends with a labelled conclusion; in between there are thirteen sections, each with its marginal head. (It is likely that the heads for the *Anniversaries* are not Donne's own, but in any case they represent well the tonal emphasis of his poems.) Once again the differences are clarified by Martz's analysis of the *Anniversaries* in terms of the formal meditation. For in effect, the main sections of *Eleonora* represent only the Eulogies of Donne's poems. The extent to which Dryden rejected Donne's Meditations—with their doctrine of history in decay and *contemptus mundi* (except for that remarkable contrast of Eleonora and the age in lines 362-70) can be readily understood by comparing the marginal heads of *Eleonora* with those of the first *Anniversary*.

Eleonora	*First Anniversary*
Of her charity.	*The entrie into the worke.*
Of her prudent management.	*What life the world hath stil.*
Of her humility.	*The sicknesse of the World.*
Of her piety.	*Impossibility of health.*
Of her various virtues.	*Shortnesse of life* [of modern
Of her conjugal virtues.	man].
Of her love to her children.	*Smalnesse of stature.*
Her care of their education.	*Decay of nature in other parts.*
Of her friendship.	*Disformity of parts.*
Reflections on the shortness of her	*Disorder in the world.*
life.	*Weaknesse in the want of corre-*
She died in her thirty-third year.	*spondence of heaven and earth.*
The manner of her death.	*Conclusion.*
Her preparedness to die.	
She died on Whitsunday night.	
Apostrophe to her soul.	
Epiphonema, or close of the poem.	

Dryden's heads are eulogistic, Donne's despairing. Dryden's show that he has Eleonora always in mind. Those to *The First Anniversary* suggest that the virtue of Elizabeth Drury was the last thing involved in his "Anatomy of the [decaying] World." As Martz shows, and as our own response to the first *Anniversary* confirms, the poem is so much about the decay of the world that the praise of even the Idea of a woman seems to be forced and, at times, even satiric. (See the section of anti-feminism, I *Ann.*, 99-110 quoted below.) Further, although Dryden's heads are not always of parallel or equal significance, they come closer to being units of subject matter and true formal divisions than Donne's. More than this, the heads form into larger groupings and reflect a development throughout the poem. The lack of relation between Donne's heads and the real structure of the poem can be fully understood by setting them against Martz's convincing demonstration of the structure of the form of a meditation. There is almost no correspondence. Finally, as we have observed, Dryden has his subject in mind always: his heads all refer to Eleonora and all invariably represent what in fact he is considering. Those to Donne's poem give no inkling that Elizabeth Drury ever existed, or that he had any concern with her. (The second *Anniversary*, which is as superior structurally as in other respects to the first, is relatively less subject to such strictures.)

Such difference in attention to the object of eulogy should not obscure certain resemblances, or certain differences greater still. Perhaps the most remarkable example of use and change of Donne is to be found in the imagery of Dryden's first eleven lines.

> As, when some great and gracious monarch dies,
> Soft whispers, first, and mournful murmurs rise
> Among the sad attendants; then the sound
> Soon gathers voice, and spreads the news around
> Thro' town and country, till the dreadful blast
> Is blown to distant colonies at last;
> Who, then, perhaps, were offering vows in vain,
> For his long life, and for his happy reign:
> So slowly, by degrees, unwilling fame ⎫
> Did matchless Eleonora's fate proclaim, ⎬
> Till public as the loss the news became. ⎭

The movement of the first eight lines—a lyric, rhymed version of Milton's style—is part of the sense and feeling of the lines. It is of course as Drydenic as anything he wrote, down to the concluding triplet, but there are recognizable echoes of Donne.

> As virtuous men passe mildly away,
>   And whisper to their soules, to goe,
> Whilst some of their sad friends doe say,
>   The breath goes now, and some say, no.
>
> ("A Valediction: forbidding mourning," 1-4)

The private scene of Donne's officious "sad friends" is translated into public terms, but the contrast between the good and the ignorant is the same. With this echo is fused another, from the comparable section—the Introduction—of the first *Anniversary*.

> But as in states doubtfull of future heires,
> When sicknesse without remedie empaires
> The present Prince, they're loth it should be said,
> The Prince doth languish, or the Prince is dead:
> So mankinde feeling now a generall thaw,
> A strong example gone, equall to law,
> The Cyment which did faithfully compact,
> And glue all vertues, now resolv'd, and slack'd,
> Thought it some blasphemy to say sh'was dead,
> Or that our weaknesse was discovered
> In that confession. (I *Ann.*, 43-53)

These harmonious, energetic lines must have appealed to Dryden. Donne's princely image—which changes to another, of religious heresy, amplifying the sense of loss—becomes in Dryden that of a monarch and the offering of pagan, Roman vows, again suggesting a loss whose true extent is unknown. Dryden's borrowings are, however, rarely amenable to simple description. Seven years earlier, in 1685, he had written for *Threnodia Augustalis* two sections (16-28 and 119-159) describing in similar terms the progress of news of Charles' sickness and apparent recovery. And section IX of the Anne Killigrew *Ode* treats the ignorance of her death on the part of her distant brother in a way obviously like that of lines six and seven of *Eleonora*. Like all poets, Dryden frequently echoes himself; and like Donne among others, he often weaves a tissue of diverse allusions almost impossible to unravel.

Since Dryden's purpose was to praise the Countess of Abingdon, the metaphors he employed are naturally amplifying, enlarging figures.

They represent a realm of value that is true and attracts his belief, whether or not the person to whom the figures induce comparison is worthy of them. Rather, the significant thing is that his style seldom falters. There is indeed one dreadful couplet: "The nation felt it [the death of Eleonora] in th' extremest parts, / With eyes o'erflowing, and with bleeding hearts" (12-13). That is simply foolish, though less so than Donne's review of the sufferings of a world without the idealized Elizabeth Drury: "This great consumption to a fever turn'd, / And so the world had fits" (I *Ann.*, 19-20). If Dryden stumbles and Donne falls, it is because the problem of tone is the crucial one in panegyric. For *Eleonora*, Dryden chose a tone eschewing the elegiac, which suggests some personal involvement, if only of a theoretical kind, and sought instead that of the panegyric. The choice enabled him to speak entirely of his subject (except for the personal note, the *poëta loquitur* towards the end). By so choosing, he availed himself of several realms of value that he could share with his readers, since the loss is always to be considered in terms of the values held by civilized men.

What the decision meant for metaphor can be readily understood by reference to the sources of his metaphors. Some are taken from native literary sources (chiefly Donne), others from the classics (chiefly Virgil); some from important areas of contemporary experience (royalty, science); and others from religion (the Bible and Christian tradition).[7] The areas of choice are remarkably close to those of *Mac-Flecknoe*, a poem of inverted panegyric, but the handling of the metaphors is obviously different. The poem opens with Eleonora's death compared to that of some "great and gracious monarch," and in view of the resemblances of the passage to those in *Threnodia Augustalis*, it seems likely enough that the echo of Donne in these lines is fused with a depth of political feeling that could permit Dryden, to some extent, to mourn Eleonora sincerely. Royalty, science, and religion are his paler emotional equivalents to Donne's decay.

The handling of imagery in *Eleonora* more closely resembles that in *MacFlecknoe* in the use made of religious figures. If anything, the religious metaphors of the later poem are more dominant than in the earlier, although—perhaps *because*—they do not function in the same degree of integration as a "controlling metaphor." There are some thirteen echoes of, or allusions to the Bible, almost equally divided between the two Testaments.[8] Although it may seem curious that the

Old Testament should play so large a role in the poem, the explanation is simple enough. It rather than the New Testament comprehends those matters of character, society, government, and history with which Dryden's poetry is chiefly concerned. *Eleonora* is a public poem, with its heroine an example for all women and men, both in her personal virtue and in her observance of duties at once social and religious.* To say the religious images in *Eleonora* resemble those in *MacFlecknoe* is to say that they often function as allusions. To call them allusions is to say that most of them make little sense unless their scriptural context is recalled along with the few details given: this fact will make it necessary to distinguish them from the echoes of Donne. The first such echo compares Eleonora's provisions for the poor with God's benefaction of manna to Israel in the wilderness.

> For, while she liv'd, they slept in peace by night,
> Secure of bread, as of returning light;
> And with such firm dependence on the day,
> That need grew pamper'd, and forgot to pray:
> So sure the dole, so ready at their call,
> They stood prepar'd to see the manna fall. (16-21; cf. Numbers xi.)

The pampered poor are of course compared to the murmuring Israelites, an episode Dryden had already found useful as a comparison for the disgruntled English.[9] Yet the allusion, slowly built up in the passage, is mingled with the image of the sun for Eleonora. She is the "returning light" of those dependent on her, trustworthy as the succession of days. From the simile ("as . . . light") in one couplet, Dryden's imagistic logic moves to the metaphor "day" as the first rhyme-word of the next couplet. The parallelism of light-day is further heightened by contrast of both of the words with "night," in the first line of the passage. But the most daring aspect of the allusion lies buried; if the dependent poor are Israelites, then their benefactress is God, a comparison strengthened by the interwoven light imagery, which is a traditional emblem for divine Providence. Donne might have attributed the principle of "coherence" to Elizabeth Drury, ascribing to her all manner of astonishing powers, but he had not gone this far. It is revealing to see how

---

* In the "Epistle Dedicatory," Noyes, p. 271, Dryden's remarks about Abingdon show that his conception of him is also public: he contrasts Abingdon favorably with other English lords.

Dryden manages such comparisons in his poem, escaping the "blasphemy" attributed to Donne by Ben Jonson and Louis Martz.*

One of the ways in which Dryden avoids *the effect* of blasphemy is by burying such comparisons. Although the technique can be observed in the allusion to the granting of manna, it is clearer in the double allusion of a single couplet. (37-38).

> He, who could touch her garment, was as sure,
> As the first Christians of th' apostles' cure.

The simile appears to echo the cures effected by St. Peter (Acts ix. 32-43), and Christ's charge to all the Apostles before His death to heal the sick (Luke ix. 1-2) is no doubt also involved. Yet the first line is an allusion comparing Eleonora to Christ: "they . . . besought him that they might touch if it were but the border of his garment: and as many as touched him were made whole" (Mark vi. 56). Much of the effect of blasphemy is avoided by making the comparison explicitly with the Apostles and allowing the allusion to imply without statement. To be sure many of the allusions do not raise the problem. But there are enough throughout the poem to suggest that Dryden placed himself in yet a larger difficulty. It was not enough to avoid the effect of blasphemy in such passages; a way was necessary to transcend blasphemy itself, however hidden it might be in imagery or in other biblical comparisons.

Strangely enough, the solution does not become truly clear until that point later in the poem where he comes closest to the effect of blasphemy. The passage (295-300) differs from the majority of the biblical metaphors in not being an allusion to the Bible but a more general recollection of it. Both the text and the marginal note, "She died in her thirty-third year," are involved.

* Jonson's well-known declaration "That Donnes Anniversaries were profane and full of blasphemies: that he told Mr. Done if it had been written of the Virgin Marie it had been something" can most readily be found in Grierson's ed., II, 187. Martz (p. 233) finds the imagery "extravagant" in the *First Anniversary*, "even blasphemous," not on religious but literary grounds (whatever that distinction may mean for blasphemy) since "the imagery is not supported by the poem as a whole." This is precisely the difference between the more hyperbolic metaphors of Donne and those of Dryden—Dryden's relate to the conception and the execution of the whole poem. It should be said that Frank Manley in *John Donne: The Anniversaries* (Baltimore, 1963) argues that Hebrew and neo-Platonic traditions of wisdom literature give the *Anniversaries* a thematic unity. I cannot see that he proves the connection; his excellent notes refer to nearly everything else (including two or three of Dryden's borrowings) but these traditions.

But more will wonder at so short an age,
To find a blank beyond the thirtieth page;
And with a pious fear begin to doubt
The piece imperfect, and the rest torn out.
But 't was her Savior's time; and, could there be
A copy near th' original, 't was she.

The "pious fear" of "her fellow saints" examining "fate's eternal book" recording her life is precisely the fear of blasphemy—that she is another Christ. Obviously the dilemma is of the poet's own creating; he wishes to have the comparison without the charge of profaning scriptures.*

Dryden's salvation from the risk of blasphemy is, most simply put, neo-Platonic. Eleonora is a "copy" of Christ, a type or, as his working title shows, a "pattern." Christ, God, the Holy Spirit, the Apostles—all of whom she resembles in the allusions—are the Ideas of which she is the most perfect mortal embodiment. By clarifying the nature of his comparisons only toward the end of the poem, Dryden gets the maximum force from his comparisons; the clarification itself draws upon the convenience of neo-Platonism to obviate real blasphemy. Thereafter in the poem he exploits the larger metaphor of the poem, Eleonora as the pattern of the divine and near divine. She is compared to Enoch and Elijah—so pure is she that, like them, she may have been assumed directly into Heaven (338-39). And the echoes that follow in the remaining thirty-seven lines are chiefly to Donne rather than the Bible, adding yet another element of safety.

The neo-Platonism that provides the basis for conceiving of Eleonora as a type or pattern of God, the apostles, or the prophets has certain resemblances to some kinds of typology found in earlier seventeenth-century literature. Donne, for example, examines the results of the death of his Idea of a woman in terms of the concept of microcosm and macrocosm, the latter having a relation to the former that approaches the neo-Platonic relations between the Idea and the phenomenon in a manner like Dryden's concept of the pattern. At other times it is difficult to know just how far one is to proceed along old lines.

---

* Like many of the allusions, the marginal note to line 331, "She died on Whitsunday night," poses the same problem in its association of Eleonora with the day the Holy Spirit descended as the Paraclete.

> So sure the dole, so ready at their call,
> They stood prepar'd to see the manna fall.
>   Such multitudes she fed, she cloth'd, she nurs'd,
> That she herself might fear her wanting first.
> Of her five talents, other five she made;
> Heav'n, that had largely giv'n, was largely paid . . .
>
> . . . .
>
> Heav'n saw, he safely might increase his poor,
> And trust their sustenance with her so well,
> As not to be at charge of miracle.
> None could be needy, whom she saw, or knew;
> All in the compass of her sphere she drew:
> He, who could touch her garment, was as sure,
> As the first Christians of th' apostles' cure.   (20-25; 33-39)

Seven or eight lines dealing with motivation have been omitted from this section on Eleonora's charity; what remains has been already glanced at and now may be pursued to raise new questions. The lines on the manna (20-21) imply that she is Godlike in providence; the succeeding line seems to be a comparison to Christ—His feeding of the multitude with the miracle of loaves and fishes, for example. Dryden shifts throughout the passage from metaphor to plain statement, as also from open comparison to comparison buried in allusion: and the metaphors function in terms of biblical allusion, making her sometimes a type of the divine. Thus, Godlike she provides manna; Christlike she feeds the multitudes; but she is a real woman in having exhaustible riches (23). Then she becomes the most highly endowed of the servants in the parable of the talents (Matthew xxv. 14-21). Thereafter she is a kind of efficient cause of Heaven's bounty, saving the necessity of abrogating natural laws with a latter-day miracle; yet immediately thereafter (38-39) she is granted the power to work miracles in the buried comparison to Christ and the explicit reference to the Apostles.

Such fluctuations provide the poem with an opportunity for wit and the possibility of varying means of amplification through metaphor. But throughout this passage the metaphoric principle remains the same: Eleonora is a type of the extraordinarily good or the divine. This basic theme of Eleonora as a pattern of the divine and the good controls much of the imagery, tone, and meaning of the poem; it governs much of the structural procedure. Much, but not all, since the pattern motif works in a second way, as a few lines will show.

> A second Eve, but by no crime accurs'd;
> As beauteous, not as brittle as the first.
> Had she been first, still Paradise had bin,
> And death had found no entrance by her sin:
> So she not only had preserv'd from ill
> Her sex and ours, but liv'd their pattern still. (170-75)

Most of this passage treats her as a type of Eve. So strong in fact is the antifeminist tradition to which Dryden's own inclination leads him to respond here, that she (the single exception) is superior to "our Mother." But the conclusion points another way altogether: she is not only a pattern *of* Eve (or God, or Christ, or the Apostles) but also *for* the rest of humanity. In this, she is also treated neo-Platonically, but now as the Idea of which her fellow human beings may, hopefully, become earthly types, just as she in her turn is a type of yet higher beings. The remark quoted earlier from the epistle dedicatory shows Dryden's exactitude. He "intended" the poem "not for an elegy, but a panegyric —a kind of apotheosis, indeed."

It is this concept of Eleonora as a pattern in a double sense, a pattern of and a pattern for, that is the central idea and organizing principle of the poem. It governs the nature of the praise, keeps the esthetic distance public and, in one way or another, gives all the major metaphors their logic. Dryden's success in using the concept of a dual pattern to give his poem a structural logic can best be understood by reference to the *Anniversaries*. Donne, too, has his passage on Eve—it is one echoed in *Eleonora*.

> [Ruin] labour'd to frustrate
> Even Gods purpose; and made woman, sent
> For mans reliefe, cause of his languishment.
> They were to good ends, and they are so still,
> But accessory, and principall in ill;
> For that first marriage was our funerall:
> One woman at one blow, then kill'd us all,
> And singly, one by one, they kill us now.
> We doe delightfully our selves allow
> To that consumption; and profusely blinde,
> Wee kill our selves to propagate our kinde. (*1 Ann.*, 100-110)

"How witty's ruine!" as Donne says, and how witty he is. But what is the connection between such antifeminist, faintly indecent wit and the presumed subject of his poem—the Idea of a woman? His wit undercuts his praise of Elizabeth Drury and, in its categorical dismissal of women, very much tarnishes the Idea. It requires no great indulgence on our part to forgive such wit. But Dryden's excess in calling Eleonora a better Eve, which also requires suspension of disbelief, only strengthens his conception—the antifeminism merely amplifies his one ideal pattern.

If Dryden echoed Donne with a difference in such a passage, he also echoed other lines in the *Anniversaries* that were more to his purpose. His "So she [Eve] not only had preserv'd from ill / Her sex and ours, but liv'd their pattern still" expresses the way in which she is the double pattern and in so doing recalls Donne.

> She that was best, and first originall
> Of all faire copies . . . (*I Ann.*, 227-28)
> . . . .
> Shee whose example they must all implore,
> Who would or doe, or thinke well, and confesse
> That all the vertuous Actions they expresse,
> Are but a new, and worse edition
> Of her some one thought, or one action . . . (*II Ann.*, 306-10)

This is the most common use Donne makes of neo-Platonism in the eulogistic sections of the *Anniversaries*. The meditative passages, especially in the *First Anniversary*, differ in treating her less as a pattern of superior beings than as principles (coherence, "just supply") lost with her.

To Dryden, a poet with so strong an imagination for the structural conception of poetry, this control was but second nature. Yet he was not content to rest with a dual principle governing the whole, for his final metaphor of Eleonora as a pattern is one in which the force of metaphor weakens, or strengthens, into accurate description and assured conclusion. Line 291 speaks of "her fellow saints," and the "Apostrophe to her Soul" (340-58) is rendered into a prayer to a saint for intercession.

> O happy soul! if thou canst view from high,
> Where thou art all intelligence, all eye,
> *If looking up to God, or down to us . . .*
> Give 'em [her family], as much as mortal eyes can bear,
> A transient view of thy full glories there;
> That they with mod'rate sorrow may sustain
> And mollify their losses in thy gain. (340-42; 352-55)

The passage is kept general enough not to ruffle any Protestant sensibilities with talk of saints and invocations, but the line following the passage makes clear enough with its "great saint" just how Eleonora is now conceived. As a saint she has her excess of merits entitling her to comparison with the divine: she is a pattern of the divine. Also as a saint she is a pattern for others and a source of relief to them. (This dual sense in which she is a pattern is made clear by the line I have italicized.) The many guises in which she has appeared throughout the poem were but metaphorical—ways of appreciating her exceptional virtue. Yet even here Dryden startles us with "thou art all intelligence, all eye," a conceit at once sudden and natural (and also borrowed from Donne—*II Ann.*, 200). "Intelligence" relates in a special sense to the "soul" of an angel. (The intelligent is of course the highest of man's three souls, and angels were often considered as intelligences of stars, intermediaries between the pagan astrology and Christian thought.) "Intelligence" relates in another traditional association to "eye," which is both the organ of sense commonly related to reason and the starting point in this passage for imagery of sight.

The last metaphor for Eleonora, that of a saint, turns out to be in a sense no metaphor at all. It is possible to take it literally. Partly because the concept of a "saint" is capable of being understood in general, weakened senses as well as in the strict sense, and partly because it is the climactic and a less hyperbolic metaphor in a long series establishing her as a pattern, the comparison of Eleonora to a saint takes on both a finality and a justice that render it the most effective of all. If it is truest in a sense because it is least metaphorical, it is also truest because it comprehends both of her functions as a pattern into one status, as had not been possible in the earlier comparisons. Donne had sought ever more climactic and powerful roles for his idea of a woman. Dryden begins with metaphors more startling in import and adapts them to a last figure that reconciles us to earlier claims by altering them. More importantly, the final metaphor of the saint suggests that the whole metaphorical process has not been a matter of rhetorical amplification, but simply the "truth." The idea of sainthood is capable of being treated in typological metaphors of Old Testament figures, the Apostles, and even the three persons of the Trinity. At the end of the poem we are led, then, to review the earlier comparisons in a new light. It becomes difficult to say whether the final metaphor of the saint renders all into truth, or whether the truth is not the most decisive metaphor of all. Donne begins with a real girl who becomes progressively more wholly rarefied into a metaphorical tenor. The *Anniversaries* so successfully drive a semantic wedge between Elizabeth Drury and what she is supposed to represent that we are left with a purely formal girl and a metaphorical tenor of greater interest and application to the life of the poet than to her. Dryden begins with the maximum divergence between his metaphorical vehicles and tenors—the most public figure, the king, represents a wholly private life; divinity, the human. By the end of the poem, we are led to believe that the distance has been abolished. By becoming a dual pattern, of the divine and for her fellow men, Eleonora absorbs the metaphors of the poem into her own truth.

It is not enough for Dryden that a poem should possess a discernible structure; it must have complex inner relationships, governing ideas and metaphors. And most importantly, it must move, not in the way that Donne's brilliant exercises in process do, but to ends defined and determined by the nature of the movement. Dryden seldom therefore writes of that exalted *now* and *here* to which Donne absorbs all else. In Dryden's poetry, the *now* is related to what is contemporary in a more extensive, less intensive world; its meaning grows in the exploration of its past and future. The *here* is an important realistic matter requiring specification. Neither the *here* nor the *now* takes on real importance unless it participates in the grandeur of history or of eternity: "For but a now did heav'n and earth divide" (306). Dryden's control over his poetry and his manipulation of orders of time in allusion can be seen most readily in the way the poem's epigraph, the famous comment of the Sybil to Æneas, is made to relate to the poem:

> Superas evadere ad auras,
> Hoc opus, hic labor est. Pauci, quos æquus amavit
> Juppiter, aut ardens evexit ad æthera virtus,
> Dis geniti potuere. (*Æneid*, VI, 128-31)

> "The gates of hell are open night and day;
> Smooth the descent, and easy is the way:
> But to return, and view the cheerful skies,
> In this the task and mighty labor lies.
> To few great Jupiter imparts this grace,
> And those of shining worth and heav'nly race." (*Æneis*, VI, 192-97)

In *Eleonora* Virgil (who was long used to such treatment) is Christianized and neo-Platonized. Like all mortals, Eleonora descends, but like only the blessed few specially rich in divine grace she rises again to the world of light. Far from forgetting his epigraph, Dryden uses the sixth Æneid for two classical types of Eleonora: Anchises and Cybele (197-202). Both comprehend the future in the present, even as the technique of allusion recalls the past.

The examples given of Dryden's echoes show him levying upon three sources for allusion—Donne, the Bible, and Virgil. The differences among the three are less important to a consideration of his metaphorical technique than the degree of recognition the echoes can be thought to evoke. The case of Virgil is the simplest, and most like the allusive practice in *MacFlecknoe* or *Absalom and Achitophel*. The Virgilian echoes are clearly meant to be recognized, and the recognition serves as a means for evaluation by the standards it establishes. Shadwell is compared to Ascanius and dismissed with laughter. Eleonora is compared to Anchises and Cybele and found to fit the valued patterns. This form of evaluative allusion is that which Dryden usually practices. But it is not a form that is adhered to by all the allusions to the Bible, much less by those to Donne. Several of the biblical allusions are clear, are meant to be comprehended and to evaluate. Others are buried in a context leading us in other directions, as that to the cure of those touching Christ's robe. Yet others approach blasphemy so nearly that their evaluative power would recoil upon the poet, had he not fitted them into his special structural strategy guaranteeing that their thematic force was freed in terming Eleonora a saint at the crucial moment. This form of allusion is practiced by Dryden on relatively few occasions, chiefly when he employs unusually complex means to overcome problems of tone. The most familiar example is that of the opening lines of *Absalom and Achitophel*; less familiar examples abound in *The Hind and the Panther*.

The echoes of Donne are simpler than this in employment but more difficult to characterize with assurance as allusions, as the term is usually understood. Allusion differs from mere borrowing or use of materials precisely in the reader's awareness of the echo. One doubts that Dryden could have expected his readers to recall Donne, who had sunk farther in popular estimation than Cowley or Cleveland—certainly he was less well known. Yet in the Epistle Dedicatory Dryden speaks of him pointedly and respectfully, almost inviting comparison. To an extent difficult to calculate the echoes carry with them the eulogistic aura of the passages they recall, as if the difference between Dryden's stylistic practice in this poem from that elsewhere in his work would alert readers familiar with his usual styles. Moreover, ill-printed though they are, the mid-century and Restoration volumes of Donne's poems bespeak a certain currency.

The question of how much Dryden counted upon his readers to recognize echoes of Donne—how far he could expect echoes to perform as allusions—is, then, not easily decided, and the examples of "versification" of Donne by Pope and others in the next century clarify the problem very little. It is one, however, which seems to date from the time of Dryden's conversion and his turning in his poetry to areas of thought that seem likely to have been unknown to many of his readers. The sacred zoölogical lore and typological metaphors of *The Hind and the Panther* illustrate the problem well. To Montague and Prior, who "transversed" that poem, as to many readers since, unfamiliarity with older kinds and sources of metaphor prevented any ready understanding of Dryden's technique.

If one effect of his conversion was to lead him back to older modes of thought and kinds of metaphor that antedate even Milton, it seems that another was to give him an increasing sense of isolation in his age, that led him, even while he continued to write poetry as wholly public as *Eleonora*, to a kind of private allusive style which even more than *Absalom and Achitophel* required his readers to have some manner of key to unlock certain compartments of his meaning. One cannot be sure, but it does seem unlikely that mention of "Doctor Donne" in the Epistle Dedicatory was sufficient to apprise his readers of echoes whose recognition brought the force of allusion. What is more certain is that the echoes, or allusions, serve a consistent purpose that falls somewhere between mere borrowing and evaluation. They may be called descriptive allusions, since their function is more modest than that of the usual metaphorical strength released by his recognizable allusions. Descriptive allusion requires only a sense that Donne had written with similar praise of a young woman he had not known, and that sense is provided by the Epistle Dedicatory. Donne's historical position was probably at once too remote and yet too near to allow for more. He was more remote in time than Cleveland and Cowley, more remote in estimation than Milton.

He was too near to be a classic in the usual sense applied to Ovid or Virgil. He was not even unavailable enough to require translation, as were Chaucer and Boccaccio in *Fables*. Yet in the return to consideration and translation of earlier writers and ways of thought which is a feature of the writing of the last fifteen years of his life, Dryden must have enjoyed returning to Donne. Aging, and like men immemorially, feeling himself alone, he returned to a kind of poetry he had enjoyed and practiced in his early years. Comparison of it with his earliest poems shows that, like most old men, he came to create a world different from that of his younger years. Unlike most old men, he reacted here as throughout the last years of his life with enthusiasm rather than with sadness. In a special sense he was indeed "transported by the multitude and variety of [his] similitudes," of allusions that took him to metaphoric techniques at once old and new in his poetry. What little passion there is in *Eleonora* is not for its object, the Countess of Abingdon, but is that of an old man reviewing his youth and his art. We could have used more of such feeling, even at the expense of concern with its formal subject, even to the loss of some of that concinnity which had become habitual with him. No one will deny that Dryden speaks very well in poetry, even in *Eleonora*. What we can deny the poem has, for all its "pindaric" gestures and Donnean metaphors, is the power to capture our feelings with a true poetic music.

Themes and Variations

PART THREE

Varieties of Lyric Poetry

CHAPTER VII

The costly feast, the carol, and the dance,
Minstrels, and music, poetry, and play.
        —*Palamon and Arcite,* II.

"In lyrical poetry, Dryden must be allowed to have no equal," said Sir Walter Scott in a judgment that may seem more a milestone than a monument of English taste.[1] By some definitions Dryden is scarcely a lyric poet at all. If lyric poetry is the product of a private exaltation autobiographical in reference and but little a product of human reason, then he is more the lyric poet in passages of his historical poems, satires, and religious poems than in those prized by Scott. But there are of course many varieties of lyricism. Pindar's public odes, Virgil's "Messianic Eclogue," Lucretius' hymn to Venus, Ovid's fictional love situations, Spenser's epithalamia, and Milton's *Lycidas* are the proper springs of Dryden's lyric inspiration. In his lyric poetry as in theirs, powerful emotions might at times overflow, but such welling was not merely spontaneous. It was rather an intellectual articulation of feeling than an emotional development of ideas. Scott's judgment makes no sense at all if we bring to Dryden's lyric poetry only post-Romantic expectations, and little more if those of private poetry written earlier in the seventeenth century. All his lyric poems are in some respect radically public in their mode or in their circumstances of uttering. This fact determines their limitations and their triumphs. It explains why classical rather than medieval or late modern lyricism is the best analogue.

So protean is lyricism that it is difficult to define its limits—among Dryden's own lyrics we find song, elegy, ode, masque, and opera. The set pieces of *Annus Mirabilis* or *All for Love,* the *confessio* in the first part of *The Hind and the Panther,* and the indictment of the age at the end of *Eleonora* have lyric qualities. On the other hand, *Threnodia Augustalis,* his first original poem in pindarics, seems to be in most other respects a historical poem. Once all such allowances have been made for variety or special qualities, it remains true that the subjects of his lyric poetry are the common ones of love, death, and other exalted experience. It is of course Dryden's special handling of such subjects that puts his seal upon the usual lyric staples.

As in other modes, so in lyricism he began with earlier fashion. The "Song" from *The Indian Emperour* (1665) recalls numerous Jacobean lyrics.

I

Ah fading joy, how quickly art thou past!
   Yet we thy ruin haste.
As if the cares of human life were few,
   We seek out new:
And follow fate, which would too fast pursue.

II

See how on every bough the birds express
   In their sweet notes their happiness.
They all enjoy, and nothing spare;
   But on their mother Nature lay their care:
Why then should man, the lord of all below,
   Such troubles choose to know,
As none of all his subjects undergo?

III

Hark, hark, the waters fall, fall, fall,
   And with a murmuring sound
Dash, dash upon the ground,
   To gentle slumbers call.

The generalized ethical theme coupled with sensuous languor was not to be characteristic of what Pope termed Dryden's "energy divine." The wit is also ill defined. For although to "follow fate, which would too fast pursue" obviously means to seek out that which is, to one's ruin, seeking one out itself, the opposition between *follow* and *pursue* is unclear. The relation of the third stanza to the rest of the poem is also far from clear outside the play. The poem suggests the sort of lyrics Dryden might have written had he been born not in the year Donne died, but in the year Donne himself was born.

Most of the songs from the plays are love poems, defined (after *The*

Indian Emperour) in terms of certain kinds of passionate experience and into certain predications about those kinds. They are written for a variety of song and dance measures. In their variety and consistency of views of love, the four songs from *An Evening's Love* (1668) anticipate the love poetry of Dryden's whole career. It is of course a personal love poetry—personal not to the poet but to the individuals of the songs, as sometimes also to characters in the plays. Like most songs in plays, they are set off by a degree of greater artifice from the artifice of the plays, in order to make plain the greater esthetic distance. Still, they must comprise the only considerable body of love poems that never tempt one to use the author's name to designate the speaker of the poems. The lyrics are in this sense entirely dramatic, and their drama is also that of clearly definable situations, of stages in the course of an affair of passion. Dryden seems to look, bemused, from a detached vantage point, almost from the theater wings, upon the passions of others, to model roles upon what he sees and so to set into motion his actors and actresses. The effect would be altogether artificial, if he did not seem after all to have interest in what was going on and if the language were not at once so colloquial and so pure. The combination of flushed faces and veins filled with cold water is strange. So is the fact that the closer an affair comes to its sexual climax the more lilting the measure is apt to be, as the second song from *An Evening's Love* exemplifies.

> When, with a sigh, she accords me the blessing,
>   And her eyes twinkle 'twixt pleasure and pain,
> Ah, what a joy 't is, beyond all expressing,
>   Ah what a joy to hear: "Shall we again?"   (13-16)

It is not easy to characterize the tone, if by that we mean Dryden's own attitude here toward sexual pleasure. Just how much "joy" is conveyed by the lyric measure? If the lyric poems were of this kind alone we would surely say that we feel uneasy with the air of detachment from the passions of others, at the haling out from private shadows and into the public day of the private and intimate passions of others. Some have concluded with Dr. Johnson that Dryden's was indeed not one of those gentle bosoms. Others that he enjoyed sexual excitement.

Before judging we must consider other songs which, even at the risk of being thought oversolemn, I propose to treat with the seriousness given the songs of Shakespeare or Blake. The third song from *An*

Evening's Love is very similar in its measure and in leading by stages to sexual union. It differs, however, in incorporating the detached view more wholly within the involved sexual viewpoint. The speaker is a woman recounting a past event, which itself adds to the distance, but she also tells in two stanzas how she has repulsed her lover's advances by laughing out. In the third she has yielded—and there is other laughter.

> I knew 't was his passion that caus'd all his fears,
>   And therefore I pitied his case;
> I whisper'd him softly: "There's nobody near,"
>   And laid my cheek close to his face:
> But as he grew bolder and bolder,
>   A shepherd came by us and saw,
> And just as our bliss we began with a kiss,
>   He laugh'd out with: "A ha ha ha ha!"

Strong sexual emotion, like any other, withers under laughter. We feel even less at ease with this poem, since we are caught between the "bliss" of the lovers and the laughter of the onlooker. Neither provides much basis for equanimity in the presence of the other. Yet both are integral to the whole, which is constituted of sophisticated realism and pastoral idealism. Sylvia and Amyntas woo in the environment of flowers and the nightingale. The onlooker is a "shepherd." The difference between the two poles of the experience can best be shown in exaggeration by that remarkable poem of Rochester's, "A Song. To Cloris," which begins, "Fair *Cloris* in a Pig-Stye lay, / Her tender Herd lay by her." In short, the pastoral is as much a controlling metaphor here as is religion in *MacFlecknoe;* both play in ironic fashion with the experience created by the poem. Of course Dryden did not consider the pastoral to have the evaluative force of religion. Yet the pastoral is traditionally appropriate to love—but not this kind of love, we protest. The difference between the usual pastoral ideal and the real action here is that of the laughter. Once again it is a question of tone. Is love regarded as something ideal? Is it only a physical passion? Or is it a joke in which all men are involved?

The answer is that it is all three, with the balance seeming to shift from poem to poem. If the ecstasy is somewhat questionable while it is still ecstasy, it is wonderful in anticipation and regretted in those poems reflecting back upon the experience of love. The first song shows regret in the difference between its first and last stanzas.

I

You charm'd me not with that fair face,
    Tho' it was all divine:
To be another's is the grace
    That makes me wish you mine.

IV

Now, every friend is turn'd a foe,
    In hope to get our store;
And passion makes us cowards grow,
    Which made us brave before.

Many of Dryden's best known songs are of this kind. Passion turns out, after all, to disappoint, but it is better to have lost than never to have loved at all. Or so the songs of this kind seem to say. Yet again it is not quite so simple. The regretful songs are prevailingly far purer in diction, often with few images, perfected in cadence, and indeed more "classic" in line. Quite simply they are often better songs. The fact suggests that the regret over love is to Dryden the truer, deeper experience, as one of his best known lyrics, the song from *The Spanish Friar* (1680) well shows.

I

Farewell, ungrateful traitor!
    Farewell, my perjur'd swain!
Let never injur'd creature
    Believe a man again.
The pleasure of possessing
Surpasses all expressing,
But 't is too short a blessing,
    And love too long a pain.

II

'T is easy to deceive us,
    In pity of your pain;
But when we love, you leave us
    To rail at you in vain.
Before we have descried it,
There is no bliss beside it;
But she that once has tried it,
    Will never love again.

III

The passion you pretended,
  Was only to obtain;
But when the charm is ended,
  The charmer you disdain.
Your love by ours we measure,
Till we have lost our treasure;
But dying is a pleasure,
  When living is a pain.

Love is "too long a pain." Yet several passages show it is also incomparably attractive "Before we have descried it." Moreover, "The pleasure of possessing / Surpasses all expressing." As the situation in the play shows (Olympia is said to complain of Bireno's leaving her), and as the phrase, "perjur'd swain," suggests, the pastoral metaphor is operative. Unfortunately for Olympia, the pastoral world is made to admit its enemies, time and change. In these songs, Dryden's lovers do indeed seize the day; but it passes, and they reflect that though it brought joy it brings remorse.

The first song from *An Evening's Love* shows, very nearly explicitly, that the developing psychology of love is what most interests Dryden. The fact that such an emphasis is so to speak midway between the experience and the ethics of passion accounts for the uneasiness we feel with the songs of consummation and the detachment of all. Some of the best songs are those, relatively less known, which focus precisely upon the psychology. In them ecstasy and ethics are never far off, but these two interests are absorbed by the dominant psychological emphasis. The fourth song from *An Evening's Love* is just such a poem.

I

DAMON.   Celimena, of my heart,
              None shall e'er bereave you:
           If with your good leave I may
           Quarrel with you once a day,
              I will never leave you.

II

CELIMENA.   Passion's but an empty name
              Where respect is wanting:
           Damon, you mistake your aim;
           Hang your heart, and burn your flame,
              If you must be ranting.

III

DAMON.   Love as dull and muddy is
                       As decaying liquor:
              Anger sets it on the lees,
              And refines it by degrees,
                       Till it works it quicker.

IV

CELIMENA. Love by quarrels to beget
                       Wisely you endeavor;
              With a grave physician's wit,
              Who, to cure an ague fit,
                       Put me in a fever.

V

DAMON.   Anger rouses love to fight,
                       And his only bait is:
              'T is the spur to dull delight,
              And is but an eager bite,
                       When desire at height is.

VI

CELIMENA. If such drops of heat can fall
                       In our wooing weather;
              If such drops of heat can fall,
              We shall have the devil and all
                       When we come together.

The pastoral names are once again poised against an unpastoral awareness of time and sophisticated motivations. Within the larger poising,
the attitudes of Damon and Celimena are also opposed. The two are one
of those "gay couples" who seek with bargaining to come to terms with
each other and thereby define ideas of love and human nature. Damon
pleads his idealism on a sophisticated condition—he needs a daily
"quarrel," "anger," "an eager bite." It would be difficult to say
whether the pastoralism admits the unpastoral, or the sophisticate a
genuineness of passion.

Celimena's argument reveals something very similar, although opposed. She accuses Damon of "ranting," of using "an empty name"—
mere words—in pretending to a "passion" lacking .in "respect." In
pastoral terms, she argues the necessity of moral idealism to make love
true love. And yet she too rejects a central feature of the pastoral, its
highflown language. There are few wittier dismissals of the diction of

all English pastoral love poetry than her "Hang your heart, and burn your flame." The next three stanzas show Damon continuing in his psychological theorizing and Celimena in her practical rejection of it. The imagery is that of "feeding" stale wine, of cure of disease, and of cavalry warfare. The last stanza leaves us we scarcely know where. But it is perfectly clear that for all of her sparring, Celimena fully assumes that they will "come together." The heat of their present verbal warfare will be as nothing to the pleasing battle of physical love.

The poem has, then, one of those turns in direction which often mark Dryden's love songs. We are left wondering at the end of the journey about what our destination has been. It becomes clear in looking back over the poem that Celimena is most concerned with distinguishing between words and the thing itself, love. Or rather, it is passion and respect, not love and words, that she desires. This characterization of her seems very true of women. Equally just is the character of Damon, who requires a sexual activity, even a limited warfare, "once a day" which will allow him to maintain delight and fidelity. By the reversal at the end of the song Dryden seems to suggest that the displays of femininity and masculinity together clarify the relation between the couple and, more-over, lead it forward to its consummation. The naturalism opposed to the pastoral asks us to consider the psychological and physical aspects of love—Celimena's *passion* and Damon's *eager bite*. The pastoral requires us to consider the ideal aspects of love—Damon's formal diction and Celimena's *respect*. At the same time, while the naturalistic gives the poem a putative naughtiness, the pastoral allows passion to function normatively by generalizing the case of the two lovers. By itself the physical excludes us; it leads the woman into compliance, the chamber, or undress. Dryden's song was sung upon the stage; its pastoral suggests the out-of-doors. It admits the passion by setting its bounds. Without the use of pastoralism as a controlling metaphor, a wholly different strategy would be necessary to admit the wider realism and the psychological truth of the poem.

The debate of Damon and Celimena well shows the strength of passion without idealized ecstasy and of eagerness without tenderness which so typifies Dryden's love poetry. The strength of feeling grows as much from a resolved, or suspended, tension of values conveyed by the psychological examination of love. It is not the quasi-pastoral alone that is the vehicle of such tension, useful as that controlling metaphor proved to be for Dryden and his contemporaries. The song from *Cleomenes* (1692) shows that strangely taut rhythms might convey as much.

I

No, no, poor suff'ring heart, no change endeavor,
Choose to sustain the smart, rather than leave her;
My ravish'd eyes behold such charms about her,
I can die with her, but not live without her;
One tender sigh of hers to see me languish,   5
Will more than pay the price of my past anguish:
Beware, O cruel fair, how you smile on me,
'T was a kind look of yours that has undone me.

II

Love has in store for me one happy minute,
And she will end my pain, who did begin it;   10
Then no day void of bliss, or pleasure, leaving,
Ages shall slide away without perceiving:
Cupid shall guard the door, the more to please us,
And keep out Time and Death, when they would seize us;
Time and Death shall depart, and say, in flying,   15
Love has found out a way to live by dying.

It would be difficult to imagine another rhythm possessing such a sense of struggle with such grace. The syntax is natural, the language colloquial; and yet across that naturalness is cut the tension of the song rhythm. It might be argued that the poem was written for some special kind of music (it was in fact set by Purcell) that would slacken the tension of the verse. But even with appropriate music, the tension remains: the tones of the two stanzas are directly opposed. If we consider the verse tension appropriate to the first stanza, then it is very strange in the second with its hope. If we imagine the anxiety of the second transformed in the graceful cadence of a song, then the first stanza is very strange. We must accept the tension as the basis of the whole. So read, the first stanza appropriately employs the charged verse to convey an agony of feeling: "No, no, poor suff'ring heart, no change endeavor . . ." We leave the rhythms of the first stanza for the words of the second. In themselves these involve a poise of contraries—the conventional "one happy minute" of the first line and the cessation or transcendence of time in the subsequent lines. The poise is expressed most clearly in the last line of all, "Love has found out a way to live by dying," which obviously plays upon the conventional ambiguity of "die" in its normal and sexual meanings. The sexual dying of a moment's ecstasy is well enough "a way to live" in the sense of providing an agreeable way to spend one's time. But it is inadequate as a way of overcoming "Time and Death," which are twice mentioned within two lines.

The tension between such conceptions of living and dying, of the moment and of Time, resembles that between the appropriateness of the struggling verse rhythm for the first stanza and its inappropriateness for the second. We cannot convince ourselves that triumph is so easy. The only way out of the dilemma would seem to be to consider a divided awareness in the speaker. To the extent that he is a lover used to the conventional terms and given to such warnings as, "O cruel fair," sexual dying may be considered an adequate way to life. For such a person, the second stanza is a hyperbole like that of the seduction poem—but unconvincingly addressed to himself rather than to the lady. Whether we consider the man also to be aware of his subjection to time and death, or merely a person subject to them and unaware, the second stanza carries no conviction that the experience of love is anything more than a transitory thing. To some extent the song reviews the affirmation in *All for Love*, deciding now that the "happy minute" is wholly inadequate to a world of "Time and Death." Yet we are left finally with no alternative than to find "ages" in the "happy minute," to discover in sexual joy the only means, however sadly inadequate, to mitigate inevitable time and death. It is not in this case the element of pastoral idealism but a disturbing, throbbing cadence in the verse itself that conveys half the experience of the poem.

Sometimes it is rather a situation that conveys the "truth" of love, which is the subject of the remarkable "Song for a Girl" in Dryden's last play, *Love Triumphant* (1694).

I

Young I am, and yet unskill'd
How to make a lover yield;
How to keep, or how to gain,
When to love, and when to feign.

II

Take me, take me, some of you,
While I yet am young and true;

Ere I can my soul disguise,
Heave my breasts, and roll my eyes.

III

Stay not till I learn the way,
How to lie, and to betray:
He that has me first, is blest,
For I may deceive the rest.

IV

Could I find a blooming youth,
Full of love, and full of truth,
Brisk, and of a jaunty mien,
I should long to be fifteen.

This is heady stuff. Youth is opposed to skill, love to feigning; love and
truth are associated with youth, in thought as well as in rhyme. Yet
what might be in some way condoned as a libidinousness natural to an
older woman is disturbing when made the condition of the innocence
of a girl not yet fifteen. In the older woman it might require reprobation
but not explanation. As it is, we are treated to something more fundamental than witty paradox. There is a real shock to the reader, or
listener, in "Take me, take me, *some* of you." Even more disturbing,
because it so clearly involves the awareness of the girl as well as of the
reader, is: "He that has me first is blest, / For I may deceive the rest."
What follows seems about to say: If only I could find someone dashing,
young, and true, I would be true to him. Nothing so easy is allowed us:
"I should long to be fifteen." The young girl is caught between a moral
anguish longing for *truth* and the onset of sexual desires. There is no
certainty that she will be promiscuous and no doubt that she longs for
physical love. We are impelled to ask, after such youth, what age? The
answer can be given in terms of the verbs of the first stanza, and even
more economically by reference to the first performance of the play.
The song was written for young Miss Cross, at this date like Mrs.
Bracegirdle, an actress of exceptional voice and unblemished reputation. The second stanza plays upon the theatrical situation. The shock-
ing "Take me . . . some of you" makes sense and takes poignancy from
the public situation; the invitation is and is not extended to the men in
the audience.

It is revealing to recall *MacFlecknoe*. As the girl says here, she will
one day need to learn as a human being (and of course as an actress)

to "disguise" "my soul," to "Heave my breasts, and roll my eyes."
Actresses need to learn to represent feelings. Is this poem really about
life or only about a theater like that one in *MacFlecknoe*,

> Where queens are form'd, and future heroes bred;
> Where unfledg'd actors learn to laugh and cry,
> Where infant punks their tender voices try?

The comparison shows how much more lyrical the tone of the song is.
Whatever the feelings of some men in the audience upon hearing Miss
Cross's inviting voice, they are rejected. They cannot fit the conditions
of the last stanza. The distressed idealism as well as the purity of the
sexual desire of the young girl seem very true of most young adolescents.
They are disturbing motives, in themselves and more so together, to
readers whose greater age permits them neither to maintain an idealism
in the face of such shock nor to remain immune to the titillation of the
experience. It is a "Song for a Girl" because without such a speaker the
experience of the poem is shattered. It is also a poem for adults, who
would like to think that *youth*, *love*, *truth*, *feigning*, and *longing* to be
fifteen are different from this. Conscious of the sophistication and mixed
motives of our own personalities, we seek to immure youth in an innocence not our own. It is an effort Dryden will not permit us. His
girl is no less human than we, although her humanity is conveyed by a
more starkly poised set of motives than we are normally aware of.

Dryden's subordination of the claims of passion and of ethics to the
psychology of love has the effect of making his love songs seem somewhat remote from other treatments of the subject, and perhaps from
the subject itself. The habit in the songs of assessing rather than presenting experience is in some ways like the psychological self-conscious-
ness of the twentieth century, although its particulars are those of the
seventeenth. Donne and Suckling, Burton and Browne, Gassendi and
Descartes set some of the norms of psychological examination inherited by the Restoration, which altered them to some extent by
combining them with viewpoints taken from neo-Epicureanism. Dryden's interests in Lucretius are well known. So are some of his disagreements with neo-Epicureanism.* Yet on balance he was affected. Of all

---

* Dryden translated the 4th Book of *De Rerum Natura*, "Concerning the Nature
of Love" (Noyes, pp. 188-92) as well as other sections. His reservations were the
usual Christian ones, with certain personal features as treated below.

his friends, Dr. Walter Charleton was the one most identified with the somewhat suspect neo-Epicurean cause, and his writings during the 1650's and 1660's therefore reveal something of the context of Dryden's ideas about love. It may be argued that a single volume, *The Ephesian and Cimmerian Matrons*, referred to briefly in an earlier chapter, provides a better context for the literature of passion in the Restoration than any other readily to be found.[2] *The Ephesian Matron* by Charleton plays upon a dual interest, a mild sexual titillation and a philosophical naturalism. So much can be shown by the prefatory epistle.

> As for her *Religion*, I confess also, I can give you no certain account of it, because (contrary to the custom of most of her sex) she is very reserved in that particular. Yet, if I may have the liberty of conjecturing from some Actions of hers, I should take her to be of old *Epicurus's* Faith, following the simple dictates of *mother-Nature*, and living by the plain rule of her own *Inclinations;* as holding it a contradiction, *to be born under one Law, and to another bound.*[3]

Charleton is one of the most important proponents in the day of an Epicureanism modified to conform to Christianity. Perhaps it should be put the other way about. His description of the Matron is therefore praise of a kind, adapting as we have seen in considering the opening lines of *Absalom and Achitophel*, neo-Epicureanism to ideas of Christian liberty. If the wit leaves us somewhat nervous, the reason is evident soon after.

> For her *Humour*, you will find her in all things a *perfect Woman*, a little subject to *changes*, seldom out of *extreams; weeping* and *smiling* in a breath, leaping at once out of a *Charnel-house* into a *Nuptial-bed;* soon quitting a violent *grief* for a good *Husband* lately *deceased*, for . . . solace in the embraces of a *new Love.*[4]

The psychological has absorbed the passionate and the ethical.

The tale itself is at once erotic and cynical. There is a hypothetical espousal by "some witty *Disciple*" of Epicurus" of ideas disparaging "the *excellency* and *immortallity* of that noble essence, *the reasonable soul*" (p. 22) and a rejection of such a "weak and prevaricating *Epicurean*" (p. 24 ff.). The argument really modifies Epicureanism rather than refutes it, however, by accommodating to the naturalistic idea of men's motives an argument that there are two souls: "the one [is] *Rational,* or *Intellectual,* and *Incorruptible,* as being of divine Original. . . . The other only *Sensitive* . . . [is] the common . . . Tye, betwixt the celestial and incorporeal . . . and the terrestriall and corporeal nature of the Body."[5] Since the tone of the story emphasizes sensation rather than ratiocination, it is obvious that Charleton's rejection of Epicureanism is but partial. His aim in adapting such a story to Epicurean naturalism can best be understood by the later interruptions (pp. 56-69), which are even given titles: "Of Love determined" and "Of Platonick love." Although the former allows for "*Charity,*" its chief purpose is to show "Love and Lust to be still one and the same thing, as I have proved it to be" (p. 62). Charleton gives five reasons for rejecting the seventeenth-century version of Platonic love. It is unclassical in its heterosexuality. Modern "Platoniques" are young and burning rather than "superannuated" like Socrates. The moderns seek to "*Learn,*" i.e., to experience, rather than to teach. And modern women "are for the most part *Married* to others, and so ought to propagate Virtue, (if they have so much as to spare) rather in their Husbands and Children than in Strangers" (pp. 66-67). As in many Restoration comedies and in some of the poems of Rochester, Charleton's naturalism here is a means of exposing pretended idealism for what it is, a hypocritical mask for self-indulgence.

If Charleton gives us the ancestry in philosophy and attitude of Etherege's Dorimant or Wycherley's Horner, he does not provide us with the whole of their plays. There is another half to them, and to the volume containing Charleton's story in this edition. One "P. M. Gent." furnished a second story, *The Cimmerian Matron,* which is less a story of human frailty than of deliberate, even malignant, lust.[6] By the same token, the idealism of the prefatory epistle and the treatise, "The Mysteries and Miracles of Love" (pp. 33-77), is gentler, more tolerant of human nature than the comparable theorizing in the first story. As with Charleton, then, as so often on the Restoration stage, there is here a tension in attitude. Equally, the two essays on love appended to the stories are opposed. "P. M." rejects Charleton's claiming "*Love* to be so *juvenile* and sooty an Argument."[7] He cites philosophers, and a wide assortment of divines—Heliodorus, Æneas Silvius, Robert Burton, Jeremy Taylor, and others—who either found love worthy of study or who wrote stories like these of the matrons. He has no difficulty in finding biblical precedents, either. The point of the treatise on "The Mysteries and Miracles of Love" is that to love is so human that reprobation is vain and unnecessary. The reductive paraphrase certainly fails to convey the fine mixture of condescension and approbation toward the subject. How relevant it is to Dryden's songs can be judged, however, by comparing two remarks with the debate between Damon and Celimena or with the second stanza of the tense song from *Cleomenes*.

> Notwithstanding Love be thus immortal, as being the proper affection of an immortal Soul [so confuting Charleton's equation of love and lust], and devoted to an eternal Object, Good: yet can I not deny, but it is a kind of *Death*. For, who is ignorant that Lovers die as often as they kiss, or bid adieu. . . . Here's all the difference, the delight of *sensual* love is therefore furious, short of duration, and subject to decay: the *Platonique* depending solely upon the Mind, whose powers are perpetual, is therefore calme, of one equal tenour, and everlasting. (pp. 65 and 74)

He ends with *"Heroick Passion,"* touching upon numerous matters of interest to attitudes expressed in Restoration drama. Only one, the relation between art and nature, is closely concerned with the background to Dryden's songs. The author rejects Charleton's charge of the hypocrisy of idealism by admitting it as Dryden admits the pastoral:

> we account it an excellency in a Painter, to make his pieces fairer than the Originals; and among the many praises deservedly ascribed to our incomparable *Mr. Lely*,* this is not the least, that his curious pencil can at pleasure not only follow the finest lines of Nature, but sweeten them; at once both imitate and excell the life. Why then do you condemn the same in a Lover? it is indeed an excess in both; of Art in one; of Affection in the other: and, in my opinion, equally commendable.[8]

The two stories and their commentaries provide four attitudes toward love. The story of the Ephesian Matron possesses an eroticism in the titillating and a modified neo-Epicureanism in the philosophizing comments. The first questions the idealistic hypocrisy that love is more than lust. The tale of the Cimmerian matron has a repulsiveness in its

* *"Mr. Lely"* is of course Peter Lely, later knighted, a leading Court painter of the day.

sordid events, but a tolerance in the reaction to them. Contrary to the tone of the story, the "remarks" question a love that is no more than passion. At the same time, just as the titillation seems out of place in a purely naturalistic approach, so the tolerance is ill-sorted with a sordid tale. Just as all four elements are present with others in Restoration comedy, so the four together provide a background, though not a description, for Dryden's songs. In his case, love is not separated so wholly from other considerations—commerce, divinity, war—which suggest a more humanistic than philosophical consideration. He also refuses to simplify to such an extent, and sexual passion is treated with such others as pride, anger, jealousy, and despair. The attention is taken to worlds beyond the sophisticated adult world of the two tales to those of childhood or the pastoral. But like the stories, Dryden's songs are concerned with the nature and role of sexual passion in human life.

His point of view is at once more normal in its acceptance of passion and more detached in its regard of it. The acceptance argues both a felt personal attraction and a seventeenth-century concern with kinds of experience best expressed in lyric poetry. It is of a piece with the treatment of passionate will in the plays, because like the plays his love lyrics suggest a deeper involvement with such emotional forces in human nature than the themes of his other nondramatic poetry readily indicate. But the detachment implies a degree of negative judgment— upon the enjoyment or status of passion as an indulgence of the will— which admits ethical claims that otherwise often seem to have been forgot. It is true that not even in the plays of which they are a part does he allow reason so far to be subordinate as in the songs. Yet for that very reason, the claims of the heart are given fuller and more positive hearing in the plays than in the mixed tones of the songs. These are after all best regarded as variations on the larger issues of the plays, allowing the passionate will of man a greater hearing in matters of love, but a more grudging judgment.

The songs of Dryden also have in common their being written to be set to music and their concern with the passions. As the major odes written for St. Cecilia's Day show, Dryden felt these two elements closely related. The songs have other features more or less in common— the experimentation with a wide variety of rhythms, purity of diction, avoidance of complex verbal figures, use of controlling metaphors, and recourse to ironic conceptions. Many of them, as the examples chosen indicate, strongly stress some manner of time sequence. Although ideas and other elements often leave us with the impression that love is a state rather than a process, the working of ideas upon each other and the manipulation of verbs commonly set forth a development towards a given end. At its simplest and most erotic, the development is little more than a narration, and therefore in the past tense, leading to the end of sexual union.[9] For such poems the warmest interest one can sometimes muster is in their handling of song measures. In more complex versions, the temporal sequence is at once satisfying and crucial to the song's meaning. Such skill is of true importance, because it is related to the justice of Dryden's treatment of love in songs like "Celimena, of my heart" or "Song for a Girl." The temporal sequence related to the experience and meaning of the poem is also a poetic principle that relates the songs to his other lyrics and his historical concern.

Of the other subjects commonly treated by lyric poetry, Dryden's other major single subject is death. If we include among his lyric poems his epitaphs, memorial poems, pastoral elegies, and epicedes, the number of poems on the subject must be put very high. Among them is one of the poems most admired in our century, "To the Memory of Mr. Old-ham" (1684). It has a special place among his poems on death by reason of the depth of its mourning for a loss.

> Farewell, too little, and too lately known,
> Whom I began to think and call my own:
> For sure our souls were near allied, and thine
> Cast in the same poetic mold with mine.
> One common note on either lyre did strike, 5
> And knaves and fools we both abhorr'd alike.
> To the same goal did both our studies drive;
> The last set out the soonest did arrive.
> Thus Nisus fell upon the slippery place,
> While his young friend perform'd and won the race. 10
> O early ripe! to thy abundant store
> What could advancing age have added more?
> It might (what nature never gives the young)
> Have taught the numbers of thy native tongue.
> But satire needs not those, and wit will shine 15
> Thro' the harsh cadence of a rugged line:
> A noble error, and but seldom made,
> When poets are by too much force betray'd.

> Thy generous fruits, tho' gather'd ere their prime,
> Still shew'd a quickness; and maturing time   20
> But mellows what we write to the dull sweets of rhyme.
> Once more, hail and farewell; farewell, thou young,
> But ah too short, Marcellus of our tongue;
> Thy brows with ivy, and with laurels bound;
> But fate and gloomy night encompass thee around.   25

The structure of the poem is not unlike that of the songs and other poems. The first ten lines develop the nature of the poet's relationship to Oldham, so conveying a sense of real loss.[10] The next eleven evaluate Oldham's achievement, and the last four bid ritual farewell. We have gone from past to present to the verge of an aborted future and the pity of the actual—a temporal scheme we have seen before.

What seems so simple, however—the nature of the relationship between the two men—is altered subtly in successive treatments of it, and chiefly by metaphorical means when something slightly different seems overtly to be meant. At first Oldham is but recently, and not well, known (1). Then he seems to have become a son, "my own" (2). Next they are brother poets and, in particular, satirists (3-6). Lines 7-10 introduce the first Virgilian allusion, to the story of Nisus and Euryalus at the funeral games of Anchises in the *Æneid*, V (see Dryden's *Æneis*, V, 373-441). We should observe that the allusion shows that what has been won is *priority*, not quality. The race is that to create modern English satire.

The stress upon Oldham's priority suggests both Dryden's own late coming to satire (he was fifty when *The Medal* appeared) and leads to thoughts of the younger poet's early ripeness, the subject of lines 11-21. These lines possess that quiet wit by which the implicit is made to control and alter the overt. The imagery of ripeness is particularly beautiful. The lines convey as well amplitude ("abundant store," "generous fruits") and vitality ("too much force" and a "quickness," meaning vitality as well as earliness and hearkening back to the race imagery). These are warm tributes to Oldham. They provide overt and, as far as they go, real bases for admiration.

The qualification comes in three stages, with three poetic issues: the necessity of observing poetic "numbers" (12-16), the desirability of working everything into a passion (17-18), and the advantage of experience in art (19-21). Oldham's satire is deliberately and notoriously rough, even cacophonous at times. Dryden justifies this in one of his virtuoso effects: "wit will shine / Thro' the harsh cadence of a rugged line." The wit is evident. So is the real grace of cadence beneath the appearance of roughness. This is not Oldham's way of being "rugged," nor is it related to the charge raised by the lines, "the numbers of *thy native tongue*" which Oldham had not learnt (12-14). Oldham had yet to learn his English, says Dryden gently, displaying how to write ruggedly in that tongue without loss of sense or cadence. Another characteristic of Oldham's is his effort to load every rift, not so much with ore as with gunpowder. Melodrama, savage indignation, and exclamation are legitimate satiric resources, but in Oldham's style the strain is evident. If such an excess is to be preferred to insipidity, as Dryden's lines say, it is also true that it is his verb that gets the rhyme: "by too much force *betray'd*."

The benefits of experience bring Dryden back to the past tense (from the present with its generalization), if only for a line and a half. Oldham's fruits *had* "quickness"—early ripeness and vitality. But the quick is now dead, and the surviving poets go on maturing: "time / But mellows what we write to the dull sweets of rhyme." The skillful triplet, called yet more to our attention by an alexandrine, ends in its smooth, slow way by raising the issue this section of the poem has seemed to ignore in speaking of real and potential achievement. Oldham is dead. The remembrance of the fact softens the irony of the preceding passage. It is *we*, the living, upon whom the mellowing and maturing force of time now has its effect. The second section concludes by making the tone of the passage not so much laudatory as pensive, not so much ironic as concerned in a quiet, reflective way with many things. The distance between the *our* of the third line and the *we* of the twentieth is that between Oldham and Dryden on the one hand, and the dead Oldham and us the living on the other.

The new relation is developed in the last four lines. Oldham is now the "Marcellus of our tongue" (22). The distance between Dryden and us on the one side with Oldham on the other is continued and increases as the Roman tribute, the *ave atque vale*, is given and as Oldham fades into the "gloomy night." As "our tongue" recalls "thy native tongue" in the previous passage, so the natural imagery there is recast in the "ivy" and "laurels." The effect of the middle section has not been to lessen grief—its wit is too subtly and much too softly modulated for that—

but to lead to a redefinition of the relationship of the two men. We are brought at last to their true relationship: Oldham is the Marcellus to Dryden's Augustus.* The last two lines develop the Virgilian passage alluded to (*Æneid*, VI, 866) and a long last line as Oldham is encompassed in a dignified death. This is the point of funeral elegies—that someone has died. But unlike almost all others, this really stresses the fact only in the last line. The effect of its introductory "But" is therefore unusually strong, and the tone might have gone out of control without the Virgilian allusion and the earlier wit to control it. A second important effect of the allusion is to redefine the role of Dryden, who becomes Augustus mourning his most promising successor. Characteristically the poem becomes most highly personal when most public; it is most full of feeling when most reliant upon "technique," and most direct when employing allusion. Because it is also true that the "gloomy night" is lightened by the brightness of the Virgilian allusion, Oldham fades from sight among the living and appears forever in a new version of Roman history. These are the combinations Dryden had failed to sustain in *Eleonora*. It is not likely that he knew Oldham all that well, but he did have some acquaintance with him, enough to judge the man and see in him what was personally important to himself.

The "Ode on the Death of Mr. Henry Purcell" (1696), Dryden's last work of any importance before his *Virgil* appeared in the next year, is in certain respects like the poem to Oldham. In both Dryden is writing of the untimely death of a younger artist whom he had admired. (Oldham had been but thirty, Purcell was thirty-seven). There are some important differences, however. Purcell had already achieved greatness—he is still often called England's greatest composer—and as a composer was best celebrated in a poem written for a musical setting. Perhaps the combination was the cause, perhaps not, but the *Ode* to Purcell is one of Dryden's most lyric, least intellectual works in a major form. It is written for singing and for instrumentation, with a clear sense of the possibilities afforded by such a performance. The poem is more lovely than thoughtful, more musical than endowed with that inner structure of meanings found in his other odes. Yet it has qualities of special interest.

---

* The "hail and farewell" has suggested to so many readers Catullus' poem on his brother's death that I must be wrong in thinking it alludes to Æneas on the death of Pallas, so giving a transition between the Nisus-Euryalus and Augustus-Marcellus allusions. In his analysis of the poem, Hoffman, pp. 93-97, suggests that Dryden's Marcellus merges the nephew of Augustus with Marcus Claudius Marcellus, both of whom appear in *Æneid*, VI.

One of them is its tone, which can best be judged by comparison with the lines in *Lycidas* that Dryden uses at two points. The first echoed passage contains Milton's traditional elegiac blame for the responsibility, which is then withdrawn.

> Where were ye Nymphs when the remorseless deep
> Clos'd o'er the head of your lov'd *Lycidas*? . . .
> Ay me, I fondly dream!
> Had ye been there — for what could that have done?
> What could the Muse herself that *Orpheus* bore,
> The Muse herself, for her enchanting son
> Whom Universal nature did lament,
> When by the rout that made the hideous roar,
> His gory visage down the stream was sent,
> Down the swift *Hebrus* to the *Lesbian* shore? (50-51, 56-63)

Dryden's passage shows no grief.

> We beg not hell our Orpheus to restore:
>   Had he been there,
>   Their sovereigns' fear
>   Had sent him back before.
> The pow'r of harmony too well they know:
> He long ere this had tun'd their jarring sphere,
>   And left no hell below. (16-22)

Milton's elegy is both greater and longer, in both respects encompassing far more. Apart from this, the significance of the comparison is that it shows what the poem on Oldham does not of Dryden's usual practice. Lycidas is mourned because he is so sadly assumed into a larger world. Purcell is a triumphantly valued part of it. Milton's blameful address to the Nymphs, "Had *ye* been there," becomes an assured, "Had *he* been there." Milton maintains the pastoral convention; Dryden speaks of him in distinction to us the living. Milton's subjunctive conveys a better might-have-been, Dryden's a sense of triumph: Hell would have become harmonious and ceased to be Hell, and in any case *our* Orpheus is not there. (Where he has gone is left to the next stanza to treat.) Dryden chooses not to fill in the human world around his Orpheus as Milton does about his. Instead he is more factual, attentive to historic truth. This can be understood in his reason for calling Purcell *our Orpheus*. Milton's reason had been a watery death and a pastoral convenience in identifying the shepherd with the musician. Dryden, who knew the pastoral conventions as well as anyone, seems to refuse to use them except where they are unexpected, as controlling metaphors in songs such as those we have seen. But he has good reasons to consider Purcell an Orpheus. There is a real connection in music, which is used as the intellectual center of the poem. More importantly Purcell was also commonly referred to as the English or British Orpheus, as the title of the selected edition of his music, *Orpheus Britannicus* (1698), shows. We observe again how Dryden's metaphors grow from some kind of established truth.

Dryden's tone in this passage is, then, clearer, brighter, more appropriate, and less complex than Milton's. Most important of all, Dryden speaks of achievement, not loss. His conception is not of inexplicable loss but of explicable grandeur, less of death than of immortality. He dwells upon harmony, which is treated as a musical fact, as a creative, beneficent force (in opposition to the evil force of discord), and of harmony in terms recalling a long tradition from his own day back to classical times. By contrast, Milton is concerned with emotional loss, and his repetitions are incantatory in aim. We can understand the difference by comparing the two poets' visions of the dead men in heaven. Lycidas

> . . . hears the unexpressive nuptial Song,
> In the blest Kingdoms meek of joy and love.
> There entertain him all the Saints above,
> In solemn troops, and sweet Societies
> That sing, and singing in their glory move,
> And wipe the tears for ever from his eyes. (176-81)

Dryden's concern is with a dramatic event such almost as he and Purcell might have collaborated to produce in a masque or opera.

> The heav'nly choir, who heard his notes from high,
> Let down the scale of music from the sky:
>   They handed him along,
> And all the way he taught, and all the way they sung. (23-26)

Instead of presenting a triumph as rich in its sudden affirmation as in its earlier grief, Dryden shows Purcell's triumphant rise to heaven. His means is appropriately musical. Plate IV shows a scale of music, looking enough like a ladder or staircase to be scaled, but made up of harmonic intervals and so a proper conceit for rising by tonal steps. His poem is based upon life and achievement, Milton's upon death, loss, and glorification. Little reconciliation is necessary for Dryden; for Milton the important problem lies in achieving it naturally.

The *Ode* differs in tone from *Lycidas* for the same reason that it differs from the poem to Oldham. Inevitably loss requires a different response from that accorded to great achievement. Far from ending his poem with death, Dryden does not seem to conceive of Purcell as one dead, whatever the title suggests. Purcell merely "retir'd" from earth and moved to heaven. The last stanza shows that everyone has benefited—the angels, other composers who now can live secure, and even the *gods*. Dryden's proper subject is the potential achievement of excellence in art, his affirmation that of a faith in the centrality of art to life. There is a steady rise in tone and idea—from birds to rival musicians, to Purcell on earth, in hell, and in heaven. Such ability is shown in time—the temporal sequence of the poem—but since it is divine, or more properly, *godlike*, it rises above time. This treatment of Purcell's death produces a poem different from, and inferior, to *Lycidas*. To compare it with Dryden's other works, this *Ode* resembles *Eleonora* as much as any in its mingling of weak with strong passages. But it is more assured in its view of Purcell: he is an artist, and Dryden is an artist. The tribute is personally genuine as that to Eleonora could not possibly be.

The poems to Oldham and Purcell deal not only with death but with life, and not only with life but with art. In each case art is associated with life, with vitality, even with reality. Art might tune hell away. And both follow the basic pattern of temporal sequence which we have seen in Dryden's poetry. The virtues and subjects of both, with much greater exercise of his powers, are to be found in the *Ode* to Anne Killigrew (1685 or 1686). To Dr. Johnson "undoubtedly the noblest ode that our language has ever produced," it is a poem whose very excellences have divided critics.[11] It is not surprising, therefore, that there has been little agreement about what the poem may be considered to mean. Van Doren comes to his conclusion in description of the first stanza: "its music is the profoundest and longest-sustained in Dryden, and its grammar is regal."[12] The title of Ruth Wallerstein's essay, "On the Death of Mrs. Killigrew: the Perfecting of a Genre," perfectly mirrors her purpose.[13] Dryden is obviously not an easy poet, but when

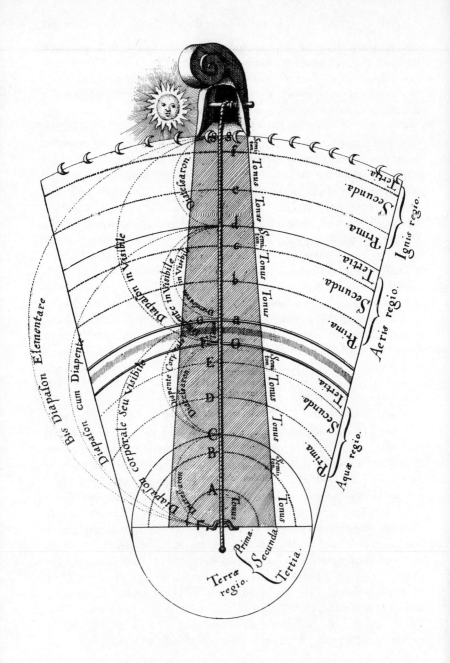

a poem almost two hundred lines long is praised for the profundity of its music (in one part), the regality of its grammar, and the perfection of its genre, we may wonder if there are not other matters to be spoken of.

Since Dryden's is a poetry that considers ideas seriously, it is necessary to consider—identify, characterize, and relate—the ideas in the poetry. E. M. W. Tillyard is one of the few modern critics of the poem to address himself to the question of the nature of its subject and of its ideas. He concludes that the subject is not Anne Killigrew in actuality but in ideal; and not as an ideal so much for her womanhood as for her art. He speaks of the poem's "enthusiasm for the arts" and its concern "with what should be, not with what is."[14] The nature of that ideal is conveyed by Hoffman's excellent analysis of the celestial or divine attributes of Anne and of the movement of the poem.

> There is a cycle in the positions of the imagery, from a postmortal heavenly existence to a premortal heavenly existence, to incarnation in a succession of earthly poets down the ages of history, to incarnation in Anne, the life of Anne, the death of Anne, and then finally, come full circle, back to the post-mortal heavenly state; the cycle involves the progress of a soul, not an individual soul but a great and continuing soul. In the last stanza the cycle and *sæcula sæculorum* are done away with the sounding of *the Golden Trump.*[15]

Tillyard is much more emphatic upon the terrestrial aspects of the poem, its "belief in civilisation" as also in "social and political order."[16] Whatever the proper focus, it is obvious that ideas are related to structure and to value. We may follow Hoffman's example and consider first the structure.

The poems to Eleonora, to Oldham, and to Purcell have shown that at their simplest they deal with the career of the person dead. It is necessary therefore to treat the structure of the Anne Killigrew *Ode* in terms of her career, to remember that such a person really lived. The

---

PLATE IV   *The Scale of Music.* From Robert Fludd, *Utriusque Cosmi . . . Historia* (1617). The ladder-like designation of harmonic intervals represents that scaled by Purcell in Dryden's *Ode*, iii. Reproduced by permission of The Huntington Library, San Marino, California.

first stanza is an exordium celebrating the poetess become a saint. As in the Purcell, the reconciliation with the death of the artist is the premise from which the poem begins, rather than the aim sought. Similarly, the last stanza is a triumphant chorus of hope and faith. In the first stanza Anne Killigrew dwells in the heavens while man continues to work out his life upon earth. In the last she is the "harbinger of heav'n," is the vanguard of men rising in hosannas "to the new morning" of eternity. (Such a change in status would seem to be something of a demotion.) The stanzas between deal with her earthly life antecedent in time to the "now" and the present tense of the first stanza. The middle section of the poem is therefore largely in the past tense. The present tense of the first stanza is also antecedent to the Day of Judgment treated in the last. More specifically, the middle stanzas, II-IX, deal with Anne Killigrew's youth (II-III), career (IV-VII), and death (VIII-IX). The proportioning is very symmetrical. To speak in yet more detail, the first of these middle parts deals (II) with her ancestry and the second (III) with the joy of her birth.

Dryden's great artistic problem arose with the next section, which deals with her career. It did not then nor does it today require a critic of his powers to see that Anne Killigrew is a most inconsiderable poet. His first move is therefore to introduce an issue complicating and redefining the artistic issue. Artistic quality is merged with ethical quality. Having established her ethical superiority, he sweeps us on with the presumption of artistic superiority. Or so its seems. As in the *Oldham*, however, there is some ironic qualification. We need not think that anything so rough as satire is directed at Anne Killigrew, but the praise is either too simple or not simple enough.

> Art she had none, yet wanted none;
> For nature did that want supply:
> So rich in treasures of her own,
> She might our boasted stores defy:
> Such noble vigor did her verse adorn
> That it seem'd borrow'd, where 't was only born. (71-76)

It is the same praise that altered the relation between Dryden and Oldham. And again on the question of morality:

> Each test, and ev'ry light, her Muse will bear,
> Tho' Epictetus with his lamp were there.

Ev'n love (for love sometimes her Muse express'd)
Was but a *lambent flame* which play'd about her breast,
Light as the vapors of a morning dream:
So cold herself, whilst she such warmth express'd,
'T was Cupid bathing in Diana's stream. (81-87)

The image of the stream recalls the conclusion of the preceding stanza: "Her Arethusian stream remains unsoil'd / Unmix'd with foreign filth, and undefil'd" (68-69). But if that be the case, how did Cupid get there? And would it not be much more appropriate, given the imagery of the *flame* that plays about her cold breast—a chastity of Diana within the flame of love—to treat the situation as that of Diana bathing in Cupid's stream? I do not wish to overstress the ironic undertones, which act more to control than to qualify; but they must be admitted on principle, just as we must see that Anne Killigrew's position at the end of the poem is more human, less ideal, than it is at the beginning. In any case, it is necessary not to make too much of Dryden's qualification of the praise. It is directed at Anne's mortality rather than at her immortality, which is what the poem is more centrally concerned with. And if the qualification is to some extent ironic, it only adds evidence that the praise is only formally of Anne Killigrew in herself.

Emerging so well from the moral test of "Epictetus with his lamp,"* Anne Killigrew is considered for her career in painting, of which we observe that more is said than of her poetry. The eighth and ninth stanzas deal with her death and its effects upon her (VIII), upon her brother (IX, 164-73) and upon the heavens (IX, 174-77), so leading us to the time "When in mid-air the golden trump shall sound" (178). On the Day of Judgment she will lead "the choir" of poets, showing the way to heaven. She is rewarded for a good life in such a way that it seems to be a reward for her excellence in art. The emphasis upon the heavenly is indeed a very astute one on Dryden's part, since it enables him to celebrate the life of a dead person as something continuing, to distinguish between art and morality in such ways that they are usefully confused, and to avoid considering Anne Killigrew purely as a human artist. By mingling description of her state with description of

---

* It is amusing that numerous critics have triumphed over Dryden for giving Diogenes' lamp to Epictetus. As Derrick showed in his edition long ago, Dryden had a passage in Lucian in mind. There would be no point in introducing the tub-sitting cynic into this poem.

her achievements, what she had done is immeasurably amplified, and
what she is in herself is transformed.

Tillyard recognized that such a treatment of Anne rendered her but
the formal subject of the poem. Indeed he goes too far in rejecting that
foundation in specific detail from which Dryden's larger subjects and
implications arise. The "biography" of Anne Killigrew is part of the
"civilisation" that Tillyard so rightly discovers as a major subject of the
poem. The central subject is, however, one between the more limited
formal subject and the civilization. It is the nature and role of artistic
genius. The poem accordingly has a structural development in which
the more fundamental ideas are implied by, and made parallel to, the
structure of the poem in terms of Anne Killigrew's life. (It is something
like the relation of chronology and functional structure in *Absalom and
Achitophel.*) The first stanza treats the connections between the timeless ideal ("thy ceiestial song" in heaven) and its earthly equivalent ("a
mortal muse"). The relation is nearly that of Platonic idea to phenomenon, and no more than anyone else was Anne Killigrew superior to
other phenomenal embodiments of that "celestial" ideal:

> Hear then a mortal Muse thy praise rehearse,
>   In no ignoble verse;
> But such as thy own voice did practice here. (16-18)

Since such commerce between the *celestial* and the *mortal* is at once
mysterious and of the utmost importance to his theme, Dryden devotes
his next two stanzas (II-III) to exploring it. We can speak of this in
terms of its religious imagery and classical allusions, but in simpler terms
Dryden is dealing with the mysterious origins of poetic genius, and
with the connection between the gift itself and the individual who
possesses it. These are subjects that engage, as nothing can in *Eleonora* or
the ode to Purcell to such an extent, his committed interest as a man
and as a poet. The next two stanzas (IV-V) examine the nature of
artistic genius in terms of the ideal and the common actuality, just as the
following two (VI and VII) deal with less and more satisfactory norms
of art. These two groups of central stanzas are therefore related, but
their complexity calls for separate treatment.

The fourth stanza deals with the profanation of the ideal in the
actual: "O gracious God! how far have we / Profan'd thy heav'nly gift
of poesy" (56-57); and with the debasement of the eternal (60-61) in

the historical (63). The fifth stanza deals with some of the paradoxes we associate with artistic genius: the "naturalness" of great art (71-74), the virile creativity of the artists and yet the seemingly spontaneous creation of the work (75-76); the tension between inner and environmental causes (77-79). It concludes by developing the paradox that artists can deal with matters foreign to them without loss of integrity. The specific instance is of a chaste poet dealing with passion, but the principle is capable of extension. These are important subjects, and interesting ones as well. If neither their importance nor interest, in themselves, renders this *Ode* greater than that to Purcell, there can be no doubt that Dryden has *made* these subjects of far greater interest and importance to us in this poem than in that to Purcell, or even to Oldham.

It seems to me psychologically understandable and just that the death of even so very minor a poet as Anne Killigrew should have urged upon Dryden questions such as these. It is easier to come to terms with them at the death of such a person than at the death of a Milton. His death is both too much of a loss and, because of the achievements of a lifetime, too great in implication to allow us free speculation into such matters. The death of any artist of such greatness does not lead us to concern ourselves with the nature of artistic genius so much as with the nature of his genius. Anne Killigrew was more useful in being not only the daughter of a friend but also a suitable vehicle for larger subjects.

Stanzas VI and VII move from poetry to the graphic arts, and from religious or moral imagery to royal and political. The wider implications of artistic genius are now considered, just as biographically these stanzas turn to Anne Killigrew's paintings and her relations with the Court. Artistic genius is now developed in two sets of terms—in a political or national version, and in a divinely creative version. Often thought to be rather limp stanzas, these two are in fact as complex, if not as exalted, as the others. At least we must see what they deal with. The political metaphor is most obvious in the sixth stanza, the religious at the end of the sixth and the beginning of the seventh. It is essential to see between the two stanzas an important distinction governing the tone. The references in the sixth are French, those in the seventh English. So it is that Anne Killigrew turns from "that mighty government" of poetry "to the next realm," which is both France and painting, and in particular to French styles of "classical" painting. The political metaphor is extended first by allusion to Louis XIV, whose conquests were even then being consolidated with the device of the *"chamber of dependences"* (or dependencies). This conquest is a *triumph* (105), but of a certain kind. "The *sylvan* scenes" with nymphs, satyrs, reflections, and ruins have earned Dryden some criticism for too artificial a description of nature. That is precisely his point. Although the virtues of the schools of Claude Lorrain and Nicolas Poussin have in our time been recognized once more, Dryden treats them as interesting but inferior. It is this kind of painting that was the fashion in France and which would in the next century especially be the fashion in England. Dryden treats it with mixed attitudes, as one of the lines out of context may be used to show: "tho' defac'd, the wonder of the eye." His introduction and conclusion to this section on French classicism in painting are also not altogether clear in import.

> Her pencil drew whate'er her soul design'd,
> And oft the happy draught surpass'd the image in her mind.
>
> . . . .
>
> So strange a concourse ne'er was seen before,
> But when the peopled ark the whole creation bore. (106-07, 125-26)

The problem is to sort out the attitudes with proper tact. Such art is a continental, and in particular a French achievement, imaged by the predatory victories of Louis XIV, whom Dryden here as elsewhere treats as a tyrannic conqueror.* In the same way that that "most Christian king" is an inferior version of Dryden's ideal of monarchy, so such continental painting is a parody of his ideal of art. The nature of those ideals and their best representatives appear in the next stanza, where James II and Queen Mary of Este are opposed to the wholly implied Louis XIV of the earlier stanza, just as the wholly implied English school of portrait art is opposed to the carefully described classical painting of the continent. There is no ironic qualification, no undertow of questioning in this stanza. James II is warlike, as kings should be (especially kings with such neighbors), but he does not attempt to conquer other

---

* Something of the nature of the view of French art held in England can be gained from Elizabeth Manwaring, *Italian Landscape in Eighteenth Century England* (New York, 1925). Any catalogue of paintings by Claude Lorrain, Nicolas Poussin, or by their schools, would include scenes like those Dryden mentions. Dryden's Francophobia, like his distaste for priests, admitted exceptions, but he nowhere, to my knowledge, has a good word for Louis XIV, even after his conversion. See *Hind*, 1974-76 and 2164-75; III, 680-82, 870-81.

nations. Queen Mary represents beauty, an English beauty which is as much superior in its actuality to the classical nymphs as is English art to French, or English government to French. The auxiliary imagery of nymphs, or "heroines," is even the same, though its meaning is different.

> . . . nymphs of brightest form appear
> . . . .
> [She] Before a train of heroines was seen,
> In beauty foremost, as in rank the queen. (116, 140-41)

The French version of creative power involves "nature, art, bold fiction." It creates, or more properly, conserves the "strange" variety of life as "when the peopled ark the whole creation bore." So much for the rather contrived French artistic microcosm for life. "The scene then chang'd." Indeed it has, from "the next realm" to England. The parallel between English portrait painting and French landscape painting (or "perspectives") shows the differences and superiority of the English. For all the talk of "conquerors" (in a simile) and of the "peopled ark" (in a metaphor) the world of French painting is unreal, attractive enough (108-19), and historically rich (120-22), but by comparison dehumanized. England possesses real people, and it is man who is the proper concern of art: "Our martial king," "Our Phoenix queen," and a "train of heroines." The conclusions of the two stanzas are difficult in themselves and in relation. That of the seventh is spectacular:

> Thus nothing to her *genius* was denied,
>   But like a ball of fire the further thrown,
>   Still with a greater blaze she shone,
> And her bright soul broke out on ev'ry side.
> What next she had design'd, Heaven only knows;
> To such immod'rate growth her conquest rose
> That fate alone its progress could oppose. (142-48)

This is opposed to the image of the ark, which Cowley had made a metaphor for artistic wit. The contrast appears to be one between artistic genius considered in terms of the nature it treats or conserves (in the ark), and the genius as a force of its own. The imagery of light has, from its use earlier in the poem, associations of beauty, goodness, and celestial or divine nature. But this last section of stanza VII also has the function of transition to stanza VIII, and thus is not precisely comparable. We are not meant to associate the light imagery with God as in *Religio Laici* or *The Hind and the Panther*. Nor are we meant to take the clause, "Heaven only knows" in the modern sense, any more than "immod'rate growth" is necessarily wrong. (See *Absalom and Achitophel*, 847).

Whatever religious implications may be intended here, those earlier in the stanza are clearer and more important for their contrast with the ark of the preceding stanza. The portrait of the king strikes the viewer's "sight with reverence." His "high-designing-thoughts" are "figur'd" in Anne Killigrew's portrait of him by a kind of "magic." Appropriately enough, it is Queen Mary who is the important symbol of the artistic-English-sacred power. It would seem that in name as well as description she is compared to the Virgin: in "her matchless grace" (*plena gratia*), in her "heav'nly," "peerless" qualities; in her receiving her crown "from sacred hands"; and in being queen of a train (140-41). Such a comparison would have pleased so devout, even fanatic a person as Queen Mary, and it is probably the only place in Dryden's works where it is possible to discover a reference to the Virgin. These two stanzas show the power of art to conquer various realms of nature or, at its best, to reveal the inward reality. The former alternative is to be found in Anne Killigrew's "French" painting, and is less desirable; it is the graphic equivalent of "What nature, art, bold fiction, e'er durst frame." The latter and superior art is found in her English painting, which is "not content t' express [the] outward part," and which more nearly approaches poetry and religion.

The loss involved in her death, which is to say the death of the artist —is treated in stanzas VIII and IX. The former of these has what is for Dryden an unusual indulgence in wit for the sheer joy of wit, without that further purpose served by all details which usually marks his poetry. The whole stanza, while not unmoving, manages a surprisingly unruffled composure at what is in effect the death-scene. The wit purges sentiment, and by purging enforces it. It is also an exercise of the prerogative of the free sensibility.

> In earth the much-lamented virgin lies!
> . . . .
> [Destiny], like a harden'd felon, took a pride
>   To work more mischievously slow,

And plunder'd first, and then destroy'd.

. . . .

     But thus Orinda died:
Heav'n, by the same disease, did both translate;
As equal were their souls, so equal was their fate. (152, 157-59,
                           162-64)

Anne Killigrew is dead of smallpox. There is a difference between Dryden's exclamation quoted (152) and such a possible alternative as "In earth the much lamented poet lies!" That felon smallpox, the agent of Destiny, the "fate" which alone could quench the furious "blaze" of her light (144-48), then destroys her beauty and her life. The thought of the smallpox as God's means of translating two poets is wittily played, one meaning acting to control the other. Similarly, the comparison of such "equal" poets as Katherine Philips and Anne Killigrew is a control and an evaluation. Indeed, Anne Killigrew benefits as an artist by the comparison, and it is amusing to recall that Mrs. Philips was the "Matchless Orinda." Like her, Anne is matchless in individuality and as a person who is an artist. Such a current of wit will not be to everyone's taste, but the stanza serves more than one purpose. It settles the extent of Anne Killigrew's gifts. It *places* her: she belongs to the rank of poets in which Orinda appears, a judgment a long time in coming, in spite of earlier hints. It also enables us to treat hereafter the two related subjects as separate subjects: the formal subject, Anne Killigrew, can now be treated in terms of the loss of such a person to her family, and she may be freely praised with the hyperbole due on the occasion of death. The real subject, artistic genius, is similarly freed from its imperfect representation in Anne Killigrew. Finally, the mixed tone makes certain that the disaster of her death does not darken the triumph of artistic genius. Had Dryden dwelt upon the ideas and mood of the line, "Not wit, nor piety could fate prevent," the balance of the poem would have been lost, and the triumph of artistic genius would have yielded to the elegy for an individual.

The eighth stanza wittily describes the public loss of a beauty that had created beauty. In the next, Dryden conveys the loss more movingly in the person of Anne Killigrew's brother Henry, a naval captain and later admiral. The irony which had never been too far away in earlier parts of the poem, nor ever too close, and which had entered the poem

as an obvious factor in the wit of the preceding stanza, is now the means
at once of restraining and intensifying human feeling. The brother
should not pray for early return.

> Ah, generous youth, that wish forbear,
> The winds too soon will waft thee here!
> Slack all thy sails, and fear to come,
> Alas, thou know'st not, thou art wreck'd at home! (168-71)

He is urged to consult the propitious Pleiades, "the constellation which
is traditionally associated with the navigation of the seas . . . [and whose
name] is derived from the Greek verb *to sail*."[17]

Appropriate as it is, the celestial image takes our attention up from
the seas to "mid-air" on the Day of Judgment, when "the golden trump
shall sound, / To raise the nations underground." It is an extraordinary
passage. Henry Killigrew might sail home by his sister's star, so avoiding
being emotionally shipwrecked by her death. And the visual star image
yields to the celestial trumpet, to a sound affecting the personal and
political state of those buried "nations." Poets will hear the music first.
Since although born in time, artistic genius transcends time, the power of
the poets in being able to confer immortality entitles them to lead the
way to eternity.

> The sacred poets first shall hear the sound,   ⎫
> And foremost from the tomb shall bound,   ⎬
> For they are cover'd with the lightest ground;   ⎭
> And straight, with inborn vigor, on the wing,
> Like mounting larks, to the new morning sing. (188-92)

The whole passage is made to bear upon that last verb. The exercise of
song, of artistic power, is the proof that artistic genius is the least mortal
of human gifts, and nearest the divine creative power.

The poem *To the Pious Memory of the Accomplish'd Young Lady,
Mrs. Anne Killigrew* is about her and her gifts ("Excellent in the Two
Sister-Arts of Poesy and Painting"). It is able to speak to its subject as
Eleonora cannot. Rather than treating the "idea of a woman," however,
it celebrates Dryden's faith in the dignity and power of artistic genius.
By following the life and career of the daughter of a friend, Dryden is
able to pay personal tribute and to introduce his real subject of concern.
By questioning the abilities of Anne Killigrew in unobtrusive ways, he

is able to shift the subject to what more wholly interests him. By beginning with Anne's death and presumed translation to heaven, he is able to introduce the crucial celestial imagery: the imagery of stars and music in the first and last pairs of stanzas must be compared. Stars and music, music earthly and music divine—in such images, and in the magnificent power of the style of the *Ode* we have Dryden's own illustration of the faith he has affirmed in human capacity.

The Killigrew *Ode* appeared late in 1685 or early in 1686. It is Dryden's statement of faith in his art, whose ideal he and others may have at times abused. Apart from an informal epistle to Etherege and a poem dedicatory to a translation by a friend, this is the last poem he wrote before his other great statement of faith, *The Hind and the Panther*. It is worth reading the *Ode* as a preparatory affirmation for the religious poem, since in both he moves from the natural, the worldly, the imperfect in which art is perforce involved and in which it must even rejoice, to the transcendent supernatural realm into which (ordered) imagination in the *Ode* and (rational) faith only can take us. Both poems are somewhat uneven, either too tightly or too loosely woven, but both also fuse and order the three temporal concerns whose development marks most of his finest poetry. The mortal Anne Killigrew provides the basis for a subject in which he may feel personally involved. The power of art to gain immortality uses her as a symbol of that which arouses his strongest hopes for what may be done in time and may transcend it. And the eternal realm to which Anne Killigrew has gone subsumes by directing the other two. Death is a subject that may be referred to all three orders of time, but when Dryden considers it in their terms his funeral poems become celebrations of life. Such an emphasis does not imply an incapacity for grief. The poem to Oldham belies that. The emphasis does, however, suggest a degree of assurance in the relations between death and life or loss and achievement that marks most of his work. His prayer for the "mind" of the dead Charles II shows the balance.

IX

Amidst that silent show'r, the royal mind
  An easy passage found,
And left its sacred earth behind;
    Nor murmuring groan express'd, nor laboring sound,

Nor any least tumultuous breath:
Calm was his life, and quiet was his death.
Soft as those gentle whispers were,
In which th' Almighty did appear;
By the still voice the prophet knew him there.
That peace which made thy prosperous reign to shine,
That peace thou leav'st to thy imperial line,
That peace, O happy shade, be ever thine!

And in a later stanza of *Threnodia Augustalis* (1685), he celebrates the civilized gain of an era with a fervor much the same as that in the Anne Killigrew *Ode*.

XIII

As when the newborn Phœnix takes his way,
His rich paternal regions to survey,
Of airy choristers a numerous train
Attend his wondrous progress o'er the plain;
So, rising from his father's urn,
So glorious did our Charles return:
Th' officious Muses came along,
A gay harmonious choir, like angels ever young;
(The Muse that mourns him now, his happy triumph sung.)
Even *they* could thrive in his auspicious reign;
  And such a plenteous crop they bore
Of purest and well-winnow'd grain,
  As Britain never knew before.
Tho' little was their hire, and light their gain,
Yet somewhat to their share he threw;
Fed from his hand, they sung and flew,
Like birds of Paradise, that liv'd on morning dew.

These lyric passages from a historical ode, like the temporal concern of his lyrics, illustrate the extent to which his personal values led to exaltation. Love was only questionably admissible to him, because its eruptive strength of passion and will might subvert a harmonious scheme by raising the moment above meaningful time. It seems significant that Charles is praised for his "royal mind" and that his capacity for love is ignored. The ironies of the opening of *Absalom and Achitophel* have no place in triumph. Similarly Anne Killigrew is praised for the chasteness of her life and the powers of that artistic imagination in which she shared. It is in such affirmations that Dryden's lyric poetry finds its greatest strength and its clearest connection with other nondramatic poems.

Alexander's Feast (1697), the second of his poems for St. Cecilia's Day, is however the lyric poem that is likely to continue to give the widest pleasure. It is the poem Scott felt to be the greatest of its kind; and every reader must be astonished at the extraordinary show of easy, irrepressible vigor by a poet approaching seventy. It is probably the most evenly successful of all his poems. Even the shift in the ending is more one of musical key than of quality. Yet the reason for the general admiration of the poem is surely that although it possesses the concinnity of Dryden's greatest work with an unsurpassed realization of certain musical possibilities of the language, the richness for once does not draw upon ideas so much as upon an almost dramatic representation of action. It is, for Dryden, an easy poem. That the action represented is wittily deprecated and judged inferior to other ways of life does not seem to matter so much, since it does not really affect the way in which the poet and we share in the festive welter of human life. But the ironies must be heard.

The subjects of the poem, like those of its three rivals for our chief interest among the greater lyrics, are implied by its full title: *Alexander's Feast; Or, the Power of Music; An Ode in Honor of St. Cecilia's Day.* The occasion, the Feast of St. Cecilia on November 22nd, gives us the formal subject and heroine of the poem. "The costly feast" of the poem itself makes Alexander and human action the center of our attention. The "Power of Music" suggests the crucial role of Timotheus and the governing subject of the poem, which is the superiority of the artist to the man of action. It is not quite that simple. It would be better to say that the subject concerns the role played by art in determining our ideals of action and our actions themselves, as also the mingled detachment and involvement of the artist in the kinds of actions he associated with. Once more, as in a lesser way in the *Killigrew Ode*, the metaphor is that of music. The phrase in the title, "The Power of Music," scarcely differs from the phrase in the Purcell Ode, "The pow'r of harmony." The proper epigraph for the action of the poem was given by the earlier *Song for St. Cecilia's Day:* "What passion cannot music raise and quell!"

The first stanza is wholly festive and magnificent, if a bit given to orotundity in its periphrases for Alexander: "Philip's warlike son" and "The godlike hero." (Alexander's name is not once given in the poem itself.) In this beginning, action is crowned with ceremony and ritual. Alexander sits at center and "Aloft in awful state," with "His valiant peers . . . plac'd around," and "The lovely Thais, by his side." The dominant imagery is floral. The one suggestion of the laughing, good-natured, and altogether effective irony which Dryden develops later appears in the simile for Thais, who "Sate *like* a blooming Eastern bride." The directive power of the simile reminds us that she is a courtesan. Not that we much mind.

The second stanza introduces Timotheus by name, placing him yet higher than Alexander and surrounding him by the orchestral equivalent of Alexander's warriors. Touching his lyre into notes, he starts the music with a song summarized by subsequent lines. As in the Killigrew *Ode* and in some other poems, the opening lines of *Alexander's Feast* have provided an overture, and the succeeding stanza (or passage) leads to the chronological or historical beginning of the action. (Some poems of course omit the overture or combine it with the beginning of the temporal progression.) We are led now by Timotheus to history and biography, which will be developed in such a way that our attitudes and ideas follow the poet's through the account of action and on to a transcendent ending.

The action of the poem moves forward from the line, "The song began from Jove" (25), which means that the story of Alexander's life begins *with* Jove's rape of Olympia and her conception of Alexander, as well as that Timotheus' music begins *from* Jove, is divine in its power over human lives. From the line introducing the first music heard at the feast, the theme of the poem is evident in the treatment of origin. Timotheus' songs or his music take Alexander from birth (in this stanza) to the soldier's life and the military achievements of Alexander's youth (III and IV), to love (V), and to the ritual, religious responsibilities of the Greeks to their dead (VI). In each stanza Timotheus the musician plays upon Alexander, the instrument of his virtuosity. After the first stanza, only the fourth begins with consideration of Alexander ("Sooth'd with the sound, the king grew vain") rather than Timotheus. The irony directed towards "Philip's warlike son" is apparent enough in his being an instrument manipulated at will. But Dryden enjoys making it clearer. When in the second stanza everyone hears Timotheus tell of their leader's divinity on his father's side, an amusing enough myth in itself, they shout, "A present deity!"

"A present deity," the vaulted roofs rebound:
>   With *ravish'd* ears
>   The monarch hears,
>   *Assumes* the god,
>   *Affects* to nod,
And *seems* to shake the spheres. (36-41)

The italicized words need no more comment than the comparable later passages.

>   Sooth'd with the sound, the king grew vain;
>   Fought all his battles o'er again;
>   And thrice he routed all his foes; and thrice he slew the slain.
>   (66-68)

. . . .

>   With downcast looks the joyless victor sate,
>   Revolving in his alter'd soul
>   The various turns of chance below;
>   And, now and then, a sigh he stole;
>   And tears began to flow. (84-88)

. . . .

>   The prince, unable to conceal his pain,
>   Gaz'd on the fair
>   Who caus'd his care,
>   And sigh'd and look'd, sigh'd and look'd,
>   Sigh'd and look'd, and sigh'd again:
>   At length, with love and wine at once oppress'd,
>   The vanquish'd victor sunk upon her breast. (109-15)

What is important here is the high-spirited tone, the laughter of *Mac-Flecknoe* which echoes in these lines for almost the last time in Dryden's poetry. After a brief intermission (Alexander is able to raise himself from Thais while it is still dark), the "godlike hero" is awakened for the night attack upon "the Persian abodes, / And glitt'ring temples of their hostile gods." The religious emphasis leads on to St. Cecilia in the last stanza.

Our condescension, and Dryden's, to Alexander is the source of our affection for him. The man of action, perhaps the greatest man of action in the Western world, seems almost a child. We judge from a height like that of Timotheus, although without losing a genuine sympathy and concern. Only the dourest puritan would go unstirred by the hedonism of the first and third stanzas. The fate of the betrayed "Darius great and good" forecasts tragic possibilities for kings that a Jacobite like Dryden knew only too well. Moreover, just as the private world may seem at times maudlin and self-indulgent, so the public world of the ancients at times only brings the heart a wearied revulsion that excites within us a real sympathy for Alexander. It is of course Timotheus who is singing.

> "War," he sung, "is toil and trouble;   ;
> Honor, but an empty bubble;
>> Never ending, still beginning,
> Fighting still, and still destroying." (99-102)

Dryden recognizes that retreat to the private concerns of love may seem at times the only answer to such senseless activity.

Stanza VI is in some ways the most inspired of all. Timotheus arouses Alexander to the razing of the Persian buildings and the sacking of the temples. The rushing out into the night after the sleep following Alexander's satiety with Thais and wine is magnificently imagined:

> The princes applaud, with a furious joy;
> And the king seiz'd a flambeau with zeal to destroy;
>> Thais led the way,
>> To light him to his prey,
> And, like another Helen, fir'd another Troy. (146-50)

The effortless mastery of a great range of metric rhythms provides—in the changes from the all but too simple anapestic run, to the grave hesitation of the next two lines, and to the majesty of the last line—a rhythmical equivalent of the ideas, their complement in an experience conveying a conception of human nature and history.

For these lines do consign Alexander and Timotheus to history. It is past, the heroic action of the race, and so too those artistic ideals which had inspired it. The sudden distancing is a technique like that Keats was to use at the close of *The Eve of St. Agnes* in order to prevent the

---

PLATE V   *The Tuneful Voice was Heard from High.* From Robert Fludd's *Historia.* Reproduced by permission of The Huntington Library, San Marino, California.

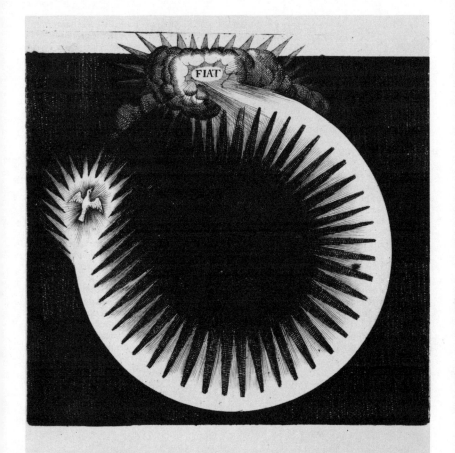

CAPUT. III.

De tribus prioribus creationis diebus.

IFFICILIS videtur cognitio dispositionis dierum ante Solis creationem factæ, cùm inter ipsos quoque Patres Theologos differentia haud exigua de dierum illorum natura oriatur. Nam *Basilius, Damascenus,* & alii *Græci* volunt, quod lux illa facta primo die causaverit diem per emissionem luminis, noctem verò per retractionem illius voluntate divina factam. Sed *Doctores*

G   *Latini*

Quid, mortalis, eras, et ubi, quum maxima terræ   Materies quam prima Chaos, cum machina formis   Sidera, cœlicolumq; chorus miratus inhæsit,
Fundamenta Deus posua? cœcumque resoluit   Est distincta suas? quam laudibus omnia nostris   Iubilaq; aligeri cecinerunt læta ministri?   Iob ca.38.

wrong sort of moral question from being raised. Dryden's is another purpose.

> Thus, long ago,
> Ere heaving bellows learn'd to blow,
> While organs yet were mute;
> Timotheus, to his breathing flute,
> And sounding lyre,
> Could swell the soul to rage, or kindle soft desire. (155-60)

The past, art and its action, yield to a finer art and action: "At last, divine Cecilia came, / Inventress of the vocal frame." (161-62). The distancing is necessary, as for Keats, but also as with *The Eve of St. Agnes*, it is not altogether satisfactory. The last few lines were objected to by Dr. Johnson for containing a false analogy. But the real problem is that St. Cecilia replaces Timotheus without our gaining a replacement for Alexander and his actions. If getting an angel down from heaven is all the gain from the loss of Alexander, most of us would be willing to admit St. Cecilia's moral and inventive superiority and long for the good old days of Alexander and Timotheus. Of course, it does not really matter that Dryden and Keats attempt so to manipulate our responses at the end. As long as they close in such a way that what has gone before is not really contradicted, we will read the poems with indulgence, enjoying what goes before for its picture of humanity or of young love.

Alexander's Feast is one of the several symptoms of Dryden's assertion of his own values, of the dignity of his art, and of his personal integrity during the years after the Revolution which had brought William and Mary (unlawfully in his view) to the throne. (One wonders whether had it been Charles or James on the throne instead of William, Dryden would have written such a line as, "The king seiz'd a flambeau with zeal to destroy.") In the two years following his conversion, Dryden wrote three of his major works—the Killigrew *Ode, The Hind and*

PLATE VI   *From Heavenly Harmony / This Universal Frame Began*. In illustration of Job, xxxviii: 4-7, partially quoted here. From the interleaved Bible, Vol. II, in the British Museum. Reproduced by permission of the Trustees of the British Museum.

the Panther, and the *Song for St. Cecilia's Day* (1687). Twice in these years, in *The Hind and the Panther* and the *Song,* he treated the creation of the world. In the Killigrew *Ode* and in the *Song* he twice gave a vision of the last days.[18] Both the poems themselves, and the fact that two of them are lyric and one a confession of faith, show that although his conversion was motivated by a desire to save his soul, its effect upon his writing was to invest his poetry with an even greater personal intensity than before. As, before his conversion, the Killigrew *Ode* is his first statement of faith—in himself as an artist—and as *The Hind and the Panther* sets forth his religious faith, so the *Song for St. Cecilia's Day* caps the affirmations by praising, in its controlling metaphor of harmony, the complex of the mortal, immortal, and eternal disposition of history. In no other poem was he able to set forth his most deeply held values with such economy and simple grace. Absorbing as it does a number of traditions of thought, the ode yet orders them with ease into a new structure.

The sequence of the poem is that of the temporal order with strong historical implications. The opening stanza deals with the creation of the world, an exalted moment whose intellectual and visual terms can be appreciated by examination of Plates V and VI with their biblical and harmonic bases. The concluding stanza, which is a "Grand Chorus" rather than the "tuneful voice" of God creating the world, deals with the dissolution of the earth and the Day of Judgment, as Plate VII shows in another biblical illustration. Creation and Judgment Day are at once parts of history and the hinges of eternity. History proper, the record of man's doings in time upon earth, begins just after the first stanza, whose last word, *Man,* leads into history and time; for as Plate VIII shows, in the traditional view of the harmony of the creation man is at once the lowest on the harmonic scale and the basic diapason or end of the creation. Similarly, this human or historical sequence of stanzas in the *Song* ends with the last word of the seventh stanza, *heav'n.* To anyone who takes the first and last stanzas seriously, the problem posed by the poem is not precisely structural, however. It is one of meaning and interest. Without question, the middle stanzas lack the interest and power of the others. Yet they fit into the purpose of the poem by contributing to its temporal development. On the analogy of other odes, including *Threnodia Augustalis,* we would expect the *Song* to deal with its subject in a temporal sequence, and the middle section therefore with man's life in historical time. So it does, metaphorically.

The metaphor of course relates to music: "What passion cannot Music raise and quell!" The raising of the passions by music involves theories of speculative music developed out of classical writings through neo-Platonic theories during the Renaissance. Since, as Plate VIII shows, man is himself a part of the celestial harmony, a properly struck chord should vibrate as much in him as in a tuning fork. Dryden's first metaphorical step was to relate passions to instruments, as earlier writers had tended to relate them to such classical, but otherwise altogether uncertain, modes as the Lydian or Dorian. By extension, the Trumpet and Drum easily represent not just martial passions, but also war. His next, and most important step, was to order the appearance of the instruments into something like a chronological or historical sequence. Jubal's invention of "the chorded shell" gives us the first musical instrument (Genesis iv. 21). It is succeeded by the trumpet and drum, the flute and the lute, the newly introduced violin, whose sound is "sharp" to English ears accustomed to the viol, and at last by the organ.

The sequence is clearly from the most simple and primitive to the most complex. It is close enough to actual chronology to represent human history in the terms Dryden likes to treat in his lyrics: an artistic progress piece representing civilization. But this sequence is evocative of another, suggesting a more purely human and evaluative historical development. The progress piece of musical instruments is paralleled by a progress piece of the passions, beginning with the primitive awe raised by Jubal's shell, proceeding through the martial and amatory passions aroused by appropriate instruments, to the "holy love" inspired by the organ. To stress the historical nature of the double sequence, Dryden has manipulated his tenses into a basic past-present-future sequence. Creation belongs to the past, history to the present, Judgment to the future.

It is not quite that simple. The organ is out of place, in order to let its invention provide the climax of the poem. More importantly, the second and seventh stanzas are in the past tense, although they are part of the historical sequence. The reason for this can be seen in their use of the Jubal typology and in the fact that only in these two stanzas are human individuals named. Orpheus and St. Cecilia are Jubal's descendants; at least the Vulgate describes him: "ipse fuit pater canentium cithara et organo," which is obviously of greater significance to the poem than the English version of 1611. Dryden names these individuals and makes them seem almost mythic. It is not their legendary character that is important, however. The significant thing is their human individuality by contrast to all else in the poem, their creativity, and their being set off by such devices as differing verb tenses. What Jubal, Orpheus, and St. Cecilia represent beyond their musical achievements is immortality, and this third order of time, growing from the historical, is used by Dryden on either side of the purely historical and mortal as a kind of parenthesis outside it and yet inside that yet greater parenthesis of the poem, the eternal.

This closely ordered pattern of the poem is very like the older ideas Dryden levies upon in suggesting hierarchies and intellectual harmonies. It even seems like them in their static quality, that timeless air so well shown by Plate VIII, or developed in terms of the *musica humana* and *musica mundana* discussed by John Hollander in *The Untuning of the Sky*.[19] This element in the poem is very like the typologies of sacred zoögraphy in *The Hind and the Panther* both in its static, timeless character and in being drawn from sources in Christian humanism and classical thought antedating the most vital forms of thought in the works of his contemporaries or even in those of earlier poets. But Dryden is not content with the static, as his double progress pieces show, and as can be shown further by his emphasis upon creation and dissolution, before or after which all was or shall be changed. By shifting attention from the timeless truth of the system to its origins, history, and end, Dryden has given the old views a new life and, it may be said, some modernity. His care in bringing together such divergent strains can best be appreciated by the function and fulfillment of the repeated line "What passion cannot Music raise and quell!" Part of the historical time sequence of the progress pieces, part also of a stanza dealing with man's immortal achievement, it seems only to govern the following five stanzas. Yet in none of these has Dryden properly treated (as he did later throughout *Alexander's Feast*) the powers of music to *quell* the passions. Only in the Grand Chorus are the passions quelled, but there climactically as the trumpet of Judgment Day sounds. This, the second trumpet of the poem, completes the progress piece of the instruments and passions by transcendence from mortality and immortality to eternity. In such fashion, the poem picks up a dynamism, for all its static traditional thought and symbolism. The structural movement leads to climax, taking even the movement of history yet farther on in a sudden upward surge. In the same fashion, the controlling metaphor of music in its symbolic embodiment of harmony is at once kept consistent and given a process of development.

Although it is remarkably simple in appearance, the *Song for St. Cecilia's Day* has very complex workings. The complexity involves not only structural articulation in itself but also the disposition of materials so traditional that it seems fruitless to seek individual sources. Yet some effort must be made to indicate the intellectual streams absorbed by Dryden's tides. The beginning of these beginnings lies somewhere in the unrecoverable past, but Plato's *Timaeus* is probably the most influential of all accounts apart from that in Genesis. As Benjamin Jowett said of the *Timaeus*, "In the supposed depths of this dialogue the neo-Platonists found hidden meanings and connections with the Jewish and Christian Scriptures, and out of them they elicited doctrines quite at variance with the spirit of Plato."[20] Even without the neo-Platonic shadows, the *Timaeus* contains a good deal of what may be called the dark side of Plato. Its long account of the creation is divided into two parallel accounts, the first dealing with the heavenly Creator and his creation of the universe. The second and shorter account of the creation focuses upon man. Although in this section the body and its diseases occupy the greatest space, the beginning emphasizes man's immortal soul, which involves reason, and his mortal soul, which consists of passion and desire. Matters would be very simple if we could assume this dialogue to be Dryden's source. Yet, as other presumed sources for the poem show, there are many analogues introducing religious elements with the musical metaphor.[21] The account of the creation in Job xxxviii (especially 7), itself affected by many layers of interpretation, is important to Dryden's conception of harmony as a creative force, as the accompanying illustration (Plate VI) of verses 6 and 7 shows. They read:

> Whereupon are the foundations [of the earth] fastened? or who laid the corners thereof; When the morning stars sang together and all the sons of God shouted for joy.

It is not easy to decide, much less with certainty, what were Dryden's Platonic, or neo-Platonic, sources. There is, however, an inherent probability that his going to Cambridge when those he later called "our dreaming Platonists" were flourishing was significant for his understanding of Platonism. The probability that he was influenced by the

Cambridge Platonists is strengthened by the nature of his references to Platonism. He held that "A Man must be deeply conversant in the Platonick philosophy" if he were to employ the spiritual "Machines" which he himself hoped to use in a modern epic, and that it was "the principles of Platonic philosophy as it is now Christianised" that necessarily must be drawn upon.[22] It is difficult to believe that he could have had in mind any men other than the Cambridge Platonists. It is not so much their doctrinal views which, apart from their belief in the supremacy of reason he came mostly to reject, as their way of figurative thought that appears to have remained influential in his mind. A passage from a sermon preached by Ralph Cudworth before the Commons in 1647 shows a kind of metaphorical thought like that in the *Song for St. Cecilia's Day*.

> Yet we are all this while, but like dead Instruments of Musick, that sound sweetly and harmoniously, when they are onely struck, and played upon from without, by the Musicians Hand, who hath the Theory and *Law* of Musick, *living* within himself. But the Second, the *living* Law of the Gospel, the *Law of the Spirit of Life* within us, is as if the *Soul of Musick*, should incorporate it self with the Instrument, and live in the Strings, and make them of their own accord, without any touch, or impulse from without, daunce up and down, and warble out their harmonies.[23]

In addition, as I suggested in an earlier chapter, Dryden's use of controlling metaphors to suggest steadfast values seems to involve Platonism: whether in satire or in panegyric, he compares the individual event or person in time to ideal values or beings above time. To the extent that what is involved is a distinction between a temporal and a "supernal realm," it would seem that Dryden is using Platonism in the very metaphorical act. I think it impossible to exclude an element of Platonism, but it must be added not only that it is a *use* that need not imply deep commitment, but also that numerous other elements are involved. The comparison of Charles II to David, to God the Father, and to God the Son in *Absalom and Achitophel* may owe something in its metaphorical practice to Platonic and neo-Platonic ways of thought. But the typologies themselves could come to a seventeenth-century poet from purely political sources or biblical glosses. Moreover, the *Song for St. Cecilia's Day* draws upon scientific thought that is owed to sources very different from Platonism. Neo-Epicureanism was of special importance (and itself influenced by other ways of thought) in giving more detailed explanation of the workings of the Creator in making the world.

Even an anti-Epicurean like John Fell, Bishop of Oxford, found it necessary to glance at Epicurus and Lucretius when he concerned himself with the origin of the world, its development in human history, and its dissolution—the three movements of Dryden's *Song*.

> But the truth is, the Origen of the World is a matter so notorious, that even *Epicurus* and his followers could not over-look it; and thought it a less absurdity to make a casual concourse of Atomes, produce all the powers, the motion, the beauty, and the order of the World, then to imagin it to have no beginning. And to this they were induced not only by attending the chain of causes . . . but more particularly, from the observation of those evident marks of newness, which appear every where thro-out the world; and which are substantially urg'd by the Epicurean Apostle *Lucretius* in his 5 Book. I mean the growth of Arts and Sciences, the plantation of Countries, the date of Histories, the Analogy of Languages, and the like.[24]

Creation, human history, and "The Character of the Last Daies," to use the title of Fell's sermon—these are obviously the *foci* of Dryden's poem. Fell indicates with perfect assurance the learned conception of the *De Rerum Natura* of Lucretius as a poem dealing with origin and development. How relevant this conception is to Dryden's poem can be judged by a perusal of Book V. The resemblance in detail can be shown by comparing with Dryden's first stanza the passage in Thomas Creech's translation of Lucretius giving the creation of the world in terms of Epicurean atomism.

> But yet no *glittering Sun*, no *twinckling Star*,
> No *Heaven*, no roaring *Sea*, no *Earth*, no *Air*,
> Nor anything *like these* did *then* appear,
> But a *vast Heap*; and from this mighty Mass
> Each part retir'd, and took his *proper* place;
> *Agreeing* Seeds combin'd, each *Atom* ran
> And sought his *like*, and so the Frame *began*.[25]

Shortly thereafter Lucretius develops, as Fell indicates, what is in effect a progress piece version of human history (Creech, pp. 168-84).

Neither Fell, Creech, nor John Evelyn—who was the first to translate Lucretius into English substantially—is an Epicurean. Dryden is not either, but the adaptation of certain neo-Epicurean ideas marks the writing of most of his career as we know it. (Of course he also translated parts of Lucretius.) It is perfectly easy to show that most of the philosophical thought in Dryden's poem can be found in writings of his friend Dr. Walter Charleton (not that it can be found nowhere else). For example, the combination in the first stanza of a theory of creation involving both the atoms described by Lucretius and the four elements ("cold, and hot, and moist, and dry") must strike some readers as being somewhat eclectic, to put it no higher. Charleton has explained the relation between atoms and elements in his *Physiologia Epicuro-Gassendo-Charltoniana: or a Fabrick of Science Natural, Upon the Hypothesis of Atoms* (London, 1654):

> Patrons of Atoms do not . . . deny the Existence of those four Elements [which he terms Heat, Cold, Humidity, and Siccity] admitted by most Philosophers: but allow them to be *Elementa Secundaria*, Elements Elementated, *i.e.* consisting of Atoms, as their First and Highest Principles. (p. 100)

The very order of Dryden's account follows the temporal logic here: first atoms, then elements. (And since they proceed from the fiat of God's "tuneful voice," the whole is under Christian control.) Charleton shows how the neo-Epicurean doctrine could also be accommodated to Christianity of a kind. For although he is a proficient in neo-Epicureanism,

> as a proficient in the Sacred School of *Moses,* I may answer; that the fruitful *Fiat* of God [Dryden's "tuneful voice"], out of the Tohu, or infinite space of Nothing, called up a sufficient stock of the First Matter, for the fabrication of the World in the most excellent Form, which he had Idea'd in his own omniscient intellect from Eternity. (p. 103)

PLATE VII   *Music Shall Untune the Sky*. As in the *Song for St. Cecilia's Day*, the trumpet sounds; the dead and living are altered; and, to the right, "this crumbling pageant" is "devoured." The inscription is taken from Matthew xxv: 31-32. From the interleaved Bible, Vol. IV, in the British Museum. Reproduced by permission of the Trustees of the British Museum.

Cum venerit filius hominis tunc congregabuntur ante eum omnes gentes terræ et seperabit
iustos ab iniustis sicut separat pastor oues ab hoedis ﹔ G. L. fode excudebat

M. d. vos inuentor

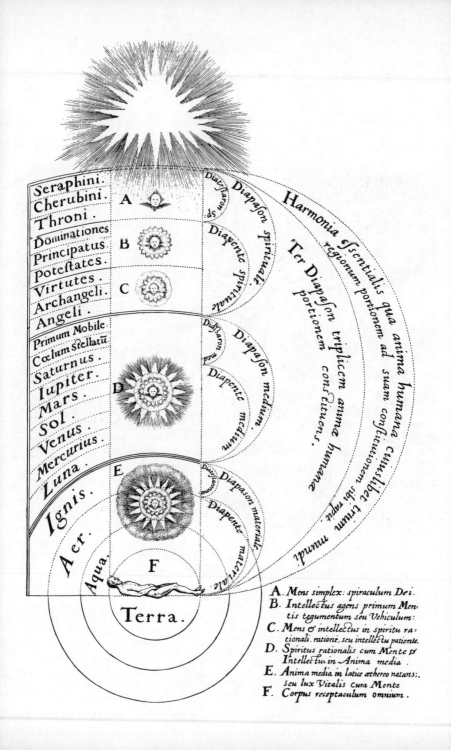

Seraphini.
Cherubini.
Throni.
Dominationes
Principatus.
Potestates.
Virtutes.
Archangeli.
Angeli.
Primum Mobile.
Cœlum stellatū
Saturnus.
Iupiter.
Mars.
Sol.
Venus.
Mercurius.
Luna.
Ignis.
Aer.
Aqua.
Terra.

A
B
C
D
E
F

Diapason
Diapason spiritualis
Diapente spiritualis
Diapason
Diapason medium.
Diapente medium.
Diapason materialis
Diapente materiali

Harmonia essentialis qua anima humana cuiuslibet regionum portionem ad suam constitutionem sibi rapit.

Ter Diapason triplicem animæ humanæ portionem constituens.

A. *Mens simplex: spiraculum Dei.*
B. *Intellectus agens primum Mentis tegumentum seu Vehiculum:*
C. *Mens & intellectus in spiritu rationali. ratione, seu intellectu patiente.*
D. *Spiritus rationalis cum Mente & Intellectu in Anima media.*
E. *Anima media in latice æthereo natans; seu lux Vitalis cum Mente*
F. *Corpus receptaculum omnium.*

We recall the stanza from the conclusion of the progress-piece in *Annus Mirabilis*, on the Royal Society:

> O truly Royal! who behold the law
>   And rule of beings in your Maker's mind;
> And thence, like limbecs, rich ideas draw,
>   To fit the level'd use of humankind. (661-64)

And we observe that Charleton, too, conceives of a God whose essence is wisdom or reason, rather than will, and see that by using God's "tuneful voice" as the creative force in the *Song*, Dryden has managed to bring together the divine "*Fiat*," "omniscient intellect," and a sense of action in words sung to music and beginning the sustaining harmony of the universe.

In 1687 Dryden was far more orthodox than Dr. Charleton in the fifties and sixties. Yet as Charleton shows, there is available to Dryden a strain of neo-Epicureanism far different from that which came into English thought with libertinism at the same period. This strain of Charleton's at least was consonant with neo-Platonism, Aristotelianism, and Christian orthodoxy. Charleton may have been eclectic (Dryden certainly was, in common with other poets), but he was aware of the questions that might be asked of a proponent of neo-Epicureanism. He was also aware of the possibility of heresy in the doctrine. And yet he felt free to adapt it to his own Christian belief, which would seem to be proto-Deist. The best evidence of his defense of himself is his translation, and selective espousal, of *Epicurus's Morals* (London, 1656). Like Charleton, Dryden may have found even Epicurean heresy adaptable to orthodoxy; in Charleton's prefatory apology (sig. b4r), one group of those denying the immortality of the soul is described in terms that seem to gloss the famous conceit in the Grand Chorus of the *Song for St. Cecilia's Day*. This group

---

PLATE VIII   *The Diapason Closing Full in Man.* From Robert Fludd's *Historia*. Dryden's *diapason* is shown here in its harmonic and philosophical implications. Reproduced by permission of The Huntington Library, San Marino, California.

conceived of the soule of man to be only a certain harmony, not of Musicall sounds, but a contemperation of parts, humours, and qualities, and consequently, that as of Musicall Harmony, nothing can remain after the sounds are vanished, so of the soul nothing can remain, after death hath destroyed that harmonious Contemperation of parts, humours, and qualities from whence it did result.

"The living [shall] die." It was Dryden's own orthodoxy that furnished the other more important half of the conceit: "The dead shall live."

The musical metaphor of harmony is without doubt more orthodox in its associations than is neo-Epicureanism. Equally, neo-Epicureanism is by far the more capable of application to the physical, scientific world. Dryden had no need to agree with all that Charleton said, any more than Charleton with all of the tenets of neo-Epicureanism.* An adaptor as always of a wide variety of learned material, Dryden shaped the dissident elements into his own firmly held orthodox harmony of ideas. This is as true of his conceptions of time and eternity as of other matters in the *Song for St. Cecilia's Day*. Once again, Dr. Charleton may be taken to epitomize scientific or philosophic thought in the century. He distinguishes between the two orders of time in "Of Time and Eternity" in his *Physiologia*. If time is an infinite succession, how does it differ from eternity? To give but one of his conclusions: "*Time* and *Eternity* differ from each other, in no other respect, than that Eternity is an indefinite duration, and Time . . . a certain *part* of the infinite duration, commencing at the Creation, and determining at the Dissolution of the World."[26] The resemblance with Dryden's poem needs no stress.

Neo-Platonism, traditions of speculative music, earlier poetic treatments of harmony, glosses upon crucial passages of Scripture, biblical iconography, and neo-Epicurean scientific thought are drawn into the ode and shaped, under the controlling metaphor of harmony, as also by the developing sequence of Creation, progress-pieces, and Judgment Day, into the three orders of time to which Dryden recurred throughout his career. The historical or mortal; the immortal rising from, yet above, that; and the eternal, teleological orders—these are fundamental to his thought. His songs and the poem on Oldham emphasize the first, the

---

* Dryden does disagree on details. In *Physiologia*, I, ii. Sect. 2., Dr. Charleton rejects the plurality of worlds, concluding that "this World is the Universe." As *Eleonora*, 79-82, shows, Dryden was clearly excited by the idea.

funeral poems (including that on Oldham) treat the second, and the major odes develop the third. It can be seen that his lyric poetry gives, as it were, musical versions of some of the major themes of his plays and his nondramatic poetry, apart from the lyrics. The songs emphasize forces that captivate and mislead the will, as their plays show in larger contexts; and, whatever the pleasures of anticipation, the songs commonly show the reason of regret.

In their emphasis upon immortal achievement, the funeral poems necessarily dwell more upon praise than upon mourning. Men and women whose lives are remarkable for the "doing of great deeds and the speaking of great words" are given their public due for personal achievement. The tone is public, with merely private concerns cancelled by the fact of death. To the degree, however, that Oldham and Anne Killigrew are but mortal—that is, not immortal—Dryden mourns death as a loss. The tension between their private mortality and their personal immortality is such that it requires considerable tact on his part to set the balance properly. The tension and balance are set in *Alexander's Feast* by the provision of three heroes—Alexander, Timotheus, and St. Cecilia—with Alexander himself retaining a poetic tension in the vectors of his public grandeur and his private weaknesses. The enduring regard readers have felt for the poem to Oldham and for *Alexander's Feast* suggests that Dryden reaches the widest audience and strikes most deeply into human experience when the tension is strongest, when the mortal and private best serve as considerable counterpoise to the immortal. Certainly the ode on Purcell pales beside these poems. Yet there will always remain some of us who prefer the greater sublimity of the *Killigrew Ode* and the *Song for St. Cecilia's Day* in their concern with eternity. The concern with the three modes of mortal history, immortality, and eternity in these two poems undoubtedly created unusual tensions and the need for extremely complex balances, as also thematic movements, that had their effect in an unevenness not to be found in the poem on Oldham or in *Alexander's Feast*. The choice between them is probably unnecessary, but since it has always been made, it can be characterized as one between a consistency of poetic realization with a wealth of human detail and warmth, and a grandeur of style accompanied by unevenness and a certain remoteness from human detail. Something of the same choice is offered between *Absalom and Achito-*

phel and *The Hind and the Panther.* If it is unfortunate that the choice should be thought necessary, the alternatives are such that neither choice need cause regret.

Of all Dryden's lyric poems, the songs are the least substantial. They give their due pleasure but, unlike the plays which include them, they do not raise important issues in important ways. Some of their interest and most of their limitations stem from the way they create a real world inhabited by literary shepherds, or a pastoral world in which real men and women find their humanity curtailed. If Dryden had been able to crown his career as he had wished, it would in effect have been by developing the narrative methods of *Annus Mirabilis* into a romance epic on the subject of Arthur or Edward the Black Prince.[27] He would have sought to give the epic new life by modifying the tradition of Tasso and Spenser with history.* Had he done so, the songs would seem even less important. But circumstances under Charles, James, and William and Mary forestalled such hopes, denied that dream he shared with earlier Renaissance writers. If he found it possible to give the dream a certain reality by his translation of Virgil (1697), in the closing years of his life, the epic clearly lay beyond his powers and outside the possibilities afforded by circumstance. His interests in human action, in narrative poetry, and in raising an admirable large structural edifice remained, however. And out of these interests grew the last great work of his life, the *Fables* (1700). With that combination of translations and original poems done, only the "Secular Masque" for *The Pilgrim* (1700), a last lyric reviewing his century, lay between him and death. But he could look back upon at least partially fulfilled hopes to write a great narrative poetry. This, with his fully realized creation of lyric poetry, marks him as a writer imbued with the ideals of the late Renaissance. If they showed nothing else, his lyrics would yet reveal the fact that he was wholly a part of his century and not of the next.

* Dryden's historical plans are clear from his saying, "I would have taken occasion to represent my living friends and patrons of the noblest families, and also shadowed the events of future ages, in the succession of our imperial line." The temporal scheme is that discussed throughout this chapter.

Thematic Variation and Structure in *Fables*

CHAPTER VIII

He match'd their beauties, where they most excel;
Of love sung better, and of arms as well.
—*To the Duchess of Ormond*

Dryden's poetry includes nearly 38,500 translated lines (his prose, almost two thousand pages), and it has been said that "For every line of original nondramatic poetry he wrote two lines of translation from a foreign poet."[1] Among the translations, the *Virgil* (1697) holds pride of place, but Ovid occupied him throughout his career, and he translated as well all of Persius, much of Juvenal and Lucretius, and some of Horace. From Greek he rendered parts of the *Iliad* and Theocritus; from Italian, Boccaccio; and from French, various writers of plays and prose. It appears that he also read Dutch and Spanish, although the evidence is not wholly clear. In sheer bulk, his translations demand consideration in any study of his poetry. Their quality is such that every modern critic who has studied them in detail has come away at least with admiration and commonly with the conviction that they are the greatest English versions of their authors. The theories of translation Dryden espoused and put into practice have long been praised. To be sure, these are judgments requiring confirmation or qualification through continuing study, which alone can arrive at answers to such questions as that of his command of Spanish or details of his rendering of Boccaccio. Yet we shall always wish to understand the larger features of his translations—the interpretations of authors given by translations, the dominant themes Dryden impressed upon the originals, and the virtues or defects as poetry evident in Dryden's versions. These

questions are best studied in the *Virgil* or the *Fables,* his largest entities
as translations. Views of the *Virgil* have varied considerably over the
past three centuries, but the attention to it in our own time has praised
Dryden as much for the larger as for the more detailed qualities. The
Fables has benefited less from close examination but, on the other hand,
it has been held in persistently high regard. All have felt that the continuing maturation, or mellowing, of Dryden's style culminated in a
special warmth, in an old man's benignity and practiced ease.

Although the *Fables* is as fitting a crown to half a century of poetry
as any writer might wish, many who subscribed to the sumptuous volume
must have been astonished in 1700 to discover Mr. Dryden arguing in his
fine rambling way that Chaucer was a greater writer than Ovid or
Boccaccio. The Preface is at once personal and critical, modest and
proud. It is unmistakably characteristic.

> By the mercy of God, I am already come within twenty years of
> ["fourscore and eight"]; a cripple in my limbs, but what decays are
> in my mind the reader must determine. I think myself as vigorous as
> ever in the faculties of my soul, excepting only my memory, which is
> not impaired to any great degree; and if I lose not more of it, I have
> no great reason to complain. What judgment I had increases rather
> than diminishes; and thoughts, such as they are, come crowding in so
> fast upon me, that my only difficulty is to choose or to reject; to run
> them into verse, or to give them the other harmony of prose.[2]

Here is that other harmony he speaks of, and here too that tendency to
speak of John Dryden. "He may be thought to mention himself too
frequently," Dr. Johnson said; "but while he forces himself upon our
esteem, we cannot refuse him to stand high in his own."[3]

In any other writer we should find it odd to discover such personal
revelation in the introduction to a volume consisting largely of translations. Not the least important basis of Dryden's importance as critic
and translator, however, is the degree to which his personality does
become engaged with that of the writer by whom he is so much taken.
One cannot but be amused by the way in which he time and time again
discovers that the writer whom he is studying at the moment has a
soul more like his own than any other. In the Preface, it is not Ovid,
Chaucer, or Boccaccio who so engages him, but Homer. Plainly, the
first book of the *Iliad* was launched in the *Fables* as the first move in a
plan to translate the whole. At the same time, the Preface in effect bids

farewell to Ovid, who most often throughout his career engages his attentions as translator, and in its most memorable passages inaugurates Chaucerian criticism.[4]

Everything about the *Fables* has the marks, not of translation as it is commonly conceived, but of deep personal involvement. The nature of such an engagement with the authors translated in the *Fables* can be understood by giving added weight to Dryden's figure of *harmony*. The word is one which appears repeatedly in his poetry, and it is itself an apt conception of the character of his poetry at its best. It conveys a unity achieved from highly diverse elements, a concept of order which is dynamic rather than fixed, and, as the poems upon music reveal, a symbol of creative energy. It would be very uncharacteristic indeed if a collection that engaged him personally to the degree the Preface reveals he was engaged in the *Fables* did not have a special, original harmony.

To urge so much is not to deny that our impression of the *Fables* is apt to be one of variety to the point of disorder. If here, too, there is God's plenty, it is not at once manifest what the divine intentions may have been. There are two complimentary poems, one to the Duchess of Ormond, the other to John Driden of Chesterton. There are two poems written earlier: *Alexander's Feast* and *The Monument to a Fair Maiden Lady*. There are five translations of Chaucerian poems, including *The Flower and the Leaf*, then still thought canonical. There are three stories from Boccaccio, the first book of the *Iliad*, and eight selections from Ovid's *Metamorphoses*. It is small wonder that some of Dryden's best editors, notably Scott and Christie, set about to furnish a scheme that they thought made better sense. Scott put the poem to John Driden among a group of epistles, the poem to the Duchess of Ormond under the heading, "Fables.—Tales from Chaucer," as an introductory piece. Chaucer appears in one of the volumes of poems, as does Boccaccio, under "Fables.—Translations from Boccace." Ovid and Homer appear in the volumes of "Translations," where they are brought together with Dryden's other translations from their works at different periods of his career. If such an arrangement is itself confusing, the motive behind it is not far to seek. Scott must have wondered why Dryden did not employ in the *Fables* a more natural order of poems, according to their original authorship, if nothing else. The question is a fair one. But one cannot come to the *Fables* written at the end of Dryden's life without the strong conviction that, whatever his faults of carelessness with details, his powers of design are not to be questioned. It is a sound principle that with him, as with any other poet, we should assume he knew what he was doing. Dr. Johnson put it higher: "Perhaps no nation ever produced a writer that enriched his language with such variety of models."[5] The problem is to discover what variety of model, and then what dynamism of order, Dryden gave to his *Fables*.

That Dryden sought some unifying conception cannot be doubted, as his title shows. It suggests, for example, that the Chaucerian poems are not to be regarded as "tales" in distinction to the poems of Ovid. In fact, in a letter to Pepys dated 14 July 1699, Dryden informs this devotee of Chaucer that he is translating "Fables from Ovid," "Novills from Boccace," and "Tales from Chaucer."[6] Since in the Preface to the *Fables* he speaks of the "ribaldry" in many of Chaucer's "novels,"[7] it can be seen that in one instance or another he has referred to the Chaucerian poems as tales, novels, and fables. That the generic term finally chosen was, on this slim evidence, merely the most attractive, or possibly the most inclusive, may be conceded. But as further consideration shows, it was perfectly natural for him to seek a single term to encompass his variety of materials.

Although most of the poems in the *Fables* are those which we would readily classify as narratives, there are some considerable exceptions. The two complimentary poems, certain passages added by Dryden to his originals, and the more philosophical selection from the last, or fifteenth, book of the *Metamorphoses*—"Of the Pythagorean Philosophy"—do not fit with modern notions of narrative poetry at all. His conception was, however, that of the *narratio* of the Roman rhetoricians. Cicero, Quintilian, and others are at one in distinguishing three subtypes of *narratio*. There was *fabula*, "which is not merely not true but has little resemblance to the truth" (non a veritate modo sed etiam a forma veritatis remota). There was *argumentum*, "which, though not true, has yet a certain verisimilitude" (falsum sed vero simile). And there was *historia*, "exposition of actual fact" (in qua est gestae rei expositio).[8] Each type was associated with a literary form, and each was connected with the rhetorician's art. Of the three, *argumentum* is the most protean. Associated especially with comedy, it was constantly slipping into other technical and general meanings in the writings of the Roman rhetoricians themselves.[9]

For our purposes the tendency of *argumentum* to become associated with argument and exposition is the most important. Since the term is used in the rhetorical manuals, it was inevitable that they should suggest its connection with persuasive and dissuasive writing. Such was the reason for introducing the discussion to begin with. Similarly, ideas connected with the root meaning for *arguere*, "maintain" or "prove," kept alive the expository sense of "argument." It is the expository sense that includes the philosophical passages added by Dryden or treated by Ovid in his last book—which otherwise seems no more than an expository appendage to narratives; and the rhetorically persuasive that accounts for the panegyrics upon the Duchess of Ormond and John Driden, as well as for various satiric additions to a number of poems in the *Fables*. Once again it is possible to see how, given three terms—now fable, argument, and history—Dryden chose for his title the one that was the most attractive and usable. More importantly, it is clear that the entire range of poems in the *Fables* is comprehended in the traditional conception of narrative. It is in this quite clear and basic sense that we may speak without doubt of the unity of conception of the whole.

Of course, such a unity in no way accounts for the appearance of utter casualness in the order of the *Fables*. It is small wonder that Scott took matters into his own hands when he observed, at one juncture, the tale of the incest of *Cinyras and Myrrha* followed by *The First Book of Homer's Ilias*, and that by *The Cock and the Fox*, Dryden's version of "The Nun's Priest's Tale"; or, at another stage, Dryden moving his reader from *The Speeches of Ajax and Ulysses out of Ovid* to the *Wife of Bath, Her Tale* and thence to *Of the Pythagorean Philosophy*. Yet the very appearance of disorder should lead us to ask about Dryden's purpose. His *Miscellanies*, with their more conventional organization are not called *Fables*, nor is this called as perhaps it might have been, a miscellany. (Yet even the miscellanies, and especially the second, *Sylvae*, show a far from casual arrangement.) To discover his means of integration it is necessary only to ask the question and to read through the *Fables* in order, preferably with the original texts to show the nature of Dryden's additions and changes. What one discovers is a connection of the separate fables on the basis of the shared emphases of juxtaposed works. Such connections vary—they are chiefly those of subject, motif, and situation—and in any event the *Fables* is not a completely integrated whole. But the arrangement is not casual, and there is no disorder. It is, moreover, beyond dispute that the connecting of one fable to another sometimes leads to a series treating of a subject like love, and to a yet larger reiteration of subjects and themes into a developing whole.

The nature of the connections established between one poem and the next is best shown by their author. The poem *To Her Grace the Duchess of Ormond with the Following Poem of Palamon and Arcite* suggests in its very title some manner of relationship between the two. Its first thirty-nine lines establish a mythical or historical connection between it and Dryden's version of "The Knight's Tale." It is a historical metaphor of the kind he loved so much.

> O true Plantagenet, O race divine,
> (For beauty still is fatal [destined] to the line,)
> Had Chaucer liv'd that angel face to view,
> Sure he had drawn his Emily from you;
> Or had you liv'd to judge the doubtful right,
> Your noble Palamon had been the knight;
> And conqu'ring Theseus from his side had sent
> Your gen'rous lord, to guide the Theban government.
> Time shall accomplish that; and I shall see
> A Palamon in him, in you an Emily. (30-39)

The last two lines could scarcely be clearer. The preceding show that as the Duchess is to be read into Emily (and *vice versa*), so is the Duke into Palamon. (Dryden refrains from speaking of an Arcite for obvious reasons.) What is especially interesting is the unspoken identification of "conqu'ring Theseus" with William III. Since Ormond was appointed by William (as his grandfather, "Barzillai," had been by earlier kings on three occasions) to high post in Ireland, time would indeed see him go to guide the Irish government, the Thebes to England's Athens. The separation suggested here alludes to the fact that the Duchess had preceded Ormond to Ireland. Dryden regrets the loss of so remarkably beautiful a woman, but is sure that her famous beauty has removed the agonies of the Irish civil wars.

> The waste of civil wars, their towns destroy'd,
> Pales unhonor'd, Ceres unemploy'd,
> Were all forgot; and one triumphant day
> Wip'd all the tears of three campaigns away.
> Blood, rapines, massacres, were cheaply bought,
> So mighty recompense your beauty brought. (64-69)

The lines provide a constellation of varied meanings. The panegyric is obvious, as also the sympathy for Irish suffering. *Pales* and *Ceres* continue the Athens-Thebes context, and the conclusion recalls the famous passage in the *Iliad* where the beauty of Helen seemed ample recompense to the suffering Trojans. Ireland is still ancient Thebes.

Such a set of analogies is one that we are meant to carry into the opening section at least of *Palamon and Arcite,* where we discover that Dryden's Theseus, once again a conquerer, is far more cruel, and responsible, in war than Chaucer's "worthy duc." The passage in Chaucer (A 1001-1011) is little more than a transition from his opening scene to Palamon and Arcite.

> Whan that this worthy duc, this Theseus,
> Hath Creon slayn, and wonne Thebes thus,
> Stille in that feeld he took al nyght his reste,
> And dide with al the contree as hym leste.
>   To ransake in the taas of bodyes dede,
> Hem for to strepe of harneys and of wede,
> The pilours diden bisynesse and cure
> After the bataille and disconfiture.
> And so bifel that in the taas they founde,
> Thurgh-girt with many a grevous blody wounde,
> Two yonge knyghtes liggynge by and by . . .

The equivalent passage in Dryden is longer and grimmer (I, 123-42). I must stress that here, as elsewhere in this chapter, comparison or specific comment indicates a debt by Dryden to the original author, and where such signs of indebtedness are lacking, the passages are Dryden's wholly or in significant part. The amount of change he introduces is truly remarkable. He begins,

> The process of the war I need not tell,
> How Theseus conquer'd, and how Creon fell;
> Or after, how by storm the walls were won,
> Or how the victor sack'd and burn'd the town . . .
>   Thus when the victor chief had Creon slain,
> And conquer'd Thebes, he pitch'd upon the plain
> His mighty camp, and, when the day return'd,
> The country wasted, and the hamlets burn'd,
> And left the pillagers, to rapine bred,
> Without control to strip and spoil the dead.
>   There, in a heap of slain, among the rest
> Two youthful knights they found beneath a load oppress'd . . .

Theseus is made the active force and is in effect given responsibility for the terrible wasting of the country. It is very much the "conqu'ring" Theseus of the poem to the Duchess—a brilliant and merciless soldier. The epithet, "conqu'ring," is twice echoed in the passage from *Palamon and Arcite* and, with the identification, makes Dryden's estimate of William clear. He is a soldier, and the only right to the English throne that he can justly claim is that of William I. The title of conqueror is one which only a very few of William's supporters cared to give him, since in common royalist theory it is the poor best that a usurper could claim.

The connection between the first two poems is, then, very clear and surprisingly detailed, although it would be unwise to seek a thorough-going contemporary analogy in *Palamon and Arcite*. To attempt as much would be to strain a most delicate fabric. Not even Dryden could risk a systematic and unfavorable picture of William. Moreover, it seems doubtful that he would have wished to, even though his *Palamon and Arcite* connects at its other end with the poem to *John Driden*, which is laden with discussion of the proper principles of English constitutional theory. It is enough to make a connection, allow the story its autonomous play, and seek a connection with another story. General subjects and themes might be raised repeatedly, but it would have been undesirable and no doubt impossible to develop a systematic historical metaphor like that in *Absalom and Achitophel* through twenty varied stories.

There are other kinds of evidence, or symptoms, of Dryden's concern to integrate the several "fables" into one whole. That his mind was occupied with such matters can be understood from the headnotes he supplies to many of the selections from Ovid. In these he seems to feel a strong necessity to relate his selection to what has gone before in the *Metamorphoses*. *The Twelfth Book of Ovid His Metamorphoses* has a long note, "Connection to the End of the Eleventh Book." *Ceyx and Alcyone* has a headnote with a yet more revealing, if more confusing, head: "Connection of This Fable with the Former." What is meant is not the connection of *Ceyx and Alcyone* with *Theodore and Honoria* in Dryden's own *Fables* but with the preceding story in Ovid. Yet it is not such symptoms but comparison of the original with the translated texts that reveals the best evidence of the methods and purposes of Dryden's integration. A very simple example can be found at the beginning of *The Flower and the Leaf*, which follows *Ceyx and Alcyone*. Ovid's story ends with the metamorphosis of Ceyx and Alcyone into kingfishers breeding in the halcyon winter days. She is

> A wintry queen: her sire at length is kind,
> Calms ev'ry storm, and hushes ev'ry wind;
> Prepares his empire for his daughter's ease,
> And for his hatching nephews smooths the seas. (496-99)

In the first stanza of the original of *The Flower and the Leaf* Dryden found:

> When that Phœbus his chair of gold so hie
> Had whirlid up the sterrie sky aloft,
> And in the Bole was entrid certainly,
> When shouris sote of rain descendid soft,
> Causing the ground fele timis and oft
> Up for to give many an wholesome air,
> And every plain was yclothid faire . . .

Was there not some possibility of devising a transition from the winter of Ovid's poem to the spring of the next? Dryden's first nineteen lines develop the original stanza into some of his loveliest nature poetry, but not until the transition has been made. (Material from the *original* is italicized.)

> Now turning from the wintry signs, *the sun*
> His course exalted thro' the Ram had run,
> And, *whirling up the skies, his chariot drove*
> *Thro' Taurus* and the lightsome realms of love. (1-4)

The transition, and its deliberate development, are obvious. Such obvious transitions may be called linkings as opposed to the more usual conections made between subject matter, motif, and character which constitute the chief means of integrating in the *Fables*.

How these means function can be shown partly by negative reasoning. Dryden had translated more of the eleventh book of the *Metamorphoses* than is in the *Fables*. He uses Ovid's lovely story of Ceyx and Alcyone (*Meta.*, XI, 410-748), placing it between *Theodore and Honoria* and *The Flower and the Leaf*. Although tragic, *Ceyx and Alcyone* is sufficiently idealistic to make the transition beautifully. But Dryden also translated the story immediately following his "Ceyx and Alcyone." This is his "Æsacus transform'd into a Cormorant," (*Meta.*, XI, 749-95). The translation is very spirited and witty, but Dryden did not include it in the *Fables*. Had it followed *Ceyx and Alcyone*, its tale of Æsacus' love for the nymph Hesperie, her flight and death from snakebite, his attempted suicide, and his transformation into a cormorant would have broken the tonal and substantitive transition to *The Flower and the Leaf*. The sequence would have been interrupted. It is possible that Dryden translated the story of Æsacus at some earlier date. If so, however, it is strange that he had not published earlier. It is in fact one of his few posthumously published poems, printed in *Ovid's Metamorphoses in Fifteen Books. Translated by the Most Eminent Hands* (1717). It appears to be a left-over from the *Fables*, short enough to have been copied down or received among Dryden's papers. In any event, every reader can see how beautifully the *Fables* now moves from *Theodore and Honoria* to *Ceyx and Alcyone* to *The Flower and the Leaf*, as also how awkward the inclusion of the story of Æsacus would be.

It is possible to examine in considerable detail each poem as a transition between those that precede and follow. But this is something readers will choose to do for themselves. A schematic résumé will be less attractive but simpler and sufficient here. What follows is, therefore, a table of the poems and their connections, emphasizing those of subject and of a mechanical nature. The larger thematic relations will be discussed subsequently.

Duchess of Ormond

1-39, 64-69 develop the identification of the Duchess of Ormond with Chaucer's Emily, of the Duke with Palamon, and of William III with Theseus. Thebes becomes Ireland, Athens England.

Palamon and Arcite

CONNECTION. The identifications (see preceding) developed in terms of Theseus (William) and the plundering conquest of Thebes (Ireland) are treated in 123-40, a passage altered by Dryden. Also, the inter-related subjects of arms and love introduced in the *Ormond* are explored throughout this poem.

To my Honour'd Kinsman, John Driden

CONNECTION. The issue of the happy life, the blessed mode of living. *Palamon and Arcite* shows the search for it in arms and love, with the necessity of reconciliation to life's tragedy (see *Palamon*, III, 1024-97). *Kinsman* shows that not the active but the country life, not arms but civic duty, not war but peace, provide the best possibilities for the happy life. *Link*. Use of the word *blest* or related forms in the last 4 lines of *Palamon* (added by Dryden) and first of *Kinsman*.

Meleager and Atalanta

CONNECTION. The hunt of the Calydonian Boar here relates to the hunting of the *Kinsman* (50-66), whose prey is called (63) the "emblem of human life." The hunt of the boar is here called a war (179), and the two hunts are so set off as metaphors of peaceful and warlike life.

Sigismunda and Guiscardo

CONNECTION. The story offers another pair of lovers and their trials, with the tyrant Tancred paralleling Althea and Diana in the former poem in wishing to exact revenge on a son and a race of people. The issue of justice and punishment is raised in the story over these matters, and Dryden adds the marriage of Sigismunda and Guiscardo.

Baucis and Philemon

CONNECTION. The examination of a pair in love continues, now in an idyll of marriage, for which the addition of marriage to the preceding story has been a preparation. The issue of justice is again treated, with the reward of virtue being shown by the treatment of Baucis and Philemon by Jove and Hermes, and with the punishment of evil, by the destruction of the inhospitable other Phrygians. Justice is further expressed in the metamorphosis of Baucis and Philemon into trees.

Pygmalion and the Statue

CONNECTION. The examination of a pair in love continues. Although a happy story, it involves Pygmalion's initial desire to be unmarried, and an unnatural love for a statue; the problem is solved by the metamorphosis of the statue into the woman, again upon request through the action of a deity.

Cinyras and Myrrha

CONNECTION. The examination of a pair in love continues, with Myrrha's unnatural love for her father developing as a further step from Pygmalion's for a statue. As the headnote to the preceding poem shows, Cinyras and Myrrha are also descendants of Pygmalion. The action here also ends in a transformation—of Myrrha into a tree.

The First Book of Homer's Ilias

CONNECTION. Dryden's added last line to the preceding, tells how Adonis, by arousing the anguish of love in Venus, "reveng'd his mother's fires" of passion. Similar amorous disturbances upset the Grecian chiefs, lead to the desire to achieve revenge upon Troy for the rape of Helen and, in the main action of this book, Agamemnon "to revenge himself upon Achilles" for the loss of Chryseis by seizing Briseis (headnote). Dryden extends with addition the close of the book with its quarrel between Jove and Juno.

The Cock and the Fox

CONNECTION. Both this and the preceding involve debates between the characters. Dryden expands both the debate between Jove and Juno and that between Chanticleer and Partlet. The former ends (in Dryden's version) without lovemaking in bed, linking the Greek story with that of Chanticleer and Partlet, who are unable to make love on their narrow roost (421-24).

Theodore and Honoria

CONNECTION. Another pair of lovers is treated and, as in the preceding story, the plot centers about a vision (Dryden even adds here a passage on dreams, 221-30) which Honoria, unlike Partlet, believes—and so saves herself.

Ceyx and Alcyone

CONNECTION. Again a pair of lovers is treated, the ultimate happiness of the preceding story being the starting-point of this. The prophecy by Alcyone of her husband's death and the vision sent her by Juno parallel the visions and dreams of the two preceding stories.

The Flower and the Leaf

CONNECTION. The poem shares with the preceding the central feature of vision or dream. Dryden has made the connection firmer by his alteration of the medieval vision into a dream vision and by the initial link of the seasons. Such a transition is one to a new tone for the subject dealt with in the last few poems: it is now "the lightsome realms of love" (Dryden's addition, 4).

Alexander's Feast

CONNECTION. The vision of the chaste and the passionate knights with their ladies and at joust in *The Flower and The Leaf* reintroduces the mingled subject of love and arms which is treated, in this ode, in terms of Alexander, whose wars and whose love for the courtesan Thais relate particularly to the passionate Knights of the Flower. Dryden's expansion of the reference to the Nine Worthies in that poem (535-39) perhaps prepares for the consideration of Alexander, who is one of them; and, as in the preceding poem, so here the action takes place at night.

The Twelfth Book of Ovid His Metamorphoses

CONNECTION. The mingled subject of arms and love continues, the story of the Trojan War and its cause in Paris' action (5 ff.) relating to the Persian wars of Alexander and his love for Thais. The last action of the preceding and the first here involve the classical religious requirements of burying and honoring the dead.

The Speeches of Ajax and Ulysses

CONNECTION. This story from the beginning of *Meta.*, XIII, naturally connects with the end of Book XII, leading to events after the Trojan war.

The Wife of Bath, Her Tale

CONNECTION. In both this and the preceding, wisdom or skill triumphs over brutal strength: "And eloquence o'er brutal strength prevail'd" (592 of the preceding). Here the hag's skill with magic (Dryden, unlike Chaucer, makes her a proficient in the art) and her wisdom win her the knight who had ravished a girl.

Of the Pythagorean Philosophy (From *Meta.*, XV)

CONNECTION. There is a link in the idea of governing domestically in the preceding poem (e.g., 546, the last line), and publically in the initial praise of Numa here. But the real connection is between the philosophical nature of this selection and the long philosophical passage added or changed by Dryden towards the end of the preceding

(386-484), which also introduces Roman history for examples of virtue (448 ff.).

The Character of a Good Parson

CONNECTION. Dryden adds to the end of the preceding poem ten lines mingling matters religious with political (with a comparison of Numa to Charles II—see *Threnodia Augustalis*, 465 ff.). This passage leads into the religious and political imitation (with contemporary allusions) of Chaucer's character of the Parson. Dryden's numerous additions and changes make the imitation very like the preceding, except that Christianity here replaces the pagan philosophy there.

The Monument of a Fair Maiden Lady (Noyes, p. 735)

CONNECTION. As the Parson represents the male, ecclesiastical, and public ideal of the good life, so the Maiden Lady exemplifies the female, lay, and private ideal. Grace or charity are exemplified by both characters, but not amorous love or, of course, arms.

Cymon and Iphigenia

CONNECTION. The ideal, celibate lives shown in the two preceding poems are contrasted with "real" lives admitting love. The bridge between two such contrasted subjects is provided by forty-one lines ("Poëta loquitur") at the beginning of this poem. In it Dryden rejects the strict view of divines that love is "folly," arguing that it "Awakes the sleepy vigor of the soul, / And, brushing o'er, adds motion to the pool" (29-30); the same water-passion image is used near the close of *Maiden Lady*, "A soul so calm, it knew not ebbs or flows; / Which passion could but curl, not discompose" (32-33). That "passion" ennobles is at least the official theme of *Cymon*.

There can be little doubt that Dryden deliberately integrates, or at least connects, the poems in the *Fables*. It is equally clear that some of the connections are more firmly made than others. Some might wish to add other kinds of links to the résumé just given, and some might choose to extend the kind of historical allegory found in the first two poems throughout the whole of the *Fables*. But it may again be insisted upon that any reader who sits down with the complete *Fables* and their originals will quickly see how Dryden's changes are part of a general practice leading to the principles of integration.

Something further of the nature of both the principles and the practice can be understood by consideration of the probable origins of Dryden's conception. Surely he was led to create a unified whole from the disparate poems by the examples of the larger works in which they had already appeared. Setting aside his own poems and the *Iliad* as special cases, we see that what comprise the great majority of the poems come from three sources which are themselves made up of autonomous, disparate materials integrated by various formal devices. It is easy to see how fictional frames like those of *The Canterbury Tales* or the *Decameron* might have interested him and, equally, why they were of no use to him. Such frames would have subjected works that are after all translations to a context too much his own. (This should not prevent our seeing that the *Ormond* is in its way an introductory and governing overture for the whole of the *Fables*.)

It was the *Metamorphoses* which provided Dryden not only with the most stories but also the best model. It both showed that there was no need of a formal frame and suggested numerous ways of connecting stories. No one who reads Dryden's lengthy headnotes to the Ovidian poems can mistake the care with which he had studied the details of Ovid's connections. Indeed, his headnotes show more concern with connective techniques and transitions than any other translation known to me. The same attention to form has led him to introduce into *The Cock and the Fox* an allusion to the Wife of Bath (569-70) which anticipates modern scholarly concern with interconnected tales like those of the "marriage group."

The *Metamorphoses* provided a very workable model. In them we discover that Ovid's conception of narrative is almost as various as that represented in the *Fables*. The section on the Pythagorean philosophy in Book XV is the obvious example of the inclusion of "argument," and the recounting of Roman history towards the end of the work gave Dryden ample precedent for his historical passages. If it is impossible to discover satiric touches in Ovid, Book XV does contain the obverse of satire, panegyric. Satire apart, every literary mode to be found in the *Fables* may be found with ease in the *Metamorphoses*. There is of course no reason to prove the most obvious—that Ovid makes use of *fabula*— but it does seem significant that whatever distinctions our own conceptions of the credible might hold, it is often most difficult to judge what Ovid would have thought fable and what history. The same is true of Dryden, because as the poem to the Duchess of Ormond most readily shows, and as numerous other passages confirm, in the *Fables* history is apt to merge with myth or to live as much in a metaphor for a fictional plot as in itself.

There is nothing unprecedented in this, as *Absalom and Achitophel*, *The Medal*, *The Hind and the Panther*, or indeed numerous other poems show. But there is a difference in emphasis. Until about 1685 the historical metaphors are more often analogies for other historical sequences. "Real" history stands for "real" history, David is as truly David as a figure for Charles II. After about 1685 the historical metaphors more often come to involve the panegyrical, the fabulous, and the mythopoeic. The "chamber of dependences" devised by Louis XIV represents Anne Killigrew's invasion of the sister-arts of poesy; the history of the English Reformation is a tale of a Lion, a Panther, and other beasts; and the total history of man can be represented in a progress piece of musical instruments in an ode for St. Cecilia's Day. One cannot fail to be struck by the fact that this development seems to accompany Dryden's conversion. This momentous event in his personal life seems to have brought him access to richer—some would say more Baroque—kinds and uses of metaphor.

In certain respects the *Fables* is the most fabulous and magical of all his works, and at the same time it is one of his very most neoclassical because most wholly indebted for conception to a classical author. In the *Fables* Dryden makes no attempt to retain the order of the works of Chaucer and Boccaccio in the original larger works; but he *does* retain the order of Ovid's stories, seemingly as a kind of sketch for the full canvas of the *Fables* or, to use his own metaphor, as the plan for building. We read the Preface to the *Fables* most often for its criticism of Chaucer. Dryden in it suggests that he is turning from other interests to Homer. But as for other great English poets, so for him Ovid is the classical writer he recurs to most often during his career, and there is no cause for wonder that the *Metamorphoses* should prove to be the model for the *Fables*.*

What Dryden considered to be the important subjects and themes

---

* When this book was at the printer's, a study of the *Metamorphoses* appeared, analyzing its structure in a way confirming Dryden's sense of its unity and revealing the appropriateness of his using it as an inspiration for the structural principle of *Fables*. The book is *Ovid as an Epic Poet* by Brooks Otis (Cambridge, 1966). See *The Times Literary Supplement*, 28 July 1966, pp. 664-65.

of the *Metamorphoses* is a question whose answer can only be inferred, and a reader who is not himself intimate with classical studies can but speculate about present-day conceptions of Ovid's dominant concerns. Such admissions made, it seems possible to suggest certain resemblances in subject and theme between the *Fables* and the *Metamorphoses* and to discover important differences. In his first four lines Ovid emphasizes his concern with change, invokes the gods for aid (since they were the authors of the transformations), and states his intention of beginning with the creation of the world and progressing thence to his own day. It is often not easy to follow that temporal progression in the *Metamorphoses*, although he does begin, as he says, and does end with Augustus. The gods play a very important role, but it is not quite that which Ovid seems to suggest. They may be the authors of change, but in the sense of their being given to disagreements among themselves and often acting on a terrestrial stage they seem almost as much immersed in changes as the human beings whose lives they affect. There is no doubt that Ovid is concerned with change, even obsessed by it. It is natural that his last book should be devoted for the most part to an attempt to provide a philosophical basis for it. The Pythagorean philosophy, as Dryden calls it, is one which is capable of giving comfort to those for whom the idea of change is an obsession—at least it shows that change is a universal law related to other laws.

Dryden's concern with such matters is obvious. His last work, *The Secular Masque*, seems almost a lyrical, dramatic redaction of sections in the first book of the *Metamorphoses*, and the attitude with which he regards the changes witnessed in his century has an Ovidian sadness. What is different in the *Fables* is the emphasis. Significantly, he is interested in changes in fortune rather than in form, with the human condition in time and with human destiny rather than with the Ovidian emphasis upon the bewildering alterations in men and nature. The shift in emphasis in regarding the human is accompanied by a similar change in the conception of the divine. I find it most difficult to characterize Ovid's attitudes toward the Olympian deities, but it is perfectly clear how Dryden regards them. They are either simply pagan and false, or humanistic equivalents for the Christian God. Their false pagan nature is stressed as early in the *Fables* as *Palamon and Arcite*, where Dryden repeatedly emphasizes the Chaucerian point that Venus, Mars, and Diana are pagan, even to the point of adding that the human characters in the story worship at their *fanes*. The humanistic conception can also be observed in *Palamon and Arcite*, since in his additions to the speeches of Egeus and Theseus towards the end of his third book he develops that Stoicism which Christian humanism found congenial in so many ways.

Similarly, his alterations of Ovid in *Of the Pythagorean Philosophy* are so numerous that it is clear that in spite of the undoubted fascination which Pythagorean and Platonic conceptions held for him, the changes which they related in both the physical and metaphysical realms are those he associated with man in this world, while he placed a serene faith in a transcendent God. In like fashion he shares Ovid's concern with history from its beginnings to the present (and in fact beyond into eternity). Although he of course finds it impossible to introduce into the *Fables* the sustained sequence of history that Ovid proposed to himself, he has no difficulty in giving expression to his historical interests in his numerous interpolated passages, allusions, and allegories. As always with Dryden's models, Ovid's *Metamorphoses* is less a model to be followed than an inspiration for original creation.

The *Fables* must, therefore, be considered in its own terms. Appropriately enough, when Dryden appears before the reader he does so as a poet rather than as a translator. The first forty-one lines of *Cymon and Iphigenia* are labelled with a "Poëta loquitur." Functioning partly to bridge a poem on a Maiden Lady and another on high passion, these lines also bring Dryden to speak to the Duchess of Ormond, with whom the *Fables* had begun. We are back full circle to that lovely and mythopoeic poem in which he introduces in one fashion or another the subjects he develops throughout the *Fables*. By relating them to the Duchess, Dryden is able to treat love, arms, history, directed change, and religion. Of these subjects, love and arms are the most prominent. They occur sometimes together as in *Palamon and Arcite* or *Alexander's Feast,* sometimes separately as in a story or two from Boccaccio or in much of Ovid's account of the Trojan War. Usually, however, where one is to be found so is the other, and neither is far away, even when Dryden's theme is that of the good life (*Honour'd Kinsman, Good Parson, Fair Maiden Lady*). One or the other may be deprecated, but to speak of the Maiden Lady's immunity to passion is to raise the subject.

The importance of these subjects is clear enough in even a casual reading of the *Fables*. Dryden seeks, however, to make the probable certain. He begins his poem to the Duchess of Ormond by announcing the subjects and making a comparison between the Duchess and Chaucer's Emily, between Homer and Chaucer, and between the ancient and the Chaucerian achievement.

> Madam,
> The bard who first adorn'd our native tongue,
> Tun'd to his British lyre this ancient song;
> Which Homer might without a blush rehearse,
> And leaves a doubtful palm in Virgil's verse;
> He match'd their beauties, where they most excel;
> Of love sung better, and of arms as well.
>   Vouchsafe, illustrious Ormond, to behold
> What pow'r the charms of beauty had of old;
> Nor wonder if such deeds of arms were done,
> Inspir'd by two fair eyes, that sparkled like your own. (1-10)

In the passage introduced into the beginning of *Cymon and Iphigenia* Dryden returns to the subject of the influence of love (which is of course the point of the story that follows).

> Love, studious how to please, improves our parts
> With polish'd manners, and adorns with arts.
> Love first invented verse, and form'd the rhyme,
> The motion measur'd, harmoniz'd the chime;
> To lib'ral acts inlarg'd the narrow-soul'd,
> Soften'd the fierce, and made the coward bold;
> The world, when waste, he peopled with increase,
> And warring nations reconcil'd in peace.
> Ormond, the first, and all the fair may find,
> In this one legend, to their fame design'd,
> When beauty fires the blood, how love exalts the mind. (31-41)

Such glances as that toward Ovid's history of man's survival of the deluge in *Metamorphoses* (Ovid, Book I; 37 here) take away some of the ecstasy of love, or some of the passion of Dryden's statement, by placing love in such a larger realm of experience that it has become more a principle creative of good than an impulsive instinct. In the story of *Cymon and Iphigenia* the general, beneficent conception dominates the beginning but yields to homicide and the carrying-off of Iphigenia and Cassandra on their very wedding day. It is not surprising that arms and war come back into the story.

A war ensues, the Cretans own their cause,
Stiff to defend their hospitable laws:
Both parties lose by turns; and neither wins,
Till peace propounded by a truce begins.
The kindred of the slain forgive the deed,
But a short exile must for show precede:
The term expir'd, from Candia they remove,
And happy each at home enjoys his love. (633-40)

So the *Fables* ends. War, as one line here shows is something "neither wins," a lesson taught Alexander by Timotheus, and to be learned more explicitly by the fate of Ajax. Nowhere in the *Fables* do arms bring happiness, although they do show what was once called greatness of mind. Like his other important narratives—*Annus Mirabilis*, *The Medal*, *Absalom and Achitophel*, and *The Hind and the Panther*—those of the *Fables* are highly pacific in tone. The syntax in the passage just quoted may well be loose, but there is a certain significance in "neither wins, / Till peace propounded by a truce begins." Where there is only strife, an undefeated warrior like Ajax turns mad at the end and takes his own life. What the good life may be in the active, civic realm, is shown in the poem to John Driden, which governs this aspect of the *Fables* as that to the Duchess of Ormond does the whole. It is a life of *peace*, a word used often in the poem and applied as much to all human history as to that portion of it Dryden had himself witnessed.

Enough for Europe has our Albion fought:
Let us enjoy the peace our blood has bought.
When once the Persian king was put to flight,
The weary Macedons refus'd to fight,
Themselves their own mortality confess'd,
And left the son of Jove to quarrel for the rest.
  Ev'n victors are by victories undone;
Thus Hannibal, with foreign laurels won,
To Carthage was recall'd, too late to keep his own. (158-66)

The allusion to Alexander ("the son of Jove"), reminds us once again that in *Alexander's Feast* the bellicose emotions are called a "madness" (69), and Timotheus will have little of it.

"War," he sung, "is toil and trouble;
Honor, but an empty bubble;
  Never ending, still beginning,
Fighting still, and still destroying." (99-102)

The life of arms is an exciting one in the *Fables*, and its major exemplars usually get praise and sympathy. But as a way of life it is vain or tragic. The Virgilian tone for *horrida bella* had not been absent from *Annus Mirabilis*, but here in the *Fables* there is (in spite of Dryden's preference for Homer in the Preface) a sadness and yearning for peace like that which most readers have found in the *Æneid*.

Man at arms is tragic, or would be, if the proper response were not at heart Stoic:

> Sunt hic etiam sua præmia laudi,
> Sunt lacrimæ rerum, et mentem mortalia tangunt.
> *Solve metus.*

Dismiss your fear. Get on with the human necessity to do what can be done. So Theseus advises at the end of *Palamon and Arcite*. The human activity treated most often in the *Fables* is of course love, which Dryden presents in so many versions and in so many contexts that it may claim to be the most important subject of the whole. If man at arms is tragic, man in love is comic, but comic in a very wide sense indeed. At one end we see the Maiden Lady, who has charity but not *eros;* at another end of the ideal we have Baucis and Philemon, models of conjugal felicity and truth. We also observe the incestuous Myrrha, the "wretched" Sigismonda and Guiscardo, the amorous Chanticleer, or the Greek chieftains falling out over women at the beginning of the *Iliad*. The *Honour'd Kinsman* shows John Driden active in sports of the field and happy for not being in love. Truly, "love's the subject of the comic Muse" (*Cymon*, 24), but in the *Fables* the concept of comedy is that of the *comédie humaine*. In such variety we see that Chaucerian, divine plenty which leads Dryden to hint at the outset of the poem to the Duchess of Ormond that as the succession was from Homer to Virgil to Chaucer, so indeed does the succession continue from Chaucer to Dryden. (See 1-39). In recasting the love stories for the *Fables*, Dryden is concerned to make the motivations of the characters fit their person-alities and their actions. So that whether incest, married love, violent love, or indeed the love of the Duke and Duchess of Ormond is touched upon, the prevailing aim in the disparate stories is not so much to depict an ideal as a reality. The integrated attitudes emerge, as is usual in his poetry, from the whole. Myrrha is obsessed, Baucis and Philemon think first of each other, Cymon rapes Iphigenia out of her husband's hands, and the Duke of Ormond needs a son. Dryden seeks to convey the truth of love every bit as much as the truth of arms, and there will be many who will think that he has succeeded in the "comic" subject more wholly than in the tragic. But those who think so will not be as new to what Chaucer calls "that art" as Cymon, or inhabit the same world as Keats's Madeline.

One reason why the picture of love in the *Fables* differs from that in *The Eve of St. Agnes* is that in the *Fables* neither love nor lovers can exist in a life apart from all other concerns. The private concerns of passion or tenderness are but part of the whole pleasure and duty of man. Often love is involved with arms; indeed, it is commonly the cause of strife involving families or nations. Put differently, it is equally true that the public life of arms or civil endeavor is shown to involve private desires. The mingling of public and private experience gives rise to a poetic world unlike that Dryden had created earlier in his career. As *All for Love* shows, the plays often treat both realms, but usually in conflict. *The Hind and the Panther*, as also *Religio Laici*, comes closest to the *Fables* in combining public and private interests, but they are otherwise so different as to be hardly comparable. And in any event, their concerns are so harmonious with the public in their terms of expression as to be more properly termed personal than private. In other respects, however, the *Fables* deals with a problem which Dryden addresses himself to repeatedly, that of the good life. "Good life be now my task," he resolves in *The Hind and the Panther*, but throughout his career he had in effect asked the question in *The Pilgrim's Progress* and in Cowley's "Dangers of an Honest Man in Much Company": not perhaps "whither shall we fly," but "what shall we do?" It is indeed a question that exercised his century, and if Bunyan's road was shown him by the inner light, or if Cowley's led to an ambiguously happy retirement, Dryden's was the high way of Christian humanism. His solution to the problem is not at once as clear because it is more complex; but because it is more complex it is also more satisfying.

The solution involves the consolations of philosophy. Consolation is necessary if war brings misery as well as achievement, and if love is too often a passion that disturbs the mind. There are some partial answers. Baucis and Philemon, the Good Parson, the Widow mistress of Chanticleer, or the Maiden Lady achieve the good life but at the cost of denying part of its fullness. Chanticleer observes that the industrious, poor widow "sits cow'ring o'er a kitchen fire; / I draw fresh air, and nature's works admire" (463-64). Each of these partial answers represents a kind of life which most men cannot or would not attain. A different kind of partial answer is given by that kind of philosophical attention to the principles of things that Dryden introduces into Palamon's prayer to Venus (*Palamon*, III, 129 ff.), where Chaucer's thoughts are heightened by the infusion of the opening lines of Lucretius' *De Rerum Natura*. Lucretius appealed to Dryden without satisfying him. Knowledge of the universal principle has its benefits, but where, as in the story of *Palamon and Arcite*, the very constitution of things includes years of suffering, death, and loss, the consolation is imperfect. Arcite loses the woman he has striven for and even won by test of arms; by Arcite's death Theseus and the others lose one whom they love and admire.

It is the uncertain human estate, man's changing fortune, that requires consolation. The answer in *Palamon and Arcite* is a Roman answer, but Roman in the sense of that Stoicism which the humanists found more congenial with Christianity than the Epicureanism of Lucretius. As has been noted, Dryden introduces Stoicism into the two important speeches of *Palamon and Arcite*, that of Egeus (III, 877-90) and that of Theseus (III, 1024-1134). In the latter he adds considerably to Chaucer, and, as more than one person has felt, both the translated and the added portions are superior to Chaucer. In these lines we find some of Dryden's most moving poetry, and in that fact we observe something of the claims levied upon his feelings by Stoicism.

If finally the Stoicism is also inadequate, the reason seems to be that he has been too much moved by Ovid's preoccupation with change. Among his many additions, adaptations, and changes in *Of the Pythagorean Philosophy* is the very moving and revealing line, "For time, no more than streams, is at a stay" (268). The counsels of Stoicism might answer the changes one observes in one's own affairs, but they were an insufficient defense against a world fluid with change. Ovid touched Dryden with Platonic and Pythagorean conceptions of an eternal reality underlying changing forms without giving him the answer he sought. His dissatisfaction, if that is not a misleading word, with Ovid can be partly judged by the fact that he is unwilling to close the *Fables*, as Ovid had the *Metamorphoses*, with such philosophy. He goes on to two specifically Christian ideal figures in the Good Parson and the Maiden Lady. More than that, he insists with the last story, *Cymon and Iphegenia*, that philosophic generalization of such kind is no substitute for the vitality of real life, however imperfect that may be.

To one concerned so greatly with change, the affirmation of immortality—of the survival of achievement and good name in time—is no adequate solution. Dryden was debarred from affirming as he had often in earlier poems, those supreme human achievements that gain immortality and transcend time. As other additions to *Of the Pythagorean Philosophy* reveal, if change is a preoccupation, the stream of time will bear human achievements away.

> And every moment alters what is done,
> And innovates some act till then unknown. (276-77)

All the world's a stage, with "The shifted scene for some new show employ'd" (389). Yet what if change were directed? What if we should speak, not of time and metamorphosis, but of fate and fortune?

These are questions which in some form clearly now weighed upon Dryden's mind as they had not done since early in his career. They are also questions raised by Chaucer in his "Nun's Priest's Tale." It is startling to discover in Dryden's *Cock and the Fox* that he has actually increased Chaucer's concern with determined events, and elsewhere in the *Fables* that the concern with fate vies strongly with that other problem, the possibility of meaningless flux in the world. It may well seem paradoxical, even contradictory, to discover that both mutability and a deterministic fate challenge a man's intellect and his faith. Yet so it is with Dryden. There is a fine ironic passage added in *The Cock and the Fox* on the doom of Chanticleer. No doubt the irony applies to Chanticleer, but then he is man as well as Cock, and the first two lines especially possess too much force to be merely ironic.

> Alas, what stay is there in human state,
> Or who can shun inevitable fate?
> The doom was written, the decree was past,
> Ere the foundations of the world were cast!
> In Aries tho' the sun exalted stood,
> His patron planet to procure his good;
> Yet Saturn was his mortal foe, and he,
> In Libra rais'd, oppos'd the same degree:
> The rays both good and bad, of equal pow'r,
> Each thwarting other, made a mingled hour. (675-84)

The lack of stay "in human state" yields to concern with fate. But since the fate is transmitted from its decree before time began through the planets, it is possible that fate may be "mingled." Given such definition of the problem, change is but the temporal aspect of a fate existing outside of time.

In other additions in *The Cock and the Fox* Dryden seems for the first time to examine certain aspects of his conception of the nature of God that he had hitherto put in abeyance. Believing God's essence to be wisdom or reason rather than will, he could believe (in the context of sixteenth and seventeenth-century religious thought) that he did not need to share the concern of the Calvinists and other voluntarists with the problem of free will. Now, however, he explicitly recognizes that a wise God foresees in His knowledge, that divine prescience may lead to deterministic conclusions almost as directly as divine voluntarism.

> For what [God] first foresaw, he must ordain,
> Or its eternal prescience may be vain:
> As bad for us as prescience had not bin;
> For first, or last, he's author of the sin.
> And who says that, let the blaspheming man
> Say worse ev'n of the devil, if he can.
> For how can that eternal pow'r be just,
> To punish man, who sins because he must?
> Or how can he reward a virtuous deed,
> Which is not done by us, but first decreed? (513-22)

Curiously, the very consideration of God's essential reason in this context has led to the introduction, as so rarely in Dryden, of what he knew to be one of His attributes: will, "eternal pow'r." Having come to this personal dilemma over that question of freedom and necessity which has exercised so many minds, Dryden was not likely to discover a solution that has eluded the philosophers. He begins his affirmation by developing Chaucer's distinction between strict and conditional necessity.

> Thus galley slaves tug willing at their oar, ⎫
> Consent to work, in prospect of the shore, ⎬
> But would not work at all if not constrain'd before. ⎭
> That other does not liberty constrain,
> But man may either act or may refrain.
> Heav'n made us agents free to good or ill,
> And forc'd it not, tho' he foresaw the will.
> Freedom was first bestow'd on human race,
> And prescience only held the second place. (533-41)

It would be useless, and for me impossible, to sort out the details of the logic, although it does seem generally that as God has His essence and His attributes, so the human condition is essentially ("first") free and only attributively ("the second place") determined. Dryden himself seems to doubt his logic and in the lines following turns to his conception of God's merciful goodness. The affirmation is really one of faith, with divine power in effect deliberately limiting itself.

> If [God] could make such agents wholly free,
> I not dispute, the point's too high for me;
> For Heav'n's unfathom'd pow'r what man can sound,
> Or put to his omnipotence a bound?
> He made us to his image all agree;
> That image is the soul, and that must be,
> Or not the Maker's image, or be free.   (542-48)

Characteristically, Dryden had cast a light forward toward this passage by stressing earlier in *The Cock and the Fox* that other attribute of a wise God, grace: "Good Heav'n, whose darling attribute we find / Is boundless grace, and mercy to mankind." (281-82). Grace, or mercy, is also Dryden's darling attribute, so that it is no surprise to discover that after he has dwelt upon the ideas *Of the Pythagorean Philosophy* he should emphasize in both the Good Parson's life and in God's treatment of man the operation of grace as the normative feature. He begins with the Parson.

> . . . on eternal mercy [he] lov'd to dwell.
> He taught the gospel rather than the law,
> And forc'd himself to drive, but lov'd to draw:
> For fear but freezes minds; but love, like heat,
> Exhales the soul sublime, to seek her native seat.
>   To threats the stubborn sinner oft is hard,
> Wrapp'd in his crimes, against the storm prepar'd;
> But, when the milder beams of mercy play,
> He melts, and throws his cumbrous cloak away.
>   Lightnings and thunder (heav'n's artillery)
> As harbingers before th' Almighty fly:
> Those but proclaim his style, and disappear;
> The stiller sound succeeds, and, God is there.[10]

In this lovely, benign, and indeed gracious passage, the soft, almost noiseless English rain of God's grace falling on the just and the unjust is the refreshment of man, and the far happier equivalent to being lost in the stream of time.

Because such matters were so important to him, Dryden seems never to have hesitated to introduce general "argument" into his poetry, any more than had Chaucer, Spenser, Chapman, or Milton. But he does always relate them to the whole, whether that be governed by a larger argument, metaphor, plot, or all together. Like Chaucer, he comes to consider determinism on the evidence of dreams in *The Cock and the Fox*. Unlike Chaucer, he sees another issue in the problem. He introduces a play between fancy or imagination and reason. Partlet is given to what is apparently private reason; in any event, like the Socinian Fox of *The Hind and the Panther*, she denies the supernatural. Chanticleer's (and Dryden's) first consideration seems almost Chaucerian, because it involves reason and experience: "Some truths are not by reason to be tried, / But we have sure experience for our guide" (207-08). Like his forefather Chauntecleer, Chanticleer then tells the stories of events foretold in dreams and visions. One ill-advised dreamer "At length to cure himself by reason tries," declaring, "'T was but a vision still, and visions are but vain" (237-242). The event proves him wrong, as does the death by shipwreck of the young merchant who argues against his more believing companion.

> "Stay, who will stay; for me no fears restrain,
> Who follow Mercury the god of gain.
> Let each man do as to his fancy seems;
> I wait not, I, till you have better dreams.
> Dreams are but interludes which fancy makes;
> When monarch Reason sleeps, this mimic wakes;
> Compounds a medley of disjointed things,
> A mob of cobblers, and a court of kings.
> Light fumes are merry, grosser fumes are sad;
> Both are the reasonable soul run mad:
> And many monstrous forms in sleep we see,
> That neither were, nor are, nor e'er can be.
> Sometimes forgotten things long cast behind
> Rush forward in the brain, and come to mind.
> The nurse's legends are for truths receiv'd,
> And the man dreams but what the boy believ'd.
> Sometimes we but rehearse a former play; ⎫
> The night restores our actions done by day, ⎬
> As hounds in sleep will open for their prey. ⎭
> In short the farce of dreams is of a piece,
> Chimeras all; and more absurd, or less." (321-41)

If it be argued that it is only too easy to read such poetry in disregard
of the irony—as it is to take Theseus' remarks on the imagination out of
their context in *A Midsummer Night's Dream*—it must be admitted
that Dryden's emotions are aroused. More than that, he never abuses
reason wholly, nor without a specific context in which its claims are
pushed too far. Here, however, the event shows that the merchant has
claimed too much for reason. Similarly, Chanticleer's dream is shown
to predict the future truly. We may most temperately conclude that
Dryden is aware of the folly that may come of trying to attribute significance to dreams but yet that he holds that there is in man a faculty
of imagination, "fancy," that is capable in some realms of achieving
more than reason.

The imagination in *The Cock and the Fox* is largely confined to the
matter of dreams, showing that it is able to give man a glimpse of the
future. It shows as well that all is not mere change and, what is most
significant, it is the human faculty perceiving that divine justice depends
upon divine grace. Dryden begins with lines we have met with.

> Good Heav'n, whose darling attribute we find
> Is boundless grace, and mercy to mankind,
> Abhors the cruel, and the deeds of night
> By wondrous ways reveals in open light;
> Murther may pass unpunish'd for a time,
> But tardy justice will o'ertake the crime.
> And oft a speedier pain the guilty feels;
> The hue and cry of Heav'n pursues him at the heels. (281-88)

The passage is crucial to Dryden's version. The last two lines are something of a forecast of their own in their image of the hounds after the
fox; the end of the poem is already in sight. More importantly, reason
and imagination are reconciled. The "deeds of night" are revealed to
the dreamer, whose vision appears at night, revealed to his imagination;
this, through the operation of divine grace, makes them known to the
"open light" of reason. The line describing God's workings—"By
wondrous ways reveals in open light"—is very nearly emblematic in
imagery. In merely human terms, the passage shows how the imagination
may inform the reason of truths unknown and unknowable to it. What
is largely a psychological matter here becomes theological in the passage
on prescience and freedom. What is imagination in dreams is faith in
affirming man's freedom. What is revealed here is obscure until faith
presents it in reason's open light. What is affirmed there is the gracious

goodness of a wise God who is also "Almighty." One is pleased to see that Dryden follows Chaucer in giving Chanticleer artistic gifts, another use of the imagination, and feels it appropriate to the spirit of Chaucer's tale that Chanticleer's imagination should be the agency ("his fancy wrought," 757) that saves him at last from the Fox.

For once in Dryden's poetry, the more intellectual themes of the *Fables* are easier to discuss than the use made of history, which is not to say that history is unimportant. The complex relation between the poem to the Duchess of Ormond and the *Palamon and Arcite* makes clear how particular and how broad the historical subject may be. The particulars are usually easier to understand, once they have been discovered. The most familiar example of particular historical allusion in these poems is probably that in the last thirty-five lines of the *Character of a Good Parson*. The passage is strongly royalist, affirmative of passive obedience, and critical of the divines who took the oath of allegiance to William and Mary. The sentiments are very much those of a Jacobite. Since the poem is a professed imitation, and since the genre was one which commonly provided contemporary substitutions or allusions, its references to events between 1688 and 1700 are not surprising. It is therefore more revelatory of the historical cast of the *Fables* that Dryden should be given to similar passages in other poems ostensibly translations—as in *Palamon and Arcite*—and that many small touches should confirm the historical emphasis of his thought. In *The Cock and the Fox*, for example, he follows Chaucer's irony in describing in mock elevation the hens' lamentations when Chanticleer is hent by the Fox. But he adds a line whose characteristic ring has serious overtones—"And all the Punic glories at an end" (709). The Fox is of course no Scipio, and Chanticleer's imagination saves his little Carthage from obliteration. The history remains serious, while the event described is the more ridiculous.

The most straightforward history in the *Fables* is to be found in the poem to John Driden. The sketch of King William's War, the wish for peace, and the statement of principles of government are as serious as anything Dryden ever wrote on a historical subject. The passage on government (171-94) is probably more theoretical, possibly less immediately "poetic" than the more famous passage in *Absalom and Achitophel*, but it is the clearest, surest statement of his lifetime. He seems to have thought so, because he wrote to Montague that he offered "it as a Memorial of my own Principles to all Posterity."[11] Its chief features are again those of the Clarendon Settlement. The English Con-

stitution consists of King, Parliament, and Law; each element con-
tributes in its way to efficiency, balance, and liberty. What is new is a
greater dynamism—the imagery is not only architectural as before, but
dominantly fluid.

> A patriot both the king and country serves;
> Prerogative and privilege preserves:
> Of each our laws the certain limit show;
> One must not ebb, nor t'other overflow.
> Betwixt the prince and parliament we stand;   ⎫
> The barriers of the state on either hand: ⎬
> May neither overflow, for then they drown the land! ⎭
> When both are full, they feed our blest abode;
> Like those that water'd once the paradise of God. (171-79)

In peace it is the parliament that should exercise the greater sovereignty,
in war and times of danger, the throne. We recall that in *Absalom and
Achitophel* Dryden had recognized that there were some good men who
thought the king's power too great. They opposed David mistakenly,
but not venally. Yet the best protest is not in rebellion but in the dignified suffering of John Driden's "grandsire," who refused "to lend the
king against his laws," went to prison and "In bonds retain'd his birthright liberty" (see 180-94). As always with Dryden, the principles are
royalist and conservative. They are perhaps obsolescent. They are also
dignified, reasonable and, *mutatis mutandis*, sufficiently alive to describe
the working constitution of the government of the United States.

   Dryden's view of government is also one which he attributes to Athens
under Theseus at the end of *Palamon and Arcite*—at the end Theseus
has changed from a usurping tyrant to all that an English monarch
should be. In proposing the marriage of Palamon and Emily he is suggesting something "For which already I have gain'd th' assent / Of my
free people in full parliament" (III, 1121-22; the lines provide another
link between *Palamon* and *Honour'd Kinsman*). *Palamon and Arcite*
shows in this example and in the quite different conception of Theseus
at the beginning of the poem how very difficult it is to define the dominant historical motif of the *Fables*. The poem begins and ends with
metaphors for contemporary English history, but the metaphors work
to establish what seem incompatible themes. The incompatibility poses
no insoluble problems in itself, but it does raise the question of the historical function of the more than two thousand lines between the initial
and concluding historical metaphors. Unless I am mistaken, the body of

the poem—like most of the poems in the *Fables*—possesses no continuing historical analogy like that in *Absalom and Achitophel*. Had Dryden found enough support to write his long-cherished epic, such a sustained historical analogy would have been feasible. As it is, the historical analogies of the *Fables* seem intermittent, like Spenser's in *The Faerie Queene*. They are notes sounded from time to time, echoing with sufficient reverberation to jar upon the ear with the suggestion at times of discord. The metaphor is Dryden's from the passage of Theseus acting "in full parliament." And like his Theseus, we may conclude on other grounds that the seemingly discordant historical analogies "As jarring notes in harmony conclude" (1118).

The other grounds imply acceptance of a conception of narrative as history with large elements of fable and *argumentum*. By relating stories supposed to have happened at various times, Dryden is able to create a shifting historical pageant of man at arms and in love—amplified by man's engagement in other human activities and by concern with recurrent human problems. The effect is very different from that of *The Canterbury Tales* or the *Decameron*, in which the frame fixes a time of reference for the whole. Nor is the effect like that of "The Monk's Tale," in which there are numerous stories of "historical" events, since the Monk deals with parallel and therefore highly static tragedies of the medieval kind. Once again, the closest analogy is to the *Metamorphoses*, except that there Ovid intends a historical or chronological progression throughout his fifteen books. Dryden is for once (apart from his lyric poems, where in any case there is usually a temporal structure underlying the allusions to a variety of historical segments) unsystematic. We recur yet again to the obvious fact that however much he might seek to integrate the *Fables*, their material is so various that systematic chronological arrangement was undesirable and probably impossible. Certain kinds of intellectual rigor characteristic of his poetry were out of the question.

It appears to me that the relaxation of narrative is one cause of the wide popularity of the *Fables* in his day, and a reason why, given their mature style, many have since found in them much to admire with special warmth. Late in his life Dryden is returning to what seems a simpler art than that he had practiced in his great eighties. Not since *Annus Mirabilis*, or in their different way the plays, had he allowed himself the pleasures of what we think of as simple narrative, the telling of a good story. *MacFlecknoe, Absalom and Achitophel, The Medal,* and

The Hind and the Panther infuse so much meaning, so much metaphor, into plots that the narrative seems to dissolve. Now, late in life, his powers undiminished, he brings the ripe experience of a lifetime to bear upon a number of stories that are in themselves worth the telling. It is rather as though Pope had sung his more narrative songs of innocence at the end of his career instead of writing then his great epistles, satires, and the *Dunciad*. It is curious that Pope's career is very nearly the reverse of Dryden's in this respect. His fables, and there are a number of them, his *Rape of the Lock*, and his *Eloisa to Abelard* come near the beginning, Dryden's at the end. Of course no man can, when his experience is ripest, sing simply of innocence. Dryden of all writers is no exception. He chose to integrate his collection in a new way, infused into the many poems a great deal of intermittent history and even more religious and philosophical "argument."

The result is once again *sui generis*, the effect no less grand for seeming less controlled. To describe that effect it is necessary to take into account the ease of telling, the mellow style, and the comprehensiveness conveyed with such seeming artlessness by the shifting historical scenery of the *Fables*. What appears to be thrust upon Dryden by necessity is translated by careful purpose into a special virtue. If it was impossible to make narrative relate history, it was possible to incorporate history into narrative and enrich it with fable and argument. The effect is one, then, to be gained by reading through the *Fables* from beginning to end, inserting into modern editions in their proper places *Alexander's Feast* and *The Monument of a Fair Maiden Lady*. Although a reading of the whole is the only one that will convey to the full the particular achievement of the *Fables*, Dryden has often suggested (it would have been out of character not to do so) the nature of the whole in significant parts. The whole of the poem to the Duchess of Ormond is just such a part and one, moreover, whose beauty grows with each reading. Speaking at the end of the poem of her recovery from illness, Dryden rises steadily in tone to his conclusion.

> Blest be the pow'r which has at once restor'd
> The hopes of lost succession to your lord;
> Joy to the first and last of each degree,
> Virtue to courts, and, what I long'd to see,
> To you the Graces, and the Muse to me.
> O daughter of the rose, whose cheeks unite
> The diff'ring titles of the red and white;

Who heav'n's alternate beauty well display,
The blush of morning, and the milky way,
Whose face is paradise, but fenc'd from sin:
For God in either eye has plac'd a cherubin.
   All is your lord's alone; ev'n absent, he
Employs the care of chaste Penelope.
For him you waste in tears your widow'd hours,
For him your curious needle paints the flow'rs;
Such works of old imperial dames were taught;
Such, for Ascanius, fair Elisa wrought.
   The soft recesses of your hours improve
The three fair pledges of your happy love:
All other parts of pious duty done,
You owe your Ormond nothing but a son;
To fill in future times his father's place,
And wear the garter of his mother's race. (146-68)

These lines reveal one of Dryden's styles at its best. Personal at once in reference to the Duchess and himself, allusive to English, Greek, and Roman history, allusive to religious matters, descriptive of the hopes of a noble family in yet their common humanity, combining the two chief subjects of arms or chivalry and of love, in all these respects the passage gives us the *Fables* in miniature. The effect is not one of unsystematic writing but of variety merged into a whole—both by microcosmic representations of the total work and by recurrent subjects and symbols. It is a spacious imagination that comprehends the shifting times of the allusions into the enduring present of the verbs.

The passage, the poem, and the *Fables* are in such sense mythopoeic, creative of myth from numerous stories that combine their shifting emphases into a whole that pictures man seeking now this way now that, now in ancient and now in modern times, to find for himself the good life. He fails, he succeeds; he fails again, and succeeds yet once more. One story is connected to the next by devices of integration and by the similarity shown in juxtaposition. More than that, the repeated treatment of efforts to find the good life in arms, in love, in public or private endeavor, in the family or in the government takes on meaning by recurrence. The meaning deepens with reference to contemporary events and, more significantly, by treatment of the subjects of change and fortune suggested by the varied stories. If we have Dryden's most considered opinions upon the English Constitution, we have also his most explicit treatment of Platonism and Pythagoreanism along with neo-

Epicurean and Stoic colorings. Governing all, as God beneficently governs His creatures, is Dryden's affirmation of a wise God whose "darling attribute," grace, frees man from any fear that might arise from consideration of that other divine attribute, omnipotent will.

It is a lovely mythology, and no less so for being by turns fabulous and true, or rather fabulous and true together as mythologies properly must be. Its tone is characteristically questioning, realistic, delighted, and affirmative. Of the tonal elements the second and third deserve some little attention. As with Chaucer's "smale foules . . . / That slepen al the nyght with open eye," the realism and the delight are often mingled. In *The Cock and the Fox* Dryden seems to have the barnyard more vividly in mind than Chaucer himself.

> Lay Madam Partlet basking in the sun,
> Breast-high in sand; her sisters, in a row,
> Enjoy'd the beams above, the warmth below. (574-76)

The delight in the world as it is includes the universe as it is known to the new science, which he draws upon for an anachronistic addition to *Of the Pythagorean Philosophy:* "The dance of planets round the radiant sun" (94). This is the real world, the Copernican universe, in which the delight man may take is sufficient to endow it with the magic attributed by earlier poets to the old, Ptolemaic system. As the single line shows, the real and the mythic are in Dryden's poetry never far apart. Even when the imagery grows conceited, when spring is treated by complex metonymy as the emergence of life from within to the out-of-doors, the joy is real.

> When first the tender blades of grass appear,
> And buds, that yet the blast of Eurus fear,
> Stand at the door of life, and doubt to clothe the year;
> Till gentle heat and soft repeated rains
> Make the green blood to dance within their veins:
> Then, at their call, embolden'd out they come,
> And swell the gems and burst the narrow room;
> Broader and broader yet, their blooms display,
> Salute the welcome sun, and entertain the day.
> Then from their breathing souls the sweets repair
> To scent the skies, and purge th' unwholesome air;
> Joy spreads the heart, and, with a general song,
> Spring issues out and leads the jolly months along.
>   (*The Flower and the Leaf,* 7-19)

Only those who have chosen not to stand close enough to Dryden* to see what is there would doubt that the imagery of "soft repeated rains / Make the green blood to dance within their veins" is his. Here as elsewhere, his love of the particulars and peculiarities of closely observed life refashioned by the imagination mingle with general thematic conceptions. It is, after all, a joy which "spreads the heart," a joy that accounts for all that can be seen to be foolish, vain, wrong, and tragic in human life, and yet remains joy. Such affirmation, holding or held by ideas, beliefs, and structural design, resembles nothing else so much in Dryden's earlier work as *The Hind and the Panther*, more intellectually remote as that poem often is. For Dryden, the greatest wealth of detail swelled in his mind when it was conceived within the most complex or original structural schemes. If it is quite possible to exaggerate the degree of structural integration in the *Fables*, that is a peril which has not always affrighted Dryden's readers.

Other comparisons show as much without reducing the appeal of the mythopoeic beauty of the *Fables*. One of the most striking modern discoveries of literary scholarship of the seventeenth century has been the discernment of the use of the formal religious meditation to achieve ways of ordering individual poems and groups of poems. Dryden's model was the *Metamorphoses* rather than the meditation, and although the materials at his disposal did not permit the extraordinary degree of integration that has been discovered in George Herbert's poems in *The Temple*, Ovid may be thought a more workable model for bringing together narrative poems. Not Dryden, not even Herbert, carried integration of disparate poems to the lengths possible in poetry. Nor were they the first, if I may bring into discussion of Dryden some seemingly exotic information.

From the tenth through the fourteenth centuries, Japanese Court poets were devising methods of integrating sequences of their own poems and anthologies of poems by many authors into yet more wholly unified wholes. Dryden integrated twenty poems of over 11,500 lines; one Japanese collection integrates, and far more complexly, almost 2,800 short poems comprising very nearly 14,000 lines.[12] Neither diminishes the achievement of the other, and each makes that of the other seem less idiosyncratic. What Dryden has done may be conveyed by an ex-

* See the epigraph to *Absalom*: "Si propius stes / Te capiet magis" (If you stand closer, you will be more taken).

pression of his own, though with less of its Latin meaning. He has conceived a work made up of translations in such a way that they are not translations but *transfusions* of various older poems with new purposes. The originality and affirmation make the *Fables* what it is.

These are qualities always to be esteemed in literature. They are remarkable in a poet nearing the end of his lifetime and of a career stretching back over four decades of highly varied achievement. Perhaps it is the varied nature of his works, or perhaps the complexity that underlies the surface, or perhaps it is the necessity of understanding his wholes before the significance of their parts is clear—whatever the cause, none can deny that assessment of Dryden and his poetry, of the *Fables* no less than *The Hind and the Panther*, has proven difficult. Dr. Johnson, who admired without liking *The Hind and the Panther*, and who had little patience with the *Fables*, may yet be quoted at length to describe the beauty of this last extended work of Dryden's life.

> Perhaps no nation ever produced a writer that enriched his language with such variety of models. To him we owe the improvement, perhaps the completion of our metre, the refinement of our language, and much of the correctness of our sentiments. By him we were taught "sapere et fari," to think naturally and express forcibly. . . . He shewed us the true bounds of a translator's liberty. What was said of Rome, adorned by Augustus, may be applied by an easy metaphor to English poetry embellished by Dryden, "lateritiam invenit, marmoream reliquit," he found it brick, and he left it marble.[13]

If Dr. Johnson's handsome tribute will bear alteration, one can only urge that it is not marble but life with which Dryden leaves us, seeking for one's own easy metaphor to describe his place in the history of our poetry his praise of Charles II in *Threnodia Augustalis*, XII.

> Amidst the peaceful triumphs of his reign,
>   What wonder if the kindly beams he shed
> Reviv'd the drooping arts again;
>   If Science rais'd her head,
>   And soft Humanity that from rebellion fled! . . .
> The royal husbandman appear'd,
>   And plow'd, and sow'd, and till'd;
> The thorns he rooted out, the rubbish clear'd,
>   And bless'd th' obedient field:
> When, straight, a double harvest rose;

Such as the swarthy Indian mows;
Or happier climates near the line,
Or Paradise manur'd and dress'd by hands divine.

His poetry possesses some characteristic faults, especially of unevenness and carelessness. These may be readily forgiven for its virtues. It also possesses, especially in that intellectual remoteness revealed by comparison with the achievements of the Romantic poets, limitations that are more serious. Yet his achievement is a highly varied and dignified late expression of Christian humanism, and those who answer to his charge that we stand closer to it will continue to be taken by it. Dr. Johnson must after all speak the last words for such of us. Concluding his parallel of Pope and Dryden in the *Life* of Pope, he says,

> if the reader should suspect me, as I suspect myself, of some partial fondness for the memory of Dryden, let him not too hastily condemn me, for meditation and inquiry may, perhaps, show him the reasonableness of my determination.

BIBLIOGRAPHY
NOTES
INDEX

BIBLIOGRAPHY

The titles include works cited in the book, standard works, and important modern studies. Inclusion does not necessarily imply agreement nor omission anything other than oversight. Unless otherwise specified, London is the place of publication.

I. BIBLIOGRAPHY, CONCORDANCE

Macdonald, Hugh. *John Dryden: A Bibliography of Early Editions and of Drydeniana.* Oxford, 1939.

Monk, Samuel Holt. "Dryden Studies: A Survey, 1920-1945," *ELH*, XIV (1947), 46-63.

———. *John Dryden: A List of Critical Studies Published from 1895 to 1948.* Minneapolis, 1950.

Montgomery, Guy, *et al. Concordance to the Poetical Works of John Dryden.* Berkeley and Los Angeles, 1957.

Osborn, James M. "Macdonald's Bibliography of Dryden: An Annotated Check List of Selected American Libraries," *MP*, XXXIX (1941), 69-98, 197-212; XL (1942), 313-19.

II. BIOGRAPHY

Congreve, William. See the Epistle Dedicatory in his *Dramatic Works of John Dryden*, I. (Given below.)

Johnson, Samuel. *Lives of the English Poets.* G. B. Hill, ed. 3 vols. Oxford, 1905. [See the lives of Dryden and of Pope.]

Malone, Edmund. See the *Life* in his *Critical and Miscellaneous Prose Works of John Dryden*, I. (Given below.)

Osborn, James M. *John Dryden: Some Biographical Facts and Problems.* New York, 1940.

Saintsbury, George. *Dryden* (English Men of Letters Series). New York, 1881.

Scott, Sir Walter. See his "Life of Dryden" in *Works of John Dryden*, I. (Given below.)

Ward, Charles E. *The Life of John Dryden.* Chapel Hill, 1961.

III. IMPORTANT AND USEFUL EDITIONS OF DRYDEN'S WORKS

Christie, W. D., ed. *Dryden* [Selected Poems]. 5th ed., rev. by C. H. Firth. Oxford, 1926.

——, ed. *The Poetical Works of John Dryden.* 1870.

Congreve, William, ed. *The Dramatick Works of John Dryden.* 6 vols. 1717.

Day, Cyrus Lawrence, ed. *The Songs of John Dryden.* Cambridge, Mass., 1932.

Frost, William, ed. *Selected Works of John Dryden.* New York and Toronto, 1953.

Gardner, William Bradford, ed. *The Prologues and Epilogues of John Dryden.* New York, 1951.

Hooker, Edward N., H. T. Swedenberg, Jr., *et al.*, eds. *The Works of John Dryden.* Berkeley and Los Angeles. In progress: published to date, I (1956) and VIII (1962).

Kinsley, James. ed. *The Poems of John Dryden.* 4 vols. Oxford, 1958.

Legouis, Pierre. *Dryden: Poèmes choisis.* Paris, 1946.

Malone, Edmund, ed. *The Critical and Miscellaneous Prose Works of John Dryden.* 3 vols. 1800.

Nettleton, George H. and Arthur E. Case, eds. *British Dramatists from Dryden to Sheridan.* Boston, 1939. [Contains well edited texts of *The Conquest of Granada*, Part I, and *All for Love.*]

Noyes, George R., ed. *The Poetical Works of Dryden.* rev. ed. Cambridge, Mass., 1950.

Scott, Sir Walter and George Saintsbury, eds. *The Works of John Dryden.* 18 vols. 1882-1892.

Summers, Montague, ed. [Dryden's] *Dramatic Works.* 6 vols. 1931-32.

Ward, Charles E., ed. *The Letters of John Dryden, With Letters Addressed to Him.* Durham, 1942.

Watson, George, ed. *John Dryden: Of Dramatic Poesy and Other Critical Essays.* 2 vols. 1962.

Williams, W. H., ed. *Dryden: The Hind and the Panther.* 1900.

IV. OTHER EDITIONS, STUDIES

Amarasinghe, Upali. *Dryden and Pope in the Early Nineteenth Century.* Cambridge, 1962.

Anon. *The Fables of Young Æsop.* 1700.

Augustine, Saint. *The City of God.* R. V. G. Trasker, ed. 2 vols. Everyman. 1945.

Arendt, Hannah. *The Human Condition.* Garden City, New York, 1959.

Baker, Herschel. *The Wars of Truth.* Cambridge, Mass., 1952.

Bates, Stuart. *Modern Translation.* Oxford, 1936.

Benson, Donald R. "Theology and Politics in Dryden's Conversion," *SEL,* IV (1964), 393-412.

Biblia Sacra Cum Glossa Ordinaria [and *postillae* of Nicholas de Lira]. 6 vols. Antwerp, 1617.

Boas, George. *The Happy Beast in French Thought of the Seventeenth Century*. Baltimore, 1933.

Bottkol, J. M. J. "Dryden's Latin Scholarship," *MP*, XL (1943), 241-55.

Bredvold, Louis I. *The Intellectual Milieu of John Dryden*. Ann Arbor, 1934.

Brennecke, Ernest, Jr. "Dryden's Odes and Draghi's Music." *PMLA*, XLIX (1934), 1-36.

Bronson, Bertrand H. "Some Aspects of Music and Literature in the Eighteenth Century," *Music & Literature . . . Papers Delivered . . . at the Second Clark Library Seminar*. Los Angeles, [1954], pp. 22-55.

Brooks, Harold F. "A Bibliography of John Oldham." *Proceedings and Papers of the Oxford Bibliographical Society*, V (1936), 1-38.

Brower, Reuben A. "An Allusion to Europe: Dryden and Tradition." *ELH*, XIX (1952), 38-48.

———. "Dryden's Epic Manner and Virgil." *PMLA*, LV (1940), 119-38.

———. "Dryden's Poetic Diction and Virgil." *PQ*, XVIII (1939), 211-17.

Brower, Robert and Earl Miner. *Japanese Court Poetry*. Stanford, 1961.

Burnet, Gilbert. "Two Cases of Conscience." In S. Macky, ed. *Memoirs of the Secret Service of John Macky*. 1733. Second Appendix, xxiv-xxxiii.

Cassirer, Ernst. *The Platonic Renaissance in England*. Austin, 1953.

Chambers, A. B. "*Absalom and Achitophel:* Christ and Satan." *MLN*, LXXIV (1959), 592-96.

[Charleton, Walter]. *Epicurus' Morals*. 1656.

———. *Exercitationes de Differentiis & Nominibus Animalium*. Oxford, 1677.

———. *Physiologia Epicuro-Gassendo-Charltoniana: or a Fabrick of Science Natural, Upon the Hypothesis of Atoms*. 1654.

———. [Henry Carey?] *Natural History of the Passions*. n.p., 1674.

——— and P. M. *The Ephesian and Cimmerian Matrons*. 1668.

Chaucer, Geoffrey. *The Works of Geoffrey Chaucer*. Ed. F. N. Robinson. 2nd ed. Cambridge, Mass., 1961.

Chiasson, Elias J. "Dryden's Apparent Scepticism in *Religio Laici*." *Harvard Theological Review*, LIV (1961), 207-21.

Cicero. *De Inventione*. H. M. Hubbel, ed., Loeb ed. 1949.

Cowley, Abraham. *English Writings*. A. R. Waller, ed. 2 vols. Cambridge, 1905-1906.

Creech, Thomas, trans. *Lucretius, De Rerum Natura*. Second ed. Oxford, 1683.

Cressy, Hugh-Paulin de. *Exomologesis*. Rev. ed. Paris, 1653.

D., E. *A Treatise of Humilitie*. 1654.

Dahlberg, Charles. "Chaucer's Cock and Fox." *JEGP*, LIII (1954), 277-90.

Davies, Godfrey. "The Conclusion of Dryden's 'Absalom and Achitophel.' " *HLQ*, X (1946), 69-82.

de Sola Pinto, Vivian. "Rochester and Dryden." *Renaissance and Modern Studies*, V (1961), 29-48.

Dick, Oliver Lawson, ed. *Aubrey's Brief Lives.* 1960.

Donovan, Mortimer. "The *Moralite* of the Nun's Preste's Sermon." *JEGP*, LII (1953), 498-508.

Eames, Marian. "John Ogilby and his Aesop." *BNYPL*, LXV (1961), 73-88.

Eliot, Thomas Stearns. *Homage to John Dryden.* 1924.

———. *John Dryden: The Poet, the Dramatist, the Critic.* New York, 1932.

———. *Selected Essays.* 1950.

Elliott, Robert C. "The Shape of Utopia." *ELH*, XXX (1963), 317-34.

Feder, Lillian. "John Dryden's Use of Classical Rhetoric." *PMLA*, LXIX (1954), 1258-78.

Fell, John. "The Character of the Last Daies," [a sermon preached] "in Oxford . . . 1675." 1676.

Ferguson, Robert. *No Protestant-Plot.* [Three Parts, authorship not wholly certain] 1681, 1682.

Fludd, Robert. *Utriusque Cosmi Maioris scilicet et Minoris Metaphysica, Physica, atque Technica Historia.* Oppenheim, 1617. [Volume I concerns the macrocosm, II the microcosm; other works are sometimes included as subsequent volumes.]

Franzius, Wolfgang. *Historia Animalium Sacra.* Wittenberg, 1612.

———. *The History of Brutes.* Trans. N. W. [of the first part of the preceding work]. 1670.

Freedman, Morris. "Dryden's Miniature Epic." *JEGP*, LVII (1958), 211-19.

———. "Milton and Dryden on Rhyme." *HLQ*, XXIV (1961), 337-44.

Freeman, Rosemary. *English Emblem Books.* 1948.

Frost, William. *Dryden and the Art of Translation.* New Haven, 1955. Yale Studies in English 128.

Fujimura, Thomas H. "Dryden's *Religio Laici:* An Anglican Poem." *PMLA*, LXXVI (1961), 205-17.

Gagen, Jean. "Love and Honor in Dryden's Heroic Plays." *PMLA*, LXXVII (1962), 208-20.

Grierson, Herbert J. C. *The Poems of John Donne.* 2 vols. Oxford, 1912.

H., B. *Emblemata Sacra.* ?Amsterdam, 1631.

Hagstrum, Jean H. *The Sister Arts: The Tradition of Literary Pictorialism . . . from Dryden to Gray.* Chicago, 1958.

Heiserman, A. R. "Satire in the *Utopia.*" *PMLA*, LXXVIII (1963), 163-74.

Hemphill, George. "Dryden's Heroic Line." *PMLA*, LXXII (1957), 863-79.

Hoffman, Arthur W. *John Dryden's Imagery.* Gainesville, Florida, 1962.

Hollander, John. *The Untuning of the Sky: Ideas of Music in English Poetry, 1500-1700.* Princeton, 1961.

Hooker, Edward N. "The Purpose of Dryden's *Annus Mirabilis.*" *HLQ*, X (1946), 49-67.

Hooker, Helene M. "Dryden's *Georgics* and English Predecessors," *HLQ*, IX (1945-46), 273-310.

Hooker, Richard. *The Laws of Ecclesiastical Polity.* Everyman. 2 vols. n.d.

Jack, Ian. *Augustan Satire . . . 1660-1750.* Oxford, 1952.

Johnson, Samuel. The lives, "Dryden" and "Pope" in *The Lives of the English Poets*. (Given above, II.)

——. *Notes to Shakespeare*. Ed. Arthur Sherbo. Los Angeles, 1956-58.

Jones, Richard Foster. "The Originality of *Absalom and Achitophel*," *MLN*, XLVI (1931), 211-18.

Jones, Thomas, ed. "A Catalogue of Tracts for and against Popery (Published in or about the Reign of James II)." *Remains* of the Chetham Society (Manchester). Vols. XLVIII (1859) and LXIV (1865).

Kantorowicz, Ernst. *The King's Two Bodies: A Study in Medieval Political Theology*. Princeton, 1957.

Kaufmann, R. J., ed. Introduction ("On the Poetics of Terminal Tragedy"), *All for Love*. San Francisco, 1962.

Keast, William R., comp. and ed. *Seventeenth-Century English Poetry*. New York, 1962.

Kermode, Frank. "Dissociation of Sensibility," *Kenyon Review*, XIX (1957), 169-94.

——. *Romantic Image*. 1961.

Kinsley, James. "Dryden and the Art of Praise." *English Studies*, XXXIV (1953), 57-64.

Korn, A. L. "*MacFlecknoe* and Cowley's *Davideis*." *HLQ*, XIV (1951), 99-127.

La Fontaine, Jean de. *Fables Choisies*. Paris, 1668.

Levine, Jay Arnold. "The Status of the Verse Epistle Before Pope." *SP*, LIX (1962), 658-84.

——. "John Dryden's Epistle to John Driden," *JEGP*, LXIII (1964), 450-74.

Lord, George deForest. *Poems on Affairs of State . . . 1660-1678*. New Haven, 1963.

Lovejoy, Arthur O. *Essays in the History of Ideas*. Baltimore, 1948.

Lowell, James Russell. "Dryden," *The Writings of James Russell Lowell*. 11 vols., III. Boston, 1890.

Lowell, Robert. ΠΑΝΖΩΟΡΥΚΤΟΛΟΓΙΑ, SIVE *Panzoologico-mineralogica. Or a Complete History of Animals and Minerals*. Oxford, 1661.

Maimbourg, Louis. *The History of the League*. Trans. with a Postscript by Dryden. 1684.

Manley, Frank, ed. *John Donne: The Anniversaries*. Baltimore, 1963.

Manwaring, Elizabeth. *Italian Landscape in Eighteenth Century England*. New York, 1925.

Martz, Louis L. *The Poetry of Meditation*. New Haven, 1954. Yale Studies in English 125.

McFadden, George. "Elkanah Settle and the Genesis of *MacFlecknoe*," *PQ*, XLIII (1964), 55-72.

Miller, Clarence H. "The Styles of *The Hind and the Panther*." *JEGP*, LXI, (1962), 511-27.

Milton, John. *Complete Poems and Major Prose.* Merritt Y. Hughes, ed., New York, 1957.

Miner, Earl. "Dryden and the Issue of Human Progress." *PQ*, XL (1961), 120-29.

———. "Some Characteristics of Dryden's Use of Metaphor." *SEL*, II (1962), 309-20.

———. "The Wolf's Progress in *The Hind and the Panther.*" *BNYPL*, LXVII (1963), 512-16.

Murakami, Shikō. "Reverence for Human Nature—The Poetry of Dryden and Pope." *The Journal of the Faculty of Letters, Osaka University*, X (1963), i-vi, 1-84.

Nevo, Ruth. *The Dial of Virtue: A Study of Poems on Affairs of State in the Seventeenth Century.* Princeton, 1963.

Osborn, Scott C. "Heroical Love in Dryden's Heroic Plays." *PMLA*, LXXIII (1948), 480-90.

Ogilby, John. *The Fables of Æsop* [and] *Æsopics.* 1668.

Ovid. *Metamorphoses.* F. T. Miller, ed., 2 vols. Loeb ed. 1951.

———. *Ovid's Metamorphoses in Fifteen Books. Translated by the Most Eminent Hands.* Samuel Garth, ed. 1717.

Patrick, Simon. "A Sermon Preached . . . Before His Highness the Prince of Orange" [20 Jan. 1668/9]. 1689.

Phædrus. *Phædri . . . Fabularum Æsopiarum Libri Quinque.* Amsterdam, 1667.

Philipott, Thomas, Robert Codring, and Robert Barlow. *Æsop's Fables.* 1666.

Phillips, James E. "Poetry and Music in the Seventeenth Century." *Music & Literature . . . Papers Delivered . . . at the Second Clark Library Seminar.* Los Angeles, [1954], pp. 1-21.

Plato. *The Dialogues of Plato.* Ed. Benjamin Jowett. 5 vols. Oxford, 1897.

Price, Martin. *To the Palace of Wisdom: Studies in Order and Design from Dryden to Blake.* New York, 1964.

Prince, F. T. "Dryden Redivivus." *Review of English Literature*, I (1960), 71-79.

Prior, Moody E. *The Language of Tragedy.* New York, 1947.

Proudfoot, L. *Dryden's Æneid and its Seventeenth Century Predecessors.* Manchester, 1960.

Pseudo-Cicero. *Ad C. Herennium de Ratione Dicendi.* Harry Caplan, ed. Loeb ed. 1954.

Purcell, Henry. *Orpheus Britannicus.* 1698.

Quintilian. *Institutio Oratoria.* H. E. Butler, ed. 4 vols. 1953.

Roper, Alan H. "Dryden and the Stuart Succession." Unpub. diss. Johns Hopkins University, 1961.

———. "Dryden's *Medal* and the Divine Analogy." *ELH*, XXIX (1962), 396-417.

Røstvig, Maren-Sofie. *The Happy Man.* 2 vols. rev. ed. Oxford, 1962.

Salmon, J. H. M. *The French Religious Wars in English Political Thought.* Oxford, 1959.

Schilling, Bernard N., comp. and ed. *Dryden: A Collection of Critical Essays.* Englewood Cliffs, New Jersey, 1963.

——. *Dryden and the Conservative Myth.* New Haven, 1961.

Smith, David Nichol. *John Dryden.* Cambridge, 1950.

Smith, John Harrington. *The Gay Couple in Restoration Comedy.* Cambridge, Mass., 1948.

Spedding, J. R., L. Ellis, and D. D. Heath, eds. *The Works of Francis Bacon.* 7 vols. 1857-59.

Stapleton, Thomas. *Thomae Stapletoni, . . . Opera quae Extant Omnia.* 4 vols. Paris, 1670.

Stillingfleet, Edward. *Works.* 2 vols. 1710.

Sutherland, W. O. S., Jr. "Dryden's Use of Popular Imagery in *The Medal.*" *University of Texas Studies in English,* XXXV (1956), 123-34.

Swedenberg, H. T., Jr. "England's Joy: *Astraea Redux* in its Setting." *SP,* L (1953), 30-44.

——. *The Theory of the Epic in England, 1650-1800.* Berkeley and Los Angeles, 1944.

Sylvester, Joshua, trans. *Divine Weekes and Works of . . . Du Bartas.* 1605.

Tavard, George H. *Holy Writ or Holy Church.* 1959.

Tillyard, E. M. W. *Five Poems, 1470-1870.* 1948.

——. *Poetry Direct and Oblique.* 1934.

Topsell, Edward. *History of Four-Footed Beasts.* 1658.

Underwood, Dale. *Etherege and the Seventeenth-Century Comedy of Manners.* New Haven, 1957. Yale Studies in English 135.

Van Doren, Mark. *John Dryden: A Study of His Poetry.* New York, 1946. [Originally *The Poetry of John Dryden.* New York, 1920.]

Verrall, A. W. *Lectures on Dryden.* Cambridge, 1914.

Waith, Eugene M. *The Herculean Hero in Marlowe, Chapman, Shakespeare and Dryden.* New York, 1962.

Wallerstein, Ruth. "On the Death of Mrs. Killigrew: The Perfecting of a Genre." *SP,* XLIV (1947), 519-28.

——. *Studies in Seventeenth-Century Poetic.* Madison, 1950.

——. "The Development of the Rhetoric and Metre of the Heroic Couplet, Especially in 1625-1645." *PMLA,* L (1935), 166-209.

——. "To Madness Near Allied: Shaftesbury and His Place in the Design and Thought of *Absalom and Achitophel.*" *HLQ,* VI (1943), 445-71.

Wasserman, Earl R. "Dryden's Epistle to Charleton." *JEGP,* LV (1956), 201-12.

Whitaker, William. *A Disputation on Holy Scriptures, against the Papists, Especially Bellarmine and Stapleton.* 1588. Trans. and ed. by William Fitzgerald. Parker Society, vol. 26.

Williams, W. H. " 'Palamon and Arcite' and the 'Knightes Tale.' " *Modern Language Review,* IX (1914), 161-72, 309-23.

Williamson, George. "The Rhetorical Pattern of Neoclassical Wit." *MP*, XXXIII (1935), 55-81.

Wilmot, John, Earl of Rochester. *Poems*. Vivian de Sola Pinto, ed. 1953.

Winterbottom, John A. "The Development of the Hero in Dryden's Tragedies." *JEGP*, LII (1953), 161-73.

———. "The Place of Hobbesian Ideas in Dryden's Tragedies." *JEGP*, LVII (1958), 665-83.

———. "Stoicism in Dryden's Tragedies." *JEGP*, LXI (1962), 868-83.

Woodhead, Abraham [?]. *A Rational Account of Roman Catholicks Concerning the Ecclesiastical Guide in Controversies on Religion*. 1673.

Yates, Frances A. *The French Academies of the Sixteenth Century*. 1947.

NOTES

I. PERSONALITY AND PUBLIC EXPERIENCE:
Annus Mirabilis

1. See Ruth Wallerstein, "On the Death of Mrs. Killigrew: The Perfecting of a Genre," *SP*, XLIV (1947), 519-28, which discusses the Hastings poem at some length.
2. Watson, I, 95.
3. Watson, I, 101-102.
4. *Hind*, III, 508-510; 1802-1804. Throughout this book citations of *The Hind and the Panther* are given to part and lines within the three parts, and also to the consecutive numbering of Noyes, followed in the *Concordance*.
5. Watson, II, 32.
6. The contemporary background is fully sketched in *Works*, I, 258-59. The relation of the second half of the poem to Dryden's political ideas is excellently set forth in the unpublished dissertation by Alan H. Roper, "Dryden and the Stuart Succession" (Johns Hopkins University, 1961).
7. See *Works*, I, 316.
8. See *Works*, I, 316.
9. See Herschel Baker, *The Wars of Truth* (Cambridge, Mass., 1952), Chs. I, III, IV, and VII; also Elias J. Chiasson, "Dryden's Apparent Scepticism in *Religio Laici*," *Harvard Theological Review* LIV (1961), 207-21; and Alan H. Roper, "Dryden's *Medal* and the Divine Analogy," *ELH*, XXIX (Dec., 1962), 396-417. Baker's background is excellent, but without the guidance of Chiasson and Roper it is impossible to see Dryden aright in it. On Dryden's adherence to the "realist" or "rationalist" tradition of Aquinas and Hooker, see below, especially ch. V.
10. See Roper, "Dryden's *Medal*," pp. 407-14, and Dryden's phrasing: "the law / And rule of beings in your Maker's mind" (661-62).
11. Ward, *Letters*, p. 35, dating the letter 1691.
12. See Ch. VII, and Earl Miner, "Dryden and the Issue of Human Progress," *PQ*, XL (1961), 120-29.
13. The role of Cleveland, the nature of Restoration political verse, and the use of historical metaphors in the century are discussed in three useful books: Ruth Nevo, *The Dial of Virtue* (Princeton, 1963); *Poems on Affairs of State*, vol. I, ed. by George deForest Lord (New Haven, 1963), with an Introduction giving *Annus Mirabilis* a sure historical context; and J. H. M.

Salmon, *The French Religious Wars in English Political Thought* (Oxford, 1959), an excellent study.

II. DRAMA OF THE WILL:
All for Love

1. *An Evening's Love*, first song, 1-8. Dryden's lyric poetry is considered in Chapter VII.

2. See John A. Winterbottom, "The Place of Hobbesian Ideas in Dryden's Tragedies," *JEGP*, LVII (1958), 665-83, which shows that place to be in the purely dramatic characterization of persons we are not led to respect; and "Stoicism in Dryden's Tragedies," *JEGP*, LXI (1962), 868-83, which shows Dryden's values to be like those of dramatists earlier in the centry.

3. "Of Heroic Plays," prefixed to *The Conquest of Granada*, Watson, I, 158.

4. Heroical love is described in traditional terms by Robert Burton, *Anatomy of Melancholy*, Part III, Sect. II, and is discussed by Scott C. Osborn, "Heroical Love in Dryden's Heroic Drama," *PMLA*, LXXIII (1958), 480-90.

5. "Of Heroic Plays," Watson, I, 163.

6. The suggestion is that of Eugene M. Waith in *The Herculean Hero* (New York and London, 1962). He also stresses the romantic element, as "a characteristic Renaissance addition to the classical model of the Herculean hero" (p. 72).

7. Preface, Watson, I, 222.

8. Watson, II, 202.

9. Ward, *Letters*, p. 54.

10. Noyes, pp. xxiii, xxv.

11. "Prologue," 19-20, to the Davenant-Dryden *Tempest*.

12. Watson, I, 221.

13. II, i; Scott-Saintsbury, VII, 359.

14. IV, iii; Scott-Saintsbury, VII, 436.

15. V, i; Scott-Saintsbury, VII, 466.

16. John Harrington Smith, *The Gay Couple in Restoration Comedy* (Cambridge, Mass., 1948), p. 70, on *Marriage A-la-Mode*.

III. METAPHOR AND VALUES:
Macflecknoe

1. For an excellent analysis of such comparisons in the *Congreve*, see Hoffman, *Dryden's Imagery*, pp. 133-38.

2. See Watson, II, 91-92.

3. Dryden's Virgilian allusions have never been fully investigated, but aspects of his practice are treated by J. M. J. Bottkol in "Dryden's Latin Scholarship," *MP*, XL (1943), 241-55. There are many examples of the

literary effects gained by such allusions in William Frost, *Dryden and the Art of Translation* (New Haven, 1955) and in the articles by Reuben Brower cited in the Bibliography. Morris Freedman has written on Dryden's echoes and use of Milton in *Absalom* (see Bibliography) and is preparing a study of the subject.

4. See A. R. Heiserman, "Satire in the *Utopia*," *PMLA*, LXXVIII (1963), 163-74; and Robert C. Elliott, "The Shape of Utopia," *ELH*, XXX (1963), 317-34; Elliott is preparing a paper on the relations between the two genres, extending his analysis of *Utopia* as a formal satire into discussion of the generic affinities of utopian and satiric writing.

IV. METAPHORICAL HISTORY:
Absalom and Achitophel

1. Watson, II, 4.

2. For the currency of such thinking, see E. N. Hooker, "The Purpose of Dryden's *Annus Mirabilis*," *HLQ*, X (1946), 49-67; and *Works*, I, 257-59.

3. *Lives*, ed. G. B. Hill, I, 436-37.

4. Whitaker's remarks are to be found in *A Disputation on Holy Scriptures, against the Papists, Especially Bellarmine and Stapleton* (1588), trans. and ed. by the Rev. William Fitzgerald, Parker Society, vol. 26. The quotations and paraphrases that follow in the text are from pp. 402-10.

5. The doctrine of the two bodies of the king is basic to passages of *Threnodia Augustalis* (1685). It is a belief amply studied by Ernst H. Kantorowicz, *The King's Two Bodies: A Study in Medieval Political Theology* (Princeton, 1957). Although references to the concept can be found in Tory pamphlets during the 1680's, a readier illustration is the title page of Hobbes' *Leviathan* (1661, reproduced in the ed. of Michael Oakeshott [Oxford, 1960], p. 1).

6. Edward Stillingfleet, *Works* (1711, etc.), 2 vols., II, Part Two, Preface, 151. I have reversed italic and roman usage.

7. Stillingfleet, *Works*, II, Part Two, 194 (Ch. II, secs. 10-11).

8. The "Two Cases" of Burnet are printed in *Memoirs of the Secret Service of John Macky*, ed. S. Macky (1733), second Appendix, pp. xxiv-xxxiii.

9. There is an excellent discussion of libertinism in French and English thought and the drama in Dale Underwood, *Etherege and the Seventeenth-Century Comedy of Manners* (New Haven, 1957). Dryden's use of neo-Epicurean thought and its relation to his treatment of history are discussed at greater length in Chapter VII.

10. Charleton's story is best read in an edition reprinting it with another curious story of philosophizing eroticism: *The Ephesian and Cimmerian Matrons* (London, 1668). They are discussed in greater detail in Chapter VII.

11. *Ephesian and Cimmerian Matrons*, sig. A3ʳ. Italic and roman usages are reversed.

12. Morris Freedman argues in "Dryden's Miniature Epic," *JEGP*, LVII (1958), 211-19, for a large number of allusions to Milton's epics. If specific instances may be open to question, most of those he gives are not.

13. Dryden's connections between Satan, Achitophel, and Shaftesbury are grown a commonplace. They are well handled, for example, by Ian Jack, *Augustan Satire ... 1660-1750* (Oxford, 1952). In "Dryden's Miniature Epic," Freedman develops both Jack's remarks and those of R. F. Jones in "The Originality of *Absalom and Achitophel*." The discussion is amplified by Bernard N. Schilling, *Dryden and the Conservative Myth*.

14. E. D., *A Treatise of Humilitie* (London, 1654).

15. Schilling, *Dryden and the Conservative Myth*, pp. 277 and 281. Some of Dryden's best students have been misled into thinking Achitophel the center of the poem. Ruth Wallerstein, for example, in "To Madness Near Allied: Shaftsbury and His Place in the Design and Thought of *Absalom and Achitophel*," *HLQ*, VI (1943), 445-71, learnedly traces Dryden's ideas back to Plato and Aristotle, ignoring the Bible, biblical commentary, and royalist theory. Schilling is especially useful in setting such basic matters straight.

16. Schilling is, I believe, the first to insist upon this important point: *Dryden and the Conservative Myth*, pp. 147-48.

17. For Dryden on the forms of history, see Watson, II, 5-8.

18. The genre of the poem has seemed a problem to most critics. Various solutions are offered (and referred to in the text) by: A. W. Verrall, *Lectures on Dryden* (Cambridge, 1914), p. 59; R. F. Jones, "The Originality of Absalom and Achitophel"; E. M. W. Tillyard, *Poetry Direct and Oblique* (London, 1934), pp. 81-82; Morris Freedman, "Dryden's Miniature Epic," which summarizes other views; and Bernard N. Schilling, *Dryden and the Conservative Myth*, pp. 1-15, 291-306. Dryden himself gave (Watson, II, 115) *MacFlecknoe* and *Absalom and Achitophel* as examples of Varronian mixed satire, with reference to the character of Zimri. He also spoke of the *Hind* as a satire (Noyes, pp. 216 and 218). In such remarks he appears to typify the whole by passages and by characteristic rhetorical effects. The distinction can be seen by comparison with Pope's *Epistles*, which have even greater infusions of satire, while retaining another generic mode.

V. FAITH AND FABLE IN
The Hind and the Panther

1. *Lives*, ed. G. B. Hill, I, 442: "what can be more absurd?" Dr. Johnson asks, giving a number of examples where beasts break out of character. He concludes with praise of Dryden's knowledge and style (I, 446).

2. W. D. Christie, *Dryden*, 5th ed. (1892) p. xxxvi. In his Globe edition of 1870, Christie had censured Dryden's conversion but called the *Hind* "the most brilliant perhaps of all Dryden's poems" (p. ix).

3. F. T. Prince, "Dryden Redivivus," *Review of English Literature*, I (1960), pp. 71, 76, 77, 78. In "The Styles of *The Hind and the Panther*,"

(*JEGP*, LXI [1962], 511-27), Clarence H. Miller attempts, vainly I think, to distinguish the styles of the three Parts of the *Hind*. I, at least, cannot accept his distinction, understand Dryden's, or provide any of my own.

4. It should be said again that my citations of lines in the *Hind* give both the numbering of Noyes, which is continuous throughout the three parts, and the more common separate numbering by parts: 2350-447; III, 1059-1156. Citations of the first part, of course, present no problem, since both systems there give the same numbering.

5. F. T. Prince, "Dryden Redivivus," p. 74.

6. Dr. Johnson, *Lives*, ed. G. B. Hill, I, 446.

7. For example, see 794 ff., 800 ff., 818, 822 ff., 824-25 (a reference to the fable of The Fox and the Cat, with their different tricks to elude pursuit), 837 ff., 860 f., and 881 ff.—covering a hundred lines. (These passages are in II: 222 ff., 228 ff., 246, 250 ff., 252-53, 265 ff., 288 f., 309 ff.)

8. *Thomae Stapletoni, ... Opera quae Extant Omnia*, 4 vols. (Paris, 1670), IV. Stapleton was the most widely known of the earlier English Catholic controversialists.

9. Specific instances will be cited in *Works*, III.

10. Augustine, *The City of God*, ed. R. V. G. Trasker, 2 vols. (Everyman ed., 1945), II, p. 95 (XV. 27). The interpretation of the ark is in XV. 26.

11. I, 245-81; the passage is discussed below.

12. See the epistle dedicatory to the *Æneis*, Watson, II, 240.

13. Rosemary Freeman, *English Emblem Books* (London, 1948), stresses the deterioration of emblem subjects and treatment (if not always of graphic techniques) in Holland and England. Too limited a definition of emblematic modes obscures the continuity and development in such thought. See Jean Hagstrum, *The Sister Arts* (Chicago, 1958), and John Hollander, *The Untuning of the Sky* (Princeton, 1961).

14. The passage is I, 438-47. The fables are those of "The Husbandman and the Wood," "The Gourd and the Pine," and "The Sun and Wind and the Traveler."

15. See *Phædri ... Fabularum Æsopiarum Libri Quinque* (Amsterdam, 1667), e.g., III, Prol. There were of course numerous editions.

16. Ogilby's version was published 1651, etc. See Marian Eames, "John Ogilby and his Æsop," *BNYPL*, LXV (1961), pp. 73-88, and my Introduction to the reprint of Ogilby's *Æsop* (Los Angeles, 1965) for information about the editions. Dryden may also have known the trilingual *Æsop's Fables* by Thomas Philipott and Robert Codring, with excellent illustrations by Robert Barlow (London, 1666). This has a long life of Æsop (lacking in Ogilby) and like Ogilby at times makes specific, and often general, social applications.

17. See the article by Marian Eames, *supra*, n. 21.

18. The best seventeenth-century catalogue of such authors I have encountered is in Robert Lowell, ΠΑΝΖΩΟΡΥΚΤΟΛΟΓΙΑ, *SIVE Panzoologico-mineralogica. Or a Complete History of Animals and Minerals* (Oxford,

1661). Dryden's friend Dr. Walter Charleton attempted to classify animals by types in *Gualteri Charletoni Exercitationes de Differentiis & Nominibus Animalium*, 2nd ed. (Oxford, 1677).

19. Edward Topsell, *History of Four-Footed Beasts* (1658; 1st ed. 1607), sig. A7ʳ.

20. Topsell, sig. A7ʳ-7ᵛ.

21. Topsell, p. 573. Numerous natural historians mention the first possibility, but only Topsell among those I have read, the second. Unaware of the second, some of Dryden's editors have needlessly assumed a confusion on his part.

22. The Amsterdam edition is in Trinity College, Cambridge. (There were at least six editions by 1665.) I have examined a number of sacred zoögraphies and numerous natural histories. None, not even Topsell's, is so consistently close to Dryden's poem.

23. Franzius, *The History of Brutes* (London, 1670), pp. 116-17 on the Hart; p. 159 on the Wolf. This translation includes only the section in *Historia* on quadrupeds.

24. Franzius, *History*, pp. 137, 146, 147.

25. Cf. Dryden: "The Swallow, privileg'd . . . as man's familiar guest . . . Is well to chancels and to chimneys known . . . This merry chorister" (1721-29; III, 427-35).

26. See Louis I. Bredvold, *The Intellectual Milieu of John Dryden* (Ann Arbor, 1934, 1956), Appendix D, pp. 160 ff., on "English Catholic Opinion in the Reign of James II."

27. For these two interpretations, see Franzius, *Historia*, p. 513.

28. The typology is so well known that even Franzius spends relatively little space developing it. For his comparisons between the Dove and the Church, see "De Columbis," *Historia*, 460-71.

29. See Mortimer Donovan, "The *Moralite* of the Nun's Preste's Sermon," *JEGP*, LII (1953), 498 ff. and Charles Dahlberg, "Chaucer's Cock and Fox," *JEGP*, LIII (1954), 277 ff.

30. This progression in *Rel. Laici* is well discussed by Hoffman, *John Dryden's Imagery*, Chap. III, whence I have taken it.

31. The nature of these issues is best discovered by study of the religious views of the century. There have been some excellent recent discussions. The best general background is that of Baker, *Wars of Truth*, Chs. I, IV, V, and VII. Baker makes the usual mistake, however, of assuming the death by midcentury of ideas, assumptions, and beliefs very much alive in Dryden. He should be corrected by two excellent articles, that of Chiasson, "Dryden's Apparent Scepticism in *Religio Laici*," *Harvard Theological Review*, LIV (1961), 207-21, and Alan H. Roper, "Dryden's *Medal* and the Divine Analogy," *ELH*, XXIX (1962), 396-417.

32. Richard Hooker, *Of the Laws of Ecclesiastical Polity*, 2 vols., Everyman's Library (n. d.) I, xv, 4. Herschel Baker (*The Wars of Truth*, pp. 90-91) well quotes Hooker's sentence as an example of assumption of "the axiom

of knowledge," of faith in man's rational capacity supporting "the traditional dignity of man." The articles by Fujimura, Chiasson, and Roper cited above and in the Bibliography will be found to assess Dryden's stand more persuasively than the traditional view stemming from Louis I. Bredvold, *The Intellectual Milieu of John Dryden*.

33. See Baker, *Wars of Truth*, pp. 4-6, Chap. III, and Index, s. v. Voluntarism; also Roper, "Dryden's Medal and the Divine Analogy."

34. See Hannah Arendt, *The Human Condition*, Chaps. I and II, esp. pp. 23-27 for Aristotle's distinctions. See also Chaps. I and VIII of this book for further discussion and for the relation of these matters to public poetry and Dryden's historical views. Proof of the date of these lines involves minute glossing and the obvious importance of the passage to Part I. The glossing must await the publication of *Works*, III.

35. The most complex of these matters is the subject of the resolution of faith, touched upon here by Cressy. The most complete and systematic account of Catholic doctrine in English during the Restoration is that by Abraham Woodhead (other authorship sometimes suggested), *A Rational Account of Roman Catholics Concerning the Ecclesiastical Guide in Controversies on Religion*, 2nd ed. (n.p., 1673). See especially Discourse III, Chap. XI, ". . . The Resolution of Faith"; and pp. 419-48. "The Principal Contents in the Explications Concerning the Resolution of Faith."

36. These quotations on a rational faith are from the superior revised edition of Cressy, *Exomologesis*, Sect. 2, Chap. XXXVIII, pp. 306-07. Dryden refers to Cressy in the Preface to *Rel. Laici*, objecting to his "saying" concerning the deposing doctrine (Noyes, p. 160). I have not found Cressy supporting the deposing doctrine in his writings. It may be that I have missed it, or that "saying" suggests an oral or reported remark. Dryden may very well have met him.

37. Cressy, *Exomologesis*, pp. 308-09. Cf. Dryden, I, 61 ff.; cf. 761 ff. II, 189 ff.

38. The background of this issue from patristic to Elizabethan times is well treated by George H. Tavard, *Holy Writ or Holy Church* (London, 1959), from which much of my description is taken.

39. Peck's *Catalogue*, very much amplified by help from various sources and his own research, is printed by Thomas Jones, ed., "A Catalogue of Tracts for and Against Popery (Published in or about the Reign of James II)," *Remains* of the Chetham Society (Manchester), XLVIII (1859) and LXIV (1865). Strongly Anglican in attitude and perforce incomplete, this "Catalogue" remains indispensable.

40. The distinction between "Eternity Versus Immortality" in Greek thought and its relation to the distinction between Theōria and action are well treated by Hannah Arendt, *The Human Condition*, pp. 18-21. See also the discussion of Dryden's use of similar distinctions borrowed from neo-Epicureanism, Chap. VII, below.

41. Arendt, *The Human Condition*, p. 19, discussing Greek conceptions

of immortality. The quotation in her phrase, "a 'divine' nature," parallels Dryden's phrase for the Hind's "young," who, "half human, half divine," are parts of "the deathless plant." Miss Arendt relates such a conception to the "active" life and to public values.

42. From Dr. Johnson's *Notes to Shakespeare*, ed. Arthur Sherbo, *Romeo and Juliet*, Augustan Reprint Society, no. 73, p. 155; Dr. Johnson's words— "acute, argumentative, comprehensive, and sublime"—will be found in his "General Observations" at the end of the play.

VI. METAPHORICAL TRANSPORT AS
SURROGATE FOR FEELING: *Eleonora*

1. The passages in Dryden which seem to me to have close parallels in Donne's poems on Elizabeth Drury are as follows, Dryden's lines being cited in italic numbers, Donne's in roman. *1-11: I Ann.*, 43-54. *40-42: I Ann.*, 399-406. *75-82: I Ann.*, 69-78. *90-96: II Ann.*, 417-24. *126-33: I Ann.*, 9-10. *136-39: Ecclogue*, 149-50. *154-57: II Ann.*, 127-30. *174-75: I Ann.*, 227-29; see also *II Ann.*, 306-307 and for the word and something of the idea of "pattern" as in Dryden, "Canonization," 44-45. *257-62: I Ann.*, 1-8; see also title of *II Ann.*, "Of the Progresse of the Soule." *291-300: Funerall Elegie*, 83-90, 101-102. *301-304: Fun. Elegie*, 73-75. *317-22:* "Valediction: forbidding mourning," 1-4. *327-28: II Ann.*, 460-62. *330: Fun. Elegie*, 75. *375-76: I Ann.*, 473-74. Two other examples are given in the text.

2. The text used throughout for Donne is Herbert J. C. Grierson, ed., *The Poems of John Donne*, 2 vols. (Oxford, 1958 reprinting).

3. Noyes, p. 276. As Noyes remarks, the poem's resemblances in phrasing to *Eleonora* suggest composition at a nearly contemporaneous date.

4. Noyes, pp. 276-78. The poem's date has not been established. I suggest that the resemblance of phrasing in 78-80 to *Purcell*, 22-30, with the common echo of *Lycidas*, may possibly indicate its composition ca. 1698.

5. Noyes, p. 270. Conversely, *Threnodia Augustalis*, Dryden's first original poem in the irregular "Pindaric" stanzas is closer to heroic poetry in tone.

6. The distant parallels or doubtful echoes of Donne are as follows (see n. 1 for method of citation). *37: I Ann.*, 251-57; *II Ann.*, 507-508; "Valediction: forbidding mourning," 25-36. *46-47: I Ann.*, 413-16. *116-25: II Ann.*, 449-67. *143-53: I Ann.*, 259-60; *II Ann.*, 189-206. *158: II Ann.*, 123-26. *166-73: I Ann.*, 100-106; 179-82. *191: II Ann.*, 160-62. *220-30: II Ann.*, 223-25. *270-300: Funerall Elegie*, 78-106. *313-14:* "Song" (Sweetest Love), 37-40—see rhyme-words, 38-39. *362-70:* general resemblances to the meditative sections of *I Ann.* *377: II Ann.*, 43; 527-28.

7. There are other sources as well, chiefly Fontenelle's *Plurality of Worlds* and the poems of Robert Gould who, as one patronized by Abingdon and supported at his country seat, wrote a number of poems touching upon Lady Abingdon.

8. One or two of Dryden's undoubted biblical allusions have been noted

by his editors, but a fuller list is necessary. (For the method of citing, see n. 1). *19-20:* Numbers xi. *24-25:* Matthew xxv. 14-21. *30-31:* I Timothy vi. 17-19. *37-38:* Mark vi. 56; Acts ix. 32-43. *52-55:* Matthew xxv. 35-40. *71-74:* Genesis xli. *91-96:* Isaiah ii. 12-17. *118-19:* Deuteronomy xv. 1-18. *135:* Exodus xxxiii. 18-23. *176-80:* Ephesians v. 22-25. *207-10:* Exodus xvi. 11-18. *322-28:* Matthew xxv. 1-7. *338-39:* Genesis v. 24 and II Kings ii. 11. There is in addition such use of general biblical and traditional elements as comparisons with Eve and with Christ's age at death.

9. See *The Medal*, 131. God's benefaction of manna to Israel, a conventional emblem for His Providence, is one of Dryden's favorite biblical events for allusion. He had alluded to it in poetry some seven times before *Eleonora* and as recently as *Threnodia Augustalis* and *Britannia Rediviva*.

VII. VARIETIES OF LYRIC POETRY

1. Sir Walter Scott, Scott-Saintsbury, *Works*, I, 409.

2. Dr. Charleton adapted the first from the *Satyricon* of Petronius and first published it in 1659. The second story is by "P. M.," whom I cannot identify. (It may be Charleton himself.) Both works appeared in several guises or editions. In addition to those cited by Wing in his *Short Title Catalogue*, the rambling verses of Ogilby's version (*Æsopics*, 1668, pp. 197-231) should be mentioned. The story had a continental vogue as well.

3. *Matrons*, sig. A3^r-A3^v. The quotations from the prefatory "Letter . . . to a Person of Honour" reverse roman and italic usage.

4. *Matrons*, sig. A3^v-A4^r. Such inconsistency of behavior reflects commonplaces about women, but in Charleton's extremes we are reminded of Pope's *Epistle to a Lady, Of the Characters of Women*.

5. *Matrons*, pp. 24-25. The same ideas are treated at greater length, and more orthodoxly, in Charleton's *Natural History of the Passions* (London, 1674; sometimes attributed to Henry Carey). In these works as also in his *Physiologia* (London, 1654) and *Epicurus's Morals* (London, 1656), both of which are introduced later in this chapter, Charleton brings neo-Epicureanism into harmony with Christian theism.

6. There is an initial title page for both works, and a separate one for the second; separate pagination, but continuous signature numbers.

7. *Matrons*, sig. G2^v.

8. *Matrons*, p. 54.

9. See for example the "Rondelay," "Chloe found Amyntas lying," Noyes, p. 407.

10. As Jay Levine implies in his "Status of the Verse Epistle Before Pope," *SP*, LIX (1962), 658-84, the elegy is often related to the epistle form, in which a major convention is the relation established between the writer and the person addressed. Not much is known of the exact nature of Dryden's relations with Oldham beyond what the poem sets forth. What is known is summarized by Harold F. Brooks in his excellent article, "A Bibliography

of John Oldham," *Proceedings and Papers of the Oxford Bibliographical Society*, V (1936), 1-38. Congreve's testimony to Dryden's warm relationships with younger writers may be recalled to explain something of the tone of this poem.

11. *Lives*, ed. G. B. Hill, I, 439. Dr. Johnson, Warton (in Pope's *Works*, I, 213), Scott, and more recently Van Doren, Ruth Wallerstein, and E. M. W. Tillyard seem able to agree about little except that certain stanzas are vastly superior (or inferior) to others. The works are cited below or in the Bibliography.

12. Van Doren, *John Dryden: A Study of His Poetry* (New York, 1946), p. 199.

13. Ruth Wallerstein, *SP*, XLIV (1947), 519-28. The essay is reprinted in William R. Keast's compilation, *Seventeenth-Century English Poetry* (New York, 1962).

14. Tillyard, *Five Poems* (London, 1948) pp. 49-65, quoted from p. 52.

15. Hoffman, *John Dryden's Imagery*, pp. 99-128. The quotation from this, one of Hoffman's excellent close analyses, is from p. 116.

16. Tillyard is quoted from pp. 52-53. He is also very good on "The Status of the Arts" (pp. 61-62).

17. Hoffman, p. 115. This shipwreck should be compared with that in *Annus Mirabilis*, 137-40. Here the tone is more assured; the irony is personal, not general and, as the *Killigrew Ode* shows throughout, death is transcended with less agony than is shown in the earlier poem.

18. The creation passages are: *Hind*, I, 251-62; *Song*, 1-15. The passages on the Day of Judgment are: *Killigrew*, 178-92; *Song*, 55-63.

19. John Hollander, *The Untuning of the Sky: Ideas of Music in English Poetry, 1500-1700* (Princeton, 1961), surveys in detail musical theory and symbolism from classical times and discusses Dryden in his last chapter. See also James E. Phillips and Bertrand H. Bronson, *Music & Literature . . . Papers Delivered . . . at the Second Clark Library Seminar* (Los Angeles, [1954]). Poly-historians like Robert Fludd, *Utriusque Cosmi . . . Historia* (Oppenheim, 1617), dilate upon the conception underlying Dryden's middle stanzas. Man microcosmically displays the macrocosmic harmony of the rest of creation. "The diapason [closes] full in man," both as the harmonic sixth of God's creation and as the most harmonious of His creatures because most like Him.

20. Benjamin Jowett, ed., *The Dialogues of Plato*, 5 vols. (Oxford, 1892), III, 342. My summary of the *Timaeus* is based on his translation.

21. See n. 23. The poems supposed to be Dryden's sources could be multiplied many times over. Kinsley (IV, 1990-91) sums up the most often cited analogues: Milton, "At a Solemn Music," 21-24; *On the Morning of Christ's Nativity*, 117 ff., and *Par. Lost*, II, 898; III, 708-15. Also Katherine Philips, "L'Accord du Bien"; Jonson, "The Musicall Strife," 21-24; and Cowley, *The Resurrection*, stanza ii.

22. Ward, *Letters*, p. 71; Watson, II, 88. The subject is treated at length

by H. T. Swedenberg, Jr., *The Theory of the Epic in England, 1650-1800* (Berkeley and Los Angeles, 1944), Chapter XI.

23. Quoted from Ernst Cassirer, *The Platonic Renaissance in England* (Austin, 1953), p. 34.

24. "The Character of the Last Daies," pp. 7-8. The pamphlet indicates that the sermon was preached before Charles II "At the Theatre in Oxford . . . 1675." Dryden very possibly heard it. As is well known, Du Bartas was motivated in part by a desire to provide a Christian alternative to Lucretius and, with other hexaemeral writers, was influenced by *De Rerum Natura*.

25. Thomas Creech, *Lucretius, De Rerum Natura*, 2nd ed. (Oxford, 1683), p. 153.

26. Charleton, *Physiologia*, p. 79.

27. See Watson, II, 91-92.

VIII. THEMATIC VARIATION AND STRUCTURE
IN *Fables*

1. The estimate of lines and pages of translation is mine, the words in the quotation those of William Frost, *Dryden and the Art of Translation* (New Haven, 1955), p. 1. Frost concerns himself chiefly with Dryden's treatment of Virgil, Chaucer, and Juvenal. J. M. J. Bottkol, "Dryden's Latin Scholarship," *MP*, XL (1943), 241-55, demonstrates Dryden's command of Latin and classical scholarship in the century, and discusses certain features of his practice. Helene M. Hooker, "Dryden's *Georgics* and English Predecessors," *HLQ*, IX (1945-46), 273-310, discusses his use of earlier versions. L. Proudfoot, *Dryden's Æneid and its Seventeenth Century Predecessors* (Manchester, 1960), explores the subject of its title and also more general aspects of Dryden's art as translator. It must be significant that the best studies should concern the *Virgil*.

2. Watson, II, 272.

3. *Lives*, ed. G. B. Hill, I, 418.

4. Dryden's conception and treatment of Chaucer in *Fables* are subjects I discuss in an essay in *Studies in Criticism and Esthetics 1660-1800: Essays in Honor of Samuel H. Monk* (Minneapolis, 1966).

5. *Lives*, ed. G. B. Hill, I, 469.

6. Ward, *Letters*, p. 115; Watson, II, 263-64.

7. Watson, II, 285.

8. Quintilian, *Institutio Oratoria*, II. iv. See also V. x. The translations are those of H. E. Butler in the Loeb ed. of the *Institutes* (4 vols. [London and Cambridge, Mass., 1953], I, 225). See also Cicero, *De Inventione*, I. xix, and the pseudo-Ciceronian *Ad C. Herennium de Ratione Dicendi*, I, viii. The general subject is examined by Lillian Feder, "John Dryden's Use of Classical Rhetoric," *PMLA*, LXIX (1954), 1258-78.

9. See for example *Institutes*, V, x-xii, xiv; IX, iv, 135, 138; or an *index verborum*. The plural, *argumenta*, seems always to stress the rhetorical

(persuasive, dissuasive) meaning; the expository sense appears to me to develop in Quintilian out of his ideas about the nature of the proper style for argument—the plain as opposed to that more elevated for such other parts of orations as the *exordium*. Even if rhetorical theory had not supported such a definition, Dryden would have been likely to introduce expository or philosophical argument—as he does in the passage on government in *Absalom*. Moreover, as will be shown, Ovid's *Metamorphoses*, XV provided a clear precedent.

10. The passage is 29-41. The image of the sinner wrapping himself against the wind and removing his cloak in the sun's warmth is adapted from the Æsopian tale of the sun, the wind, and the traveller. Dryden had alluded to the fable in *The Hind and the Panther*: See Ch. V, n. 14.

11. Ward, *Letters*, p. 120. Jay Arnold Levine, "John Dryden's Epistle to John Driden," *JEGP*, LXIII (1964), 450-74, examines in detail certain features of the thought and structure of the poem.

12. See Robert H. Brower and Earl Miner, *Japanese Court Poetry* (Stanford, 1961), pp. 319-29, 403-13, and 491-93. In all likelihood, my time spent studying Japanese played as much a role in my view of *Fables* as the work by Martz and others on the formal meditation in seventeenth-century poetic practice.

13. *Lives*, ed. G. B. Hill, I, 469.

INDEX

Entries cover the text and the notes. Only general topics are entered under Dryden's name; the titles of his works are entered separately (titles in *Fables* are also entered separately). Titles of works by other writers will be found, when they are specified, under the author's name. Pages of most extended discussion of a work, topic, or author are given first.

A selected list of MIDLAND BOOKS

(continued on next page)

MIDLAND BOOKS